Whenever she felt inclined to feel sorry for herself, Kate would look at little Jean McKay, so pregnant that she could barely walk.

Provisions were running low. The rest of the party couldn't stop and wait for the McKays, so Kate and Angus McKay helped Jean toward a copse of spruce trees off to one side while the rest headed on. Kate laid in some thick-needled boughs on its floor and covered them over with a blanket. Together they helped Jean down on top.

There was nothing more she could do for them; she was no midwife. Suddenly she unknotted the muffler around her neck and peeled off her Sunday shawl.

"To wrap your baby bunting in."

"Oh, Katy, no, we could never—"

"You can and you will."

She trudged back across the spruce copse to hurry after the others.

Also by Alfred Silver
Published by Ballantine Books:

LORD OF THE PLAINS

RED
RIVER
STORY

Alfred Silver

BALLANTINE BOOKS • NEW YORK

Library of Congress Catalog Card Number: 86-92095

ISBN 0-345-36562-3

Manufactured in the United States of America

First Trade Edition: April 1988
First Mass Market Edition: May 1990

For Maria and Jacob,
whose stories gave me a glimmer of understanding of this one,
and for Pam and Jane and all good midwives.

AUTHOR'S NOTE

The people in this story all lived. The major events in their lives are documented in court transcripts, parish records, brittle-leaved old journals, and items filed away in the corners of archives. But this isn't a history book. These aren't the kind of people that history gets written about. There are gaps between the points in their lives at which the current of events swept them into the recording eye. I've tried to connect the points with straight lines. As a general rule, it can be assumed that the more outrageous coincidences, glaring ironies, and flamboyant dramatic gestures are the ones I never would have had the bare-faced gall to invent.

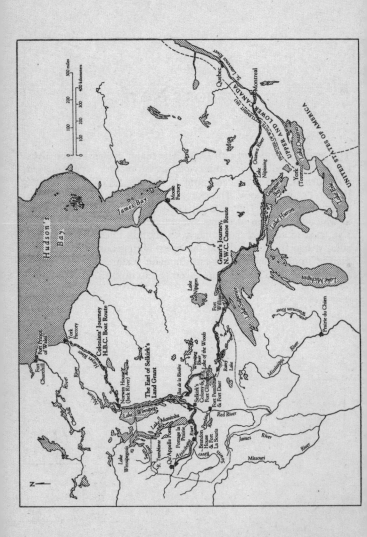

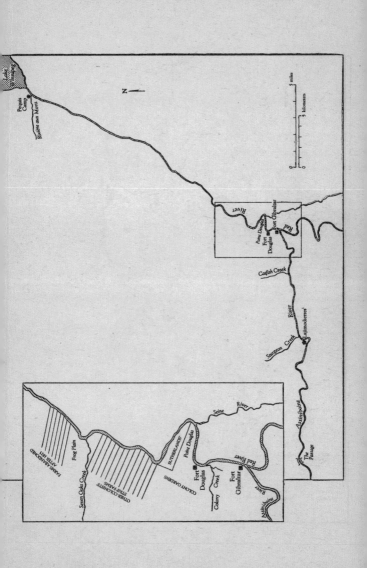

GLOSSARY

avant—in fur trade parlance, the bow paddler of a canoe, responsible for piloting the fragile, birchbark-skinned craft around snags.

Ban mhorhair Chataibh—Gaelic name for the Countess of Sutherland; "The Chieftainess of Our Clan."

the *Beurla*—Gaelic term for the English language.

bheag—Gaelic for "small."

bois brulé—French Canadian term for the mixed-bloods of the northwest; literally "scorched wood."

bourgeois—in Montreal fur-trade parlance, the "bourgeois" was the trader in charge, whether of a fort or a canoe brigade.

canot de maître—literally "boss canoe," capable of carrying four tons of cargo and a crew of sixteen.

canot du nord—literally "canoe of the north," sized for five to eight paddlers.

cehlidh—Gaelic; an evening gathering of neighbors to trade songs and stories and dance the night away.

clanna—Gaelic for "children."

Company of Adventurers—"The Governor and Company of Adventurers Trading into Hudson's Bay"; also referred to as "The English Company" because their headquarters and warehouses were in London; also "Gentleman Adventurers"; "Company of Gentlemen and Adventurers"; and various unflattering variations coined by nor'westers.

curragh—Gaelic, a small, skin-covered boat; anglicized to "coracle."

dalles—literally French "cobblestones"; fur trade usage denoted a treacherous stretch of rapids through a narrow rocky channel.

engagé—French for "enlisted man"; in fur trade usage an *engagé* was a man who had signed on for a term as a voyageur with the North West Company.

factor—Scots usage denoted a steward or an agent. A Hudson's Bay Company factor was the officer responsible for a given area, hence "York Factory," "Moose Factory," etc.

galettes—French, unleavened wheat cakes; the French version of bannock.

gouvernail—the stern paddler and steersman of a freight canoe. Like the *avants*, the *gouvernails* would be *engagés* of long standing; the noncommissioned officers of the North West Company.

HBC—abbreviation of Hudson's Bay Company.

homme du nord—literally "man of the north." In North West Company parlance an *homme du nord* was a man who worked the *canot du nord* route and consequently wintered in the *pays d'en haut*.

jardinière—French for "gardener"; contemptuously diminutive for "farmer."

jeunes gens—literally "the young men"; in the early nineteenth century it specifically referred to the generation of *bois brulé* whose numbers suddenly made them a distinct race of their own.

métis—French, literally "crossbreed" or "mongrel." Twentieth-century usage sometimes uses "métis" as exclusively French-Indian, but in the early nineteenth century many métis were named Grant, Fraser, MacGillivray, etc.

milieu—French translation is literally "middle." In the North West Company, a *milieu* was a canoe paddler who was neither an *avant* nor a *gouvernail*, a grunt engagé.

moonias—Algonkian/Cree for a man from the east, a tenderfoot. One theory is that the word originated by Crees attempting to pronounce "Montréaliste" as a French Canadian voyageur would have pronounced it.

Nor'westers—used to denote the men of the North West Fur Trading Company, derisively referred to by Hudson's Bay Company men as "the Canadian Pedlars."

pays d'en haut—French, literally "the high country"; referring to the country upriver from Fort William and across the height of land separating the Atlantic watershed from the Arctic watershed; consequently the northwest third of North America.

Peguis—Ojibway for "leaves the lodges of his enemies in ashes."

pemmican—from Cree, literally "pounded meat." Usually buffalo meat, smoked and hammered to a powder and mixed with boiled fat, frequently flavored with wild berries. Bags of pemmican have been dug up after lying buried for decades, and eaten with no adverse effects.

pièce—the standard transport package of North West Company freight, whether furs or trade goods. A single pièce weighed approximately ninety pounds and was wrapped in canvas or rawhide, about the same as a bag of pemmican.

rubaboo—a stew made of fried chunks of pemmican and whatever else comes to hand.

Rupertsland—literally "Rupert's Land," named after Prince Rupert of the Rhine, Charles II's revered Cavalier cousin and the first Governor of the Company of Adventurers. The Royal Charter of 1670 gave Rupert's company exclusive dominion over all lands drained by rivers flowing into Hudson's Bay. In HBC jargon, "Rupertsland" is roughly equivalent to the Nor'westers' "pays d'en haut."

shagganappi—Algonkian cree, meaning literally "rawhide thong." Usually referred specifically to the spiral-cut green buffalo hide used in the *pays d'en haut* for everything from braiding whips to binding cartwheels. It also came to mean anything scruffy, rough or jury-rigged, as "a shagganappi pony."

shian—Gaelic for "hill"; usually carrying connotations of a "Faerie hill" where the "men of peace"—the Sidh (sheedh) dwelt. Hence Ban sidh—"banshee," as the "ban" in "Ban mhorhair Chataibh" denotes a female Chief. "Shian dhu" would be "the dark hill," as Dublin is Blackpool.

shlanje fha, shlanje mhor (relatively phonetic spelling)—Gaelic; "shlanje" is "health," "fha" is "long," "mhor" could be roughly translated as "great"—Ban *mhor*hair Chataibh.

strath—Gaelic for "valley."

thubhairt—Gaelic for "said."

trùir—Gaelic for "three."

usquebaugh—Gaelic for "the water of life"; whiskey.

PART ONE

THE CLEARANCES

CHAPTER 1

They lived on the rim of the world. The Romans had built a wall to keep them there. The stones had tumbled down and the Romans had gone, but the wall still stood, the line between civilization and the Highlanders.

They still squatted in their stone huts, speaking a mist-shrouded Stone Age language that in all the centuries had passed only three words into civilized tongues: whiskey, clan, and blackmail. They still sang their songs together as they mowed the barley, as they herded shaggy cattle through mountain rivers flecked with ice chips, as they danced barefoot around peat fires through the endless winter nights—songs that clanged against the human ear like the screeling of gulls or the whistling of ospreys.

On a spring day in 1813, a Highland woman sat perched on a mossy rock talking earnestly to a black cat. In a tall race she was too tall for a woman. Her pinch-cheeked, raw winter pallor was plumed with a thick, long, glinting mane of red Viking gold.

The cat was listening attentively, or at least it was gazing intently, head cocked to one side, at the chunk of white, crumbly cheese she held just out of reach. Whenever his attention began to wander, she would break off a nibble-sized morsel with long, ungainly fingers and ferry it to his mouth, whereupon he grew rapt once more.

She was speaking English, of a sort: "Sit you . . . still-ly, MacCrimmon!" She fed him another crumb of cheese, peeking back over her shoulder to make sure no one in her family saw her feeding an animal who was supposed to earn his living by keeping the cottage mouseless. "Else who am I to—for? . . . make my practicing for . . . to?"

She was aware that her *s*'s were still coming out *sh*'s. The blunt, harsh consonants of the English still eluded her. She told herself that it was bound to take time to teach an old tongue new tricks. She no longer thought of her tongue as young, any more than any

3

other part of her. Twenty-nine years in the Highlands could scour off a lot of peach fuzz.

She waggled her finger pedagogically at the cat. "The Reverend Mister Ross *thubhairt—say*-ed you do know the *Beurla*—the English." The Reverend Mister James Ross had begun her English tutoring by explaining to her that all cats spoke two words of English—"now" and "me." "Would you to make a kirk minister into a . . ." She groped for the English word.

From down the hillside, a male voice called her name, breaking in on her effort. She stood up and waved her arms over her head, calling back a reply. A peewit burst up out of the ground cover in front of her, flapping and screaming, green wings batting together frantically. MacCrimmon slithered forward through the bracken.

She popped the last of the cheese into her mouth and started down the slope, not too annoyed at the excuse to shift back into the language she thought in. The man shading his eyes to look up to her was old Donald Gunn. "A good day to you, Miss Kate MacPherson."

"And to you, Mister Gunn." She scrabbled over the hummock at the foot of the slope and fetched up beside him on the peaty bank of Kildonan Burn.

Mister Gunn kept his eyes trained up the hillside. He said: "Who was it up there with you, then? Tell him to come out—I am not a gossip."

"No one. I was sitting alone, watching the clouds."

"I heard you talking. . . ."

"I have a few years yet to go, I should hope, before I reach the age of talking to myself, Mister Gunn."

The black cat came up over the hummock behind her. Mister Gunn looked from her to MacCrimmon and back again. His eyes slitted, and his hand surreptitiously formed itself into the horned sign. He said warily: "Alex Sutherland said would you come along down to the river—there is a man there we can get no sense from, and we know you have been learning the *Beurla*."

Kate accompanied him along Kildonan Burn to the place where it came out into the valley and hurled itself into the black waters of the Ulidh. There was a crowd of crofters and their wives and children standing there. In front of them, beside a thick-waisted pony, there was a thick-waisted man in a blue greatcoat, peering across the river at the fields on the other side. He clutched a pencil and a pasteboard-bound notebook in his stubby hands, and a brass spyglass hung from a cord around his neck. Whatever he was studying on the other shore, he spent as much time glancing nervously over his shoulder at the murmuring locals.

At the head of the straggle of crofters was a wiry man with grizzled hair—Three-Fingered Alex Sutherland. When Donald Gunn had said "Alex Sutherland," Kate had thought he'd meant Red Alex Sutherland. Three-Fingered Alex Sutherland raised his eponymous right hand when he saw her coming and started toward her. "A good day to you, Katy."

"And to you, Uncle Alex. Mister Gunn said that you wanted me to come."

"Yes, and thank you. We have been trying to ask this gentleman here what he is about with his glass and pencil, but it appears he has no Gaelic." He said it in the same commiserating tone that he might have said: "He has no arms or legs."

"I am afraid my English is nothing to marvel at yet, but I will try what I can do." She started across the gap of open ground between the clump of crofters and the thick-waisted gentleman. He stopped scribbling in his notebook and angled his head around slightly, just far enough to see her out of the corner of his eye while still giving the impression that his attention was focused in front of him. With each step she took, his shoulders inched up closer to his ears.

She decided to stop halfway before he choked off his windpipe and asphyxiated himself. She waggled her tongue across the tips of her top teeth to limber it up for the *s*'s, took in a deep breath, and called out in the *Beurla*: "Excuse me, sir!"

He whirled around. "You speak English! Thank Christ!"

"I have not much English, sir, but enough to say my mind without I need to take the name from the Lord to vain."

"Oh—of course, yes, pardon me. It was just such a relief to me after . . ." He rolled his eyes in the direction of her friends and neighbors and then hissed at her: "What do they want from me?"

"They want . . . *we* want . . . to be knowing what do you be doing here with your . . . your . . ." She gestured at his spyglass and his notebook.

"Oh. Oh!" He began to shake with laughter. "Of course—merely the fabled curiosity. And I thought . . . well, never mind what I thought. You may tell your people, Mrs. . . ."

"*Miss* MacPherson."

"Ah, of course—*Miss* MacPherson—oh, and my name is Reid. . . ."

"How will you do, Mister Reid?"

"How will I do what? Oh, of course— How *do* you do, Miss MacPherson. Now, *what* I am doing is attempting to calculate how many sheep can live here."

"How many pardon me?"

"Sheep." He curled his forefingers on either side of his forehead and said: "Baa."

"Yes, so. You do not needing your"—she gestured again at his spyglass and notebook—"to be knowing that. My uncle Alex Sutherland there have *trùir*—three sheeps, and old Mister Donald Gunn have four . . . no, he eated the wee one. . . . Then Robert Sutherland there have—"

"No, no." Mister Reid laughed indulgently. "You misconstrue me. I do not mean how many sheep live here *now*—I mean how many sheep *can* live here, after you go."

"After I . . . pardon me?"

"Not you—you! *You*," circling his hand inclusively. "After you go—leave—move away." He waggled his fingers in a shooing gesture. "Mister Sellar swore to me he'd posted the eviction notices. . . ."

Three-Fingered Alex Sutherland said: "What does he say?" She told him. The murmuring suddenly grew louder and uglier. The front rank of the crowd began to edge forward. Mister Reid bent down and picked up a stout walking stick lying at his feet and waved it at them, backing away. Old Donald Gunn took the stick away from him. Mary Sutherland snatched the notebook and started ripping out the pages. Mister Reid backed over the lip of the bank and dropped into the Ulidh.

They tried to pull him out, but he flailed his fists at their hands and backed in deeper. He got a surprised look on his face when the current took hold of him. He bobbed downstream, batting and kicking at the water and gurgling for help. They jogged along the bank beside him, Colin Sutherland leading the pony, Mister Gunn carrying the walking stick, Mary Sutherland fluttering loose pages out of the notebook over her shoulder into the wind, and Kate MacPherson shouting in her halting English that if he could just manage to keep his head above water, the current would fetch him up safe in the shallows.

When the current swept Mister Reid in toward shore at the bend, he found his footing and stood, still up to his thick waist in snow-fed mountain river, sputtering and shivering, his ruined riding boots slipping on the slick rocks of the riverbed. The crofters swarmed down the bank and called and beckoned to him to come out before he caught his death, but he wouldn't budge.

Three-Fingered Alex Sutherland waded in to help him out. Mister Reid took a half step back, bellowed, and struck at him with his fists. Three fingers or not, Kate's uncle Alex could still make a fist of his own. He applied it to the soft spot between Mister Reid's eyebrows, and Mister Reid grew docile.

They carried Mister Reid up the bank, chafed his wrists to bring the circulation back, sat him on his pony with his walking stick in one hand and the empty pasteboard covers of his notebook in the other, switched the pony's pudgy bottom with a branch of dead heather, and waved good-bye to him as he jounced down the valley the way he'd come. That night, at Red Alex Sutherland's *cehlidh*— the traditional gathering of neighbors to entertain each other—they spent more time arguing over the eviction notices than they did singing and dancing and telling stories. The notices had been nailed up in March, one copy for every hut in the parish of Kildonan. After a month of rain and mist and the tail end of the snow, they were only gray pieces of smudged pulp.

They might as well have been illegible to start with, even with Kate MacPherson and a smattering of others to cipher out the *Beurla*:

> *And whereas Elizabeth Gordon, Countess of Sutherland, Heritable Proprietor of the Land, hath shewn that the Title of Possession of said sub-tenant will expire at and against the term of Whitsunday in the year one thousand eight hundred and thirteen, and thereupon issuing a Warning of Ejection . . .*

The words added up to a non-thing, a nonsense song without a tune. The crofters of Kildonan parish had puzzled them over and then consigned them in their minds to that netherworld of foreign activity that had no bearing on grinding oatmeal, making cheese, patching the thatch, or gathering the cattle for the spring migration up to the mountain pastures.

But the incident with Mister Reid had brought the notices back to mind. Kate MacPherson and her parents and brothers and sisters and nieces and nephews and neighbors sat chewing the question over in Red Alex Sutherland's cottage, the young ones squatting on the floor and the older generation ensconced on the short-legged chairs designed to keep their sitters' heads below the hovering cloud of peat smoke.

The woman who was known to the civilized world as the Countess of Sutherland was to them *Ban mhorhair Chataibh*—the "Chieftainness of Our Clan." They paid rent to her and revered her, but she didn't own the land any more than she owned them. The Clan and the Chief and the land that the Clan had carved out and defended were all one entity. It had been that way since the hand of God moved over the waters.

Kate raised a large laugh from the assembled company by suggesting that the idea of *Ban mhorhair Chataibh* replacing her *clanna*, her children, with sheep was about as likely as Kate's father tucking a ewe into her bed and driving her out into the heather. Her father raised an immensely larger laugh by arching his eyebrows, scratching his beard, and saying: "Hmmm . . ."

A very few days after the *cehlidh*, the expected reassurance arrived. It was an open invitation from *Ban mhorhair Chataibh* to anyone in the parish of Kildonan who felt disturbed or confused by the recent notices to come down to Dunrobin Castle on a given day to voice their concerns and have them resolved.

On the morning of the appointed day Kate rose before the sun and stole out of the family sleeping room with her bundle of clothing. She built up the fire, broke a loaf of bannock into bits for breakfast, and scoured out the pot that little Annie had promised to wash out last night.

When the work was done, she put on her black Sabbath skirt belled out with blue petticoats and her dark blue linen Sabbath blouse. With the broach that the tinker had fashioned from the metal of a broken spoon, she fastened on her ringshawl, so called because a yard-wide shawl of good combed wool should be fine enough to be drawn through a wedding ring. The shawl was as soft as cats' ears and quite fetching, she thought, with its crosshatching of red and green on a cream-white ground. It was a pity she'd have to spoil the effect by covering it over with her old black-and-green plaid of coarse wool, the one that served her for coat and blanket and rain gear. But freezing her udders off—such as they were—hiking over the hills would be even more of a pity.

She was pulling on her stockings when the rest of the family stumbled out of their boxbeds. Halfway through breakfast, John was informed that he would have to stay behind to mind Annie and the littler ones.

"It is not fair! Katy should stay. Why do I have to be the one to stay?"

"One of you must stay," said their mother. "It makes no bones to me which one."

Their father said: "Argue it out amongst yourselves."

"It is not fair!"

"True, arguing against your sister does not seem like a fair proposition. You could take her out in the yard and go three falls against her—but I would not recommend it."

By the time Kate and her parents reached the bank of the Ulidh, there were men and women and adolescent children trickling out of the cottages all down the valley, the women in dark skirts and blouses under plaids of red and blazing yellow and blue-black and green and heather purple, their heads covered with tight-laced frilled mutches or the old style splayed curtches. Both varieties of cap were starched whiter than the snowcap on Ben Griam Mor. Kate MacPherson and the other spinsters and single girls covered their heads with a fold of their plaids. Kate had been a baby when the news had come to Kildonan that the laws banning the tartan and the belted plaid had been repealed. Her granny had been among the few old women who could still remember how to dye the yarn and weave the patterns.

They forded the Ulidh at Shian Dhu. Robert Gunn had brought his pipes. When he got winded they sang walking songs. Between the walking songs the thrushes and the blackbirds sang. The primroses were beginning to bloom, and wild thyme savoried the air. Across the hillsides spread a pale pink-purple mist of heather buds.

They hiked past Learable Hill with the row of standing stones their ancestors had set in place when Homer was a boy. A few stones still showed the fish and axe symbols of the Picts, but most of those had been incorporated into Celtic crosses after St. Donnan.

Where the Ulidh bent east on its last leg down to the sea, they abandoned the valley and cut south through Glen Loth, whose mouth had marked the boundary for the old Viking settlement of Helmsdale. It was the Vikings who'd christened their country Sutherland—the southern province—although its coasts were chewed by the polar seas.

As Glen Loth sloped upward to pass between Ben Dobhrain and Ben ne Meilich, they walked past scattered shielings—the beehive-shaped stone huts where their young people had tended the herds and each other through three thousand years.

At Lothbeg they turned southwest along the new road bordering the North Sea, toward Brora and Golspie and Dunrobin Castle, where Clan Sutherland had stood behind their Chief against the Young Pretender in 1745.

When they reached Brora they had come fifteen miles across the hills, and some of the older folk wanted a pause to catch their breath. They sat down among the shore rocks next to Brora and unwrapped bannock and cheese and unstoppered bottles of water and usquebaugh. John Gunn came at a dog trot up the road from Brora and shouted at them: "You must turn back! Go back to your homes—there are sheriff's officers and bailiffs at Dunrobin Castle. They have run out the cannons and sent for the soldiers at Fort George. They say you have run out the fiery cross and are coming down with claymores to sack the town."

"To *what*?"

"We were none of us born when the Disarming Acts came down. No one here has ever seen a claymore!"

"Now, now . . ." said old Donald Gunn. "When I was ten . . . or was it twelve. . . ?"

John Gunn shouted over the general murmur: "*I* know that—but the rumors have been flying and layering on top of each other ever since Mister Reid said you tried to murder him. The invitation to come to the castle was bait to flush out the troublemakers."

"*Ban mhorhair Chataibh* would never—"

"The Countess is in London. Go back to your homes for the sake of your lives. God knows what they mean to do."

Three-Fingered Alex Sutherland was for going on regardless, and fifty of Kate's neighbors went with him. She stood up and started after them, then hesitated and looked back to those who would wait at Brora. Her parents had stood up as well. Her father was beckoning to her anxiously. Her mother yelled: "Have you lost your wits, girl? Get back here!"

Kate turned and ran along the road toward Dunrobin Castle. The crowd skirted warily around the hedges bordering the ornamental gardens, whispering like children stealing apples. At the far end of the long avenue of oak trees, spilling out of the stableyard, was a milling mob of men and horses.

Someone suggested that they should go on to Golspie—the town they'd supposedly come to sack—rather than walking head on into whatever was waiting for them, and in the innyard at Golspie they felt safe to let their voices rise above a hush again. They were arguing back and forth about whom to believe and what to do when they heard a thudding of boots and hoofbeats coming along the road from the castle.

Someone said: "The soldiers!"

William Sutherland said: "That does not sound like regular troops to me."

The horses trotted into the innyard—not shaggy little Highland ponies, but long-legged, sleek-coated English hunters. They were carrying estate managers and sheriff's officers and a collection of kirk ministers. Behind them marched a double line of stablemen and groundskeepers from the estate, and bailiffs who yesterday had been wharf porters or tavern drink cadgers. They carried pick handles or knotted oak cudgels or broad, brass-buckled belts wrapped around their fists.

The horsemen fanned out in a line across the front of the innyard. The bailiffs filled the gaps. The crofters edged back toward the wall of the inn. The heels of Kate's Sunday shoes crunched down on something. She looked back and saw that she was backing onto a midden of broken glass and paving stones. Something her old dead granny had told her suddenly sprang to mind. She kicked off her shoe, peeled off the stocking, and filled the toe of it with pebbles and bits of glass. A couple of the other women followed her lead.

At the midpoint of the line of horsemen was a fox-faced fellow in a bottle-green coat: Patrick Sellar, the Countess of Sutherland's factor. He leaned up in his stirrups and called in a high, sharp, nasal voice: "You people are all to disperse immediately! This is an unlawful assembly." The Reverend Mister James Ross, he of the soft eyes and the way with cats and spinsters, translated into Gaelic.

There was a shuffling silence for a moment, then they began to shout back, overlapping each other:

"Aye, so you can set upon us one at a time on the road home!"

"We came to see *Ban mhorhair Chataibh*, not you!"

"We did no harm to Mister Reid—he would have drowned but for us!"

Patrick Sellar turned his head toward his battery of ministers. They each took their say in turn. The Reverend Mister James Ross's sermon was essentially the same as that of his fellows: "What you are doing is wickedness and the sin of pride! Would you set yourselves above the lawful authorities that the Lord of heaven has placed over you? You shame me. You shame yourselves. I see the flames of hellfire climbing up around your ankles."

When the ministers had finished, Patrick Sellar unfolded a piece of paper and began to read from it in English. Kate managed to pick out a phrase here and there, but the convolutions of the Riot Act were a bit much for her.

A new sound came up under Patrick Sellar's voice, another contingent of booted feet approaching from the west. It was immediately apparent that William Sutherland hadn't been just prattling. The ragged thumping of the bailiffs' approach from the castle had borne no resemblance to this perfectly cadenced, menacing pulse beat. As the marching grew louder other sounds became discernible within it: drums and hooves and the clattering of gun carriages.

There was a rush to escape from the innyard. Kate was swept along with the current. Patrick Sellar swung his horse aside, opening a gap to let them pass. Winding toward them along the road from Dornoch was a long ribbon of red coats and pipe-clayed cross-belts, with a dancing gleam above it of bayonets flickering in the sun. The soldiers were coming at a quick march, the horses of the artillery train trotting to keep up.

The army chased them up the coast road back to Brora, jog-trotting and jabbing at them with bayonets. Kate scissored her stiff legs frantically to keep ahead; all the resiliency had been worn out of her knees by the walk across the hills.

The people waiting at Brora started to run when they saw the soldiers coming. Some of the older folk dropped behind and had to be half carried. The soldiers barked behind them like beagles in at the kill.

Kate's mother tripped and stumbled. Kate grabbed one elbow and her father the other. They dragged her along, choking on the dust. A voice behind her ear growled: "Let her drop—learn how the Frogs make wine."

CHAPTER 2

 Under an orange moon four junior clerks were slumped against their luggage on the steps of the North West Fur Trading Company's warehouse at the corner of St. Thérèse and

Vaudreuil streets in the city of Montreal. Three of them were curled up docilely with their hats pulled down over their eyes. The fourth stood up, walked out into the cobbled street, and peered in both directions. He thrust his hands in his pockets and took to pacing back and forth, his boot heels ringing echoes off the stone walls of the buildings.

He was dressed in the best that the tailors of Edinburgh and Montreal could make. Tucked seamlessly into his cuffed, calf-high boots was a pair of cream-yellow doeskin breeches. Overlapping the waistband was a gray double-breasted waistcoat with a brown broadcloth tailcoat buttoned over it. His neck and shirtfront were enveloped in a cunningly tied arrangement consisting of a high collar, a ruffled white lawn neckcloth, and a broad green bow of satin ribbon. Against the perils of a spring night he'd added a sand-colored coachman's coat with double-caped shoulders.

His head was bare, allowing the breeze coming up off the river to ruffle his hair. When the moonlight struck his face, a passerby of a literary bent might have been struck at first glance by the resemblance to the portraits of the young Robert Burns. On a second look, though, the cheekbones were a bit too heavy and prominent and the hair several shades too dark—black and glossy and thick. The eyes had a definite almond slant to them that had never come out of the British Isles. They were large and dark, the irises as black as the pupils, giving the disturbing impression that they would remain opaque and unreadable no matter how direct and level their gaze.

One of the other three clerks creaked up off the steps and stumbled out onto the street. With a young man of standard size for comparison, all resemblance to Romantic poets living or dead vanished. The almond-eyed junior clerk was only somewhat taller than average, but the breadth and depth and apparent weight of his head and upper body were extraordinary, even though at age nineteen the frame hadn't yet filled out.

The second junior clerk grumped: "For God's sake, Grant, it's difficult enough to snatch a few winks as it is—I thought you people were supposed to walk softly." The black eyes swiveled sideways to intersect with the blue. "I was only making a joke, for God's sake. Can't you allow a fellow a little leeway for a sense of humor?"

Grant turned his gaze back down the black void of Vaudreuil Street, not terribly pleased with his ability to intimidate junior clerks half a head shorter than he was.

He had learned that it was a waste of breath to explain that he'd been taken from his mother's people when he was too young to remember anything. The same fool he'd explain it to today would come around tomorrow asking him how to start a fire by rubbing two sticks together. He had also learned that the instant glamour attached to his exotic origins—whether by the boys in the boarding school in Montreal or the young Scots gentry in the dormitory of Inverness College or the junior clerks in the counting house of the North West Fur Trading Company—was the same variety of glamour they might attach to a two-headed dog.

At last the carriage came clattering and grinding out of the shadows. Grant snatched up his valise, his chocolate-brown, brushed beaver top hat, and his factory-bright waxed walnut guncase and prodded the other two awake. What with shepherding the somnambulant into the carriage and piling their luggage on around them, Grant got stuck with the front passenger seat, back to back with the driver.

He watched the moonlit face of the North West Company's central warehouse jounce away and diminish until it was enfolded by the night. It seemed impossible that less than a year had passed since the morning he'd puked up his breakfast on the warehouse floor. The other new boys had all been terribly amused. Not that they weren't gagging and retching and wax-faced themselves, but it had tickled their fancy to learn that his bloodlines hadn't inured him to the effluvia of half-cured pelts and green hides and rancid castor.

Grant shook off the memory. He leaned forward across the stack of traveling gear and shook Lewis's knee to wake him. "Be a good fellow, Lewis, and exchange places with me—I get vertigo from looking back."

Lewis widened his eyes to slits and bleared around at the overpopulated compartment, legs and shoulders jammed between valises and hatboxes and fly-rod cases. "For God's sake, Grant—how? I mean to say, there's no room for a fellow to . . ."

Grant leaned sideways, flipped the door catch, and batted the door open. He swiveled up out of his seat, poked his foot onto the wrought-iron stepdown, and swung his body out into the ether, hanging backward with his hands hooked on the rim on either side of the doorway. The carriage slanted toward him, bouncing crazily on its springs. The driver roared archaic French curses. The shadows whizzed by.

"For God's sake, Grant . . ."

"There, you've got room to move now, Lewis. Be a good fellow and exchange places with me." Lewis moved. Grant swung back into the carriage, flipped the door shut, and settled down onto the seat Lewis had vacated.

The first glint of dawn began to lighten the sky enough to show they'd left the city of Montreal behind. The dark outlines of roadside inns and the gleam of the whitewashed habitant cottages on the riverfront farms began to emerge from the gloom. Lewis's eyes eased half-open again. He suddenly sprang fully awake and shouted into the driver's ear in utilitarian French: "The sun's coming up! The sun's up and we aren't there yet!"

The driver growled over his shoulder: "So what? So we get there late and they leave without you—so what? So you don't get the chance to end up a pincushion with no hair. Or in some bear's stomach. Or your best friend's stomach come February. Oh, they say it's a grand life in the *pays d'en haut*."

In North West Company usage, *pays d'en haut* was never translated, even in conversations in English or Gaelic. The literal meaning of the words was "the high country," but the *pays d'en haut* also meant the wild country, the land where fortunes were made, and the killing grounds.

When the carriage turned south at the crossroads to Lachine, the golden halo of the sun was just poking over the trees. The wharves were a scramble of color and sound: stocky men in bright shirts and sashes hoisting bales, tall men in tailcoats and top hats flapping their arms and pointing in different directions, habitant women in red-and-yellow-striped skirts and high-crowned straw caps clustering together. Every one of them was shouting, in Canadian French and Gaelic and English and a pinch of Ojibway. The focus of the whole human swarm was the main wharf and the four craft bobbing alongside it. Each canoe was about forty feet long by six feet broad at the midthwarts. Their skins were made of irregular sheets of orange amber flecked with pale yellow, the seams outlined in gleaming black veins. The amber plates glowed in the sun, flashing in the places where the waves had splashed them slick. From their widest breadth at the waist, their bodies tapered evenly to the prow and stern, where the two sides of the hull came together in a curled white upsweep painted with blue and red and yellow and green swirls and stylized bird's heads that could easily be either Celtic or Ojibway.

The coachman pulled up his carriage load of junior clerks at the edge of the melee. Three of them leaped down, snatched up their luggage, and sprinted for the wharf. Grant hung back. The company had paid the carriage's hire, but perhaps it was customary to tip the driver. There were a few coins in his waistcoat pocket. He thumbed one out, a shilling by the feel—it seemed vulgar to look. As he extended it up to the driver, he wondered if he might get it thrown back in his face if it was too little, but he had already started the gesture.

The driver took it from his hand, grunted, and tucked it in his hatband. Perhaps it was too much. Perhaps when the coachman got back to the stable he'd buy a round for the ostlers and have a good laugh at the fresh-peeled junior clerk who got all concerned about impressing the hired help.

With his rifle case in one hand and valise in the other, Grant threaded his way to the wharf as briskly as he could without breaking into an undignified trot. He got there just in time to hear Mister Henderson, the bourgeois of the brigade, say to Lewis and the others: "Load yourselves in. One of you to each *canot de maître*, I don't care who in which, so long as you're ready to embark in two minutes."

The other three junior clerks were already bustling down the wharf. Grant followed in their wake as they dropped off and ensconced themselves in separate canoes. The only one left was at the far end of the wharf. He set his guncase and valise down on the dock and crouched down on one foot, lifting his other boot over the lip of the wharf and stretching his leg down to find a purchase on the floor of the canoe between the bobbing cargo bales. Someone grabbed a fistful of the shoulder of his coat from behind and yanked hard, sprawling him backward across the dock.

It was Mister Henderson, twisting his handful of fabric and shaking his finger in Grant's face. "Have you no goddamned brains at all? I don't have enough on my plate without some goddamned *moonias* sinking us at the wharf? Put your feet on *those*," jabbing his finger at the interior of the canoe.

Grant looked to see what "those" might be. In the spaces between paddlers and the stacks of stowed freight, the inside of the hull showed as stripped birchbark under a skeleton of cedar ribs spaced a foot or so apart. Laid on top of the ribs and underneath the cargo were four long poles that appeared to run the length of the boat. Grant said: "The poles?"

"Yes, the bloody poles, you bloody *moonias*! Unless you want to put your foot right through the bark and lose us a day patching it. You'd be bloody popular when I told the crew we'd have to shave a day off rendezvous at Fort William because of you. Wouldn't you look jolly up a tree with fifty angry voyageurs baying around the . . . Trottier! Where'd you learn to stack *pièces* like that?" He charged off.

One of the paddlers reached up to take Grant's gear, stowing it among the other four tons of cargo, all bundled into ninety-pound *pièces*. Grant stepped in gingerly and sat as comfortably as he could, leaning his back against the midthwart. He turned his head to gaze out across the river, so as not to have to catch the eye of anyone who'd witnessed his humiliation, and surreptitiously brought one hand up to fiddle his collar and neckcloth back into order. He was aware of Mister Henderson climbing down off the wharf and set-tling in beside him, but he didn't turn his head.

In each canoe, the *milieus* cocked their paddles over the gun-wales, the *gouvernail* propped his long steering paddle out against the stern, the *avant* leaned up and forward over the bow. Mister Henderson barked: "*Allons!*" The painters were cast off. The guide—the *avant* of the bourgeois's canoe—looked back over his brigade and swung his arm ahead. As the *milieus'* backs dipped forward in unison and the paddle blades dipped into the river, the *chanteur*—paid twice the *milieus'* wage for his prodigious voice and memory, sang out:

"*Au près de ma blonde . . .*"

The rest of the brigade joined in on the response line, synchro-nizing their paddle-strokes to the rhythm of the song. The singing also served to drown out the wailing of the wives and mothers and children running onto the wharf as the brigade picked up momen-tum.

"*Qu'il fait bon, fait bon, fait bon.*
"*Au près de ma blonde, qu'il fait bon dormir.*"

The brigade swung north through the Lake of Two Mountains and into the broad, black, green-lipped mouth of the Ottawa River. Ten days took them up the Ottawa and the Mattawa and across the muddy sinkholes of La Vase. The work started before dawn and ended at dusk—the voyageurs' work. It was the voyageurs who did the paddling and the voyageurs who climbed into the water to drag the canoes through stretches where the current was stronger than their paddles; at the portages, from one river to another or around cataracts, it was the voyageurs who carried the canoes and the cargo—one ninety-pound *pièce* slung onto a bent back by a tumpline around the forehead and another wedged in between the

top of the first *pièce* and the back of the neck, then a shuffling jog
trot along the portage path. They laughed and sang and made bets
on who could carry more weight farther and measured distance in
"pipes," the periodic occasions when the bourgeois allowed them
to ship their paddles long enough to recharge their tobacco censers.

The gentlemen stretched their backs against the midthwarts and
traded stories and wrote in their journals and brushed their hats and
massaged the cramps in their legs and daydreamed while they
watched the shoreline tangle of birch and pine and spruce and amber moss and mist-patinated black rock drifting by. At muddy land-
falls the voyageurs carried them ashore to keep their calfskin boots
from harm.

Here and there along the riverbank or beside the portage trails
there were white wooden crosses poking out of the bush, singly or
in clumps. Grant didn't like to draw attention to himself by asking
questions, especially of such a generous-mannered soul as Mister
Henderson, but as their canoe went past another clump of crosses
on a rocky point, he gestured toward them as diffidently as he could
manage and said: "Indians?"

The bourgeois's head came up from his penny novel. "Indians?
Where?"

"No, the crosses—are they men killed in Indian attacks?"

"Christ, now I've lost my bloody place. Voyageurs don't die of
Indian attacks, they die from drowning or strangulated hernias.
'Indian attacks'! Bloody *moonias*. Would you attack your green-
grocer's delivery boy or the water carrier? Well, out in the *pays
d'en haut*, maybe the Blackfoot and the Sioux. But you'd know
more about that than I would, wouldn't you?"

The brigade nosed in to land for another portage. While the
cargo was being unshipped and the voyageurs' backs loaded up,
Grant uncased his rifle and loaded it up with birdshot. He wanted
to get across to the other side of the portage before the invasion of
humans scared the waterfowl into hiding. It wasn't just the lure of
wood duck for dinner, he wanted to be somewhere alone and do
something autonomously, even if it was only a five-minute walk.

A couple of voyageurs got packed up and dog-trotted ahead of
him. He loped along behind them. The path was fringed with the
fraying white columns of birch trunks crowded by stubby bushes;
yellow-green leaves mingling with blue-black needles. The forest
air tasted soft and fragrant after the cold, clear river air; the forest
sounds felt muffled and soothing against his eardrums after the

harsh-edged rock-water roar. Even a black squirrel's indignant screeching was absorbed.

The path of the portage suddenly angled up along the steep crest of a ridge. The voyageurs ahead of him slowed to a grunting plod. The rest of the line caught up. With the ground falling away on both sides and the undergrowth hemming in tight, Grant was stuck in the file of beasts of burden. If the portage was long enough to warrant a rest stop at the top of the ridge, though, he would still be able to get to the next body of water ahead of them.

The grade was terraced with uneven steps, determined by the natural stair lifts of tree roots and the decades of weighted moccasin soles. The first brigade of each year flattened the green shoots into the soft brown mat of decaying leaves and needles, but each spring they came up again.

The voyageur ahead of Grant was slowing down, each step growing more ponderous, each grunt deepening. Before they set out across portages, a lot of the older voyageurs—like the one plodding in front of Grant—would unknot their prism-patterned woven sashes from around their waists and wind them tightly around groin and abdomen like a pressure dressing.

There was something familiar about the pattern on this one's sash; perhaps he was one of the *milieus* from Mister Henderson's canoe. Given that they all sported the same thick black hair and beard, and that they seemed to have been hired by body build— short legs to take up minimal space in the boats, medium height and arm length to even out the paddle strokes—about the only way to tell them apart was by sash pattern.

The ascent grew steeper, and the voyageur in front of Grant stumped even slower. There were grumblings in the line behind. Somebody growled at "Patrice" to hump it harder. A sort of fable that Grant had heard once suddenly came back to him. An old Indian and his oldest wife had been sitting in the sun watching a colony of ants lugging grubs and seedpods over a hummock from one nest to another. Suddenly the ants and the burdens and the hummock began to grow. They grew and grew until the old Indian and his wife found they were watching a line of white men bent under *pièces* of trade goods and furs and oversized canoes.

The curious thing was that Grant couldn't for the life of him come up with anyone in his past who might have told him such a story, and he was quite sure it wasn't a product of his own imagination. He was absorbed in puzzling that out when he was suddenly brought back to the present by a scream of pain.

The voyageur ahead of him jackknifed and fell backward. Grant
looked up out of his reverie to see four hundred pounds of packs
and human pack mule descending on him.

His arms acted on their own, throwing up the rifle with one hand
braced on the stock and the other on the barrel. The weight had
only just teetered back past the balance point; if it had had any
momentum, he couldn't have hoped to affect it. As the back of the
lower *pièce* hit his rifle, he angled it sideways and pushed off. There
was an instant when he thought that his elbows and shoulders and
wrists were going to snap like the joints of a dead branch; then the
pièces and the man strapped to them crashed away through the
undergrowth on the side of the ridge.

Grant's eyes caught a single frame of distorted features between
the black thickets of hair and beard. Then there was only a pinwheeling, bouncing bundle of arms and legs and the willow shoots
snapping back up into place behind it. From far below there was a
dull thump, and the screams stopped.

He propped his rifle against a tree and scrambled down the ridge,
digging the sides of his boots into the soft loam, clutching at branch
ends and projecting roots to keep his balance. The voyageur had
fetched up against a dead tree at the base of the slope. He was bent
around it like a feather bolster flung down across a bedstead. The
air reeked of rum; one of the *pièces* must have had a keg in it that
had burst with the impact. The point of a shilling-the-dozen trade
knife had punched its way out through the canvas.

Grant moved closer, the boggy ground sucking at his boots. The
face had a blue-red tinge to it. It had never occurred to him that
eyeballs were that large; he would've thought that once they were
bugged out that big they would pop out. Between grimacing, thick-
furred lips, the yellow teeth stuck out like a dead rat's.

He had a notion that he could find out whether there was still
any life by putting his fingers against the throat to feel for a pulse,
but he couldn't bring himself to do it. He wondered if his father
had looked like that at the end, and his mother, and whether he
would have felt the same revulsion at the thought of touching them.

There was a sound of thicket-crashing from up the slope and a
pattering of pebbles and pellets of earth. The rest of the train of
voyageurs had unloaded their burdens and started down the ridge
face after him. One of them pushed past him and crouched beside
the body bent around the tree. After a moment he called over his
shoulder to the others: *"Il est mort."*

There was a guttural murmuring among the crowd of voyageurs

standing behind Grant. Two words were repeated: "Patrice" and "*la hernie.*" Mister Henderson puffed his way down the slope, looked things over, and detailed some men to dig a hole and some to take apart the *pièces* and repack what goods were salvageable.

It seemed to Grant that the pack of bearded men standing behind him and the group busying themselves over the body, even the trio scrambling back up the slope to fetch the shovels, were slipping surreptitious glances at him. He wanted one of them to accuse him so that he could point out that if Patrice hadn't been killed by the fall, he would have lingered for hours in the agony of the burst hernia. He wanted them to consider that if he hadn't pushed Patrice over the drop, the whole line of them would have gone down like dominoes, each with a hundred and eighty pounds of freight strapped to his back. But he knew that at the instant he'd seen Patrice fall back at him and had thrown his rifle up, the only bones he'd been thinking of were his own. From the hard glint of their glances, they knew it as well.

CHAPTER 3

Above Ben Dubhain the morning star stood out alone. The outlines of three long black stone cottages huddled near Kildonan Burn began to separate themselves from the black ground of fields radiating behind them. One of the hut doors jounced open, and a tall woman with a smoke-grimed plaid wrapped around her body stooped out into the morning.

Kate MacPherson set off for the burn lugging a rope-handled oak-stave bucket that John had been supposed to fill the night before. The bracken brushed her legs with dew. This had been the first year since she could toddle that she hadn't taken part with the other girls in the Beltane ritual of washing her face with dew. She had decided that it was high time she acknowledged that she'd crossed the line between single girl and spinster.

This was also the first year since she was twelve that she hadn't gone up to spend her summer in the shieling. John had stayed behind as well, to help their father with the peat cutting. There was a niggling twinge at the back of her mind—it was somehow important that Beltane was long past.

Her half-awake ruminations and her zigzag progress to the burn were suddenly broken off by the sound of an unearthly shrieking coming toward her. The light had grown just strong enough to show mare's tails of morning mist hovering over the bracken and furze. Streaking through them in long bounds was a leftover patch of midnight—her cat. A gray streak was slashing at his tail. No matter how often they interbred with domestic strays, the wild cats of the Highlands always came out brindled gray.

MacCrimmon squealed around her legs like a racehorse rounding the turning pole and kept on going toward the cottage. She swung her bucket at the gray thing chasing him. It twisted out of the way in midleap and came down in front of her. She could hear it spitting and hissing, but the light was still too dim to make out anything except a gray blot.

She pushed the bucket at it like a shield. "Shoo. Get away with you." The spitting and growling were suddenly cut off as it turned away from her and flounced off through the ferns. She looked back toward the cottage, just in time to see the black streak of Mac-Crimmon scooting through the door she'd left ajar. He would find himself an unobtrusive place to hide; he'd become adept at it on snowy nights when she had smuggled him inside. His color helped.

Quite awake now, she climbed down to the burn, the callus-padded soles of her feet gripping the fissures on the slick shore rocks. The rattling stream threw up a fine spray to join with the mist. She crouched forward and splashed the bucket into the water. Suddenly she remembered what was significant about the number of weeks that had passed since Beltane. It meant that Whitsuntide had also passed—the date that had been on the eviction notices. So her father had been right: the eviction notices had never meant anything, and the long run from the soldiers had been for nothing.

She hauled the bucket out full and dripping and stood with the heather-rope handle clasped in both hands, the weight of the water dragging down pleasantly on shoulders made for stooking barley and wearing yokes. Ducks hidden in the mist quacked softly. There was the splash of a salmon or an otter. The first stirrings of the morning breeze fluttered the dense wool of the plaid against her thighs and whipped a swatch of hair into the corner of her mouth. She spat it out.

There was someone on the other side of the burn. In the half light it was difficult to make out details, but it appeared to be an old woman hunched over a washing tub, gray and indistinct through the drifting shrouds of mist. Kate told herself that it was only a trick of the dawn twilight. There was no habitation on the other side of the burn. And even if there had been, no one came out to do their washing by starlight. She told herself that she was still half dreaming after all. But all the same, the hairs on the backs of her hands and forearms were standing up and dancing.

Of all the creatures out of the old tales—the water horses and faerie warriors and rock-fisted mountain ghosts—the most horrible to encounter was the frail old woman called the fairy washer-woman. She would be seen on the day of a battle scrubbing the blood from a shirt, and wife or mother or sweetheart or sister would recognize it as one she had sewn with her own hands.

Kate had no patience for those kinds of stories. But there was something on the other side of the burn, the bony hands slapping and scrubbing a lump of wet cloth on a rock. The cloth was dark, though, not white shirt linen. It appeared to be a length of plaid— the night-blue, pine-green pattern with red-and-white crosshatch-ing that was the favorite of Clan Sutherland.

There was a harsh-edged drumming sound coming from the direction of the Ulidh. Kate turned her head to look. A line of haloed spheres of light was moving through the air. The sun poked over the hills, showing her a row of horsemen carrying torches, riding in single file. Their shod hooves clattered sparks from the shore rocks and drummed over beds of moss.

She turned back to look across the burn. There was nothing there but a juniper bush with a few dead branches. The horsemen plunged past between her and the cottage and swerved inland from the burn.

She climbed up the peat bank and hurried back as fast as she could without spilling the bucket. Her father was outside the door, buttoning his trousers and blinking, his bonnet clapped on crook-edly over his patchy black hair. In front of him was a line of tall horses ranked stirrup to stirrup. On their backs were the same sheriff's officers and bailiffs who had cordoned off the innyard at Golspie. At the midpoint of the line were the Reverend Mister James Ross and Patrick Sellar, the Countess of Sutherland's fox-faced factor.

Kate's mother came out herding John, still rubbing sleep from his eyes with the back of one gangly wrist, and dragging along little Betsy. Mister MacBeth and Mister Sutherland emerged from their own doors with the remnants of their families who weren't up at the shielings.

The Reverend Mister Ross said in an anguished voice: "Why are you still here?"

Kate's father blinked at him and mumbled: "Where else would we be?"

The Reverend Mister Ross turned his startled-doe's eyes on her. She became aware that there was nothing covering her body but a loose-draped length of plaid. The Reverend Mister Ross said, "Did you not read the paper?"

She set down her bucket to free both hands for clutching the plaid around her more securely. "Which paper?"

"*That* paper." One hand stabbed distractedly at the bit of rain-lashed gray pulp still plastered to the doorpost.

"Of course I read the paper. That is why we marched down to Dunrobin. But Whitsuntide is passed now."

"And so is the time when you should have been gone from here!" He got hold of himself and settled back down onto the saddle. "The Countess has new crofts for you, along the seashore at Helmsdale. She is building a herring fishery. . . ."

Mister MacBeth growled: "We live here."

Kate's mother said: "We know nothing of the sea. My husband has never set foot in a boat in his life except the little curraghs on the Ulidh."

Kate said: "Why should we leave?"

The Reverend Mister Ross opened his mouth and closed it a few times, then got out: "It is the law!" But nothing more would come. It didn't appear to be helping him that Mister Sellar's cold, colorless eyes were fastened on him with a detached amusement.

Patrick Sellar didn't need to know the language to see that things weren't going quite the way the Reverend Mister Ross might have represented them. He said in English: "Tell them they are tres-passing."

Kate shouted in English: "We are not trespassing!" She struggled to find more English words, but the only ones that would come were "*You* are trespassing!"

Mister Sellar turned a look on her that he might have turned on a parrot that suddenly squawked out his name. Kate's father asked her what the sassenach had said. When she'd told him he puffed up red and bellowed at Sellar in Gaelic: "This strath belongs to Clan Sutherland, damn you! My great-granny nursed my grandda and the Chief's son side by side! Since the time of Robert Bruce we have—"

Patrick Sellar merely tugged a gold half-hunter out of his pocket, snapped it open, and glanced at the face, and Donald MacPherson's belligerence collapsed suddenly. Sellar said: "Tell them they have one minute to clear out their belongings." One of the bailiffs raised his torch higher and nudged his horse forward. Sellar barked, "Wait!" but kept his eyes on the face of his watch.

Mister Ross leaned forward toward his parishioners. "Please. You must take your things out of the house if you wish to save anything. You must respect the law. This is all for your own best sakes. Would I have come here with them if it was not?"

Kate's mother suddenly turned and ran into the cottage. Kate followed after her. Her mother had yanked down the wickerwork creel for hauling peat and was frantically scooping things into it— the fish pot, the crusty remnants of their last cheese making, the puckered leather purse her father kept hidden in a cranny by the hearth . . .

She came up behind her mother and laid her hands gently on her shoulders. "Do not let them fret you so easy, Mother, they can-not—"

Her mother turned on her, showing her teeth. "Are you walking in your sleep, girl, or just bone stupid? They can do anything they want with the likes of us. Get in and dress yourself and gather up what you can. Go!"

Kate ran into the sleeping room and fumbled in the gloom for her everyday skirt hanging on a peg beside her bed. She was just pulling her blouse on over it when she heard her mother yelling in the other room—at John by the tone: "Scoop the grain out of the bins. No, all in one sack, it does not matter. Hurry!"

Kate snatched up every article of cloth within reach—John's plaid, their father's Sunday trousers, their mother's shawl . . . Her mother would want her to save the remarkable porcelain chamberpot that her father had brought from the cattle fair at Inverness. She fished for it in the nook under their bed. Her hand bumped against it. It was still full and warm.

She was trying to decide whether to pull it out and empty it out the window or leave it where it was, when something soft brushed against the back of her hand. MacCrimmon. She groped for him, and he moved away. She reached in farther. He yowled and swiped his claws across the back of her hand.

It didn't hurt. She was aware that there was pain in her hand, just as she was aware of the panic and the shouting in the other room, but none of it touched her. She was observing from some walled-in, misty reverie. She pulled her hand back out from under the bed and looked at the blood-seeping scratches. MacCrimmon would find his own way out.

There was a sharp, acrid taste at the back of her mouth and a hissing sound overhead. They had set the thatch on fire. She ran out of the sleeping room, the soles of her feet slapping on the clay floor. Her mother was in a corner away from the door, struggling to dismantle the spinning wheel, oblivious to the smoke billowing downward. Kate got one hand free from her armfuls of clothing and tugged at her mother's elbow. "Leave that!"

Her mother shook off her hand. "My granddad made this for my gran. My mother watched her tug it out of their burning cottage when the Campbells and the English soldiers came after Culloden. Get out, I will not be far behind you. Drag the pot with you."

The big iron pot had been swung down from its hook over the hearth and sat just inside the threshold, filled with kitchen implements and tools and the family Bible. Kate hooked her elbow through the handle and dragged it outside. There was a bailiff standing on the wanderer's stone beside the doorway, working his torch up into the thatch.

John came and helped her drag the pot over to the peat creel and the half-filled sack beside it. Mister MacBeth and Mister Sutherland were chasing the plough ponies out of the burning byre. The MacBeths' cottage was in full flame, Mrs. MacBeth squalling by the stack of furniture. John took up a position by their father, waiting for him to do something, but Donald MacPherson stood with his arms hanging slack and his mouth open, staring at the ground. The Reverend Mister Ross had turned his horse and was watching the sun crawl higher over the shoulder of Ben Dubhain.

The flames had begun to eat their way into the layer of divots below the thatch. One of the stone weights that held the thatch in place fell to the ground. Kate shrieked, "Mother!" and started for the door. John caught her and held her back, both of them shrieking for their mother. She didn't come out.

Kate took a step back, and he let her go. She snatched up the bucket of water she'd brought from the burn and ran to the front of the house. She swung the bucket back and hurled the water up onto the roof. One small patch of flame sputtered momentarily and then flared up stronger than before, spewing up jets of steam to join with the smoke. A few of the horsemen laughed.

The whole slope of the thatch was a mass of flame now. The roof tree groaned and shuddered, and the whole mass sagged inward. Kate's mother came out of the doorway clutching the pieces of her spinning wheel wrapped in the tablecloth. A black streak shot out past her ankles, its yellow eyes as big as cartwheels and every hair on its body standing on end. The roof tree gave way, and the roof collapsed inward, fluming up clouds of black smoke and flying embers.

Kate made a grab for MacCrimmon. He slipped past her and bounded away between the legs of the horses. Patrick Sellar leaned down from his saddle and scooped him up. As he swung himself back into the saddle his right arm kept going, lofting MacCrimmon in a high arc over the front wall of the cottage into the flames.

MacCrimmon seemed to drift down slowly, screaming and gyrating and trying to run on the air until he disappeared.

Kate ran at Patrick Sellar, swinging the bucket over her head by its rope handle. One of the bailiffs drew a horse pistol from the scabbard on his saddle. As she ran past he leaned forward and swung out his arm. With no discernible malice, in the same manner that Patrick Sellar had thrown the cat, he laid the foot-long steel barrel into the point where the hinge of her jaw met the earlobe.

Chapter 4

Above Ben Dubhain, Mars was standing sentry-go for the evening star. On the eastern shoulder a spare man in a faded red tunic and dark regimental kilt was struggling upward through the heather, his right knee showing a marked reluctance to bend resiliently. Although his lips were clamped together in a thin line, in his mind he was carrying on a very lively conversation.

If he didn't catch sight of a certain one-sided pine tree, he thought, before he lost what little light was left, he would have no choice but to hunker down among the rocks and gorse bushes and wait for morning. Well, not exactly no choice—he had the option of blundering ahead blindly up into the crags and breaking his neck.

The little pine tree he was looking for was lopsided because it stood at the mouth of a rift where the winds roared up and down. He had seen the tree a hundred times in the days before he'd marched off for a soldier. Trees could change in ten years.

Even the gully might have changed. Once it had cut through the arm of the hill and come out at Glen Loth near the point where the glen opened into the valley of the Ulidh. He'd gone back and forth through it often in his youth, helping his uncle Robert convey the liquid fruits of his science and art to the back door of the inn at Golspie. Uncle Robert had been strangely reluctant to move the ponies along the King's Highway.

The shortcut through the hills would put him at his parents' door a day earlier than following the curve of the coast road. It would also save him the price of a night at the inn. He was forced to admit that there might be a small grain of truth in the character that his messmates had given him—that of a parsimonious bastard who would rather night march ten miles over broken country than spend a shilling on a warm bed and a cold supper. Not that he couldn't have found a corner by the fire at any crofter's door along the way, but Private Alexander Sutherland of the Forty-second Highlanders liked to keep to himself. Ex-private, he reminded himself, dragging his steadily stiffening right knee up another step.

His ruminations were suddenly interrupted by signals from the lower half of his body that he had just walked into a gorse bush. He skipped backward in a highly unsoldierly fashion, picking out the prickles that had managed to bury their heads in his thighs even through the thick wool folds of his kilt.

When his attention returned to the wider world, he saw, off to his right, half a pine tree with its bald side facing toward a gully in the hillside. Not that he'd doubted for a moment that he'd find it. Now just a quick jaunt down the familiar path, a midnight knock on the door, and the return of the prodigal—with all thirty of the gold guineas inside his shirt still intact.

The gully quickly narrowed and deepened into a rift. He reassured himself, as the walls inched in closer, that it would never get narrower than the width of a pony with a keg slung on either side. The crack of sky above him was black and starry, although, strangely, there still appeared to be a few ripples of red in the clouds that drifted across the stars. He would have thought the sun was long down.

The evening wind came scouring fiercely up the gully from the strath. There was a strange taste in it, smoky and sharp. It would be just his luck to be coming down the gully on a night when the revenue officers had built a bonfire at the other end to smoke out smugglers. He came out into the open and stopped dead in midstep.

The valley was burning. From one end to the other every cottage, every rick, every cow byre, was in flames or reduced to a bed of coals. He had seen valleys full of farms in flames before, in Spain. But those had been foreign homes.

He stumbled on blindly down the slope, his night sight burned out by the fires. He skirted past a dozen burning cottages. There were no squads of crofters trying to damp the flames, no wandering cattle; the only living things he saw were the fires.

He came out by Craggie Water next to the ash grove where he and Lizzie Gunn used to meet by moonlight. The cottage on the other shore sent bright red-and-gold ribbons across the choppy black surface of the water. There was a path through the trees that he didn't need to see; he'd walked or toddled or run down it every day of his life until he'd gone to be a soldier. At the end of the path was the place he'd pictured a thousand times in the last ten years, the place he would return to if he came out of the army alive, the place he remembered every time he scrawled laboriously across an envelope with half his pay inside: "Mister Alex. Sutherland, by Craggie Water, Parish of Kildonan, County Sutherland, Scotland."

The front of the cottage had fallen in. The other three walls were now the facings for a blast furnace. He moved in as close as he could, the heat searing his face. The layers of turf between the layers of still standing stones glowed with a slow-burning fire.

There was only one possible explanation: the French. For fifteen years now there had been sentinels and gun emplacements and beacons along the southeast coast of England, watching for the French to invade across the Channel. It would be perfect Bonaparte sleight of hand to land in Scotland and come down from the north.

Around the bivouac fires in the peninsular campaign, Private Alexander Sutherland had shaken his head uncomprehendingly at the stories of what the Spaniards did to French stragglers. Suddenly the stories seemed to make sense.

There was a noise in the bracken behind him. He dropped to the ground and scrabbled a few yards off to one side. A human figure, silhouetted against the glow of the fire, came to the place where he'd been standing and looked from side to side. He reached up under the back of his tunic, drew out the little flat-pommeled kidney knife, and pulled himself forward with his elbows through the drooping fronds of fern.

The figure turned toward him. Ex-Private Sutherland sprang forward, hitting it gut high with his shoulder and coming down on top of it. He jerked the head back by its long hair and brought the knife in toward the throat, the blade flashing in the firelight.

A long squeal came out in Gaelic: "I have no money—do not murder me, for the love of God!"

He just managed to stop the knife. Climbing to his feet, he yanked the Gaelic-speaking creature upright and turned its face toward the light. It was an old man with terror-stricken watery-blue eyes.

"Have you no sense at all, sneaking up behind people in the dark?"

"I meant no harm, Sergeant—merely a poor starving old man hoping for some scraps that might have been left behind, a few crumbs of bannock, a bit of oatmeal . . ."

"Looting."

"No, sir, Captain, Your Honor—only an old man burnt off his croft like all the others."

"Stop calling me those names, I am not an officer."

"Of course not, no, I can see that now—just a plain Highland soldier laddie who would never cut an old man that never did no harm to him."

There was something familiar about the old man. Subtracting ten hard years from those scraggle-boned features . . . "Donald Gunn."

Donald Gunn tried to draw his head in like a turtle. His hand slipped surreptitiously into the horned sign against the evil eye.

"You have nothing to fear from me, Mister Gunn. I am only Sandy Sutherland, that you used to sit on your knee and tell ghost stories to."

"Sandy Sutherland?"

"Alex Sutherland's son."

"Alex Sutherland . . . ?" Mister Gunn wormed his eyebrows together. "Red Alex Sutherland or Alex Sutherland of Learable Hill?"

"*This* Alex Sutherland," jabbing his finger at the flames. "Three-Fingered Alex Sutherland, that lived in this house before the French burned him out."

"French? What French?"

"The French invasion."

"A French invasion? As if our troubles were not miserable enough . . . Wait—not young Sandy that used to play the fiddle, that went off to fight the French?"

"The same."

Mister Gunn grabbed Sandy's right hand in both of his. "And here you are home with all your arms and legs, thank God. Though what a homecoming for you."

"Do you know where my parents are—and my brothers and sisters? Are they safe?"

"I should expect they have all gone down to DunUlidh with the rest. Safe? Ah, Sandy, that I should be the one to tell you . . . Your mother, she tried to stop them, and they beat her with their clubs. Your father did his best to hold her back. . . ."

"Hold *her* back?"

"Do not think ill of your father, lad. There were so many of them . . . and they bashed him something cruel as he was pulling her away. Your brothers had to carry him."

It took Sandy a moment before he could speak again. "Do they mean to hold the French at DunUlidh, then? I have heard no gunfire."

"I cannot say. I have not seen the French."

"Where were you when they burned your home?"

"Standing in my potato field watching them. If the curse I put on them has any—"

"Then you have seen the French."

"I told you: *I . . . have . . . seen . . . no . . . French.*"

"It was the French soldiers who burned you out."

"Who told you that?"

"No one. I worked it out for myself."

"If that is an example of your brainpower, no wonder you never became an officer. *Ban mhorhair Chataibh* burned our homes."

"Ban mhorhair?"

The old man nodded. It occurred to Sandy that Mister Gunn might not be quite right in the head. "Why would she burn off her own clan?" he asked.

"She has found herself a new clan—a better clan. They toil not, nor do they reap, but they grow their rent money straight out of the skin of their backs. Baa-ks." He took hold of the cuff of Sandy's uniform tunic. "Come with me. They did not burn the mill. There are pockets of flour in the cracks of the floor. When that is eaten we can learn to practice cannibalism on our new clan brothers and their wives."

It was Sandy's turn to edge away, subtly working his sleeve out of the old man's grasp. "I have to find my family."

"Go along, then. You are young, you still think that you have a life ahead of you. You will learn in time that it was taken from you before ever you were born.'' But it was the old man who left, slipping away from the fire glow and disappearing into the night. He called once out of the dark: "Sandy!"

Sandy turned in the direction of the voice.

"Welcome home."

There was nothing he could do until daylight. He found a rock to put his back against and settled down in the warmth from the fire.

The flames died, but the embers would last through the night and more—searing yellow whites and delicate ghost shades of red and orange and wine blue. He felt like a tree that had grown up bowed around a boulder and suddenly found the boulder rolled away.

With the light of the sun breaking over Ben Dubhain, Sandy realized that his joints were aching and his belly was sore. Two fragile red deer, nosing stealthily into enemy territory, broke and ran when he creaked slowly to his feet. He watched them bound into the hills. They would be back. By the end of the summer, when the new grass had grown tall enough in the ash beds to hide the tumbled stones, the deer and the foxes and the conies would be no more wary of this place than they were in the high corries.

He set off at a brisk, mechanical pace to march himself awake. He waded across Craggie Water and headed north, away from DunUlidh and the sea. He passed through the flat meadow where the Kildonan boys used to start off their New Year's shinty game against the boys from the next parish.

At the north end of the meadow was the kirk. The Reverend Mister James Ross was standing in the steeple shadow, watching a gang of men break down the low stone wall that marked the eastern boundary of the land that the Countess's great-great-grandfather had granted to the kirk. The workmen spoke to each other in English and guttural Lowland Scots.

"Mister Ross, sir, it is me, Sandy Sutherland—Alex Sutherland's eldest . . ."

"Of course, yes, good day to you, Sandy. Are you done with soldiering, then?"

"Or soldiering is done with me. What has happened here, sir—all the houses burning and everyone fled . . . ?"

"I tried to tell them, Sandy, you must believe me. I did my best, but they would not listen until their homes were burnt around their ears."

"Who did this?"

"The Countess's agents, and the officers of the law. There was no other way to make them leave."

"Why . . . why should they leave? They live here. . . ."

"*Lived,* Sandy. They were the Countess's tenants. The Countess decided the land would be more productive given over to the raising of sheep."

"Productive?"

"The strath is hers by right."

"It is *Clan Sutherland's* by right!" The Reverend Mister Ross's face assumed a soft, disappointed head-pat of a smile. "Forgive me, sir, I forget myself. . . ." Sandy looked over at the laborers working their crowbars in between the stones. "I suppose you have troubles of your own as well, sir. Where will you go?"

"Go? I will stay here. The men who come to tend the flocks will need a shepherd of their own."

"But after they pull down the kirk . . ."

"Pull down the kirk? Pull down the kirk? Who said they were going to pull down the kirk? Who told you that?"

"They are already starting on the wall of the yard."

"Oh!" The Reverend Mister Ross laughed, then exhaled and put his hand on his heart and laughed again. "Oh, Sandy, you did give me a turn. Not that I mistrust Mister Sellar's word, of course, but . . . No, they are only pulling down the wall to put it up again, farther to the east. The Countess kindly decided that the field next door, that was Colin Sutherland's, should be added to the kirk-yard."

There was a buzzing in Sandy's ears and something pressing against the bridge of his nose. He rubbed his fingertips between his eyebrows. "That was Colin Sutherland's?"

"Yes. Black-haired Colin Sutherland, who married Moira Sutherland from up the loch. I will need to put in a vegetable garden of my own now, and—"

Sandy's right arm swung up and out. The Reverend Mister James Ross was suddenly sitting on the ground with a drop of blood showing at the corner of his mouth and another seeping out of one nostril. His strayed lamb was standing above him, rubbing back and forth the stinging knuckles of his right hand.

The workmen started toward them with a kind of hesitant outrage, and Sandy backed away. A couple of the workmen knelt down beside the Reverend Mister Ross. The others advanced on Sandy cautiously—anyone who would strike a man of the cloth was liable to do anything. Sandy's heel caught against an alder root. He stumbled, righted himself, and set off at the best approximation of a run the Frenchman's bayonet had left him—an irregular, chest-pounding hop, with his left leg springing and his right leg thumping down like a lump of wood.

CHAPTER 5

Grant was crouched on a pebbled beach on the north shore of Lake Superior, shaving his face by the light of the setting sun. He never had time to attend to it in the morning, given that the brigade's routine was to roll up the tents and launch the canoes at sunrise, stopping for breakfast once the voyageurs had had a couple of hours to paddle up an appetite. It wasn't exactly a hedgehog growth that he had to contend with, but its very sparseness made him more fastidious. He dipped the razor in the lake and swirled off the lather. Remarkable that anything with such a pretty tinge of turquoise could be so cold.

He cocked his polished-steel traveling mirror to one side so he could see back over his shoulder. The canoes were laid out slantwise on the shore. The *avants* and *gouvernails* were going over the hulls as they did every night, applying a patch here and there with the spare rolls of bark and coils of white pine root, sealing them over with spruce gum. The *milieus* were smoking their pipes and drinking their tea and waiting for the cook to ready the *galettes* and the invariable soup of pork fat and dried peas or corn. With thousands of miles of wilderness to cover between thaw and freeze-up, the North West Fur Trading Company's brigades didn't lay over for hunting expeditions.

The eyes that had looked at Grant over Patrice's body were still watching his back. He shifted the mirror back to catch his own reflection. The razor scraped and scratched and dragged across the last stretch of lathered skin. He still hadn't gotten the knack of stropping the blade properly. Perhaps it was one of those skills that only came with time. Or perhaps it was the cold water that made the blade grate across his neck like a rusty rake.

The face in the mirror was too pretty, he thought. But when he came back from his seven years' apprenticeship in the *pays d'en haut*, it would be weathered and strong, perhaps with a scar over one eye. . . .

He packed away his shaving gear, splashed the lather ridges off his face, and wiped himself clean with his linen handkerchief. He stood up to survey the lake, the layers of rounded pebbles crunching pleasantly under his boot soles. They would have called it an inland sea on any continent of civilized proportions. The setting sun was hanging out soft banners of peach and muted orange, turning the water into lavender silk, with a few black, pine-spiked granite islands for contrast. It was difficult to believe that this inviting, placid sheet of pastel water could whip into a slate-gray, killing rage as suddenly as it had that morning.

He walked back up to his tent, tossed his shaving kit into his valise, and uncased his rifle. He loaded it up with birdshot, as he had at every camping place where they'd landed before full dark and at every long portage. And every time but two, when they were climbing back into the canoes again, he would fire the load off into the air. The two exceptions had been a large rodent that had proved to be inedible and a brace of Canada geese.

As he tramped off, Mister Henderson called after him: "If you get yourself lost, don't expect us to come looking."

Grant waved his hand over his shoulder. He wanted to say, "You tucked into the geese quick enough," but he didn't.

He found a gap in the tangled wall of bush and threaded his way along the patches of open ground between the tamaracks and ground-hugging dwarf cedars. At first there was sand underfoot, then matted rotting needles and crumbling deadfalls. There was a rise of moss-covered boulders that he clambered over. He came down into a miniature canyon.

The floor of the sheltered bowl was covered with a curious growth, a kind of soft-bodied coral, except that the colors were lunar green and a pallid blue gray. In places there were cylinder and cone shapes rising out of the undulating carpet. The air was still, although the trees around the rim rustled in the evening breeze off the lake.

His boots sank in up to the ankles. With each step there was a sensation of a thin base underneath that, if it gave way, would sink his leg down into squirming, shapeless things that were never meant to see the light of day. A breath of wind managed to sneak down over the walls.

Suddenly he stopped and raised his head. He wasn't quite sure at first what his body had reacted to. The air had carried in a smell of something balsamy, with a taste of green wood in it and a wild spice. He found it curious that a smell could be both feral and sweet . . . even more curious that it should freeze him in his tracks and that the skin under his armpits should have started to crawl.

He turned his head into the breeze, toward the open end of the cul-de-sac off to his right. There was a stand of green trees, with smooth greenish bark that had the furrowed black ridges of the paper birch but not the fraying.

As soon as he'd stopped moving, the mosquitoes had begun to rise. They settled onto his neck and ears, around his eyes, along his wrists where they projected past his coatsleeves. Those that came too late for prime real estate made do with drilling through the fabric of his trousers. He brushed at them absentmindedly, then slapped at them as they settled thicker, then bestirred himself to walk again. But once he'd stopped long enough for the first platoon to settle, the damage had been done. The palms of his hands were slick with smashed corpses and his own stolen blood, but they kept on coming. He headed back the way he'd come with a purposeful stride, quite aware what a ludicrous figure he'd cut breaking into a run to escape a few bothersome insects. He did run, though— scrambling over the rocks and swatting his way through the bush in a breakneck charge for the beach, where the breeze from the lake would drive them off.

As he burst back out into the open he dug his heels in and braked hard, slowing to what he hoped was a dignified saunter. But the men on the beach were all looking out toward the mouth of the bay, some of them pointing, and not even his crashing turned their heads.

The water had gone red and black now, flickering as highlight and shadow traded places with each ripple of the waves. There was one shadow that stayed constant—the silhouette of an express canoe. It was very different from the *canots de maître* that made up the brigade—shorter by a third and narrower by half. Over the past month Grant had developed a certain fraternal pride about their *canots de maître*—surprisingly agile and fragile considering the weight they carried—but this one transformed them into fat scows. The canoe turned toward them, skimming over the waves they'd lumbered through, the portside paddles glinting in the sun.

The crew of Mister Henderson's brigade hurried down in a body to the shoreline. Grant hung back. Given the rake in the beach, he could see more from twenty yards behind the crowd than he would from the midst of it.

As the express canoe shot into the shallows, its paddles were shipped in perfect unison. Two of the *milieus* on either side leaped out into the water and made chairs of their arms for the two top-hatted gentry at the midthwarts. The clerk in Grant noted that by rights the gentlemen ought to weigh two tons apiece, given that it was costing the company as much to transport them to Fort William as the entire cargo of one of Mister Henderson's *canots de maître*— probably more.

Even in the hazy light of the dying sun there was no mistaking one of the gentlemen passengers: six feet tall, coppery Byronic ringlets and side whiskers curling out beyond his hat brim, and a chin and chest like the prow of an eighty-gun ship of the line. The emperor of the Northwest: Chief Superintendent MacGillivray.

Although on paper the North West Fur Trading Company was a loose consortium of a number of autonomous firms, in practice the separate companies only entered into things when it came to div-vying up the astronomical profits. Ever since old Simon MacTavish died, the kingpin had been Mister William MacGillivray—which made him one of the half-dozen most powerful individuals on the North American continent. John Jacob Astor wasn't even in the running.

After a bit of jawing on the lakeshore, the crowd split off in two directions—Mister Henderson's brigade returning to camp and the newcomers moving down the beach to set up their own camp. The upshot that drifted back to Grant was that Mister MacGillivray had invited the gentlemen of Mister Henderson's brigade to join him for dinner, and that the voyageurs would be issued a regale of rum from Mister MacGillivray's stores. Mister Henderson was utterly ossified by the question of what treat in his own private stores might be a worthy contribution to the occasion.

Grant removed the load from his rifle rather than attracting at-tention to himself by firing it off, poured the birdshot back into his shot pouch, and laid them both to bed in the lovely hand-crafted case that Messrs. Tatham & Egg of London supplied with their .54 caliber sporting guns. He dug out his shaving mirror again and a clean white neckcloth, which he tied as artfully as he could in the dying light. By the time Mister Henderson had decided on his lone still-sealed bottle of illicit French brandy, the voyageurs were all drinking their toasts to Mister MacGillivray, and it was time to fall in with the parade down to the far end of the beach.

There were two fires there, a subtly flamed bed of coals that Mister MacGillivray's cook was fussing over and a high, crackling auto-da-fé affair shooting thumb-sized sparks toward the stars. Mister Henderson steered for the second fire. The two express canoe gentry stood up in its light. Mister Henderson presented his gold-leafed, dusty bottle to Mister MacGillivray with a smug flourish.

Mister MacGillivray raised one eyebrow and said abstractedly: "Hm? Ah, I see. . . . Thank you, Henderson.

"Cuthbert! There you are, lad! Good to see you! I was certain you were with this brigade, but I didn't see you in the mob at the shore."

Grant tried to keep his grin self-deprecatory, hunching his shoulders under the onslaught of the handshaking and back thumping. "Considering the crush on the shore, sir," he said, "and the fact that you must have been traveling since dawn, I thought it best I wait a little before paying my respects."

The great man's traveling companion stepped forward. He was nearly as tall as the chief superintendent, but not as broad, and his curls were grizzled yellow gold instead of grizzling copper. "Hello, Cuthbert, do you remember me?"

"With perfect clarity, Mister McKenzie. You did me the honor of standing in at my christening, along with Mister MacGillivray." William MacGillivray was the executor of Cuthbert Grant Senior's estate, and his brother had brought the orphaned Grant down from the *pays d'en haut* to Montreal twelve years before.

"What a remarkable memory," said Mister McKenzie. "I can't say I remember the vaguest impression of my christening—though you weren't exactly an infant at yours, were you?" He suddenly jogged Mister MacGillivray in the ribs. "I suppose we'd best not arouse speculation as to which of us was standing in for which parent."

Grant wondered for an instant if that was meant as some sort of slur on his parents but decided not. Roderick McKenzie had the reputation of being the best-hearted man in the fur trade, not to mention the best read, which was a good deal easier to accomplish.

Grant wasn't unaware that Mister Henderson was chewing pieces out of his tongue at the treatment the senior partners were giving his favorite pissing pole among the junior clerks. Between that and the jellied mutton and the fresh perch and the boiled potatoes and the onion soup and the cheeses and the shortbread and the tea and the claret, he began to feel that he might learn to resign himself to his remaining two score and ten within this vale of tears.

"I had forgotten," said Mister MacGillivray, a hush descending immediately, "how tasty good plain fare can be after a day out on the lake in a canoe. The galley on the *Nancy* spoiled me rotten."

"If it's any consolation to you," Mister McKenzie said, "you can be certain old Paquin isn't pampering the gentlemen of the Royal Navy as he did you."

One of the other junior clerks asked how the war was going. The chief superintendent said: "Good and bad. I shall treasure all my days the expression on the American commander's face at Michilimackinac when we knocked on his front gate, showed him our cannons, and informed him that his government had declared war on us. And would he please be so good as to surrender before we blew his fort to hell."

Mister McKenzie raised his long-stemmed wineglass and said: "Here's to J. J. Astor."

"Just so." Mister MacGillivray did the same, and they both drank. "The American Fur Company, you see," he explained to the mystified clerks, "had a certain amount of goods stored with us. So before the ink was dry on his government's declaration of war, certainly long before the American war office got around to composing its despatches, Mister Astor had informed us. Business is business."

"And war"—Mister McKenzie smiled—"is war."

"Just so." Mister MacGillivray nodded gravely.

One of the senior clerks said: "It can't last long now. When they invaded they were only facing volunteers and garrison troops. Wait till the Yankees find themselves face to face with the British grenadiers."

"It might have slipped your mind," Grant said, "but the British grenadiers are a mite preoccupied in Europe with Bonaparte. It certainly hadn't slipped the Americans' minds when they made the decision to declare war." Did both Mister MacGillivray and Mister McKenzie glance toward him with expressions of positive appraisal? In the flaring circle of warmth around the fire, the lake slapping on the shore, a tin cup of brandy in his hand, it was possible to imagine all good things.

Mister McKenzie poured out another round of Mister Henderson's hoarded treasure. The stories continued to go around—or back and forth, since it was Mister MacGillivray and Mister McKenzie who did most of the talking. They spoke of the old days of the splinter companies, when old Simon MacTavish would hire an entire crew for a summer just to travel up a competitor's route felling trees across portages and chopping open beaver dams next to camping spots.

Grant leaned back against the storm-polished driftwood log behind him and ground his hips back and forth to wear a deeper hollow into the bed of wave-smoothed pebbles. There was an owl booming its night watch pleasantly somewhere not far beyond the curtain of bush. Or perhaps it was some foreign animal that only sounded like a Scottish owl.

He heard his name spoken and leaned forward attentively, then realized that Mister MacGillivray had been telling a story about his father. It was too late to catch the gist. Mister MacGillivray asked Henderson: "Did you know Grant? Old Cuthbert Grant? Jesus, 'old' Grant; how time passes."

"No, I'm afraid I never had the pleasure. Although I heard the name often, of course."

Mister McKenzie said: "How could Henderson have known him? Henderson's never been west of Fort William, and Grant stayed in the *pays d'en haut* for fifteen years. Then, when he finally did decide to head back to civilization—"

"Yes, of course," Mister MacGillivray cut him off. "Poor old fellow."

Grant had made up a romance about his parents—that his mother was the reason his father had stayed in the *pays d'en haut* for so much longer than his term. Received wisdom had it that Indian women didn't transplant well into white society. Consequently, when an *hivernant*—a wintering partner—ascended to the board in Montreal, he usually left his country family in the west and started a new one in the east. Given the alternatives of either abandoning his wife or condemning her to misery in an alien environment, Grant's father had chosen to stay.

Of course there was the possibility that the company hadn't had enough faith in his ability to offer him promotion to the board, but the respect with which the senior partners spoke of him belied that. Grant was quite sure that when his father had set out on the trip east he never finished, he was already years overdue for his seat on the board, his membership in the Beaver Club, his white porticoed mansion on the slope of Mount Royal . . .

Something in that train of thought made Grant veer off. Mister McKenzie said: "Do you remember much of your father, Cuthbert?"

"Nothing at all, sir."

"Nothing?"

"Nothing to speak of. I have one fragmentary memory of an incident that I suppose took place in one of the store sheds of—" He realized that if he went on any further, he was going to have to tell the whole embarrassing story, so he stopped.

"Yes?" said Mister MacGillivray. "In one of the store sheds . . . ? And your father was there?"

"Yes, sir."

Another pause went by, and then Mister McKenzie began to laugh. "Believe me, we would not consider it too forward of you to contribute a few more details."

Mister MacGillivray said: "Although your instincts are commendable, Cuthbert. It's a wise policy to adopt in one's youth—keep your mouth shut and your hands in your pockets, and you'll prosper."

"Don't mislead the lad, Will. If I recall, the way we prospered was by keeping our mouths shut and our hands in other people's pockets."

Mister MacGillivray didn't laugh. He said: "So, Cuthbert, you were in one of the store sheds at one of your father's posts . . ."

"Yes, sir. I, uh, couldn't have been more than four or five years of age, six at the most—a mere child. I had . . . heard, you see, that the reason the beaver pelts were so valuable was because they were used in the civilized world to make hats. There were a number of beaver pelts stacked up in the shed waiting to be pressed into *pièces*. So I, you see, I took a little hand-sized trade mirror, and I took one of the pelts and I—ha, ha—I, um, tried it out—flopping it flat over my head, and that didn't look right, then holding the edges together like a cone or a toque—ha, ha—" He wondered if the fire was growing hotter or whether the scalded feeling in his cheeks came from the brandy.

"So then the door opened, and my father came in and asked what I was doing, and I told him and he laughed and explained it to me—that the hat makers didn't use the pelts as such but scraped off the hairs to make a kind of felt cloth, because beaver hairs have minute hooks that link together.

"Other than that single incident, I'm afraid I was too young for any impressions to register on my mind. After my baptism in Montreal, I can remember with relative clarity; before that there is nothing."

Mister McKenzie said: "Isn't that curious. Memory is such a

peculiar faculty. My memory always gave me the impression that you were, oh, seven or eight years old at the baptism, so mine is just as jumbled up as—''

"Not at all. I was eight years old."

"Eight?" Mister McKenzie looked at him strangely. "And you remember nothing before then?"

With a certain amount of resentment, Grant said: "Nothing."

In the morning, hustle as they might, the voyageurs of Mister Henderson's brigade got their camp broken down and loaded just in time to see the knife-keeled beauty of the express canoe round the point at the west end of the bay. They would meet up again at Fort William—just above the eye of the distorted wolf's head that was Lake Superior on the maps.

They followed in the vanished ripples of Mister MacGillivray's wake through long days, hugging the shoreline, making occasional quick sprints across open water under clear skies, progressing through the fog as through a dream with the *avants* leaning out from the prows holding torches. Grant was struck by the fact that a certain copper-haired junior clerk had passed this same way for *his* first term in the *pays d'en haut* a quarter century ago. Will MacGillivray would have been sitting in a *canot de maître* just like this one, the voyageurs might have been singing the exact same song, he would have been feeling the same sensation of insignificance as they inched around the skirts of the black cliffs, unaware that Chief Superintendant Simon MacTavish was already preparing a place for him at the table in the boardroom. As it had been with old Simon MacTavish, Chief Superintendant MacGillivray had no legitimate male heirs. The tradition had been established of informally adopting a promising young man, bringing him up through the ranks, grooming him . . .

The entire crew of all four canoes suddenly burst into laughter. For a stomach-turning instant, Grant thought he'd been thinking aloud. But they were only laughing at the joke in the last couplet of the song—with the same full-throated enthusiasm that they'd laughed on the three or four dozen previous times this trip.

CHAPTER 6

On the sloping cliffs that flanked the fishing village at the mouth of the river Ulidh, the black ruins of Helmsdale Castle stood brooding. Between the tumbled stones of the castle, along the beach and dotted here and there on the less sheer portions of the incline, there were makeshift shelters of driftwood and shore rocks and scraps of sailcloth. Inside them the remnants of the parish of Kildonan huddled in their thousands.

Kate MacPherson sat on a kelp-streaked rock with her long legs folded in front of her, her chin propped on her knees, staring dully out over the North Sea. The bruise under her ear was healing slowly. Her body was finding it difficult to keep itself upright, much less repair damage. She had been living by and large on handfuls of millet soaked in cattle blood. Once a day her father would open up a vein on the shoulder of one of their animals and then seal it up again with mud. At night Kate would sneak off into the hills behind DunUlidh with her brothers and bring back clods of dirt hidden in baskets or the folds of their plaids, trying to build up a deep-enough skin over the rocks and sand to plant potatoes. And now the cattle were beginning to die, for even they couldn't eat sand.

She had spent the morning scrabbling among the tidepools looking for shellfish. When Ian Sutherland lost his footing and was swept out to sea by a wave, she had merely stood watching while the others ran along the shoreline shouting and keening. No amount of wailing and arm waving had so far managed to bring anyone back, whether from the sea or from disease.

Her father still had a few coins knotted into the tail of his shirt, but if he spent them on food, he would have nothing when the Countess of Sutherland's agents came to collect the rents for living on her seashore. In DunUlidh market today, the price of a single potato was what a bushel had cost last week. There were cattle agents up from Inverness who would be glad to buy her father's

43

entire shaggy-forelocked, sprung-ribbed herd for enough money to feed his family for three days.

Kate could feel herself sliding further into a dull-eyed, listless apathy. Perhaps when she had sunk far enough she would join the line of scarecrows drifting down the coast road toward Glasgow City and the wool mills and the soot-grimed tenements. Or perhaps by that time Mister Sellar and his improvers would have built their herring factory and would kindly put her to work for what wages they decided.

The tide was beginning to come in, the long rollers rippling back from Germany. She was abstractly aware that her sense of smell was taking in the salt air and the dank kelp, that her eyes were seeing the green-gray surf break in and recede, that her ears were hearing the hiss and roar of the waves and the cries of the seagulls. But none of them seemed any more substantial than the phrases of old *cehlidh* songs that her mind's ear was fabricating.

Finally she came to the realization that the music was coming from outside of her, somewhere off to her left. She climbed down from her rock and worked her way between the slippery, house-high boulders of the shoreline. Away from the surf, the music became louder—a single fiddle playing the songs of her childhood. And playing them none too adroitly. A wall of boulders blocked her path. She hitched her way up the side of one, pulled herself forward on her belly to the sun-warmed crown, and there below her was her musician.

He was sitting with his back to a driftwood stump—a scrawny specimen in a Black Watch kilt and frayed-seamed red tunic, plodding with painful concentration through "Kishmul's Galley." She tried to angle around to get a look at his features, but all she could see was the back of his neck and one freckled ear poking out from tousled, pale brown hair. Then he bobbed his head sideways. She ducked her head down, but his eyes were closed in tight-lipped, childish intentness to the task at hand. The nose was thin and sharp, the eyelashes darker than the hair, the bones of the face somehow birdlike, light and frail looking.

If she'd come across him a month ago, she wouldn't have recognized him. Ten years had passed since she'd seen him last, and he'd been only one of the dozens of children she'd grown up with—running half-wild up and down the banks of the Ulidh until they reached an age when they could be trusted to herd cattle. They all blended together now in a dimly remembered mass that she was more likely to associate with the current runny-nosed crop of urchins than with the harsh-voiced, pinch-faced parents those distant boys and girls had grown into.

But Alexander Sutherland's name had figured in a lot of conversations since they'd come down to DunUlidh. There was a certain comfort in clucking over someone whose troubles are greater than one's own, and Alexander Sutherland was one of the few that the Kildonan crofters could take that comfort from these days—home from ten years fighting his country's enemies to find his father beaten to death by his country's lawful authorities.

She corrected herself on the "beaten to death." The death certificate had said that Three-Fingered Alex Sutherland had died of natural causes and made no mention of the fact that one side of his skull had been cracked in like an eggshell.

The fiddle was grinding haltingly through the demonic lilt of "The King of the Faeries" when her elbow dislodged a rattle of pebbles. He stopped playing, stood up, and turned around, the color of his tunic seeping up into his cheeks.

Her first thought was to sink down through the fabric of the rock. When that failed to work she decided to brazen it out. She turned and slid down the face of the boulder feet first. The hem of her skirt squeezed up between the surface of the boulder and the fronts of her legs almost to the point of indecency, but at last her toes touched the ground and she let herself drop.

She turned to face him, shaking out her skirt. He was holding the fiddle and the bow in one long-fingered hand against the breast of his tunic. She gave him what she hoped was a mollifying smile and said: "You do not play half-bad for a beginner."

"I began to play the fiddle when I was eight years old."

"Oh. Well . . . it was only that the one tune seemed a trifle . . . you understand, a trifle . . . halting."

The hue in his face went a few shades darker. "I do not recall issuing invitations to judge a recital."

She crossed her arms and looked down, then forced herself to look right at him. "You would be Alexander Sutherland, then."

His spine stiffened. "Would I?"

"You look to be the same lad Donald Gunn's bull chased into the Ulidh—a little longer in the legs, perhaps."

His chin jutted out farther. Perhaps he didn't think it ladylike to speak of legs. Or perhaps she hadn't chosen the best incident to remind him of—he'd been a little younger and smaller than the rest of the pack, and they'd had a tendency to dupe him into things such as slinging stones at Mister Gunn's bull. Or perhaps he'd found some other reason to take offense. She'd never had much success at smoothing ruffled feathers, although she'd been born with an uncanny knack for ruffling them.

He said: "Kate MacPherson."

She nodded. They focused their attention on the interesting rock formations behind each other's shoulders. She said: "I was very sorry to hear about your father." As the words were leaving her mouth, she became aware of how inane they sounded. "Forgive me, I realize it is a lame—"

"It was kind of you to say so," he said stiffly. "I am done here. You can have the place to yourself. Good day to you."

As he turned to step over the stump of driftwood, the hem of his kilt hitched up to show the ridges of scar tissue on his right knee. His progress across the shore rocks was awkward and lopsided. It was then that she remembered the other detail of the stories about Alexander Sutherland's homecoming—that he'd come back a little lame.

CHAPTER 7

The gentlemen of Mister Henderson's brigade shifted canoes from day to day, to vary their options for conversation. When the brigade reached Thunder Bay Grant was ensconced beside one of the senior clerks. The canoes progressed slowly along the shore of a massive prone rock monolith looming out of the waves. The senior clerk said: "That's the famous Sleeping Giant."

"The famous which?"

"Sleeping Giant. The Ojibway have a manitou named Nanabouzho. He lost his hunting luck in one particularly grim winter. Every night when he came home empty-handed, his starving wife would give him the sharp side of her tongue, until one night he'd had enough and gave her the back of his hand. He hit her harder than he meant to and killed her. When he saw what he'd done he went mad with grief and ran blindly through the forest until he tripped at the edge of the lake here and fell in. He begged the waters to turn him into stone so he wouldn't feel any more. It does have a certain primitive poetry to it, don't you think?''

Grant shrugged. What the company wanted from the Indians wasn't their Stone Age poetry. As the prow of their canoe rounded the feet of the Sleeping Giant—or perhaps the head, it was difficult to tell; Nanabouzho had weathered some over the years—Grant fought the urge to kneel up and gawk over the heads of the paddlers. Fortunately they were bending their backs so hard into the last sprint that his view of Fort William was pretty much unobstructed anyway.

After a thousand miles of rock and spruce and lichen and willow swamps, the sight of Fort William was like a good roundhouse axe handle between the eyes. Some hand larger than Nanabouzho's had scooped a hole out of the wilderness and set in its place a quarter-mile-wide swath of wharf in front of manicured vegetable gardens, cattle barns, a sheep cote, a schooner-sized dry dock, trimmed shade trees, wheat fields, and a fifteen-foot-high palisade surrounding the shingled roofs of several dozen buildings that any Scottish mayor would have been proud of.

The cannons in the corner bastions and in the guardhouse over the main gate puffed out a salute, the syncopated booms trailing out across the water. Out of the gates came a milling horde of eye-searing rendezvous shirts, fur caps, top hats, sober broadcloth coats belted with delirium tremens sashes, beaded buckskins and fringed white doeskin skirts, feathers and brass earhoops, and tartan waistcoats.

While the bow and stern lines were still being tied, the bales of cargo bounced out as though on springs, and the passengers were manhandled ashore. From the midst of the melee on the wharf, Grant's eyes were drawn upward to a few thin columns of smoke from the wooded ridge above and behind the fort. At the base of the smoke was a scattering of white cones with minute stick figures moving in silhouette against them. Mister Henderson had stopped beside him and followed his eyes. Grant said: "Indians?"

"No. *Hommes du nord.*" His tone of voice suggested that he would have been more comfortable with a scalping party of Sioux. He pasted on a convivial smile. "Well, Cuthbert, I might not get the chance when it comes time for me to start back, or for you to start north, so I'll say good-bye now." He stuck out his hand and pumped Grant's up and down. "It's been a pleasure having you in my brigade. Good luck in the *pays d'en haut*. When you come back to Montreal do pay me a call.''

"I will, sir. Thank you." Perhaps he wasn't such a bad fellow after all. One of the fort agents took the new arrivals in tow. Grant was swept along through the gates, between the guardhouse and the apothecary, along a row of brick warehouses, and into a broad, moccasin-tamped square with three wide, gabled, square-beam buildings at its head. They crossed the square on a diagonal, threading their way through knots of arguers and laborers and drinkers and loungers, all gabbling away in the fur trade patois of which every third word was some Indian dialect.

At the corner of the square was a fourth whitewashed, adzed-log building, smaller than the three gabled buildings. The entranceway was two doors wide but appeared to suffer from permanent congestion nonetheless. Inside were benches and tables, a rough plank floor, and a bar counter, all crammed with voyageurs and a smattering of Indian women. A few pugnacious greetings got shouted at the new brigade, mostly at the *engagés* but a few at the clerks.

The fat Canadian behind the bar presented each of them with a loaf of white bread, a half pound of butter, and a gill of rum. Grant didn't quite know what he was supposed to do with them, but as it appeared to be some sort of tradition, he figured he'd at least take a few bites to join in the spirit. After two months of no bread but pan-fired *galettes* and stale biscuits, the first bite tasted surprisingly good. He kept ripping off soft, crisp-crusted chunks, slathering them with butter, and popping them in his mouth until he was scraping the last of the butter off the dish with the crunchy heel. As for the rum, the first few swallows went down a little rough, but after that it was easy.

The air inside the room suddenly seemed very stale. He made his way out through the crush at the door and stood with his back against the outside wall to steady himself. Eventually the heart palpitations stopped. A year as an apprentice clerk in Montreal had given him a good foundation in the fundamentals of ingesting alcohol—rumor had it that Mister MacGillivray had been scraped off a few of the same floors in his youth—but four ounces of Jamaica rum in ten minutes was still a bit of a shock.

He was having a good time watching and listening when it occurred to him that his eavesdropping might be a bit conspicuous. He pushed away from the wall and set off walking at a pace just businesslike enough to give the impression that he was going somewhere. His wanderings taught him that the voyageurs called the grog shop the *cantine salope*—the "whores' tavern,"—and that only a couple of brigades of *hommes du nord* had arrived so far; many more were expected in the next few days.

An *homme du nord* was, literally, a "man of the north," but the phrase had a lot of other implications. They were the voyageurs who worked the canoe brigades north and west from Fort William and consequently wintered in the *pays d'en haut*. Some of them were *engagés* for a season, some of them lived their lives out there. The evolution of the *hommes du nord* was an inevitable offshoot of the system that the company had invented to move goods across thousands of miles of bush country waterways in a short traveling season. Every spring, while the brigades were starting northwest from Montreal with loads of trade goods and supplies, there were brigades of *hommes du nord* starting southeast simultaneously— from the Athabasca, from Lake Nipigon, from Fort des Prairies, from Red River—with the winter's fur harvest. At Fort William the brigades met and exchanged cargoes while the wintering partners and the Montreal partners were parleying in the Great Hall. Then they all charged off in their separate directions to get dug in before the ice set in again.

Grant had drifted his way around into the central square again, wondering where he was supposed to be, what he was supposed to be doing, and what had happened to his luggage. The company wasn't paying him to be a tourist. There was a man in a rust-colored tailcoat striding across the square in a path about to intersect with his—a broad-chested, golden-maned, side-whiskered veteran at least a head taller than anyone else in sight.

"Excuse me, sir. . . ?"

The boots stomped to a halt. "Yes?"

"I just arrived with Mister Henderson's brigade, and I'm afraid I'm not absolutely certain where—"

"You're Cuthbert Grant's boy, aren't you? Duncan Cameron." A paw thrust forward.

"How do you do."

"Damned well, that's how I do, and I'm sure you will yourself. So, bloody grocer-clerk Henderson didn't show you where to settle your traps, hm? The clerks get put up in the barracks just west of the Great Hall."

"The Great Hall?"

Mister Cameron laughed like a clog dance on a bass drum. "Of course, damned stupid of me—how would you know that? That's the Great Hall"—sweeping his arm toward the verandahed building in the middle of the three at the head of the square—"and that one beside it is your billet. I have to stump along now, but no doubt we'll meet again at dinner. Pleasure to meet you.''

"And you, sir."

The barracks building was bisected by a narrow corridor down its length, with doorways dotted along both sides, some of them flanked by little heaps of dirty laundry. Through one of the laundryless doorways, Grant caught sight of his rifle case.

Two feet inside the doorway was the end of a head-high partition separating two mirror-image cubicles. His cassette was at the foot of the bed that his rifle case and valise had been dumped on top of. There was a narrow bed with white sheets and gray blankets, a tiny, parchment-paned window, and a couple of rough plank shelves with a candlestick on one end. He unlocked the cassette and just managed to fill up both shelves and the pegs on the walls with his possessions: three pairs of woolen trousers, four linen shirts and two wool, one black broadcloth tailcoat and three waistcoats, cased pistols, compass, sheath knife, woolen stockings, eight bars of Meechem Bros. Hand & Body Soap, a box of toothbrushes, ten tins of Pymm's Teeth Powder, black riding boots, two cambric neckcloths, a dozen handkerchiefs, a white meerschaum pipe, and books with their pages still uncut—the new Coleridge, Jane Austen, Robert Burns, Henry Fielding, *The Complete Shakespeare, The Compleat Angler, Anabasis* in the original, and Mr. Defoe's *The Amorous Adventures of Moll Flanders*. He thought for a moment someone had stolen his winter coat and then remembered that after packing and repacking for three hours he'd decided that carrying a winter coat to the fur country was dimmer than coals to Newcastle.

He changed into clean clothing and spare boots and piled his mud-stained traveling clothes and boots outside the door, then lay down on the bed to wait for the hall sounds to tell him it was time for dinner.

The smell of clean sheets and the feel of even a thin, hair-stuffed pallet cushioning his body lulled him into a half sleep. He wondered if he'd made a mistake in putting his muddy boots out and heard the voices in his mind's ear—"*Mister* Grant was expecting a bootblack; will somebody kindly convey our apologies to *Mister* Grant and tell him that west of bloody Edinburgh we clean our own stinking boots"—but he left them there.

He drifted between memories and daydreams. He found himself wandering up a road outside Grantown-on-Spey, the ancient stronghold of Clan Grant, where he'd been put up at a distant cousin's between college terms. It was his first summer there, and he wanted to look at Castle Grant, the new Georgian manor house that had been built in the heart of the pine forest by good Sir James Grant.

The larks were singing, the long-needled pines were emitting a soft whispering and a sweet, green smell. He was standing at the edge of the graveled carriage drive, staring up at the white marble wonder, when a gamekeeper crunched up to shoo him away. "I am entitled to be here; I'm a Grant. My name is Cuthbert Grant."

"Well la-de-fucking-da. My name is Ian Grant, and the man that keeps the public house is Henry Grant, and the tart that scours out his chamberpots is Lizzie Grant. Clear off before I boot your little black Grant ass up around your Grant ears."

There was a thumping of boots along the corridor. Grant swung his boots off the bed and fell in with the parade for dinner. The mounds of dirty clothing had disappeared, including his traveling boots. In the open square were half a dozen laundry tubs with an Ojibway girl standing in each, trampling away with skirts hiked up, the sunlight gleaming off taut, wet, tawny legs. Grant's second thought was that he hoped that wasn't the way they were planning to clean his boots.

In the Great Hall, two hundred clerks, agents, partners, guides, and other members of the higher orders of the North West Fur Trading Company sat down to dine on roast beef and moose nose and beaver tail and trout and wild rice and fresh carrots and wild parsnips under the life-sized and larger portraits of Simon Mac-Tavish and William MacGillivray and Sir Alexander Mackenzie and a full-length rendition of Nelson at Trafalgar. Word had it that the vast empty space along the west wall would be filled next year by David Thompson's map of the company's territories and explorations—north as far as the Frozen Ocean and west to the Pacific.

The conversation was of the war with the Americans, of the competition against the Hudson's Bay Company, of toes frozen off in the *pays d'en haut* and pickled in jars of brandy for conversation pieces, of traders scalped and their wives raped to death, of profits and losses and of the belt-tightening they would have to practice in case the war interfered with the company's lines of supply.

When dinner was done, the tables were cleared away, the front doors were flung open, and a kilted piper marched in braying "The Road to the Isles." On his heels came a dozen voyageurs with fiddles under their arms followed by a wide stream of boatmen, trappers, and Ojibway women, all dressed to the teeth in their separate versions of barbaric splendor. In a moment the Great Hall was a mass of dancers reeling, jigging, quadrilling, and scalp dancing in the light from a hundred candles and the tree trunk in the ox-sized fireplace.

Grant backed himself into a shadowed corner and set to picking out the great men of the company. Some of them were jouncing away with the wildest of the dancers, and some of them were already at the stage of propping up the mantelpiece. Mister McKenzie gave him a nod and a wink. Mister Cameron raised his glass in his direction.

The sight in front of him needed only minor alterations in some costume details and complexions, and rough-cut stone rather than rough-cut logs in the background wall, to resemble a scene from one of Mister Walter Scott's epics of the great days of the clans or the songs of Ossian. Grant tried to think why his eyes should be so moist. He had to blink repeatedly to keep from embarrassing himself. It wasn't the drink—he'd been a good deal drunker in the past without feeling this dangerously emotional.

By some unspoken agreement, at about midnight the rank and file spilled out into the square, leaving the senior partners to their single malts and strategies. The dancing carried on under the stars around a Visigoth-sized bonfire.

Two voyageurs in front of Grant were arguing over something; the subject was superfluous—the point was that one of them was an *homme du nord* and the other a *mangeur du lard*, a distinctly unflattering reference to the pork fat soup that the men of the eastern brigades were fed on. Immediately they were at each other with fists and feet and knees. Grant skirted away as a ring formed around them and went to dip his cup in one of the barrels of watered rum on the rim of the circle of dancers. At the hub of the wheel there were three fiddlers sawing through the vitals of ''The King of the Faeries.''

The dancing Ojibway women appeared to come in two distinct varieties: dew-eyed forest flowers and seamed-leather, barrel-bellied harpies. About three years made the difference. Among the first variety was a girl in a white doeskin dress with a red and teal-blue porcupine quill design on the bodice. It seemed to Grant that she kept glancing his way. His eyes couldn't quite manage to trap hers, so he couldn't be certain. He had no uncertainty whatever, though, about the aesthetic effect of the supple bouncing underneath the quill work and the butter-soft fringed leather skewing around her hips. He broke into the circle beside her and did his best to accommodate the music with a series of movements that were not quite a jig and not quite a reel and not quite a punch-drunk shuffle.

She kept tossing her head to shake away the crow's wing of hair folding down across her left eye, black eyes darting slyly at him from between black lashes, skin like poured russet gold . . . The head tossing was a pretty gesture, but he was considering asking her to stop it—for some reason it was upsetting to his body's equilibrium. Suddenly she began to waver in front of him, focusing and unfocusing. The music and shouted singing folded back on itself, tipping him into vertigo. He stumbled away from her, into the dark on the lee side of the building that housed the Great Hall.

After spewing up a cup or two of watered rum and various entrées, he was surprised at how much better he felt, although he was still weak and gasping, leaning one hand against the wall. He got the distinct impression that he could hear another song being sung in competition with the chorale coming from the square. This one was an old voyageur song as well and equally drunken. It appeared to be coming from inside the Great Hall. He found a windowsill and peered over it.

They were sitting on the floor, cross-legged or kneeling, the partners, the agents, the chief superintendent, in a double line paralleling the fireplace. Some of them held walking sticks, one had the fireplace tongs, another the poker, two others the halves of a knee-snapped broom. They were bellowing out one of the more obscene voyageur songs, the one that ended with "Dead? I thought she was English!" paddling away with their walking sticks and fireplace tools. When Roderick McKenzie lost his balance and fell sideways off his knees, they all made a great to-do about saving him from drowning without swamping the canoe.

Grant ducked back down before they could see him and made his way to the square, trying to reconcile what he'd just seen with the men whose dinner conversation had been of pounds sterling in the tens of thousands, chartering ships from England and pressuring the imperial government to arrange reciprocal agreements with the East India Company.

His Ojibway girl was occupied with a voyageur now, her fingers entangled in his droopy mustache. When she saw Grant she broke away from the Canadian, laughing, and ran across the trampled grass toward him. Her hands butted up against his chest, large hands for such narrow wrists. She started to say something in Ojibway, checked herself, and laughed, covering her mouth with one hand, then started again with a bit less of an alcohol slur. Enunciated or not, her words meant nothing to him. But her meaning wasn't difficult to divine, not while her hand was slipping inside his coat to pull him to her and her knee pressing against the inside of his thigh.

She was jerked away from him. The abandoned voyageur had hold of her right wrist. Grant snatched hold of the left one. They tugged at her, which seemed silly, especially since the man on the other end earned his living by paddling a canoe sixteen hours a day.

Through the tendrils of his droopy mustache, the Canadian growled, "You better get yourself off to your bed, young gentle-man. Your friends had the sense to do that long ago."

Without letting go of the warm brown wrist, Grant glanced around and found there wasn't a frock coat or a top hat to be seen, only bright-colored calico and beaded deerskin. At the edge of the firelight one man was whacking at another with a barrel stave. Just past them was a pair of knees up on either side of a pair of squirming buttocks.

A ring of voyageurs was beginning to form around their tug-of-war. Although not one of them was taller than the end of Grant's nose, they all had shoulders like Clydesdales and a nasty sheen over their eyes. One of them said: "It's too late for him to get in. They barred the doors to keep us out."

The droopy-mustached one said unpleasantly: "Maybe if you pound real hard and call for help, your friends will unbar the door for you." He yanked the girl toward him, tearing her wrist out of Grant's grasp. The firelight glinted off the pommel of a big, ugly-looking sheath knife snuggled into his waist sash.

Grant tried to swallow enough saliva to rinse away the sand coating his throat. A lunatic impulse came to mind. His right hand snaked out and plucked at the decorative steel bulb at the top of the knife handle. The voyageur's knife appeared to leap into his hand obligingly.

His body sometimes acted with such swiftness and precision that no one, including himself, could quite say how an incident had happened. It never failed to give him a happy little thrill of accom-plishment, whether it happened while he was fencing or riding or boxing or scrambling over the rock bluffs behind Inverness. He looked to the voyageur to see if any of the same pleasure at his adroitness had communicated itself. The eyes above the droopy mustache had definitely grown very thoughtful. Grant took the girl's pulse-warm wrist again and said to the voyageur: "You are quite right, it is past my bedtime. Thank you so much for reminding me.''

He led her into the gap between the Great Hall and the clerks' barracks. He wondered whether he should keep the knife with him in case the droopy-mustached one pursued them, then realized that *it* would be the reason to be pursued—it was one thing to steal a girl for an evening, especially with so many of them around, but another thing entirely to make off with a man's knife. He thrust it into a corner beam just before they stepped into the shadows.

As soon as they'd rounded the back corner of the Great Hall, she grabbed him, shoved him up against the wall, and planted her wet mouth over his, her fingers squeezing between their bodies into his trousers. He put his hands on her shoulders and pushed her back, shaking his head. The look she gave him was compounded of shock and insult and disorientation. He took her hand, led her to the postern gate in the southeast corner of the palisade, and out past the icehouse and the barns into the open fields.

A starry night and a half moon, enough light to throw crescent shadows underneath her breasts as she shucked the dress off over her head. The doeskin made a soft hissing sound when it fell into the grass.

She lay on her back and moved her right hand down between her legs. He threw off his coat and settled onto his knees between hers, unbuttoning his trousers. He reached down to help her, but she pushed his hand away and spread herself open with two fingers until he'd slipped in. Both the chambermaid in Grantown-on-Spey and Madelaine at Montreal's Le Coq d'Or had expected him to effect arrangements. He held her shoulders and laid his cheek against her forehead, breathing in the musky smell of her hair. They pounded out the message to the stars that they were alive and well until the Great Bear shambled over the horizon.

The morning came with a large rock pounding doggedly inside Grant's head. They were lying in an open pasture with her dress half under them and his coat half covering them. Three spotted cows were studying them from twenty yards away, jaws working under dim brown eyes. Grant struggled to his feet and headed down to the shore, each footfall sending tremors through his eggshell skull. He got down on all fours and shoved his face into the water. It took near drowning to convince him that human beings weren't meant to drink with their heads immersed.

He came back to where he'd left his coat, rubbing one hand back over his hair to squeeze out the water. She was still sleeping. When he lifted the coat off her she rolled over on the grass, dragging the dress along to cover her against the cool of the morning.

He hadn't walked more than four steps when she called out: "Grant!" He turned back, surprised that she knew his name. She was propped up on one arm, the dress puddled in her lap, her eyes slitted against the light. Her other arm was held out in front of her, the thumb rubbing back and forth across the palm.

Not certain whether he was more repulsed by her or by himself, he dug into his pockets and found one lone, forgotten shilling. He walked back and put it in her hand. She closed her hand and lay down again without looking at it, asleep before she hit the ground.

He walked back toward the fort, picking up his pace as the increasing intensity of light—and therefore the pain in his head—reminded him that he should have been at work in the counting house at dawn. He could hear the words already or read them behind the eyes that would turn to him when he rumpled in reeking of rum: "The Indian blood coming out in him, it always does sooner or later. . . ."

He had almost reached the postern gate when something to his right caught his eye and held it. He stopped and turned his head in that direction, then veered away from the fort. On the other side of the vegetable gardens and the pasture, tucked in among the mossbanks and pine groves at the base of the ridge, was a fenced graveyard with a number of whitewashed wooden markers. Toward the back was a bleached gray, split-armed cross with barely discernible letters:

CU HBE T GR N   17 2–1 99.

He wondered whether he had stood beside the grave before. When he'd come east from the *pays d'en haut* as part of the cargo manifest for the brigade of 1801—"Item, 1 pièce Martin Pelts; item, 1 Halfbreed Childe . . ."—there would have been a layover at Fort William before the transfer to the Montreal brigade. Perhaps Roderick McKenzie or one of the MacGillivrays had walked him out here to show him where his father lay. But then again, it wouldn't have required an immense leap of intuition to guess that he would find his father's grave in the cemetery of the fort they'd brought his body to.

A puff of wind carried him a wisp of that same sweet, wild, resiny smell that had been so curiously disturbing in the hollow in the woods on the north shore. The taste was unmistakable. He turned to face into the wind.

It was only the ghost of a breeze, but one stand of trees was quivering as though their own private gale were howling in from Thunder Bay. The silver undersides of the leaves turned up to glint and shimmer in a flash of sunlight. Along with their scent, the breeze carried him a sibilant, dry-husk rattling like the fingers of the dead.

Other people were coming into the cemetery—Mister Mac-Gillivray and an Indian woman. She looked plump and suety but prim in a cotton Sunday-service dress. Grant assumed that she was Susan, the Cree woman who had borne Mr. MacGillivray's children during his apprenticeship. He tried to picture her twenty-five years ago with her red-haired junior clerk, snowed in along the Athabasca.

Mister MacGillivray seemed startled to see him. He murmured something to Susan and then walked toward him while she struck off toward the south part of the graveyard. Grant tried to summon up an expression of alertness.

"Well, Cuthbert, I should have expected that I might see you here."

Grant nodded abruptly.

With a bit of a twinkle, Mister MacGillivray said: "A touch the worse for wear this morning?" As he tried to sputter out some reply, Mister MacGillivray took a little silver flask from his coat pocket. "It's nothing to be ashamed of. If you try and live by the shorter catechism out here, they'll find you hanging from your roof tree come spring." He filled the belled-out cap of the flask and held it out to him. "Just knock this down and hold it in, it'll steady your hand. But only one, mind. The morning you need two is the morning you start looking for another line of work."

Amazingly, once he'd held it down long enough, the whiskey did make the surface of the planet an almost tolerable place. Grant was making polite "thank you" and "good-day, sir" noises and backing off toward his morning's work when Mister MacGillivray said: "You've heard something, I should expect, of the Earl of Selkirk's plan to establish a colony of Highland crofters at Red River on land granted by the Hudson's Bay Company?"

"Something, sir, not a great deal."

"What do you think your people will think of it?"

Grant blinked at him. "My people?"

"The half-breeds."

Grant felt as if he'd been slapped. "I don't know, sir. It's been more than ten years since . . ." He was starting to say "since I was a half-breed," but amended it to ". . . since I left."

"Hm, of course, yes. Well, when you do get back to the *pays d'en haut*, Cuthbert, that is something you might do for me—just keep a weather ear out for how your . . . how the métis are taking to this idea of farmers moving in on top of them. Will you do that for me?"

"Of course, sir."

"Good lad." He looked up at the sun. "I suppose they'll be missing you in the counting house. Tell them you were held up talking to me."

CHAPTER 8

At low tide the sea gave DunUlidh back a quarter-mile-wide strip of slime-covered boulders, sand-choked basins of saltwater, and clumps of purple-green kelp. One early morning a thousand refugees from the parish of Kildonan stood gathered there, facing inland. With their hunched-in shoulders and dark rags of clothing, they might have been mistaken from a distance for a flock of jackdaws.

The focus of the crowd was a big man in a blue broadcloth tailcoat, fawn trousers, and cuffed calfskin boots, standing on a boulder at the high-tide line. In the manner of the Caesars, a tight, thick cap of wine-red lovelocks framed his balding forehead, although he'd added a fierce pair of side whiskers to modernize the effect. It was said that he was a man from the right side of the Highland line, but there was something indisputably alien about him, the skin burnt brown by some harsher sun.

In a booming voice he said in Gaelic: "My name is Colin Robertson. I was born in Stornoway on the island of Lewis, but I have lived most of my life as a fur trader in North America. I am here on behalf of the Earl of Selkirk—and on behalf of yourselves, for that matter.

"The Governor and Company of Adventurers Trading into Hudson's Bay has granted to Lord Selkirk, for a sum of money and other considerations, a piece of land in the heart of North America that is larger than the entire area of the British Islands. He means to found a colony there that will be a refuge for the people of the Highlands who are being driven off their homes. He has appointed a governor who went out two years ago with a crew of men to build a settlement at the forks of the Red River.

"We are ready now to bring out young married couples to start settling, although we are willing to take a few unmarried young men and women as well. Each head of a household will be given a lease on a piece of land that he can work toward owning—Lord Selkirk believes that a man works harder for himself than he would for anybody else. The land around the Forks is open prairie—all a man needs to do is burn the grass off and then sow his crops.

"We have chartered two ships that will be sailing for North America in a few weeks. Those who are selected will be asked to pay a nominal passage. In cases of extreme destitution the passage money can be deferred and held against your account until the first crop is in. That is the nub of what I came to tell you. If you have any questions you want answered, ask them now."

There was a long, shuffling silence as the Kildonan crofters responded in the time-honored fashion of Highlanders confronted with a stranger: stand relatively still and peer back impassively. The silence stretched out until a female voice in the middle of the crowd called out: "How much is this 'nominal passage money'?" Heads in the front ranks craned around to see who the brassy woman was.

Kate MacPherson crossed her arms and kept her eyes fixed on Colin Robertson, affecting not to see the disapproving faces. They all had questions, but they would have stood there staring at his boots until the tide came in and drowned them all.

Colin Robertson's eyes found her. He said: "Ten guineas." It was more than her father's annual rent on their old croft.

Now that one of the congregation had pried open its jaws without any fatal effects, the questions came thick and furious. How bad were the winters? How long was the voyage? How dry was the soil? How savage were the red Indians? A male voice from somewhere behind Kate called out: "You make it all sound very cozy, but the letters in the *Inverness Journal* say different." She turned her head and stood up on her toes to look over the heads behind her, but she couldn't see who had spoken. Although the Gaelic sounded natural enough on his tongue, there was something in the lilt that was foreign to County Sutherland.

They'd all read the letters in the journal or had heard them read aloud. They were published once or twice a week, more so in the last two weeks, and signed "A Highlander." "A Highlander" was distraught at the sugary stories about Rupertsland that Lord Selkirk's agents had been telling to his fellow Highlanders and wanted them to know of his own experiences there—starvation and drought and winters so cold that the wolves froze to death if they ventured out of their dens on a bad day, not to mention the red Indians.

Colin Robertson said: "Any bald-face liar can write a letter and sign himself 'A Highlander.' Lord Selkirk has made inquiries to find out who this 'Highlander' is, but he keeps himself well hid. I can tell you for a certainty, though, who pays this 'Highlander' to write his letters. There is a gentleman—I use the term loosely—named William MacGillivray who is the chief pirate of a group of illegal peddlers in the Hudson's Bay territories who style themselves the North West Fur Trading Company. I know them well because when I first went out to North America I was employed with them for a time, before I learned what they were. . . ."

"Before you were fired!" the voice with the curious lilt called out.

Colin Robertson blew up like a six-foot rooster, hopping between the impulse to jump down and plunge into the crowd and the impulse to stand on his tiptoes to see where the voice was coming from. "Who is that man? Where is he?" Kate's head turned with all the others to the heading of the voice's last sounding. There was a bit of milling around, but it appeared that he had managed to melt himself into the crowd.

It took a moment for Colin Robertson to compose himself. "You see what their tactics are! The North West Company cowards are willing to go to any lengths—short of showing themselves—to keep you out of Rupertsland because they are afraid—and rightly so—that the rule of law will inevitably follow settlement. They have no legal right to be there. All the country drained by rivers flowing into Hudson's Bay was deeded to the Hudson's Bay Company by good King Charles Stuart."

Colin Robertson continued to answer questions for another hour, salting in enough references to inevitable hardships to soothe their Calvinist-influenced vision of life. When the questions started repeating themselves, he said: "Well, I can see the tide starting to come in. I will be at the inn in Golspie through the coming week.

None of you need me to tell you what kind of a life you can expect on this side of the ocean. Anyone who wants something different had best come see me soon—there will be only so many places on the ships."

He bounded down off his rock and headed for the tall bay horse tethered farther up the beach. Kate watched him from her place in the thinning crowd, his boots eating up the stretch of beach between him and his horse in half a dozen strides. She wondered what kind of place this Rupertsland must be to take an Orkney fisherman's boy and rear him into this big impossible creature stomping heedlessly through the cobwebs of the past.

He had worked his boot into the stirrup when he suddenly stopped and looked back over his shoulder at a scarecrow in the tattered remnants of a Highland soldier's uniform. Kate was too far away to hear their voices, but it appeared that Colin Robertson was trying to beg off any further questions, while Alexander Sutherland was insistent, jabbing his forefinger into the palm of his hand. Colin Robertson grudgingly consented to listen, asked a couple of questions of his own, then pumped his bent leg straight in the stirrup and thudded into the saddle. They spat into the palms of their hands, and Colin Robertson leaned down from his high horse to shake on it—whatever it was.

That evening, under their makeshift hovel that kept off the worst of the rain, around a smoldering fire of damp driftwood, Kate's mother and father and the older boys chewed over Colin Robertson's proposal. They nudged it, pecked at it, and pushed it around in circles like a family of rooks with a dry bone.

Kate said: "I will go."

They stopped and looked at her. Her father said: "Go where?"

"To North America."

Her mother growled: "That is a daft thing to say. You cannot go blundering off alone among a bunch of savages."

"I would not have to go alone. John could come with me."

John just sat staring into the yellow flecks of flame without volunteering a syllable. But something in his attitude of listening had changed.

Her father said: "We have no money for the passage."

"Sell some of the cattle, before they starve to death. Two mouths less to feed here would make it easier for you."

Her mother said: "We would never see you again."

Kate began a reply to that, but something in the tone of her mother's voice made it difficult to control her own. She took a long breath in and let it out slowly, then said levelly: "Once John and I have built a farm and got a harvest in, we will send money for the rest of you to come and join us."

Her father said: "Leave Sutherland?"

"You have been thrown out already! Has it not sunk into you that all of that is gone? What do they have to do to you—"

"You will not use that tone of voice when speaking to your father!"

Her father said: "The winters there . . . they say the rivers freeze down to the bottom for six months of the year. How could you live? And the wild Indians, and the great bears . . . They say that—"

"Who says? 'A Highlander'? The sneak thieves Mister Robertson spoke of?"

Her mother said: "Donald McKay came back to live in Dun-Ulidh. And they say his half-Indian nephew is with him now as well. We will call on them tomorrow. Once you hear the truth of what this place is like, that will be the end of it."

"Mister McKay always spoke very fondly of his years in Rupertsland."

"As a single man in the fur trade. He will sing a different tune about families and women and children trying to make homes there, unless I miss my guess."

She did. Old Donald McKay said: "The Forks of the Red, where they're building their settlement, may well be the best farmland in the world. That's my old stomping grounds just downstream from Brandon House, which my brother, God rest his soul, and me founded for the HBC—Here Before Christ. Oh, pardon me. Ahem. Yes, beautiful country, grass up to your . . . armpits, as far as your eyes can see. Think what it would do with wheat. You can ask John Richards"—patting his nephew's wrist—"he's the factor now at Brandon House. He can tell you if I'm stretching the truth. Go on, tell them—am I lying?"

John Richards McKay was quite the most exotic-looking human being Kate had ever seen—the blond hair and blue eyes of the northern Highlands amalgamated with the coppery skin and hatchet features of an alien race. He opened his mouth to speak, but his uncle jumped back in: "Cree and Saulteaux there—wouldn't hurt a fly unless it was Sioux. And the game—buffalo, quail, deer . . . Fishing that'd break a poacher's heart, there's so little sport to it. 'Course the winters are a bitch—I mean, a bastard—I mean . . ."

Kate said: "Can they be any worse than the winters in the Highlands?"

Mister McKay squinted his ancient eyes at her and blew out a long exhalation through puckered lips. "Oh, yes, Miss Mac-Pherson; oh, my, yes. Freeze your ti-oes off. You can beat 'em, but they're mean—kill you quick or grind you down. You see, even though we're farther north here, the winters don't get so cold because of . . . something to do with the ocean—don't ask me to explain it, John Richards is the one with the education. And at the Forks of the Red there ain't nothing between you and the North Pole but thousands of miles of prairie and ice fields so the wind can get a run at you. But the summers! You ain't ever seen sunlight before!"

"Actually," said John Richards McKay, "I would feel I had been remiss if I did not enlighten you about some facets of the situation at Red River that have developed since my uncle's time. There are two factors you should consider. Imprimis—" He held up the index finger of his right hand. "Imprimis, Lord Selkirk might have done better in his choice of a governor. It may well be that Miles MacDonell was an exemplary junior officer during his military career, but the authority he's been given as governor seems to be a bit too much for him. Secundo—" He extended his second finger. "In the whole of Rupertsland, which is an area equal in size to half the continent of Europe, there is not one officer of the law."

After a few pleasantries, the McKays escorted them to the door. Donald McKay had come home to retire in the parish of Kildonan, then moved to DunUlidh when the eviction notices went up. The only exterior sign that the cottage wasn't just another herring fisherman's was a pair of antlers over the front door that dwarfed the crown of any roe deer Kate had seen in the high corries of Sutherland. She asked the old man: "Are those from the buffalo, then?"

"Which?"

"The antlers," gesturing with her chin toward the face of the cottage.

"Buffalo? No, no—buffalo have horns, like a cow—well, not like any cow you've ever . . . Those are wapiti. Elk. Think of the biggest stag you ever saw, then double it." He squinted out over the rocks and the gray water and sighed. "Thirty years I spent dreaming of home. What a fool."

His nephew said: "Come back with me."

"What? Look at me!" He brandished his two canes.

On the walk back, her mother said: "I trust this puts that foolishness out of your mind."

"What foolishness?"

"This foolishness of running off to North America."

"Not in the least."

"Did you not hear the man? He said they have no law there!"

"Oh, aye, Mother, whereas we have plenty of law here."

Whether it was caused by Colin Robertson, or John Richards McKay, or by the sudden destruction of what had been an iron-bound future, Kate found her thoughts drifting into ruts that she had weaned her mind away from years ago. She'd learned that they always led her to the same sterile what-ifs: what if she hadn't stropped her wit so gleefully on Duncan Sutherland, or if she'd let Ian MacBeth put his hand a little farther up her skirt before she'd knocked him down? In daylight she could always remind herself that the children Duncan Sutherland had fathered were the whiniest brats she'd ever seen, and that Ian MacBeth still had the foulest breath of any man she'd ever met under the age of sixty. But sometimes when she woke up in the middle of the night, those weren't the thoughts that came to mind.

When the dawn had just begun to separate the sea from the sky, she shook John awake and got him on his feet for the walk to Golspie. Even at that, there were a hundred others waiting at the inn ahead of them. By the time the Earl of Selkirk's agents were ready to start taking down names, there were seven hundred. With a certain bitterness, Kate wondered where the other six hundred and fifty had been the last time she'd stood in the innyard at Golspie, and what would have happened to the Royal Fusiliers if they'd been here.

A table and chairs were carried out of the public room and set up by the door. Two men sat down with pens and ink bottles and sheafs of paper. One of them was a young man with a set of bristling side whiskers that he must have scalped off an old sea captain, judging by the peach fuzz on the rest of his face. The word drifted back down the line that he was Archibald MacDonald, the Earl of Selkirk's protégé, who was on his way to take up administrative duties in the colony. The other was a Doctor LaSerre, who would be in command of the current contingent of colonists.

About a dozen places ahead of Catherine in the line was Alexander Sutherland, flanked by a younger brother and sister. She was close enough to hear the exchange when they got up to the table.

"Name?"

"Alexander Sutherland."

"Age?"

"Twenty-four."

She burst out laughing, then smothered it as best she could and looked up at the sky. She knew she had a few years on him, but if he was twenty-four, she was the Empress Josephine. When her laughter had subsided she drifted her gaze back down the line behind her and then at the ones who'd already been listed and were wandering away. With very few exceptions all were in their late teens and early twenties, as robust and resilient looking as anyone could expect in a line of refugee crofters.

"Name?"

"Catherine MacPherson."

"Age?"

"Twenty-four."

Between the two ships that the Earl of Selkirk had chartered, there was room for two hundred and fifty. Then word came that one of the ships had been condemned as unseaworthy—the harbormaster at Stromness was a cousin to a certain Mister MacGillivray. That left room for only ninety-three. Thirty-three single men and twenty unmarried women were grafted to the complement of families and young married couples. The oldest of the spinster women, at twenty-four years of age, was Catherine MacPherson, traveling under the care of her brother John.

When the word came that they were, in fact, accepted, Kate finally began to consider that it wasn't just a fishing expedition to the loch that she'd bullied her brother into this time. But then, when she thought back over the years, she realized John had never allowed himself to be bullied into anything unless it was something he'd wanted to do. That way, if the curragh tipped over, he had someone to blame.

The ninety-three were to convene at Thurso on the north coast, where the Orkney boats would ferry them to the deep-water harbor at Stromness. Some were making their way to Thurso as passengers on fishing boats, but it cost no money to walk—up the valley of the Ulidh to the foot of Strath Naver and down to the waiting boats. They were to sail from Stromness on the *Prince of Wales*, in company with the *Eddystone*, a Hudson's Bay Company transport ferrying company cargo and company employees, including John Richards McKay. They would be escorted as far as Iceland by HMS *Brazen* in case some French or American privateer had some momentary lapse of memory as to who ruled the waves.

Kate and John strode north along the east bank of the Ulidh with their bundles slung over their shoulders. It was one of those slate-skied days when the hills seemed luminescent. The heather was in full bloom, and herds of black-faced sheep skipped over the knolls. In the alder bushes and the long shore reeds the sedge warblers were singing. John was crying, which helped Kate to keep her jaw set firm.

The rest of the family had walked them to the edge of DunUlidh, handing over the sailcloth-wrapped bundles they'd carried turn-about until it was time for them to turn back. There was nothing any of them could do there except to kiss and cry and keen as if at a wake and throw their arms around each other and promise to send letters by next spring's ships.

Kate's bundle was heavier than it had been when she'd packed it in the evening. She knew that her mother had snuck something else into it during the night when she'd thought Kate was asleep. With each step it made a curious clunking sound, as of pieces of wood knocking together.

She tried to get John to join in singing to get his mind off the scene back at DunUlidh:

Oh, the summertime is coming
And the leaves are sweetly turning
And the wild mountain thyme
Grows around the purple heather . . .

She realized she was only making it worse.

When they came to the place where Kildonan Burn trickled into the Ulidh, she turned east and led John to the cottage where they'd lived all their lives. There was nothing left but piles of charred rubble. She set down her bundle and untied the string. On the top was the palm-sized japaned tin box she kept her sewing needles in. She had taken the needles out last night, wrapped them in a scrap of cloth, and stowed them at the bottom of the bundle.

Now she slid back the lid on the box, scraped together a little mound of earth with her fingertips, and scooped it into the box. Before she wrapped the bundle together again, she rummaged through to find out what her mother had put in. Wrapped up in her Sunday shawl were a few lengths of old hand-turned doweling. Underneath was a wooden frame.

She grabbed John's bundle and started tearing at the string. "Here, leave that, that's mine. . . ." But by then she had it open. Wedged in among John's things was the wooden wheel that fitted to the dowels and frame. Her mother had known she would have guessed from the feel if she'd put the wheel in her bundle. Under-neath the wheel was her granny's Bible.

Kate put her tin box back and tied the bundles up again. She slung hers on her shoulder and stood up to start off again.

John said: "No. I will go back."

"Back to *what*?" He didn't have an answer, but he shook his head anyway. She stuck out her hand. "Take hold of it, Johnny." He crossed his arms glumly and looked down at the ground. "Take it!"

She led him north through the green graveyard that had been Kildonan parish. There were still crofters in Strath Naver. *Ban mhorhair Chataibh* and Patrick Sellar would get around to them. The last thing she saw of the valley of the River Ulidh was a pair of ospreys circling through the clouds around Ben Griam Mor. It was said that they mated for life and always came back to the same nest in the spring.

CHAPTER 9

The sun was climbing over the Sleeping Giant. In the woods across the river, unseen hordes of songbirds and squirrels were laying their claims to the day. Grant stood on the wharf with his forearms resting on the head of his rifle case while the voyageurs of Duncan Cameron's brigade revolved around him as though he were one of the anchoring hubs of a human conveyor belt.

Except for half a dozen *mangeurs du lard* who had taken a notion once they'd got to Fort William to sign on for a season in the *pays d'en haut*—exchanging their status as veterans of the Montreal run for that of *mooniases* like Grant—the forty men of the brigade were all *hommes du nord*. They tended to be rangier than the *mangeurs du lard* and darker, with less incidence of facial hair and more of high cheekbones, hawk noses, and black eyes.

On Grant's left hand was a line of hunched beasts of burden plodding *pièces* of trade goods to the waiting canoes. On his right hand was a line of light-footed, laughing colts bounding back toward the steadily diminishing consignment of cargo stacked at the base of the wharf. It seemed to Grant that one of them called something out to him as he jogged by. It sounded like "whop-son."

He turned around to face the returning line and picked out the fellow as he plodded back under two *pièces*—a dark, slim specimen of about his own age, with a translucent attempt at a mustache and eyes that were curiously like a snake's—if there was such a thing as a companionable snake. As he approached Grant he grinned and grunted out the word again. This time it was definitely *wappeston*, which meant nothing to him whatever.

The bent back straightened itself minutely, bringing the companionable snake's eyes to within a couple of feet of the level of his own. The grin strained itself a fraction wider and out of it came again: *"Wappeston!"* Grant gave him his best approximation of a cool stare, which was a good deal colder than he imagined. The companionable expression disappeared.

A shade tree uprooted itself and stepped between Grant and the sun. It was Duncan Cameron, folding the manifest sheets into a waterproof valise, the back light making a halo of his golden mane. "Seems we're about ready to get under weigh. First day is always late. You can stow your gear in the lead canoe and ride with me."

The *canots du nord* were half the size of the *canots de maître*. They had the same smell, compounded of wet birch, spruce gum, and cedar, but a different feel to them. As they moved out into midchannel, Grant could feel the changes in water temperature and current through the light skin and resilient cage of cedar ribs. He felt as if he were riding in the breast of a swallow on the currents of the wind.

The paddlers started up a song that was a different version of one Mister Henderson's brigade had sung—more ingenuously obscene. They were working upstream on the Kaministiquia River.

Mister Cameron creaked his back against the midthwart and stretched out his long legs to cross his ankles on the *pièces* stowed in front of him. Because of the narrowness of the *canots du nord* and the wideness of Mister Cameron's shoulders, Grant sat behind instead of beside him. The leonine blond head lolled back and groaned: "I don't believe I would have lived through one more night of rendezvousing. We're going to be next-door neighbors, Grant—no more than two hundred miles as the crow flies. I've been shifted from Nipigon to Bas de la Rivière—any longer than a few years at one post and your brain starts to seep out your ears like a cheese left in the sun. You'll be pleased to know you're assigned to your old stomping grounds along the Qu'Appelle.''

"My which?''

"Your old haunts. 'Course Fort Tremblante is gone—in between the Indians' drifting and the Hudson's Bay bastards setting up upstream every chance they get, we spend more time tearing down and slapping up forts than we do trading furs.''

Grant tried to assess what "Fort Tremblante" was supposed to mean. "Fort of the Quakers?''

Cameron exploded with laughter and slapped his beefy paw on his thigh, then looked back over his shoulder and stopped laughing. "Oh, sorry, I thought you were . . . damned funny, though, even if you didn't mean it. Fort de la Rivière Tremblante . . . ? It was your father's post when you were growing up. *Tremblante*, as in the trees.'' He looked up and down the riot of trees along the riverbank and then thrust out his arm to point. "There! Those trees. *Tremblantes*.''

In among the richer greens of oak and pine and maple, there was a patch of paler trees with smooth, gray-green bark, their heart-shaped leaves quivering in the breeze and rippling their silver undersides to the sun. Over the splash and roll of the river it was impossible to hear anything so subtle as the rattling of the leaves one against the other, but Grant knew it was there. He said: "Do they, by chance . . . Would they, the *tremblantes*, happen to have a . . . a curious odor to them? A perfume?''

"Perfume? Not so's you'd notice, perhaps a little in the spring. . . . Ah—you're thinking of the poplars. Well, they're both poplars. Very much alike, except the *tremblantes* shimmer, and the balsam poplars have the scent. You'll find them together all across the prairies, wherever there's a slough or a stream, just about every place there's water there's poplars.'' The big right hand suddenly slapped down on the rim of the canoe, bringing an anguished glance back from the guide in the prow. "Ha! There, you see? You do remember!'' He dropped his head back over the midthwart to give Grant a wink under an upside-down grin. Grant didn't grin back.

Three days upriver they passed a cave mouth that the winds hooted and howled through, at the foot of a long, rocky gorge with a waterfall at the end—white silk roaring straight down a broken-toothed plunge of black rock. The palette inside the gorge was dark and deep: the green and amber moss and red-scaled pine bushes and black walls all gleaming with a patina of fine mist.

The portage went up a steep, slick trail along the side of the falls.

Grant fell in with the line of moccasined pack animals, in front of four headless figures under a turtled canoe and behind a surprisingly scrawny *homme du nord* gasping under two *pièces*. It was Alex Fraser, the snake-eyed one who had spoken the Indian word to him back on the wharf. Through observation and eavesdropping, Grant had come to the conclusion that this was Alex Fraser's first season as a voyageur—although it seemed like a contradiction that someone could have lived out his whole life in the *pays d'en haut* and still be as much of a *moonias* as he was himself.

Fraser's lead foot slipped off the slick edge of the next step in the rock. The *pièces* on his back shuddered and wavered, teetering him on the edge of the foam diving down to the rocks below. Grant put his hands out and steadied the lower *pièce*. Fraser found his balance again and grunted back into his gasping ascent. Grant sneaked one cupped hand under the base of the *pièce* and surreptitiously boosted it with all the strength he could get into his forearm, holding it until they got to the crest of the slope. He didn't imagine it took a great deal of the weight off, but it was something.

Above the falls the country changed. The thick-trunked, broadcapped forest they'd been winding through became a tangled mass of twisted, gnarled bush and jumbled rock faces. At the first camp past the falls, word went around that the fresh meat they'd stocked in at Fort William had all been eaten. The *engagés* started up a chant of *"rubaboo, rubaboo,"* rubbing their bellies and sticking out their tongues as though they were gagging. The tin plate the cook handed Grant was filled with a species of floury broth lapping island chunks of water-logged shoe leather and floating bits of onion. The cubes of shoe leather turned out to be some kind of meat, smoky and chewy and gamy. Mister Cameron flopped down on the deadfall he was leaning on, spooning mouthfuls of the same concoction off his own plate. Grant asked him what it was.

"*Rubaboo.*"

"Ah. And what is a *rubaboo*? Some manner of quadruped?"

Mister Cameron laughed in midswallow, shooting a bite of half-pulped meat onto his plate. He wiped his chin with the back of his wrist, popped the ejaculated chunk back into his mouth, and said: "I never know when you're pulling my leg, Grant. *Rubaboo* is pemmican stew. Hmm . . . '*Rubaboo* is pemmican stew,' not bad."

"I see. And pemmican is . . . ?"

"Now I know you're pulling my leg."

"Not at all. I've seen the word on manifest lists, of course, but . . ."

"You don't remember the taste?"

"Mister Cameron, if pemmican is another instance of the many things that are supposedly familiar to me from my long years as a wild Indian, I am forced to repeat for the ten thousandth time—"

"Don't get your sporran in a knot, son. Pemmican is cured buffalo meat—dried and pounded to shreds and bagged in tallow. Sometimes they use venison, but buffalo lasts best. So long as you keep the bags from getting waterlogged it'll last forever, or a lot longer than you or I will, at least. And it's concentrated—daily rations for an *homme du nord* are eight pounds of fresh meat or a pound and a half of pemmican. If the Plains tribes hadn't invented pemmican, the company of so-called gentlemen and squat-to-piss adventurers traipsing into Hudson's Bay'd sleep a lot easier."

"Why?"

"They can run their provisions into the bay by the shipload, straight into the heart of the fur country. We have to be paddling back and forth between Fort William and the Athabasca every summer. And without pemmican we sure as hell wouldn't."

"So in a sense, then"—Grant couldn't help but smile at the aptness of the analogy he was about to come out with—"pemmican is to the North West Company what coal is to Mr. Blake's dark, satanic mills."

Mister Cameron thought about it for a moment. "Which mills?"

"Likely"—Grant had to forcibly pull in the corners of his mouth to get the words out—"likely the James Mills from Mister Blake's point of observation." It was quite the most delightfully double-edged pun, cutting both William Blake and Jeremy Bentham's Utilitarians at the same stroke.

Mister Cameron said: "Well, it's an early morning tomorrow. . . ."

The mornings blended into one another; long days paddling or lining the canoes upstream or hauling the cargo through the bush. And then Grant came out at the end of yet another long portage of shadowed thickets and tumbled granite ridges to find an astounding phenomenon waiting at the other end: a body of water that flowed in the direction they were traveling.

According to the science of cartography, they had just crossed over the height of land that separated the Atlantic watershed from the river system flowing north and west. According to the Royal Charter of the Governor and Company of Adventurers Trading into Hudson's Bay, they had just crossed out of Upper Canada into Rupertsland, the HBC's private preserves, and were now trespassing.

According to the Earl of Selkirk's land grant, they had just crossed the southeastern boundary of Assiniboia and were now under the jurisdiction of his governor. According to North West Company tradition, they had just crossed into the *pays d'en haut*, and every *moonias* in the party was about to be initiated into the fraternity of *les hommes du nord*.

Mister Cameron distributed a tot of rum to all the men who were already *hommes du nord*. While they were downing that, the guide—with a great deal of consultation and advice from the other veterans—selected a well-needled cedar bough and amputated it with his skinning knife. Then he walked toward the lakeshore whipping his bough through the air for a warm-up. The first *moonias* was brought forward.

The *mangeur du lard* was made to kneel on a rock jutting over the water. The guide dipped his cedar bough in the lake and worked the *moonias* over until he was thoroughly baptised in the waters of the *pays d'en haut*. Then the new *homme du nord* was given his tot of rum and made to pledge that he would never step aside for a *mangeur du lard*, never let a *moonias* cross into the *pays d'en haut* without being initiated, and never fuck another voyageur's wife without her permission.

Grant hung back by the inland edge of the clearing and watched the guide and his brother *avants* pounce one by one on the other junior clerks and the green *mangeurs du lard*. It looked to be a painless enough ceremony. And it was certainly providing a good deal of harmless amusement to the veterans. There was a strain of self-mockery running through their performance, as though the ceremony were a kind of solemn-faced joke that only those who'd been through it were allowed to laugh at. All in all, there was no reason why the back of his neck should have knotted up like a cluster of gnarled pine roots.

The guide finished up the last of the *mangeurs du lard* and was about to throw his branch of office in the water when he caught sight of Grant. He pointed him out gleefully, and one of the other *avants* trotted across the moss- and lichen-encrusted rock campsite to fetch him. Grant took a half step back, shaking his head. The *avant* nodded his head, laughing happily at how well Grant was playing his part—at least half the fun lay in the reluctance of the initiates. He put his hand on Grant's shoulder. Grant shrugged it off. The laugh faded. He reached for the shoulder again, and Grant batted it away.

The wind-scarred face of the *avant*, burnt the same red-black color as an old bloodstain, lost all its good humor. Over his shoulder, Grant could see two of the new *hommes du nord*—the ones who had come west with Mister Henderson's brigade—turning their heads toward him and murmuring to the others.

The *avant* took another step in toward him. Grant stepped back, wondering why he was digging in his heels against a bit of harmless idiocy. He said: *"Je suis un homme du nord."* The *avant* stopped and squinted at him, wrestling with the question of whether Grant was trying to be insulting.

The bull-moose bellow of Duncan Cameron's voice came down: "Mister Grant is certainly within his rights. I know for a certainty he's wintered seven years along the Qu'Appelle. If that doesn't qualify him as an *homme du nord*, there's a lot of you are going to have to line up to get christened again." He poured out one last measure of rum, and they all drank loudly to the boys of the north.

Grant didn't join them. He moved down to the shore out of sight of the camp and sat on his heels looking out over the water. The sky to the west had broken up into irregular stained-glass shards of red and black and a blue like the back of a swallow. There was a woodpecker hammering in the woods behind him. Something splashed out on the lake, leaving ripples.

Discounting the stopover at Fort William, it had been nine weeks of solid traveling since he'd left Lachine. Nine weeks of dawn-to-sunset crawling across this armored backbone of the continent, clinging like blind men to the guides who claimed to know the difference between Roderick McKenzie's route and the thousands of identical deer paths and stream mouths, every one of which was the gateway to an endless labyrinth of tangled deadfalls and granite and mosquito hatcheries.

From the far side of the lake echoed a brazen, maniacal, fluting laugh that would have sent St. Augustine diving for his *Pocket Guide to Agents of the Fiend Known to Inhabit Lonely Wildernesses*. Grant knew that it was only the bird known in Gaelic as the rain goose, which British naturalists called the great northern diver and the North Americans called a loon. But for all his ornithology, his breath had grown just as scant and tremulous as any superstitious old mystic's.

He had to face the fact that he was doing and saying and feeling things that he couldn't account for. Nothing beyond the pale, perhaps, but he didn't much care for it. He didn't care for it at all.

Chapter 10

Kate was soaring lazily above the slate-blue steel mirror of Loch An Ruathair watching for the silver spark of a fish beneath the waves. Her arched white wings reflected on the water in fragmented segments, their bands of black blending in and disappearing. An identical reflection grew beside hers as another osprey arced down and skimmed across the surface of the water. Someone was shaking her shoulder and calling her name.

She came back slowly to the creaking and swaying of the ship and the thick, dank smells of the cargo hold where ninety-three Highland crofters had been battened in for fourteen days. Ninety-one, she reminded herself. Hugh MacDonald and William Sutherland had been commended to the waves, dead of the fever.

According to Doctor LaSerre, it was typhus. Whatever it was, it didn't seem to affect her like the others, so she'd been doing what she could to help—holding the basin to catch the blood let out by Doctor LaSerre's lancet, bathing the sick with cold water to bring their fever down, spooning barley broth down their throats.

The hand shaking her shoulder grew more insistent. "Katy, please, you must wake up!" She opened her eyes to the flat round face of Catherine Sutherland, bouncing between light and shade with the swinging of the two feeble lanterns suspended overhead. The braid-framed, bannocklike features bore no resemblance to the older brother's—Alexander, the awkward fiddler.

The fact that Kate had opened her eyes only mollified Catherine Sutherland for a moment. She started shaking her shoulder again. "Katy, are you awake now?"

"Hmm."

"Please. Doctor LaSerre, he—"

"I know." Someone had packed her jaw in jelly while she was sleeping. She flexed it and cracked the hinges. "I know. Time to take my turn again. . . ."

"No. There is something wrong with him. Just after you lay

down. He fell. We laid him on a bed, but I cannot wake him now. He is dreadful hot."

Kate sat up and threw off the plaid draped over her legs. "Where is he?"

"There," pointing at the far end of the hold. "We laid him on Willy's bed."

"You *what*? You put him on—" She cut herself off. It was criminally stupid to have laid the doctor down on blankets soaked with a dead man's fever sweat, but she wondered how clear her own thinking would have been if it was her baby brother they'd just slid into the ocean. She jacked herself up to her feet and picked her way down the hold between the pallets of the sick and dying and their bundles of possessions. By now the sailor's gait of rolling from the hips to accommodate the swaying of the ship was second nature to her.

Beside the ragged bit of sailcloth that Catherine Sutherland had tacked up for a curtain around her younger brother's bed there was a young man squatted on the deck flipping frantically through the pages of a book. It registered peripherally that the young man was Archibald MacDonald, the side-whiskered protégé of Lord Selkirk. She assumed that the book was a Bible.

She jerked up the curtain. Doctor LaSerre was lying on his back with his chin jutting upward, his lips drawn back from his teeth. She placed her hand gingerly across his forehead. The skin was wet with sweat, but not—as Catherine had led her to expect—hot. It was clammy and cold. She put her hand under his shirt and pressed the left side of his chest—the soft, fatty muscle giving way beneath her fingers like a cushion. She took her hand away and lined her fingertips along the side of his throat, below the jaw, as he had showed her to do. She said: "He is dead."

Archibald MacDonald said: "Not necessarily. I have almost collated the symptoms. . . ."

She looked down. It wasn't a Bible, it was a medical book. "Bugger your symptoms. He is dead."

Archibald MacDonald closed his book and rose slowly to his feet. He squared his shoulders and said grimly: "Then I am in command." He turned his head to survey the length of the hold and his new responsibilities. Kate followed his gaze.

The swinging bars of light and shadow made of it a shifting magic-lantern show: slack scarecrows sitting up with their forearms draped across their knees, parched bundles of bones stretched on their backs staring up at nothing, men with drained faces pulling up the coverings that their wives threw back off in pendulum response . . . all underscored with the hissing and grunting and gabbling of delirium. Somewhere in the shadows a woman was crooning "The Garten Mother's Lullaby," intermittently overborne by a male voice bellowing.

Kate swung her gaze back to Archibald MacDonald. His eyes were stretched open like a ewe giving birth. He licked his lips as though he were about to say something, but for a moment nothing came out. When it did it was: "We will . . . what we will do is . . . we shall . . ."

Within a few days Kate had lost all notion of the past or the future, or of any world outside this sealed-in, bobbing communal coffin. The universe was constituted of clammy limbs hot to the touch, the damp rags and the buckets of seawater, the bleeding lancet, and the clumsy hands of helpers even less adept than she.

By far the worst of all her patients was Alexander Sutherland. His sister told her that he'd once had something called Walcheren fever—named after some campaign in Flanders—that had become chronic and was more responsible for his discharge from the army than the wound in his knee. Whether that was compounding the typhus or for some other reason, he had sunk immediately into a delirium crisis that wouldn't end. But he refused to die.

His fever dreams seemed much more torturous than those of her other patients. He would thrash his limbs about and gyrate and bark out nonsense phrases or words in foreign languages. One of them— *guerrilla*—was explained to her by Robert Gunn, the piper, as a Spanish word that had been brought back to Britain by the soldiers of the peninsular campaign. He said it meant "the little war," which seemed to her to be a pretty fair description of what she went through every time it came Alexander Sutherland's turn to be spoon-fed or swabbed down.

She was passing by his pallet one day—or night, she'd given up trying to differentiate—when she noticed he was actually sleeping calmly. She was lugging her bucket of water and rags up to the bow end of the hold to start her rounds, but this was too rare an opportunity to pass up. She squatted down beside him, jerked the grimy plaid that covered his body down to his waist, wrung out one of the rags floating in the bucket, and went to work. His torso was emaciated, the collarbones and ribs and tendons of his arms pushing out through the skin. The fever flush in his face made his hair appear lighter, more golden, sticking to his forehead in damp curls.

He started to shiver. She kept at it with a callousness that would have surprised her a week ago. Doctor LaSerre had said that cold swabbing would bring the fever down, and that was that. As the cold worked its way in, he began to moan. His right hand came up and tried to brush away her hand and the wet rag, but there was no strength left in it.

His moans began to form themselves into words. "Cold . . . Sergeant . . . can't . . . Rest by the . . . did and where is he now? . . . ice in her hair . . . Flower of the roadway—soft as silk but feel it through your boot soles—step we gaily on we go, heel for heel and toe . . ." He was crying, the tears eking their way out between his eyelids.

As though it had no connection to the man inside the body, his right hand began to edge across the rough ticking of his pallet, the fingers stretching out lazily and then curling, pulling the hand along behind it like a crab with one set of legs crushed. When it came to the far edge of the pallet, the fingers reached over the rim, scrabbling for something underneath. They came out with the edge of a folded piece of paper and pressed it securely to the palm.

His breathing grew more regular and deep. Kate dropped the rag back in the bucket and dried her hands on her skirt. They were red and numb and cracked from the saltwater, but with so many mouths and throats burnt dry with fever, freshwater was far too precious to waste on skin. She drew the plaid back up to cover his body. The arm that had stretched out to reach the piece of paper lay uncovered. The hand had gone slack, the fingers falling away from the projecting corner of the paper. She took hold of his wrist, raised the edge of the plaid, and pushed his arm in underneath it.

As she lowered the covering her eyes traveled to the piece of paper still poking up between the edge of the thin mattress and the curved planking of the hull. She glanced around to see if anyone was watching her, then reached across Alexander Sutherland and tugged the paper free.

It unfolded awkwardly, a stiff vellum parchment folded twice across its width. Her eyes were drawn down immediately, skipping past the lines of writing to the red wax seal with a signet ring impression at the bottom of the page. Beside it was a flowery signature in a grand hand. She had never been clever at deciphering the more exotic flourishes of penmanship; most of her reading had been the plain, clear print of hymn books and Bibles. But once she'd puzzled out the capitals in the signature, the rest of the letters leaped into focus—Thomas Douglas, Earl of Selkirk.

The paper suddenly vanished with a crackling tear, replaced like
a conjuring trick with Alexander Sutherland's sharp-toothed face.
"Thief! Do you think me that far gone that you can . . ." And then
John Bannerman was behind him, with his thick hands pulling the
thin shoulders back.

John Bannerman was of her little brother's generation—as all
single males seemed to be—an earnest boy with green eyes, red
hair, and milk-white skin, but a broad back and big hands despite
the delicacy of his coloring. The fever had hardly touched him, and
he'd enlisted himself right from the first in the Archibald MacDonald Memorial We Hope Nursing Corps.

Alexander Sutherland's eyes were already clouding over; the
clarity had only been a momentary aberration. John Bannerman
eased him back down onto the bed, one clawed hand still clutching
the paper to his chest, and Kate covered him.

CHAPTER 11

Rainy River and Rainy Lake both lived up to their appel-
lations. The *engagés* simply shucked their shirts, tucked
them under the *pièces,* and kept on paddling. The gentlemen kept
dry as best they could with bits of tarpaulin and oilcloth. Rainy
River opened out into Lake of the Woods. For three days they
wound through shallow shoreline inlets that miraculously transformed themselves into broad channels between islands. It was a
world of clouds of mist and clouds of waterbirds, of green-black
water and black-trunked spruce and peeling-ivory birch, of crag-
ended shore boulders of white or black or gray with veins of pink
and green and red and blue.

They camped on island inlets or sheltered outcroppings of the
shoreline. Whether on cedar-needle carpets or sandy beaches or
mossy cul-de-sacs, Grant wasn't sleeping many nights through.
There were strange, half-human creatures peopling his dreams,
bear's heads stuck on human necks and wolves with hands. They
called to him in words he didn't understand. Darting in and out

of their shadows was a small, lithe, black-and-brown thing—something like an otter or a monkey, Grant could never get it to stay still long enough to tell. Sometimes he chased it and sometimes it chased him. He could think of no good reason why, even in his dreams, he should be afraid of such a winsome little thing. But whenever it moved toward him, he would back away. If it kept on coming, he would turn and run.

Lake of the Woods emptied into the Winnipeg River. In among the *engagés'* conversations, Grant began to hear a word—*dalles*—that he didn't know. Which was curious, since his French vocabulary was three times the size of any of theirs. The closest he could think of was the French *dalle*, for a paving stone or gravestone. . . . A low rumbling came from the north, the direction the river flowed in. The guide fished out a spare paddle from the bow and passed it back to Mister Cameron. Cameron grinned over his shoulder at Grant's expression of offended propriety. "Everybody paddles through the *dalles*. If we don't move faster than the water, the *gouvernail*'s got no steerageway. If he can't steer, the *dalles* will spit us out the other end like *rubaboo*."

He seemed remarkably jaunty for that grim a prediction. A manic sheen was forming over his eyes, and a narrow flush brushed along each cheek from the wings of his nostrils. Something of the same mood seemed to have overtaken the *engagés*, who were bending a little harder into their strokes. Their song had petered out even though they had barely touched on verse fourteen.

There was a tap on Grant's shoulder. He turned his head and found himself facing the pommel of a paddle that the *gouvernail* was holding by the blade. He took it obediently and did his best to copy the grip of the professionals. Mister Cameron said: "Just plant it in like a shovel and try to keep in time." The rumbling grew louder. The river spun around a bend into a narrow, rock-walled channel and exploded into white froth.

Grant dug his paddle in hard. The *milieus* had already finished their stroke and were chopping at the water again. He gave up trying to match them and just scooped at the water as fast as he could. There was white foam as high as the gunwales and jagged white walls gleaming with quartz flakes on either side. The guide was skewed out over the front of the canoe like a figurehead, hugging the prow, waving his free arm, and bellowing over the roar of the rapids: *"Droit, droit, droit—à gauche! À gauche!"* The *gouvernail* was up in a standing crouch in the stern, leaning his body into the shaft of the steering paddle.

A granite fang that would have disemboweled a naval frigate shot
by, bumping Grant's paddle blade against the eggshell skin of the
canoe. The wind whipped his hair against his ears, and the water
tried to yank the paddle out of his hand with every stroke. If the
guide blinked, if the *gouvernail* misheard one syllable, if any one
of the paddlers let up on the sprint, they would all be shredded on
the rocks.

The guide began to scream louder, whipping his hand in an arc
behind his back. Grant felt a suffocating urge to lean up to see what
the guide was screaming about or to look back and make sure that
the *gouvernail* was paying attention. He stomped down hard on
both urges and kept paddling.

They skipped down two long terraces of foam and missed a
series of rock spines by about the width of a clergyman's mind.
Grant was sure his eyes had registered, on the base of the last
spine, a tiny olive-gray bird with stick legs and a nose like a tooth-
pick, darting merrily through the maelstrom.

Then the walls dropped away, and the canoe splashed down onto
a placid, green-glass pond with water lilies crowding its edges.
Grant let his wooden arms go slack and started to lean back. Mister
Cameron barked: "Not yet!" He leaped back to his jig-time paddling until the *gouvernail* allowed them to ease up. As they did, the
second canoe in the brigade blew out of the *dalles* like a shell out
of a cannon. Had they slowed down any earlier, its prow would
now be having carnal relations with their stern.

Grant propped his paddle across the gunwales, leaned back
against the *pièce* behind him, and laughed. He couldn't think of
what there was to laugh about, but he kept doing it. Mister Cameron
looked back over his shoulder and grinned. "Well, damn me for a
sassenach, you really do have a heart in there somewhere," he said.

Grant sat up stiffly and composed himself. There was another
low rumbling up ahead.

The river kept it up for three days, alternating between fast water
and insanely fast water. The pad at the join of the fingers on Grant's
right hand grew blisters where the curved tip of the paddle pommel
pressed against it. The blisters broke and welled up again and turned
green. His arms stayed attached to his shoulders with glue and spit.
His legs started to atrophy from being cramped up tense beneath
him. The muscles in his back felt like a cowhide that had been
tanned and stripped and braided into buggy whips with the cow
still in it. But if he'd had time to think of it, he would have been

grateful to the river, because when it came time to camp at night he would gobble down his plate of *rubaboo*, drop onto his blankets and leap through a dreamless sleep to the safe dawn and the guide hollering "Levé!" and kicking down tentpoles.

The river Winnipeg finally exhausted itself and spread its banks to become Lake Winnipeg. The lake stretched over the north horizon, a placid steel blue with flat, sandy shorelines. After weeks of being hemmed in by evergreens and granite ridges, it was a lot of sky to look at. On the lakeshore west of the rivermouth stood the North West Company post of Bas de la Rivière Winnipeg.

As the brigade offloaded the cargo and drew the canoes up on the beach, a motley group of worn-out *engagés* and brown-skinned women and children shambled out the palisade gates. One of them, a reedy specimen with hound-dog eyes and a wispy jaw beard, actually had the temerity to approach the fort's new bourgeois while he was busy trying to sort out the jumbled *pièces* into the order on the manifest sheets. "Monsieur Cameron . . ."

"Hm? Oh, *bonjour*, Falcon. Nomading it this summer? Be a good fellow and back off the beach while we're getting the cargo sorted out. Come up and see me for a dram once I get settled in." Falcon retreated with a dejected droop. Mister Cameron called the crew together and numbered off the dozen *pièces* that were to go into the fort. "Cover the rest over with tarpaulin and leave a guard. No use hauling them off the beach; you'd just have to haul them back again tomorrow morning."

One of the *gouvernails* said: "*Tomorrow* morning?"

"Yes, *tomorrow* morning. Unless you plan to haul them over the last leg on ice skates."

The *engagés* looked far from happy, but they did what they'd been told and kept their grumbling to themselves. Grant wondered whether their obedience was due to some inbred respect for authority, or to the force of Mister Cameron's personality, or to the force implied in Mister Cameron's hands—which looked to have been designed for poleaxing Highland cattle without a poleax. He was beginning to form the impression that it was a combination of all three.

"Come along, Grant, we'll see where we can get you settled for the night."

They were almost at the gate when the droopy, hound-dog-eyed fellow intercepted them. "Monsieur Cameron, I was—"

"Later, Falcon"—the bourgeois brushed past him—"Give us a

chance to get perched. Crippled Christ on a crooked crutch, once these people get the whiff of a chance to cadge a drink . . .''

Grant glanced back over his shoulder. Alex Fraser the snake-eyed had come over to Falcon the hound-dog-eyed. The two of them murmured with their heads together, then shot a look at the backs of the receding gentlemen. Curiously, it seemed to Grant that they had been discussing him.

Within the perimeter of Fort Bas de la Rivière were a couple of rectangular warehouses with a square cabin between them and a number of low sheds and outbuildings snuggled up against the palisade to save the trouble of building one wall. Mister Cameron proceeded toward the door of the cabin between the warehouses. The roof shingles were covered over with moss, and the lone window had no shutter, although it wasn't likely that many flies got past the cobwebs. The door itself was hanging inwards by one leather hinge. The bourgeois put his boot to it, and the other hinge gave way.

Mister Cameron disappeared into the interior, bellowing and—by the sounds of things—hurling pieces of furniture about. Grant hung back discreetly, standing in the dusty, weed-choked courtyard, letting his eyes drift over the face of the cabin. Despite the dilapidation there was something surprisingly cozy about it and inexplicably familiar. It was nothing but an adzed-log cabin with a cedar shake roof of eccentric but serviceable design. He could line out quite clearly in his mind the details of its construction but couldn't explain the effect that its appearance had on him. It was rather as if, in the illustrated dictionary of his mind, the little copper-plate reproduction beside the word ''home'' was of an adzed-log cabin with exactly such a roof.

A flock of fort *engagés* and Indian women went running past Grant into the cabin. After an entr'acte chorus of bellows and apologies they came running back out again, dispersed in all directions, and then converged on the cabin again bearing brooms and buckets and carpenter's tools.

Duncan Cameron came out smiling. ''Well, a few minutes and the place should be habitable.''

The hound-dog-eyed fellow called Falcon drifted forward across the compound. ''Monsieur Cameron . . .''

''Damn it, Falcon, you're charming enough company, but I will not be in any mood for company until I've found a place to settle my ass and filled my belly.''

"Yes, sir." The eyes drooped lower, the eyebrows elevated, and the upper lip puffed out like a bullfrog's throat. He turned to go.

"No, wait a moment. Do you know where Neskisho Sutherland is?"

"Yes."

"Good. Be a good fellow and fetch her for me, no one else seems to . . . Well?"

Falcon was still standing there. "It would take some time."

"Yes, yes, all right, I know you're not on the lists this season. I'll make it worth your while."

The eyebrows elevated even higher. "It would take a long time."

"Then the sooner you get started . . ."

"Maybe till, oh . . . next spring."

"What?"

"She's out around the Fishing Lakes on the Qu'Appelle. . . ."

"She's *where*? She signed on to guide from Bas de la Rivière to the Qu'Appelle—I have the papers with her mark on them! I'll break her!"

"She's doing that already, starting with her leg. Her horse fell on her. I told her she was getting too fat, but she—"

"Wonderful. Delightful. What the hell am I supposed to do for a guide?"

"Me."

"You?"

"That's why I'm here instead of back with my wife and my new baby. Neskisho asked me to take her job for her."

"You've never even been a *milieu*!"

"That's why I thought I'd do well as a guide—guides don't have to paddle or carry anything."

Mister Cameron laughed. He looked at the sky and then back at Falcon. "Well, you know the country, there's no question about that. And if Neskisho thought you could do it . . . But you'd better be very clear about one thing—any item on the manifest list that doesn't make it to its destination is coming off your wage. At retail prices. Oh, and do you swim?" Falcon shot him an appalled look. "Good. Because if one of those canoes runs into a rock and sinks, you'll be better off going down with it. This is the bourgeois of your brigade, Mister Grant."

The hound-dog eyes drifted over to Grant and rested for an instant before the nod of acknowledgment. They had taken on an opaque cast, with something lurking that could have been amusement or malice or anything in between.

Mister Cameron's last sentence suddenly registered on Grant. "The bourgeois?"

"Yes. I'll stay on here, of course, especially seeing the deplorable condition MacLeod's left the place in."

"But I've never—I don't even know the route. . . ."

"Nothing to it—three days south to the head of the lake, turn left up the Red, three days to the Forks, turn right up the Assiniboine, eight days to Portage la Prairie, another eight to Brandon House—skip the turnoff up the Souris—six days to Fort Montagne à la Bosse, bear to your right, six days to the Qu'Appelle, turn left, and two days puts you at Fort Esperance. Or thereabouts." He winked at Grant's mask of horror. "Don't worry, that's Falcon's job."

Falcon said: "Not Esperance."

Mister Cameron said: "That's what the trip sheet says."

"They broke down Esperance to move upstream where the Hudson's Bay put a new post. Now it's Fort John."

"John? Fort John? What kind of a flat-ale excuse for a name is Fort John?"

"For John Pritchard, the bourgeois."

"Ah. Well, I'll tell you what, Falcon. If Little Pritchard is going to be Mister Grant's introduction to the *pays d'en haut*, maybe you'd be good enough to drop by whenever you're in the area and sprinkle on a pound or two of salt."

Falcon said: "Introduction?" Grant looked at him sharply, but the eyes remained opaque.

Sitting in the bourgeois's renovated cabin in front of the fire—banked up to discourage the blackflies from infiltrating down the chimney—the three of them puffed on their pipes and belched up recent memories of venison and wild rice and Indian parsnips. Mister Cameron said to Falcon: "How are the *jardinières* progressing?"

"I came overland, not by the Forks, so I didn't see. From what I hear, though, they got new barracks buildings up and more seeds in the ground than last year. I hear their sheep didn't make it through the winter. . . ." He threw back his head, gave a lifelike rendition of a wolf howl, then rolled his eyes happily and licked his lips.

Mister Cameron shook his head and let out an angry sigh. "If those bastards have their way, you'll be driven off before you get to be much older—or yoked together to pull their ploughs."

Grant said: "Which bastards?"

"That bloody Bible peer Selkirk and his colony of *jardinières*."

Grant stuck his pipe back in his mouth. The Highland Clearances, or the "Improvements," as the champions of progressiveness called it, had been a subject of much academic debate during his last year at Inverness. Grant had been as prone to pompous pamphlet quoting as any other senior classman, until he'd come across a family of what he'd taken to be beggars by the side of the road. He'd dug a few pennies out of his pocket. The chief scarecrow had looked down at the coins in Grant's hand, then stared levelly into his eyes and said: "We are not beggars, we are MacLeods of Assynt—or we were. God knows what we are now, but we are not beggars. Bless you, though, for your kind heart."

Despite his best intentions, Grant tugged the pipe back out of his mouth and said: " 'Bastards' is not a word I would apply to the crofters who have been driven off their homes, nor to the man who is trying to help them."

"Och, aye." Mister Cameron slid into Gaelic, a lilting burr spiced with manful melancholia. "We cannot but feel pity for the poor, proud, put-upon people. Those of the Flowers o' the Forest who were not trodden under at Culloden and Flodden are now to be torn out by the roots. But the Earl of Selkirk and the company of indenturers are only bringing them across the ocean to use them."

Falcon cocked an eyebrow at Grant and jerked his pipe stem at Mister Cameron. "Is he talking garlic again?"

"Gaelic," Mister Cameron corrected him.

Falcon shrugged. He said to Grant: "Another cup of wine and he'll start telling you stories about his childhood in the misty highlands of . . . Schenectady, New York."

Mister Cameron laid one hand on his heart and said: "I'm not ashamed that we were forced to flee to the Colonies. But by the time we left the Highlands I had already reached the age of eighteen."

Falcon said: "Weeks?"

Mister Cameron said: "Months." And then the two of them burst into laughter. When it was done, Mister Cameron carried on in French: "It makes no difference when I left, my heart's still in the Highlands. Just as yours is still in Paris. . . ."

"Paris?" Falcon started laughing again.

"Well, Montreal, then."

"Why should I give a damn about Montreal? This is my home— the *pays d'en haut*."

"Ah, but for how long?" Mister Cameron winked at Falcon gravely and passed the bottle around one more time. "If I were you, Falcon, I'd start teaching my newborn son to speak Gaelic—no, English, rather, the men that run the colony and the Company of Dentures are far more comfortable in English, and those are the men your son is going to have to take orders from once that colony gets its claws in.''

Falcon shrugged. ''They leave us alone, we leave them alone.''

Mister Cameron leaned back, pursed his lips into a crooked smile, and nodded his head slowly.

CHAPTER 12

Kate was standing on the foredeck of the *Prince of Wales*, watching the gray pencil line in the distance swell gradually into a shoreline. The old tub's prow shuddered after each head-on wave, like a dim bull trying conclusions with an oak tree. There was no sign of the sails of the *Eddystone* in the whole circle of the horizon. She assumed it had gone on ahead and was already at anchor in the harbor at York Factory, somewhere along that charcoal-sketch line. She'd managed to get out of one of the sailors that HMS *Brazen* had finished its escort assignment and turned back somewhere around the tip of Greenland. The crew weren't much for making conversation—a third of them were still down with the fever.

After weeks below deck, Kate felt a bit drunk on crisp, salted air and the immeasurable expanse of gray water and blue sky.

A hand came down beside hers on the rail. She turned her head, expecting to find John Bannerman. Instead, it was Alexander Sutherland, looking like Lazarus the day after—and smelling the part as well. She wondered if she did, too, now that there was fresh air for contrast. He had a woolen coat drawn tight around his throat and civilian trousers and boots underneath. His eyes were on her when she turned, and he nodded. ''Miss MacPherson,'' he said, then looked past her at the shoreline.

''I am glad to see you on your feet, Mister Sutherland.''

"Thank you." He kept his eyes directed at the shore. "Not only for saying so, but for making it possible."

"It is entirely your own doing, Mister Sutherland. If I had it in me to cure anyone, your brother and the others would still be alive."

He didn't seem to have anything further to say, but neither did he move away. She began to get a little annoyed. If the order of the day was to stand silently watching the shoreline grow, she much preferred to do it alone. Suddenly he said: "I remember very little of the time since we left Stromness—which I suppose is as good a way to spend six weeks in a cargo hold as any—but it does leave me with a certain niggling . . . I do hope that . . . It is a bit embarrassing, you see. Out of the little that I do remember, I find it impossible to tell for certain which of it actually took place. I do hope, though, that I did not do or say anything that might have been poor repayment for the comfort you were trying to . . . Sometimes, you see, in a fever a man can—well, it is one thing in a military hospital, where all the surgeons and attendants are hardened to that sort of thing, but—"

"Mister Sutherland, I can assure you that you neither did nor said anything untoward."

He let out a sigh of relief. "Good."

"And even if you had, what kind of a Christian would I be to hold a grudge against a man for what he said or did when he was half-mad with fever?"

He laughed oddly. "What kind of a Christian indeed?" It was enough to pull her head around again, given that she wasn't aware of having said anything to amuse. His face was disfigured with a hard-bitten ghost of a smile. She turned away again.

A moment earlier she might easily have taken offense or demanded an explanation, but his fumbling apology had reminded her of something. "Oh, by the by, Mister Sutherland, I was wondering . . . There was . . . on a day when I was bathing you, and you were having a dream about—oh, I do not know what, you said something about 'ice in her hair' or some such—if I am prying, do tell me so—but I could not help but notice at the time that there was a . . ."

"I do not remember the occasion, but I certainly know what the dream must have been about."

"What I meant to ask was—"

"You are not prying, although it is not a pretty story. It was Corunna—'Not a drum was heard, not a funeral note as his corse to the rampart we carried . . .' Grand stuff, hm? The glorious

burial of the glorious Sir John Moore at the glorious battle of Corunna. . . ."

"To tell the truth, Mister Sutherland, I was only—"

"No, no, I do not mind speaking of it. We had chased the
Frenchies through the mountains into Spain, and then the generals
heard that Bonaparte had come from France to take command. So
we turned and ran. They called it a strategic retreat, but after the
first two days the Grand Army of the Peninsula was a pack of rat-
eyed beggars, leaving our wounded to die in the snow.

"There was a woman named Jane Barlowe. She had been married to a corporal killed in Flanders, and then followed the regiment
as a laundrywoman for a time, and then married Sergeant Barlowe
on the march into Spain. Somewhere during the retreat to Corunna
she fell in one of the quagmires in the path. I am quite certain it
was her. By the time I came up to her she had sunk in up to her
chin. I am quite certain she was dead. We used the top of her head
for a stepping-stone."

Kate decided not to ask about the piece of paper with Lord Selkirk's seal after all. They stood looking at the oncoming shore,
gripping the rail hard with each descent down the breast of a wave.
After a moment he said: "I should not like to leave you with the
impression, Miss MacPherson, that I mean any disrespect to the
other men who were there. God knows there was enough of that
when we got back from Spain. It seems civilians can only see the
soldiers that march to war for them in one of two lights—either as
glorious, gilded heroes or contemptible louts. There is no denying
that we ran like scared rats all the way to the sea. But when it came
time to hold the French at Corunna, we by-God did."

The ship nosed down into a particularly steep trough. The high
crest of the next wave flung itself across the ship's blunt prow,
drenching them with cold seawater. They were both thrown forward against the rail. It bisected Kate just above the hips, thudding
hard into her midriff and knocking the breath out of her. There was
nothing to stop the momentum of her upper body. She found herself
staring straight down into black water. Her feet left the deck.

Alexander Sutherland's hand locked on to her arm and held her.
She got back on her feet, found her breath again, and gave him a
perfunctory nod of thanks. She was quite sure she wouldn't have
fallen any farther, even without his hand.

A shout went up from the afterdeck. The sailors swarmed up the
ratlines and began to furl the sails. The anchor rattled down into
the bay, sending up a geyser as it entered the water. The boat

winches were whizzing away already, the ship's boats smacking onto the waves and then bobbing and nuzzling against the side of the ship.

Alexander Sutherland went to find his sister, and Kate went to find her brother. The sick were being carried up from below decks. It would take two boat relays to get the passengers off. Archibald MacDonald was quivering in the throes of another decision—would he look more the man in charge by leading the first party ashore or by staying on board to supervise the disembarking? He decided to stay behind.

Kate and her brother got into the lead boat, and as it pushed off from the ship, Robert Gunn stood up in the prow with his feet braced wide, pumped his pipes alive, and cracked the air with the triumphal strains of "Johnny Cope." Kate craned her neck to one side to see around him.

The coxswain had set a surprisingly fast stroke. They were coming into the mouth of a river. The dun-colored blur of the shoreline was quickly diversifying itself into low bluffs sloping up from the bay, gray soil matted between gray rocks with a few clumps of grayish weed growth. Beyond the crest of the banks were the tops of a few gaunt little ridges dotted with twisted, stunted bushes.

Her brother, perched beside her on the bench, said dourly: "It does not look like much of a country for growing potatoes."

"Red River and the colony are eight hundred miles south of here, John. Climates and landscapes have been known to change in eight hundred miles."

A flat-crowned plateau dominated the landscape on the right-hand side of the inlet. As the sailors' oars drove the boats in through the rivermouth, the plateau became a sprawling, man-made stone edifice bristling with guns. But the sailors rowed right past it. Kate could see now that a great many of the stones were tumbled down, and that there were weeds growing among the ones still in place. The guns were rusty and skewed out of the ports. Suddenly John wailed plaintively: "Where is the *Eddystone*?" She didn't have an answer.

The boats turned in toward the south shore of the river. There was a log-palisaded fort above the bank. From the flagpole above it floated and snapped an elephantine blue, red, and white Union Jack with the letters "HBC" emblazoned across it in gold.

The instant the boats crunched up against the shore, the sailors hurried the settlers off, practically throwing the sick ones out of the boats. As soon as the passengers were out, the boats hustled back toward the ship to shuttle off the rest of the colonists and cargo. Kate found herself lurching awkwardly along the beach, her legs expecting the land to sway with the motion of the waves. Except for those who were still incapacitated with fever, sitting huddled together in a plaid-wrapped clump, all the others were engaged in the same dance—stumbling and reeling like drunks, laughing at themselves and at each other.

Robert Gunn was the worst. He was bound and determined to announce their landfall with another pibroch, but a piper needs to stride back and forth to play properly. Kate finally sat down, she was laughing so hard at him. At the top of the ridge behind the beach, she saw three motionless figures silhouetted against the evening sky, one with a rifle crooked in its arms, another with a long feather jutting out sideways from the crown of its head.

There was a rough path angling down the face of the bluff. The figure that came trundling down was a complete surprise to Kate. She hadn't expected that all the residents of Rupertsland would be dressed in matted furs and birchbark shoes, perhaps, but it was almost a disappointment to see a trim-shaven man in a broadcloth tailcoat, spit-polished riding boots, and a wide-brimmed felt hat of the pattern favored by country parsons. He stomped to a halt at the foot of the path, and bawled out: "Who's in charge here?"

When no one else moved forward, Alexander Sutherland limped into the breach with his army English and said: "Doctor LaSerre was the officer commanding, but he died on the transport. We are the Red River expedition."

"The what?"

"The party for Lord Selkirk's colony. Our orders were to disembark at York Factory, where boats and guides would transport us up to the colony."

"Then what the hell are you doing here?"

Alexander Sutherland blinked at him and then started again, enunciating his English more crisply: "Our orders were to disembark at York Factory and—"

A frantic shouting came off the water behind him. The boats were coming in to shore again. Archibald MacDonald was standing in the prow of the lead boat, waving his arms and shouting—in the unfortunate falsetto that his voice tended to leap into whenever he grew excited—that he would be there to take charge in a moment. As the boat touched the shore he leaped off and ran forward to establish his authority. Once on the stationary surface, he took three wobbly jumps and went chin first into the pebbly clay.

The man in the parson's hat said to Alexander Sutherland: "That's bloody wonderful for you, mate, but if I were you, I'd go back and check the level of the rum barrel and then whiff the breath of whoever's navigating that barge of glued-together old dog turds out there. This is Fort Churchill. He's missed York Factory by two hundred miles."

CHAPTER 13

The prow of the bourgeois's canoe charged toward a solid tangle of marsh grass and spike-rooted, foundered snags. The guide, a certain twenty-year-old half-breed drifter, sat in the prow with his wispy chin resting on his right hand, fluttering his left hand to his right or to his left to direct the *gouvernail*'s paddle blade. The bourgeois, a certain nineteen-year-old junior clerk, sat bending the midthwart with his back, his teeth clenching his lower lip and his hands gripping the rims on either side.

A battery of ducks and other waterfowl flapped out of the marsh in a panic at the imminent collision. A great blue heron flapped majestically, awkwardly, over the rest of the flock. The first reeds hissed and scratched against the prow. The canoe shot through them, past the end of a drowned oak tree, and into a clear channel that would become the Red River.

Falcon turned his back to the bow and slumped down with his forearms draped lazily across his knees, clucking one corner of his mouth and bobbing his head. He said: "How about that. I always wondered how they found the channel from the lake side."

As cavalierly as he could, Grant said: "How do they?"

Falcon shrugged his shoulders and his eyebrows. "Seems like blind luck to me."

Grant laughed, as everyone always did. Pierre Falcon—"Pierriche" to the crew—seemed incapable of arousing resentment. Scar-toothed *gouvernails* twice his age didn't mind taking directions from him. The *chanteur* had seemed delighted when Falcon usurped his position to lead the crew in a thirteen-verse ditty ending with

Qui en a composé ce chanson?
Pierre Falcon, le bon garçon.

Although the bourgeois was ultimately responsible for the brigade, Grant had learned by the end of their first day out that a large portion of his job consisted of guessing which command decision his guide was fishing for:

"Should we camp here, Mister Grant, or keep on till the sand spit?"

"How much farther is it to the sand spit, Falcon?"

"Two pipes, maybe two and a half."

"Is the sand spit a good campsite?"

"Wet year like this, Mister Grant, may be a lot of sandflies."

"Perhaps, then, we should stop here if you—"

"Mister Grant says we camp here!"

Upstream from the delta was a creek feeding into the Red from the west, with an Indian encampment beside it. The rickety lodges, the trash piles of bones and fish heads heaped up behind them, and the naked brown children playing in the garbage aroused a kind of detached revulsion in Grant. Falcon said: "That's Chief Peguis's Bungee band. Funny they haven't moved out onto the lake for the fishing. The creek is Rivière aux Morts. They say a lot of different stories about how it got to be called that, but I know the true one.

"Long years ago there was a Bungee girl who was pretty and young, and there were two men of her tribe that wanted her. They were both big warriors, and it looked like they were going to fight over her regardless which one she decided on. But there was a French trader wintering with them, and he said they should play the moccasin game, and whoever lost would step aside, instead of one of them getting killed.

"So they agreed to that, and one night they sat down in the Chief's lodge to play the moccasin game, with the French trader to be the judge. They played all through the night and the next day and into the next night, and whenever one of them got almost far enough ahead to make a winner, the other one would catch up and get past him. Both of them would more and more often say the other was cheating or the game wasn't right, but the trader would always say it looked fair to him. They got more and more mad, and finally one of them took out his knife and so did the other one, and they jumped on each other, and in the end they were both dead. The funny thing was, after it all the French trader took the girl for his woman. I guess he felt sorry for her. Or maybe it was a Scotch trader, I get them mixed up.''

The Red was a different species of river from the clear, fast-flowing waters of the spruce rock country. It was muddy and wide and slow, but still strong enough to give the paddlers a fight working against the current. The banks were clay slopes thick with tall awnings of oak and maple and elm, the spaces between their trunks crowded with wolf willow and red hazel wands.

That night after dinner, Grant leaned his back against a poplar trunk. A few starlit curls of froth showed on the black, burbling ribbon of the river. The coals of the smudge fire glowed softly, its mosquito-chasing smoke pervasive and sharp. Two of his *engagés* were still awake, one of them holding up a pine-knot torch while the other dabbed melted spruce gum on a puckering seam. The other three canoes lay angled on their sides, sails splayed over them for sleeping awnings. The far edge of the torchlight just caught the front of the bourgeois's tent.

The western quarter of the sky was still glowing with sunset, showing the wall of trees on the other shore. The wall seemed to Grant more like a curtain that could be whisked away. Something crouched behind it, he thought, waiting for him. Over his head, the leaves of the quaking aspens made the dry, crackling rustle of whispering ghosts. If he just listened long enough, he would be able to understand what they were saying to him. There was a phrase he could almost hear already, one he had heard somewhere before.

He told himself that he was obviously in need of a night's sleep. He pushed off from the tree trunk and crossed the campsite, nodding good night to the *engagés*. He crawled into his tent, shrugged out of his clothes, and rolled himself up in his blankets. But the lazy murmuring of the prairie river wasn't loud enough to drown out the rustling of the leaves. Now he could hear what they were whispering. The hum of the river and the rattle of the leaves became a musical chant with the clatter of sticks and drums and a smoky, dark picture of two lines of squatting, black-maned creatures. The word the voices called out to him was *wappeston*.

Before they got under way in the morning, the *engagés* trimmed their beards, hauled out their bright-colored rendezvous shirts, and knotted ribbons in their hair. When the sun reached its zenith the brigade began to pass an occasional old shanty on the east side of the river and bright, new-built cabins on the west shore. Grant said: "The Earl of Selkirk's colony?"

Falcon pointed his thumb at the new cabins and grunted assent, then turned to the weather-whitened ones on the east bank. "But not those. Those are one-time *engagés* who worked out their terms and then decided they liked it better here than back where they came from."

The river horseshoed around a wooded point thrusting out from the west bank. On the upstream shoulder, as unexpected as a brass band on camel back, were squared-off fields of yellow grain and green rows of potatoes, radiating from a cluster of whitewashed barracks buildings with an HBC-emblazoned Union Jack fluttering overhead. Lord Selkirk's colony and the Hudson's Bay Company appeared to be one and the same.

In the field hemming the shore were a dozen sunburnt white men working with hoes. One of them took off his raggedy straw hat and waved it at them, shouting cheerily in Gaelic: "Good day to you, you gibbering, piss-swilling, half-nigger sons of bitches."

A few of Grant's paddlers took the friendly tone at face value and called back greetings in French or Cree. Grant tipped his hat and shouted back merrily in Gaelic: "And a good day to you, sir— I pray that your mother enjoyed being humped by the blind hog that sired you, for I am certain that the hog did not." The hat dropped out of the man's hand, and a couple of his fellow field hands laughed.

The fields gave way again to the green wall of riverside bush. Above the tangled crowns of burl oak and poplars, another flag appeared—a white ground with the letters "NW" in blue. A mile upstream from the HBC establishment, the woods on the west bank came to another abrupt end. Falcon explained that both companies cleared off the bush and trees for several hundred yards around their posts, partly to get building materials and firewood, partly to create campsites for their customers, and partly to leave an open field of fire. In fur trade jargon the cleared land was known as the "plantation."

This particular plantation was dotted with tall cones of gleaming white decorated with bright-colored pictographs. A pack of black-maned, brown-limbed children broke away from these tents and ran raggedly along the riverbank, keeping pace with the brigade.

Beyond the tents stood the high log palisades of Fort Gibraltar. A swivel gun went off in one of the bastions flanking the front gate. The *gouvernails* leaned hard on their steering paddles, and the brigade hove in to shore.

The bank above the landing place had been worn down to a broad, easy slope between the steeper banks on either side. As Grant started up, there was a jingling sound off to his right. He turned. Behind the giggling knot of children on the crest of the bank was one of their fathers or uncles. He was sitting on a shaggy yellow pony with circles of green pigment around its eyes and brass bells on its harness. Above his loincloth and fringed leggings he wore nothing but a necklace of slick white animal bones and teeth interspersed with white feathers. His body was sun-polished mahogany with two ugly-looking scars on the pectorals. His right arm was stretched out, holding a short-barreled musket decorated with feathers and brass studs, the heel of the butt propped on his thigh. The opaque expression carved on his features, the permanent-looking curl of his lips, the rigidly erect posture, were a gauntlet whipped across the face of the world. It was as though the water he drank and the air he breathed were composed of equal parts of ferocity and pride.

Grant turned away from him and continued up the bank. At the top, the protective wall of shoreline woods had been cut away, and whatever was waiting for him on the other side would have its chance.

There was nothing. Beyond the palisade of Fort Gibraltar was a sun-seared, gently waving ocean of grass, dotted with archipelagoes of clustered trees fading into the haze of the distance. The sight sucked the air out of his lungs. A man could run in a straight line until he couldn't run any longer, then walk until his legs gave out, then keep crawling until he died, and he wouldn't have traveled the width of a scratch across that landscape.

"Funny they should call it Gibraltar, eh?"

Grant jumped like a startled cat. Falcon went on blithely, "Le Bras Croché said when he built it that Gibraltar was the only name to call it, but I never understood. The old Gibraltar is an island or something, isn't it?"

"Gibraltar is a mountain at the mouth of the Mediterranean Sea—one-half of what the old Greeks called the Pillars of Heracles. Whoever controls Gibraltar owns the Mediterranean."

"How about that? Le Bras Croché always had a sense of humor. You see—" He pointed with his arm along the muddy river winding westward. "The Assiniboine." He swung his arm into alignment with the much wider stream flowing up from the south: "The Red. And the Red as well," jerking his thumb over his shoulder at the joined river they'd just traveled up, forming the tail of the crooked "Y" of prairie rivers.

"The Sioux used to bring summer raiding parties and hide out there"—Falcon indicated the point of land between the joining of the rivers—"because anybody going east, north, or south from the plains had to paddle past here."

"So whoever controls the Forks of the Red owns the *pays d'en haut*."

"I don't know about that, but the Sioux found that perching over there and seeing who came along beat the hell out of working trap lines."

A wheezing voice behind them said: "Pierre."

They turned to find a fat, pallid man in moccasins and broadcloth. Falcon shook the extended hand. "Hello, John. Surprised to see us make it this far with such a dim excuse for a guide? This is Mister Grant—Mister Wills."

The puffy hand settled into Grant's like an overripe mushroom. "How d'you do? Albert! Get a crew together and . . ." He waved his arm vaguely at Grant's *engagés* struggling up the bank hunched under *pièces* and canoes. "Mister . . . Grant, was it? You did say *Grant*?"

Grant nodded. If it was his Christian name Wills was fishing for, he could whistle for it. Grant had no intention of allowing it to be "Mister Wills" and "Cuthbert"—and he had even less intention of chumming it up with "John." The buried pig's eyes squinted at him. "First time in the *pays d'en* bloody *haut*, Mister Grant?"

"This is my first season as an *hivernant*, Mister Wills."

"Well . . . come along, then, we'll have a little tot and a jaw before supper. My Albert can sort out the cargo."

Falcon fell in on Wills's other flank. Grant was a bit put off by the breach of etiquette—in proper form the two bourgeois should start off behind closed doors and then allow the guide to join them once they'd exchanged their higher planes of gossip. But etiquette had already been shredded by that "Pierre" and "John."

The bourgeois' quarters at Fort Gibraltar were a long way from a shanty in the pines. The house was sixty-some feet long, built of eight-inch-square beams, with a main room dominated by a massive stone fireplace. Skins of grizzly bear and antelope lay draped across the floor or pegged to the walls between painted buffalo-hide shields, feathered war clubs, and etchings of Pall Mall clipped out of the illustrated magazines. On a chair pulled close to the sunlight coming through four palm-sized panes of imported glass sat a sinewy, dark-haired woman in a woolen dress, pricking needlepoint onto the toepiece of a moccasin.

She set her work aside as they came in and took Falcon's hand without rising from her chair, in the accepted chatelaine manner. "*Bonjour*, Pierre, what a pleasant surprise to see you here."

"Pleasant surprise for me to make it here, Josephte."

Wills said: "Mister Grant, this is my" —Grant was expecting "daughter"— "wife, Mrs. Wills."

She was up on her feet. "Mister . . . *Grant*?"

"How do you do?"

She didn't seem to even see his proffered hand. Her hands had gone up to her chin, the fingertips pressing against her thin lower lip. She said in a whisper: "Cuthbert?"

As parlor tricks go, it was pretty impressive. He was about to congratulate her and ask how she'd done it when she flung herself on him, arms twining around his neck. He managed to disengage her before he'd suffocated. He moved back. "Forgive me, madame, I'm afraid you have the advantage of me."

She put her hands up to his cheeks. There were actual tears in her eyes. "It's me, Cuthbert—Josephte!"

"Josephte?" He gave the prescribed polite little chuckle of drawing room confusion. He looked from Falcon to Wills, shrugging his shoulders.

Her voice took on a primmer, more acerbic tone. "Your sister, Josephte." Her transported smile was fading swiftly.

"My sister? I'm afraid you must be mistaking me for—"

"No—your name is Cuthbert Grant, your father's name was Cuthbert Grant, you were born at Fort Tremblante north of the Qu'Appelle two years before I, they took you east after our father died, then took you and our older brother, James, to Scotland, James died there in an accident . . . Am I getting warmer?"

"Ah. Well. Yes, I suppose you are, then . . . my sister. Forgive me, it was so long ago." He gave her hands a fraternal squeeze as an excuse to step back farther. "What a pleasant surprise to encounter you again. Well, I say *again,* although . . . ha ha." He looked to Falcon and Wills again. Neither of them smiled back.

Dinner wasn't particularly convivial. A small brown boy tussled in. Mrs. Wills sat him on her knee and introduced him to "Uncle Cuthbert." She kept prattling on about people with outlandish Indian-sounding names and childhood incidents that meant nothing whatsoever to him. He was perfectly happy to answer her questions about Inverness and Montreal, and she seemed appropriately awed, but even that wore thin after a while. Finally she deflected her attention onto Falcon and a conversation concerning someone named Mary, who appeared to be Falcon's wife and the mother of his child. But even then Mrs. Wills kept glancing at Grant as though there were something in her conversation with Falcon that should be drawing him in as well.

He was just as happy to fade back and get some breathing space. He couldn't quite fathom Falcon's folly at getting himself saddled with a wife and child so early in life—especially when there were wheezing relics like Wills just waiting to keel over and leave a niche for a younger man to rise in the company. But far more germane was the question of why his sister—there seemed to be no way around the fact that she was his sister—should be able to remember a period of time that he couldn't, even though she'd informed him she was two years younger. Finally he hit upon the obvious explanation: his years away from the *pays d'en haut* had been crammed full of events and scenes in the wide world, while between her childhood and the present she had experienced only the drab round of backwoods life.

He got the brigade back in the water at first light the next morning. The *engagés* seemed to feel that they were due a layover at Fort Gibraltar. Whether they were or whether they'd just hoped to take advantage of their baby bourgeois, he didn't really care.

Getting clear of Mrs. Wills wasn't the escape he hoped it would be. The suffocated feeling didn't leave him. His dreams and the creatures in them grew steadily more baroque. In the mornings he would shuffle out of his tent unrested and flop into the canoe for another day of stifling sunlight, palming muddy river water up to his mouth or onto his forehead. His replies to Falcon's leading questions shrank to monosyllables and then to grunts and wordless nods. Every loop and twist and winding of the river seemed to carry him deeper into some queasy netherworld where spells had power.

A week upstream they came to Fort La Souris, perched at the mouth of the Souris River flowing up from the south, facing the Hudson's Bay Company's Brandon House on the north bank of the Assiniboine. Grant got enough of a grip on himself to shave and dig into his cassette for a clean shirt and a presentable neckcloth for dinner with the bourgeois, but what he said or heard over the course of the evening was as murky as his dreams.

The night after embarking from La Souris, he huddled shivering in his blankets in his tent. Except for taking off his boots, he no longer undressed for bed. He slipped into a dreamscape where he peered from a blind through cattails and marsh grass at a black-maned monkey otter. It skimmed nose first down a mud slide and spattered through the shallows on the far shore. The dream moved on through shifts of time and place and incongruities, until Grant found himself sitting on a big chair in the headmaster's chambers at Castle Grant, signing policy instructions to the Montreal partners with a sharpened canoe paddle dipped in a bowl of ink. He turned to call over his shoulder for more ink and came nose to nose with the slippery little dark creature. The shock of their noses touching jolted through his mind. His head walloped the ground and bounced. Awake, he put both hands on his skull to make sure it was still attached. He lay staring at the roof of his tent for a while and then climbed out into the night.

Falcon was the only one awake, puffing his pipe by the campfire. Grant sat down on the other side, a blanket draped over his shoulders. He sneaked glances at Falcon across the flames. Falcon's eyes would be on the fire, or the stars, or studying the bowl of his pipe. There were furtive splashes in the river that had nothing to do with the constant ripple of the current; furtive rustles in the bush that had nothing to do with the constant whispering of the trees.

Finally Grant said: "Do you know anything, by chance, of the Cree language, or the Bungee?"

"Both are much the same. I spoke them both before I learn French, and a long time before English."

"There are some words, or phrases, that keep recurring in my mind. Quite probably they're only nonsense syllables—the way a string of meaningless sounds will sometimes get stuck in one's head and chase its own tail . . . Most likely that's all they are. But it did occur to me that they might be scraps of memory, from . . . another time . . ."

"What are they?"

"One is"—he labored his mouth awkwardly around the uncouth sounds—*"Neso-utim-pisikwa."*

Falcon started to laugh and then coughed around his pipe smoke. "Well, yes, that would be Cree for sure. But . . ." He ducked his head and made a clucking noise with the corner of his mouth. "It seem a strange thing someone should pick to remember. It mean two dogs . . ." He made a circle with the thumb and forefinger of his left hand and poked the pipe stem in and out of it. *"A foutre."*

"Copulating?"

"Well, I don't know about that, but fucking for sure. 'Two dogs fucking'—*Neso-utim-pisikwa.*"

Grant laughed and scratched the back of his head. "Well, there you have it—nonsense syllables. I suppose if one knew enough languages, every series of random sounds would turn out to mean something in one of them.''

Falcon ducked his head and made the clucking noise again. "May be."

"Well, there is no possible reason for a phrase like that to have stuck in my memory.''

"Funny thing." Falcon sucked out another puff of smoke. "It seem to me there was a Cree from the Qu'Appelle name of Neso-Utim-Pisikwa.''

"Named Two Dogs Fucking?" Grant laughed.

"Well, may be somebody had a medicine vision, or somebody make a joke on him, or some other reason. I knew a Blackfoot once called Woman Dressed Like a Tree. There is another funny thing, too—most of the Plains tribes people change their name often, but Two Dogs kept his always. I guess nobody mix him up with someone else.''

A fragmented vision seeped into Grant's mind's eye—a slope-shouldered figure holding the halter of a gray pony, walking it in circles to its right and then its left, the long, tattoo-dotted arm moving in time to low, monosyllabic commands.

"It seem to me," Falcon went on, "when I think of him that this Two Dogs got himself caught by the Sioux up on the Pembina a couple year ago. Not a pretty way to go. And what was the other?''

"The other?''

"You said there was two word you remember.''

"Oh. Yes. Yes, the other one was, uhm, what was it now? Oh, yes . . . *Wappeston*." Falcon stuck the pipe back in his mouth and tongued it thoughtfully. Grant said quickly: "Well, there, that explodes the entire theory, doesn't it? Nothing more than a handful of nonsense syllables strung together in—''

"No." Falcon's eyes had taken on the same opaque look they'd worn when Grant had first been introduced to him. "No, it is Cree. It mean white ermine.''

"Ermine?''

"The weasel, you know, in the winter, when it's white.''

"Well, well. How curious." It seemed that a large pair of hands was pressing in against his sternum and his backbone like a bellows, making it a bit difficult to take a full breath. "Etymology is a curious science, isn't it? The study of the origins of words. For instance, the word . . ." He paused to cough out the straw that seemed to have lodged itself in his throat. "The word 'panic.' The

word 'panic' comes from the Greek 'Pan'—the god of the woods
and the wild places. It seems that when these . . . highly civilized
Greeks strayed too far from their civilized cities . . . into the wild
places, they might start to hear the music of the pipes. Pan's pipes,
you see, not the bag kind, ha ha. The music made them . . . dis-
oriented, you see, a kind of vertigo. 'Panic.' Perhaps they weren't
quite so civilized as they liked to believe.''

"Or may be too civilized for their good.''

CHAPTER 14

The captain of the fat barque *Prince of Wales* hadn't been
dipping into the rum barrel or looking at the wrong map
when he'd anchored at Fort Churchill instead of York Factory. The
information finally filtered down to the flotsam and jetsam on the
shore of Hudson's Bay that the captain had decided somewhere
around Hudson's Straits to disembark them at the closest landfall.
One rumor had it that he thought by getting rid of them he'd get rid
of the fever, another that he'd been paid by the North West Fur
Trading Company to abandon them.

Sandy Sutherland would have liked to be able to say that he had
never seen such a monumental balls-up in his life, but after ten
years in the British army . . . They weren't allowed into the fort
for fear of the fever, they couldn't go back on the ship, and there
were no boats waiting here to take them inland. And there was no
denying the fact that the leaves on the few nonevergreen bushes
were already turning color. But at least nobody was shooting at
him. There was nothing for it but to keep fed and warm and dry
and get as comfortable as possible while the high command sorted
it all out.

While others were amusing themselves with shaking their fists
and ranting at the clouds, Sandy was scavenging bits of driftwood
and a length of old sailcloth to make a shelter. He rigged a lean-to
up against two long crates that the sailors had stacked away from
the bay and called his sister over to line it with whatever blankets

and plaids they had in their bundles. There were a few sacks of
oatmeal left in the stores from the voyage, and word came down
that the fort people would be happy to provide them with further
provisions and charge them to Lord Selkirk's account with the company.

It looked, though, as if his major problem would have nothing
to do with food and shelter. He'd thrown away his old regimentals
back at Stromness, and he still hadn't adjusted to civilian clothes.
After ten years in a kilt, trousers seemed like the most constricting
invention the human mind had ever hit upon.

By sunset the beach was dotted with cheery cooking fires in front
of shelters that would hold up under anything less than a full gale.
But looking out across them, Sandy couldn't shake the feeling that
they'd come all this way to wind up back where they'd started
on the beach at DunUlidh—except at DunUlidh they hadn't been
on the brink of an arctic winter.

For six days they watched the boats go back and forth between
the *Prince of Wales* and Fort Churchill, refitting and reprovisioning
the ship for the voyage home. On the seventh day an open boat with
a square sail came scudding out of the south, bearing the chief
factor from York Factory. The boat passed by the rivermouth and
steered straight for the anchored barque. The chief factor grappled
up the ship's ladder and kicked open the door to the captain's cabin.

When the chief factor stomped out of the captain's cabin minutes
later, he rattled back down the ship's ladder and pointed his crew
toward the ragged piles of debris on the shore. "All right! Here!
Come along! Gather yourselves together here!" He was waving his
arms and bellowing before the boat's nose grounded on the shore.
"I don't have the whole season to spend sorting out your messes!"

Sandy joined in with the crowd gravitating toward the mastiff-
voiced terrier barking from the prow of the boat, "Get your traps
together. The crew will load you back on board the ship. We'll set
sail by midday for York Factory."

There was a raggedy cheer, and the flock started to disperse.
Then Archibald MacDonald called out: "Would it not be simpler,
sir, to take the boats from here?"

"To what? To what? To what?" The chief factor jumped down
from his pulpit onto the beach, bawling and pawing at the ground
like a wounded bull.

Unperturbed, Archibald MacDonald went on, "If you could persuade your men in Fort Churchill to supply us with boats and guides,

we could set off immediately up this river, rather than wasting days traveling down to York Factory. Wouldn't that be a better plan?''

"Oh, that would be a lovely plan. That would be a bleeding dilly of a goddamned clever bloody plan. Because this is the dammit-to-hell lovely Churchill River, isn't it? And at York Factory they have the bleeding Hayes River, don't they? Or when you want to get to bloody Glasgow do you set off on the Edinburgh High Road? I bet you do.''

It was a long way past midday by the time they got loaded on again, and the sails finally snapped to life in the last glow of the setting sun. Sandy was standing with his sister at the port rail, as much out of the sailors' way as possible. His attention was directed toward the starboard rail, where Kate MacPherson was standing with her brother and John Bannerman. As the ship gained momentum Sandy absentmindedly patted his sister's shoulder, although his eyes remained on Kate MacPherson. "There, you see?" he said. "No use in railing at mix-ups. If you just save your breath and bide your time, things usually sort themsel—'' There was a grinding crunch from the bow, and the ship stopped dead. All the articles riding on it that weren't fastened to the deck—crates of freight, barrels of provisions, human beings—kept moving.

Sandy picked himself up off the deck and helped his sister to do the same. He looked over toward the starboard rail. John Bannerman was helping Kate MacPherson back onto her feet. Sandy didn't find it a pretty sight—John Bannerman's hands on her, that is.

Catherine said: "What is it? What has happened?''

"You know as much as I do. Wait here, I will go see what I can hear.'' He drifted back toward the quarterdeck in the time-honored private soldier manner—"Who, me, sir? Just studying the clouds. . . .''

The chief factor was standing with his feet braced wide and his chin threatening to impale the captain's breastbone. "What kind of a feeble bloody apology for a ship's bleeding captain can't get his lovely goddamned boat out of a bloody harbor?''

"The sandbar.'' The captain elevated his shoulders and held out the palms of his hands for the gypsies in heaven to read. "We've grounded on the sandbar.''

"I know we've grounded on the bleeding damn-your-so-called-eyes sandbar. I don't need a bleeding deep-sea sailor to tell me that—or to do it, for that matter. I could've grounded us myself, and I don't draw a salary to navigate.''

"Well, if you insist on trying to ride roughshod over the tides . . .''

Steam seemed to rise off the chief factor's forehead, but he only ground his molars a few times and damped his voice down to a consultative level: "What do we do now?"

"We'll have to disembark the passengers, to lighten the ship in the water, and then load them on again once the tide has floated her clear." The chief factor turned his head and opened his jaws to bellow—when the captain added: "We'll have to take off the cargo as well."

The chief factor whipped his head back around to peer suspiciously at the captain. "The cargo?"

"Definitely. We'll never float her clear with that much ballast." The captain turned to stare at something in the rigging overhead that appeared to demand his immediate attention.

So it was back into the boats and onto the beach again. While most of the colonists rolled themselves up in plaids or blankets and bits of canvas or oilcloth to settle in for the night, Sandy and a dozen others got dragooned into helping the sailors manhandle the cargo out of the boats. He took some comfort from the fact that no one else could have gotten much sleep till they were done, what with the cursing and thumping and crate kicking. The last thing he saw after finally worming his way in beside his sister was the black silhouette of the ship out in the harbor, dancing with red and amber torchlight as the captain drove his crew to be ready for the morning tide.

He was in a tavern somewhere in Europe with a gypsy girl sitting on his knee. Things were just getting interesting when another woman started elbowing him in the ribs and calling his name. He turned to push the other woman away. It appeared at first to be Kate MacPherson, and then not. The darkness parted, and he was peering up into the flat, round, braid-framed face of his sister, Catherine. "Alexander! Wake up! Wake up and look at this!"

She was sitting up, with the layers of their wool-and-canvas cocoon spilling off her, letting the cold air charge in on him. He tried to pull the covers back around his shoulders—if she wanted to freeze, that was her business. But she threw them back and pushed at him harder. "No! Wake up and *look* at this!"

He rolled over onto his stomach and peered out at the bay, following her outstretched arm. She was pointing at nothing so far as he could tell. There was gray sky and gray water and a few curls of white that might have been distant whitecaps or the fins of beluga whales. It was definitely not worth waking a man up for.

Suddenly he rose to his knees and shaded his eyes against the sun. The slate-colored water rolled on pristinely to the horizon, unbroken by mast or hull or sail. There wasn't even a floating spar to show where the *Prince of Wales* might have gone down. The tips of the waves were ruffled playfully by a steady wind from the south, a wind that could have carried even that old tub halfway back to Hudson's Straits by now. He wondered whether the sudden chill came from inside him or if there was a taste of snow in the air.

CHAPTER 15

The banks of the Assiniboine gradually rose up two hundred feet high and spread themselves wide to make a valley for the river to wind through—or, as Falcon explained it, the valley walls that had been there all along, miles out of sight, gradually narrowed in. Grant didn't particularly care which it was. His grip on what was real and what wasn't seemed to have disintegrated utterly. Sometimes when he was certain it was broad daylight and he was sitting in a perfectly substantial *canot du nord* paddled by living *engagés*, he could see the otter-skinned creature of his dreams turning lithe handsprings along the shore.

And a second dream image had begun to haunt him, dangling in front of his eyes like a mesmerist's watch case: a pair of soft buttery slippers of russet gold with flower petals—pink and glossy red and glossy yellow—on the soles.

The brigade turned into the Qu'Appelle River, which flowed into the Assiniboine from the west through a valley of its own, the walls closer together and more sheer than the Assiniboine's. The water was more green-black than muddy brown. The floor of the valley was flat, the banks flush and straight and low. What with its uniform width and squared banks, the Qu'Appelle might have been cut with a chisel by some canal-building god—except that its switchbacks and lunatic meanderings, like a coiled satin ribbon looped haphazardly between the valley walls, belied the rumor that gods were supposed to hold their liquor better.

Falcon said: "They call it the Qu'Appelle—'The River That

Calls'—because the Crees say there is a lost spirit that wanders up and down the river, calling. If you hear it once, no matter how far away you go it still calls you back to—''

"Whoever it was, Falcon, who informed you that I came here to compile a collection of native folk stories was either pulling your leg or suffering under a ludicrous misapprehension of his own.''

Falcon shut his mouth. Grant leaned back and clicked his eyes from side to side. Although the tops of both walls were shaved-off plateaus, they presented two utterly different landscapes. The north slope was scraped next-to-naked, the brown folds of its runoff-seamed skin showing between shriveled tufts of buffalo grass and sage and a few thin stands of poplars along creek gulleys. The south wall was thick with trees, patches of them already showing gold and brown and red among the green. He wondered if the explanation was that the arid north wall got the full force of the summer sun. He opened his mouth to ask Falcon, then remembered what he'd just said to him and closed his mouth.

The sun beat down, diffusing his thoughts and senses. He took his hat off, wondering if the sun would do his mind the kindness it had done the north wall of the valley—wither all the sprouting tendrils and burn it dry.

Two forts faced each other across a shallow spot in the river—Fort John on the left and the Hudson's Bay Company's Fort Qu'Appelle on the right. The brigade angled in toward the left bank, and Grant climbed out onto the shore. Green grasses and stalks of sweet clover wrapped themselves around his legs to pull him down into the earth.

The fort gate opened, and a crew of *engagés* came out to help his men unload. They were led by an insubstantial-looking Englishman with an immense store of enthusiasm—rubbing his hands together and calling to Grant: "Well, well, here you are, here you are, well, well. John Pritchard''—he stuck out his hand—"and you'd be young Cuthbert Grant.''

It wasn't until after Mister Pritchard had finished pumping his hand that Grant remembered to nod that yes, he was young Cuthbert Grant. By that time Pritchard was already off on another tangent. "No trouble, I expect? No, I shouldn't think so—no canoes foundered, no *pièces* lost?''

Grant remembered the manifest sheets in the trip box. He took out the key from his waistcoat pocket and handed it to Mister Pritchard.

"What's that? Oh, of course. Plenty of time for that. So what do you think of the *pays d'en haut*?"

Grant shrugged. "A thousand miles of riverbanks."

"How's that? Oh. Oh, yes, I see. I suppose you don't get to see much but the shore bush. That's darned funny, actually. 'A thousand miles of . . .' Well, there you are, Falcon! . . ."

Grant stopped listening. He wondered if there was a polite way of asking Mister Pritchard just to show him his quarters and lock the door from the outside until he felt like coming out. When he returned from his musings, Pritchard was saying to Falcon: "I should think we'll have a kick-up tonight if the brigade hasn't had a layover since Fort William. I'm sure McGillis will be glad to lend you his fiddle if—"

"No. I'll draw my salary and head off, if you can loan me a horse."

"Of course, yes, silly of me, I should've realized you'd want to . . . Say!" Mister Pritchard turned to Grant. "Why don't you go with him. We can get the cargo sorted out without you—no, we can! And you can bring the other horse back. Give you a chance to see the country—I mean, besides the riverbanks—and get a look at Tremblante again. And you'll want to see Mary anyway. . . ."

"Mary?"

"Mary—your sister, Mary. Falcon's wife."

Grant turned his head to look at Falcon. Falcon's face was impassive, and his hound-dog eyes stayed fixed on Mister Pritchard. Grant had never noticed before how thin Falcon's neck was. If he picked him up and shook him long enough, Falcon would be bound to explain it all to him.

"So why don't you?" asked Mr. Pritchard.

"Why don't I what?"

"Go with Falcon. . . ."

Falcon picked two horses out of the paddock behind the fort—a black and a bay—and saddled them. Both were scruffy, primeval-looking beasts, with thick fur, deep chests, and squared-off heads. Falcon handed him the reins of the black. The saddle was just a home-sewn affair of rough hide enveloped around a few coils of horsehair or straw for padding. He got his boot into a stirrup, grabbed a handful of the coarse black mane, and vaulted aboard.

They crossed the river at the ford, rounded the Hudson's Bay fort, and headed across the flat basin toward the north slope of the valley. Grant said: "Why didn't you tell me you were married to my sister?"

"You never asked me."

"How many sisters do I have?"

"Three. Marguerite's married to François Morin. Mary is the youngest. It was having her that killed your mother."

Falcon headed up the slope on a long diagonal to ease the steepness of the incline. The dry, powdery soil crumbled under the horses' hooves. Dust-filmed grass tufts broke off with a delicate crunch. Grant kept his eyes trained upward where the land dipped into the sky. When his horse lurched up across the rim, he reined it in. Spread out in front of him was a gently waving tableland rolling out to the far horizon. It shifted and rustled with the wind— blue-green and silver-green grasses, red hazel wands, silver-blue ash bushes, purple thistles, mint-green clover, pale gold wild oats. The blue of the sky deepened from a delicate cornflower shade directly overhead to the band of triple-dyed royal blue along the horizon.

The landscape wasn't all that different from the sea of grass and tree islands that he'd looked out at from beside Fort Gibraltar—a bit more of a roll to it, a little drier, perhaps, a bit less green. But the suffocating feeling was gone. Not that his breath was coming steady and even, but what was interfering with it was a distinct tingle of anticipation.

Falcon was growing smaller ahead of him. Grant jogged his horse with his boot heels and it set off in a spine-jarring approximation of a trot after Falcon. There was a blackbird singing in a stand of willows off to his right. The smell of sage came up from the leaves bruised under his horse's hooves. Grant only registered them peripherally. He was wrestling for a definition of what had changed—in him or the landscape—that he should have lost that feeling of futility and insignificance in the face of the immensity of the grasslands.

Falcon looked back over his shoulder and said: "What are you laughing at?"

"Was I laughing?"

Grant's horse's gait was smoothing out, which was a good thing. Paradoxically, he was finding it more difficult to maintain his seat on the saddle, which was not. It appeared that his horse had somehow worked itself up into a gallop. As they went past Falcon, his horse did the same, but there was no mystery as to how that had happened—Pierriche was whipping at its haunches with his hat. Grant vised his knees tight against his horse's rib cage and punched it with his heels, leaning his body forward and shouting nonsense syllables into its ears. Falcon drew even with him. Both of them were laughing now, the wind of their passage whipping the spittle out of their mouths.

In the midst of miles of scrub grass there was an immense lone oak spreading its crown out to the sun. When they drew even with it, Falcon slowed his horse to a walk. Grant gratefully followed suit. All four of them were hauling in air with long, deep sighs. Falcon said: "Did you see that tree there?"

"Difficult not to."

"Well remember what it looks like from the north, for when you're coming back, so you can find your way."

"All I'll have to do is head for the valley . . ."

"What valley?"

Grant looked back over his shoulder. Beyond the oak tree there was nothing but a long, unbroken roll of grasses and poplar islands all the way to the base of the sky. "Is it over the horizon?"

"No, no—we haven't gone that far yet. But it—" he held his hands up vertically and brought the palms together, "disappears. Landmarks that go down don't help you much until you're standing on top of them. Ask Le Corpé."

"Ask the dead?"

"Le Corpé is what the Crees call Pritchard, 'cause he lost his horse out on the prairie once and wandered lost till when finally a hunting party stumbled across him they thought he was a walking dead man."

That was the difference Grant had been trying to define—the horse. The same vast openness that made a man with his boots rooted to the ground feel so futile was an infinity of possibilities to a man on horseback, a world for the taking. Perhaps it had partly to do with the higher vantage point that let him see further, but the major difference was that where a man on foot might walk forever in any direction without finding his home, a horseman could ride forever without leaving his home.

Falcon said: "It fools you, this country. It looks simple, but it ain't."

"Like the color."

"The which?"

"The color," sweeping his arm out to encompass the prairie. "One can't say exactly what color it is, because all the strands of different colors are constantly changing."

Falcon cocked one eyebrow and gave an "if you say so" nod, but he didn't seem displeased. He jogged his horse back into a trot.

By the time they stopped for the night, every muscle, bone, and organ in Grant's body felt as if the horse had been riding him. With his belly filled with buffalo steak that Mister Pritchard had provided from the fort's icehouse and Falcon had roasted over the fire, he rolled himself into a blanket and was immediately asleep.

He came awake staring up at the stars. He hadn't been jolted awake, or scared awake; his eyelids had just eased themselves open. The skies full of stars that he'd seen since he'd left Lachine, from the riverbank or lakeshore camps, had been only fragments. The clarity of each star was enough to punch a hole through a steel breastplate.

He sat up. Staring straight ahead with his eyes no more than three feet off the earth, there were still stars. He was sitting on a flat black plate with a bowl of stars turned over it.

It might have been he'd slept most of the night and only sat up for the last half hour; it might've been the other way around. He watched the rim of the sun rip open the belly of the eastern sky and crawl up through the blood. As the purple bled away to blue, the ducks on hidden ponds and songbirds in the ground cover came to life. The strange thing was that he felt slightly more rested than Mister Washington Irving's Van Winkle and a lot less lost.

Falcon woke up and started a fire with some flaking brown plates that he called buffalo chips. He went off toward a nearby stand of scrub and came back with his hat full of black-tinged berries, which he fried up in a pan with bannock dough. Grant ate his entire share and then coaxed his brother-in-law into frying up three more.

Halfway through the morning's ride they came across a herd of pronghorn antelope that skipped away on fragile legs with plump rumps showing white. Grant watched the summer-fattened white flags bounce away, grinned, and said: *"Cambrai."*

Falcon said: "That's what we call them. How did you know that?"

Grant shrugged and kept on riding. Somewhere far back in his mind was a ghostly shred of guilt, as though he'd surrendered something of himself. But overriding all was a feeling that he had hurled himself off a high cliff and discovered that the air bore him up. He was soaring. He couldn't stop laughing.

As the sun grew higher he shrugged off his coat and strapped it into the long rawhide fringes depending from the back of his saddle. His collar was choking him. He unfastened his neck band and let his collar hang open.

They came over a rise to a broad, curved ridge sweeping down like the heel of a spoon. Falcon slapped his horse into a gallop, careening down through the ridge grass. Grant punched his pony with his heels and charged after him, assuming it was another impromptu race. But Falcon didn't look back at him. He had clapped his hat back on his head and was standing in his stirrups and craning his neck forward.

When Grant saw what Falcon was making for, he pulled back on the bridle and let his horse slow to a walk. At the base of the ridge was a grove of poplar trees, the trembling silver scales already dotted with autumn gold, split by a stream. The apexes of three white cones showed between the trees.

He rounded a knoll and found the remains of a small log palisade, leaning and tumbled in, and the sun-bleached bones of a log house that had long ago collapsed upon itself. He followed Falcon's path along the bank of La Rivière Tremblante until he came to the edge of the clearing around the horseshoe of tents.

There was a milling crowd of people around Falcon. Some had black hair, some red hair or blond, others chestnut; skin shades varied from yellow gold all the way to mahogany. They were dressed in everything from loincloths to corduroy trousers, from bead-worked black velvet waistcoats and embroidered antelope skin jackets to ermine-tail-tasseled hunting shirts and rawhide headbands. Grant wondered at the variety before his eyes: satin ribbons and brass earhoops, copper armbands and quillwork bracelets, silk scarves and antler-handled sheath knives and necklaces of silver coins. But it seemed there were two elements common to all of them. The first was that not one of them could be identified as a member of any previously defined race, not Gallic or Indian or Scots or English. The second was that there was a freedom, in their movements and expressions and laughter, that would have singled them out as aliens in any society that had fear or history to live up to.

The crowd split open, and Falcon came through it toward him, his arm around a black-haired girl who was trying to find a way to wrap her body around his and walk at the same time. The tribe fell in behind him.

Grant kicked his boots out of the stirrups. Falcon stopped beside his horse and swung his arm up with a flourish. The young woman looked up at him shyly, then giggled and put her hand over her mouth. She looked back quizzically at Falcon, then her head suddenly snapped back around. The hammered-copper lips fell open, and the big black eyes moistened over. She said: ''Wappeston?''

Grant slid down awkwardly off his saddle. She was on him before his boots hit the ground, weeping and squeezing his ribs and enveloping his neck with kisses and his mouth and nose in soft black waves of hair. He wrapped his arms around his baby sister's back and lifted her off the ground. To his unspeakable embarrassment, he discovered that he was crying, too—and not wistful, manly tears, but gulping, stuffed-nose, gurgling sobs. Nobody seemed to mind.

PART TWO

WAPPESTON

CHAPTER 16

The half-breed child called Wappeston had awakened early. He wormed his way out from between the buffalo robes that he and his sisters were snuggled into—a bit too snug since baby Mary had got big enough to be freed from her mossbag and cradleboard. His sisters were still called by their white names. Neso-Utim-Pisikwa, Two Dogs Fucking, their mother's long-armed brother who had taken them into his family, had given him the name Wappéston because his skin went so white in the winter and his hands were so fast at the moccasin game.

He slithered into his leggings and moccasins, then tugged his loincloth through the thong and shrugged over his head his buffalo calf hide floppy hunting shirt with the scratchy wool on the inside. If it grew warm enough later in the day, he would turn it inside out. Neso-Utim-Pisikwa's oldest wife, Horse Catcher Woman, had decided that the spring had come on enough to take down the inner curtain of white-clay-softened buffalo hide that hung through the winter from the inside of the tent poles, so that the cold air coming in off the outside wall went up over their heads and out the smokehole. It seemed to Wappeston that she'd rushed it by a moon or two.

By the time Wappeston was dressed, Two Dogs Fucking's daughter, Holds Fast Woman, had crawled out of the mound of furs on the other side of the hearth and was kneeling by the square of ground at the back of the tent that no one ever stepped on, burning a swatch of sweetgrass and talking to the manitou.

Wappeston pushed aside the skin flap covering the circular entrance and slipped outside. He could see his breath. He pretended for a moment that he was a grown man smoking tobacco in a council—a pipe-stem bearer and the custodian of a sacred bundle. No, two sacred bundles.

Horse Catcher Woman was kneeling on the ground beside her cooking fire, stirring something in the iron pot that Wappeston's father had given to her before he went away to where the sun rises. Wappeston ran over to her, batting his forearms against the sides of his rib cage, and stood by the fire sucking in deep nostril drafts of stewing antelope. She didn't get the hint, or chose to not take it.

"Horse Catcher Woman, I'm awake!"

"I can see that. Unless you're walking in your dreams." She pinched out a few savory leaves from one of the rawhide envelopes lying in the grass beside her and crumbled them into the stew.

"I'm hungry."

"You'll stay hungry for a while yet. That's what you get for not staying in bed until the men have made up their minds whether they want more to piss or sleep."

"But I had to get awake early today. Walks Sideways and me are going to follow the big boys when they go to learn from the birds how to dance."

"They'll take a stick to your head if they catch you."

"They won't. But Walks Sideways will come soon and then I'll have to go and I'll die if I go off with nothing to eat and it smells so good, Horse Catcher Woman, you make such good things to eat, that if I don't swallow all the time I talk the juice will run out my mouth and down my chin and freeze 'cause it's so cold outside."

"You throw as much shit out of your mouth as your other end." But she was smiling nonetheless. "It isn't cooked yet."

"How do you know if somebody doesn't taste it?"

"Oh, sure, one breath you say I cook so good the water comes out of your cheeks enough to drown you, and the next breath you say I can't tell when meat's raw until someone bites it and pukes." But she brought out a carved-horn spoon and handed it to him. He scooped out a cube of meat and juice and sucked it into his mouth and bit down with his back teeth. The inside was cold and raw and bloody, and the outside was very hot. He burned his tongue and had to chug air in and out of his mouth.

He ladled up a dozen or so spoonfuls, blowing on each one, until his belly was belled out and warm, and then handed the spoon back to Horse Catcher Woman and told her she was right, it wasn't cooked yet, and ran away.

He ran around the back of the tents, past the string of horses and the young men guarding them, until he got to the far side of the camp and the otter-pattern tent where Walks Sideways lived. Even at eight years of age, Wappeston knew that the tent paintings weren't just arbitrary decorations, that the otter pattern—like the green star pattern and the dancing antelope pattern—was unique and bought or handed down from the previous owner to the family that lived in that tent now.

The mother of Walks Sideways, Big Plume Woman, crawled clumsily out of the entranceway and manipulated the two long poles of the butterfly-wing flaps that directed the smokehole's draft. A billow of black smoke belched out from the top of the tent, and she crawled back inside.

After the first puff, no more smoke came out. Wappeston lay down in the sweetgrass to watch. Big Plume Woman heaved herself out again and switched the bases of the poles around so that the high flaps faced more toward the sun. She crawled back in. There were a couple of coughs of black smoke and then no more. After a moment Walks Sideways and his father and grandfather and brothers and sisters and aunts and uncles came spewing out of the tent gasping and choking and rubbing their eyes. Big Plume Woman followed after them, took hold of the poles, and switched them around so the flaps faced away from the sun. The father of Walks Sideways aimed a kick at her, flopping his little dingus up against his big belly, but he missed.

By now Wappeston was rolling from side to side in the long grass, laughing. Big Plume Woman reached her arm inside the tent, came out with a stick of kindling, and ran toward him. He ran away. It appeared to be a law of nature that human beings' sense of humor diminished in direct proportion to the deepening of the furrows on their faces and the widening of their waists.

Walks Sideways met him in the willow bushes fringing the stream that ran behind the camp. They watched until they saw the big boys—half a dozen of them—striking off across the prairie, then sneaked along behind them, running hunched over through the sweet clover and wild roses and flinging themselves onto the ground whenever one of the older boys turned his head to look back.

They could hear the booming of the prairie chickens' mating display from half a mile away. The older boys dropped down in the tall grass and crawled forward. Wappeston and Walks Sideways watched them watching the prairie chicken strut and fluff its feathers and shake the big orange air bladders puffed out beside its throat. Farther on, by a stand of spruce trees in a coulee, they watched the older boys watching a grouse prance back and forth and bat its wings against its chest. But the best part was watching the older boys try out their new steps, chanting and hopping stiff-legged and arching their spines and puffing out their chests and shaking their heads from side to side. It was also the most dangerous part, since if the older boys heard them laughing, they'd come after them.

Once the older boys had moved on Wappeston and Walks Sideways laughed themselves sick, beating their fists on the ground and kicking their moccasins up at the air. Once they'd got their breath back they tried to imitate the older boys imitating the birds and collapsed again.

By now they were both hungry, and since it was still too early in the year for berries, they headed home.

"Wappeston!" It was Horse Catcher Woman. "Get into the tent. Le Bras Croché came to see you."

He forgot about being hungry and ran. Le Bras Croché had worked for his father and had taken his place at the trading fort. He was sitting on a buffalo robe, lounging against a willow backrest that Horse Catcher Woman had woven for Neso-Utim-Pisikwa, smoking tobacco with him and the father of Walks Sideways and the other important men. He was a wizened little man with a withered arm, which was what *le bras croché* meant in one of the white languages that Wappeston couldn't keep straight.

The strange thing was that Wappeston's sisters were there as well. It was unusual enough that Wappeston should be allowed into the tent when the men were passing the pipe around, much less girl children. Wappeston sat down next to them. They edged a little closer to him but knew better than to drape themselves over him under the circumstances.

He sat quietly while the men carried on their conversation about pelts and pemmican and who the Assiniboines might side with if the Sioux did come north in strength. Finally Two Dogs Fucking turned to Wappeston and said: "Le Bras Croché is going to take you to your father's country."

"My father's country?"

"Well, first," Le Bras Croché said, "to the fort so you'll be there when Duncan MacGillivray's brigade comes in from the Athabasca. He'll take you in hand to Fort William, and then one of the east brigades will take you to Montreal in time to start school—the same school your brother's in. You can likely board with him. How'll that be, eh? How long's it been since you seen him? Two years?"

Wappeston thought about that. "Three summers. He went away the year before my father."

"Well . . . and then when you finish school in Montreal, both you and James are going to go to college in Scotland, in your father's country. How'll that be, eh?''

"I can't."

"Can't? Can't? You don't have to worry about 'can't'—it's all arranged. Don't you want to see your brother? Don't you want to go to your father's country?"

"Yes . . ." Although there were, in fact, several contradictory "wants," but that wasn't the issue. "I can't. I don't have the right moccasins."

Le Bras Croché laughed, not unkindly. "Well, buy 'em! You can buy all the moccasins you want, or shoes or boots or gold stilts, for that matter. You're a rich man—or you will be when you grow up. Matter of fact, unless I miss my guess, you'll be even richer then, after William MacGillivray's done managing your father's money. You tell me what you think you need, and I'll take care of it for you."

"Moccasins with flowers on the bottom."

"Huh?"

"When my father went away, he went from a place a long ways from here, so I didn't see him go. But I saw when my mother went away, and she went to where my father went, and she had to wear moccasins with flowers on the bottom when she went."

"Huh?"

Two Dogs Fucking said in a soft voice to Le Bras Croché: "Burial moccasins. With beadwork on the soles."

"If you're going to take me to the country where my father is, and where my mother is, I'll have to have moccasins with flowers on the bottom."

Grant had expected that when the time came for him to ride back to Fort John, he'd have to ride alone. Instead he brought with him an eight-year-old half-breed orphan who'd been lost for eleven years.

CHAPTER 17

Fort John was the headquarters for the Qu'Appelle department and the central depot for a good many outlying posts. There was a lot of work for a junior clerk to do—a brigade load of supplies to be docketed, inventoried, and stored and then parceled out among the packhorse trains of *engagés* delegated to various outposts for the winter. A *moonias* had many skills to learn, such as how to run a fur press—a tall device resembling a guillotine that compressed pelts into *pièces*. The trapping season wouldn't truly get under way until the first snow, but in the meanwhile there were bands of Plains Cree and Assiniboines drifting in with pemmican and dried meat from the autumn buffalo hunt.

Grant and John Pritchard were sitting on a couple of upturned kegs in the autumn sun, resting their backs against the front wall of the bourgeois's quarters cum trading store that was the center of Fort John. A few red-and-yellow leaves drifted in over the palisade.

"Tell me about the colony," said Mister Pritchard after a few moments of companionable silence.

"Colony?"

"Lord Selkirk's colony at Red River."

"I don't know the least thing about it."

"You must have seen it this summer, coming past the Forks. I was stuck here all season. Have they got any buildings up?"

Grant tried to call up a picture. It wasn't a time he much liked to remember. "It seems to me there were half a dozen or so rather large barrackslike affairs, to the best of my memory."

"And crops? Were they getting crops in?"

"There were a number of plots of land with rows of plants; I'm afraid my knowledge of gardening is sketchy at best."

Pritchard sighed enthusiastically. "If you'd been out here as long as I have, you'd've given them a lot more than a passing glance. What they're doing is monumental. Wherever I'm posted I always put in a patch of potatoes and a few rows of turnips, and what comes up is— No, come see, I can't explain it. . . ."

Pritchard was positively gyrating with anticipation as he led Grant around the icehouse. Tucked in behind it was a square of black earth with three lines of dark green bushy plants and one of plants with long, leafy stocks. Mister Pritchard squatted down and dug his fingers into one of the hillocks of earth. "Here, look at this." He handed what he'd dug up to Grant. "Have you ever seen the like?"

Grant was under the impression that he had. It looked remarkably like a common, garden-variety brown potato, except with the root tendrils still attached and beads of earth clinging all around. But he did his best to be astounded.

"And I don't even manure them! They just come out of the ground like that! Once Lord Selkirk's colonists get a couple of harvests in and word gets back to the old country, where they're still trying to scratch a living out of farmed-out plots of dust, you're going to see something. They could really make something of this country."

As they came back around the front of the icehouse, two *engagés* went pounding by on horseback, waving rifles and shouting at the gatekeeper to let them out. A great many of the fort's personnel had been making similar exits over the last few days and not coming back. Grant gestured in their direction and said to his bourgeois: "Are they only signed on for the summer traveling season, then?"

"What? Good Lord, no—where would they go? They'd die— that isn't Trois Rivières or Lachine out there. Well, if they were métis or freemen, of course, that'd be another thing. . . . No, they'll be back after they've taken their try at the buffalo herds. Provided they don't get scalped, in which case the company saves their wages. There won't be much to do around here for the next few weeks, anyway, now that we've got the inventory socked away. If somebody didn't have to be the bourgeois, I'd go off with them myself— and frankly, if I wasn't such a shoddy excuse for a horseman. . . . Say, why don't you go? There's still a few that haven't started off yet—I'm sure they'd be glad to take you along."

"I didn't think the company was paying me to go on hunting parties."

"No, you can! Don't worry, the company'll get its money's worth out of you over the winter. Hey there—Bostonais! Bostonais!"

The gentleman lumbering across the courtyard in front of them was almost as broad as he was tall. Beneath a blunt, flat nose and cheekbones like boulders, the lower half of his face was covered by a thick black forest of beard growth. The eyes were mere inferences between the crests of the cheekbones and the jutting eyebrow ridges. Bostonais Pangman was supposedly employed as an interpreter, but Grant had yet to hear him speak two words in any language.

He didn't speak now, either. At the mention of his name, he simply stopped and turned and waited, as though he half expected that the bourgeois had only called out his name as part of the process of identifying the local flora and fauna to the new junior clerk.

Mister Pritchard said: "When are you going off to join the hunt?"

Bostonais looked up at the sun, sniffed the air, wrinkled his forehead, and shrugged.

"Would you be willing to take Mister Grant along with you?"

Bostonais moved his feet in order to turn his head toward Mister Grant. His gaze wasn't particularly unfriendly, but then neither was it particularly human. From somewhere behind the beard came a surprisingly soft-edged bass rumble: "You got a good gun?" Grant nodded. "You ride?" Grant nodded again.

Mister Pritchard said: "Do we have a good buffalo runner with the fort herd that you could cut out for Mister Grant?"

Bostonais thought about it. Far back within the caverns of his eyes appeared a tiny gleam. He nodded his head slowly. "I come get you some morning."

Two mornings later Grant was asleep at the back of the storehouse where they'd partitioned off a space for him, when the back door flew open and bounced against the wall. Bostonais said: "You coming?"

"What? Oh—yes . . . just a moment." He pulled his clothes on groggily, pushing his feet through the wrong pants legs and then starting over. Finally he grabbed his rifle and coat, rolled his blankets up, and started for the door. At the last moment he ducked back in, snatched the pistols out of their case, and shoved them in his belt.

Bostonais was sitting on a standard-sized saddle pony that looked stunted underneath him, holding the leads of two packhorses and the bridle of a world-weary spotted pony. His eyes fixed themselves on the pistols. "You ain't going to kill no buffalo with them."

"I wasn't intending to." The spotted horse gave out a put-upon sigh as Grant climbed aboard. The packhorses weren't carrying enough between them to constitute a single full load. Perhaps they'd been brought along to carry the spotted horse when it got tired.

They rode west along the floor of the valley. Bostonais didn't say a word all morning, and Grant decided he'd be damned if he was going to try and initiate a conversation. Or ask for a rest halt. By the time the sun had reached its zenith, his stomach was starting to digest itself and his legs felt like a wishbone stretched between two horribly indecisive giants.

Finally Bostonais pulled up his horse by a copse of scrub oak and said: "We stop here and eat." His idea of eating turned out to be a chew on a stick of jerked venison and a pull on the water bottle, but Grant's legs were so delighted to see each other that the complaints from his stomach hardly registered. The spotted horse lolled its head around and rolled its eyes sadly as he put his boot back in the stirrup.

They rode on until the sun was dipping behind the rim of the valley, putting a hazy glow into the red and yellow leaves. The river had widened out into a crooked lake covering half the width of the valley's flat floor. Bostonais turned in along a deer path through the woods. When it emerged a mile later in a small clearing on the shore, Bostonais got down off his horse and pointed at Grant's rifle. "Maybe you load that up with birdshot we don't have *rubaboo* for supper," he said.

A little farther along from the campsite, the shoreline disappeared—the lake and the shore blending into a marsh of tangled cattails and drowned willows. Grant fought his way along from hummock to hummock. Although he could hear the adenoidal chortling and murmuring of ducks and grebes and widgeons all around him, they stayed hidden in the reeds. But there was a white swan cruising an inlet of clear water, snapping at tadpoles in the shallows. He hesitated, then called himself a *moonias* for passing up a fresh dinner just because it was pretty and raised the gun stock to his cheek.

When the gun went off the air exploded with hundreds of fat ducks flapping out of the reeds and flying away. He considered reloading, but by the time he got himself ready for another shot, they'd all have flown out of range or be back under cover. So he waded out into the lake, his boots sinking into the silt and cold water seeping in over the stylishly cuffed tops. He picked up the swan by its neck, the frothy white back feathers drenched with red.

By the time he got it back to camp, Bostonais already had a fire going and had stripped down and hobbled the horses. He looked up and said: "You hold her in the water she'll be easier to pluck. You always hate to kill the pretty ones, but you got to eat."

"I suppose they're all pretty when you see them up close."

"I s'pose."

Grant had managed to get the swan half-stripped, pulling an scraping with his fingers and the edge of his knife, when he hea an unfamiliar voice behind him. He looked over his shoulder. Bo tonais was still crouched by the fire breaking up dry branches. (the other side of the fire were five mounted Indians lined side l side across the end of the clearing.

They were all young men, their hair gleaming with bear's greas dressed in loincloths and moccasins, paint and weapons, and m much else. One of them—face painted with side-by-side stripes pink and orange and lime green—was talking at Bostonais with arrogant cheerfulness. Grant's grasp of Cree had started to con back to him in snatches, but this was a different language entirel He let the swan drop on the ground and stood up, leaning h shoulder against the trunk of a poplar tree—the same tree he ha leaned his rifle up against. He wished he had reloaded it after shoc ing the swan but at the same time wondered whether he was ju being a hysterical *moonias* in envisioning massacres every time saw an Indian. He crossed his arms and tucked his hands in behin his armpits to stop them from shaking.

The stripe-faced one slid down off his horse and took a coup of steps in toward the campsite, still prattling on at Bostonais a gesturing grandly at their hobbled horses. Grant didn't need know the language to understand that he was complimenting the on their fine string.

The Indian stopped a couple of feet in front of Bostonais an gazed at all the riches displayed around the camp. He dragged h eyes back to Bostonais and mimed a pipe and tobacco. Bostona shook his head. The striped face slumped in heartfelt commiser tion at two men who appeared to be so wealthy but couldn't eve afford a pipeful of tobacco. His four friends just sat their hors quietly, watching.

Grant had seen the same exact performance a hundred tim before—in schoolyards or warehouses or dormitories—the prefe or head junior clerk toying convivially with the new fish while th line of hooded eyes watched and waited. But prefects and war house bullies didn't carry muskets and stone-headed warclubs an feathered spears. Behind his crossed arms Grant was working th palms of his hands back and forth against the fabric of his shirt blot the sweat off, but there was so much pouring down from h armpits now that it had become a futile gesture. Bostonais just kept nonchalantly tearing little branches off big branches.

Stripe-face asked Bostonais another question, miming a drink. Bostonais shook his head and stood up, but only to get more effective leverage on the thick limb of dead oak he was debranching. Again the Indian's face sank into sorrowful commiseration, but then it suddenly brightened into a caricature of happy inspiration— perhaps the unfortunate half-breed gentlemen really did have tobacco and rum somewhere in their gear, only they didn't know it; he would help them look for it.

He started across the clearing toward their pile of saddlebags and packhorse panniers, moving on a path that would take him past Bostonais about five feet to his right. He was halfway through his third step when Bostonais's right arm swung straight out from the shoulder, bringing the thick end of the oak limb against the back of his neck in an explosion of splinters and bits of bark. Strangely, although it was a blunt object hitting flesh, the sound was more of a crunch than a thump. Stripe-face's head snapped back farther than Grant would have thought a human neck could bend, and he fell to the ground like a bag of old bones. The only part of Bostonais's body that had moved was his arm—he hadn't even turned his head to see where the branch would hit.

There was an outburst of noise from the other four Indians— ejaculated syllables, shying horses—and then an instant of utter silence as they decided what to do next. During that instant, Grant picked up his rifle and cocked it.

The double click of the hammer going back rang surprisingly loud across the silence. The four Indians turned to look at him. The fifth one hadn't moved since he'd hit the ground. Bostonais crouched down beside the fire, nonchalantly stirring the coals with the end of his club, but incidentally putting himself in a position where he could see both Grant and the Indians out of the corners of his eyes.

One of the remaining four Indians moved his horse forward a bit; he kept his eyes on Grant but spoke out of the side of his mouth at the other three. It didn't take a clairvoyant to guess that he was pointing out that Grant's rifle could only fire once, which was incorrect—at the moment it wouldn't fire at all.

With as authentic an imitation of Bostonais's nonchalance as he could muster, Grant walked over to the spot where his blankets were laid out. He eased himself down cross-legged, keeping the muzzle of his rifle trained toward the horsemen. Draped over the blankets was his coat. He propped the butt of the rifle against his hip, took his left hand off the stock, and jerked aside his coat. Under it were his pistols. Four pairs of black eyes went down to the pistols and then back up to his face.

Bostonais left the fire and stretched out his arm to take hold of the halter of the riderless Indian pony. He led it a few paces forward, then stooped to pick up the limp body of its rider and drape it over the saddlepad. He turned the horse around and pushed it back toward the others. The lead Indian took hold of the halter, and they rode off in single file down the deer path.

When they were gone, Grant slumped down on his blankets, caught his breath, and then busied himself with his rifle. Bostonais went to the swan at the edge of the lake and took over the plucking. He growled over his shoulder: "We keep on just like we're going to stay the night here, but once it's dark we move on." Then his head jerked back over his shoulder as he realized that Grant was loading the rifle. He went back to the business of stripping the swan, white feathers puffing up in clouds, but a curious sound had started up somewhere within his chest. It sounded to Grant like two empty coconuts rolling around together on a wooden platter. Finally he concluded that it was the sound of Bostonais laughing.

CHAPTER 18

Kate MacPherson and the other stranded colonists were told there was no alternative: they would have to spend the winter at Fort Churchill and resume their journey in the spring. There was no room for an extra ninety people inside the fort. The chief factor lent them axes and a guide to lead Sandy Sutherland and John MacPherson and John Bannerman and a dozen others to a place upriver where he said there was a sheltered hollow they could put up barracks in.

Kate slept in her sailcloth shelter on the beach and every day trekked inland to the temporary hospital that Doctor Abel Edwards, the man Doctor LaSerre had been meant to replace, had improvised in a tumbledown cabin a mile from the fort. She was helping Doctor

Edwards with the fever victims when Archibald MacDonald stumped in flapping his arms against the cold. "They've made a good start on the housing. I've told the rest of the party to be ready to march off to Churchill Creek in the morning."

"Oh, you have, have you?" Doctor Edwards sealed off the vein of a patient he was bleeding and put away his lancet. "Well, I suppose it's not a bad decision. The sooner they get dug in there, the better. Rinse out the basin for me, Miss MacPherson." He rolled down his sleeves and reached for his coat. "We can spend the afternoon going through the crates to see what might be useful."

Archibald MacDonald said: "Which crates?"

"The crates of farm implements and so on that came on the *Prince of Wales*."

"Those crates are for delivery to the governor at Red River!"

"So are these people. If there's anything in those crates that might give them a better chance of surviving long enough to get there, I'm sure the governor won't quibble about a few broken cargo seals."

"I won't have it."

"You won't what?" The doctor began to laugh. "You won't what?"

"I won't have it. I have been placed in charge of—"

"*I'm* in charge."

"No, *I'm* in charge. Lord Selkirk placed me as second in command to Doctor LaSerre, and when he passed on I therefore became—"

"And we all saw how well that went. You misplaced the ship and got them stuck here for the winter. The governor entrusted me with keeping these people alive until the spring, and that's what I intend to do. And I don't care how many tea parties you've had with Lord and Lady Selkirk. Now leave it go and we'll not say another word about it."

Much to Kate's disappointment, that's what Archibald MacDonald did. When the men in charge had gone she filled up the water jugs and then set off after them.

The tarpaulins that had been pegged over the cargo crates were thrown off. A few men with crowbars were prying up slats, with knots of their fellow refugees peering over their shoulders. A number of the fort Indians—what the fur trade people called the home guard—were watching from a distance, along with a few of the officers' half-breed wives and children.

One of the men with crowbars was John Bannerman, he of the
red hair and green eyes. "Good afternoon, John. I thought you
were busy building our winter shelters."

"Oh, hello, Katy. A number of us came down to help with
moving everyone up in the morning."

"What have you got there?"

"Your guess is as good as mine so far." He pushed down too
hard on the end of the crowbar and split the slat. "Oh, well . . ."

It was a crate of muskets. He took one out, and the muzzle came
close to her nose. She ducked away. "Be careful. . . ."

"He could not hurt you with that, unless he clubbed you over
the head with it." It was Alexander Sutherland. He took the musket
out of John Bannerman's hands. "The barrel is packed full with
grease, and there is neither flint nor powder." He shook his head.
"The generations of our ancestors that must be spinning in their
graves at the thought of grown Highlanders who know nothing of
handling weapons. . . ."

Kate pointed to another crate and said to John Bannerman: "Try
that one."

Inside it was a pair of small brass cannons. In the crates beside
it they found cutlasses, bayonets, several sets of manacles, but no
hoes or axes or plowshares. Kate said to Archibald MacDonald:
"They put the wrong cargo aboard. This is a shipment for a penal
colony."

In the aggrieved tones of the recently violated, he replied: "I
can assure you, Miss MacPherson, that the cargo I supervised from
wharfside to disembarking was the consignment to the colony, and
these crates are they."

"Then just what kind of bloody-minded idiots has Lord Selkirk
got running his colony?" asked Alexander Sutherland.

Archibald MacDonald said stiffly: "Lord Selkirk and I have every
confidence in Governor MacDonell's ability to assess the needs of
the colony."

"Well, you had better pray you are wrong. Because if Governor
MacDonell had good reason to order in *this* kind of shit . . ." He
couldn't seem to find words strong enough to finish, so he threw
the musket back in the crate and stomped off lopsidedly.

There was frost on the ground the next morning. They set off in
a body, the sick leaning on their healthier brothers and sisters,
following a short, dark, bow-legged Indian in tartan trousers. He
led them fifteen miles over hummocks of lichened granite and

around the edges of surprisingly green, inviting meadows that he called "muskeg." Kate came to the conclusion that they were this country's version of peat bogs.

The hollow around Churchill Creek turned out to be sheltered enough from the bay winds to grow actual trees. There were four long barracks made of logs and clay that were nearly ready to be roofed and a separate cabin for Mister Archibald MacDonald. There was also a little hut off to one side that Alexander Sutherland was building for himself and his sister.

The healthy men were put to work finishing the construction, the sick of both sexes were sat down to tie nets for snagging quail, and the able-bodied women were sent out to pick the cranberries that grew along the borders of the muskeg.

Kate was off with Catherine Sutherland, whose brother's sudden emergence from one of the listless indisposed to man in charge had retwigged her curiosity about the "incident of the sealed paper." She looked around to make sure that the other berry pluckers were out of earshot, then said in as artless a voice as she could muster: "Oh, by the by, Catherine, the funniest little thing just came to mind. Why it should stick in my mind, I couldn't say, but . . . It seems to me that when we were on the ship, I was walking along between the sickbeds one day and there was a piece of paper had fallen off someone's bed. I picked it up and put it back and never thought any more of it until today. But it suddenly came back to me, and I wondered if I had put it on the right bed. It seemed to me it was your brother's bed—your brother Alexander, that is. Do you know of your brother having any such thing—a piece of paper with a red seal on it?"

"A red seal?"

"Yes, a red wax seal, as from a signet ring. The kind that an Earl might use, or a Duke, I suppose, or a magistrate or—"

"No. You must have put it on the wrong bed."

She wondered if Catherine might be lying—perhaps her brother had told her to keep it secret. But then Catherine Sutherland had never been able to keep a secret. "How strange. I was certain it was your brother's. Are you quite sure that—"

There was a roar like the kraken waking, and a gleaming white mountain erupted in the middle of the creek in front of them, sheets of water cascading off its summit. Its details were obscured by the geyser it had thrown up, giving Kate the impression that it was one of the white whales from the bay that had somehow blundered upriver. Then she saw the claws.

A crowd of men came running from the construction site, carrying the muskets that Alexander Sutherland had shown them how to load. They took up positions on the bank and raised their guns. The bear held its ground in the middle of the creek, roaring and slapping at the air.

The tartan-trewed Indian ran in between them, waving his arms and pushing at the gun barrels: "No! Bad! Bad! Wait a time!"

As some of the muskets edged down skeptically, the Indian turned and moved slowly toward the bear, rapping the back of his knife blade on his musket barrel and shouting and stamping his feet at the edge of the water. The bear increased the volume of its roaring and gave a demonstration of how high it could stretch its paws.

Kate's heart had calmed down enough to allow her vision to pick out details on the bear—the agate-black beads of eyes, the rubbery black tip of the snout, and the creamy, wrist-deep fur. The bear gave one last bark at the Indian, then splashed down onto all fours, turned its nose upstream—only its wedge-shaped face and puffball ears above the water—and paddled away against the current.

The Indian turned back and grinned with his eyes while his mouth scowled. "Bad time. No meat on bear. All other . . ." He waved his arm inclusively at the late-autumn landscape. "Fat time now. But ice bear lean time till ice time. Wait in water till ice time. On big water"—he pointed in the direction of the bay—"big bear wait."

If their bear had been chased from the bay by the bigger bears downstream, Kate didn't want to meet them. The Indian went on, pointing at the spot in the creek their bear had called home. "Bear!" He held up his right hand with the thumb extended as its head and the fingers dangling down as legs. Then he held up his left fist in a recumbent position. "Not so big bear." He trotted his right hand along until it collided with the left fist upstream. The two hands flurried against each other, then the left hand ran away farther upstream, and their bear settled in in its place.

Alexander Sutherland said: "There might not have been much meat on him, but there was some."

"May be." The Indian shrugged. "But not so much."

Kate said: "So if we simply . . ." She mimed his action of banging a knife blade against a rifle barrel and gave out a few ululations. "If we simply make noise, they will run away?"

"Some . . . time . . ." The Indian appeared to be wrestling with a concept that was over their heads. "Some time yes, but some time bear . . ." He opened his mouth and snapped his jaws in the

air, then stuck out his right arm and drew a line across it where it
joined his shoulder. He made his eyes small and bearlike again and
chewed thoughtfully, with the abstract look of a being concentrating its attention on its palate and taste buds.

The men began to drift away the way they'd come. Catherine
Sutherland went with them. Kate couldn't really blame her—the
largest predator in the parish of Kildonan, excluding the human
ones, was a wild cat. But she'd be damned if she was going to
spend the next six months bolted into a log barracks.

She had just gotten herself settled back into berry picking when
there was a loud splashing from the creek and a series of guttural
boomings like a walrus belching into a rain barrel. A white maelstrom came churning down the creek.

The firing squad reassembled itself quickly. The bear feinted a
series of rushes out of the water, and the Indian shouted at it from
the bank again. This time the bear came out of the water straight
at him with astounding speed. The Indian threw up his musket and
fired. The rest of them all fired at once.

When the smoke had blown away, the bear was stretched out on
its belly with its head pillowed on one paw, hind legs floating on
the water, its white coat spattered with blood. Of the dozen or so
who had fired, Kate wondered if half of them had hit the bear.

The Indian pushed at the bear's body with the butt of his gun.
The body looked less bulky now than when it was alive—a sinewy
old man in a fur coat two sizes too large. Still, the black-padded
paw was larger than Kate's head. She said: "Is it the same that we
chased off earlier?"

The Indian grunted and nodded his head, then jerked his thumb
upstream and said thoughtfully "May be next bear not so not-so-
big after all."

CHAPTER 19

 Farther up along the Fishing Lakes of the valley of the
Qu'Appelle, Grant followed Bostonais through a copse of

low-canopied oaks that opened out into a clearing by a bay. There
was a low, broad cabin of rough-squared logs layered with clay and
a slanting roof of matted sod. A haze of smoke drifted over from
the far side of the cabin. There was a lithe, dark, black-eyed woman
there, tending a firebed under a lattice rack of green saplings shingled over with gutted fish. A baby in a beaded leather bag strapped
to a cradleboard hung gurgling from a tree limb out of range of the
smoke.

Mary all but dragged Grant off his horse to hug and kiss him.
Pierriche was in the cabin, prowling the walls with a birchbark
bucket of wet clay, peering for rays of sunshine that would be arctic
winds and snow in a month or so. There was a baked-clay fireplace
on one wall, cooking implements and traps and fish nets on the
others. The floor was tamped earth with bearskins and buffalo robes
strewn here and there for furniture.

After dinner they lounged along the lakeshore. The sun was still
warm and late setting, but autumn was far enough along that there
was no need for a smudge fire. Grant said to the Falcons: "How
far back does your property extend?"

"Property?"

"Yes—is it just this stretch of lakeshore, or do you own the stand
of trees inland?"

Falcon laughed. "This ain't Montreal, Wappeston—this is the
pays d'en haut. Me and Mary thought this looked like a good place
to spend a couple seasons. None of the Chiefs around here use it
for a campsite, so we put up a house. The Cree don't mind because
of Mary's mother, and my mother was Assiniboine, so *they* leave
us alone. After one more winter, though, I think the trapping won't
be so good. Either I've thinned them out too much, or they're
getting wise to all my tricks. So maybe next summer we'll find a
spot along the Turtle River, or the Pembina. Around the Forks of
the Red maybe would've been good but, you know"—he
shrugged—*"les jardinières."*

In the morning they set off, cutting southwest out of the valley
of the Qu'Appelle—Grant and Bostonais and Falcon and Mary and
their son strapped to his mother's back. Late in the afternoon they
rode into a campsite where three other métis lounged around the
fire: Alex Fraser, the snake-eyed voyageur from Duncan Cameron's
brigade, and Marguerite née Grant with her husband, François Morin. By now Grant could remember his sisters quite clearly and
delighted and embarrassed Marguerite by reminding her of the time
she'd painted the dog with their uncle's face pigments.

The amalgamated party drifted westwards, traveling in single file along coulees and streambeds. The country grew drier. Ground-hugging nubs of cactus appeared in spots between the brown tufts of grass. The sage grew up into woody bushes instead of the soft-stemmed plants along the Qu'Appelle.

By a green-skinned slough alive with late-migrating ducks, they came across two other hunters—Bonhomme Montour and William Shaw. Grant was beginning to accept the fact that these chance encounters in the middle of thousands of miles of rolling prairie were appointments made last spring; that the exact equivalant of one Montreal clerk saying to another, "I'll meet you at the corner of St. Vincente and the Main tonight at ten-fifteen sharp," was one *pays d'en haut* half-breed saying to another, "Meet you at Medicine Dog Coulee at half-past the Moon of the Yellow Leaves."

The two new additions helped to put a little slack in the scouting duties. Fortunately the scouting was done in pairs, so Grant was allowed to feel he was pulling his weight despite the fact that he had only the vaguest idea how to get back to the main party if he did find buffalo sign—assuming he knew what buffalo sign was. He'd always heard that buffalo traveled in immense herds, but these "expert" hunters didn't seem to be having much luck finding them.

At night they would build a fire in a low gully and sit around trading stories and singing songs that tasted of woodsmoke and sweetgrass—mostly led by Falcon. After one in particular—which ended with a couplet identifying the writer as Falcon—Grant said: "Do you think you might give me a copy of that sometime to read?" Falcon suddenly looked embarrassed and mumbled something unintelligible, shaking his head. "Oh. Oh, of course, how stupid of me. I would be more than happy to write it down for you sometime if you would care to dictate. . . ."

Mary said: "Pierriche can write as good as you. Maybe they didn't send him across the ocean to college, but his father took him back to Montreal to go to school."

Falcon said: "Songs aren't for writing down on paper like poetry—you kill them that way. Songs are for singing."

Halfway through the next morning, Mary threw up her arm and pointed ahead. "Pierriche! There, you see? Bonhomme and Shaw . . ." On a high ridge to the west, there were two riders crisscrossing in silhouette.

Looking a bit miffed that his wife's eyes had picked them out first, Falcon said, "I see," then called over his shoulder, "Let's go!'' and kicked his horse. The men started forward at a trot, leaving the women and packhorses behind.

The trot soon built to a canter. Bostonais and François were taking off their coats and hats and bundling them up to tie behind their saddles as they rode. The colors and outlines of the landscape had suddenly become richer and sharper. Falcon and Alex Fraser were talking, as much to themselves as to each other, more or less nonsensical observations. Grant couldn't hear either of them clearly for the drumming in his ears. He had the impression that the same sound was in the ears of all the others. Even the weary old spotted nag that Bostonais had picked out for him back at Fort John was pricking up its ears.

Bonhomme Montour and William Shaw were waiting for them at the base of the ridge. They all dismounted, did a last-chance check of flints, and slung their powder horns down off their shoulders. Then, much to Grant's surprise, they opened up their shot pouches and started popping musket balls into their mouths.

Falcon said to him: ''What you do is fill your cheeks with musket balls, take your rifle in one hand and your powder flask in the other, and after you've fired you recharge your gun with the powder, spit in a musket ball—the spit wads down the powder—and there you are. Nothing to it.''

''Nothing to it,'' François echoed, ''unless the gun gets too hot and blows up in your hand.''

Bonhomme Montour said: ''Or your horse gets gored and falls.''

William Shaw said: ''Or trips in a gopher hole and falls.''

François smiled: ''And then the buffalo make *rubaboo* out of you. 'Cause by the time you get into the herd, they're all gonna be running like the women who see Bostonais coming.''

Grant lined the musket balls in against his molars, the lead taste filling his mouth. He mumbled around them, ''How do I guide the horse with both hands occupied?''

Falcon said: ''Don't you worry about that. As long as he's a buffalo runner you just worry about holding on.'' He turned to Bostonais. ''You did get him a buffalo runner, didn't you?''

Bostonais grunted in the affirmative with a distinct note of malicious glee. Falcon shot a hard look at Grant's horse, then glanced back at Bostonais. ''Not Le Père?'' Bostonais seemed not to hear him. Falcon let out a long string of Cree that was too quick for Grant to follow, although ''Le Père'' was salted through it liberally.

''Ready!'' François Morin gargled out through his musket balls, springing onto his horse.

Grant turned around to mount Le Père. The horse's slumping posture hadn't changed, but the eyes seemed to have gotten bigger than Grant had ever seen them, and there was something twitching under the spotted skin of one shoulder.

They spread out in a skirmish line and nudged their horses up the ridge. As they came over the crest, Grant had a fraction of a second of paralysis.

The landscape spread out in front of him had the same shape as the terrain they'd been traveling through—scooped-out hill banks and corrugated ridges—but it was covered to the horizon with undulating brown fur. A few fragmentary images registered—a bull rolling on its back and splashing dust up with its hooves, a fawn-colored calf bouncing on stiff legs and butting at its mother's belly, a platoon of wolves skirting along the brown coastline. Then he was busy scrabbling to regain possession of the saddle after being thrown back and almost off by Le Père's sudden leap forward.

The horse that could barely wheeze its way up to a trot hit full gallop within its first three strides, cutting straight down the slope and into the herd. The first few buffalo began to run. Their impulse radiated out through the animals around them. The entire continental shelf of buffalo was in stampede, tails up, heads down, horns tossing. . . . and Grant was in the middle of it.

Le Père came up beside a buffalo and matched its pace. The buffalo tried to shear off, but the press of bodies kept it from altering its course and the horse stayed with it. Grant gazed down in wonder at the mountainous head with its blue-black horns, the thick-wooled churning shoulders, the curiously delicate, crop-furred hips.

Le Père was whinnying shrilly—almost, it seemed, in exasperation. Suddenly Grant remembered the rifle. He sloped the barrel down across the crook of his left arm, the muzzle not more than a foot from the buffalo's shoulder, and pulled the trigger. There was an instant of gelled time, compounded of a flash of sparks, a burst of smoke, a crack of sound—and then the buffalo had somersaulted into oblivion and Le Père strained forward to the next.

With his left hand, Grant jammed the nipple of the powder flask into the jouncing mouth of the barrel and shook in a charge, praying to whatever gods cared to listen that he hadn't dumped in too much. He swung the muzzle up to his mouth and fought to spit in a musket ball without knocking out his front teeth. That accomplished, he propped the rifle across his lap and scattered a bit of powder across the priming pan. By this time there was another buffalo beside him, Le Père synchronizing its hoofbeats perfectly. Grant simply raised

the gunstock off his lap—the barrel still resting on his left thigh—
wrenched back the cock, and pulled the trigger.

That was the last intact frame he could isolate. After that his
sense of time spiraled down with the other five senses into a swirling
pool of dust eddies, distant human silhouettes mounted above the
dark sea, horse sweat and foam-flecked brown bodies, churning
thunder, bellows and grunts and blood. The inner surfaces of his
legs had melded into the heaving ribs of the horse; there was no
skin separating the inside of his hand from the gunstock.

Just when he'd grown accustomed to the notion that this roiling
dream time was all there'd ever been, the fabric of the world changed
once again. The rolling thunder grew duller, the sea Le Père was
charging through changed color and dropped lower. It took Grant
a moment to realize that they had run entirely through the herd and
broken out at the crest of the black-foamed tidal wave.

There was one buffalo keeping pace with Le Père, running far
out in front of the others. Without the crush of bodies to block the
view of the full body profile, it wasn't difficult to tell that this one
was a cow. She was six feet tall at the hunch of her shoulders and
a yard across between the tips of her horns.

Le Père edged in close beside her to give his gunner a clean shot,
following the zigzag open-country run like a well-matched dancing
partner. Grant kept expecting her hooves to catch on her long,
trailing beard, but they never did. He hadn't gotten around to reloading from his last shot, so he charged the gun with powder and
worked the last musket ball around to the front of his mouth.

As he eased the muzzle up in front of him, his eyes fixed onto
three puckered furrows of scar tissue running along the old cow's
back. A cougar or a bear had got hold of her not too long ago, but
she had lived to tell the tale. One round, opalescent, muddy-black
eye stared out sideways at Le Père from the wool-vined, crag-boned
head. Inside the snorting, straining ton of bone and muscle, the eye
was surprisingly placid, as though she knew there was nothing she
could do now but run until the bullet took her. Cow or not, she was
old and tough—boil her for a week and she'd still grind the tops off
human molars.

Grant turned his head away from the mouth of the rifle and spat
out the musket ball. Resting his weight on the right stirrup, he
stretched his body out as far as he could and just managed to extend
his right arm far enough to tap the tip of the rifle barrel on top of
the cow's head; just once, counting coup. As the muzzle bounced
back up off the springy crown of wool, his right stirrup girth broke.

The ground leaped up to embrace him. He let go of his powder flask and clutched the soft rim of the saddle with his left hand, his left knee still hooked across Le Père's back, the prairie bouncing up and down within a foot of his eyes, lashing his face with dry grass stalks. With the shift in weight, Le Père stumbled and then righted himself—but the shock almost dislodged Grant's frail hold. He dragged himself back up onto the saddle. The horse screamed shrilly, and Grant looked back. The front rank of the herd had caught up with them. One horn had raked Le Père's left flank, leaving a long bloody gash. Grant flailed back at the horns with his rifle.

Le Père was wheezing, losing his wind. Ahead and to their right was a low, steep-sided knoll. Grant kicked Le Père with his right heel to angle him in that direction, beating at his haunches with the rifle barrel. It didn't seem possible that he could keep in front of the herd on a diagonal when they'd already caught up with him at a straight run, but he did, whistling like a broken bellows. He reached the knoll just ahead of the horns and scrambled up the sandy slope. His momentum carried them almost to the crest, but then he lost his footing and slid back.

Grant tumbled forward over Le Père's outstretched neck and landed safely. He whipped his arm back and grabbed hold of the bridle, pulling with all his strength. The horse's panicked eyes riveted onto his, but he could feel them both slipping. When the first horn punched into Le Père's flank, the jolt traveled all the way up through his body and down Grant's arm. Le Père screamed and fell sideways, dragging Grant to the edge of the knoll. He let go of the reins. Le Père sank down under the hooves and disappeared.

The sun had slid halfway down its western arc when Bostonais and Falcon found Grant, still sitting on top of the knoll with his arms around his knees. The tail end of the herd had passed by long ago. The plain was dotted with carcasses, and clumps of women and children were working at the butchering.

Bostonais stood at the edge of the knoll looking down at the remnants of Le Père. The black-mopped head shook itself from side to side. "Poor son of a bitch," he murmured.

Falcon said: "Almost two." Bostonais wheeled on him, but Falcon stood his ground, reedy arms crossed, staring back levelly.

Grant worked his way up to his feet and wiped at the dried-out rivulets carved through the dust caked on his face. He said: "I guess it takes a damned green *moonias* to cry over a horse."

Bostonais looked away. He shook his head again and mumbled:
"No."

CHAPTER 20

By the time Grant and Bostonais got back to Fort John
with their loaded packhorses—Grant on a grey pony from
Falcon's string—the leaves were whirling off the trees. Grant was
despatched with two *engagés* to spend the winter managing a place
called Boucher's Post, seventy miles to the north. Once the snow
settled in, it might as well have been seven hundred.

Boucher's Post consisted of two low log shanties and a horse
corral, perched on the edge of a broad plateau of naked prairie.
Who Boucher was and what he'd done to have this place named
after him, Grant never heard.

The smaller of the two cabins was the *engagés'* quarters. Through
the front door of the other was an open area in front of a counter
of hand-sawn planks. Behind the counter were long shelves and
stacked bales and barrels of trade goods that were gradually replaced by layers of furs and bags of pemmican. As an afterthought,
back beyond the farthest end of the stock shelves, was a clay hearth
and a small cleared space where the bourgeois, Mister Grant, made
his bed. Even with two *engagés* to order about, the bourgeois's days
were made up of enough straining at the fur press, hoisting *pièces*
onto high shelves and wrestling tempestuous customers to flop him
onto his bed like a rag doll every night.

Grant was standing behind the counter in his waistcoat and shirt-
sleeves, cutting open the back seam of his broadcloth tailcoat. After
three months of working like a horse and eating like two, the coat's
fit across his upper back and chest was snugger than a sausage skin.
As he snicked his way through the stitches with his pocketknife,
he carried on a running monologue in his head, about everything
and nothing in particular. He'd gotten into the habit of carrying on
interior conversations with himself for the simple reason that there
was no one else to talk to.

Suddenly the fort dogs began to howl, a frantic wailing punctuated with short, sharp canine curses that increased steadily in volume. Grant put down his pocketknife and reached up for the massive buffalo coat hanging from a peg on the wall. He'd paid a Cree woman at Fort John to knock it together for him out of one of the pelts he'd brought back from his hunt with Bostonais. It was clumsy and awkward and a little bit musty, but it did the job.

He hefted the coat down and shrugged it over his shoulders, then popped open the door and stepped into a jolting amalgam of wind and cold and white light. It didn't seem right that a sun that bright could cast so little heat.

Stretching out to the horizon was a sparkling white wind-whipped world with a few pitiful gray fingers of willow bushes spoiling the integrity of its crust. It wasn't possible that anything could live out there, but four blanket-clad figures were snowshoeing unhurriedly toward him, trailed by a pair of dogs dragging a toboggan.

As the foreign dogs hove into the yard, the Boucher's Post pack came tearing out from between the two cabins. The toboggan dogs leaped forward to meet the charge. Houle, one of the *engagés*, came out of the cabin with a dog whip and helped the Indians beat back the melee into its separate components.

Grant kicked at the snow that had sifted in across the threshold and went back inside. He slung his buffalo coat back onto its peg and cleared his tailoring off the countertop. The door jerked open again, and Houle came in trailing four windblown Cree—a middle-aged man, an old woman, a young woman, and an adolescent boy. None of them were carrying furs or sacks of pemmican to trade.

Houle introduced Mister Grant to Chief Starblanket and repeated the formula in Cree for the Chief's benefit. Grant had a sneaking suspicion that he was looking at the entirety of Chief Starblanket's band, but he kept it to himself. He brought out the dog-eared ledger from under the counter and flipped through it. There was no listing for Chief Starblanket. Houle explained to him that the Chief had changed his name.

"When?"

Houle shrugged.

"What from?"

"La Tête Verte."

There were two pages of scrawled entries under that heading. The hands of Grant's various predecessors had recorded a long list of goods advanced on credit, none of which had been canceled out. The last entry came at the end of last season, when it was noted that La Tête Verte had been seen taking his furs into the Hudson's Bay Company's Fort Qu'Appelle.

The Chief launched into an excited harangue in Cree. At the end of it, Houle said: "He say there ain't no La Tête Verte no more. He had a vision, and now he is Starblanket."

"Ah. Ask him what he wants here."

"He want you to start a new account for Starblanket."

Grant burst out laughing. The Chief mounted up upon his dignity and began to orate again. Before he'd got three words out, the dog erupted again, much louder this time. Houle stuck his head out the door and called back: "*Carriole.*" Grant took his coat down off the peg, jerked his head at Houle to watch the counter, and went outside.

There was a team of four dogs coming up from the south, pulling a *carriole* with a man inside. Essentially, a *carriole* was a tapered high-prowed toboggan under a built-up wooden framework covered with stretched hides. The effect was not unlike an overgrown Turkish slipper. The passenger sat in the heel with his legs stretched out in the toe, padded and insulated with blankets and buffalo robes. The driver ran along behind on snowshoes. In this case the driver was Bostonais Pangman.

By the time the sled slid to a halt in the yard, there was a boiling mass of dogs in front of it—the post dogs and Chief Starblanket' dogs and the *carriole* team all scrumming in together. Bourassa, Grant's second *engagé*, came out of his cabin, and he and Bostonais waded in with the butt ends of their whips, Bostonais plucking out dogs by the scruff of the neck and one-handing them over his shoulder.

The passenger in the *carriole* turned out to be John Pritchard. Grant led them all back into the trading shed. When Chief Starblanket saw Pritchard he went for him like a raven to dead meat, complaining volubly that the *moonias* clerk didn't understand the ways of the *pays d'en haut* and of Cree medicine, but now that La Corpé was here . . . Mister Pritchard waved him off. "Mister Grant is in charge here," he said, and stood back to watch.

The Chief reluctantly turned back to Grant and picked up the oration that the dogs had cut off. "The heart of the young bourgeois is small. When he has seen more moons than there are leaves on the willow tree, he will not laugh at the medicine ways of the Cree. The heart of La Tête Verte was black and hard and shrivelled with the smoke of old fires. But the heart of Chief Starblanket is clean and white, as clean and white as fresh snow in the moonlight."

as clean and white as a page of the white man's paper with no writing on it.''

He paused for Houle to translate. Instead Grant cut in in Cree. "You confuse the North West Company with the men from Hudson's Bay. We understand and respect the medicine ways of the Cree. Chief Starblanket has made great medicine, and La Tête Verte is no more. See, these marks here''—he pointed to "La Tête Verte" scrawled across the top of the page—"are La Tête Verte." He dipped his pen in the inkwell and crossed out the words. "La Tête Verte is no more. In his place we write 'Staarrbllaannket.' Hm, seems you owe us forty beaver plews, Chief Starblanket."

Chief Starblanket looked extremely sour. The old woman who'd come in with him looked like she was about to come over the counter and bite out Grant's liver. The young woman and the Chief's adolescent son kept impassive and in the background. It seemed a safe bet that the boy was the Chief's son; two such noses couldn't be accounted for otherwise.

Chief Starblanket said: "We will die of hunger before I can pay you back forty beaver plews. How can I hunt? I have no gunpowder and no musket balls, my traps are rusting . . ."

Grant considered pointing out that several hundred generations of Chief Starblanket's ancestors had managed to hunt well enough without gunpowder and steel traps in the days before the fur companies arrived, but that didn't sound exactly like sound business practice. He said: "If you were to bring in something you could trade, to bring down the total of what you owe us, I might be able to advance you a few goods against what you'll bring in over the winter. But as it stands, it would look to Le Corpé like I'm giving away the company's trade goods for nothing."

Chief Starblanket turned and grunted at the young woman and waved toward the door. She went outside. Grant assumed that she was the Chief's wife, although she was decidedly too young to be the mother of an adolescent son, even in the *pays d'en haut*. But in the *pays d'en haut* a certain fluctuation in the components of family units wasn't at all uncommon.

She came back in lugging a string of a dozen or so sleek furs. Starblanket pointed her to lay them on the counter. Grant poured out two cups of heavily watered high wine and pushed one across the counter, raising his own in the established pretrading ritual. Instead of taking up the cup in front of him, Starblanket shook his head and asked Grant for another as well. Grant splashed a dollop from the keg into another cup. Starblanket handed it to the old woman and only then drank from his own. So, wine for the Chief and wine for his mother but no wine for his wife.

Grant went through the furs, toting them up in his head. All transactions were calculated in "made beaver plews." One black fox equaled two beaver, three martens equaled one, and so on. Chief Starblanket's furs tallied up to eighteen beaver. The Chief said he'd trade them for two pounds of powder, six pounds of shot, two fathoms of carrot tobacco, six No. 2 traps, and a keg of high wine. Grant said that he would give him one pound of powder, two pounds of shot, one carrot of tobacco, and three No. 2 traps.

While Chief Starblanket was mulling that over, Bostonais stepped toward the young woman and said something to her in a language Grant had never heard before. She sprang out with a long, enthusiastic outpouring in what sounded to be the same language, although it was salted through with a repeated series of syllables that sounded a good deal like "Mackenzie."

Starblanket's droopy yellow eyes traveled from the young woman to Bostonais and the other North West Company men and back again. Suddenly he brightened and barked in English: "May be got 'nother thing to trade!" He took hold of the young woman's skirt and yanked it up above her waist. She tried to push his hand down, squirming and blushing, but the old woman gave her a clout with the heel of her fist, and after that she just stood there with her head down and her eyes closed. Chief Starblanket switched back to Cree: "Do we have a trade? Twenty musket balls and a keg of high wine . . ."

Grant said, "No. We've done trading," and went back among the shelves to fetch the traps. Bourassa looked disappointed.

When Starblanket's band had gone out, Mister Pritchard said to Bostonais: "What did she say to you?"

"She's Blood, not Cree. Or half Blood. She said her father was a trader, but she lived her life with her mother's tribe in the foothills of the Shining Mountains. Some years back she got grabbed by a raiding party and sold for a slave."

"Why was she saying 'Mackenzie'?"

"She says that was her father's name."

"Sir Alexander?"

Bostonais shrugged. "Lot of Mackenzies that might have been her father. Or maybe her mother just picked the name out 'cause she thought it was good medicine."

Mister Pritchard persisted, "But it *could* be that her father is Sir Alexander Mack—"

"So what?" Bostonais exploded, flailing his arms out and advancing on Mister Pritchard. "Then what? So what?"

Mister Pritchard backed away. Bostonais turned away from him and leaned his back against the counter. Grant reached down for two fresh cups and dipped them full of high wine, contemplating the fact that "so what" could also be said about being the child of Peter Pangman. Peter Pangman was one of the senior partners of the company, long since retired from the *pays d'en haut* to his estate outside of Montreal. All he'd bequeathed to his son when he'd left him behind had been the nickname "Bostonais," because the old man had originally hailed from Massachusetts.

After a few sips of high wine had brought back his cheer, Mister Pritchard said: "What we came up here for, Cuthbert, was to bring you back to Fort John for the New Year's fete."

"That's enormously good of you, Mister Pritchard, but how can I?" He gestured at his log-walled responsibilities.

"No, you can! You'll only need to take one *engagé* along to manage the team. The other one can stay behind and mind the store."

Houle and Bourassa drew lots, and Houle lost. Bostonais took him aside and said: "It would be a very sad thing for my friend Mister Grant to come back and find that while he was gone you'd broke into the rum barrel or traded all the stock away to Cree girls for waxing the lizard. And what makes my friends sad makes me very sad." Houle nodded his head vigorously and then shook his head even more vigorously, just to be sure.

They set off at dawn, which that late in the year was well into the morning. Mister Pritchard and Mister Grant rode bundled in their *carrioles*—or the company's *carrioles*—while Bourassa and Bostonais trotted along on snowshoes, snapping their long whips over the dogs. When they stopped for dinner, Grant and Mister Pritchard huddled shivering by the fire while Bostonais and Bourassa lounged lazily in the snow, puffing their pipes. Perhaps being a gentleman, thought Grant, wasn't all it was cracked up to be.

When they reached Fort John, Grant found Falcon and Mary waiting for him, along with Marguerite and François Morin. Even Josephte had come west from the Forks of the Red.

Grant had left his half-bisected black broadcloth coat back at Fort Boucher. Unfortunately, his chocolate-brown one didn't fit any less tightly. But at least it was in one piece, even though it strained his shoulders back and stuck his chest out like a puffer pigeon.

As he crossed the courtyard to the warehouse where the kick-up was to take place, Grant was surprised to see the front gates swing open and the men from the Hudson's Bay post across the river come trooping in. Falcon said: "Last year Fort Qu'Appelle was the host, this year it's Fort John's turn."

For the first hour Grant felt a bit seasick with the overwhelming crush of people—upward of fifty human beings in the same place at once. But the wine helped him adjust—there were open kegs and kettles of punch lined all along the trellised tables. Dotted in between were platters of beaver tail, moose nose, buffalo tongue, antelope rump, and smoked sturgeon—even a soggy attempt at a plum pudding. The extravagance would probably mean short rations at the tail end of March, but square meals in March wouldn't be much practical use if you'd cut your throat in February for lack of a midwinter kick-up.

Bostonais was nackered to the eyeholes, dancing cumbrously with two Cree girls who couldn't have been more than fifteen. One of the Hudson's Bay Company's Orkney servants bumped into his back. Bostonais swung around, threw him backward on the floor, and drew out the long sheath knife tucked into the high top of his moccasin. The dancing stopped, and the dancers pressed away from them.

Grant pushed his way forward through the circle. He passed one of the Hudson's Bay men holding another Orkneyman back, shaking his head and hissing: "Bostonais Pangman." The Orkneyman that Bostonais had knocked down was still on the floor, scrabbling backward with his heels and elbows. Bostonais was weaving toward him in a half crouch, the knife circling lazily in his right hand.

Grant took hold of Bostonais's right wrist with both hands, barely circling the circumference, and raised it up over his head. "Hey, Bostonais . . . Bostonais! Haven't you got better things to do?"

The clouded eyes focused on him slowly, then Bostonais began to put his strength into his knife arm to bring it down. Grant strained against it. There was a rending, tearing sound behind him. He looked over his shoulder. His tailcoat had split up the back.

Bostonais laughed and flung his arms around him, then stretched them out again and grabbed the two Cree girls and bowled them and Grant toward the door. Once they'd got outside, Bostonais let go of Grant and took hold of the nearest girl. He picked her up and held her against the log wall, snuffling his beard against her neck. She laughed and dug her fingers into his shoulders and bit the top of his head. The other girl was standing back from Grant expectantly, swaying a little, daring him from under drooping lids.

Drunk or not, it was a damned cold night. Grant grabbed a handful of Bostonais's shirt and tugged. "Come on." He led them around the side of the warehouse to the yard where Bostonais and Bourassa had left the *carrioles*. The passenger orifice was just wide enough to slide the girl in among the musty flaps of buffalo robes and then work in on top of her. The opening on the other *carriole* wasn't any wider and Bostonais was, but that was his problem.

Her mouth tasted of wine and moose meat. Both their backs had to arch a bit to fit within the shape of the *carriole*—hers forward and his back. She took his hand and pushed it through the neck slit of her dress onto her breast. His hand was numb with cold, but he cupped it as well as he could. She shrieked with laughter at the icy clasp, pulling back from him with her torso while her hips pushed forward. His hand grew warmer. She started a low moan at the back of her throat and began to thrash around, but for all her thrusting and clutching there was an eerie shyness to her; whenever her eyes crossed his, they seemed to shrink back. It disturbed him for a moment. He solved it by ducking his head down into the hollow of her shoulder and closing his eyes.

When he went back inside, he encountered his three sisters murmuring by the doorway. All six eyes swiveled toward him. Mary's were twinkling with amusement. Josephte's were glinting slits. Marguerite's were the same vacuously luminous soft pools whose lids he had kissed in the autumn. Josephte said: "Is that what they took Papa's money for in your fancy college—to teach you to act like an animal?"

"There was no need to teach me that, Josephte. After all, that is what we are: intelligent animals. All our attempts to deny the noun only succeed in canceling out the adjective."

It seemed doubtful that Mary's vocabulary would have had any occasion to assimilate "noun" and "adjective," but she put her hands up over her mouth and giggled like little tinkling bells. Then she scurried around behind him and fussed with his split-seamed coat, saying that she would have to make him one that fit.

CHAPTER 21

Kate stood on the lip of the moon-white crater that housed the huddle of huts beside the mouth of Churchill Creek, watching the Merry Dancers ripple across the night sky. She'd been told that the Indians called them the Ghost Dance, and they did seem more ghostly here in Rupertsland than merry. Perhaps it was because back home they'd always been framed and limited by the hills. Here the entirety of creation consisted of the blue-white sweep of rippled snow and the glittering black vault of the sky. Between them danced the mountain ranges of colored light, flickering and coalescing in sheets that blotted out the stars.

Or perhaps it was the clarity of the air that made them seem eerier. It was so sharp and crystalline here. On nights when the moon was full she'd sometimes fancied she could see the ruined stone fort on the shore of the bay fifteen miles away, or a quarter inch inside her heart. The colors were much stronger here—wine and blood and glacial moss green and a sea-cove blue, all vibrantly luminescent. Back home the colors had been as pallid as the pale reflections now racing across the snow at her feet—ghostly echoes of ghost lights.

She informed herself that she was getting herself into a state, and that she had things to do. She had been on her way to make her rounds with a pot of strained grouse-and-barley broth when she'd veered off out of the hollow to get a clear view of the lights. If she stood there much longer, she'd have a potful of brown ice, so she bustled back down into the tiny pocket of human habitation. Tending the sick didn't strike her as altruistic; it kept her mind off listening to the wheels of the world ticking another half-year off her life.

John Bannerman was in the end cubicle of one of the four communal longhouses. Doctor Edwards said he had consumption. Whatever it was, it had put a glinting sheen over his green eyes and

146

a hollow rattle in his chest. She sat down on the edge of his pallet and unwrapped her old shawl from around the pot of broth.

She was guiding the spoon to his mouth when he was suddenly wrenched upright by a fit of coughing. His body bumped against hers, knocking the spoon from her grasp. There was nothing she could do but hold him while he gasped for breath, his head and one arm draped limply across her shoulder. His body was unnaturally warm, the heat from his skin radiating through the thick wool of her blouse into her shoulder and breasts. The blanket had fallen down around his hips. The cream-white skin of his back was mottled with patches of red.

The spasms stopped and left him lying drained against her. Gradually the hoarse rattling in his chest slowed to regular intervals. The arm draped over her shoulder came to life, crooking across her upper back and pressing her to him. She tried to push him away gently, but he pulled her to him tighter. "Katy, Katy . . ." His voice was soft and low.

"Leave go of me now, John." She tried again to free herself. "You need to rest now, you are ill."

"I am not ill, Katy," he said matter-of-factly, "I am dying." He was rubbing his cheek against the side of her neck. His hands and forearms moved up and down her back with a kind of reverent hunger.

"You are not dying. A month from now you will be leaping through the snowdrifts chasing pretty girls your own age."

"No." He had shifted himself around so that one hip was pressed against hers. "I will never leave this bed alive."

"I will make damn sure of it if you do not let go of me."

"I am not a child. . . ."

"I can see that!" She didn't feel quite sure of where she was. There was something about the clinging sensation of his hands that made her feel she was suffocating.

"No, I *am* still a child. I do not want to die a child. . . ." He began to kiss her ear, wildly, blindly, his voice indecently close as though he were whispering from behind her eardrum. "You have been so kind to me, Katy. I love you."

She worked her hands up between them, palms against his chest. "Oh, surely—'I love you, whatever-your-name-is, just come with me out behind the cowshed!' Now leave go!" She pushed him violently away. His arms tore clear of her, and he fell back on the bed. His eyes flicked up at her once, then he turned his head away and put one arm across his face. She covered him up with the blanket, made certain of the fire, took up her pot of broth, and went away.

The next two nights she came as usual to spoon-feed him. She never said a word about that night, and neither did he. He swallowed his soup obediently and grunted in reply to her questions. On the third night he was lying with his back to the doorway, the blanket bunched around his waist. In the moonlight streaming through the open doorway, the skin of his back looked unnaturally white. When she touched his shoulder to turn him over, it was stone cold.

The earth had been like a sheet of rock since late October. They sewed John Bannerman in a piece of canvas and laid him with the others in the jury-rigged deathhouse to wait for spring.

There didn't seem to be much question that the next to join them would be Alexander Sutherland. His remission hadn't lasted long, as though the fever had taken a step back to wait until he began to believe that he'd beaten it, then gleefully leapt on him again. His sister had nursed him at first, but now she was sick as well.

Kate went to look in on them one night. With five hours of sunlight a day, "night" had become a rather abstract term, but that had been the way of winters in the parish of Kildonan as well. She pushed open their hut door and found them both asleep on either side of a dying fire. She slipped in as quietly as she could and fed the fire a few more bits of wood. A spruce branch oozing with resin flared up, filling the hut with dancing light and a sweet, wild smell. Catherine Sutherland rolled over and sniffled, then slipped back into sleep. Her brother was shivering in his sleep. Kate rearranged his blanket over him; he continued to shiver. She shrugged off the blanket that she'd taken to wearing outside and laid it over him, but still he shivered. At last she stripped off her shawl and draped it over his chest and shoulders. But it didn't make any difference—and there were no more blankets to add on.

She glanced across the fire at Catherine. The girl was still snoring peacefully through one half-plugged nostril. Quietly Kate raised the edge of Alexander Sutherland's blankets and slipped in beside him.

She lay stiff and prim, flat on her back, hands folded over her breast, and waited for the heat from her body to build up under the blankets and warm him. She waited until she could feel the sweat beading out at the insides of her elbows and the backs of her knees, but he kept on shivering, stretched out on his back with his eyes closed and his teeth clenched and rattling against each other.

She stole another look at his sister's back. It hadn't moved. Kate shifted onto her side—holding her edge of the blanket so the cold air wouldn't get in at him—and then reached across his torso and pinned down the blankets on his side while she lifted her right leg over him. Straddling above him, she slid her knees back and bent her arms until her elbows touched the bed. When she felt the fabric at the front of her blouse brushing up against her skin, she stopped. She held herself in place above him, her weight resting on her elbows and forearms and on her knees and the arches of her feet.

Although her overall length had been somewhat diminished by the bends at her knees and hips, her toes still stretched down past his heels while her eyes were exactly level with his. She reminded herself that she'd always been a great horse of a girl, and there was no reason to have expected that to change.

Her hair, which was wound up in a loose plait, chose that moment to come unbound. One thick, long lock slid down beside his cheek, the firelight catching glints of red Viking gold, and brushed across his nose. He gave out a reflexive sneeze and jerked his head to one side, but his eyes stayed closed. She moved her head to brush the hair from his face.

It seemed impossible that anyone with such fragile features could have lived through ten years in the British army. Perhaps that frail look had only crept in near the end of his service, with the wound in his knee and the fever. His shivers finally subsided into the even breathing of a deep sleep. The air had grown very warm under his blankets.

His right hand came up off the bed and settled against her waist. His eyelids fluttered but didn't open. Kate's upper arms and the muscles on the small of her back were beginning to ache from holding herself poised. It seemed the most natural thing in the world to let her body sink down onto his. As her knees slid down her skirt snaked up, until the insides of her legs up to the middle of her thighs were resting bare against his warm skin.

Still in his fever trance, he ran his hands gently across the fabric covering her back. One of them started tugging at the bottom of her blouse until it came untucked. Kate raised her torso slightly, and his hands pushed up the blouse. She lay back down, her breasts and rib cage settling softly onto his chest. It seemed strange that the sensation of her belly and breasts touching someone else's skin could be both exhilarating and dreamlike.

His hands kept tugging at her blouse. She raised her arms off the bed and stretched them in front of her, as though diving into a deep pool. The rough wool snicked up over her shoulders, slid down her arms, and slipped to the floor.

Her hair had unwound itself completely as the blouse passed over it. She shook it out and watched it tumble down to frame his face. His eyes were still closed, his head rolling slowly from one side to the other. His lips were moving silently, as though his mind were sending words to his mouth that lost their edges in the fog. Something of his fever trance had communicated itself to Kate. She felt enveloped in a thick, flame-lit fog that buffered her from preachers and pulpits, from dirty songs about soldiers and maidenheads, from the clucking of cold, dutiful spinsters.

She put a hand between them and fumbled clumsily. Part of her was surprised that she could touch herself and a man so brazenly, but most of her was concentrating on the task at hand. He eased her over onto her back and took control. His eyes were open now but glazed, unfocused, his movements slow and somnambulant. The touch of his fingers was blunt but unhurried, parting gently.

At first there was only rough, scraping pain, but that changed. She realized that her eyes were closed and opened them. He was farther away—still moving inside her, but he'd propped his torso up on one elbow and was looking down at her. Gentle fingers brushed the hair back from her forehead. His eyes were clear now, piercing through the fever haze. She could see her own reflection, minuscule but fully detailed, in the round black mirrors of his eyes. She closed her eyes again and clung to Alexander Sutherland as he pumped his life out into her.

CHAPTER 22

"Did you hear that?"

Grant squinted up, trying to focus his eyes on Falcon, then realized that wasn't going to sharpen his hearing any. He started to push himself up off the floor, but his hand caught on the cuff of his new coat and spilled him back down again.

They were lounging on a mat of buffalo robes in front of the clay hearth that separated the Boucher's Post bourgeois's quarters from the trade goods and furs horseshoed around it. Falcon had drifted in that evening to trade a few fox furs. It would have been easier for him to take them straight to Fort John, but why not keep it in the family? He'd also brought the coat that his wife had made for her brother. It was fashioned of white antelope skin and tailored to copy an English riding coat a few years out of date—except that the original had had to do without multicolored quillwork and embroidered black velvet collar and cuffs.

Falcon was sitting up with his head cocked, peering at the stock shelves beyond the border of the firelight. Before Grant could manage a renewed effort at adapting a posture of alertness, Pierriche puffed his upper lip, let the air out with a self-deprecating pop, and leaned back down.

Suddenly Grant felt a gust of cold air seep in across the floor, then a furtive noise coming from among the rows of stock shelves. He stood up, all drowsiness gone, and peered into the shadows. The silhouette of a squared-off buffalo rampant detached itself from the others and said: "Boom boom, you're both dead."

Grant scooped up a tin cup and threw it. Bostonais snatched it out of the air and lumbered forward to see if they had anything to put in it. Falcon said: "I thought you were down at the Forks of the Red."

"I was. The governor of the *jardinières* made a proclamation, and Monsieur Wills paid me to bring it to Pritchard." He tossed off the rum in the cup and handed it to Grant to refill, then stomped the snow off his moccasins and shrugged off his buffalo coat. Grant handed him the topped-up cup. "Pritchard wanted me to bring it to you."

"Bring what to me?"

"The proclamation," fishing inside his smoked-hide shirt and coming out with a dilapidated square of paper.

While Bostonais and Pierriche talked among themselves, Grant leaned back to catch the firelight on the paper. The sentences were run on and the paragraphs crammed together—some clerk's word-for-word copy rather than the proclamation itself. Grant read it through once, then once again, for he couldn't believe his eyes. The Governor of Lord Selkirk's Colony hereby prohibited any party from exporting any provisions—"flesh, grain, or vegetable"—from the Colony's Territories, except under special license from the Governor. Any criminals attempting to export provisions illegally would be placed under arrest and said provisions confiscated, with the

Governor's assurance that all confiscated provisions would be compensated for at rates determined by the Governor.

Grant's wrist went slack as he blinked up at the shadows; then he handed the paper to Falcon. He looked across at Bostonais, who was engrossed in lighting his pipe with a splinter from the hearth. Grant said: "Is he insane?" Bostonais looked at Grant over the flaring pipe bowl and raised an eyebrow.

Falcon handed the paper back to Grant and said: "I guess they're having a hard winter and want to make sure they don't starve. There ain't much good hunting around the Forks anymore anyway. . . ."

"He doesn't mean the Forks of the Red." Grant brandished the paper. "The land grant that the Company of Dentures gave Lord Selkirk for his colony extends from Rainy Lake to Fort Qu'Appelle and from the headwaters of the Red River to the foot of Lake Winnipeg."

Falcon looked dubious, then began to laugh. "So the governor is going to tell the Sioux what they can or can't hunt? And all the grizzly bears will have to get licenses. . . ."

Bostonais allowed the corners of his mustache to raise slightly on either side of his pipe stem, but otherwise he remained about as expressive as a gnarl of pine roots. Grant said to him: "Pemmican, isn't it?"

Bostonais raised his eyes up off the bowl of his pipe and said: "That would do it. The country you said is theirs is all the buffalo country—at least all the buffalo grounds we can get at without giving our heads to the Blackfoot or the Sioux."

"I didn't say it was theirs—I said the Hudson's Bay Company and the Earl of Selkirk said it was theirs."

Falcon said: "Well, let them say whatever they want. . . ."

"Oh, really?" said Grant. "Do you plan to go out after the herd again this summer? I wouldn't bother—because according to what this says, there's no point in the North West Company buying your pemmican, because they can't use it to provision their brigades."

Falcon sat up. "No . . ."

"Yes! What the hell do you think this proclamation is supposed to accomplish? For that matter, what's the whole bloody colony been created to accomplish: the complete destruction of the North West Company. Christ—and there I was at Bas de la Rivière last summer telling Duncan Cameron that Lord Selkirk should be sainted for helping the poor dispossessed crofters. . . ."

Falcon refilled his cup and said: "You worry too much, Wappeston. I'll give you that it's a stupid proclamation, and I don't care for this governor coming in here and telling us where we can or can't hunt any more than you do. But think about it—there ain't no good reason why this colony would want to see the North West Company knocked on the head."

"No? Try this for a reason—the major stockholders of the Company of Adventurers Trading into Hudson's Bay are the Earl of Selkirk and his wife's brother."

"Oh." Falcon angled up his sketchy eyebrows and said unconcernedly: "Well, I guess that's a good reason."

Grant had to get up and walk around. There were too many currents whirling in on him at once. Suddenly he turned toward Bostonais. "Why did Mister Pritchard ask you to bring the proclamation to me? I mean, of course, it's certainly of concern to any employee of the company, but I presume he didn't send out runners to every outlying post. . . ."

Falcon said with a sly smirk: "Pritchard prob'ly has . . . *personal* reasons for wanting to turn it over to you."

Grant said: "What do you mean?"

"Years ago Pritchard got moony-eyed over a half-Cree girl called Catherine MacGillivray. He wanted to quit the company and go home to England or east to the Canadas and make a farm and take her with him. But she wouldn't leave the *pays d'en haut*, and Le Corpé wouldn't give in to being a trader all his life. So she married someone else. Now that husband's rubbed out." He looked up at Grant and winked. "Maybe Le Corpé ain't dead yet."

Grant said: "Catherine *MacGillivray*? She wouldn't be the daughter of . . ." His eyes caught Bostonais's, and he decided to drop it.

Bostonais upended the square-shouldered, green-glass bottle they'd been pouring their rum from and shook out the last few drops, then angled its bottom toward the fire and peered down its neck. Grant took it out of his hand and went down the gloomy passage between the stock shelves, filled it from the keg behind the counter, and brought it back.

Soon they were laughing and singing songs and telling stories, and Grant felt a bit abashed that he'd gotten so heated up about the pemmican proclamation. Not that he was ashamed of his tribal loyalty to the North West Company, or to the free hunters like Bostonais and Falcon. But it did seem a tad silly in retrospect. The Earl of Selkirk's governor could issue all the proclamations he wanted. If any of them became a real threat to the North West Fur Trading Company or the freedom of the *pays d'en haut*, the William

MacGillivrays and Bostonais Pangmans of the world were perfectly capable of chewing up the governor *and* his colony and picking their teeth with the bones.

CHAPTER 23

Kate couldn't decide which was more surprising about Archibald MacDonald's singing voice: that it was a rich deep baritone, or that it was pleasantly tuneful. She found both aspects disappointing. She preferred her ridiculous creatures to be all of a piece; life was simpler that way.

He was singing the "Lament for Glencoe," which was appropriate for a MacDonald of Glencoe. Robert Gunn was puffing up his pipes to take the next turn. All the inhabitants of the Churchill Creek camp were amicably shoehorned into one of the long communal cabins, listening to the music and the stories and taking their turns—all except the half dozen or so who were too close to death to be moved from their beds.

She closed her eyes and drifted in memory, floating on the waves of melody and melancholy, until she fetched up on the blanket-covered spruce-bough bed in Alexander Sutherland's hut. She opened her eyes immediately, blushing and glancing around to see if anyone was looking at her.

In the days that had passed since that night, she had barely thought of it. She had locked it away in its own private casket—a small, enclosed artifact that years from now she might take out to look at now and again. There was no need for her to worry at it with her mind's sharp little teeth. It was hers alone.

Archibald MacDonald finished his song, and Robert Gunn stepped forward. The people sitting on the floor in front of the fire cleared a path for him to stride back and forth in. Just as he had fitted the mouth of the chanter into his, her brother John hissed: "Ssh! Wait!" Robert Gunn glared at him, but John didn't wither. "Ssh! Listen!"

Robert Gunn unpuffed his cheeks and cocked his head. At first there was only the sound of the fire and the wind outside. Then the voice of the wind seemed to swell and take on depth, a consonant-less, echoing moan with no clear point of origin. It was joined by another voice, and then another, in arcane, fluctuating harmonies that multiplied the voices twelvefold. Kate had heard them more than once that winter, but never that many or that close. Back home, when the howling of wolves had been mentioned in one of the old stories, she'd always imagined a sound like a group of oversized dogs. This bore no more resemblance to dogs' howling than the Great Highland Pipes did to a chorus of penny-whistles.

Willy Gunn said: "My father is out there!" He turned on Archibald MacDonald. "Thanks to you."

"Thanks to me? How is it thanks to me? I never ordered him to—"

"No! You merely told him he would have to stay behind with the others when the time came for us to set off for York Factory. What did you expect him to do, lie down and wave good-bye?"

"It was entirely his own idea to go tramping about in all weathers to prove he was up to the journey. I told him they would all meet up with us at Red River regardless."

The plan was that the youngest and healthiest would march overland to York Factory, to be ready to start upriver as soon as the ice broke on the river Hayes. Those who waited at Churchill until the bay was clear enough to travel to York Factory by boat would probably not reach Red River until the end of the summer.

Kate said: "Perhaps he went all the way to the fort today, and decided to stay the night."

Suddenly they heard something moving through the snow along the outside wall. The footfalls seemed too heavy to be wolves, but the rhythm wasn't right for a two-legged creature, and there was a strange dragging sound between the steps.

Kate's eyes moved with everyone else's along the wall, following the sounds of the creature outside. As it neared the entrance, the door jiggled and shivered and then jerked open. Catherine Sutherland came in with Alexander leaning on her shoulder. He looked weak and tired, but a long way from dying. He had a healthy flush along each cheek from the walk through the cold air and his fiddle wrapped in a swatch of blanket cloth under his arm. He said: "What gave you the idea that I was going to let you get away with holding a *cehlidh* without me?"

There was much back slapping and handshaking. Kate felt as though every stitch of clothing had been stripped from her body.

She wanted to find something to cover herself with, to sneak off to her own little cubicle of privacy in the barracks next door. But the doorway was completely enveloped with people, with him in the middle. She rose to her feet as surreptitiously as possible and retreated into the shadows of a far corner.

The *cehlidh* got under way again. He took his turn along with the others, contributing a rather feeble version of "The Skye Boat Song," which everyone received enthusiastically. He appeared to be a bit distracted, his eyes scanning the crowd. She sank down lower.

Suddenly the door of the cabin jounced open again, and in through a cloud of snow came old Alex Gunn, wheezing hard but beaming. "Thirty miles! Thirty miles since morning, back and forth from here to the fort. If you still think I am too old and infirm, Mister Archibald MacDonald, to keep up with your marchers, I will race you there and back tomorrow."

What with bustling him over to the fire and stripping off his coat and asking him all manner of excited questions about his trip, Kate thought she might have a chance to get safely to the door. She sneaked along next to the wall. As she was pushing the door open, a male voice called after her. She flung the door shut behind her and hurried off down the path.

There was a lot of work to hide in over the next week. The women and children were sewing extra pairs of mittens and making snowshoes under the direction of one of the Indian women from the fort. The men were making sleds, supervised by the fort carpenter.

A guide arrived from York Factory—an Indian who spoke Gaelic with a Skye accent—riding in a curious contraption called a dog *carriole*. Archibald MacDonald immediately requisitioned it to transport his private possessions. On the morning of April 6, fifty-one Kildonan crofters lined up behind the guide on snowshoes. All the men in the party were pulling sledges piled up with bundles of possessions and bags of provisions, except for the guide and Archibald MacDonald and Robert Gunn—who flared his pipes out and let go with "Scotland the Brave."

A good portion of the distance they covered on the first day was accomplished by pitching face forward. Legs tended to cramp from the sudden exertion after winter's inactivity and from the unnatural contortions required to hold their snowshoe bindings in place. But they were moving, not being moved, and that was a grand thing.

On the second day they marched six abreast, which was much more efficient than walking stretched out in single file. Kate trudged beside Robert Gunn, self-delegated to snatch the pipes out of his hands when he tripped over his snowshoes. In the evenings she helped Archibald MacDonald with the people who had gone snow-blind or were helpless with stomach cramps after scooping up mouthfuls of snow to refresh themselves. After the first few days she was taking her turn with the men pulling sleds.

Whenever she felt inclined to feel sorry for herself, she'd look at little Jean McKay, so pregnant that she could barely walk. The McKays were in a race against time—trying to reach York Factory before their first child decided to come out and face the world. On the afternoon of the fifth day, it became apparent that they'd lost.

Provisions were running low. The rest of the party couldn't stop and wait for the McKays, so Kate and Angus McKay helped Jean toward a copse of spruce trees off to one side while the rest headed on. Angus cut a wedge-shaped opening at the base of a cone-shaped tree, then Kate laid in some thick-needled boughs on its floor and covered them over with a blanket. Together they helped Jean down on top.

There was the sound of a gunshot in the distance, but no time to waste on guessing. Kate shooed Angus into the spruce den with his wife and then did her best to close in the front of it. The picture ought to have seemed pathetic: a scared, sweating, swollen-bellied girl, teeth clenched and moaning, leaning back against the arms of her terrified husband. But in some irrational corner of her mind, Kate felt consumed with envy.

There was nothing more she could do for them; she was no midwife. Suddenly she unknotted the muffler around her neck and peeled off her Sunday shawl. She thrust it through the branches at them.

"No, no, Katy, we will be warm enough—"

"To wrap your baby bunting in."

"Oh, Katy, no, we could never—"

"You can and you will. Good afternoon."

She trudged back across the spruce copse to hurry after the others. Just before she came out into the open she heard the crunch of snowshoes from beyond the last fringe of trees. She remembered the gunshot and stood as still as she could, breathing shallowly.

Around the tree in front of her, following her trail, came Alexander Sutherland, carrying a musket in one mittened hand and a dead ptarmigan dangling from the other. He stopped when he saw her and held up the dead bird, pointing with the gun barrel at the brown mottling of feathers freckling the white. "Sure sign that spring is on the way," he said, grinning.

When she didn't reply, the cheerful smile on his face slipped a notch or two. He said: "Where are the McKays?" She nodded back over her shoulder.

He dropped the ptarmigan down in front of the spruce tree with the lattice gate of boughs, saying: "Angus, I brought something for your suppers," then came back to Kate. He said: "We had best be getting along if we hope to catch up with the others before nightfall."

The snow had taken on the same milky-gray cast as the sky. Around the horizon, gusts of wind kicked up a fine powder, making a blur of earth and sky. The only feature in the landscape was the long, broad, beaten-down path stretching out before them. From all that her eyes could tell her, she and Sandy Sutherland were walking on a bridge through a dull white void that had no up or down or substance to it.

He stumped along breezily despite the slight hitch in his stride, giving the maddening impression that he was merely out for an afternoon ramble and a spot of shooting. She glanced at him a couple of times—he'd given up trying to stay shaven, and the whiskers around his mouth were rimed with white, as were the tips of his eyelashes and the rims of his eyebrows.

They walked in silence for a time, punctuated by the sounds of the webbed frames pushing down in the snow, the rustle of his trousers and her skirt, the hiss of breath, all crispened by the cold. Then he said: "Would you care to walk behind? The track would be a little firmer then, a little easier for you."

"I was about to ask you the same question."

He let another long silence lapse, then said: "I seem, Miss MacPherson, to have done something wrong."

"Whatever might have given you that impression, Mister Sutherland?"

"At first I thought it might have been what I did on that last night you came to nurse me, but then I reminded myself that it was not entirely my doing."

"You had no part in it at all."

"No? It seemed to me that I did."

Her cheeks felt hot despite the blizzard in the wind. There was a presumption of intimacy in his voice that she would have been glad to do without. "What I meant, Mister Sutherland, was that you had no part in the blame. You were not in your right mind, and besides that, you are a man.''

"I suppose that it is very Christian of you to absolve me of any guilt I might have been feeling, Miss MacPherson, except that I have not been feeling any.''

"Naturally—you are a man.''

"If I feel no recriminations toward you and you feel none toward me, then where does the blame come in? What happened between us concerns you and me and no one else.''

"Except those you told the story to.''

"Those I what? Why would I do a thing like that?''

"You are a man.''

"You keep repeating that as though it should mean something to me. The fact that I am a man does not mean I have to brag about private matters, any more than being a woman means you have to gossip about them.''

A cluster of black dots appeared in the distance—they were beginning to catch up. "I cannot fail but notice, Miss MacPherson, that even though I have assured you that I did not blather what happened between us, the air is still considerably colder than it would be if I was walking alone.''

"I appreciate your discretion. That does not change what happened.''

"I would not want it changed.''

"Naturally, you are a—''

"I know, I know, a man. And you are a woman. Neither of which are facts to be ashamed of.''

"Mister Sutherland, there are matters that I do not care to talk about with strangers.''

She picked up her pace, but he managed to keep up with her, swinging his right snowshoe along with wide sweeps of his stiff leg. For a gratifying moment all was silent, but for the crunch of snow and the sound of their breathing—cold white clouds puffing out with each exhalation. The earth and sky had begun to separate themselves now, as the sun crawled down the horizon. The snow had taken on a ghostly blue glow, brighter than the dimming pearl and dove gray of the sky.

Suddenly Kate stopped dead and turned around, waddling the snowshoes in a half circle. "Forgive me, Mister Sutherland, that was a cruel and thoughtless thing for me to say. I apologize.''

He moved toward her, raising one hand to wave away her apology. "Probably it served me right for prying into your private—''

The turned-up noses of his snowshoes butted into hers and
stopped him. She had a momentary vision of two gawky, emaciated
creatures on great, splayed feet trying to reach each other. She gave
him a businesslike nod to acknowledge the exchange of apologies,
then turned to march on. Unfortunately, the toes of his snowshoes
had overlapped hers, and they snagged. Her body kept going, but
her feet stayed behind.

He caught hold of her elbow and held her while she regained her
balance. With a supercilious smile he said: "You will not get away
from me that easily, Miss MacPherson." She shrugged off his hand
and picked up her feet.

The black dots ahead began to take on the shape of human beings. She could hear his snowshoes crunching up behind her at
double time, then synchronizing with her own as he settled in
alongside her. He said: "What I said before . . . I had meant only
to suggest that you should think no worse of yourself than . . . than
you do of Jean McKay, for instance. After all, everyone knows that
before she and Angus ever became husband and wife—"

"Jean McKay has nothing to be ashamed of. Whatever she and
Angus may have done while they were courting, they are married
now."

He thought about that for a moment and then said: "So you
would feel differently about what happened between us that night
if you were to become my wife?"

"Don't be daft."

He must have seen her point, because he didn't say another word.

Three days farther on, the provisions ran out. They were still a
ways from York Factory. All of them were more or less accustomed
to hiking hungry over the hills of home, but here there was another
factor at work. Once their bodies' furnaces had nothing left to burn,
the cold began to dig in its claws.

Near the end of the day, a dark blot appeared ahead of them
along their line of march. As they grew closer it appeared to be a
head-high, cone-shaped tent with two people squatting in front. It
turned out to be a pyramid of dead ptarmigans and grouse. The
squatting figures stood up as the guide approached them—two
stocky, dark men with shotguns. They clapped the guide on the
shoulder and spoke to him in a guttural tongue. The guide waved
his flock toward the pyramid of birds. The chief factor might not
much care for Lord Selkirk's colonists, but damned if he was going
to let them starve to death within his jurisdiction.

* * *

Two days later they tramped into York Factory with Robert Gunn piping "The Black Bear" and the rest of them doing their best to give out the impression that the walk from Fort Churchill had been a breezy constitutional. A mile from the stockade sat a cluster of empty log shanties that Miles MacDonell, Lord Selkirk's governor, had built to shelter the first contingent for the colony three years earlier. The chief factor magnanimously gave them the use of the musty, slump-roofed sheds until the boats were ready to take them upstream.

After a few days Jean and Angus McKay wandered in, looking haggard and hungry but beaming over their new son. For no good reason, Kate found herself avoiding them. She came to the conclusion that she was in a strange frame of mind. She felt flushed all the time and hazy. Perhaps it was an effect of spring. The snow had grown porous. The naked willow bushes on the riverbank turned amber with rising sap, then sprouted silver-gray furred buds softer than any velvet. Wedge-shaped flights of geese flew over, with wild cries she heard in her blood. The ice was breaking on the river.

CHAPTER 24

As the first crocuses pushed their purple heads up through the snow, the inhabitants of the *pays d'en haut* began gratefully to slough out of their winter coats, effectively putting an end to the trapping season. The trading season had one final, furious month of bartering and tallying. There were only a few thin patches of snow left on the shaded banks of coulees when Grant and Houle and Bourassa loaded up the proceeds of the season at Boucher's Post and headed south to Fort John, trailed by a flock of sled dogs.

John Pritchard was in the courtyard, ankle deep in mud, absentmindedly supervising a crew of *engagés* that was bundling bales of pressed furs into *pièces*. He didn't even glance at Grant's tally sheets, just handed them over his shoulder to an attendant clerk.

"You'll have to join me this evening for my last supper in Fort John—I'll be starting east with the brigade in the morning. We were only waiting for the last of the outposts to come in."

Grant had a sudden twinge of apprehension, which must have shown on his face because Mister Pritchard quickly added: "No, no! No shame in being the last in. I only wish some of the others could be half that conscientious about squeezing the last pelt and pound of pemmican out of their territory."

The quarters at Fort John were crammed to the ceiling poles. Grant managed to find an unoccupied bed. He shaved and dressed, combining his beaded coat with those of his shirts and waistcoats that had best weathered the winter. In his personal order for goods to be imported against *hivernants'* accounts, he had set down a dozen linen shirts, but it would be the autumn after next before they came.

He scraped the top layer of mud off his boots and started back across the quagmire as the sun touched down on the rim of the valley wall. The inside of the bourgeois's house had changed considerably since he'd seen it last. It had lost the bare, disheveled look of a mere sleeping quarters. There was a small black-haired woman stirring a pot over the fire, kneeling on the hearth with her cooking utensils and herbs spread out beside her.

Mister Pritchard said: "My wife, Catherine—Mister Cuthbert Grant."

She looked up at him shyly, then lowered her eyelids and ducked her head. He said: "How do you do, Mrs. Pritchard." He assumed this was the Catherine MacGillivray Falcon had mentioned. He couldn't for the life of him see anything in her that would have so distracted Mister Pritchard; she seemed rather vacant and soft and edgeless, something like a lightly browned dumpling. But when he ended his greeting, she flashed him a smile complete with brown dimples and sunlit hazel eyes that would have melted the cap off Ben Lomond.

They sat down to a thick rabbit stew flavored with wild mint and sage. Grant thought he'd try throwing in another "Mrs. Pritchard" to see if it would get the same response as the first time. It did, but this time Mister Pritchard added uncomfortably: "Well . . . not really 'Mrs. Pritchard' yet, not in the true sense . . . only *au façon de la pays*, since there are no clergy or functionaries empowered to perform marriages hereabouts. So, although of course in my mind Catherine is my wife, it is not strictly true to say 'Mrs. Pritchard' in a legal sense. . . ."

"Scots law," Grant said, "recognizes any mutual exchange of vows as a valid marriage, regardless of licenses or clergy." The smile she flashed at him this time would have burnt the icecaps off the entire Grampian Range.

Mister Pritchard said: "Oh, really? Curious customs they choose to hang on to, the Scots. . . . At any rate, the governor at Red River is undoubtedly empowered to perform marriages. So as soon as Catherine and I get settled in at the colony . . ."

Grant choked on a lump of turnip. "Excuse me—I . . . ahem—that is to say—before you get settled in *where*?"

"The colony. Oh—didn't I tell you? I'm resigning the company. Catherine will come with me to the Forks and stay on there—I haven't spoken to the governor yet, but I'm certain he won't mind letting out a plot of farmland to a couple who know the *pays d'en haut* as well as Catherine and I do. Then I'll go on to Fort William and settle out my account with the company and come back to the Forks with the fall brigade. Within a couple of years—three, at the most—we'll have acres of wheatfields up to your chin, and vegetable gardens to make the proudest farmer in Somersetshire weep for shame."

Grant's immediate inclination was to ask Mister Pritchard if he'd lost his mind, but that seemed impolitic. Besides, Pritchard's revelation opened a subject that was far more interesting. In an attempt at nonchalance, Grant said: "So who, then, will . . . since you are leaving . . . who will—um, take your place here?"

"At Fort John? Hard to say—there's at least half a dozen old hands scattered across country who'd rather winter here on the Qu'Appelle."

"Ah."

"I suppose the partners will go through a good deal of fuss over it at Fort William. I won't have much say in it. But then"—Mister Pritchard grinned ingenuously—"it's no longer my concern."

"So when you leave with the brigade, should I go back to Boucher's Post or—"

"Good Lord, no. There's no point in sending anyone back there until next season. Oh—that reminds me, though: Bostonais Pangman is camped downriver by the site of old Fort Esperance. It's always difficult to be exactly sure what he's got in mind, but I did get the impression that he was waiting for you to come in so he could head east with you for the summer hunt along the Pembina."

"I should think the company wouldn't be pleased if I were to—"

"Actually . . ." Mister Pritchard's eyes focused on some vague spot above Grant's head. "Actually . . . the impression I got from the correspondence with the partners was that they wouldn't take it at all amiss if you were to while away the summer adding to the pemmican stores at Fort Gibraltar."

The savory chunks of rabbit in Grant's stomach suddenly congealed into lumps of ice. So that was that—after weighing his performance at Boucher's Post over the winter, the company would just as soon he packed himself off to hunt buffalo with the other half-breeds. All through his life, whenever he'd been commended by schoolmasters or flattered by senior partners, he'd had the chilling suspicion that all those figures of wisdom and authority might be mistaken. And now he'd proved it. The worst of it was that he'd done his best at Boucher's Post, and that he didn't even have the capacity to see what he'd done wrong.

Mister Pritchard cleared his throat uncomfortably and pursed his lips. "I don't mean to presume on my experience and your lack of same, Cuthbert, but if you will permit me . . . were I you, I would think of talking to Governor MacDonell myself. I'm sure the colony would have a place for you."

"Oh?"

"Yes! Yes, yes—I would. You see, Cuthbert . . ." Mister Pritchard cleared his throat again. "You see—I don't believe I'm talking out of turn or divulging inside information, especially considering that I am no longer inside the company, for all practical purposes . . . but I believe that we are about to enter a period of violent change here in the *pays d'en haut*. And there is no question that the Montreal partners are expecting you to play a very large part in—"

"They what? I mean—pardon me?"

"The company, whatever it is they're planning, definitely has its eyes on you and is expecting you to play some kind of major role in . . ."

Grant didn't even hear the rest. The lumps in his stomach instantaneously warmed and thawed. The birds of spring were singing. Mister MacGillivray was in his heaven, all was right with the world.

That night Grant slept very little, if at all, and climbed out of his bed feeling rested. He picked out a horse from the company string and rode southeast along the valley floor. By the tip of a knoll crowned with the stumps of what had once been the palisades of Fort Esperance, he found a hobbled horse grazing and a bearded

biped sleeping on the sunlit riverbank with a fish line tied around
the toe of each moccasin. Grant climbed down off his horse and
slunk noiselessly up to the riverbank, one hand out to tug on the
fish lines. Without lifting his hat brim to look, Bostonais growled:
"Ha ha. Good joke."

The prairie burst alive with spring. After five months battened
in against the winter, it was intoxicating to ride free through the
new grass and exploding blossoms, camping wherever fancy struck
them, swimming their horses across the river whenever it got in
their way. They stopped over at Fort La Souris, one of the many
extant North West Fur Trading Company posts that had first been
established by the late Cuthbert Grant.

Since the brigades would take a few more weeks to wind their
way downstream, Grant and Bostonais brought the first news from
upriver. To the inhabitants of Fort La Souris, it was as good an
excuse for a kick-up as they'd had since New Year's. The chief
trader from the Hudson's Bay Company's Brandon House came
across the river for the evening's festivities.

It was unusual for a half-breed to command an HBC post, but
John Richards McKay had helped his father and uncle run Brandon
House for years, so it had seemed logical to let him sub in as a
stopgap when Donald McKay retired to County Sutherland. He'd
been stopping that gap for six years now, with the exception of the
season he'd spent with his uncle in Scotland.

When John Richards McKay came across the ford in the Assiniboine to meet the son of old Cuthbert Grant, he brought with him
an odd-shaped, blanket-wrapped bundle under one arm. Grant
thought at first glance that it might be a firearm of some sort but
didn't spare it a second glance because the chief trader had also
brought along his sister.

John Richards and Bethsy McKay were quite the most exotic-
looking pair of human beings that Grant had ever seen. Both had
gold hair and copper skin, but John Richards McKay had his father's
blue eyes while Bethsy's were black like her mother's. The blue
eyes in that coloring were startling; the black were mesmerizing.
She had on a dress made out of doeskin and green velvet and wore
beaded moccasins over white silk stockings. From her appearance,
Grant would have guessed she was younger than he was; from her
assurance somewhat older.

The McKays and Grant and Bostonais sat down to dinner with
the bourgeois and his clerks and interpreters, all interacting with the

shy conviviality of people who spent months on end without seeing
a face they didn't know intimately except on the other side of a
trading counter. Miss McKay sat next to her brother, who was
across the table from Grant. She didn't speak much, and when she
did, it was in a clear-edged, soft-voweled alto.

John Richards McKay had spent two years in college at Edinburgh and had heard about Grant's education through fur trade
gossip. Neither of them had been excessively diligent scholars, but
there was a certain pleasure in being able to communicate beyond
the fundamentals. However, although his conversation was osten-
sibly with John Richards McKay, Grant found himself much more
interested in McKay's sister. On occasion he would let his eyes drift
across to her quadrant of the table. Sometimes her attention was
gratifyingly focused on her brother—and thus, at least by implication, on the charming young man to whom her brother was talking.
Other times she appeared to be paying a distressing amount of
attention to the clerk sitting beside her.

The vast quantities of wine Grant was pouring down his throat
only burnished up the soft-buffed glow on everything his eyes
touched. There was a wonderful clarity to his thoughts and to every
fire-lit object and facial feature, as though all had been outlined in
sharp black penstrokes.

John Richards was telling him ruefully about the firm resolution
he made every autumn to read the complete plays of Shakespeare
over the winter—only to find the book still lying open at the same
prologue every spring. With the world weariness of twenty years
of life and as many ounces of wine, Grant sighed wistfully and
said: " 'Had we but world enough, and time . . .' "

Bethsy McKay said: " 'This coyness, Lady, were no crime.' "

Grant was surprised enough to look straight at her. There was a
certain coyness in her expression, and a certain something else. He
glanced back at her brother. John Richards was looking at her as
well, and askance. He said: "Wherever did you come across that?"

She shrugged prettily. "It must be from one of the poems you
read to me while I was darning your socks."

"I can assure you that I never read you *that*. Unless I assumed
you weren't listening." He turned back to Grant. "See what comes
of teaching them to read. . . ."

"I always listen to you, John. In fact, you must have read it to
me more than once, and I must have listened very carefully, because I'm certain I can remember more of it. Let me see now . . ."
She pressed her right forefinger against the pouty cushion of her

lower lip. "Yes: 'Now let us sport us while we may, And now like amorous birds of prey, Let us roll all our . . . roll all our—' Damn."

" 'Strength,' " Grant said helpfully, although he had to clear his throat to get it out. " 'Strength and all our sweetness up into one ball.' "

"Yes, yes, that's it!" She clapped her hands. " 'And tear our . . . And tear our . . .' "

" 'And tear our pleasures with rough strife, Through the iron gates of life.' "

She smiled. "Just so." Her mouth shaped itself around the vowels, showing the white tips of her teeth. "It's so pretty. Is that Shakespeare?"

He dragged his gaze back up to her eyes. "No"—he had to clear his throat again—"Andrew Marvell."

Her brother gave her a long, thoughtful look, then suddenly jerked his head around to Grant and said brightly: "Oh, by the by, they wouldn't—" He looked down at the back of his hand and flexed it lazily. "They wouldn't have happened to include fencing on your curriculum at Inverness?"

"Fencing?"

John Richards ran his forefinger along the rim of the table and said abstractedly: "Yes, fencing. You know—*en garde*, tap, tap, that sort of thing."

Grant took a mouthful of claret, rolled it around with his tongue, and then swallowed it thoughtfully. "It seems to me, now that I think of it, we did do a bit of fencing now and then." No more than eight hours a week for three years.

John Richards got up from the table and returned with the blanket-wrapped bundle he'd carried over from Brandon House. He gave the hem a jerk, and out rolled two combat épées, the latest style in fencing swords.

John Richards said: "If we could manage to get some light out in the yard, would you be interested in . . . ?"

Grant smiled, weighing the pommel in his hand, and said: " 'Tybalt, you ratcatcher, will you walk?' "

In a moment the fort's *engagés* had four fires going in the yard to mark out the corners of an elongated rectangle. John Richards stripped off his coat and handed it to his sister. Grant handed his to Bostonais. John Richards said: "Five touches?" Grant nodded.

It had been two years since he'd held a sword in his hand. It soon became obvious that John Richards McKay had kept in practice— long winter evenings up and down the warehouse floor engaging imaginary opponents. Grant's parries were too slow and wide. Even though the blades were button-tipped, when they whipped down across a taut-strained thigh or punched up against a waistcoated chest, the question of whether a touch had been scored went right out of the abstract.

They engaged and disengaged five times in quick succession, each time ending with a sting on some portion of Grant's anatomy. After the fifth touch he gave John Richards a little bow and stepped back, rolling the pommel between his fingers. The audience—*engagés*, traders, a few Indians, and Bethsy McKay—applauded and shouted their approval. They were applauding for the chief trader at Brandon House; it didn't take an intimate knowledge of fencing to see that the North West Company clerk had just been humiliated.

Grant took a drink from Bostonais's cup and called out in what he hoped was a playfully sporting voice: "Again?"

As they exchanged salutes, he reminded himself that John Richards had it all over him in terms of skill and science. All right, Wappeston, he said to himself, you're supposed to have fast hands. . . . He made three moves that were really one—bat the opponent's blade, feint at his eyes, and lunge at his midriff. Even though the feint came no nearer than six inches in front of his eyes, John Richards's instincts took over and swept his arm up, leaving his torso wide open. The breath *wooshed* out of him as Grant's point encountered his short ribs. He stepped back, massaging his rib cage, and gave Grant a little bow. Cheap trick or not, it took away his assurance in the evening's scenario.

The long blades gleamed and snicked and clashed against each other. Sweat beaded out and melted to a sheen. Grunts of exertion or pain or satisfaction blended together. Grant ceased to care whether a given exchange ended with a hit against John Richards or on himself—the point was the exhilaration of the sword dance. The scratches and bruises that were dotted all up and down his right side were only a confirmation that he was alive and young and deft and quick and utterly unfettered. John Richards was laughing as well, stepping back with a broad grin and a nod whenever Grant scored a hit, ducking his head modestly when Grant paid a return acknowledgment.

When at last they called it quits they were both leaning on their swords like canes, gasping and laughing at each other's pretensions. Bostonais came up behind Grant and draped his coat across his shoulders and handed him a drink. It seemed a happy coincidence that the faces behind every arm that clapped Grant on the back were all graced with idiot grins, that every pair of eyes that caught his were lustrous and bright, and that the brightest and blackest and most lustrous of all were Miss Bethsy McKay's. He had no idea that it all came from his own infectious joy. Throughout the long, bewildering years growing up alone in alien places, he'd kept a shell around his heart. When it had finally cracked open, what had emerged was the intact heart of a child.

CHAPTER 25

Kate cocked her armpit over the gunwale and gasped for breath as the rowers finally pulled the boats away from shore. All morning long she and every other able-bodied hand had been struggling over the shoreline boulders with a wrist-thick length of hemp cable over their shoulders, dragging the boats up a white-water section of the Hayes River.

The chief factor at York Factory had condescended to loan them six boatmen to teach them to row and two York boats that had only needed a week's worth of patching before they could be trusted in the water. What the Hudson's Bay men called a York boat had turned out to be a deckless, flat-keeled affair, thirty-five feet long from pointed bow to pointed stern. The shape put Kate in mind of a willow leaf with the ends pinched in. They were painted black up to the gunwales, with a jaunty strip of red to top them off, and smelled of paint and turpentine and of the pine tar used for their caulking. Along the floor of each boat lay a sail-wrapped wooden mast that appeared to be of no practical use whatsoever.

She dipped her hand into the river and let her arm go slack. The current carried her arm out and back, the forearm sinking under and the surface ripples licking over the inside of her elbow. Very soon her hand began to go numb; there was still ice along the shore on the shady side of the stream.

The banks were bursting with color: the dewy green of new leaves, the mauve red of hazel wands, the pale blues, pinks, and yellows of wildflowers, and here and there a slick white streak of late-rotting snow. According to one of the boatmen, this spiky jungle of granite and spruce stretched for thousands of miles to the southeast and northwest, a virtually impenetrable system of defenses between the seaways and the open country owned by the Earl of Selkirk.

The men at the oars began to sing the "Mingalay Boat Song." Most of the passengers joined in, except for Catherine Sutherland and Jean McKay. Catherine was whispering advice to the new mother on ways to cope with one of the more intimate and embarrassing aspects of being a woman wandering through the wilderness. Kate idly calculated how soon she would have to find a solution to the same problem. As the numbers of elapsed days started to mount up into the mid-forties, she chided herself for her obvious lapse of memory and started counting through again. It added up the same again, and again.

She tried to tell herself it wasn't possible. The phrase echoed back in her mind with the voices of countless idiot girls back down the corridors of time: "But we only did it once!" She hadn't felt any nausea, but they said some women didn't suffer morning sickness; her belly was as flat as ever, but they said some women didn't start to show until the third month.

Jean McKay and Catherine Sutherland tried to talk to her. She kept her eyes fixed straight ahead and grunted out nondescript replies. Time folded in on itself so that when the boats finally turned in toward the shore, she thought that only a moment had passed since she'd come to her realization. She had to look at the sinking sun to assure herself that the day was ending.

She had to hold on tight to herself to keep from pushing her way out before the others. As soon as her feet touched the shoreline, she turned away from the boats and started walking. Someone called after her, but she kept on going.

The noises of the shore camp gradually faded behind her. She stumbled and slipped a few times on the slippery rocks at the water's edge, but she kept moving. When she came to a thicket of trees that grew out into the river and cut her off, she struck up into the undergrowth and forced her way around behind them, twigs scraping at her eyes and thorns catching at her skirt.

She fought her way back to the shore on the other side and sank down on the bank with her back to a poplar trunk. As soon as she sat down the blackflies and mosquitoes came at her. She tried to slap them away, but for every one she killed three more settled

Finally she drew her knees up in front of her, bent her head down, and unfolded her shawl over herself like a shroud. They still bit at her through the layers of cloth and hair, but she could live with that. Hugging her shins in her woolen cave, she put her mind to considering ways to salvage the shambles of her life.

There was a crashing in the undergrowth. She remembered the white bears at Churchill. They said there were black bears in this part of the country. She stayed where she was, hunched down with her head bent forward across her knees, breathing through her shawl, her neck bowed like an offering. One swat of a paw, one crunch of jaws on the back of her neck, would solve it for her.

There was a pattering of pebbles nearby. "I do understand, Miss MacPherson," said the voice of Alexander Sutherland, "that the prospect of the smell of salt pork frying for yet another meal is enough to drive a person to great lengths, but do you not think this is carrying things a trifle far?"

She took a moment to steady her breathing and find what she hoped was a dry voice. "I am merely keeping the insects off. Go away."

There was a smattering of footstep sounds, then his voice came again, much closer, "Miss MacPherson," and his hand came down on her shoulder.

She was up and moving away from him, ripping the shawl off with one hand to see where she was going. He caught hold of her arm. She tried to jerk it loose, but he held fast. From behind her back he said: "Please. You have mopped away the fever sweat off me and fed me and listened to me rant in my delirium. Could you not . . . it would relieve me of an obligation if you would allow me to . . ."

She turned on him, intending to say quite calmly that there was nothing troubling her, that she had merely come out for a quiet walk in the evening air alone. What came out instead was a species of wordless howl, eyes gushing and nose plugging. He wrapped his arms around her and leaned her head on his shoulder, which required some bending on her part.

There was another bout of crashing from the undergrowth, and Archibald MacDonald's voice called: "Here, then, what seems to be the—"

She tucked her head down farther into his shoulder. From his chest came a bellow that she never would have guessed could be produced by someone so scrawny: "Get away from here!"

"See here, I do have the responsibility to—"

"Did you hear me? Clear off!"

There were more sounds of thicket crackle, definitely receding this time. She dug the handkerchief out of her sleeve and worked her hand up between them. The shoulder of his shirt was soaked through. She dabbed at it, but before long the handkerchief was too sopped to blot up any more. It probably wouldn't have worked even with a dry handkerchief.

He put his hand on the back of her neck and stroked tentatively. "Now then, what is it?"

Much to her surprise, she said: "I am pregnant." It came of its own volition, in a breathy but level voice.

There was a break in the rhythm of his hand stroking her head, then it started up again. His voice came out next to her ear but distant: "And the father will not—"

She tore herself away from him, but his hands just managed to catch her and pull her back, his arms clamping her to him while she fought. "Forgive me, I meant no—that was an idiot thing to say. Forgive me. . . ."

She felt her breathing grow calm once again and settled her head back down on his shoulder. But as the spaces between her snuffles gradually grew longer, the silence became more apparent. When he finally broke it, his voice came out with a waver that steadied as he went along:

"Miss MacPherson, it would be a great honor to me if you could find it in your heart to consider becoming my wife."

She put the damp rag back up to her face and pushed away from him. This time she managed to break free, or he let her go. She took a few steps back, blinking to clear her vision. Although she was staring straight at him, she found herself becoming aware of peripheral things—the burble of the river flowing by, the deep yellow sunset light on the leaves behind his shoulder, the spring balsam smell of the poplars—as though she were starting to return to the world after a day away. She said: "It does great credit to your upbringing, Mister Sutherland, that you have such charitable impulses. But you need not go so far for pity's sake."

His head gave an involuntary twitch backward, as though he'd taken a clip across the jaw, but his eyes stayed on her. He said: "I am in no position to throw scraps to anyone, Miss MacPherson, for they are all I have. I am well aware that there is not much to me but a lame husk that the British army has tossed aside, with no prospects beyond grubbing a few potatoes out of some patch of wilderness."

"And what do you think I am? Fiona of the Silver Rings?"

He smiled. "She is not even in the running."

"Well . . . well . . . Well, Mister Sutherland, I will consider it."

"That is as much as a man could hope for, Miss MacPherson."

CHAPTER 26

Grant and Bostonais came to a runoff swollen creek flowing into the Assiniboine from the north and got down off their horses to give them a breathe and a graze before swimming them across. Grant said: "Is this Catfish Creek?"

Bostonais shook his head. "Sturgeon Creek. Catfish is a little ways farther. Then another ways to the Forks."

The opposite bank was a miles-wide swath of magenta fireweed, blazing over the soot of one of last autumn's fires. Along the top of the water, a speckled brown-gray shore bird bounced atop an old willow-wand fish trap that the ice had mangled. Grant said: "How far is it from Fort Gibraltar down to the buffalo grounds at the Pembina?"

"Down? Up—up the Red to the Pembina."

"Down in terms of north and south. It would be down on a map."

"Maps," he said with contempt. Like any other native of the *pays d'en haut*, Bostonais could draw a reasonably accurate sand sketch of a hundred-mile journey he'd only made once, but to his mind that was different from all this ink-and-paper nonsense.

"How far is it *up* to the Pembina, then, with or without a map?"

"Depends on if you know the way. Couple days."

"Would a few days' delay make any difference to the hunting?"

"Buffalo wouldn't bitch. And the meat'd be fatter from a few more days' spring feeding; hides'd be cleaner from a few more days' scraping off the winter hair—gotta be scraped anyway, might as well let them do some of it. Summer hides ain't good for much but tents and *shagganappi*." *Shagganappi* was the thong cut out of green hides that served for rope in the *pays d'en haut*.

"Ah. You see, I was just remembering some business I'd forgotten to discuss with Mister Pritchard. I should imagine his brigade would have wound its way *down* to Brandon House—Fort La Souris, that is—within the next few days. I thought I'd ride back there and then meet up with you again at the Forks."

Bostonais chewed the insides of his cheeks and said: "Hmm."

"Would you wait for me at Fort Gibraltar?"

"May be. A few days. If I head on, you can follow me easy. Just head straight up the Red, or borrow a map."

Grant got back on his horse. Bostonais said: "Don't say hello to her for me—it would hurt your chances."

The distance that had taken them three days to ride coming east, he covered in less than two going west. It was late on the second day that he urged his horse down the slope of the high valley of the Assiniboine. He skirted around the back of Brandon House and headed for the ford to Fort La Souris. He wanted to clean himself up and change his clothes before choosing from among the several dozen reasonable excuses he'd formulated to go calling at the Hudson's Bay fort.

The ford was glutted with carts crossing against him, drivers cursing and horses whinnying and splashing and high-wheeled carts teetering precariously from side to side. The carts that had already made it across were rattling toward the opened gates of Brandon House. Most of the drivers were blond Orcadians, with a smattering of darker faces that made up the usual ratio of métis and Indians at most Hudson's Bay posts.

Grant guided his horse into the water to the left of the cart line. It picked its way along carefully, feeling with its hooves for the low-water shelf that wasn't taken up with carts and ponies and laborers pushing against mired wheels.

He was halfway across when he saw that the barrels stacked on the cart beside him had a black logo stenciled across their heads: *NW*. Without thinking, he twitched the *shagganappi* halter and snugged his horse in nose to tail beside the cart pony, effectively blocking the cart. The carter, a large, sunburned Orcadian, hauled back hard on the reins just before they collided, bellowing in Gaelic: "What the hell do you think you're doing? Clear off!"

Grant pointed at the barrels and said tentatively: "Those are North West Company property."

"Not any more they ain't—and never were, legally. Clear off!"

A few of the other laborers were working their way back toward them. Grant gestured again at the sacks and barrels and said: "Where are you taking them?"

"None of your damned business! Clear off!" The carter raised his whip over his head.

A voice behind him shouted: "Put that down! Did you hear me? Put your arm down!" It was John Richards McKay, splashing forward through the shallows along the line of carts. A brown-bearded man in high boots was striding along in his wake. "Hello, Grant. I didn't expect we'd see you again 'til fall. I know what this must look like, but it's all aboveboard. Ride over and ask John Pritchard if you don't believe me, his brigade came in last night."

"He sold it to you?"

"Not strictly speaking. It's being confiscated."

"Contraband," said the brown-bearded man.

"Clear off!" said the Orcadian, still waving his whip.

John Richards turned to the carter and said: "The company is sending out an expedition to establish a post in Blackfoot country. How would you like to go?" The Orcadian lowered his arm and sat back down on his seat.

Grant said: "I don't understand—'confiscated' . . . ?"

"By order of Sheriff Spenser of Lord Selkirk's colony."

The brown-bearded man, presumably Sheriff Spenser, said: "The governor's proclamation was quite clear; no provisions to be exported without a license. If the North West Fur Trading Company wishes to export provisions, they will have to apply for a license at Colony House."

John Richards said: "Do ride over and talk to Pritchard; you'll see it's all aboveboard. By the by, so long as you're in the vicinity, what about a rematch? Most of my bruises have healed. Well, do think it over. . . ."

Grant trotted his horse along the line of carts to the bank, then kicked it up the slope and galloped into Fort La Souris. The swivel guns were still in place on the bastions flanking the gates, but there was no one manning them. Inside the yard were two half-loaded carts, their drivers lounging on the benches. A line of *engagés* was filing out of the storehouse carrying sacks of pemmican to the carts, supervised by John Pritchard. Grant reined in his horse beside him. "What's happened here?"

"Oh, hello Cuthbert, I didn't expect to meet up with you again till we got to the Forks."

"Did they catch you by surprise? You still have time to bar the gates and save what's left."

"Certainly not, we'll do nothing of the kind. The gates were barred when they came. I opened them."

"You what?"

"It's the law."

"Law? What law? Whose law?"

"Sheriff Spenser had a warrant."

"Anybody with access to ink and paper could write you up a warrant to drop your trousers and squat on an anthill—would you do it?"

"Now you listen to me, Cuthbert—"

"Alex!" Alex Fraser was coming out of the store shed with a pemmican sack on his shoulder. He turned his snake eyes toward Grant. "It's bad enough to let yourself be robbed without putting up a fight—do you have to load up the thieves' wagons for them?" The line of loaders had stalled up behind Alex. He looked around and dumped the sack down on the ground, then leaned against the front of the shed with his arms crossed. The others began to do the same.

Pritchard said: "Now, Cuthbert, don't—"

"Don't you 'Cuthbert' me—I didn't spend five months snowed in at Boucher's Post to see you give it all away to the first ass that knocks on the gate with a piece of paper."

"They didn't take the furs, only the pemmican."

"Only the pemmican? 'Only the pemmican'? Is that what you plan to tell the *engagés* who starve to death halfway to Fort William?"

"Don't take that tone of voice with me—I'm still your bourgeois."

Grant resisted the urge to press his boot sole down on the stirrup and swing his leg forward, ramming the thick base of the stirrup into Mister Pritchard's prominent front teeth. Instead he said: "Not for much longer. But I should have guessed you'd want to use the time you have left to cozy up to your new masters." He turned his horse and rode out of the fort so he wouldn't have to watch the rest of it.

By evening he decided it must be over and came back to Fort la Souris to spend the night. His original purpose in turning back at Sturgeon Creek was now out of the question—he was too angry and too ashamed.

In the morning he stood on the palisade and watched the York boats load up on the opposite bank and head downstream. In the afternoon another brigade of *canots du nord* came down from the Swan River posts. The bourgeois was one of the wintering partners, Whitehead MacDonell, a leathery scarecrow with a mop of bleached straw. He was a cousin of Miles MacDonell, the colony governor, but he was the last man to let blood relations or proclamations stand in the way of business. He had no intention of surrendering up the cargo of his brigade to anyone except Duncan Cameron at Bas de la Rivière.

Grant left his horse at Fort la Souris and went downstream with Whitehead MacDonell's brigade. When they got to Portage la Prairie, the trader there informed them that John Wills also had knuckled under to the governor's orders, and the store sheds at Fort Gibraltar had been cleaned out. The colony people had set up a blockade with artillery above the Forks, to stop any of the brigades that tried to pass by without an inspection.

When they came to Catfish Creek, Whitehead MacDonell waved the brigade in to shore. He had the *engagés* dig a trench into the side of a wooded ridge and buried all their sacks of pemmican. He said to Grant: "The bastards have us outnumbered for now. There should be another half-dozen brigades coming in to Fort Gibraltar over the next few days. We'll see how my stiff-assed cousin likes issuing orders to the boys of the north when the odds are even."

CHAPTER 27

The little flotilla of York boats had been running before the north wind on Lake Winnipeg for three days, tacking in to shore at sunset and then scudding back out into the wind each morning. In all that time of running straight south with no end to the lake in sight, the east and west shores had been clearly visible on either hand.

The boat that Kate was in had been in the lead all morning. She looked back over her shoulder and saw the square sail of the other boat looming close, billowed out like a nine-month belly. She swung

her arm around to point at the prow edging parallel with their stern.
The rest of the passengers, who were also the rowing crew, began
to shout at the steersman to stretch out the sail or batten the belaying
pins or whatever it was one did to lay on more speed, laughing and
cheering and beating on the sides of the boat like a horse's ribs.

The steersman did just the opposite, leaning hard against the
rudder to angle them into shore, pointing to the west and yelling
across the open water at the other boat. Kate looked to her right.
Along the curved rim of the world, a line of monumental slate slabs
of cloud were bulging up across the western horizon.

Both boats turned west and ran for the shore. Kate turned to the
Orcadian behind her—one of the three experienced hands assigned
to her boat—and said: "Can we not ride it out?" She had heard
the phrase "ride out the storm" somewhere, and it sounded vaguely
nautical.

He shook his head grimly. "Not worth the chance. The lake is
shallow. Like tea in a saucer—the slightest breath on it, and it
quavers. Now if you think of a quaver two hundred miles long . . ."
He turned his hand over to show what would happen to their York
boats. "A shallow lake is plenty deep enough to drown in. As nasty
a body of water for small craft as you will ever hope to see the back
of."

The wind began to shift, blowing stiff off the shore. The Orcadian she'd been speaking to leaped up with the second one to furl
the sail while the third one shouted from his tiller post to break out
the oars. Kate could make out Alexander Sutherland in the other
boat, putting his back into it with the best of them, looking fit and
freckled and quite unlike the fever-racked invalid of recent acquaintance.

She still hadn't given him her answer. From one hour to the next
she would fluctuate from telling him "yes" to definitely deciding
that it would be a terrible mistake—as though she were in any
position to make a choice. Regardless of how often she tallied up
his favorable attributes, the fact remained that her heart didn't turn
over at the sight of him.

Jean and Angus McKay were on the bench in front of her, Jean
holding their child while Angus rowed. They seemed barely older
than children themselves, but they would have the advantage of
growing into adulthood as a married couple. If she were to marry
Alexander Sutherland, they would have to chip away at each other's
hardened edges for years until the corners matched.

The wind-lashed stormfront to the west was coming in fast. By

the time the boats reached the shore, the force of it was already
ripping dead twigs off the trees. They dragged the boats up on the
sand and went frantically to work to get the tents up. Kate was
holding up a tent pole while John ran around thrusting in tent pegs
when the wind died and the sun went out and the rain came in a
curtain of thick drops that had soaked her through to the skin before
she could stoop inside. She held open the flap while John and the
others scrambled in. Then she let it drop and started down the
beach, wet sand scrumbling up between her toes. The air was warm.
She couldn't get any wetter than she was. She began to run, tufts
of grass and reeds bowing to the rain as she flew by. She hiked her
skirts to stretch out in longer bounds. Her legs felt as if they'd been
crimped into knots under her body for months.

The sand ran out. She slowed to a walk across the pebbles and
then turned to watch the black waves flare up and crash into each
other. She was quite drunk with the power of the storm. White
branches of lightning ripped across the roof of the world. The thunder came in deep, bone-crushing vowels and exploding consonants
that felt like they would crack the planet in two.

She turned around to look inland. There was a break in the
lakeshore bush behind her, and through the gap in the trees she saw
a silver-gray, undulating carpet of wind-whipped grass, rolling out
forever without a hill or a ridge for shelter. Like a stroked cat's fur,
the prairie rippled and changed colors as the hand of the wind
passed over it. A thousand times she had imagined the kind of
country she was coming to spend the rest of her life in, but never
had she envisioned anything this immense.

"Miss MacPherson!"

She turned. It was Alexander Sutherland, thirty feet down the
shore, his clothing dripping from his shoulders and hips, hair plastered to his skull. He shouted: "Are you all right?"

"Yes."

He cupped his hand behind his ear.

"Yes!"

"Yes?"

She nodded her head up and down. "Yes!"

He nodded his head and turned to look out over the chaos of the
lake.

"Mister Sutherland!"

He turned back toward her. His mouth moved, but no sound
reached her. The wind was cranking itself up again, tearing at the
air and howling. He shouted: "Yes?"

"Did you hear what I said?"

"Yes! I mean, yes, I heard, you said 'yes'!" Then something began to dawn on him. "Did you mean just 'yes,' or did you mean 'yes'? I mean, did you mean 'yes—you were all right,' or did you mean—"

"I will not go on repeating myself, Mister Sutherland!"

He grinned like an idiot boy and blew the raindrops off his nose. "That is . . . fine. That is . . . very, very fine."

Something—it felt like a very large man with a very small fist—hit her hard on the back of the shoulder. There was a rattling from the pebbled beach around her. White marbles of ice, some as large as eyeballs, were falling from the clouds and bouncing along the ground. A small one hit her on the cheek. She put her arms up over her head, and Sandy Sutherland did the same. They ran back toward the tents, battered by falling hailstones and slipping on the ones beneath their feet. Most of the tents had caved in. The boats had been turned over on the beach, propped sideways on their bows.

They ducked in under the wooden awnings and squeezed themselves a place among the others who had abandoned the tents. The air had suddenly turned cold. Sandy draped his arm around her shoulder. It felt like a clammy tentacle wrapping around her, and she shook it off with a shudder. Barely five minutes earlier she had promised to stand up with him for all time. She decided there must be something deeply wrong inside of her to have such an inconsistent heart.

The next day they came finally to the south end of the lake. The sails were out again; the boats were driving full speed toward a tangled wall of reeds and marsh grass. Like everybody else, Kate clung to the gunwale and glanced at her neighbors to see if they thought the man at the rudder hadn't lost his mind. Then they broke through the curtain of reeds, bent stalks hissing along the sides of the hull, and were in a wide marsh with narrow, snaking channels of shallow water and clouds of shore birds. The oars had to come out again. When the channel got too narrow they were used as poles to push the boats along.

The channel broadened, and the marsh plants thinned away. They were rowing up a muddy, low-banked river against a current that was surprisingly strong considering the green-brown, stagnant look of the water. Both banks were crowded with broad-crowned trees and tangled bushes. Kate said primly to the steersman, "Which river is this?" although she, like everyone else, had already guessed the answer.

"This is the Red River, ma'am."

They rowed upstream for three days, camping at night in the woods along the bank. Near the end of the third day the undergrowth on the west bank disappeared, replaced by fields of green wheat and barley and a scattering of log shanties. The men working in the fields waved their hats and shouted at the boats in Gaelic. The river took a sharp swing to the left, swept around the tip of a wooded point, and then looped to the west. At the downstream base of the point the river turned south again, but the steersmen held the rudders straight.

The green slope of the bank in front of them was runneled with pathways worn into the clay. Above the crest there were a half dozen square-beam buildings grouped around a central square. Behind and around them were barns and sheds and vegetable gardens and horse corrals and a fenced-in pasture with a cow and a bull and two calves. A few yards farther down the bank from the landing place there was a long hump on the crest, a man-made second bank of piled-up earth, sandbags, and the mouths of cannons pointing upstream.

Robert Gunn hopped out as soon as the boats nosed into shore. He piped them up the slope with "Cock o' the North." Waiting for them in the open square was a crowd of Orcadians and Highlanders—mostly men, but with a few women and children. All of them had darker skins and paler hair than the misty sun of home would ever have given them. Some were from the parish of Kildonan. There was back slapping and weeping and much cheering.

The clanging of a bell made all turn their heads toward the roofed verandah of the building at the head of the square. There were a handful of men standing on the raised platform of the porch—straight-spined types with thrown-back shoulders and big bellies. A brown-bearded one was clanging the clapper of a bell hanging above the railing. In among the others stood Archibald MacDonald with a dispatch case under one arm. While the rest of the new arrivals had been shaking hands with new neighbors and recognizing old ones, he had followed his nose straight up the stairs to the fountainhead of authority.

The brown-bearded man stopped clanging the bell and called out: "Governor MacDonell will welcome you now." He had spoken in English, and Kate did her best to translate for those around her. He stepped back, and a square-jawed, crop-haired gentleman stepped forward and looked out over the crowd.

Governor Miles MacDonell looked to have been put together out of blocks of wood that had been cut with an axe—the planes of his face and body were all squared off, chunky, and blunt, butting up against each other at sharp angles. He dropped his jaw and unleashed a crisp, parade-ground tenor—in English: "It is very gratifying to be able to bid welcome to the Kildonan party at long last—in spite of the incompetence that kept me waiting ten months longer than you should have taken. We will soon have you settled on your own plots of land, but until then you will work in the fields of the colonial establishment—Colony Gardens, we like to call it. You will be paid wages that will be entered against your account in the colony stores.

"Every man of you will be issued a musket and a bayonet and shall drill in the parade ground for an hour every morning under the direction of Sheriff Spenser. In this country there is only one law—the strong rule. We shall not be ruled. Now I believe your Mister MacDonald has some words he would like to say to you."

Archibald MacDonald stepped forward with his dispatch case clasped to his chest and opened his mouth. Kate turned and worked her way out through the back of the crowd, leaving him to enthrall the masses. She skirted around the gun emplacement—a bit of scenery she could have done without—and trundled down the bank to see to her personal possessions. As she'd suspected, the boatmen were tossing the passengers' things into the mud so as to unload carefully the HBC-stamped crates and barrels.

She fished through the heap of plaid- and canvas-wrapped packages until she found her own. She carried it up to the crest of the bank and unwrapped it on the grass to make sure that the pieces of the spinning wheel were all intact.

There was a soft, muffled thump on the ground behind her and a muted jingle of harness. When she turned her head, she saw two men sitting on horses not five feet behind her. The horses were wild, alien-looking creatures—shaggy manes and stocky shoulders and rough-cut oval heads. As she stood up, the horsemen swept into her range of vision. They were more alien and wild looking than the horses. Both had dark skin and black hair and a wind-carved, sun-glazed look, but there the resemblance ended. One of them was built like a low mountain, with a thicket of beard and hair covering all his features. The other was younger, taller, and slighter—which didn't take much doing—and relatively smooth shaven. He had a clean-lined face and big black eyes. He leaned back in the saddle, drew his legs up, and crossed them in front of him like an Indian, except that Indians didn't usually come shod in

the latest Regency riding boots. Balancing with perfect ease on his
saddle pad, he all but knocked her over by addressing her in Gaelic:
"Welcome to the Miskouseipi, Miss . . . ."

"MacPherson."

"Ah." He smiled, his teeth a gleam of white against the sun-
soaked liquid gold of his skin. "My name is Grant." He bore no
resemblance to any of the Grants she'd known back home. None
of them had been anywhere near that tall and heavy-shouldered,
and no Grant of her acquaintance had ever had immense black eyes
with lights glinting behind them. He managed a courtly hint of a
bow with his head and shoulders, then gestured with his left hand
at the surly mountain sitting on the horse beside his. "This is my
associate, Mister Pangman."

Mister Pangman waggled his fingers at her and pronounced what
she took to be some sort of how-d'you-do formula in French. His
voice was surprisingly soft and musical, in an echoing contrabass
way.

She said: "Are you with the colony, then, Mister Grant?"

Mister Grant threw back his head and laughed with the open-
throated delight of a child. It suddenly struck her that he was, in
fact, even somewhat younger than John Bannerman had been. He
cocked his head toward Mister Pangman and said something in an
Indian dialect. Mister Pangman didn't laugh. Then he turned toward her and switched back to Gaelic. "Forgive me, Miss Mac-
Pherson—allow me to assure you that I did not laugh at you. I
should expect that, quite soon, your own people will make the
humor of the situation far more apparent to you than I could hope
to. But in answer to your question—if there is one thing you can be
certain of in this uncertain world, it is that Mister Pangman and I
are decidedly *not* with the colony. Merely part of the landscape,
we."

For some reason Kate found this young Mister Grant quite disorienting, almost intoxicating. For all his ingenuous courtliness,
there was something inside her that would not stop clanging an
alarm bell. She said: "What was that word you said? 'Welcome to
the . . .'?"

"'Miskouseipi'—the Bungee name for this place, which the first
white traders translated rather lamely as Red River. In point of fact,
the true meaning is closer to 'Blood Red River.'" He smiled again—
not coldly, but not comfortingly, either. "No doubt you have already noted, Miss MacPherson, that the color of the Red River is
more mud green than blood red. But it has run red many times in

the past. And whether Cree, Sioux, Assiniboine, French, English, or Scots, all blood runs red.''

"This is colony property! You have no right to be here."

The voice came from behind Kate, in English. She turned and discovered the brown-bearded man who'd called them to order from the governor's verandah, coming up behind her with a brace of burly Orcadians.

" 'Right'?" Grant echoed dubiously, and then, contemplatively: " 'Right . . .' What an eccentric turn of phrase you have, *Sheriff* Spenser."

Alexander Sutherland stepped up beside Kate. "Are you all right?"

"Certainly. This is Mister Grant, and Mister Pangman. And this is my fiancé, Mister Sutherland."

Grant said: "Ah, Mister Sutherland." He gave another courtly half bow, this one with a certain wryness in it. "Well, until next time." He unwound his legs and lowered his boots back into the stirrups. He leaned forward to address the governor's man and repeated, though with a very different tone, "Until next time." Then he said, "*Allons-y*, Bostonais," and turned his horse. The two of them walked their horses away, tail plumes twitching.

Sheriff Spenser murmured under his breath, as though trying the sounds of the words together: "Bostonais Pangman."

"I tried to tell you," said one of the Orcadians, "But oh, no, you—"

Alexander Sutherland said: "What does that make him if he's a Bostonais Pangman?"

"Rabid, for one thing," replied the Orcadian, "and a murderer. He killed three men out west that we know of, and God knows how many Indians."

Kate looked to the backs of the two horsemen moving leisurely away. Bostonais Pangman appeared to be teasing Grant about something; both of them were laughing. Suddenly Grant whipped his horse with the ends of his reins, and both of them broke into a gallop, charging straight for a pathway in the woods that looked barely wide enough for one of them. They reached it at the same time, but neither of them would give way. They careened down the pathway side by side, their horses jostling against each other, whipped by branches and riding down bushes, arms up to shield their faces, laughing.

CHAPTER 28

Grant stood on the north wall firing ledge of the palisade at Fort Gibraltar with Bostonais, Duncan Cameron, and Whitehead MacDonell. Mister Cameron had come up from Bas de la Rivière the day before with most of the depot's complement of *engagés* to help resolve the problem of the blockade. There were two other bourgeois in Fort Gibraltar who should have been up on the palisade with them, but John Wills was too sick to leave his bed, and John Pritchard could no longer be relied upon to fight the company's battles.

All four of them had their hands or elbows propped between the axe-sharpened points at the tops of the palisade logs, gazing over the riverside trees to the cluster of buildings downstream, which Governor MacDonell had christened "Fort Douglas." The warm, soft light of the evening sun painted the whitewashed gables an amber rose. In this country an elevation of twenty feet gave a field of vision like the summit of Ben Nevis. The trees hid the colony's earthwork gun battery, but they knew it was there.

Mister Cameron said: "Couldn't you have mentioned to your cousin, Whitehead, that calling a place a fort doesn't give it walls?" Whitehead MacDonell grunted.

Grant said: " 'Stone walls do not a prison make,' but they're damned handy for a fort."

Whitehead MacDonell said: "No need for him to've gone for stone; plenty of straight trees downstream." The others nodded and grunted in agreement.

Mister Cameron said: "Well, I suppose if someone has to make little oversights like that about their defenses, it might as well be our enemies. Not that it helps solve the current impasse. . . ." He straightened up and struck a military pose, one hand on the palisade and the other on his hip. "Perhaps we could slip past their guns in the dark of night. The moon's waning."

Whitehead MacDonell said: "With two dozen canoes? Four

dozen when the rest of the brigades come in. And what's the use of gathering all that strength here if all we're going to do is try to tiptoe past them in the dark?''

Mister Cameron pondered further. "We have our own guns guarding the gates here. We could mount them on a boat—there's a rowing boat slung up behind the icehouse.''

"Good thinking, Duncan—three cannons in a rowboat against twelve in a shore battery. If you want to captain it, I'll stand up here and wave the flag.''

Bostonais said: "Send for the buffalo hunters on the Pembina to come join us. We mount up, ride down, and burn them out. That'll be the end of it.''

Mister Cameron looked at Whitehead MacDonell. Grant thought of the driven-off crofters that he'd seen straggling aimlessly through the streets of Inverness, and the tall woman he'd spoken to on the riverbank yesterday. Mister Cameron said: "I think we can find a solution that falls on the short side of a massacre.''

Bostonais said: "What do you think they mean to do with those cannons if you try to go by? Blow you kisses?'' But he'd had his say and didn't plan to argue it further.

The one part of Bostonais's plan that appealed to Grant was the idea of coming at them on horseback from the prairie. It seemed to him that Mister MacDonell and Mister Cameron had locked their plans into a map consisting of the river and the shore battery, which was playing to the enemy's advantage. Since the guns were pointing at the river, the logical approach would be to come at them from behind. Then the governor could wave all the proclamations he wanted; *les hommes du nord* would just wave back as they paddled downstream. It seemed so obvious that he decided they must have rejected it already for some reason that was over his head.

A sudden piercing shriek came from within the compound below them—the sound an animal might make as a trap snapped on its leg. They looked behind them, then at each other. One of the *engagés* came out to the base of the palisade and called up: "It's Monsieur Wills—well, it's Madame Wills that makes the noise, but . . .''

They filed down the ladder and into the bourgeois's house, through to the sleeping quarters at the back with its stifling smell of sickness. John Wills was lying on his back with the bedclothes humped over the gargantuan swell of his belly, his face bloated and gray and his clouded eyes staring through the ceiling. His left arm dangled from the bed. Crouched on the floor with her back to the wall was Grant's sister Josephte. Her three-year-old son stood squalling beside her—more from the noises his mother was making than from any understanding of what had happened to his father.

Grant tried unsuccessfully to fathom what there might have been in that pasty, fat body that could have torn such screams from his sister. He crouched beside her and cupped his hand tentatively on the side of her bony, thin-haired head. She didn't seem to feel it. He couldn't think of anything to say to her. People died; he thought she would have been used to that by now. He said: "At the end of the summer, when I go back to the Qu'Appelle or wherever it is the company assigns me, you and little John shall come with me if you wish."

She threw one arm around his neck and clutched her son with the other, then lowered her head and sobbed into Grant's chest. He muttered: "Yes, well, all right, I'm no damned good at keeping house for myself."

They put John Wills into the ground in a corner of the fort. John Pritchard had a much traveled Book of Common Prayer stowed in his outfit, so he was still good for something. Grant stood holding up his sister, watching the mound of new-turned earth rise up over her husband, listening to John Pritchard read the same prayers over him that he must have read over a hundred others—dead simply of the *pays d'en haut*, dead of driving themselves beyond their bodies' endurance in order to squeeze out a few more shillings' profit for the partners. The gamble they all took in the North West Fur Trading Company was that they would live long enough to become partners themselves.

Mister Pritchard closed his book. Mrs. Pritchard took Josephte off Grant's arm. Grant went back to talking strategies with the living. It was unfortunate that the old had to die or lose their nerve, but if that was the way the world revolved, it was good to be young and strong.

CHAPTER 29

In the patched gray worn-through barracks tent that temporarily housed the single women, Kate MacPherson was preparing for her wedding—or being prepared, it seemed to her, like a Christmas duck. She stood patiently at the center of the trampled-grass aisle that ran between the improvised beds while Catherine Sutherland and Jean McKay and the other women fluttered around her, trying the effect of a borrowed shawl here, a ribbon there. From time to time one of them would thrust Jean's tarnished hand mirror in front of her face and ask if she was pleased. She would nod obligingly, and they would cluck maniacally and start all over again.

She found herself growing progressively more annoyed at all the bustle but tried to keep in mind that they hadn't had many celebrations to fuss over in the last year and a half. She would have much preferred to simply walk down to the governor's house with Alexander Sutherland, say the vows and sign the papers and get on with the business of living without making such a to-do. Which made it doubly annoying when one of the others would comment on how flushed her face was, or suggest that if her hands were going to keep on shaking like that, she should clasp them together when the time came. She tried to focus her attention on impersonals, on the amber pin shafts of sunlight waving and dancing when the breeze fluttered the fabric of the tent, on the honey smell of the wild roses one of the women had wound into her hair.

A male voice suddenly broke in from outside the tent door. None of them had quite realized the intimacy they had built up over the last hour until it was suddenly violated. Jean McKay actually threw one arm up in front of her bodice and the other across her hips as though a man had walked in on her naked—and then blushed when she realized what she'd done.

The voice was Sandy Sutherland's. "Is Kate MacPherson in there? I would like to speak to her."

His sister went to shoo him away and came back looking flustered. "He will not go away. I told him it is bad luck, but he—"

"Old wives' tales," Kate muttered, brushing past her to get to the tent flap.

"Wait!" Catherine Sutherland came after her with a long tartan shawl. "At least cover up your wedding clothes!"

"Cover your head, cover your head!" fluttered Jean McKay, reaching up on tiptoe to ease the shawl over the flowers without crushing them.

"If seeing me face to face is going to jolt him back to his senses, better we find out now than after we have all traipsed down to Colony House."

He was standing a discreet distance from the tent flap, in a kind of formal at-ease. He was wearing a much scrubbed linen shirt, his old coat with new brass buttons, and a pair of freshly patched green trousers that didn't quite match the coat. He blushed when he saw her and looked down at the ground, then pried his eyes back up. "Good afternoon, Miss MacPherson. Or should I say Mrs. Sutherland?"

"Not yet you should not." She forced a smile to show him that it was a little joke, but he had already lowered his eyes again. He took his hands from behind his back and came out with a folded sheet of paper. He took a deep breath and said: "I believe you have the knack of reading the *Beurla* a good deal better than I do myself. I would like you to have a read of this before you . . . before we . . . ." He flapped the paper in the general direction of the governor's house, then brought it forward.

She took it from his hand. It unfolded awkwardly, stiff vellum parchment crackling and crinkling in the still air. Two-thirds of the way down the page was the red wax signet seal and the flourished signature. She flicked her eyes up to the top of the page. "In recognition of his long years in the service of his country, and in return for the sum of ten pounds English sterling received, I do hereby deed to Alexander Sutherland, late of the 42nd Highland Regiment, and to his heirs in perpetuity, a riverfront property of ten chains in width and two miles in depth, at any place of his choosing in my Colony of Assiniboia on the banks of the Red River in Rupertsland, North America. This is a freehold deed, with no leins, lease-fees nor duties to be attached hereafter. Signed, Thomas Douglas, Earl of Selkirk."

She read it through again to make sure that was all it said. After

all her suspense, she had expected something more. She handed i
back to him without refolding it.

With a touch of impatience he said: "You understand what thi
means? Everyone else in the colony is only a leaseholder. The Earl'
agents did not want to give this to me, but I told them I would no
cross the ocean to be someone else's tenant—not after the Clear
ances." He flapped the piece of paper like a regimental standard
"This means that whatever piece of land we choose to settle on
no one can take it away from us, or from our . . . heirs, or ou
heirs' heirs. No one else knows of this, not even my sister—well
you know my sister . . . but I wanted you to see it before we . . .'
He waved his hand again in the direction of the path to the gover
nor's. "So you would know I held nothing back from—"

"I have seen it before."

He blinked at her a few times and then said: "You have what?'

"On the ship, when you were ill. You snatched it from my hand.'

His head cocked to one side, and his eyes narrowed a half squint
as though something were pressing in at his temples. "I aske
you—I asked you on the ship before we landed at Churchill. Yo
told me—"

"You asked if you had done anything untoward while you wer
ill. I told you no—I do not call it untoward for a man to get angr
when he wakes out of a fever dream and finds someone snooping
through his private papers."

His eyes stayed on her but screwed down to slits, as though trying
to pierce through a fog. Suddenly a heavy hand thumped dow
onto his shoulder. He looked behind him, straight into the thick
cornsilk mustache of Robert Gunn.

"I am come to pipe your bride to the kirk, Sandy. Or to the
governor's front steps, at any rate. You had best get stepping if yo
mean to be there to meet her."

Sandy turned obediently in the appropriate direction, and hi
legs marched him away. His feet found their way to the mouth o
the pathway through the riverside woods, carrying him through
blur of dusty green.

He had never seen anything in himself to qualify him as a prize
in the matrimonial stakes. That was why he'd held the deed back
from her for so long—it seemed too much like bribery. He'd neve
been able to understand why she'd climbed into his bed that night—
except perhaps to call it an aberrant moment of loneliness or pity
But if she had seen the deed before then . . .

He stopped walking, took himself by the scruff of the neck, an forced his senses to focus on the reality around him—the separate serrated leaves of the elm trees, fresh-scythed prairie grass, sweet clover with honey bees.

But how could she have been certain of getting pregnant from one night's lovemaking? He laughed at himself and started to walk again, folding the deed back into his coat pocket. And then it occurred to him that he only knew she was pregnant because she'd told him.

Miles MacDonell was standing on the railed verandah of the whitewashed manor house he'd had the colony servants build for him. Archibald MacDonald stood beside him with the registry ledger under one arm, happily basking in the glow of reflected authority.

Sandy stopped at the base of the porch steps. The governor looked down at him and smiled a straight-lipped smile. He said in his flat Atlantic colony English: "I was beginning to wonder if you'd changed your mind."

Sandy made an effort to return the smile, along with a companionable shrug. The governor laughed and nudged Archibald MacDonald with his elbow. Did everybody know, then?

He turned away from them and looked out over the landscape away from the river—flat prairie grass to the curve of the horizon. There seemed to be no backgrounds to this country. Every move a man made was silhouetted against the sky.

The sound of pipes drifted from the pathway through the woods along the river, playing "The Lewis Bridal Song," which had always been a favorite of his. It brought to mind a horde of red- and gold-bearded, kilted, battle-scarred giants skipping arm in arm down a mountain pathway:

Step we gaily on we go
Heel for heel and toe for toe
Arm in arm and row on row
All for Mary's wedding.

There were voices singing along with the pipes, substituting "Katy" for "Mary." Robert Gunn emerged from the bush, followed by a double line of Kildonan refugees and Red River colonists decked out in whatever finery they could lay their hands on. Beside Robert Gunn strode a tall, bashfully graceful woman with pale blue and pink flowers plaited into her red-gold hair. One of the old songs his mother used to sing to him had had a wedding in

it—when the bride came in "she shimmered like the sun." He'd
thought it was a figure of speech.

> *Plenty herring, plenty meal,*
> *Plenty peat to fill her creel,*
> *Plenty bonnie bairns as weel,*
> *That's our toast for Katy.*

CHAPTER 30

The brigades from Lake Winnipegosis and Lake Mani
toba, from the Upper Assiniboine and Souris rivers, and
from the headwaters of the Red and Pembina were all stacked up
at Fort Gibraltar. The brigades from the North and South Saskatch
ewan and the Athabasca country were stacked up at Bas de la Ri
vière; their route came down through the north end of Lake
Winnipeg and didn't pass through the Forks of the Red, but th
blockade stopped them just the same. The pemmican that was sup
posed to be waiting for them at the Bas de la Rivière depot hadn'
got past the Forks.

Every day that went by was another to be lopped off the end o
summer, when it came time for the annual race against winter o
the return trip from Fort William. Governor Miles MacDonell woul
have been happy to allow the provisioning brigades to pass on t
Bas de la Rivière any time they chose, provided they surrendere
their provisions.

Grant was supremely disappointed and confused. His view c
the world did not include the company getting strangled by on
arrogant prig throwing a quick loop around the Red River. Th
disturbing fact wasn't that the governor had been allowed to mak
his proclamation and set up his blockade, but that the compan
didn't seem to have any response except to huff and puff and wav
its arms. With John Wills dead and planted, both Whitehea
MacDonell and Duncan Cameron had assumed the demeanor c

the man in charge—except when the subject of the blockade came up, in which case each deferred to the other.

Falcon appeared from Fort Pembina, where he'd been waiting with Mary and Marguerite and her husband for Bostonais and Grant to link up with them for the summer hunt. On the outskirts of the tent village that had sprung up around Fort Gibraltar to house the spill-off of stranded *engagés*, Grant sat down with Falcon and Bostonais to smoke a few pipes of tobacco and drink a few cups of watered rum and watch the sunset paint the Assiniboine red.

Falcon said: "We can't squat waiting for you beside Fort Pembina forever. If we don't get out on the prairie soon, the herd'll be chased down to the Black Hills, and I don't fancy leaving my topknot with the Sioux."

Grant said: "I can't go until this blockade business is settled."

"Leave it to them to sort out."

"Them?"

"The fur companies. I know the North West pays you a wage, but this ain't our problem."

"No? What I told you at Boucher's Post still stands, so far as I can tell. If there was no pemmican trade and no North West Fur Trading Company, you'd find your life was changed considerably."

"The whole company isn't going to go down just because of this—or if it is, it's up to William MacGillivray and the rest of them to fix it. I don't see the partners running here from Montreal to ask you and me what to do about it."

Bostonais said: "They don't want to give in, and they don't want to fight. To hell with them. Let's go hunting."

Alex Fraser and Bonhomme Montour drifted over to their smudge fire. A little later they were joined by another member of the previous autumn's hunting party—William Shaw—in company with a very dark young man Grant hadn't met named Seraphim Lamarr and a knock-kneed old freeman named François Deschamps. In the local patois "freemen" always referred to the ex-*engagés* who'd chosen to stay in the *pays d'en haut* rather than returning to the Canadas, and never to their half-breed sons and daughters, perhaps because it was assumed that they were free. They were known as *les jeunes gens*. The French phrase meant "the young men," but there was another aspect to the *pays d'en haut* usage, the timeless shoulder shrugging of one old Chief to another after a broken truce: "You know my word is good, but what can I do about my young men?"

Grant turned away to face the prairie, half listening to the chatter around the fire, and watched a solitary oak tree turn from red-haloed green to purple-haloed blue-green to cobalt-haloed black and then disappear. The smudge fire changed from a mound of matted grass and green sticks hissing out a filter of smoke to a bed of coals and flame. But Grant's sense of disorientation didn't change. Each of those guttural, resonant voices laughing with such ease under the stars denoted someone who had lived in this wild world all his life, who had his mother's bone-deep understanding of the country in one hand and his father's steel tools and gunpowder in the other. And there were hundreds of them—thousands of them—scattered across the *pays d'en haut*. Yet some tinpot little governor moves in and starts to issue proclamations that could alter the shape of their lives, and they just shrug their shoulders. There had to be some central piece missing from the puzzle, but he just couldn't see it.

There was a bustle and a loud hallooing behind him. He stood up to look. It was Duncan Cameron and Whitehead MacDonell striding into the firelight, Mister Cameron with a pudgy little keg crooked under his arm. "I thought perhaps you might be waxing thirsty." They splintered the keg's head and dipped their cups in. After a few jokes, Mister Cameron said: "I'm surprised you allow them to do this to you."

Grant said: "Whom? Who—do what to whom?"

Falcon murmured, "Hoodoo," and chortled to himself.

"Les jardinières," nodding his head in the direction of the colony. "Coming in and robbing you of your inheritance."

Grant said: "My inheritance?"

"*Your* inheritance—all of yours. If you people don't have prior right to this country, I don't know who does."

Seraphim Lamarr said: "What people?"

"You people. *Les bois brulés.*"

Bostonais said: "What the bloody shit kind of 'people' is that supposed to be—'burnt wood'?"

Falcon said: "That isn't what it means. . . ."

"Don't tell me—you think I don't know French and Anglais? *Bois*—'wood'; *brulé*—'burnt.' "

"Sure, sure." Falcon waved away Bostonais Pangman's outrage. "That's what it means in words, but that ain't why they gave the name to us."

" 'Us'? What kind of dogshit 'us' is—"

"Well, listen and maybe you'll know, eh? Why would anyone call people that was half white and half Indian 'burnt' like 'charred,' eh? It don't make sense. But two hundred years ago, Étienne *Brulé* became the first courier *de bois* and had a Huron wife that he had children by. So there."

Duncan Cameron said: "Regardless, I still don't see why you should allow this Miles MacDonell to waltz into your country and start issuing orders."

Alex Fraser said: "What can we do about it?"

Whitehead MacDonell said: "Knock them on the head."

Bostonais perked up considerably at that, but Mister Cameron said: "The company doesn't want any part in a war, Whitehead."

Falcon said: "He's got the law, this governor."

Grant said: "What law?"

"The English law."

"What—because he says he does?"

"He is the governor, from the Earl of Selkirk"—Falcon enumerated on his fingers—"and besides that he's a captain from the English army. That sounds like the law to me."

Grant said: "And is there no law—no *right*—inherent in the fact that this is your home? This whole country," sweeping his arm toward the dark horizon. "Not your possession, but your *home*. Do you think that means less than some chain of authority coming down from some European King who beat some other European King in some European battle and among the spoils was a property deed to a continent neither one of them had ever set foot on? Whatever you want to call yourselves—*bois brulés* or métis or goddamned shiftless half-breeds—there isn't a man in Europe below the rank of Duke who wouldn't change places with you." He suddenly grew self-conscious and trailed off. All around the gleam of firelight there were black eyes trained on him intently, buckskinned shoulders hunched toward him, moccasined feet shuffling in closer out of the shadows. He would have thought they'd known all that without needing him to tell them.

CHAPTER 31

At moments when the big cloud galleons steered clear of the sun and the wind died down, Alexander Sutherland was quite prepared to swear that if he stopped working long enough and strained his ears hard enough, he'd be able to hear the juices sizzling out of the prairie grass. The vegetation seemed to be not so much ripening as baking. Sweat seeped out from under the rim of his woolen tam-o'-shanter, rivering down around his eyes. But it was the only hat he had. Better a bit of sweat than poached brains.

He was breaking furrows with a mattock. He hadn't swung a mattock since before he'd left his father's house to follow the recruiting sergeant. It was a simple enough tool, a three-foot hardwood haft fitted into a lopsided iron head. The shorter arm of the head was like an abbreviated, narrowed axe blade. The longer arm had a bit of a curve to it and a squared-off blade, a cross between a pickaxe and a shovel.

Most of the work was done with the long, curved end. He'd swing it down to bite deep into the ground, lever the end of the haft forward to break up the clods, shuffle his feet backward along the unbroken ground, and raise the mattock back up over his head. Occasionally it bit into a tangle of roots that it couldn't break through; then he'd revolve the haft and hack away at them with the axe-blade side of the head.

Lord Selkirk's agents hadn't been lying when they'd said that at Red River there were no towering forests to clear away, only prairie grass that could be burned off in an afternoon. It did make for anxious moments, beating at the fire with wet blankets to keep it from taking the whole prairie with it, and it did mean that every time Sandy shuffled his feet back to lift the mattock again, he raised puffs of soot—soot that mingled with his sweat and caked to his hands and ran into his eyes—but it did beat the decades-long process of inching a clearing out of the forest stump by stump. What Lord Selkirk's agents hadn't mentioned, or perhaps hadn't known, was that just beneath the surface of the prairie was a thick mat of intertwined roots.

He expected that the work would seem less tedious once he was clearing his own fields rather than those of the colony establishment. Archibald MacDonald, with an amateur surveyor, had been laying out lots to distribute to the new arrivals. Sandy had no intention of leaping to the first lot that came available. As eager as he was to get to work on his own place, he would have decades to regret a hasty choice.

While his muscles and his eyes went on with the work at hand, his mind slipped away to what had become its favorite occupation in the last few days—drawing out a map of the west bank of the Red River north of the Forks, adding in details gathered in his wanderings, debating the advantages and disadvantages of this unoccupied location or that one. . . .

"Mister Sutherland!" It was Sheriff Spenser, standing at the edge of the burnt-off square of land. Sandy nodded at him, gave out a polite grunt, and carried on with his work. He did appreciate the "Mister." As well as sketching out a geographical map of Lord Selkirk's colony, he'd mapped out the chain of command. New World or not, the social strata were already as calcified as *Burke's Peerage*, from the governor, his inner circle, and the Hudson's Bay factor down through the hoi polloi of colonists to the colony's indentured servants.

"Mister Sutherland! Wouldn't you rather be spending the afternoon taking a pleasant cart ride across the prairie?"

Sandy let out a noncommittal grunt that the sheriff might take for an amused response, if he so chose, and swung the mattock back up over his head.

"I mean that serious. The governor will send over one of the Orcadian laborers to do this job."

Sandy paused with the mattock at the apex of its swing and turned his head toward the sheriff. "Why would the governor do that?"

"Because you'd be a better man for another job we have in mind—most of which consists of taking a pleasant cart ride across the prairie."

Sandy carried the mattock over to a bucket of water he'd left standing by the riverbank and scooped up a couple of handfuls of tepid water to wash his face and neck. He turned to the sheriff, who had tagged along behind him. "What kind of job would I be better suited for than one of your full-time laborers?"

"It's come out that one of the North West Company canoe brigades heard about the blockade ahead of time and buried their cargo of pemmican a few miles up the Assiniboine. We've learned where it is, and we're going to confiscate it."

"Your Orcadians can dig and lift and carry as well as I can, if not a damn sight better."

"Perhaps, but you're a damned sight better at handling a musket and a bayonet, or I don't know the Black Watch."

Sandy picked up his mattock and went back into the field. Sheriff Spenser followed him. "You can have my word that the day's work will be credited to your account, if that's what you're—"

"Did you ever shove a bayonet in a man's guts and twist it free to pull it out again? If you had, you would not come asking me to do it over a few sacks of dried meat."

"It isn't the pemmican, it's the principle of the thing."

"Oh, grand. That's a much better reason."

"There isn't going to be any fighting."

"Then what difference does my soldiering make?"

"Because you know how to keep your head with a musket in your hand. The North West Company might send a party over to scare us off. If we show them a few bayonets, they'll back off, but they'd like nothing better than for one of us to lose his head and take a shot at them so they can run off squealing to the Colonial Office in London. If I have enough old soldiers with me, I'll be able to *avoid* trouble."

"Could you trust an indentured servant to make a straight furrow?"

Sheriff Spenser raised his eyebrows and ran his eyes up and down the sketchy line Sandy had carved so far, meandering around stubborn rocks and wavering from side to side in a path only its mother could call straight. Sandy laughed and walked back to the bucket, upended it, and came back to Sheriff Spenser toting the empty bucket in one hand and the mattock in the other. "Well, there is the one thing can always be said for soldiering—it kicks the green Jesus out of working for a living. Bang your drum, Sergeant."

They made their way across the green-sprigged fields and in through the compound of barracks buildings that made up the colony establishment.

Sandy split off from the sheriff to head over to the cluster of tents housing the new arrivals, on the edge of which was the sailcloth-and-spruce-bough lean-to of his honeymoon home. His wife wasn't there. He dragged out the musket and cartridge belt that had been issued to him on arrival and went back to join the sheriff.

Besides ex-Private Alexander Sutherland, the sheriff's pemmican posse was made up of ten of the colony's Orcadians and one supple-looking plainsman who was introduced as "Lajimodierre." They piled into two high-wheeled wooden carts, much like the carts that were used in the Highlands. They drove in a straight line southwest, jostling and bouncing over hummocks.

Their path intersected with the north bank of the Assiniboine. They turned west and followed it along, avoiding the more eccentric loops and twists. Ahead of them was a thick stand of trees jutting north onto the prairie. Lajimodierre said: "Catfish Creek. Past it is Sturgeon Creek, good fishing both, and past that my house and *ma femme*—my wife—and children. We come here from Fort des Prairies west when we hear about the colony."

Catfish Creek was in a low glen of interconnecting, curved ridges crowded with oak trees. Lajimodierre directed the sheriff, who directed the carts, to the base of one of the higher ridges, and then called: "Stop! Here." He bounded up to the crest of the ridge, the toes of his moccasins seeming to grip the tufts of grass. Sandy and the others followed much less nimbly. Lajimodierre was tugging at a patch of vines and dead bush that proved to have no roots. Underneath them was a stomped-down mound of freshly dug earth that smelled like a latrine. Lajimodierre cupped his hands down by his crotch and pushed his hips forward. "To keep the wolves and raccoons from digging."

The sheriff handed up a half a dozen long-handled spades. Sandy offered one to Lajimodierre, who shook his head and laughed. "No, no—I find, you dig."

It was easy digging, the ground still loose from the previous shovels. About three feet down one of the spades bit into something with a different consistency. Lajimodierre called for them to stop and jumped down into the pit, brushing away the dirt with his fingers. There was a layer of tightly packed leather bags with bits of brown wool still on them. They were heaved out one at a time and hauled down the slope and into the carts. Under the first layer was another, and then a third. It was a bit like carrying giant, fat sausages.

Sandy was heading up for his sixth load when he heard a distant low rumbling. He got up to the top of the ridge and turned to look back. The sunlit plain spread out before him all the way to the woods along the Red, the shadows of small clouds scudding across

the grass. Passing through the clouds were six horsemen fanned
out in a ragged line, galloping hard toward Catfish Creek.

During his years in the army, Sandy had seen the best horsemen
in the world—Murat's hussars and Spanish gypsy riders and the
suicidal messengers who galloped from one British general to another. He had seen cavalry charges from every angle. But seeing
the riders charging toward him now—easy and relaxed on homemade saddles tied to half-wild ponies galloping full tilt over broken
ground—he realized he'd never really seen horsemen before.

Lajimodierre stood up beside him and said: "They ride pretty,
don't they?" And then the two of them headed down the slope with
the others to get their muskets out of the carts.

Sheriff Spenser hadn't deigned to arm himself. He stood with his
arms crossed and his feet planted wide, between the carts and the
wild hunt advancing upon them. They reined their horses to a rearing halt not two paces in front of him, spattering him with pebbles
and pellets of earth. The pairs of riders on the flanks laughed and
prodded each other over the relative merits of their performance.
But they quieted down when they saw that the two men in the middle
were sitting their horses silently, gazing levelly at Sheriff Spenser.

They were the same two men Kate had been talking to on the
riverbank—Bostonais Pangman and the clean-shaven one with the
Highland name, Grant. Grant had a brace of pistols tucked into
the woven sash around his waist. The other five held muskets or
double-barreled hunting guns, either dangling loosely from one
hand or slanted crosswise athwart the pommels of their saddles.
Tucked into their sashes or hanging from their belts were hatchets
and thick-bladed skinning knives in beaded sheaths.

Bostonais Pangman's eyes shifted to Lajimodierre and stayed
there. Grant draped his reins over his pony's neck and crossed his
legs in front of him, like an Indian sitting by a campfire. He smiled
a placid Sunday-afternoon smile and drifted his eyes away from the
sheriff across the uneven line of bayonets. Sandy wondered whether
Grant hadn't realized what a precarious posture he'd put himself in
in case of trouble or whether he really didn't expect any. Perhaps
he was so sure of his agility that he knew he'd be able to get his
legs untangled before anyone could pull the trigger. Sandy also
wondered if behind that smile the blood was pounding as loudly in
Grant's ears as it was in his own.

Grant's eyes traveled back to the sheriff. With the smile still in
place, he said in English: "I do so dislike being the bearer of sad
tidings, Mister Spenser, but I'm afraid the buried treasure that you

and your friends have accidentally stumbled upon is in fact the property of the North West Fur Trading Company. We'll take charge of it from here."

"You'll do nothing of the kind."

"I'm certain that the company will provide some sort of recompense for your labor in digging it up, and for the rental of your carts, of course."

"We'll take it back ourselves, to Fort Douglas. Any provisions being illegally smuggled out of Assiniboia are immediately forfeit to the colony. You know the law."

"Regrettably, I do know the law—a good deal better than you would wish me to. For an instance, I know the colonial secretary has declared that Rupertsland is under the jurisdiction of the courts in Upper and Lower Canada. I am not aware that the Canadian courts have ratified any of Miles MacDonell's self-important edicts, or even heard of—"

"Lord Selkirk's governor is the final authority here!" For someone who'd wanted men with cool heads behind him, Sheriff Spenser was dangerously overheated himself.

With his eyes still fastened on Lajimodierre, Bostonais Pangman murmured a few words to Grant in his fur trade French-Indian dialect. Grant bit off a giddy bubble of laughter and darted his eyes along the sheriff's line of men.

Sandy murmured to Lajimodierre: "What did he say?"

"He say there ain't no law here but who shoot first. He tell Grant to stop jawing and weed us out."

The Orcadian behind them took a half step forward, growling: "Let him try, then—there's twelve of us to six of . . ." There was a brassy sound to his voice, echoing the brassy taste at the back of Sandy's mouth.

Sandy raised his arm to cut him off, but Lajimodierre had moved first, clamping his hand onto his musket stock. "Ssh—he can count as good as you, may be better. Let him come to his own decide."

Sandy was astounded to discover that he was actually trying to calculate—as though it were a rational question of debate—whether it would be better to shoot Grant first or Bostonais. It was insane that he and they should even be there, facing each other with loaded guns across a cartload of dried meat in a vast wilderness teeming with game. His breathing had accelerated into a pattern of short, shallow drafts. The smell of sage crushed beneath the cartwheels was suddenly so strong that it seemed impossible he hadn't noticed it until now. Grant's eyes had taken on an unnatural sheen, and his cocky smile looked painted on. But what was making Sandy's body knot up was the posture of Bostonais Pangman and the other four métis.

All five of them sat loose and poised and absolutely still, their faces negligently calm, their eyes focused nowhere in particular—so that any movement within their field of vision would stand out. None had moved their weapons; all of them knew from a hundred past occasions—the Sioux hand dropping down toward a war club in the middle of a parley or the wink of an eye that turned a campfire card game into knives and blood—that when the time came, it was only a flick of the wrist and pull the trigger.

When he was discharged from the army, Sandy had made a solemn promise never to carry a musket behind a fool again. And here he was doing just that: because if Sheriff Spenser honestly believed that those lazy-eyed horsemen would react to a shot fired in their direction by running to the colonial secretary, then Sheriff Spenser was more of a fool than any inbred, inherited-commissioned ensign in the entire British army.

Grant opened his mouth to speak and then closed it again, covering his lapse with a broader smile. He uncrossed his legs and straightened them down to the stirrups. "I would love to while away the afternoon discussing legal niceties with you, Mister Spenser, if I thought for one moment that your opinion or mine might have even a minuscule effect upon the final resolution. Do take good care of our pemmican until then." He jogged his reins and turned his horse.

Sandy wondered whether the other five would follow him. They appeared to be wondering the same thing. Perhaps if he had wheeled his horse quickly and galloped away, or if he had hesitated to see if they were following him, they would have stayed where they were . . . and in another moment the shooting would have started. But he turned the horse in a smooth, gradual motion and walked it away without looking back. All five of the others fell in after him. As they caught up to him he kicked his horse into a gallop, and instantaneously there was a six-man horse race—each of them laughing and calling the other names, whipping at each other's horses with their reins.

One of the colony men brandished his musket up over his head and shouted after them: "That's right, run, you lily-gutted—"

Lajimodierre spun around and shouted: "Shut your stupid mouth!"

The laborer's face went red with indignation. Sandy stepped in beside Lajimodierre and crossed his musket in front of him. A few of the other Orcadians pushed up beside their brother in an ugly knot.

Sheriff Spenser's voice cut through their grumbling: "Are you so disappointed you didn't get killed that you're going to start bayoneting each other? You still have to finish the loading before we turn home."

The knot unraveled, and the Orcadians began to stack their muskets against the carts. One of them said to Lajimodierre: "You weren't afraid of that pack of raggle arses, were you?"

"Afraid, me?" Lajimodierre looked down at his mustard-brown buckskin trousers. "These were white this morning."

The Orcadians laughed, and Lajimodierre gave them a wink and a chuckle-headed grin. But his eyes were cold.

CHAPTER 32

Grant stood in the watchtower over Fort Gibraltar, gazing across the long belt of June-green treetops at the shingled roofs of the colony. Occasionally a metallic flash broke through the leaves as the sun caught a rank of bayonets where Governor, ex-Captain, Miles MacDonell was drilling his militia of colonists and indentured servants.

The situation hadn't changed, and Grant was still smoldering with rage and shame. It was impossible to say whether the governor was acting on instructions or whether the proclamation and the blockade had been his own idea. Either way, he had to understand that the stakes on the table took the situation far beyond a few tin soldiers. For one hundred and fifty years the Hudson's Bay Company and the Montreal traders had been skirting around each other and edging farther into the *pays d'en haut*. They had grown to the point where between them they now covered the entirety of the fur country, and their annual profits had grown into the kinds of sums of money that highly civilized countries fought wars over.

Grant had no idea what he was expected to do. Should he have
started shooting at the crew of colonists digging up the pemmican?
Attack the crofters trying to build new homes behind the governor's
gun emplacement—and let people like the tall, red-haired woman
he'd met on the riverbank take their chances?

Maybe the point was that the companies were engaged in cutthroat competition but had to stop short of actually cutting throats;
any bloodshed and the British government would have no choice
but to step in. The blockade was a textbook example of leaving an
opponent with only two choices: escalate into a physical assault or
back down.

A canoe was gliding downstream on the Assiniboine, appearing
and disappearing on the narrow band of water that showed between
the treetops. Grant hadn't paid much attention to it, assuming it
was only a family of Saulteaux or Swampy Cree. But as the craft
neared him, he saw that the paddlers had thick beards and the
bright-colored shirts and sashes of *hommes du nord*, and that there
was a white-bearded man in top hat and black waistcoat leaning
against the midthwart.

Grant shouted down into the yard: "*Bateau! Bateau!* On the
Assiniboine!"

Engagés started to leap up and scramble for the gates. As he
looked back at the canoe, Grant could see now that the voyageurs
looked somewhat more raggedy than the usual run of *hommes du
nord* and the old man at the midthwarts was a shrivel-faced imp
with one withered arm.

It had been a dozen years since Le Bras Croché had handed him
over to Duncan MacGillivray for the journey east, and he hadn't
seen the old man since. At that time he hadn't known that the
French nickname the voyageurs had given him referred not only to
his withered arm, but also to a miser's hooklike grasping. He also
hadn't known that the reason John MacDonald of Garth—as Le
Bras Croché had been christened—had been suddenly elevated to
bourgeois of the largest district in the *pays d'en haut* was because
Wappeston's father had decreed it on his deathbed. It put him in
mind of his father's story of the beaver felt, hooks hooking against
hooks to make a fabric that couldn't be pulled apart.

By the time he got to the riverbank, the *engagés* were already
pulling the canoe ashore. Duncan Cameron was there, shaking the
old man's good hand and clapping him on the back. John MacDonald of Garth said: "What the hell are you whole lot doing still here?
You should be halfway to Rendezvous by now."

"Selkirk's bloody colony. Come up to the fort and I'll explain it to you over a cup of rum or two."

"Twist my arm. Ha ha ha. Twist my arm. . . ." By that time they had progressed up to the top of the bank and were walking past Grant. The old man was waggling his withered arm, doubled over with glee at his own wit. Suddenly he stopped short and peered up into Grant's face. "You're not a Grant by any chance, are you, lad?"

"That I am, sir."

"James?"

"No, sir—James died of the fever in Scotland. . . ."

"Of course, of course—bloody stupid of me. Cuthbert, then. Good to see you, lad," slapping his good hand against Grant's shoulder. "By God, by God—look at those shoulders. Look at you. Wouldn't your papa've been proud. Did you run off on your schooling, then?"

"No, sir—the company brought me out here after I'd graduated."

"By God—big as a house and a genuine education to boot. Bugger me with a froze porcupine. Come along inside, Cameron's standing the drinks. The old place doesn't look half-bad. I built this place, did you know that? Well—me and fifty *engagés*. Took us three summers. By God"—slapping Grant between the shoulder blades—"you could break me over your knee like dry kindling. Wouldn't try it, though; I've still got a few tricks left in me."

When Duncan Cameron and Whitehead MacDonell had explained the situation, Le Bras Croché sat brooding on it and then slapped his hand on the table, laughing. "Well, the joke's on me, isn't it? It was me that called this place Gibraltar, and look at this—they've knocked us on the head. Ream me out and pin me up to dry."

He sent an envoy to the governor and arranged a meeting. It was eventually agreed that the colony would return two-thirds of the confiscated pemmican and let the brigades pass downstream in return for a guarantee that the new man the company appointed would have his hunters supply the colony with fresh meat over the winter. Neither Duncan Cameron nor Whitehead was at all pleased, but within the company hierarchy John MacDonald of Garth was a long way above both of them.

Grant was holding up the gatepost with Bostonais's help, watching the last *pièces* being stowed away in the brigade, when John Pritchard came up to them with his Catherine glued to his side.

''Well, Cuthbert, we've had our differences, but it's always sad to say good-bye.''

''Not always,'' came to mind, but instead Grant shook the proffered hand and said: ''I wish you both a safe journey.''

''Oh, Catherine won't be coming with me. They'll take her in at Fort Douglas until I come back with the fall brigade. Come along now, dear. . . .''

Bostonais spat on the piece of ground they'd just vacated and said: *''Jardinières.''*

The canoes set off with the massed chorale of four brigades bellowing ''The Abbess and the Mohawk.'' John Pritchard's Catherine ran along the bank waving and wailing. Bostonais said: ''She got more reason to wail than she knows. I wouldn't want to be Pritchard when he tells them at Fort William that he's crossing over. Well, maybe now we can get some hunting done.''

''Actually, you know what I've gone and done—I've left my horse at Fort La Souris. I'll have to catch up with you on the Pembina.''

''How will you get there?''

''I can borrow a horse from the Fort Gibraltar string.''

''Mm. Then you have to leave it at Fort La Souris, ride your horse here, borrow another horse to ride back there to get the borrowed horse, leave the second borrowed horse there . . .''

''I imagine I could catch up with you within ten days, or a couple of weeks.''

''Much longer'n ten days and you'll be heading into too late.''

''You will have killed them all?''

''Killed them all . . .'' Bostonais's chest began a deep, slow rumbling. ''That's good—'Killed them all. . . .'''

CHAPTER 33

Kate was stirring their morning oatmeal over the fire when her husband crawled out of the tent. She had come to the conclusion that they were better off feeding themselves. Their wages

or working in the communal fields at Colony Gardens were cal-
ulated at one shilling a day if the colony establishment provided
heir meals or one shilling and sixpence if they fed themselves. For
ess than sixpence a day she could get enough oatmeal, barley, and
otatoes from the company stores to feed them. She had tried to
discuss it with him, but he had just shrugged his shoulders and
aid: "Do what you like."

Since they'd been married he hadn't said more than twelve words
nd half a dozen grunts in the course of a day. She'd tried to think
f what she might have done to offend him. Finally she'd had to
ccept that this must be the inevitable way of things when you
hanged from a woman to a wife. She'd made her bed, and now
he would have to lie in it. Or rather, she quipped to herself without
nuch pleasure in her cleverness, she had lain in his bed, and now
he would have to make what she could of it. Whores can't be
hoosers. There were no outward physical signs yet, but it couldn't
e much longer before they started to show.

Without a glance in her direction, he headed down to the river
o wash himself. There was a bare hint of morning mist that the
alf-risen sun was already searing away. She had never imagined
here could be a sun as hot and yellow; the stories they told about
he coldness of the winters had to be exaggerations.

When he returned from the river he didn't come toward the fire
o wait for his breakfast; he began to take their tent down. She said:
"What are you doing?"

"Taking the tent down."

"I can see that. Why?"

"To move it to our property. Or does it make more sense to you
o hike back and forth from here to there every day?"

"But where? Which place? I had no idea you had chosen a—"

"Is the breakfast ready?"

When they'd done eating she helped him break down their shelter
nd wrap their possessions into bundles they could carry on their
acks. She followed him along the path that had been cut through
he riverside bush north from Fort Douglas to the lots that had
ecently been surveyed.

Before they neared the boundary of the first homestead, he turned
ight off the path and began to force his way through the tangle of
ush and trees covering Point Douglas. "Point Douglas" was what
iovernor MacDonell had christened the tongue of land that thrust
ut east from the bank, forcing the river to loop around it. Fort
Jouglas and the blockade gun battery stood by the south shoulder

of the point, at the upstream end of the bend. The fields of colony gardens carried on straight north, their eastern border lined along the base. The newly surveyed river lots began at the downstream shoulder of the point, where the river ended its loop and continued on toward Lake Winnipeg.

She followed him into a triangular meadow, bordered on both arms by the riverside tree belt apexing at the tip of the point. Half way up the path he dropped his half of their possessions and said "I suppose this is as good a place as any to put up a temporary shelter. The first business is to clear a potato field so we'll have some kind of harvest. Then we can start work on the house. With luck, we should be able to put up a snug-enough shanty to get us through the winter and still have enough autumn to furrow a few acres for winter wheat."

"I had no idea that they were surveying lots on Point Douglas."

"Neither have I. My deed—*our* deed—says 'any place of his choosing within the Colony of Assiniboia,' although I suppose you do not need me to tell you that. No one else has settled here, and this is the place of my choosing. There is plenty of water on both sides . . ."

"But—it is so isolated from the others."

"Precisely."

She assumed he meant that when the time came he'd prefer not to have his nose rubbed too publicly in the fact of his wife producing a baby five months after their marriage, so she let it drop. He unknotted the thongs binding his tools, slung the scythe over his shoulder, and went away. She unrolled their bit of sailcloth and arranged the best sleeping awning she could, then spaded out a firepit and ringed it with rocks. She scrambled down to the river a few times to cleanse herself of the soil-salt taste of dirt and tears, then clambered back up the bank and carried on.

She had a couple of potatoes roasted just as the sun hit its zenith. He came back, set the scythe aside, and ate, then said: "Dip the bucket full in the river, then, and get your plaid."

He took up the spade and led her to the base of the point, where he had cut a swath around a broad square of grass. He set the grass on fire, and they ran back and forth along the downwind side, Kate batting at sparks with her soaked plaid and her husband frantically spading up the clumps she couldn't smother.

From the cloud of smoke behind them, a voice shouted: "What do you think you are doing?"

"What the hell does it look like?"

"But this is not one of the surveyed lots. You have not been assigned this lot." It was Archibald MacDonald.

"Back off until we get this under control, or there will be no lots to assign anyone!"

When the grass was reduced to a black, smoldering mat, her husband said: "If you can take care of this, I will take care of Mister MacDonald— We shall go over and speak to the governor, Mister MacDonald, but first I must fetch something to take along with us—just wait a moment." He went back to where they'd dropped their things, then accompanied Archibald MacDonald toward Fort Douglas.

He came back without Archibald MacDonald, looked at the squared plot of black earth she'd been patrolling, and said: "I suppose that is enough of this for one day—we should have some supper and turn in."

They had but the one mattock, and he didn't seem eager to add the cost of another to their account, so that meant he had to furrow the field on his own. In the morning she asked him where he wanted the house, then scythed down that spot while he was off hacking up the potato field. But she couldn't very well start laying down the foundation logs on her own. Once the clearing-off was done, she took the spade and paced out a convenient distance from the house site and started digging a hole for the necessary.

She had no idea how late it was until he called her name and she looked up and realized that the light behind him was red. She said: "Look! Four feet down in topsoil and still no end of it!"

He might have put on a quizzical or thoughtful expression—he was silhouetted against the sundown—but after a moment he said: "So?"

"So! In Kildonan anyone who had eighteen inches of topsoil was reckoned to be sitting on top of the richest land in the world. You chose a grand place to make a home."

Either the angle of the backlight had lowered enough or her eyes had adjusted, but she could see the tightness in his face suddenly soften and round upward. But it was only for an instant—then his features sharpened and narrowed again. He said in a cold voice, "It is past time for dinner," and turned away.

CHAPTER 34

Once the palisades of Fort Gibraltar had sunk behind the horizon, once there was nothing but a man and his horse and the open prairie and the endless immensity of sky, Grant was amazed at how released he felt. He was growing quite familiar with the country between Fort Gibraltar and Brandon House—or Fort La Souris, he corrected himself. Perhaps far too familiar, since already he knew it better than any stretch of country within his posting in the Qu'Appelle district—given that it was his fourth ride across the same ground within as many weeks.

Once the frustrations of the blockade were behind him, he felt that he could breathe again. He was beginning to suspect that the mountains around Inverness and Grantown-on-Spey, the narrow streets of Montreal, the tight-pressing forests of the east, had all been claustrophobic. Six more years under the burst-open skies of the *pays d'en haut* might not be all that miserable.

Fort La Souris turned out to be virtually empty this time of year, with only a handful of *engagés* and their families. Grant sent an *engagé* across the river to inform the chief trader at Brandon House that Mister Grant was in the area and, if Mister McKay was not otherwise engaged, would like to come calling, to converse and exchange views on the recent situation at Red River.

Since there was no bourgeois currently in residence at Fort La Souris, Grant occupied the bourgeois's quarters. He set a kettle onto the fire to give himself a soft shave and a standing bath, then buffed his boots, brushed his trousers and waistcoat, and shook out his frill-fronted dress shirt.

The *engagé* stuck his head in the door to shout that Mister McKay said Mister Grant should head over there for supper. Grant spent some time fussing together a cunningly tied arrangement of high collar and white neckcloth and wine-red silk bow ribbon, and then went out to his horse. One of the *engagés* had transferred his saddle and harness to a Fort La Souris horse.

There were only the three of them at dinner. Since Grant had last seen her, Miss McKay had acquired a curiously magnetic sheen to her lustrous-black eyes and a rose-dust flush to her cheeks. He put it down to the claret.

Even with the door standing open, the room grew uncomfortably warm. But Grant refrained from loosening his neckcloth. John Richards informed him that he and his sister might relocate in the autumn. "Not that I haven't been happy during my years at Brandon House, but one can't spend one's entire life on one little bend in the Assiniboine—"

"I suppose *one* could," she said, a golden eyebrow arching demurely.

"—so I've let it be known that I wouldn't be too distraught if the company took it in mind to post me to another district."

Grant said: "I can't imagine why you stay on with them."

"Whom?"

"The Company of Indenturers. Outside of the fact that your father and your uncle more or less left you your position here. But when you look at it, what exactly did they leave you? The most you can hope for is the occasional increase in wages until your retirement. You can never own a stake in the concern or share in the profits."

"And you think you can, with the Canadian peddlers?"

"I fail to see why not, barring some kind of accident."

"The accident already happened. Look at the color of your hand. 'All the perfumes of Arabia shall not wash it white . . .' "

"Leaving aside the question of your horrible mangling of that quote—thank you"—as John Richards refilled his glass—"you are also misapplying the English company's prejudices onto the North West Company. We can rise as high as ability allows."

"Is that the royal we or the editorial we?"

"The racial we."

"Racial? What race—the brotherhood of mongrels?"

"The métis."

"Exactly—mongrels. Or would you register the offspring of a Great Dane and a Labrador retriever in the same breed as a cross between a beagle and a fox terrier? Because that is about as much as I have in common with Bostonais Pangman or Hercule Littlenose, or you, for that matter—outside of the fact that you're almost fit to tread the same fencing mat with me."

"We all have a good deal in common, if you'd look at it."

"Certainly—we all live in the *pays d'en haut*, as do the Blackfoot

and the Cree and the Saulteaux, and the Orcadian employees of the
Hudson's Bay Company, and your company's Canadian *engagés*,
and a number of Scots and English traders, with a smattering of
Germans and Yankees. Define your terms."

"They define themselves."

"Do they now? All right—I'm half Scots and half Sioux, you're
half Scots and half Cree: does that make us part of the Dakota
nation or the Cree nation or—"

"Neither."

"What then?"

"A new nation."

"Oh, please. Where's our flag? Where's our government? Or are
you planning to elect yourself King—Cuthbert the First?"

The two of them went on amusing and abusing each other, growing steadily drunker, until both were merely growling in their sleep.
Finally Grant pulled himself up from his chair and onto his horse,
pointed it across the ford at Fort La Souris, and flopped down onto
the bourgeois's bed. He jounced awake in the gray light of dawn,
shivering and head sore and riveted to the mattress with the sickening revelation that he had spent his evening with Bethsy McKay
hollering drunkenly at her brother.

By the time he crawled out of bed, the morning was half-gone.
He cut his horse out of the herd, saddled it, and fixed a lead halter
to the borrowed horse he'd ridden from Fort Gibraltar. Whichever
way he looked at it, he'd made a fool of himself. Perhaps by autumn, when he'd pass by again on his way west, she would have
forgotten. He was crossing to the icehouse to rummage out some
traveling provisions when Bethsy McKay rode in through the gates,
her gold hair burning in the sun.

She walked her horse over to him and handed him a bundle of
red cloth. He unfolded it and found nothing wrapped inside. The
cloth itself was about four feet square, with a large white 8 sewn
onto both sides. He said: "What is it?"

"Every nation needs a flag."

Unsure of whether she was mocking him, he said: "Eight?"

"Turn it sideways."

Sideways the 8 became the ancient infinity symbol of the silhouetted snake swallowing its own tail. "What should I do with it?"

"Cut it up in pieces and stack it on the outhouse bench if you
want—it's yours."

"Of course I won't. It's— Thank you, that was very kind of

you." She was certainly touchy this morning. "Where are you going?"

"One of the fort servants killed a porcupine last week. I've soaked the quills, and now I need to gather some berries and so on for dyes—nuts and roots and berries, just like an old Cree woman. I suppose it's a lot of trouble to take when I could just use the glass beads in the warehouse, but what else do I have to do with my time? Does it look worth the trouble to you?" She hiked up the hem of her skirt to show the high tops of her moccasins, tied just below the knee. The fringed cuff had a gleaming black-and-red-and-white design of intricately woven quillwork. His attention was drawn more to the clean swell of knee and thigh growing out of it.

"You can't go traipsing off across the prairie alone."

"I've been doing it since I was twelve."

"I've just saddled my own horse . . . to take it out for a bit of a run. I could come along for company."

"Suit yourself."

The sky was a Chinese blue, with an armada of puffy white keels floating on the sky and speckling the plain with shadows. It seemed to Grant that he and Bethsy were riding across the floor of a tropic ocean while the massed fleets of French and Spanish navies lumbered overhead.

Bethsy said she needed gooseberries and cranberries to boil down to an acidic base to penetrate the quills, a moss that grew on spruce trees to make yellow dye, and hazelnut bark and a certain porous brown stone for black. She led him south along the Souris until they came to the mouth of a stream with half its pebbled bed exposed to the low-water mark of high summer. They climbed down off their horses and walked along the bank, looking for her brown stones. He kept coming up with the wrong kind, although to him they looked identical to the ones she was dropping in her pouch. The fifth or sixth time that he came up hopeful but wrong, she laughed at him and tugged at the lock of hair across his forehead: "Can't you see—this one is darker and shinier. . . ."

"I thought that was only because it was wet."

She threw his rock away and shook her head at him. "Didn't they teach you anything worthwhile at that college?"

"It doesn't seem so." As her hand drew away from his face, he almost reached for her to kiss her . . . but changed his mind. He'd thought he'd left his shyness with women somewhere east of Fort William, but apparently not. He decided it was because he was sober.

They came to a place where the banks of the stream expanded around a deeper bowl in the earth, making a miniature lake with marsh grass crowding the banks. Bethsy got back on her horse, and they cut across country, first to a spruce bog for moss and stripped hazel bark, then to a cupped ridge thicketed with berry bushes. Grant unlimbered his rifle and carried it in the crook of his arm, watching out for bears.

They filled two birchbark pails with small, hard, bright red berries. There was a curious tang to the air that irritated the back of Grant's nostrils. The horses, their reins hitched to bushes at the base of the ridge, began to nicker and stamp. Grant and Bethsy had worked their way almost to the ridge top, topping up the last inch of the birchbark buckets, when Bethsy suddenly straightened up and said: "Oh, my God."

Grant dropped his bucket and cocked his rifle, expecting to see a bear. Standing straight brought his eyes up over the top of the ridge. To the west was a thick curtain of black smoke from the earth to the sky, rippling and waving above a bright broken line of flame that stretched for miles. The wind was billowing the smoke toward them.

Grant had seen smoke from prairie fires before, but he had never been close enough to see the flames. It was said that they could move very quickly, but it was still too far away to gauge. Bethsy said: "Come on, it's moving this way." She started down the ridge, then turned back to call him. Her voice was agitated but not particularly fearful. "We'd better get back to the fort."

They wound their way down the slope between the tangles of bushes. He could taste the smoke in the air now. The horses began to whinny and rear, jerking their heads against the reins. Grant handed his bucket to Bethsy and ran down the last stretch of the ridge, leaping over the bushes in his way. The thin branches the horses were tied to gave way before he got to them. He made a grab for his horse's tail and came away with a few strands of hair. Both horses pounded away across the prairie.

Bethsy had thrown the buckets away and followed him as quickly as she could. She said: "If the wind doesn't shift, it will catch up with us long before we can reach the fort walking."

"The river?"

"The Souris, the Assiniboine's too far."

They set off walking at a brisk, Sunday-stroll pace, Grant swinging his rifle in his left hand. Bethsy's thin-soled moccasins didn't

ve her much protection, and every now and then she'd yelp and
p away from a sharp rock or a stiff stand of stubble.

The line of treetops marking the river didn't appear to be getting
y closer. Grant looked back over his shoulder. The sky above the
rry ridge was black with smoke. And then the flames burst over
e top, running down in a ragged line through the bushes, whipped
rward by the wind.

Bethsy began to run. Grant ran with her, an awkward pace half-
ay between a jog and a lope. Bethsy panted out: "We'll never
ake it."

"The stream?" About a mile ahead off to their right was the
gged line of bush along the stream they'd visited earlier.

"It isn't wide enough. The fire'll cross over."

"The pond, then—where it widened. We can wade out to the
iddle until . . ."

"Yes." She saved her breath for running.

The air around them grew hazy and thick. Birds began to burst
it of the ground cover on all sides. Half a dozen antelope bounded
'. A ground squirrel was running frantically back and forth in
ont of the entrance to its den. Grant wondered whether it would
e safe in its hole or whether the fire would suffocate it.

He looked back over his shoulder. The fire was gaining on them.
e could feel the heat now. He grabbed hold of Bethsy's hand and
n full tilt, dragging her along. Suddenly she let out a squeal of
iin and fell face forward, her hand yanking him off balance and
rawling him out in front of her. When he looked back this time,
e world was a sky-tall maw of black smoke with a lower jaw filled
ith teeth of flame. A quail hovered above the flames eating her
est, buffeting at the smoke with her wings. A moment later she
rned over in the air and plummeted to the ground.

Bethsy glanced at her right foot and gasped: "It isn't cut or
visted." She scrambled back up to her feet. Grant took her hand
id began to run again. But as soon as her right foot hit the ground
ie screamed and fell again. He threw away his rifle, picked her
», and set off at a stumbling jog toward the tangle of wolf willow
round the pond ahead.

His arms began to give way quickly, so he locked his hands
gether, making a basket rim of his arms with her drooped inside
. The air tearing into his lungs had grown as thin and rarefied as
the top of a mountain, but hot and thick with smoke. He could
el the heat singeing the fabric at the backs of his knees and the
air on his neck. There was the sound of an explosion as the fire

reached his rifle. His clasped hands began to slip apart with swe
The world in front of him jounced up and down, wavering w
heat haze and the sweat and smoke tears that he couldn't blink aw;
He knew his running had become a zigzag line, but it was only
momentum that kept him going—if he stopped to orient himse
he'd fall.

He broke through the line of willow bushes, and his boots sa
into the muck between the shore reeds. As he felt himself falli
forward, his hands snapped apart. The weight of her body dragg
his arms down. "All right, you sons of bitches," he told them, '
you've never done anything before . . ." and he surged all
strength he had left into his arms and threw her forward as he fe

There was a thin coating of water on the mud where the side
his head slapped down. The cold drops that splashed up over
face, and the taste of oxygen in the air among the reeds, broug
him half-awake. His body felt weightless and strengthless, esp
cially his arms and shoulders. He was being dragged across
mud and reeds. Bethsy had twisted one hand into the collar of
shirt behind his neck and was pulling him into the water.

By the time she got him out into the middle of the pond, he h
revived enough to get his feet under him. Standing, the wa
reached his chest but slowly rose up to his chin as his boots sa
into the ooze of the pond floor. A bedraggled badger swam p;
them as the fringe of bush along one shore of the pond burst in
flame. Between the heat and the wind and the blowing embers, t
fire had leapt the stream quickly. The pond was soon ringed wi
fire, the smoke blotting out the sun.

Bethsy pulled up the hem of her skirt from under the water a;
stretched it over her mouth and nose. Grant did the same with
handkerchief. The air he sucked through it took on the sour tas
of stagnant marsh water, but it was better than smoke. Althou;
they were no longer in danger of being burned to death, they we
a long way from safe. The fire was sucking the oxygen out of t
air, and the smoke was so thick Grant could barely make o
Bethsy's face two feet in front of him.

But gradually the smoke began to clear, and the air began to tas
sweeter. He could see Bethsy quite distinctly now—or her head,
least, which was all that showed above the murky surface of t
pond. Her hair was plastered to her head from ducking it under t
water. Her eyes and the rims of her nostrils were red.

There was still a haze around them, but it was as much stea
and mist now as smoke. He reached through it toward her, b

scovered that his boots were locked fast in the mud, so he simply
aned forward. She angled her mouth toward his. Her arms came
ound his neck as he kissed her, the tip of her tongue slipping in
etween his lips. He straightened his body again, and she came
ith him. Her bare legs, the skirt floating above them, came up
d locked behind his knees. It was she who unbuttoned his trou-
rs and pulled his shirt off over his head, leaning her body out
om his to do the same with her blouse. Then she pulled her skirt
p over her body and threw it away. Her skin was slick and warm
gainst his. He worked his hands up and down the curve of her
ack and the taut swell of her buttocks. She put one arm across his
oulders and pulled herself up above him, pushing with the backs
f her calves around his thighs, working his trousers down his legs.
he lowered herself around him, whimpering and biting her lip,
hile he stood with his feet locked in the mud. For an instant he
lt like the Colossus of Rhodes with a golden statue of Aphrodite
rawling across him.

After his final shudder they stayed as they were for a long time,
eir arms wrapped around each other and the water buoying them
p. He was quite certain that what had just happened between them
lt different from all his prior escapades, but he wasn't sure just
ow.

He thought for a moment that she was crying, then realized that
had begun to rain. She moved away from him. There was a trace
f blue around her lips—the raindrops were warmer than the water
the pond. She started toward the shore. He couldn't pull his boots
ree, although bubbles of marsh gas came up with his struggles.
inally he pulled his feet out of his boots and left them there.

She was kneeling with her back to him on the mud between the
ond and the burnt ground. Beyond her was a vast black steaming
lain with embers hissing in the rain. She had taken off her moc-
asins. Her legs were streaked with mud. He knelt beside her and
ut one arm across her shoulders. The air was quite warm, the mat
f reeds and ooze beneath his knees springy and moist.

She said: "The fires usually bring on rain; something about the
eat and the smoke going up. . . ."

"That doesn't make the vaguest approximation of sense."

"It doesn't have to make sense, it's true."

She had turned toward him to say that, bringing her body around
gainst his. It was a simple matter to wrap his arms around her and
ear her down, somewhat more complicated to work his wet trou-
ers off. The mud and water squelched up around them. She ground

herself down into it and bit his shoulder and wrapped her limb
around him like vines.

The sun came out again, sliding toward evening but still brig
and warm. Bethsy took his soaked trousers and her mud-crust
body down to the clear water and pebbled shore of the strea
Grant fished in the pond for the rest of their clothing but only fou
her long-tailed blouse.

He climbed back over the old beaver dam that had made t
pond and found Bethsy standing in the knee-high stream, her hea
back and her eyes closed, wrists behind her neck and her bac
arched, pointing her body at the sun.

She opened her eyes and turned toward him as he picked his wa
across the slick stones. He held her blouse draped artfully
accidentally in front of his groin, embarrassed that he was mo
embarrassed at his nakedness than she was at hers. Just before l
reached her they heard the sound of hooves clopping on ston
From somewhere around the twist in the stream gulley ahead
them, several horses were walking toward them.

There was no place to hide. Grant could see clearly in his mir
the five young Assiniboines that he and Bostonais had encountere
last fall, see the delight on their faces when they rounded the ber
and found him and Bethsy naked and unarmed, but he could se
no place to hide. He thought of the beaver dam—they could hide
the water behind it. He grabbed Bethsy's wrist just as the horse
came around the twist in the bank.

There were five of them. The two in front had métis trackers
their backs. Behind them rode John Richards McKay. He was lea
ing Bethsy's horse and Grant's—it must have followed hers in
Brandon House.

They stopped their horses. John Richards did his best to preten
to be looking in his sister's direction without really looking at he
His two companions were doing exactly the opposite. He sai
"Your horses . . . came in without you. I was—with the fire an
all—I was worried."

His sister said: "It's good of you to worry, John, but as you ca
see I'm still intact"—she smiled a wicked little smile—"more
less."

"Well, good—that is . . . I'd best be getting back, then." H
leaned down and looped their horses' reins around the end of
snag, then turned his horse. The other two reluctantly dragged the
eyes away and followed him.

It was sunset by the time Grant and Bethsy sleepwalked the

horses through the gates of Brandon House, the sky a cavern of purple glass raked with feathers of incandescent orange and red. The chief trader's quarters were deserted. Bethsy scraped together a stewpot full of odds and ends, and they fell on it like Huns on Rome. John Richards came in and drifted around the edges of the room as though looking for something, then finally sat down at the end of the table. Bethsy asked if he'd eaten, and he said he had.

Grant leaned back from his scraped plate and arched his shoulders over the rim of the chair back. He asked John Richards how long it would take to ride from Brandon House to the mouth of the Pembina, "following the course of the rivers so I won't lose my way."

"Oh, eight or nine days, I should expect, depending on the horse."

"Ah. I suppose then I'd best get started by the end of the week at the latest. Bostonais's waiting to meet me to go hunting. I'll have to replace my rifle—well, 'replacing' it won't be possible—I just hope they have something a notch above trade guns in stock at—"

Bethsy stood up and said crisply, "Perhaps you'd best get started now," and went to the door, leaving her gravy-encrusted plate where it lay.

"Pardon me? What do you—"

She pushed the door open and threw it shut behind her. Grant turned from the still shuddering doorframe to John Richards and elevated his shoulders and eyebrows in the universal symbol for "Women—go figure." John Richards didn't return it.

CHAPTER 35

Kate was standing on the rough and rickety excuse for a table that her husband had knocked together, its legs still upholstered with slick green poplar bark, stacking sticks to make a rough and rickety excuse for a chimney. The way people built chimneys in Rupertsland was to lay up a skeletal framework of sticks and then cover it over with a mixture of riverbank clay and chopped grass. Working her way up in sections of half a foot or so, alternating between a pile of amputated poplar branches and her bucket of wet clay, she'd just reached the broad hole they'd left open in the roof until the chimney was done.

She poked her head up through the hole and rested her arms on the rim, gazing down across the lawn of their sod roof onto the Red River flowing north from its loop around Point Douglas. The thick canopy of trees on either bank bowed in over the broad, brown lazy current ambling toward Lake Winnipeg. On the west bank, a few slim curls of smoke drifted up from the lush green to dissipate in the wind. Although she couldn't see them, she knew that hidden in among the belt of trees there were other squared-log shanties like her own, dotted every few hundred yards or so along the west bank for two miles north of Point Douglas. Along the network of paths worn through the undergrowth there would be women bustling back and forth from house to house, borrowing this and lending that and asking and giving advice on questions such as whether they were mixing in too much grass with their fireplace clay for stiffening.

The house on Point Douglas was half a mile from its nearest neighbor. Kate would have to rely on her own judgment about how much grass was needed to hold the clay in place until the fire baked it hard. If she guessed wrong and the whole contraption burst into flames halfway through February, she and her husband would have no one to blame but her.

She told herself that all the neighborly consultations going on along the west bank were only a collection of blind guesses reinforcing each other. The sooner she got the chimney built and started a fire in the hearth, the sooner she'd know if she'd guessed right or wrong. She pulled in her arms and ducked her head back down. She had just stooped forward to climb down off the table and fetch up the bucket of clay when a clawed hand dug into the pit of her stomach and twisted hard, doubling her over and dropping her down onto her knees on the tabletop. She clutched the edges of the table and held on as the claws sawed through her. When it let go, it left a serrated ache that seemed petty by comparison.

She stayed where she was—hunched on the tabletop with her legs doubled under her and her arms splayed out—teaching herself how to breathe again, groping for an explanation of the pain. Her first thought was the potatoes. For all that they'd come out of the ground as swollen and juicy as something from the old songs of lost crofters feasted under faerie hills, perhaps there was some kind of poison in the ground here that had soaked into them. Or it might be the fever that she'd nursed out of so many others finally catching up with her.

Then she laughed as it suddenly came clear to her. It was only the baby. After four months with no discomfort or outward signs, she should have been expecting that when he finally made his presence known, it would come hard. With that understanding, the character of the pain changed. She would just have to get used to it. She could feel a limpid smile taking charge of her mouth and a flush warming her cheeks, part and parcel of the whispering conspiracy between her body and the cosmos. She let go of the table and straightened up.

Something warm and glutinous seeped down between her thighs. She screamed and flung herself down flat on the tabletop, shooting her legs out behind her.

There was no one within earshot to help her. She thought of climbing down off the table and running to Surgeon White at Fort Douglas, then saw a picture of a half-formed bloody head pushing down between her running legs. She stayed where she was, her eyelids alternately flaring open and clamping shut, and tried to think between the bells clanging in her ears and the whimpering animal noises coming out of her throat.

She reached out her hands and took hold of the sides of the table again to rock it from side to side, still holding her body and her squeezed-together legs down flat on the tabletop. Finally it tipped over and spilled her onto the dirt floor. Like a beached seal, she pulled herself across the floor to the doorway, dragging her legs behind her.

There were no trees in front of the house, only a scythed patch of weeds and grass and sweet clover sloping down to the river. Holding her hips flat on the dirt threshold, she planted the palms of her hands on the ground and pushed up to the height of her arms. She peered through the green haze of decapitated grass necks. A canoe drifted around the end of the point, with two dark-skinned, black-haired men slumped lazily inside dangling fish lines. She shouted at them in Gaelic. One of them raised his hat brim languidly and glanced in her general direction, then lowered it again.

She put her weight onto her left arm, waved her right arm over her head, and tried again in English: "Here! Please! Help me!"

This time both turned their heads toward her, but that was all. She dredged her mind for any scraps of French that might have stuck there. *"Aiday!"*

They dropped their fish lines, unshipped their paddles, and

started paddling toward her. She waved them off, pointing back the way they'd come. "No! Fort Douglas! Doctor! Husband! Sutherland!" However much of that they got, they turned the prow into the current and paddled frantically upstream around the point.

She unlocked her left elbow joint and flopped down onto the dirt. She ground the side of her head back and forth against the trampled grass in front of the doorway, bits of plant stems and soil clinging to the sodden skin around her eye, and chanted in a cracked voice: "Please Lord please do not let my baby die I know he was conceived in sin I know I have been wicked and proud but he has done no harm to anyone please do not let him die."

To repay the colonial establishment for the squared and seasoned logs he'd taken from their stockpile to build the walls of his house, Sandy was working in the saw pit—a machine whose component parts consisted of a deep trench, a two-handled whipsaw, and two men. The upper man got sore forearms, a crick in his back, and stiff knees from straddling the trench. The low man got sore biceps, a crick in his neck, and all the sawdust he could eat.

The upper man he was paired with was his brother-in-law, John MacPherson. For the thousandth time that day, Sandy pulled the saw blade down to the bottom of his stroke and then relaxed his arms to let his hands ride John's stroke back up. John was standing ready, his back stooped and his hands around the saw pull, but he was gazing back over his shoulder in the direction of a distant hubbub of voices.

Sandy said breathlessly: "If you have had enough, then stand back for another man and I will work him into the ground as well." Then he looked around at the walls of the trench and added, "Though I suppose if anybody has been worked into the ground . . ."

John turned to face him with a nervous expression. "I think it may be Katy. . . ."

Sandy let go of the saw handle and reached for the lip of the trench. When John took hold of his forearm, Sandy pushed off with his good leg and half vaulted out of the trench.

A cluster of colony men was standing on the riverbank, trying to translate into Gaelic from the Gallic patois of two men shouting from a canoe. Sandy picked out something about *la maison sur la pointe* and a woman lying in the doorway. He started running. John called after him about going to fetch the doctor. He shouted back over his shoulder: "And Joan MacLeod!"

He cursed himself for not being able to run any faster than a
lop-legged hobble, and for not taking one of the Indian ponies that
the colonial establishment had offered up for sale, and for the thousand little cruelties and cold responses he'd exchanged with his wife
in their few months together. The question of whether or not she'd
read his deed back on the ship now seemed childishly spiteful.

He came out of the pathway through the woods breathing hard,
pelted across the field of green barley and over the rows of potatoes,
rounded the corner of the house, and found her lying on her belly
half out of the doorway. She raised her head as he came toward
her. Her face was puffy and wet with tears, her eyes red-rimmed
and glistening.

He sat down on the ground beside her, stretching his right leg
out stiff, and tentatively reached one hand toward her face. Her
hands came up and snatched it halfway, gripping it fiercely. She
said: "I am sorry, I am sorry . . ." The words were run together,
uncontrolled, harsh gasps puncturing the air.

He reached out his other hand to stroke her hair. "Ssh. Did I
say you had done anything you need be sorry for?" There was
something unnatural about the placement of her legs, lying stretched
out and pressed together in the shadowed interior. "Did you have
a fall?"

"No, it is the baby. . . ."

He saw now that where the shadow of the door frame cut off the
sunlight across the back of her skirt there was a stain of blood. His
body jerked backward as though to remove itself from the concept
of something dead inside the crucible of life. She snatched his hand
back and pressed it to her forehead, saying again: "I am sorry, I
am sorry . . ."

"It is not your fault. How could it be your fault? John is bringing
Joan MacLeod and the doctor. They will know what to do." He
asked her if she wanted to be carried to the bed, but she didn't want
to move until someone who knew about such things was there to
advise her. He asked her if she wanted a drink of water, but she
just clasped his hand tighter and shook her head. He asked her if
she was in pain, and she said only a little. He thought of saying that
they would have other babies but didn't; she didn't seem to want to
believe that the child inside her was beyond hope.

He twisted himself around in the dirt so she could pillow her
head on his leg. All he could do was wait, with one hand clasped
in hers and the other resting sideways on her temple to shield her
eyes from the sun. His own gaze drifted up and down the muddy

waves of the river and skimmed unseeing along the treetops of th
far shore; nothing registered in his vision until he settled once agai
on the red-gold tangles glinting in the sun and the long, large
capable hands now wrapped so limply around his own. He curse
himself again and again for being such a feeble excuse for a mar
to be able to do nothing but sit idly by, holding her hands an
wishing impotently that he could draw her pain out through ther
into his own. He wondered in horror at himself, that he could hav
spent the last month lost inside his self-induced nightmare of grasp
ing, lying women and phony pregnancies.

He heard a horse crashing through the bush behind the house
and a moment later a saddleless Indian pony burst around the cor
ner of the house. Clinging to its neck was Joan MacLeod. Clingin
to her and hauling back wildly on the nose halter was John Mac
Pherson. He managed to get the pony to stop, then slid down an
helped Joan MacLeod to the ground.

Joan MacLeod was the closest thing the colony had to a midwife
an old wise woman in the Highland tradition of herbs and poultice
and possets—a fat old badger with a waddle and a squint and a tas
for some of her own remedies. She looked down at Kate, her eye
traveling up and down the prone body, then spat and said to Sandy
"Get away."

"Is she . . . ?"

"How would I know till I look? Get away. This is women
business. You don't have the stomach for it."

Sandy eased his hand out of Kate's grip, eased his leg out from
under her head, and started toward the riverbank. John followe
him, saying: "Surgeon White is off at Gunn's. Someone went
fetch him. . . ."

Sandy tuned out John's voice to listen to Joan MacLeod behin
him saying softly: "Now, dearie, did you have a fall?" Then th
river drowned her out.

They sat on shore rocks with their hands in their pockets an
watched the river roll by. John said hesitantly: "Katy is strong. Sh
can take everything the world decides to throw at her."

"Nobody can take everything the world decides to throw
them."

There was a bellow from the top of the bank. "Stupid girl. Stu
pid, stupid, stupid girl. John MacPherson! Get up here and tak
me home." The men came timorously up the bank. "And kee
the horse slow this time—I hope your mother taught you more abou

being a horse rider than she taught your sister about being a woman.''

Kate was still lying on her stomach. Joan MacLeod had walked away from her. She turned back and kicked the ground in Kate's direction, sending a spray of dust and plant bits over her. "Get up. I told you there was nothing wrong with you except your body coming back to itself after a winter of strain and hunger.''

Sandy stepped between them and put his hand out as though to push Joan MacLeod away. She stepped back and barked at him: "Did you think she was carrying a child? I hope to Christ you were not marrying her to do the honorable thing, although nothing would surprise me from you two after this. Such a pair of full-grown fools I hope I never get galloped half to death for again. Give me a hand up here, John MacPherson. Get your back into it.''

John managed to get her up on the horse, then took the halter and walked back the way they'd come, tossing mystified looks over his shoulder. Sandy looked down at his wife. She was sitting up slowly, looking down at the ground, one hand cowling her face. She said in a small, thin voice: "I thought . . . I *knew* . . . four months without—'' She looked up at him. "What was I supposed to think?''

He didn't know. She looked away again. He turned his head and looked across the river, then back in the direction of Fort Douglas. Already a path was being worn through the weeds and bush by his comings and goings to the fort and his fields. He said: "I had best get back to work.''

CHAPTER 36

Grant came awake slowly, with not much enthusiasm and no prior intent. There was a glowing sky in front of his eyes. It was that glow, making a red light through his eyelids, that had done the damage. It did seem strange, though, now that he'd pried his eyelids open, that the sky should be a uniform milky white with a blue sun at its zenith.

His right arm was still asleep. Perhaps it had something to do
with the pony that had fallen on it. On closer inspection it wasn't a
pony after all, but a high-boned, brown-skinned girl with a mane
as thick and coarse and black as any mustang's, although a good
deal longer.

The milky-white sky with the blue sun turned out to be the inside
of a tepee glowing with diffused daylight and a bright blue circle
of sky showing through the smokehole at its apex. The girl across
his arm was Sings to Herself, daughter of the extended-family métis
hunting party that Grant and Bostonais and the Falcons had met up
with fording the Turtle River yesterday. She was lying on her back
with her half of the striped wool blanket wrapped ineffectually
around her left leg. If his eyesight and memory served him well,
her hips and breasts and mouth were wider, fuller, heavier, and
riper than Miss Bethsy McKay's. Thinking back a few hours, he
was reminded that she was also a good deal more pliant in every
way. He certainly felt a good deal tenderer toward Sings to Herself
in the same sense that one felt more tender toward a kitten than a
grown cat.

He managed to sit up, ungently jerking his wooden arm from
under Sings to Herself's gently snoring head. She didn't notice. All
over the circular patch of ground enclosed by the tent there were
fur-covered, lumpy archipelagoes and islands denoting Sings to
Herself's slumbering aunts and uncles and siblings and cousins.
Grant's arm was beginning to tingle unpleasantly and his head to
do a good deal more than tingle and a good deal more than unpleasantly. If they were still nearby the Turtle River, he might drink it.

He scraped his clothing together into a bundle and crimped his
arm across the bundle against his chest. On hand and knees like a
three-legged dog, he threaded his way between the sleepers to the
circular, flapped orifice of the tent.

It was not pleasant outside. The sun was too bright, and the birds
were singing loudly and the midsummer flowers were brutally vi-
brant. He pulled on his trousers and turned a cautious circle. In the
blue V between the two white cones there was the distant red and
white of the new flag. He wove his way toward it.

The flag was stuck to the tip of the tent where Bostonais and the
rest of the party had slept. They had breakfasted and were peeling
the skin off the tent and unhobbling the horses. Another five minutes and there wouldn't have been a flag to orient himself to.

They were fortuitously over the ridge and gone before there was
any sign of stirring around the tents of Sings to Herself's family

Not that Grant had any regrets or second thoughts, but he decidedly did not want to cope with good-byes just now. They would meet again.

They traveled southwest along the edge of what Bostonais told him was Sissiton country. It seemed that the Sissitons were allied with the Sioux, or Dakota nation, but weren't exactly Sioux or part of any other nation. It was all a bit much for him in his present state, but he was quite clear on the fact that they didn't want to run across any Sissitons or Sioux or Dakotas who considered the buffalo who roamed this section of the High Plains their property.

By noon that day Grant was already perking up. By evening of the next day he was wondering if his sleeping robes wouldn't feel a good deal less empty with Sings to Herself in them. A week earlier he would have attached the same yearning to Bethsy McKay. It occurred to him that one could only be in want of what one did not have. He suspected he was growing wise.

On the fourth day Bostonais and Falcon and François were all certain, by various signs that Grant couldn't see, that they were about to strike the trail of the herd. Before they did, though, they saw a very thin column of black smoke toward the eastern radius of the horizon. They veered in that direction, although again Grant didn't know why—he'd thought they were supposed to avoid other human inhabitants—but he kept his mouth shut and his horse in line. Falcon and François were looking grim—and Bostonais's expression was darker than usual, which was saying something. Mary and Marguerite looked harrowed and fiercely hushed any of the children who let out a peep.

The column of smoke grew wider but hazier, like a campfire dying out. The far lip of a coulee separated itself from the prairie ahead. The rest of the party reined in their horses. Bostonais, Falcon, and François dismounted and handed their reins to Alex. Grant did the same. They crouched and started walking forward. When Grant started after them, Bostonais turned and pointed him to stay where he was. He watched them make their way toward the coulee ahead, dropping to the ground and crawling for the last twenty yards. There was a moment when all three of them were prone, peering over the near edge of the gully, then Bostonais slowly stood up. The other two rose to their feet more slowly. Grant walked forward. A shift in the wind drifted the smoke, now barely a gray mist, toward him. It tasted of burned pork and singed hair.

There was one dead pony in the coulee. One of Sings to Herself's uncles had a buffalo runner that was the same yellow shade. There were other dead things around it, among the scattered bits of tent skin and broken camp gear. One of Grant's brothers-in-law, or perhaps it was Bostonais, put a hand on his arm. He shook it off and walked down the hill.

They had staked her out spread-eagled across a convenient rock. He recognized her breasts—they had slit her dress up both sides and tied it over her head. Half the length of a lance haft was sticking out of where they'd got tired of sticking up everything else they could think of.

There was a very businesslike, metallic series of sounds behind him. He stood up and turned around. The horses and the women and children had come up. Bostonais, Falcon, François, and Alex were checking their loads and their flints and strapping on their knives. Grant said: "They . . . How could they . . . Pigs . . . What kind of a world . . ."

To reach Grant's jaw with the back of his hand, Bostonais had to put the full extension of his arm behind it in an upward arc. Grant looked up from the ground, blinking away the sudden mist that had settled across his eyes. Bostonais said: "Is that what you think it should cost them—you talk them to death?"

Grant stood up. Mary was standing nearby, holding the reins of his saddle horse and the leads of his packhorse and buffalo runner. He unstrapped his new rifle, which was a long way below the standard of Messrs. Tatham & Egg but still serviceable, checked the load, and then unfastened the flap of one of the panniers on his packhorse and fished out his pistols. His brothers-in-law and Bostonais and Alex Fraser all tied the long leads of their buffalo runners to a thong at the back of their saddles before mounting their horses. Grant did the same.

They rode west, Bostonais and François periodically leaning down to scan the ground. What they were peering at just looked like scuff marks on the prairie as far as Grant could tell, but the other four came to a general agreement that the Sioux raiding party had only just moved on that morning—after their evening's entertainment—and that there were about a dozen of them. The odds didn't appear to worry anyone.

The sun was almost straight in front of them when Grant's saddle horse gave out. He did what Bostonais and François had done a few miles back—leaped down, tore off the saddle, hurled it onto his buffalo runner, and galloped on using the halter lead for reins. The drumming and jouncing of the horses didn't change. The sky

turned dark overhead while the bands of cloud rimming the horizon
went from yellow to orange to dull red. Against that red, black
silhouettes appeared—a herd of twenty or thirty horses, half of
them with riders on their backs.

There was an explosion to Grant's right—a blaze of sparks and
a burst of burned powder smell. One of the silhouetted centaur
figures up ahead somersaulted into oblivion. Grant glanced to his
right and saw Bostonais lowering his rifle. Grant held his own fire;
he knew he was nowhere near as good a shot from a gallop. Falcon
and François brought up their rifles. Several of the silhouetted
horsemen turned in their saddles and fired back on the run—red
sparks against black silhouettes against the red sky. François
grunted, "Merde!" and pitched sideways but pulled himself back
up in the saddle and kept on.

Bostonais swerved his horse to one side and leaned out from his
saddle with his rifle clubbed out by the barrel. Grant could see a
low, hunched figure moving quickly along the ground; then Bostonais's arm swung out, there was a muffled crunch, and Bostonais
was galloping ahead again, anchoring the right flank of their fanned-
out, five-wide front.

Grant brought up his rifle, picked out one of the horsemen ahead,
and—remembering the lesson Bostonais had just given—dropped
his sights and fired at the horse. The light was gone. He clamped
his rifle under his left arm, drew his pistols, and fired them both.

There was nothing ahead of them but night and stars now. They
reined their horses in, dismounted, and threw themselves onto the
ground, gasping until their breath came back. Falcon tore the left
sleeve off his shirt and tied it around François's leg. When the
moon came up they hauled themselves back up onto their saddles,
turned their horses' heads, and let them walk. On the way back,
Bostonais made them stop six times. After the first time, Grant
learned not to look.

They recovered their saddle horses along the way, all but
Falcon's, which had burst its heart. When they got back to the
coulee they found that Mary and Marguerite had wrapped the bodies up as decently as possible and dug the beginnings of a wide
grave. They built the fire up high to dig by, taking breathing spells
to stand turnabout at guard duty on the rim of the coulee. Before
the moon went down, they had filled in the hole over Sings to
Herself and her family.

When the last spadeful of earth was tamped down, they all stood
around the mound of naked earth trying to think of something to

say. Grant said: "Fear no more the heat o' the sun, Nor the furious winter's rages; Thou thy worldly task hast done, home art gone and ta'en thy wages . . ." The rest of it seemed too flippant for such a cruel death, so he shifted to "We are such stuff as dreams are made on, and our little life is rounded with a sleep."

That seemed to satisfy the others, except for Bostonais, who kicked at the side of the mound and growled: "Before you cross the river, Gray Eyes"—which was the name of Sings to Herself's father—"look back over your shoulder, and I bet you'll see the ones that did this following right on your heels. You might have to look close, though—some of them got a few pieces missing."

As soon as the sky in the east began to lighten, they moved on. Two days farther south they caught up with a segment of the herd.

The passing of the days first wore away the numbness that had surrounded the shock of finding Sings to Herself, then gradually dissipated the horror. Summer was gone by the time they wound their train of loaded-down packhorses back to Fort Pembina, facing the HBC and Selkirk colony outpost of Fort Daer across the mouth of the Pembina River. Fort Pembina was ringed with the tents of dozens of hunting parties like their own, drifting in to trade their summer harvest of pemmican and tallow and hides.

Grant's mind kept coming back to the same question. He and four other métis hunters had chased three times as many Sioux and dropped six of them while the rest kept on running. There were hundreds of métis hunters here and thousands of them scattered across the *pays d'en haut*. Why did only small family groups of métis hunters go out every summer to skulk along the edges of the Plains tribes' hunting grounds, some of them never coming back?

There appeared to be a number of varying opinions on the subject, which made for several nights of lively campfire dissertations. What Grant found most surprising, though, was that apparently it was a question no one had asked before.

one has to organize defences here, just in case. Which is sometim...

CHAPTER 37

West of Lake of the Woods, where the rivers wound through open country, news traveled faster than canoes. The *engagés* at Fort Gibraltar knew that their new bourgeois was on his way in with the fall brigade a week before he got there. Grant had come up to Fort Gibraltar and packed off Josephte and her son with the Qu'Appelle brigade and then hung on to meet her late husband's replacement.

Grant and Bostonais were leaning against the front gates of Fort Gibraltar, taking in the late August sunshine, when the shout came down from the watchtower: *"Bateaux! Sur la Rouge, à la pointe!"* *Engagés* boiled out of the gates. He and Bostonais drifted over to the riverbank to have a look. A peal of music suddenly burst out from a diabolical instrument that must have had every loon within earshot taking down its shingle.

In the prow of the lead canoe was a piper in bonnet and belted plaid. At the midthwarts was a British officer in a gold-braided scarlet tunic and a cocked hat. The officer bounded ashore and mounted the bank in long strides. As he crested the bank Grant finally recognized him, by his height and the mane of gold curls spilling out from under his hat: Duncan Cameron. "Grant! Good to see you, lad."

"And you, Mister Cameron."

"Let's make it 'Captain' Cameron, shall we?" he said, punctuating it with a wink.

"Have you left the company, then?"

"What? Not a bit of it—I'm the new bourgeois here."

"Oh. Congratulations. But . . ." He gestured feebly at the uniform.

"We all have to do our duty when our country calls. We're still at war with the bloody Yankees, you know. It may be winding down, but you never know what tricks they might get up to. Some-

231

one has to organize defenses here, just in case. Which is somethin
I've been planning to speak to you about. . . ."

"Me?"

"Just so. Come on along inside and— What's this?" He halte
his triumphal progress to peer at a somewhat weather-worn squa
of parchment nailed to the gatepost.

"Another proclamation from Governor MacDonell." This on
informed the inhabitants of the country enclosed by Lord Selkirk
land grant that it was now illegal to hunt buffalo from horsebac
Apparently the contingent of colonists who'd gone down to Fo
Daer to hunt meat hadn't had much luck—perhaps because th
métis hunters were driving the herds too far out onto the prairie
perhaps because they hadn't learned much about hunting buffalo
the Orkneys or the Scottish Highlands. The governor hadn't deigne
to include his reasons in his edict, but it wouldn't have made mu
difference if he had.

Duncan Cameron said: "I'm damned." From his tone of voi
and the expression on his face it was difficult to judge whether
was irate or delighted. "Here, you"—the red-sleeved beam of a
arm swung out to collar a passing *engagé*—"fetch me a mallet an
four nails, there's a good lad." Then he yanked down the governor
proclamation, folded it up neatly, and slipped it into an inside pock
of his uniform coat.

From the same pocket he brought out a slender, oilcloth-wrappe
packet, rather like a waterproof envelope, and flipped open the fla
Inside were several folded sheets of official-looking vellum.
selected one, snapped it open briskly, and put the packet back
his pocket, by which time the *engagé* had come pelting up with
square-headed hammer and a handful of nails. His new bourgeo
said: "I said *four* nails. Do you have any idea what it costs us
move a keg of nails here from Fort William? Well, just make su
you put the rest of them back. I'll probably mash half a dozen
them sticking this up anyway. Here, Grant, be a good fellow an
hold this in place. . . ."

Grant pinned his thumb against the top of the paper and held
there while Duncan Cameron nailed it in place. It was a captain
commission in His Majesty's Corps of Voyageurs, signed by i
colonel, the Honourable William MacGillivray. Grant had be
under the impression that the Voyageur Corps had been disbande
shortly after their first and only action at Michilimackinac, b
apparently he'd been mistaken.

"There!" Captain Cameron tossed the hammer back to the *engagé*. "Now, let's go in and have a dram and—"

"Please?" It was a female voice, coming from behind them. "Please, sirs?" Grant turned around. She was a very short, rounded, dark young woman. About five months rounded, at a rough guess. "Please . . . where John Pritchard?"

Grant said: "Of course—Mrs. Pritchard. Forgive me, I didn't . . ."

She gave him a quick, shy glimmer of a smile and ducked her head, then turned her eyes back to Duncan Cameron. "Where . . . ?"

"Little Pritchard? Montreal by now, I should expect."

"Montreal?"

"Yes. He seemed to be under the impression that he could close out his account and his shares with the company at Fort William, but of course all the back ledgers are in Montreal."

"When he come back?"

"Back? To the *pays d'en haut*? Not this season. Even if they manage to get the figures all balanced in jig time, the rivers will be frozen. And even when the traveling season starts up again, I don't know how he'd plan to go about getting here. He certainly won't be traveling in any of the company brigades since he's no longer with the company. Now, if you'll excuse us—come along, Grant."

Once they'd got past the gates and were crossing the quadrangle toward the bourgeois's house, Captain Cameron said: "It'll be a misty morning in hell before you'll see John Pritchard back in the *pays d'en haut*. I've seen Will MacGillivray rear back on his hind legs and roar from time to time, but never like this rendezvous. When it came out that Pritchard had watched them waltz into Fort La Souris and waltz back out with our provisions, and that Le Bras Croché had knuckled under to the blockade, I thought we'd have to reshingle the Great Hall."

"I suppose if Mister Pritchard's sold out his shares, he should have enough ready money to hire a guide and voyageurs to bring him back next season. . . ."

"Oh, I'm sure he could spare the cash, but he's only got one kin."

"I don't understand."

"He's planning to go over to the other side, and take with him the one thing that bloody colony's the shortest on. After fifteen years in the *pays d'en haut*, even a dunderhead like Pritchard's bound to've picked up some kind of notion of what's what out here.

So, hiring a guide and voyageurs is one thing; traveling two thousand miles through country that belongs to the people he's betrayin
is another.''

"You don't think anyone would—"

"The point isn't what I think, it's what Little Johnny Pritcha
thinks. In the short time you had together, you may have notice
that he ain't exactly the Lion of the North.''

They sat down in the bourgeois's quarters, now denuded of mo
of the wall hangings and souvenirs that had been part of John Wills
home, and Cameron called the fort cook to tap them out a pitch
of wine. "Drinking quality, mind you—not the vinegar for mixin
high wine." He had a great deal to ask Grant and was extreme
interested in how the summer hunt had gone, extremely affected b
the brutal murder of Sings to Herself and her family—"I knew o
Gray Eyes from the old days"—and extremely interested in Grant
concept of a new nation. *Engagés* and clerks and *gouvernails* ke
bustling in and out with questions about manifest lists and stowin
cargo. The bourgeois dealt with them briskly, as though they we
annoying but unavoidable interjections from a mundane world th
was far less important than his conversation with Grant.

Their circle grew a little wider. Grant would mention a name
the context of some anecdote, and Mister Cameron would sudden
snap his fingers: "Of course, Bostonais! He was standing on th
bank with you when we hove in this afternoon. Jean Claude—be
good fellow and see if Bostonais Pangman's still lurking about, an
ask him to come in and join us for a glass of wine." Then o
François Deschamps had to be hunted up, and Seraphim Lama
and Alex Fraser.

It was quite late in the evening when Captain Cameron said: "
have been empowered to do a little commissioning of my own.
Rising to his full height, he headed over to the cassettes and *pièc*
stacked along one wall. Grant had never seen so much luggage an
personal gear; the *engagés* had been bustling in and out with it a
afternoon. Half the *canots du nord* in the brigade must have bee
loaded with the bourgeois's private effects.

"As you may or may not be aware," Cameron threw over h
shoulder as he flipped through a ring of keys and studied the li
of cassettes, "it is quite customary in His Majesty's more far-flun
possessions for the officer commanding to commission officers
lead irregular troops of light cavalry or rangers from the local po
ulation, to help hold the line against foreign invasions until an a
equate force of regulars can be shipped to the scene." He unlock

a cassette, raised its lid, said, "Nope," and went on to the next.
"I have been instructed to commission four lieutenants, one for
each district of the *pays d'en haut*, to raise columns of irregular
horse from among the half-breed population—or, as Mister Grant
more aptly puts it, the 'New Nation.' Ah, here we are. . . ."

He had unlocked half a dozen cassettes by now, and the one he'd
been looking for had a length of red cloth folded over the contents.
He shook it out, and it turned into a military tunic with gold frogs
and gold braid and gold piping on the black cuffs and collar.

"Monsieur Lamarr, if you will be good enough to accept this,
and His Majesty's commission . . . And it seemed to me that Mister William Shaw would be a good choice for the English River
district, and Monsieur Bonhomme Montour for the Pembina. The
major difficulty, however, is that the logical choice for the
Qu'Appelle and Fort des Prairies troop has responded so well to
the fresh air and hearty fare of the *pays d'en haut* that we thought
we'd need two uniforms to fit across his shoulders. However, we
did manage to requisition one size triple-X wide—if you would try
this on, Mister Grant?"

It did fit across his shoulders, although he couldn't manage to
get it fastened over his chest. Captain Cameron winked and said:
"All the better to show off your lace jabot."

There was the swearing-in to do and papers to be written up.
Captain Cameron was all for rousting out one of the junior clerks,
until Grant pointed out that that was, after all, what the company
had educated him for. They found some ink and pens and paper in
a drawer, and Grant took Duncan Cameron's dictation. Seraphim
Lamarr said: "Who do you figure we'll have to defend the country
from?"

"It's more your country than anyone else's, so I suppose you'll
have some say in that."

Alex Fraser said: "Do you really think we're going to be invaded?"

"Some would say you already have been."

Another skirl of pipes came up the river two days later. Grant
climbed to the watchtower to have a look. A squadron of York boats
was rounding Point Douglas, heading in to the landing stage under
the colony's shore battery. It was difficult to pick out details at that
distance, but there seemed to be a number of women and children
salted in among the cargo.

The ladder behind him creaked under the ascent of Captain Cam-

eron, who had temporarily discarded his uniform in favor of buckskin trousers and a checked wool shirt. He looked out at the
immigrants piling onto shore and shook his head. "Another contingent next year, and the year after that . . . At this rate I shouldn't
wonder that they'll soon have taken up both banks of the Red from
the forks all the way to the lake."

"They have to go somewhere."

"I suppose. And where will the Falcons and the Bostonais Pangmans go—to the Highlands of Scotland?"

"The *pays d'en haut* is a big country."

"I suppose. I suppose that's what Sings to Herself and Gray Eyes
tried to say to the Sioux. At this rate the New Nation isn't going to
get much older. It is quite a remarkable flowering, actually—if
you'd been here as long as I have, you'd be just as astounded,
although it took your fresh eyes to point out the change. There've
always been métis in the *pays d'en haut*—or since long before my
time, at least—little pockets dotted here and there among the Plains
tribes or the flotsam and jetsam around the forts. But suddenly in
this generation—your generation—the numbers have jumped to the
point where they've become a population in themselves. Quite remarkable.

"Oh—before you head back west to take up your duties in the
Qu'Appelle, there is one little matter I'd appreciate your help in. I
have warrants for the arrest of Miles MacDonell and John Spenser,
issued by one of the justices of the peace that the courts in Lower
Canada swore in to keep order in the Indian territories. . . ."

"What have they done?"

"Who?"

"The sheriff and the governor. I didn't realize there was—"

"Done? Done? You were here at the start of the summer. They're
to be arraigned in the Canadas for unlawful seizure of private property, not to mention threatening with cannons—the list goes on and
on. MacDonell's cleverly took himself off to York Factory, but we
should be able to get Spenser without too much trouble."

It was no trouble at all. Sheriff Spenser went fishing at Catfish
Creek and got caught himself. The trouble came in transporting
him to Bas de La Rivière, where he would be held until an opportunity came up to ship him east. They set off from Fort Gibraltar
in two *canots du nord*, Captain Cameron at the midthwarts of the
first and Grant guarding Sheriff Spenser in the second. When they
came parallel to the gun battery in front of Fort Douglas, a young
man with bushy side-whiskers leaped up on top of the embrasure

and shouted: "Stop or we'll blow you out of the water!" A number of men stood up behind him, each holding a smoldering linstock over the touchhole of a cannon.

A voice behind Grant hollered in French: "Don't shoot! We'll give him back to you! Head in to shore. . . ."

"No!" Grant whipped his head around, saw it was old Jean Claude MacGregor the *gouvernail*, and said to him: "Do you panic so easy, Jean Claude?"

Both canoes were naked in the water, no more than a hundred yards from the cannons. The mouths were of various sizes, from a foot to a few inches, and their lips were of varying colors, from black cast-iron field pieces to brass swivel guns. The sloped-earth breastworks had grown quite verdant over the summer, with a smattering of purple-and-white wild asters among the green between the cannon slots.

The *milieus* of both canoes were backing water furiously to hold them hovering in place against the current. With a slight rasp of dryness in the throat, Duncan Cameron boomed out: "This man is under lawful arrest, to be delivered up to the proper authorities for trial. Would you interfere with the exercise of a duly sworn warrant of—"

"He *is* the duly sworn officer of the law here!" the side-whiskered young man screeched back. "You are nothing but kidnappers! These cannons are loaded with grapeshot! If you go one foot farther, I will give the order to fire!"

Grant was certainly no less fond of his own skin than any other man in the canoe and no less appalled or repelled by the prospect of having it shredded by grapeshot. But that very real emotion, rather than overwhelming him, remained an undercurrent. If he'd had any room in him at the moment for self-awareness, he would have been quite surprised at how clearheaded he felt. He called out: "If you let fly with your grapeshot, I suppose it will save Sheriff Spenser from going to trial, but you'll have to strain the river with a sieve to sew him back together. And how will you tell his bits from ours?"

The young man with the side-whiskers looked suddenly doubtful. He resolved it by throwing his arm up in the air and shouting: "You shall not pass!"

Sheriff Spenser screamed, "Don't fire, for the love of God!" and clasped his hands together in a praying posture. "Please, let us pass."

Captain Cameron bellowed, "Fire and be damned to you," and

swept his arm ahead. If the *milieus* had had to take a positive action to follow the implied order, they might not have done so, but all they had to do was pause in their backpaddling and consider whether to follow it or not, by which time the current had carried them on. Grant looked back over his shoulder at the young man with the side-whiskers. He was still standing on the breastworks with his arm up in the air, opening and closing his mouth like a washed-up halibut.

As Grant swiveled his head forward again, he caught a glimpse of someone standing in the shore growth on Point Douglas, a tall woman with red hair. He looked again, but by then she was hidden by the trees.

The current swept them around Point Douglas. The *gouvernails* had to attend to holding them in the midchannel, but everyone else in both canoes was free to collapse and exhale. The laughter was of the same strain, although much more so, as at the end of the *dalles*. Cameron called across at Grant: " 'Strain the river with a sieve'! Lord, Lord . . .''

Grant shouted back: " 'Fire and be damned to you'!'' The entire complement of both canoes was helpless with laughter, with the exception of John Spenser.

Captain Cameron caught his breath enough to say: "When that side-whiskered popinjay's arm went up, two thoughts bounced through my mind. The first was, Here it comes, Duncan—you'll never make old bones, and then, Hell, they ain't exactly young bones anymore.''

Grant's laughter accelerated again along with that of the *engagés*. Despite his privileged inroads to the higher reaches of the company, he had no more of an understanding of Duncan Cameron's position than they. The grizzling in Cameron's gold mane only placed him in that amorphous category of "older generation." It didn't occur to him that there were ramifications to the fact that Duncan Cameron had been an *hivernant* for twenty years.

CHAPTER 38

Kate finally gave in to the admission that it was the middle of the night. She had been lying patiently waiting for the dawn light to start seeping through the interstices in the hand-sawn clapboard shutter at the foot of the bed. She had given up trying to recapture sleep; she was too impatient. Whenever she felt the timid beast stealing close to her, she'd make a grab for it and frighten it away.

The bed wasn't helping. The crisscross ropework her husband had knotted through the frame had been a springy underpinning for the first few weeks, but gradually the ropes had begun to stretch a little and the knots to give a little until it valleyed in the middle like a hammock.

The air was warm and still underneath her husband's snoring. He was lying on his side with his back slumped half onto her. She worked her way out from under him and hauled herself up out of bed to get a drink of water. She inched her way across the belly of night that passed for the inside of their log shanty, anticipating the location of their few sticks of furniture and navigating around them to the door.

Beside the doorway was a sawed segment of tree trunk with a wooden bucket standing on it. She dipped in the tin cup hanging from a thong above it. The instant the water touched her tongue she spat it out. It was river water, left to stand overnight to let the silt sink to the bottom of the bucket. The sediment hadn't settled yet.

Not only was she still thirsty, but now her mouth tasted of clay and river sludge. There was a clear stream of cold water running over clean stones, emptying into the river between the south shoulder of Point Douglas and Fort Douglas. She was sure she'd have no trouble following the path at night; it would be less dark outside than it was in the cabin. She could take the bucket, and they would have fresh water for the morning. She wouldn't even need to fumble

239

around for something to put over her nightdress. Although there
had been a sudden frost last week that had killed most of the standing grain, it had turned summery again since then.

The air outside the closed-in cabin was cool and fresh, sweet
with the smell of scythed hay and clover. She stopped to hurl the
murky excuse for water out of the bucket and then went on her way,
swinging it in time to her long strides. The cold dew on the trampled grass stalks tickled her feet and ankles. Back toward the tip of
the point, a sliver of moon with the shadow of a circle—the new
moon in the old moon's arms—was sliding down into the waiting
fingers of the trees.

There was an intoxicating feeling of freedom, even something
slightly wicked, in walking through the dark woods in her loose
nightdress while the rest of the world slept. It was too bad there
weren't any other homes between theirs and the fort—she would
have liked to imagine some insomniac old woman glancing out the
window and catching a glimpse of the White Specter of Red River
floating through the trees. Within a week of retelling, the bucket
would have been transformed into a severed head, and within another week there would be an entire story detailing whose the head
was, how the ghastly maiden came to be carrying it, and why she'd
been condemned to wander restlessly this pathway under every
waning moon.

Her eye caught a movement in the bush beside her. She glanced
toward it. There was nothing but trees and the shadows of trees.
The moon- and starlight were so pale and deceiving that it was
difficult to tell the branches from their shadows. Something moved
again—a quick, jerky motion with an accompanying rustle of dry
leaves. She tried to recapture the movement, to go over the memory
of what her eyes had registered to determine what it was. The shapes
were indistinct enough to fit themselves to anything her imagination
chose to come up with.

She reminded herself that a moment ago she'd been amusing
herself by mocking the feverish imaginations of insomniac old
women. And then her ears started in. Suddenly the woods were
filled with scrabbling, rustling sounds and tiny high-pitched squeals.

The moon went down. She blundered head on into a screen of
solid bush where the path should be. She stepped back and tried to
retrace her steps to the pathway. The prodding ends of a clump of
willow wands stabbed into her chest and shoulders. She skirted
around it, expecting to come out on the path. In a moment the trees
and undergrowth had closed in all around her.

She set her bucket down bottom up, sat on it, and politely asked her imagination—since it was so bent on finding ways to occupy itself—to imagine a way out of the bush. What it came up with instead was a picture of her husband waking up in the middle of the night alone and rousing the entire colony to search for her with torches, and of her stumbling out of the woods in her nightdress to explain that she'd gone for a drink of water.

She decided to take up her bucket and walk. The belt of trees along the riverbank wasn't all that wide; if she could keep going in one general direction, she'd either come out on the riverbank, the open prairie, or the bank of the creek she'd set off looking for in the first place.

She set off with her free hand held in front of her face—the cliché was true, she couldn't see it—to ward off boughs. Tree roots and fallen branches tried to trip her up; twig ends snatched at her nightdress. She was beginning to shiver; the cool of the earth was working its way up through the soles of her feet.

A tiny bright light danced through the air in front of her, an amber-hot flying ember. It scooped across her vision and winked out. She told her imagination that enough was enough. Then there was another and another, bobbing and dancing and leaving ghost trails of yellow light across her night-swollen pupils. She told herself it wasn't possible, but there they were. Her imagination told her what it would feel like if one of them touched her, burning a hole in her skin or setting her hair on fire.

They were all around her now. Every time she tried to break out of the circle one would zoom in front of her. Then one suddenly appeared right in front of her nose. She swatted at it, hoping that if she hit it only a glancing blow, it wouldn't burn. There was a tiny buzzing sensation against the palm of her hand, but no heat at all. The light went out.

She started forward again. The lights skipped away from her and then vanished into the trees. She was wondering whether anyone would believe her if she told about the lights when she heard singing, soft and low and lazy, off to her right. With old stories of the Men of Peace and the Ban Sidh shrieking through her memory, she moved toward the sound. There was another light in that direction. It flickered, but it didn't move.

She came to the edge of the woods. Spread out in front of her was the black plate of the prairie with the vault of stars above it. The light was a campfire built by somebody who knew his business—just large enough to cast a glow of warmth all night long with

a minimum of feeding. The flame light showed the shapes of hobbled horses browsing beyond the fire. Around it, lounging with
their backs against saddle-padded rocks, or curled on their sides
with their heads propped on their elbows, or sitting cross-legged
staring into the fire, were half a dozen métis hunters and three of
their women. The firelight flashed on gold earrings, brass-studded
belts, and polished gun barrels. Two of the women had a gypsy
look about them: brass bracelets and embroidered velvet, bright
silk scarves wound through waves of blue-black hair. The third
woman—who looked to be no more than fifteen—wore no orna-
ments besides the beading on her white skin dress, and her black
hair hung straight. One of the cross-legged men was leading a low-
pitched song in the throaty, thick-voweled métis French that tasted
of sage and moosemeat and wildflowers.

Looking out at them through a frame of poplar leaves, they
seemed to Kate to be as much a part of the land as the rocks and
trees. She wondered if a group of Sutherlanders would have looked
that way to an Englishman or a Lowlander traveling through the
Highlands in the days when the Clans were still the Clans.

She pushed through the last fringe of bush and started toward
the fire. Heads swiveled to face the white shape floating out of the
woods toward them. One of the men reached for his shotgun, another crossed himself. A third lumbered to his feet, his looming
bulk blotting out half the firelight. Even with half his face in darkness, she recognized him by the blunt, broad nose and the massive
cheekbones jutting out of the coarse black beard.

As she drew closer, a couple of the men still sitting began to
crack jokes in French and Cree at the man who'd crossed himself,
springing laughter out of the others. She stopped in front of Bostonais Pangman and said in Gaelic: "I have lost my way. Might
you be good enough to show me the path back to the colony?"

The boulder head cocked itself to one side, but the expression
on its face didn't change. The shoulders gave a little shrug.

She turned to the others and repeated herself. They all stared
back at her blankly. She tried in English, but that got no response
either. One of the lounging men, a skinny one with eyes like a
snake's, lowered his lids and muttered something out of the side of
his mouth at the man beside him. His companion chuckled low in
his throat, but neither of them took their eyes off her. Bostonais
was standing with his arms crossed, breathing slow and deep, the
thick taste of trader's rum coming at her in waves with each exhalation. She took a half step back. The Indian-looking girl laughed

Bostonais said a few words to Kate that had a vaguely English sound to them, but somewhere between his Gallic-Cree mouth and her Gaelic ear the sense of them got lost. He lowered his arms and took a half step forward. She took a full step back. He wrinkled his forehead and took another step forward.

She thought of Bostonais's courtly, smooth-faced, Gaelic-speaking partner and snatched at a scrap of French that came to mind: *"Je desire . . . Je desire . . . Monsieur Grant."*

The entire pack burst into laughter, except for the Indian girl, who waited until the laughter had died and then said something quizzical to the man beside her. When he gave her an explanation in the same tongue, she shot a look at Kate that would have shivered a Glasgow footpad.

Bostonais, the corners of his mustache elevated, said, *"Monsieur Grant est . . ."* then waved one huge paw off across the prairie. He held one hand out palm up and waggled the fingers of the other across it in a creditable imitation of a traveling horse. He pointed emphatically at the patch of ground he was standing on, all the while muttering his thoughts aloud in French, as though his hands had to hear to translate into mime. At the end of the demonstration a full smile cracked his face in pure delight at his ability to circumvent language barriers. He lowered himself to the ground and patted the grass beside him, beckoning her to sit and wait.

Seeing no other alternative, she sat down to wait, setting her bucket beside her. Bostonais clapped himself on the chest and intoned: "Bostonais." Then he raised his eyebrows and bobbed his head at her. She responded with her name.

With the formalities out of the way, Bostonais tossed off the dregs from a tin cup sitting beside him and dipped it in a small, splintered-head keg perched a discreet distance away from the fire. As an afterthought, he snatched up an empty cup lying beside it and made a dipping motion in the air with his eyes on her and his eyebrows raised. She shook her head. He shrugged and tossed the cup back down. On inspiration, he suddenly reached across her, picked up her empty bucket, and repeated the same dipping motion, with his eyebrows raised even higher.

The rest of them could barely contain themselves at this supreme witticism, flopping helplessly on their backs and beating their fists on the earth. She could feel her spine stiffening and the prim line of her mouth drawing even tighter. When the laughter finally died she heard the muffled plodding of a horse walking slowly toward them. Bostonais rose to his feet, and the others turned their heads

in the direction of the approaching hoof falls. A spotted horse a▸
bled into the firelight, carrying an apparently saddle-weary M◉
sieur Grant.

He was wearing the same bright red uniform tunic he'd had
in the canoe two days ago. The firelight glinted off the gilt butto
and gold braid. He reined in his horse, swung one leg over its ne◖
and slid to the ground. The Indian girl was on him immediate▸
standing in close with her hands on his chest, spewing out a tongu
clicking litany containing a recurring phrase that sounded to K▸
like "whop-piss-down." Grant stood smiling with his neck be
forward and his eyelids drooping, toying with her hair and slippi▸
in interjections in the same language.

Kate waited patiently for the scene to play itself out. When
didn't look like it was going to, she stood and called out: "Mis◖
Grant."

Grant swiveled his head toward her, as did the Indian girl, bla◖
eyes flashing over a fringed deerskin shoulder. Grant glanced ▸
Bostonais. Bostonais started to explain, but Kate cut in on top ▸
him: "I have lost my way. I tried to explain it to your friends, b▸
the language, you see . . . I wonder if you might be so kind as ▸
show me my way home."

Grant had brought his eyes back to her. The lids had ceas◉
drooping. It was uncanny, seeing that Regency buck's face wi▸
those large, black, slanted almond eyes, as glistening and opaq▸
as mist-sheened stones. It was as though some utterly alien creatu▸
had put on a human mask. She shook off the inrush of old wive▸
tales of elfin knights and water horses and opened her mouth ▸
reintroduce herself. Before she could get a word out, he'd inclin▸
his head toward her and said: "A pleasure to encounter you aga▸
Miss MacPherson."

"Mrs. Sutherland."

"Ah. Nonetheless, I would be honored to escort you home.▸
He vaulted back onto the saddle and beckoned her forward. T▸
Indian girl said something to him in a guttural tone. He lean◉
down and took her chin in his hand, murmuring banter at her. S▸
cuffed at his wrist and jerked her chin away. He laughed a▸
straightened back up in the saddle.

Kate said: "All you need do is point me the way home."

"Not at all, Mrs. Sutherland. You are a stranger in our hom▸
Bostonais—*lever*, hunh?"

Bostonais fastened his hands around her waist and wafted her ▸
into the air. She just had time to hitch up the hem of her nightdre▸

with her free hand—the other was still clutching the bucket—before he came down astride the horse's haunches. Grant jogged the horse with his heels, and they moved away. She didn't need to know the language to get the gist of the hoarse pleasantries shouted after them.

"You must excuse my friends, Mrs. Sutherland—well, I don't suppose you must, but nonetheless . . . They have a somewhat more boisterous standard of propriety. Although the truth is, I found them more subdued than I'd expected. Perhaps that was your influence. Or perhaps the influence that I am under only made them appear subdued to me." Even though his head was only turned back halfway to his shoulder, she could still smell the clouds of whiskey wafting out with his words. She wondered if he uttered such high-toned convolutions when he was sober. Either way, it seemed somehow ridiculous coming from one so young.

"I should tell you where I live if you mean to take me home."

"I know where you live, Mrs. Sutherland." He twisted his head a fraction farther back toward her and, with a glint in his eye, added ingenuously: "Where else would I be meaning to take you?"

He had turned the horse onto a narrow, winding pathway through the bush. The musty smell of dying leaves mingled with the odor of horse and whiskey, leather and sweat. She had wriggled her way just far enough back from the end of the saddle that her body wouldn't brush against his, propping her free hand on the horse's haunch behind hers. The broad, warm slab of muscle rolled up and down beneath her hand with each step.

Grant's arm snaked out and eased a trailing branch aside, letting it snap back when she had passed its angle of return. She said: "I hope your kindness has not been misinterpreted by Mrs. Grant."

"Mrs. which?"

"Grant . . ."

"Who?" Then he laughed. "You mean the Bungee girl back there? Oh, dear, no, Mrs. Sutherland. She is a delightfully charming young lady in her own way, and one of the many daughters of the estimable Chief Peguis, but she is most emphatically *not* Mrs. Grant. Nor is anyone else. You may rest assured, Mrs. Sutherland, that I am decidedly unattached, at least in any formal sense. At the risk of bumping up against your civilized sensibilities, the sowing of wild oats is our major agricultural activity in the *pays d'en haut*—probably the only one the country is suited for."

She unpursed her mouth enough to say: "I thought Chief Peguis was what they call 'Saulteaux'?"

"Yes."

"But you said his daughter was 'Bungee'—or is that a word you would rather not translate in mixed company?"

"Not at all. 'Bungee' is the trader's name for their tribe, or rather for their language, which is the basis of the lingua franca of the High Plains. It was the first word any white trader ever heard in their language, and still is to this day when a *moonias* takes his first post. 'Bungee' means 'too small' or 'not enough.' You see, the native personage will lay his furs down on the counter, and the trader will make his offer, and invariably the native personage will say: 'Bungee.' "

He seemed to expect that she would express amusement at that, so she didn't. He went on: "Somewhat in the same way as the Romans named the tribes north of Hadrian's Wall as Scots, from the Latin *scottus*—'thieves' or 'brigands.' Dear, dear, Mrs. Sutherland, you must unbend your spine sometime; with a name like Grant I should be entitled to make mock of the Scots without causing offense."

She wanted to tell him that she wasn't near so prissy as all that, but the truth was that she was terrified to open her mouth for fear of what he might make of what came out of it. No matter how thoroughly she reminded herself that he was only her baby brother's age, she still didn't feel like she held the whiphand. So she held her tongue, which if she'd still been in Kildonan parish would have prompted several dozen people to circle the date on the calendar.

Although the sky remained as black as ever, the mourning doves began to flute their resonant dawn songs. She decided there must have been some subtle increase in the light: she could see the back of his ear quite clearly now, and the narrow stretch of delicate, tan skin between the root of his earlobe and the thick, straight, coarse-cut crop of black hair overlapping the gold-leafed Napoleonic collar of his uniform tunic.

They came out onto the cart track that ran between Fort Douglas and the farm plots upstream. A few tiny yellow-white embers danced through the air in the bush on the other side of the track, winking on and off. Grant said: "The fireflies are making a night of it."

Her eyes caught an opening in the bush—the path that she and her husband had worn through from the cart track to their house out on the point. She started to say, "I can find my way from here," but he had seen it at the same time.

"I had told you I would escort you home, Mrs. Sutherland, not merely the general vicinity."

The pony began to stamp and toss its head. He flicked the rein, and it took up its rolling walk again. When they came out into the strip of cleared field around the house, the dawn had advanced far enough to separate the silhouette of the cabin from the river beyond. She started to bend her right knee up to dismount and realized there wasn't a safe and dignified way for her to get down off the horse while the saddle was occupied.

His hand came back and took hold of her leg just above the knee, half on the hiked-up hem of her nightdress and half skin to skin. The hand just rested there, holding but not gripping. He twisted around to face her and said softly: "There is a traditional reward for knights-errant rescuing damsels in distress. . . ."

She could feel the heat rising up the sides of her neck. Her right arm cocked back reflexively—if she swung the bucket hard, she could probably knock him off the horse. Then he answered his own rhetorical pause: "A kiss."

She relaxed her arm and sat demurely upright, not pulling back or moving forward. It seemed innocent enough, and playful—she'd kissed many uncles and cousins in her time. She moved her head a fraction of an inch forward. He twisted his head at an angle, and leaned back. His lips were thicker than her own. They didn't clutch or press, just melded themselves softly onto hers and then let go, the thin skin clinging as they peeled apart.

He untwisted his back, raised one arm, and held it out perpendicular to his body, crooked at the elbow. "For your dismount, madam." The urge to clout him with the bucket returned, for his arrogant assurance that his arm would hold her weight. She took hold of his arm, bent her leg up between them, and brought it over to the other side of the horse. Inevitably, in doing so she exposed the length of leg that her much abused nightdress had still managed to conceal. With a bit of a smirk in his voice, Grant said: "They're nothing to be ashamed of, Mrs. Sutherland."

She slid off the horse and marched toward the house. The pony's hooves thudded softly behind her as Grant turned back the way they'd come. The doorway was a blacker rectangle in the shadowy face of the house. Her husband was standing in it. She stopped in front of him and said: "I feel such a fool."

"Oh?"

"I could not sleep, so I went to fetch some water from the burn.

I lost my way. If I had not chanced across Mister Grant and his people, I would likely still be stumbling around in the dark.''

"Mister Grant?"

"Aye, you remember—he was at the landing in the spring. The young half-breed that speaks Gaelic."

"Ah." He stood aside to let her pass. She set her bucket down on the log block beside the door and fumbled along the inside wall to find the shutter. He said: "I thought I had filled the bucket last night."

"You had, but that was river water. I thought you would like something fresher for a change."

"Ah." His voice remained bland and nondescript. "It is empty now."

"I told you, I lost my way." She managed to work the makeshift latch free and swung open the shutter, which sagged slightly on its leather hinges. A pale ghost of light leaked into the house. "What woke you?"

"I rolled over and found my wife was gone."

"Well, I am back now."

"Ah."

CHAPTER 39

Bostonais signed on for the season to provide fresh meat for Fort Gibraltar, so Grant rode west alone. He was just as glad. For some weeks now he'd been debating a decision in the rare bits of time he had to himself.

The prairie rolled away easily under his horse's hooves. The wild grasses were bent-necked with seeds, blood-purple and white-gold bearded heads hanging heavy in the sun. The oak and poplar bluffs, which showed better than any relief map where there were low spots on the baked earth to pool the runoff, were turning honey-colored. The sun was still as hot and bright as high summer, though. It was the season the traders had dubbed Indian summer, because it ran on Indian time and always showed up late.

Halfway through the morning he took off his quillworked riding coat and strapped it into the thongs at the back of his saddle pad. His uniform tunic was safely stowed in one of the panniers bouncing on his pony's withers, rolled around Bethsy's flag. When the sun reached its zenith he stripped off his shirt and tied it around his waist.

Bethsy McKay was the reason he was glad to have a few days' ride alone. Not that he hadn't already come to the same decision each time he'd been able to debate facets of the question at hand. But now he had time to look it all over at once to make sure he was doing the sensible thing.

He'd spent as much time in the company of Sings to Herself as he had with Bethsy, but there was no question which of them he missed more. As foolish as it had seemed to him last year that Falcon should have saddled himself with a wife and family so early in life, the fact was that in the *pays d'en haut* the basic necessities of life weren't all that difficult to provide; and since there wasn't much beyond the basic necessities of life that could be provided in the *pays d'en haut*, the responsibilities of being a provider weren't as onerous as in the outside world. Then, too, before the year was out he would reach his majority and come into his inheritance. A year ago it had seemed idiotic that society should have fastened upon an arbitrary number of birthdays as the magic entrance to adulthood, but now that he was fully mature he saw the wisdom of the law.

There was no question, too, that when the time came for him to leave the *pays d'en haut* Bethsy would have no trouble adjusting to the salons of Montreal and London. They might have to do a certain amount of adjusting to her. For all her outlandish ways, he couldn't envision a situation where she'd be anything but a credit to him. Whichever way he looked at it, it was a sound decision to make Bethsy McKay his wife.

Late in the afternoon of his third day out from Fort Gibraltar, he crossed the ford across the Assiniboine to Fort La Souris. He was sluicing off the travel dust in the yard trough when one of the traders ambled by to pass the time of day and mentioned in passing that there was a new chief trader across the river at Brandon House. Grant spluttered and swallowed a bit of dank and dusty trough water and said: "What's happened to the McKays—to Mister McKay, who was the chief trader?"

"They reposted him to Fort Qu'Appelle. He took his sister with him."

The three days from Fort Gibraltar to La Souris had been a pleasant interlude of solitude. The week from La Souris to the Qu'Appelle was a bit more of his own company than Grant had bargained for. The only other human beings he saw were a distant family of Plains Cree moving south along the summit of the Assiniboine valley with their possessions travoised on tent poles. Exactly the same device was used in the Highlands, except that there the poles didn't double as tent poles. In silhouette, the Cree travelers might easily have been a family of crofters dragging their piles of peat or produce to Inverness market.

The day after Grant finally turned west of the Assiniboine into the valley of the Qu'Appelle, he sighted a new fort on a knoll butting out of the south slope. A crew of shirtless brown men was swarming over the fresh cut, pink-white pointed caps of the palisade, hanging the front gates. Grant skirted past it to carry on toward Fort John, when he recognized the barley-beard thatch of Whitehead MacDonell behind the work crew. He kicked his horse up the face of the knoll.

"So there you are, Grant—I was wondering if the wolves had got you. *Haul on that line, damn you—don't pluck it like the widow plucked the parson's pecker!* Welcome to Fort Esperance the second. The house in the southeast corner is yours. I believe Mrs. Wills has already set up housekeeping."

"What happened?"

"Happened?"

"To Fort John? Surely the company doesn't need two forts in—"

"Hadn't you heard about that? *McGillis, get those goddamn hinges up there before their backs give out!* Seems last summer a gang of Stoneys took a jaunt south and burned out a village of some tribe allied with the Mandans. So this summer the Mandans and their friends came looking for them. Couldn't find the Stoneys, so they burned Fort John. Lucky for us there was only a couple of *engagés* minding the store for the summer and no trading goods to speak of."

"Ah. And the Hudson's Bay men managed to hold them off at Fort Qu'Appelle?"

"Who knows if they had to? I wouldn't put it past the Company of Dentures to've bribed the Mandans to come up here. The Hudson's Bay bastards are still trying to get back at me for when I told the Blackfoot that the English traders sneezed smallpox bugs. *What* he hell are you doing? I told you to fix the top hinge first!'' And e charged toward the gatepost.

Josephte had bedecked the cabin walls with the feathered war lubs and other geegaws that had decorated the bourgeois's quarters t Fort Gibraltar. There was a pot of fish and wild onion soup teaming on the fire. John was crawling around the dirt floor looking to dig for worms. Josephte had laid down a pile of buffalo robes nd blankets in one corner for her bed and John's and another pile n the opposite corner for the man of the house. As he was shaving is face and brushing the tangles out of his hair, he said: "Perhaps ou might find something to hang as a curtain to partition off the rea around my bed. I'll be bringing home a wife this afternoon.''

"A what?''

"Wife—you know: man, woman, cohabitation, so on.''

"Do forgive me for forgetting my place. I know I have no right o make complaints or ask questions, but I'm afraid it will take me while before being a poor relation comes natural—I'm new to t.''

Grant blew out a long sigh and looked up at the ceiling, then viped the lather off his face and went out to his horse.

He rode west along the river, enveloped in the mystic odor of a lean shirt. Both he and his horse wore fresh-brushed coats. His oots were polished, and his shaving mirror had told him that a ummer's sautéeing had brought out a trace of Byronic gypsy in his eatures. So why did he feel nervous?

Fort John was a square field of dewy-green new growth within he perimeter of the charred stump ends of the palisade, like jaws f scurvy-blackened teeth. He trotted his horse across the ford and hrough the gates of Fort Qu'Appelle. The Hudson's Bay Company ort was bustling with its own gangs of workmen, getting everything attened down and refitted before winter. John Richards McKay wung away from the crew he was supervising and strode over to Grant with his teeth displayed and his hand held out. "Grand to ee you, Grant. I expect we're going to be neighbors this winter.''

"Not as close as we might have been.'' John Richards wrinkled is forehead. Grant jerked his thumb over his shoulder in the direction of the ruins of Fort John.

"Oh, yes. Damned shame, that. Still, I suppose it could've been vorse.''

"Oh?''

"It could've been my fort.''

They both laughed. When the laugh ended Grant said: "Where
Bethsy?"

John Richards's face closed up. He suddenly discovered a pres
ing need to keep an eye on the two men repairing the fur pres
Without taking his eyes off them, he said to Grant: "She's o
riding."

"Where?"

"I couldn't say. You know my sister—wherever the impulse
the moment took her."

"She shouldn't be off on her own; she doesn't know the countr
around here. And riding alone through Assiniboine country isn
the same as it is around Brandon House."

"She wasn't—" At that moment Bethsy rode in through th
gates, followed by a white horse carrying a tall, fair-haired youn
man in a yellow coat.

She slowed her horse to a walk as she passed Grant, but sh
didn't look at him. He said: "Bethsy!"

She pulled her horse up. So did the fair-haired young man. Sh
turned her head in Grant's direction, casting about with her ey
before they finally chanced to settle on him. "Why Mister . .
Grant. I'd heard that we were going to be neighbors over the winte
and now here you are. No doubt we'll have many opportunities
chat, but if you'll excuse me for the moment, Mister Cumming
and I haven't eaten since breakfast." She jogged her horse's rib
with the heels of her high-topped moccasins.

John Richards was staring fixedly at a point halfway between th
rim of the palisade and the heads of the men ferrying barrels int
a store shed. He said, "I had best get back to work. Do be su
and drop by when things quiet down," and walked away.

CHAPTER 40

With two bodies producing heat under three wool blanket
and a buffalo robe, it was like an egg incubator inside th
bed. But Kate wasn't deceived. She poked her nose up over the ri

f the musty buffalo robe and decided it was even worse than she'd thought. She probably would have been able to see her breath if there'd been enough light inside the cabin.

By this hour of the morning on a summer day the sun would've een up for hours and so would she, bustling assiduously, but now here was no need to bustle. There wasn't much to do at all except grumble and try to keep out of each other's way. During the summer he house had only had to function as a nook for eating and sleeping, a closet opening to the world outside. But now that they were more or less imprisoned in it, she'd become painfully aware that he could cross from one corner to another in four strides.

She stole one hand up and snaked it out around the thick lip f the skinned-out hide, burrowing her fingers in among the curls f wool. The colony establishment had issued these buffalo "robes," as they were called in Rupertsland, at the first snowfall, ne to a household. She had yet to see a buffalo, but since the pelts grew wool instead of fur, she imagined some kind of oversized wild brown sheep. The underside was about as pliable as six layers f sail canvas glued together.

Her husband stirred beside her, nuzzling up against her shoulder in his sleep. Since the winter clamped down he had become a piece f furniture that, no matter where she set it, she was always walking into when she turned around again. She could no longer predict, on those occasions when he reached for her in the night, whether he was going to say something cruel to him to drive him off, or perform her wifely function dutifully, or wrap herself around him like a bitch wolf in heat. She no longer felt inclined to reach for him.

She disentangled her fingers from the curls of buffalo wool and stretched her whole arm up into the air. The cold clamped onto it and gleefully swarmed up and down its length. She swung her feet out and planted them down on the floor; they bounced back up like a marionette on springs and thrust themselves back under the covers. Whatever could have possessed her to get into bed with bare feet? she wondered. Then she remembered that today was Hogmanay, so she had washed her stockings last night and hung them up in front of the hearth to dry.

She took a deep breath and heaved herself out of bed, then padded quickly to the fireplace and shoved a handful of twigs into the ashes of last night's fire. No matter how many times she got up in the night to stoke it, the fire always sank down to a few dormant coals by morning. She blew the twigs into flame and piled on a few

sticks of kindling and a shank of split birch. She was pleased to se
their stack of firewood was growing low; it would be something
get him out of the house for a few hours.

Her stockings were still damp, but she pulled them on regardles.
As she was doing so there was a noise from the door, not exact
a knocking, just a thump like a single blow against the wood wi
some blunt object. She decided it was only a spruce bough dumpin
its load of snow, but then she heard it again. Her husband muttere
something unintelligible and dug his head under the bedcovers. Th
sound repeated itself. She went to the door and jerked it open
crack.

There was enough light outside to see by—that faint, sourceles
winter opalescence that seemed to come out of the snow as muc
as the sky. Standing close to the doorway was a gaunt, wolfis
Indian with one limp feather slanting down across his forehead an
a buffalo robe caped around his shoulders wool side in and th
whitened skin decorated with quillwork and pigment drawing.
Those details only registered peripherally; what leaped to the for
front of her vision was the knife in his hand.

He pushed the door full open, forcing her back into the room
and took a step inside. There was a loud click from behind he
The Indian stopped dead. She looked back across her shoulder. H
husband was standing in his nightshirt holding his musket at a
vance. She moved out of the way.

The Indian took a quick step backward, and his hands came u
in front of him, a long stream of Bungee words gushing out of h
mouth. His eyes latched on to the knife in his own gesticulatin
hand. He launched into an elaborate and frantic pantomime to sho
that he'd only unsheathed it to use the haft for knocking on th
door. He kept tugging at one long black forelock of hair and ho
ping up and down on one moccasined foot while pointing at th
other, which he'd raised up in the air. His pointing and tugging wa
further complicated by the fact that in the hand without the kni
he held the loop handle of a birchbark canister, which he held o
on display.

Alexander suddenly began to laugh. He tried to say somethin
to her, but he couldn't stop laughing. Finally he got out, "Fir
foot . . ." but then the laughter took him again. He got hold
himself enough to choke out, "Hogmanay—first foot," and then h
was gone again. She looked back to the Indian.

He was nodding his head vigorously, although his eyes didn
leave the muzzle of the musket still leveled in his general direction

He said, "Ommi-hay, ommi-hay," in what was obviously an attempt to get his mouth around the outlandish consonants of "Hogmanay." She still couldn't believe it, although it fitted his performance perfectly—at Hogmanay, the Gaelic New Year, it signified good luck for the year if the first foot to cross the threshold was that of a dark-haired person bearing a gift for the house.

The "ommi-hay" finished Alexander. He was laughing so hard now that he had to sit down on the hearth, hanging on to the musket with its butt propped on the floor and its barrel pointed at the ceiling. With the line of fire now safely directed away from him, the Indian began to laugh as well. Kate squeezed past him and closed the door against the cold air rushing in. He made a circle of his thumb and forefinger and placed it over his heart where the bullet might have gone in and then fluttered his fingers behind his back to show his insides splattering out, laughing a kind of baritone giggle.

He set the birchbark container on the table and pried off its lid, disclosing a dark, gelatinous liquid that smelled like stewed tree rind with a paint-thinner sauce. He grunted, "Peguis," then nodded his head. "Peguis," he repeated, and pointed from the container to them, making a drinking motion with his right hand.

Alexander forced a sickly approximation of a grateful smile and reached his hand out for the birchbark loving cup. The Indian pushed his hand away—meeting little resistance—and shook his head, curling up his lip to show his front teeth and waggling a fingertip against one.

Kate said: "Scurvy! Like the spruce tea they gave us at Churchill, for scurvy." She wiggled one of her fingers against one of her front teeth. The Indian nodded enthusiastically and broke into laughter again, as though the concept of one's teeth falling out from scurvy was even funnier—if possible—than the concept of one's insides getting splattered across the back wall over a linguistic miscue.

Alexander said unhappily: "We have nothing to give him to drink." A drop of whiskey and a bite to eat for the guest were essential parts of the first footing. He put together a series of gestures to show the Indian that they had no whiskey. He took it relatively stoically.

Kate said, "At least we can give him something to eat," and tried to sit him on one of the stools at the table. He shook her off and went back to the door, beckoning them to follow outside. She went as far as the doorway. Sitting in the snow outside was a toboggan loaded down with stoppered birchbark containers, some of them decked with green icicles of frozen leaked spruce gumbo.

The Indian pointed at the toboggan, then north toward the rest of the colony farms. He said, "Peguis say me . . ." and walked two fingers across the air. He raised up his hand in a farewell gesture.

Alexander said, "Wait!" and scurried back into the house. There were rummaging sounds and then: "Where did you put the bannock from last night?"

"In the sack—in the corner of the biscuit box."

He came back out with a broken-off bit of bannock and tried to give it to the Indian, who was obviously suspicious of their motives in trying to force a dried bit of flatbread into his mouth. Alexander said: "For luck."

The Indian suddenly brightened considerably. "Huh, luck, luck, waugh. Luck!" That particular word, with its great and mysterious religious significance to all whites, was enough to explain the most bizarre behavior. Never one to insult another culture's superstitions, he bit off a piece of the bannock and chewed it up with his mouth open to show them he was performing his ceremonial duty diligently. He swallowed with a long gulp and again held up his hand in farewell.

Alexander took hold of it and pumped it up and down, clapping him on the shoulder. After an instant's confusion, the Indian nodded and laughed and clapped him on the shoulder as well. When her husband had stepped back, Kate impulsively sprang forward and gave their first footer a quick peck on the side of the mouth. The Indian was taken aback; then he grinned broadly, cupped his hands on her shoulders, and yanked her to him, planting his mouth firmly on hers and squeezing her body against his. When he let her go she was sure she heard the pop of a bottle parting company with its cork.

The Indian stepped back toward his toboggan, beaming with pride at his quick mastery of the white man's customs. Kate closed the door and leaned against it, feeling several shades of red merry-dancing across her cheeks. Her husband was standing by the hearth with his fist over his mouth, looking down at the floor. She got the distinct impression that he was trying to avoid her eyes.

She stoked the fire and boiled up a bit of oatmeal. Excluding the occasional potato or turnip, and the even more occasional bit of bannock—the wheat that had survived the autumn frost had to be hoarded for seed—their diet since October had consisted of oatmeal and pemmican. She had found the taste of pemmican to be about what she would have expected of rock-pounded, tallow-preserved, months-old buffalo meat. The only surprise was the high ratio of hair, leaves, grass stalks, and bits of prairie.

They puttered away the morning. Her husband took out his fiddle and set to reminding his fingers how to play "MacPherson's Rant." His fingers didn't seem to have much of a memory. At midday she put on her best shawl, and he wrapped up his fiddle in a swatch of old wool, and they covered themselves in coats and blankets and bonnets and mufflers and went outside.

It was a pristine day. A light overnight snowfall had painted a feathery white skin over the drifts on either side of the path. On a day like this, all debate over whether the damp cold of home was more comfortable than the dry cold here became frivolous. "Uncomfortable" wasn't even in the running when a stiff intake of breath made the lining of one's lungs break up into crystals and patter down on top of the diaphragm with a festive tinkle.

The wind carried the sound of the pipes to them long before they reached Fort Gibraltar. They whiled away a few hundred paces in arguing whether the tune was "Johnny Dhu" or "The Hen's March Through the Midden." The south gate of the fort was propped halfway open. A lone métis stood guard, or slouched guard, with his back against the edge of the gate. He grinned at them around his pipe, exhaling the mingled scents of rum and onions and trade tobacco, and jerked his chin over his shoulder.

The nor'westers had cleared the floor of one of their warehouses. At the far end, standing in front of the ceiling-high stacks of bales and barrels, a piper and two fiddlers screeched over the crowd. On a long table there was a feast laid out of roast prairie chicken, venison, moosemeat, buffalo tongues, beaver tails, whitefish, and smoke-cured goldeye, with side bowls of carrots, potatoes, wild rice, and apples. The fort cooks kept bringing in more dishes and carrying the empty platters away. There was mulled wine, claret, rum, brandy, and what the traders called high wine.

Jean and Angus McKay were there, with their blue-eyed nine-month-old baby. Catherine Pritchard was there, with her belly swollen out farther than her swollen breasts and her hazel eyes turning wistfully toward the door as though she still expected the man who'd left her six months ago to wander through it.

Kate's brother was there, bending his head with John McIntyre and his coterie of grumblers. Alexander's sister, Catherine, was there, tied in with the knot of indentured laborers who followed

John McIntyre. John McIntyre was a squat, red-faced, snub-nosed rodent of a man who was always jabbing up his stubby forefinger and standing up for someone else's rights, whether they'd asked him to or not. He seemed to see himself as a combination of Wallace and Thomas Paine. And from the look in her moon eyes when they rested on him, so did Catherine Sutherland. Kate suspected that Alexander approved of his sister's choice of company about as much as she approved of John's, but the house on Point Douglas was a long way from the bachelors' and spinsters' barracks at Fort Douglas.

Duncan Cameron strode across the room in full sail—gold braid, gold curls, scarlet coat, white linen, and whiter teeth—nodding and winking and booming out broadside salutes in response to the waves of good cheer breaking off his prow. He had three glasses of some smoky amber liquid in his hands. Kate wondered at the expense of transporting glass to the wilderness when tin cups would have served as well.

"Mister Sutherland! Mrs. Sutherland! Last through the door but not in my heart!" His Gaelic had an eccentric twist to it, but she wondered what hers would sound like after a few decades among the sassenach. He pushed the glasses toward them. "Usquebaugh, the genuine article. Would there was enough for more than one paltry glass for each mouth, but at least it is a taste of home."

Alexander said, "Thank you, sir," and took one of the glasses with a deferential duck of his head.

Kate shook her head and said: "No, thank you."

"Do you not take liquor, Mrs. Sutherland?"

She looked down at the glasses. "Not so much."

"Easily mended." He tossed off half of one glass in a single gulp, then topped it up with half the contents of the other glass and handed the half glass to her. He winked and clinked his glass against both of theirs and said: "Here's to us, who's like us? Damned few and they're all dead." Then he threw the entire contents of his glass down his throat with no visible effect but a slight brightening of the flush on his cheeks.

Kate was pleased to see that her husband sipped his reverently. The cautious sip that she took evaporated as it touched her tongue, sending wisps of peat fires and mountain rills straight up behind her eyes.

HMS Cameron exchanged a few more pleasantries with them and then sailed on majestically, exchanging friendly salvos with the smaller craft and eventually heaving to at the group gathered around

John McIntyre and John MacPherson. His expression turned grave there, as he nodded weightily and fingered his side-whiskers in a thoughtful manner.

A number of the guests had started dancing, whooping around the floor in a lopsided reel. One of them broke away and stumbled toward Kate, his chest heaving and his eyes watering, a Gallic-looking brigand with a black, spiky mustache like a curled hedge-hog over his mouth. He thrust his arm out in a point and shouted hoarsely: "You! Hey, you, my friend! You!" She realized he was pointing past her at her husband.

Alexander said: "Lajimodierre."

"So I am. You remember." He fastened one hand onto Alex-ander's shoulder and used his arm as a crutch while he caught his breath. "Too much dance. Come along, you meet *ma femme*—my wife," and started to drag him away.

"Wait." Alexander pulled him back. "This is my wife. Mrs. Sutherland, Mister Lajimodierre."

"*Bonjour madame, et* . . . Hogmanay, uh?" He said it as though he thought it translated as "Happy New Year." "You come along, too. Meet my wife."

He led them to a corner where a woman with cornflower eyes and cornsilk hair was sitting cross-legged in a prim-necked wool dress, talking earnestly to a small boy knuckling tears off his cheeks. There was an older girl standing behind her with crossed arms and a belligerent pout. From a peg on the wall behind the girl hung an Indian cradleboard with a blond infant dozing in the beaded velvet bag strapped to it. The woman had a wiry look about her, with narrow cheekbones and a snubbed-off hook nose.

Mister Lajimodierre said: "*Marie Anne, c'est Monsieur et Ma-dame Sutherland.*"

She glanced up, gave them a perfunctory nod, and went back to lecturing her child. Lajimodierre crouched down beside her and murmured a few French sentences at her, although there were two repeated words that Kate could understand: "Bostonais" and "Grant." Mrs. Lajimodierre looked up at Alexander with renewed interest, then kissed the boy and gave him a little slap on the bottom by way of dismissal. Her husband gave her a hand up to her feet, and she focused her attention on the Sutherlands. She had even less English than her husband, but since neither of them appeared to know any Gaelic and neither Kate nor her husband had any French to speak of, they all had to struggle along in the conquerers' tongue.

Marie Anne put a hand on the pouty girl's head and said: "This

ma fille, La Reine—do a courtesy, La Reine, *comme il faut*. . . .]
call to her La Reine for she was bertha-ed *l'anniversaire* La Reine.'

"The birthday of the Queen," her husband put in.

"So, yes. *Et mon fils*, La Prairie." The boy withdrew his mois
hand from the well of his eye long enough to shake their hands. "]
call La Prairie for he was bertha-ed on the prairie. Because for yo
see when I was"—she hooped both arms out in front of her t
denote an elephantine pregnancy—"I was on a horse ride. The
horse he was *un chasseur* . . . a . . ."

Mister Lajimodierre said, "A buffalo runner," which didn'
make it any clearer.

"So, yes. We pass a buffaloes herd, and the horse he go ma
and"—she galloped her fingers through the air—"in with the buf
faloes, and they go mad. La Reine I had in a pannier on the horse
and this one in my . . ." She patted La Prairie's head with on
hand and her stomach with the other. "What can I do but hang t
the horse and pray? When we come out safe I come off the horse
and down lay on the prairie and out come . . ." She tousled L
Prairie's yellow hair and then looked over her shoulder at the pegge
and trussed baby. "Henri, he sleep."

Her husband said: "He is dead now, the horse—last summer,
hear. After so many buffalo he killed they finally killed him."

Alexander regaled the Lajimodierres with the story of the India
knocking on their door that morning. Kate was proprietarily please
to see how amusing the Lajimodierres found the story—Mister La
jimodierre translating the difficult parts for his wife—until it cam
to the part about the kiss at the end. Mrs. Lajimodierre becam
utterly helpless, hugging Kate's arm and shivering with giggles
which seemed a bit excessive.

When the laughter had finally begun to recede, Kate said, a trifl
stiffly, "I hope that I shall be able to learn to speak Ojibway, o
Bungee, someday. Can you, Mister Lajimodierre?"

"Well, it change from tribe to tribe, but yes—Ojibway, Chip
pewa, all the same, just different ways whites try to say the name.'

"It mean . . . uh . . ." Mrs. Lajimodierre puckered her mout
and pointed at it. "You know . . ."

Alexander said, "Kiss?" which sent her into another paroxysm
of laughter.

"No, it mean . . ." She went through the puckering routin
again and nudged her husband. "Jean Baptiste . . ."

"Puckered up."

"*Oui*, pucker dupp."

"As a moccasin, you know, around the front?" Mister Laji-modierre pointed at the toe of one of his moccasins by way of illustration. "'Cause when they get a prisoner, in a war, they cook him till he is all puckered up."

"They eat them?"

"Eat them? No, just cook them"—Mister Lajimodierre shrugged—"You know, for fun."

That cast a bit of a pall on Kate's image of the happy-go-lucky child of the woods with his endearing "ommi-hay." She said: "However that may be, no civilized white man could have shown more Christian charity to us than Chief Peguis has."

"Peguis, hunh." Mister Lajimodierre gave them a corrugated smile and brushed one-half of his mustache with the side of his finger. "He ain't nobody's fool, or Christian martyr, neither. He ain't come into the Red River country that long—since after I been here. His Saulteaux getting push out from the east, into Cree land and Assiniboine and Sioux. It don't hurt Peguis to have you Selkirk people on his side."

Kate felt cheated. Why wasn't it possible in the scheme of things for Chief Peguis to simply have a kind heart? Mister Lajimodierre seemed to have read her disappointment, for he added: "I don't think it cut against his grain to help you, just it come even more natural when it help his own folks at the same time. There's worse you could have for a friend than Chief Peguis." At that moment Duncan Cameron tacked in and out of the crowd nearby. Mister Lajimodierre's eyes seemed to settle on him naturally and linger there.

Whether or not it was Mister Lajimodierre's Machiavellian characterization of Chief Peguis that put the idea in her head, it seemed to Kate that as she got acquainted with Mrs. Lajimodierre, Mister Lajimodierre was throwing in encouragements and nodding to himself as though they were satisfying some agenda of his own. For all his outdoorsy simplicity, she kept seeing the fulcrum of a scale behind the bridge of his nose; everything his eyes flicked over was drawn in and weighed and balanced.

The four of them sat down to dinner in a row. What with trestles and boards added to the length of the table, and kegs and boxes added to the fort's stock of chairs, there was room for about forty to sit down at once. An impromptu series of sittings developed, with those who hadn't eaten yet, or who had gotten their second wind, waiting to pounce the instant a place was vacated. Kate had never seen so much of so many different things to eat in one place.

Before she'd sampled half of what was in front of her, she was leaning back in her chair stifling little burps.

Captain Cameron sat down at the head of the table and loaded up his plate. He made a great show of clasping his hands together reverently and lowering his head to intone:

> Some hae meat that canna eat,
> Some would eat that want it,
> But we hae meat and we can eat
> And so the Lord be thankit.

As he dug in, Kate found herself speaking, from a place that was languorous and suffused with the odors of roast game and good wine, a place where a refugee crofter's daughter was safe to be as arch as a Duchess, "It is very gracious of you, Captain Cameron, to choose to start your dinner with the Selkirk grace." His mouth had just closed around a forkful of meat, potatoes, carrots, and fish, with a curl of onion perched on top, but his eyes sought her out.

"Oh, were you not aware that the verse you recited is known as the Selkirk grace, since Robert Burns composed it at the Earl of Selkirk's dinner table?"

He chewed three times and swallowed the lot. "I did not know that, Mrs. Sutherland—well, I knew, of course, that the words had sprung from the immortal Rabbie; Lowlander or not, would that some of our own folk had had his feeling for the Highlands. But I had not known of the Selkirk story. Although that would have been the old Earl, of course; your Earl could have been no more than a bairn still studying his catechism. I am told he is a great one for studying the Scriptures, your Earl. It might have been better for all of you if he had devoted as much zeal to studying other subjects, such as geography and law."

She had the sudden disquieting impression that there was something going on she didn't understand. Mister Lajimodierre was leaning back in his chair with his eyes opaqued, gazing at a spot over the far wall. Even without the Gaelic, he seemed to be taking a very clear message from the captain's tone of voice.

Cameron had paused to moisten his throat with half a glass of claret. He went on piously: "Not that I mean to slight anyone's religion. Heaven knows in a godforsaken wilderness like this you need all the faith you can cling to. When I think of the destitution in my own heart the day I first stepped off the ship, knowing I would never see the hills of home again, never smell the heather by the loch, never hear the keening of the lone piper in the glen . . . 'Yet still the blood is strong, the heart is Highland, And we in dreams behold the Hebrides!'"

He wiped away a manly tear and fortified himself with the rest of his claret. "Aye, laugh if you will—the captain is in his cups and growing melancholy. But when I mind me of that day, when I thought the heart would break inside me . . . And *that* was when what was spread out in front of me was the grand, green, prosperous land of Upper Canada, the bustling towns, the bursting wheatfields nodding golden in the sun; when I think of you here, not only driven off your rightful homes, but then cast up here in this endless, rock-strewn, savage wilderness . . . Hamish!" he called to the piper. "Give us 'The Flowers o' the Forest.'"

The eerie, rippling strains of that most beautiful of all Highland laments drifted out over the yabbering guests, and Kate watched the pinched faces soften as the piper's song worked its long fingers into the tenderer folds of their hearts and eased them open. Captain Cameron sat wistfully marking the time with his soup spoon. As the last notes died away he refilled his glass, rose to his full height, and said in a hoarse, hushed voice that filled the hall: "To absent friends."

Every Gaelic speaker in the room stood to call back the response and drink.

The musicians broke into a livelier set of tunes, and the dancing started up again. Alexander took his fiddle up to the front of the room, stood a few paces back from the North West Company fiddlers, and shyly added in a few notes behind them. After a few tunes and a few more glasses of wine he was in the thick of things, following along on the tunes they started and even introducing one or two himself. Kate was surprised at how few sour notes he seemed to hit; maybe she had drunk more than she'd thought.

It turned out that the Lajimodierres were somehow under the same obligation she and Alexander were to show themselves at Governor MacDonell's Hogmanay regale. Reluctantly, both couples said their good-byes and then bundled themselves up against the cold, Marie Anne fussing over Alexander's coat to make sure no portion of his sweat-damp shirt was exposed to the air.

On the frozen river in front of Fort Gibraltar were half a dozen dog *carrioles*, the leaders of each team staked far enough apart to keep the dogs from getting at each other. Kate had become entranced with the *carriole* sounds of harness bells and barking and would often run outside the shanty to watch the hunters from Fort Gibraltar skim around Point Douglas. When Marie Anne learned that she had never ridden in one, she insisted that Kate take her place in the waiting sled. Lying swaddled in furs with La Reine and La Prairie at either shoulder and Henri under her chin, Kate was as excited as a child going to the fair. Eyes wide, she watched the line of dogtail plumes line up in front of her. Mister Lajimodierre unlimbered a long dog whip and popped it over the head of the lead dog, coaxing them all into motion with loud endearments.

The *carriole* gave a little lurch and then shot forward. Kate let out a squawk that the older children laughed at, and then they were all laughing, skimming over the snow, grains of soft powder blowing back into their faces. The sled bed made a constant, hollow roar and hiss, harmonizing with the soft patter of the dogs' paws. The wind-drifted waves of snow, crusted in bumps and hummocks, traveled through the springy slats of the sled bed and into her bones, creating the sensation that the *carriole* was just a thin shell of her body flying along the top side of the clouds.

Kate leaned back, rested her shoulders against the bearskin-padded framework, and allowed herself to be taken for a moment by the notion that she was Marie Anne, that the children nestled around her were her own and that this ice-clawed, wind-ripped vastness was her natural home. Then the buildings of Fort Douglas shot forward on the left bank, and Mister Lajimodierre had put his hands on the back rim of the *carriole*, dragging his body weight against it to keep the prow from climbing up the pole dog's tail. By the time the children were all extricated and the dogs staked out, Marie Anne and Alexander had caught up with them, Marie Anne laughing and brushing snow out of her hair.

One of the Orcadian laborers answered their knocking and wordlessly ushered them into Colony House. In the high-ceilinged hall that took up most of the first story, long trestle tables had been laid out like the ones at Fort Gibraltar, but there was no claret, no mulled wine, only a few dry-skinned roast grouse. At the far end of the room Robert Gunn paced back and forth, the sound of his pipes echoing back on him. At the foot of the stretch of tables a few of the colony servants stood murmuring by a keg and a pile of tin cups. At the head of the table sat Governor Miles MacDonell with Archibald MacDonald to his right and the rest of the colonial establishment standing behind. Otherwise, the room was empty.

The governor was sitting straight-backed in his chair, a tin cup balanced in the fingertips of both hands, staring at a spot an arm's length down the table. Archibald MacDonald was sitting with his shoulders up around his bristling side-whiskers and a fixed grin plastered on his face to illustrate what a delightful Hogmanay he was experiencing.

Miles MacDonell raised his head to look at them and then stood. Above the square-cut chin, the line of his mouth raised up at both corners. He nodded at them, extended his arm at the table, and then sat down again. It was said that when he'd traveled up to York Factory in the autumn, he'd been so brooding and despondent that the chief factor had confiscated his sword and pistols for a few days.

Robert Gunn let the mouthpiece of his chanter drop free and wandered over to them. He murmured: "Thank Christ to see a human face again. I could not rightly say whether I have spent the afternoon inside a madhouse or a morgue or both."

Archibald MacDonald sidled up behind him and muttered: "It would seem to me that now we have guests arrived, it would be the time to start playing, not stop."

"My throat is dry. If you want music, you play." He slapped the pipes into Archibald MacDonald's midriff and headed off toward the gang of Orcadians by the keg.

Archibald MacDonald stared down at the armful of ebony and tartan. A mournful drone wheezed out of it with the last gasps of air trapped in the folds of the bag. He looked up, and his eyes lighted on Mister Lajimodierre. He said in English: "Are you Jean Baptiste Lajimodierre?"

"Yes."

"I'm told that you are the man I should speak to about building a dog carriage."

"Dog carriage? *Carriole*?"

"Quite. What would you charge to build a fine, fast dog *carriole*, and how long would it take you?"

"Well, there are many different ways to make one, and then the decorates, all need different time to do, so cost different money. Then the dogs, I got many different young dogs, some train some not, they cost different money . . ."

Kate and Alexander left Mister Lajimodierre weighing Archibald MacDonald's purse and went to pick at one of the dried-out birds for form's sake. A few hours earlier they would have considered the birds a treat, dried out or not, but their winter-shrunken stomachs were swollen full and their mouths spoiled by the feast at Fort Gibraltar. The governor sat watching them with his fixed imitation of a cheery host.

Fortunately a few more of the colonists began to trickle in from Fort Gibraltar, many of them in a state of festiveness bordering on the incoherent. They provided enough of a diversion for the Alexander Sutherlands to slip out unobtrusively.

It was night outside, which only meant that eight hours had passed since sunrise. Crunching along the path from Fort Douglas to the shanty on the point, Alexander began to wax eloquent about Captain Cameron's delightful and generous feast. Kate said: "Very open-handed of him to give us what is ours."

"Ours?"

"Do you not remember in the summer, Governor MacDonell gave the North West men back their pemmican on their promise that the new chief at Fort Gibraltar would supply us with fresh meat? I had wondered what Mister Cameron was doing with all that his hunters were bringing in, since devil a bit of it have we seen. Now we know what he was doing with it; he was saving it up to play lord of the manor to us poor, forelock-tugging crofters."

The inside of the house was as cold as it was dark. Even the embers in the fireplace had died. Kate went to work with the tinderbox, scraping the piece of flint along the corrugated steel rod until one of the falling sparks caught in the tinder. While she was coaxing the fire alive, her husband sat slumped on one of the stools he'd knocked together in the summer, cradling his wool-wrapped fiddle in his arms.

As the flames crackled in the hearth, he unwrapped his fiddle and played one tune, "The Skye Boat Song," simple and clear and slow, just the pure notes with few trills. The long-lashed eyelids closed serenely as the firelight picked up the gold in his hair and flickered amber patches across the bones of his face. There was something in the nature of the tune passing through him—achingly lovely but without the defeated, melancholy strain she heard in too much of her people's music—something in the flowing motion of his long-fingered hands, in the firelight on his face—something in it all that transfixed her.

When the tune was done he lowered the fiddle and the bow. He looked up, and his eyes caught hers. He seemed taken aback by her expression. She looked away quickly. There was nothing there after all except the man she'd married.

CHAPTER 41

The empty eye slits in the wedge-shaped white fur mask fit perfectly over the middle two knuckles of Grant's left fist. He was standing behind the counter at Fort Esperance, absentmindedly stroking the ermine skin that Jumps High had brought in—the paws straddling his forearm, the black-dipped paintbrush tail tickling the thin skin at the crook of his elbow—while Jumps High talked to him.

"Falcon said I don't have to be a Cree no more. Is that true? I never was Cree, just my mother was, and it didn't feel right to pretend like I was Cree—but a man can't just be a tribe of his own. Not for long. Sooner or later a bunch of Cree or Assiniboine or Blackfoot are going to knock him on the head."

The delicate, thick, glass-smooth fur was coming alive under the stroking, the individual hairs standing up and crackling in the dry air, reaching to meet his fingers. Over the first half of the winter he'd grown accustomed to the fact that there were a great many young men like Jumps High. They could track a lizard through a dust storm, shoot the eyes out of a squirrel, or take on a grizzly bear with a hand axe, but inside them all was the same unease and yearning. He'd also learned that most of the things he wanted to say to them they would say for themselves if he just stood still and listened.

"I don't mind being Cree instead of Blackfoot or Dakotah or any of the other nations, but Falcon says there's going to be a New Nation and Wappeston's going to be its Chief."

"There already is a New Nation. The only question is whether it's going to take hold of its own destiny or not. And I'm not the Chief—that will be up to you and the rest of the New Nation once you decide whether you want a Chief. The English King's War Chief for the *pays d'en haut* just asked me and three others to try to get as many of the soldiers of the New Nation together to help us we could, that's my only authority. But if you decide for yourself

267

that you want there to *be* a New Nation, instead of it getting strangled at birth by the governor of *les jardinières*, then come down to
the Forks of the Red in the spring and—''

The cannons over the fort gate boomed. Grant called the junior
clerk out of the stockroom to man the counter, snatched down his
rusted-iron wolf fur winter coat off the wall peg, and went outside.

The *engagé* in the watchtower was pointing beyond the gates,
hollering, ''*L'express! L'express!*'' Clerks and *engagés* and their
wives and children were poking their heads out of doorways or
tumbling out into the snow with one sleeve of a coat on and a cap
slapped haphazardly on their heads.

The gatekeeper took down the bar and heaved open one of the
great barn doors. A *carriole* with eight dogs shot through the niche,
skating wide out of a too tight turn but managing to stay upright.
On the heels of the two snowshoed men running behind it came
the fort dogs, yelping and growling.

The express men dragged the *carriole* to a halt, dug down inside
it, and came out with a bulging rawhide bag. One of them slung it
across his shoulder and walked toward Grant. ''Mister Grant, is
Whitehead . . . ?''

''*Mister* MacDonell is on a tour of inspection around the outlying
posts. I'll take care of that.'' He slung the bag across his own
shoulder. ''Come in and warm yourselves.''

He dumped the bag out on the counter and dug through the
mound of personal letters until he found the sealed packet of company dispatches. Leaving the junior clerk to sort the letters, he took
the packet to the far end of the counter and broke the seal. In among
the sheaves of official correspondence for the bourgeois, there was
one labeled ''Cuthbert Grant, Esq.,'' from Duncan Cameron.

Lieutenant Grant,

*I hear good word of your recruitment work along the Qu'Apelle.
I think I do not exaggerate my own campaign here to say that by
the spring the jardinierès will need but a small push to see them
all pack off for good. And I know just the lads to do it.*

*Tell your jeunes gens that as soldiers of the New Nation they
can expect to be fed and uniformed here at Red River, along with
other presents. His Honourable Governorship and that ilk will
turn tail soon enough when they see you and Seraphim et al in
front of your cavalry. All their fine plans of harnessing your
ponies to their ploughs and stealing your homes from under you
and making you their servants will . . .*

"Mister Grant?"

It was the junior clerk, holding a red-wax-sealed document. "What should I do with this?"

Grant plucked it from his hand. It was addressed to "Mister John Richards McKay, Qu'Appelle House, Rupertsland" and was distinguished by the seal of the governor of Assiniboia. It wasn't unusual for the North West Company express to carry correspondence for neighboring HBC posts and vice versa, but colony dispatches was stretching the courtesy. Grant said, "I'll take care of it," thrust the company packet into his coat pocket, and went back outside. He squelched across the snow toward his quarters, rattling the edge of the dispatch for John Richards McKay and wondering what to do with it.

He hadn't been to Fort Qu'Appelle since that short, brutish encounter in the fall. On New Year's Day, when the HBC post took its turn to host the celebration, he had volunteered to stay behind and keep an eye on Fort Esperance. He could always detail one of the *engagés* to run the governor's dispatch across the river. . . .

Suddenly he snapped it hard across the side of his left hand, furious at his cowardice. He ducked into the cabin just long enough to get Josephte to dig out his saddle and bridle. He thought of changing his shirt and shaving, then decided the hell with it and took down his rifle, wrapping it in a swatch of blanket cloth against the cold.

The horse corral behind Fort Esperance was generally occupied to overflowing in the winter. The horses had enclosed themselves in a honeycomb series of individual paddocks, built by pawing the snow aside to get at the frozen grass. It was a dry winter this year, so the walls of their snow forts were barely up past their hocks. Grant picked out a black pony from the string and bridled and saddled it, catching the cinch bindings in the long hairs of its winter coat.

The Fort Qu'Appelle gatekeeper eased open the massive wooden door with a show of reluctance. As soon as the opening was wide enough to let him through, Grant kicked his horse ahead and asked the man where he might find the chief trader.

"Mister McKay is off looking over the other posts. Back maybe next week. Mister Cummings is in charge."

Grant hesitated. Given that the dispatch was addressed to John Richards McKay, Chief Trader, he could reasonably deliver it either to the chief trader's office or his quarters. He kicked his horse toward the private cabin set aside for the chief trader and his dependents, reflecting that in either place he was likely to deliver the document into the hands of Mister Cummings.

He looped his horse's reins into the doorpost ring and raised his hand to knock—then changed his mind. Instead, he lowered his hand to the latchstring, jerked the door open, and stepped inside.

She was on the far side of the room, sitting cross-legged on a buffalo robe in front of the fire, sewing a quillwork design onto a length of moosehide that looked to be cut for a rifle scabbard. There was no one else in the room. She looked up at him, held her eyes on him for an instant, then shifted them back to her fingers and went on with her work.

He said: "I came to deliver a piece of correspondence that came for your brother in our express."

"He isn't here."

"So I heard, once I'd ridden across from Esperance. I imagined I might entrust it to you to hold against his return."

"I imagine you might."

He set the dispatch on the table. She didn't raise her eyes, just kept on picking out different-colored quills from the birchbark containers ranged around her and working them into the moosehide. He wanted to pick her up and bounce her against the wall. Instead, he said: "A little gift for Mister Cummings?"

"Whom else would it be for?"

"Since it has been four months since I saw you with him, experience suggests that you would have moved further afield since then. Or do you find your natural tendencies stilted by the narrowness of the selection here?"

He was gratified to see her hands halt in midmotion. Her eyes came up but stopped just below his. There was a ribbon of red spreading across the skin above her cheeks. She said: "I should imagine you'd know a good deal more about the local selection than ever I would."

"You have an overactive imagination."

"Have I? And how were you amusing yourself last summer along the Red—humping buffalo?"

"I haven't tried it. You will have to tell me about it sometime."

He started for the door. Her voice followed after him: "Yes, now that you've run your errand, I suppose you'd best be running back to your bourgeois."

He stopped at the door. "Not to worry. As difficult as it might be to imagine, he can actually manage to wait for up to—oh, Lord, *minutes* at a time, before he gets itchy."

"I suppose anyone can when they have something to wait for."
Suddenly she stood and started for the door. "How thoughtless of
me—you are waiting for me to open this for you. I should have
realized from your failure to knock that you have trouble with the
concept of doors—having spent your childhood in a tent and all."

She pushed the door open. He started through it and then turned
back to deliver some brilliant Parthian shot. His body bumped
against hers—and they were on each other instantly, pasting tongues
together, pulling skirts up and pushing trousers down, and working
hands under collars to get at backs and breasts.

When he returned to the world at large, he realized that they
were lying on the floor in a puddle of clothing and that flakes of
snow were drifting in on them through the half-opened door. They
pulled the door shut, built the fire up, and jumped into her bed.
They confessed what idiots they'd been and exonerated each other
of blame. Then Grant rode away again on a whirling floodtide of
consciousness and memory—the rounded button of a chin softening
the point of her jaw, the musky sour-milk smell of her sweat, the
slick, warm insides of her closing around him like a fist around a
whipstock.

They were whispering edited stories of their recent pasts when
a knock sounded at the door. Bethsy leaned up in the bed and called
out: "Yes?"

"Bethsy? It's me . . . Allan."

"What do you want?"

From the ensuing pause, the question seemed to require a certain
amount of thought on his part. Finally he knocked again and called
through the door: "Are you all right?"

"All right?" Grant shouted back. "She's astounding!" They
heard no more from Allan.

After a certain amount of sleep and a certain amount of further
exploration—their bodies still weren't all that familiar to each
other—a faint, white glow began to edge into the room through the
cracks between shingles or around the door and shutters. Grant
remembered his horse and pulled on his trousers, boots, and coat
to venture outside.

The horse was still there, munching stolidly on a little heap of
hay that someone had tossed down on the snow. Someone had also
taken the bit out of his mouth and loosened the saddle girth. As for
being left out in the elements, Grant knew a Shagganappi pony
would stand pretty much where he'd been left through anything

short of a blizzard, in which case he would get a little frisky about finding the lee side of a shack to take the edge off the wind.

"Hello, Grant."

Grant turned around. It was John Richards McKay. "I thought you were off on an inspection tour?"

"The dogs got into an argument over a rabbit, and two of them got too badly chewed up to run. I'll start out again tomorrow."

"When did you get in?"

"Well . . ." He shrugged. Grant had a sudden suspicion that he'd come back the night before and had slept in the *engagés'* quarters or on the floor of the storeroom.

"Your sister will be glad to see you back safe. Come in, we'll have a cup of tea or—"

"Perhaps later. . . ."

"You do live here."

"Yes, I suppose that's true. All right, but . . ." He waggled the fingers of one mitten at the doorway. "Do you just stick your head in first and tell her I'm back."

"Announce you?"

John Richards smiled. "If you like."

Grant jogged the door open and walked into the gloom. "Your brother is back. He had some trouble with the dogs."

She got out of bed and pulled a dress on over her head, then called out: "Come in, John."

He came in and closed the door, and they kissed each other. John Richards stripped off his coat and cap and mittens and hung them from pegs on the wall. Bethsy built up the fire and fussed with tea leaves and a kettle, then asked Grant to break the ice on the water bucket. John Richards sat down at the table and looked at the sealed dispatch. Grant said: "I brought that over for you. It came in our express."

John Richards picked it up and looked it over. "I wonder what it is."

His sister called from the hearth: "You could open it and look."

He did. Grant pulled on his shirt and sat at the table while John Richards attended to the dispatch.

There appeared to be two pieces of paper, a scribbled note folded inside an official-looking document. John Richards was reading the note first. He said: "They've arrested Bostonais Pangman."

Grant said: "What?"

Still skimming the note, John Richards said: "It appears the métis hunters along the Pembina were driving the buffalo out of reach of the colony people who'd gone down there to hunt provisions. Archibald MacDonald went to the métis camp to tell them they were breaking the law by hunting from horseback, and Bostonais ran him out. They came back in force and arrested Bostonais and brought him back to Fort Douglas. They have him chained up in a shed."

Although the hearth was drawing perfectly, Grant suddenly felt as though the room were full of smoke—his lungs had to pull hard to get enough oxygen out of the air. Bethsy primly set down three china cups and a silver teapot on the table, then sat across from him. He grappled for her eyes with his, hoping to latch on to some thin thread of empathy. When she finally raised her eyes from fussing with the tea things, they were as superciliously sealed off as the grim, hard line of her mouth. He said to her, "This is different," and was surprised at the raw, husky croak that came out. "You can see that . . . ?"

She said coolly: "What is different?"

"This . . . situation. It's different from last summer."

"It is?"

"I was a fool then, running off for no good reason. But this . . . chained up in a shed in the middle of winter. You can understand that, can't you?"

"Understand which?"

"That it isn't a question of what I want to do . . ."

"Do what you want. I'll do what I want."

John Richards was studiously examining the second piece of paper, but there was no way to dismiss the fact that he was there. Grant tried to think of a polite way to ask a man to leave his own home, but it was impossible. Adopting as passionate a tone as he could muster with a third person present, he said: "What choice do I have?"

Bethsy didn't reply, but her look said quite plainly that the choice seemed obvious to her. She got up and took the kettle off the fire. John Richards came to the bottom of the sheet of paper and looked up, his face pale. He said: "You'd better read this," and handed it to Grant.

It was ornately lettered, with many calligraphic flourishes. After a rather lengthy preamble, it got to the point. All employees or agents of the North West Fur Trading Company who were doing business within the boundaries of Lord Selkirk's land grant—from Rainy River to the western edge of the Qu'Appelle district, from the narrows of Lake Winnipeg to the headwaters of the Red—were trespassing. The governor of the Selkirk colony would allow them a grace period of six months from the date of the proclamation to pack up and leave. After that, trespassers would be arrested and their property confiscated.

John Richards said: "They want me to nail it to the gate of Fort Esperance."

"You may well end up beside it."

Bethsy said: "What is it?" She had filled the teapot and sat back down. There was no trace of the woman who had melted around him in her bed an hour ago.

John Richards made an attempt to wave it off, but Grant had already handed her the notice of eviction, saying: "I believe she's moderately literate."

Bethsy read it through, then looked up at Grant with a pretty smile and said: "It looks as though you had best start hunting for another employer."

He said, "You don't really understand anything, do you?" and took it from her hand. "I'll save your brother's hide and deliver this for him."

He rode across the ice back to Fort La Souris, wrote a note for Whitehead MacDonell, and left it with the proclamation, handing it to the clerk he summarily appointed temporary bourgeois until Whitehead got back. It was high-handed and irresponsible, but Josephte would be there to give advice, and she knew at least as much about running a trading fort as her brother. He cut out the three toughest-looking ponies from the fort string, put a few sticks of jerked buffalo and a water bottle filled with rum in his coat pocket, and rode out of the gates of Esperance at a gallop, leading the spare ponies on a long Y halter.

Halfway between the mouth of the Qu'Appelle and Fort La Souris, the horse he was riding went down with its lungs frozen. He picked himself up out of the snow, stripped off the saddle and bridle, strapped them onto the next horse, and kept on going. He slept around the clock at Fort La Souris and then cut out two fresh horses. By the time he reached Fort Gibraltar, both ponies were half-dead and so was he. There were colored lights bouncing off the snow, and the wind was talking to him.

He woke up on the spare bed in Duncan Cameron's quarters. His body felt as if it had been dragged under the ice from Esperance. Through the entire insane escapade he'd been fixed on the thought that if he could reach Fort Gibraltar, Bostonais would be freed. Now that he'd arrived he had to face the fact that he had no

lea how to get him out. Duncan Cameron seemed very unhappy
bout the possibility of any kind of assault on Fort Douglas.

Grant spent the afternoon in the watchtower, studying Fort
Douglas through the flimsy latticework of naked treetops. His eyes
ept returning to four closet-shaped outhouses set in back of Colony
House. When it was dark he borrowed a double-barreled gun from
'aptain Cameron and slipped north through the riverside bush.

They would have a guard on whatever shed Bostonais was in.
No doubt they would also have some kind of sentry arrangement at
he front of Colony House, if only to illustrate the governor's au-
nority. But it seemed unlikely they would guard the necessaries.

He got in behind them without anybody raising an alarm and
hunked himself down in the snow to wait. He heard voices and
ootsteps coming out. One door opened and closed, and then an-
ther. He waited. The theory was that no one else would come out
hen all four were occupied, given a choice between waiting inside
nd standing in the snow in the middle of February.

A solitary set of footsteps came out and took possession, and
nen another. Grant cocked the hammers on the gun and took off
is right mitten. The voice of reason told him to stay in the shadows
ntil he could slip away. Instead he stood up and walked around to
he front of the necessaries.

The door to the far left outhouse opened first, and one of the
Drcadian laborers came out. Grant showed him the gun, put his
nitten to his mouth, and waved him out into the open. Then two
oors opened at once. Grant panicked for an instant, knowing he
ouldn't cover all three at the same time, but they didn't call his
luff. The fourth one tried to duck back inside when he saw the
un, but Grant managed to get his hand in between the door and
he jamb and pulled him out.

They were a good catch: three colony servants and a nervous
ttle man who seemed to think he was important. Once he'd got
hem herded well on the way to Fort Gibraltar, he stopped worrying
bout trying to shush them. Said the nervous little man: "So the
North West Company is expanding its activities to kidnapping?"

"This isn't a kidnapping. You're under arrest."

"For what?"

"For as long as it takes."

It didn't take long. The next day negotiations started, and on the
ollowing day a delegation from each fort met in the open for an
xchange of civilities followed by an exchange of prisoners. Hog-
nanay wasn't a patch on the night they brought Bostonais Pangman

home to Fort Gibraltar. It did seem strange to Grant, in the rare
moments when he wasn't fully occupied with rum and laughter,
that some of the people at the celebration were colonists. But he
had better things to do than think.

CHAPTER 42

The campfire and hearthside stories set in winter in the
pays d'en haut invariably centered around one of two major characters: cold and hunger. From May through September the
countryside was teeming with wild game and plant life, but for the
remaining seven months nine-tenths of all living things were either
hibernating or had fled south.

The fur traders' hunger stories were of snowed-in clerks reduced
to boiling down green hides and moccasins, and of whole forts kept
alive by the bourgeois's Cree wife's skill at snaring mice and rabbits. The Indians' stories were of food caches destroyed by wolverines and of children eating their dead brothers and sisters. Just
beneath the delicate lace of hoarfrost, just below the voices singing
around the fire, just behind a lover's eyes, lurked the Wendigo,
waiting for the hunger madness to set him free.

The majority of the Red River colony population trekked south
to Fort Daer to spend the remainder of the winter hunting buffalo
in the Pembina hills. Kate and Alexander Sutherland stayed on in
their shanty on Point Douglas-eking out meals from what remained
of their slim harvest and what they could buy on account from the
colony's stores, stuffing themselves once a fortnight at Captain Cameron's open-house *cehlidhs*.

Kate was standing at one end of their rickety table, trying clumsily to shave the bark off a handful of still-frozen willow twigs.
Catherine Pritchard had told her that dried willow bark could be
crumbled in among tea leaves to make the stores last longer. Kate
had spent a good portion of Captain Cameron's latest *cehlidh* wrestling through language barriers with Mrs. Pritchard. A good many
of the colony women seemed to find it terribly amusing that the

deserted half-Indian girl should refer to herself as "Mrs. Pritchard," and even more ludicrous that she'd chosen to name her baby son "John Bheag"—"Wee John." Mrs. Pritchard had promised to show Kate when summer came how to find the kinnikinnick plant whose leaves made good tea and tobacco and how to recognize the breadroot plant, a kind of wild potato.

There was a sudden hammering on the door. Kate jumped, bisecting the twig she was trying to peel. Her husband looked up from the other end of the table, where he was working away on his own bit of wood with a knife. He was trying to carve a wooden spoon with a handle that was both long enough that she wouldn't scorch her hand and sturdy enough that it wouldn't crack. Six tries so far this winter, and he still hadn't given up.

She put down her knife and went to the door. There were two men outside swaddled in lengths of blanket wool and plaid and scraps of rabbit fur: her brother and Robert Gunn, the piper. They made a great show of easy conviviality, as though they dropped in on the house on Point Douglas every second day. The fact was that Kate hardly saw her brother anymore except at Captain Cameron's *cehlidhs*.

She set the kettle on the fire and crumbled in a few shards of willow bark with a handful of tea leaves while John and Robert Gunn were knocking the snow off their boots and loosening their mufflers. Once around the table, John and Robert Gunn embarked on a rambling, generalized conversation that held up quite well until the tea was steeped.

Alexander took a tentative sip of the willow-tea concoction and shuddered, pursing his mouth unpleasantly. Robert Gunn seized the moment to look up at the ceiling and cough significantly. John stopped in midsentence, then gathered himself together and said abruptly: "We do not have to stay here."

She said: "Then go back to your barracks, you made your own invitation."

"You misunderstand me, Katy—I mean we do not have to stay here, at Red River. None of us have to."

"Where else would we go?"

"To Upper Canada."

"Why should we do that? We have homes here."

Robert Gunn snorted. John said: "Here? Do you want to spend the rest of your life trying to grow crops out of ice and . . . and jumping to attention every time Miles MacDonell belches and . . . and . . ."

Robert Gunn leaped in to help him: "And fighting the wild animals for scraps of food! Why do you think they brought us here by way of Hudson's Bay instead of from the east through Upper Canada?" He didn't wait for a reply. "Because if they'd brought us through the east, we would have seen the rich farms and prosperous towns there, and the free land for the asking—not this good-for-nothing, rock-strewn wilderness."

Alexander said dryly: "It is wondrous to hear that you have been gifted with the second sight since coming here, Robert—I do not see how else you could know so much of Upper Canada when you have never been within a thousand miles of the place."

"Captain Cameron knows Upper Canada well enough."

Kate said: "Ah, Captain Cameron."

"You will not go sneering at Captain Cameron—he has been a better friend to us than ever Miles MacDonell and his toadies."

"In my own home, Robert Gunn, I will sneer at whoever I damn please."

John got a pained look on his face. He said: "Show her the letter, Robert."

Robert Gunn dug a much handled piece of paper out of his coat pocket. Kate read it aloud for her husband's benefit.

My lads,
Not since I saw the hills of home sink into the sea and knew the truth of Lochaber No More have I been so heartsore as these last months watching you suffer so unjustly. I have been at pains to help you but thought it would be cruel to breathe a word of it and raise your hopes before I knew my efforts would bear fruit. Now I can tell you—the Legislative Council of Upper Canada has agreed to grant free land there to those of you who would see their families settled safely in a civilized country. The North West Fur Trading Company has agreed to provide you with passage east with their spring brigades, at a fee of thirty shillings per to defray expenses. The Company has been prevailed upon to wait payment in some cases till you are established there, since there is small doubt many of you have been made indigent by the fat promises of MacDonell and all that have proved so thin in the end. As for the just wages owed you, if any receipt can be got in the name of MacDonell or the Almighty Earl or especially in the name of the Hudson's Bay Company, rest assured that my friends in the North West Company will pursue them through the

*courts. That all herein written down is true, you may take the
word of*

> *Duncan Cameron, Captain,*
> *His Majesty's Voyageur Corps*
> *Officer Commanding*
> *Fort Gibraltar*

She folded the letter along its creases and put it on the table.
Robert Gunn snatched it up and slipped it back in his pocket. John
said: "I will go."

"Go where?"

"To Upper Canada."

"Don't be daft."

"He is not being daft."

"You stay out of this, Robert Gunn."

"You will not use that tone with me, woman."

"I will use whatever tone with you I please, and if it is not to
your liking, you can see the door from here. Now John, you will
not be so daft as to go running off when you have not even given
the place as much time as it took us to get here."

"I am not a child, Katy. I have thought it all through."

"Then why did you bother to come to me?" Much to her an-
noyance, it was necessary to dab her cheeks with the sleeve of her
blouse.

"To convince you to give this place up—it will only break your
hearts and your backs for nothing—and come away with us."

"No." As soon as it was out of her mouth, she realized that
there was a plural involved here and turned toward her husband,
but he didn't seem inclined to contribute a dissenting opinion.

"Try to think beyond yourself, Katy. Think of the others. Perhaps it is worth it to you to hold on here just to satisfy your own
stubbornness regardless of the consequences, but are you prepared
to have the lives of so many others on your conscience? There are
many of your neighbors who sway back and forth but might well
make up their minds to go if they saw that even you are not prepared
to fight it out here." Then he looked to her husband apologetically,
apparently as an afterthought. Perhaps it was a congenital Mac-
Pherson trait. "Not meaning, of course, Sandy, that the others do
not hold you in high respect as well, but you know my sister."

"Oh, aye, I know your sister."

"You have nothing but this Cameron's word on what you can
expect in Upper Canada."

The MacPhersons sawed it back and forth until both were exhausted. They gave it up for the present, both of them promising to think it over further, each of them meaning they expected the other to think it over further. She kissed her brother good-bye and closed the door behind him and Robert Gunn, then turned back to her husband. He had picked up his lump of wood again and was studying the grain along the roughed-out handle. She said: "You did not say much."

"There was not much to say."

Over the next ten days the snow on the roof grew porous. Then it froze again with a glasslike skin, hanging a crinoline of icicles from the eaves. With the next warm wind a shower of water droplets squeezed down through the seams between the tiles of sod. Her husband climbed up and cleared the snow off the roof, destroying her broom in the process. He bound a batch of willow twigs around the end of a bobbed sapling for a new one.

She stepped out the door one afternoon and heaved the dishwater from the bucket. She was stepping back inside when an eerie sound riveted her in place. It was both alien and familiar, like a voice heard in a dream once. When it came again she recognized it. It was a bird's song—not the squawk and twitter of the black and mousy winter birds, but a genuine song. For an instant, in among the tortured black twigs of the oak tree at the corner of the house, a puff of bright blue with a pale rose breast bounced from branch to branch before disappearing around the other side of the trunk.

She sat down on their dwindling stack of firewood and felt the tears springing down her cheeks. Now that it was over, she realized she'd been wrong about the winter. She had been afraid of its sharp, cutting teeth, but it was the grinding teeth that won past all defenses, the wearing-down effect of five months when the briefest errand outside meant bundling on layers of clothing, when there was no living thing to see but the white owls and the wolves and ravens, when the muscles never lost their tensing against the cold, even in sleep.

Sitting on the stack of firewood in the sunlight, with the wind on the other side of the cabin, she felt surprisingly warm. She closed her eyes and let the sun radiate on her eyelids. She definitely deserved a moment of self-congratulation in the sunlight, if not a full parade with pipes and drums and regimental colors.

She could hear a parade. She knew it was her imagination going overboard with relief, but still she heard pipes and horses and har-

ness bells and laughter and shouting. She opened her eyes, then
stood. Through the naked swatch of trees she could see that something curious was happening at Fort Douglas—a troop of men bustling in and out and carrying on as if it were May Day in the snow.

She picked her way forward between the tree trunks and soggier
snowdrifts to have a look. She thought at first that it might be
another party of deserters—Duncan Cameron was allowing those
colonists who were planning to leave in the spring to billet themselves at Fort Gibraltar—but they'd been sneaking off in twos and
threes, not advertising themselves in triumphal processions.

As she came to the edge of the bush, she recognized a few of
the men who'd deserted some time ago, including Robert Gunn. In
among them were the black beards and brass-studded rifles of métis
and the red coat and plumed hat of Duncan Cameron. They were
boiling in and out of the armory shed, loading the colony's winter-
stored cannons onto horse-drawn sledges—what they called "stone
boats" in the Highlands.

They finished their loading and set off singing and laughing,
dragging the sledges toward Fort Gibraltar. The last to leave were
Bostonais Pangman and Cuthbert Grant, wheeling their horses as
a rearguard. Grant saw her over his shoulder and reined in his
horse. He shouted something in French to Bostonais and, waving
him on, trotted back toward her across the half-soggy, half-
crystalline black ground.

He was dressed in a long coat made from the pelts of some
animal that had thick underfur and long guard hairs, rust orange
and black and white and badger gray. The coat hung open, showing
the bright red military tunic beneath. His skin was a good deal
whiter than it had been in the summer, with a pink flush. He stopped
his horse in front of her and bowed in his saddle. "Good morrow
to you, Mrs. Sutherland, on this fine spring afternoon."

"What is that performance about?"

"Ah—no doubt you have heard of the scheme that Mister Archibald MacDonald has hatched up while your good governor is
down at Pembina: to arm the colony schooner with the colony
artillery and blockade the river against any of you leaving for Upper
Canada."

"I have heard nothing of the kind."

"No? Well, isolated from the others as you are here, I imagine
here's a good deal that doesn't reach you. Be that as it may, it was
decided that it would be in everyone's best interest to deliver Mister
MacDonald from temptation."

"So you stole the cannons."

"Not at all. It can hardly be called thievery when Mister Mac-Donald was standing there watching us. He no doubt recognized that Captain Cameron, as an active commissioned officer in His Majesty's military forces, is the final authority here."

"No doubt he also recognized that there were two dozen of you armed to the teeth."

He opened his mouth and laughed. "No doubt; Mister Mac-Donald does appear to have a mathematical turn of mind. But I did not ride over here to parry insults with you, Mrs. Sutherland, as delightful as that might be. I merely wished to make so bold as to say that there are one or two among Lord Selkirk's colonists whose departure for Upper Canada—despite the obvious necessity . . ." The hard-polished surface of banter and politesse suddenly melted away, and for an instant the black-almond eyes were not opaque. "Whose departure I cannot but look upon with regret. Adieu, Mrs. Sutherland." He stood in his stirrups and inclined a bow that had no archness in it, then wheeled his horse to ride away.

"If by that you mean me, Mister Grant, then it will please you to know I am not leaving."

He yanked the reins hard and looked back over his shoulder. "Not what?"

"Not leaving."

He turned the horse around to face her, and once again, as had happened when she'd first met him, an alarm bell at the base of her skull began to clang. His entire posture had suddenly gone as rigid as a spring wound to the point of exploding. His eyes were like black ice. And when he spoke, his voice had altered to that of a stone statue magicked to life: "I had not taken you for a fool, Mrs. Sutherland."

"Some have, Mister Grant, but either way I am not leaving."

"Your colony is falling to pieces around you."

"What the others choose to do is their business. I did not run five thousand miles from the Countess of Sutherland to be chased out by the North West Fur Trading Company."

"Do not make the mistake of thinking of this situation as merely a war between two trading houses—although, believe me, that would be grave enough: the sums of money involved are astronomically beyond those which induced the Countess of Sutherland to do what she did to you. But if that isn't enough to make you think sense, consider this: The oldest and deepest dream of the human race is to someday return to Eden having eaten of the Tree of Knowledge.

hat is about to happen here. The New Nation can take possession
f their mothers' Eden while still retaining their fathers' knowl-
dge. Whatever sympathy we might have for you for having lost
our Eden—and there is a great deal of sympathy, believe me—do
ot make the mistake of thinking that will stop us from riding over
ou if you stand between us and ours.''

"But surely a few tiny farms in this whole vast wilderness will
ake no difference to—''

"Are you incapable of any thought at all?'' His horse shied
nder him. He yanked its head down, roaring over its rearing and
amping and squealing, "This year another hundred of you will
t out from Stromness, next year two hundred, and the year after
at? The New Nation is not fighting for a few acres of riverbank
r for a higher profit margin, it is fighting for its life. Get out of
ere while you still have the chance.'' He chopped his hand through
e air, turned away from her, and gave his horse its head.

Grant had had every intention of heading back to the Qu'Appelle
s soon as Bostonais was freed, to take up his duties as a clerk at
ort Esperance and to patch up the rift with Bethsy before it wid-
ned even further. But then there had been the business of the
olony artillery.

He was saddling his horse the next day when Captain Cameron
alled him in to talk about the housing problem. What with the
ccumulation of absconded colonists waiting for the spring bri-
ades to take them east, and more *jeunes gens* of the New Nation
rifting in every day, plus Fort Gibraltar's full complement of win-
ring *engagés*, the seams of the palisades were strained to bursting.
eraphim Lamarr, William Shaw, and Bonhomme Montour had
nown an admirable flair for recruiting war parties but didn't appear
 have any idea what to do with them once they'd been recruited.

Duncan Cameron let him know in no uncertain terms that the
rvices of another clerk at Fort Esperance were far less important
 the company at this juncture than a solution to the overcrowding
t Fort Gibraltar. At any moment somebody was going to bump
e wrong shoulder or hoist the wrong skirt, and the grand alliance
f the company and the disaffected colonists and the New Nation
as going to turn into a free-for-all.

A short ways downriver from the northernmost farm in the col-
ny, just beyond where Seven Oaks Creek flowed into the Red from
e west, was an abandoned hunters' encampment in a meadow
alled Frog Plain. Grant assembled a work party and rode down to

Frog Plain to refurbish the old cabins and knock together some new ones. He hung out Bethsy's flag from a stripped sapling nailed to the roof of the cabin he'd occupied for his own.

Within a few days Frog Plain was the base camp of the soldiers of the New Nation—running footraces and horse races, playing cards around the fire, drinking the North West Company's rum, galloping off in groups to hunt and fish, and terrorizing every white, Indian, or mixed-blood father with a daughter over the age of ten within a hundred miles. It was with a warm feeling of satisfaction that Grant recalled the Duke of Wellington's reported description of his Army of the Peninsula: "I don't know if they scare the French, but they sure as hell scare me."

None of which eased his nagging certainty that Bethsy was sitting in Fort Qu'Appelle convinced that he was doing the same thing to her now that he'd done last summer.

CHAPTER 43

Sandy was helping to put the finishing touches on the horse mill in front of Colony House. Personally he would have thought it a mite premature to devote so much effort toward solving the problem of grinding the colony's grain when they had yet to solve the problem of growing enough grain to grind, but no one had asked him his opinion.

In a world that paid any attention to logic, he wouldn't have been working on an installation at Fort Douglas, no matter how pragmatic the installation or how immediate the need; he would've been working on his own fields on Point Douglas. However, the Orcadian laborers who should have been working on the horse mill had either absconded to Fort Gibraltar or were refusing to work. It seemed that they'd signed on as colony servants for three years when they'd come across the ocean with the governor in 1812. The three years had expired, and the governor had nothing to offer them for their back wages except promissory notes—and he refused to offer them anything for the future except new contracts at the same

ld terms. John McIntyre the Liberator had spoken up for them.
Now if only Sandy could get him to speak up for his sister.

It wasn't a pure sense of community responsibility that had made
Sandy offer his services for this job. He was hoping that volunteering his labor would help remind the colonial establishment that his
sister's was impending. He hoped someday to tell Catherine that
that was how he'd come to be standing with one end of a nine-foot
oak beam crooked under his arms while John MacPherson held the
other. For all his grumbling and threats, John had yet to walk the
path upstream to Fort Gibraltar.

Governor MacDonell was stooped over Sandy's end of the beam,
peering at the capstan slot it was supposed to fit into. "Bring it up
a little . . . a *little*, I said! Now over to the right—no, the left . . .
Not that far, damn it! Inch it back to the right now . . ."

Sandy had been inching it to the right and left and up and down
for a little while longer than it took for the beam to begin dragging
a man's shoulders out of their sockets. The end of the beam had
been tapered with an adze to fit snugly into the rim on the shaft that
would turn the millstones by the power of Indian ponies plodding
in a circle yoked to the spokes.

"Sir!" Sandy grunted out. "Sir . . . I believe . . . it does
not . . . fit . . ."

"Of course it fits! Or it would if you'd hold it steady."

"Sir . . . I believe . . . it needs to be . . . shaved down . . . a
little farther . . . sir."

"Does it, now? Are you a carpenter? What if it gets shaved down
too far and it joggles in the hole, hm? Did you ever think of that?"
He slapped the beam for emphasis. "And then the carpenters would
have to start all over."

"It . . . does . . . not . . . bloody . . . fit . . . sir!"

"You watch your tone with me, mister. I could have you in irons.
All right, put it down. You there! Fetch me the master carpenter!"

John let his end of the beam drop with a thud that traveled up
through Sandy's arms. Sandy let go of his end, and the governor
marched off to oversee something else in the interim.

Sandy slumped down on the damp ground with his elbows
propped behind him. A young man and woman, both with gold
hair and coppery skin, came out of the Hudson's Bay Company
house and stood arguing with each other. Sandy's eyes, like John's,
traveled over in that direction and then stayed nailed in place—on
the woman. She was dressed in a modified hybrid of Cree and
Spanish gypsy—a black velvet skirt vined over with embroidery,

beaded moccasins and headband, and an extremely lightweight linen blouse. The design element of the cheekbones had been carried over into the breasts—all four were high, prominent, and sharply defined.

John said: "Crippled Christ on a crooked crutch! If MacDonell sent her around to tuck us in at night, he would have no trouble with desertions!"

"Had you not seen her before? She came in some days ago with her brother on the boats from the Hudson's Bay posts upriver. The lad she is talking with is her brother."

"Poor bastard."

"The governor has put him to drilling one of the defense platoons. I thought you knew him from Scotland."

"Scotland? Give your eyes a scrub and take another look at his skin and his cheekbones."

"He was there visiting his uncle, old Donald McKay. Your sister said you all went down to speak with him at DunUlidh before it was decided that you would come over here."

"No—just because they were deciding on my life does not mean they invited me to come along."

"Mister Sutherland."

Sandy looked up over his shoulder and squinted against the sun. It was Mrs. Pritchard, with her son's cradleboard slung under her arm. Before he could reply to her greeting, John jumped in with, "What is it they are arguing about?" She wrinkled her forehead. John pointed with his head at the McKays across the courtyard, abusing each other in full-throated Cree.

"Wappeston."

"What is Wappeston?"

"Many ask that this days. Mister Sutherland, I come to tell—your sister time come now."

Sandy scrambled to his feet. "How close is it?"

"Now."

"John, would you fetch Joan MacLeod from Fort Gibraltar? Here—take one of those," pointing at the pair of tethered Indian ponies waiting to be hitched to the mill spokes.

"The governor would not like—"

Already running, Sandy yelled back: "Bugger the governor. If he had not been stalling me off all week . . ." The jarring gait of his limping hop run commandeered the breath he would have used to finish the sentence.

He found his wife in back of the house, chinking cracks in the walls. She had a bucket filled with wet clay from the riverbank and was working it in between the logs using an old broken-pointed knife as an improvised trowel. Her skirt and blouse were streaked with red-gray, crusted stripes; there was even one running across her cheek into her hair.

He leaned a hand against the wall to catch his breath. "Catherine is starting her labor." She stuck the knife into a log and stood up and wiped her hands on a pulled-up tuft of grass. "If you would go to her, I will go back and fetch the governor."

They split off toward opposite shoulders of the point. When Sandy got back to Fort Douglas the governor was at the mill site talking with the carpenter, who was trying to concentrate on adzing a half inch off the beam end all around.

"Sir, could you come along with me and bring the registry book, please? It will not take above a quarter hour."

"I don't have a quarter of an hour."

"Neither does she, sir—there is no more putting off!"

"Ah, yes, I see, I see. Well, take Mister MacDonald, then, he can see to it just as well as—"

Sandy took off across the courtyard toward Colony House. The governor shouted after him: "Do you know anything of what happened to the other horse from the mill team?"

"John MacPherson took it to fetch the midwife. I told him to."

"That animal was colony property!" But by that time he was out of range of the governor's voice.

Archibald MacDonald was sitting in the governor's office inking in ledger entries. "You must come quickly for my sister and bring the registry," Sandy told him. "The governor said for you to go with me."

Instead of leaping up and starting for the door, Archibald Mac-Donald meticulously blew the ink dry on the last entry, then closed the ledger and put it back up on the shelf and took down the registry and the Church of Scotland prayer book. He reached for his hat. "Very well, then. Where is she?"

"At Robert Gunn's."

"I can't go down there!"

"The governor said!"

Archibald MacDonald took a stiff breath to steel himself, then set the books and his hat on the desk and unlocked the wall cabinet, disclosing a row of cutlasses and pistols with a chain running through the trigger guards and hilts. He stuffed a pair of pistols in his pockets and slung a cutlass baldric over his shoulder, then carefully locked everything up, retrieved his hat and books, and nodded to Sandy. "Let's go."

The house that Catherine Sutherland and John McIntyre had been living in since March, when Robert Gunn packed up his pipes and marched to Fort Gibraltar, was at the downstream end of the colony, almost to Frog Plain and the half-breed camp. A number of the other disaffected Orcadians had set up temporarily around John McIntyre, and it was not a healthy spot for colony officers to venture into.

The new leaves curtaining the path were translucent, the sunlight filtering through them a greenish gold. Archibald MacDonald kept his head up and his spine straight, although the pace he set was less than brisk. The path wound its way along the riverbank, crossing weed-covered strip farms with deserted cabins whose doors and shutters had already been scavenged for firewood. The few shanties still occupied and bustling only served to point up the number of empty ones. Sandy began to feel a little sympathy for Archibald MacDonald. Most of his aggravating qualities simply boiled down to youth, and time would cure that. "Enough of us will stick it out, Mister MacDonald. Another year or two and I will be sending passage money to my old mother and all back in Sutherland."

"That's the spirit, Mister Sutherland." Archibald MacDonald's features brightened with a slightly misty smile.

There was a loud party of men gathered around a keg of NWC high wine in front of the cabin that had been Robert Gunn's. Robert Gunn was standing with them, along with a couple of the other colonists who'd already deserted. They growled some highly disrespectful things at Archibald MacDonald, who threw his back against the wall. Juggling his books up under his left elbow, he snatched out a pistol with his left hand and drew the cutlass with his right. "I give you fair warning, the first man to raise his hand against me will never raise it again!"

They hadn't considered doing damage to any part of Archibald MacDonald except his dignity, but now that he'd brought it up . . . Those sitting on the ground climbed to their feet and fanned out in a line away from the keg. One of them bent down and picked up a fallen branch.

Sandy said: "Let us by, he means you no harm."

Robert Gunn said: "Your word means shit here, Sutherland."

The one who'd picked up the branch took it down off his shoulder and leaned on it. "Let them by. They came for John and Catherine's sake."

One of them said: "Not for John's." The others laughed and headed back to the keg.

The cabin had a dirt floor and no furniture. John McIntyre was sitting on the cold hearthstone with a cup in his hand, looking dazed. On a pile of old blankets in a corner lay Sandy's sister— moon-faced Catherine now moon-bellied as well—whimpering between slow, rhythmic grunts. Kate was kneeling on the edge of the blankets, holding her sister-in-law's hand and stroking her glistening forehead. In the assuring voice that Sandy now recognized as the one Kate used when she didn't know what the hell was going on, she was saying: "Just you hold on a while, dear, Joan MacLeod will be here before you know it."

Sandy pushed Archibald MacDonald forward. He put away his pistol and fumbled one of his books open. "We are gathered here in the sight of God and these witnesses . . ."

Late that night Mister and Mrs. McIntyre were delivered of a tiny girl. She died before they had a chance to name her. In the morning the Sutherlands and the McIntyres stood on either side of the open grave behind the cabin, waiting for the governor. He had promised to come down to read a prayer.

An Indian pony came walking along the path from Fort Douglas. There were two people on its back, and neither of them was Miles MacDonell. One of them was Catherine Pritchard. The other was a wiry, wind-burned man with a blond beard.

Mrs. Pritchard jumped down first, looking off balance without her baby. She started to say in her rudimentary Gaelic: "See, here he is—"

"Now, now," the man climbing down behind her cut in in the *Beurla*, "in English, in English."

She shifted into her extremely rudimentary English—all winter she had been working hard to learn the British white man's language and now discovered it was the wrong one. "This . . . husband, John Pritchard." She finished with a flourish of her arm and an explosion of white teeth and dimples.

Sandy had no idea what to say or do under the contradictory circumstances, whether he should express joy for the Pritchards' sake or stay somber for the McIntyres'. Apparently neither did anyone else. The first to find the proper footing was, of course, his wife. "It is a grand thing to see you back here safely at last, Mister Pritchard, but just at present, you see . . ."

"Yes, yes, I know. The governor could not come and asked if I would," drawing a battered Book of Common Prayer out of his coat pocket.

They lined up in a U around the grave. Mister Pritchard read a few prayers in English. Then they each took up a handful of earth and sifted it through their fingers, the pellets pattering and bouncing on the linen pillow slip wrapped around the baby. Sandy shoveled in the rest of the dirt, and they covered the grave with loose stones to keep the wolves from digging it up.

The Sutherlands and the Pritchards headed back toward the Douglases, Fort and Point, with Mrs. Pritchard riding on the pony and the other three walking alongside. Mrs. Pritchard seemed nervous, and her hand kept twitching at the pony's halter, as though she wanted to lash it to gallop ahead. Sandy wondered whom she'd left her baby with, then realized that that was probably the reason for her nervousness.

Once they were far enough away from the McIntyre cabin, Kate said: "Wherever did you drop from, Mister Pritchard?"

"Well, it's a long story, frankly—and a hellish long way around to get here. To put it simply, by the time I'd finally got my affairs wound up with the North West Company in Montreal, the winter had set in, so I couldn't travel the rivers—well, not that I would've regardless. The Kaministiquia route belongs to the North West Company, for all practical terms, and they . . . But fortunately for me, Colin Robertson happened to be in Montreal, on business for . . ."

Pritchard's voice faded out for a moment as Sandy's attention was drawn inward to trace the memory that had sprung up at the name "Colin Robertson." Finally he placed it at DunUlidh—the big man with the wine-colored vine-wreath hair, who had stood on the shore rock to tell the dispossessed of Kildonan parish about the Earl of Selkirk's colony and had leaned down from his horse to shake ex-Private Alexander Sutherland's hand on the bargain of a freehold deed.

John Pritchard was still relating his tale: ". . . said to myself, No, you can! and set off with the guides and porters Mister Robertson had offered me, to Moose Factory at the foot of James Bay, then straight across to Jack River House and south to the Forks— an arc over and around the North West Company's stomping grounds. It took six months, but here I am in one piece."

Kate was getting the glassy look that Sandy recognized all too well; signifying that she believed herself in the presence of some-

hing Truly Romantic. He could look forward to at least a week of
er being suddenly transported while spooning out the porridge.
She would assume he was too dull-witted to imagine that she was
daydreaming of what it would be like to be the subject of the kind
of devotion that would bring a man back across a hostile half con-
inent.

Mrs. Pritchard said, "Please," to attract her husband's atten-
ion, then pointed down the path. "Hurrying. John Bheag."

"John what?"

Kate said: "'Bheag'—it means 'little' in Gaelic. Perhaps she
means your son."

"Oh. No, you hurry along, dear, I'll catch up with you. Don't
worry, I won't get lost." He slapped the pony's rump, and it trotted
ahead of them up the path with Mrs. Pritchard peering fearfully
back over her shoulder. "She was so worried about leaving him
trussed up on his cradle board, but she refused to bring him to the
burial—some pagan superstition, no doubt." He clapped his hands
together. "There is much to be undone."

Kate said coldly: "Perhaps, Mister Pritchard, her pagan superstition had to do with the feelings of the McIntyres."

"How's that?"

"So, Mister Pritchard," Sandy jumped in, "how far is it you
figure you traveled to get back here?"

"Certainly two thousand miles, once you allow for the angle
north to Moose Factory and back down. It would have gone by a
good deal faster except that every time we laid over in a Hudson's
Bay Post I had to go through the same performance with the guides
that Colin Robertson had lent me. 'No, we can!' I'd say. 'A journey
of a thousand miles begins with the first step! Just put one foot in
front of the other, and you're on your way again! The darkest hour
is—' "

A sudden bellow of cursing erupted out of the woods beside the
path, a man's voice shouting on and on in Gaelic. Sandy ducked
into the bush to have a look, the other two following after him.

The woods turned out to be a narrow belt bordering one of the
many cleared fields of Mister Alex MacLean, the colony's resident
gentleman farmer. Mister MacLean was out in the middle of the
field, kneeling with his back to them, next to a pony lying on its
side. Behind the horse, pulled askew by its traces, was a clumsy
attempt at a plow knocked together out of a forked tree limb.

Sandy walked out across the furrows. Mister MacLean's attention was focused entirely on the bush at the other side of the field.

"Bastards! Goddamned bloody coward bastards!" He heard Sandy coming up behind him and swung his head around. There were tears in Mister MacLean's eyes. The pony's head lay pillowed in his lap, and there were three arrows and several bullet holes in its side.

CHAPTER 44

Grant rammed home the fresh load, planted his rod in the ground, rolled back up to his feet, and poked his rifle out from behind the poplar he'd chosen for cover. Before he could take aim, however, he heard another sound above the fusillade of gunfire—a distant howl of pain. He lowered his rifle and pivoted to press his back against the tree trunk. "One of them's been hit!" he shouted.

He got no response so shouted louder, revolving his head from one shoulder to the other: "I said one of them's been hit! Didn't your mothers teach you how to shoot straight?"

The firing died down. To his left and to his right, all along the line of bush across the base of Point Douglas, brown, bearded heads popped up from behind boulders or under spruce trees. Some of them looked innocent, some annoyed; some of them shrugged their shoulders or looked accusingly at the next man down the line. "I distinctly heard one of them cry out!"

Seraphim Lamarr said: "I didn't hear nothing."

Grant ran the sound back through his mind. He wasn't so sure now, perhaps it had only been a bird's squawk. Nonetheless, now that he'd started it . . . "How many times do I have to tell you? Aim for the outside edge of the window frames or shoot *high* through the windows—don't shave it too fine."

Bostonais rumbled: "Might've been a ricochet. Hard to control them."

Alex Fraser called out from his hiding place: "Some of us ain't so good at not hitting who we're shooting at!"

Someone farther down the line shouted, "You always been pretty ood at it, Alex!" which got a laugh.

Grant shouted loud enough to be heard at both ends of the line: Alex! Are you shooting to miss?"

"That's what you told us to—"

"No! That's what I told everybody *else* to do! You aim straight : them, then they'll be safe." There was laughter all up and down e line, including Alex.

Something *whunked* hard into the obverse side of the trunk Grant as leaning against, vibrating the tree and pattering down a shower f dead twiglets on his head. The muffled pops and cracks of gun-re from the other side hadn't stopped when theirs did. If anything, ey had increased. Another something *whinged* against the edge f the trunk just above Grant's shoulder and buzzed on by, spraying is cheek with splinters.

He flung himself to the ground, rolled into a spruce thicket, and red prone through the top of a window on the second story of olony House. The instant the gun butt kicked his shoulder, he ipped over onto his back, sloping the muzzle across his chest, and apped his powder flask into the mouth of the barrel. There was o necessity to reload quickly; a potshot every minute or two from e boys in the bush was more than enough to keep Miles Mac-onell's stalwarts flat on the floor. And there was really no need press his back to the earth while he was reloading; given the uality of marksmanship in Colony House, he probably would have een quite safe sitting on a tall stump. But he wanted to develop exterity at the standard métis method of reloading during a stand-g fight, and the only way to accomplish that was through prac-ce. He would never get as good at it as Bostonais and Alex Fraser, ho'd been doing it since they were weaned, but he was improving.

On this instance, though, once he'd inserted the powder and the adding and the ball, he realized that he'd left his ramrod standing the ground beside the poplar tree. He sprawled over to reach for , and something in the distance caught his eye. He looked, then t up and looked again, then started to laugh. Bostonais turned round.

The belt of brush they were using for cover backed onto the urned-off meadow that had been furrowed into fields for the farm n Point Douglas. Standing right out in the open, out of range of ray shots from Colony House but in plain view and easy range of e back of the métis line, was a man with a hoe calmly hilling fant potato plants. From their brief introduction a year ago, Grant recognized the Mister Sutherland whom the red-blond Miss MacPherson had married.

Bostonais said: "Deaf or crazy?"

"Perhaps neither. All things into account, you still can't help but admire some of them."

"I can."

From farther along the sheltering belt of trees, a foghorn voice boomed out over the gunfire: "Halloo! Hallo the fort!" The firing on both sides died down. "This is Captain Cameron! I have a duly sworn warrant for the lawful arrest of Miles MacDonell! For confiscating private property, illegal detention and abduction, and sundry other charges! If you surrender him into my custody, to be transported to Upper Canada for an impartial trial in front of magistrates appointed by the British Crown, we will leave you in peace! Otherwise, I cannot answer for the consequences!"

A hoarse, brassy tenor bellowed back from Colony House: "I have a warrant for *your* arrest, Cameron! Surrender yourself to me!"

"Your people are the ones who are suffering for this, MacDonell! If you surrender yourself to me, they have my word of honour that—"

"Your word of *what*?"

Captain Cameron stepped back out into the open, turned to Grant, and shrugged. Grant stood up and fired a bullet into the shingles of Colony House, and the shooting started up again. Captain Cameron dusted the mud off the knees of his white uniform breeches, then mounted his horse and rode the wide circuit across the prairie that would bring him back to Fort Gibraltar without coming in range of Fort Douglas.

After they'd been going at it a while longer, Grant took a look at the sun to determine whether it was time to call it a day. There was a sudden loud boom and a crash and a high-pitched scream from the direction of Colony House. The explosion sounds echoed off the river and then faded, but the screams kept up.

This time there was no question. Grant dropped his rifle and scrabbled forward on his hands and knees to the front of the bush. Curls of black smoke, glittering with sparks and wispy embers, were billowing out of a window on the second story of Colony House. Grant's snipers were shouting back and forth at each other from their hiding places:

"Mother of Christ!"

"What was it?"

"Mother of Christ!"

"A cannon! It was a cannon!"

"Don't be stupid, we took all their cannons. . . ."

"It was a cannon! I saw it—a little brass one. I saw it poke out the window, and I ducked my head down and—"

"Mother of Christ!"

"Are you hit?"

"It isn't us that's screaming, is it, idiot! It's them—they put a match to it, and the goddamn thing blew up!"

There was only a thin gray film of smoke still sifting out the window, but the screams hadn't dissipated. If anything they had grown louder and were now augmented by a cacophony of incoherent voices. Grant crawled back through the bush and stood up, brushing off the bits of grass and moss clinging to his regimental tunic. Mister Sutherland and his hoe had disappeared.

Grant picked up his rifle and called over his shoulder: "That's enough for today. Let's go home."

"No!" Among the others emerging from their hidey-holes was Seraphim Lamarr, resplendent in his own red tunic with gold frogging across the chest—perhaps more resplendent, in fact, since his could fasten. "No—why should we go back? They're all confused now. Now's the time to hit them!"

Grant said: "Hit them? I think you're the one who's confused, Seraphim. We didn't come here to kill anybody, remember? Just to scare them."

"Who decided that?"

"We did. Remember?"

Most of the others had emerged now and were standing around uncertainly, looking from Grant to Seraphim. Seraphim said: "Okay, maybe that's what we decided, but maybe I changed my mind."

"Maybe I didn't. I don't see a great deal of sport in taking potshots at people who, for all I know, are trying to sew someone's guts back in."

Bostonais said: "I like a fight as much as anyone, but if Wappeston says the smart thing for us to do now is go back to Frog Plain, then I'm going."

"Why?" Seraphim bellowed. "Look"—displaying a fistful of his tunic—"I been made a lieutenant the same as he has. That means you have to listen to me as much as him."

Bostonais said: "I don't have to listen to nobody."

"So why should you listen to him instead of me?"

"Well, for one reason, Seraphim—because if it was up to you instead of him, I'd still be sitting chained up in a woodshed, or more likely froze to death."

Grant said, "If you want to argue strategy, Seraphim, let's do it back at Frog Plain over a cup of rum," and headed off toward the horses. Bostonais went with him, and Alex Fraser and Jumps High, and enough of the others so that finally Seraphim had no choice but to fall in behind or end up looking like more of a fool than he did already.

When they galloped into the camp at Frog Plain, those of the *jeunes gens* who had stayed behind poured forward to pump them for stories—all except Pierre Falcon. Falcon was sitting cross-legged in the sun, a good hundred yards back from the melee. He was perched in front of the cabin Grant had taken for his own. He showed no inclination to move, as though the last place he'd ever want to be was where people were bandying stories about.

Grant trotted over to his brother-in-law. From twenty feet away he could see the gleam of phony innocence in the hound-dog eyes. Grant dismounted and waited for Falcon to tell him what it was he was looking so innocent about. Falcon just kept bouncing his stick up and down. "What's going on?"

"On? On? What's going on? Well: I'm sitting in the sunshine playing catch-me with a stick, the earth is getting dusty with summer, there's a little finch singing in the maple bush over there . . ."

Grant cocked his head to one side and squinted at his brother-in-law. Falcon looked at a dust speck overhead, at the brown river rolling by, at the ears of Grant's horse, everywhere except back over his shoulder at the cabin door. Grant stepped past him and butted the door open with the heel of his hand.

The interior of the cabin was dark. Beyond the crooked patch of light coming in through the door, someone stood up with a jangle of bracelets. Something in the movement told him who it was. He started to shout her name and leap forward, then remembered the circumstances under which they'd parted. He restrained himself and reached back to push the door closed.

In a matter-of-fact voice she said: "I'm pregnant. Should I marry you or one of the others?"

"Others?" As always with her, the instant she opened her mouth he was shooting down white water through the *dalles*. "What do you mean, 'others'?"

"The others who would like to."

He sat on a buffalo robe by the hearth and pressed two fingers to his right temple.

"Well?"

"You don't give a man much time to think."

"A woman doesn't have much time."

By way of conversation he said: "I was planning to ask you in the fall, but then there was Cummings."

She knelt down in front of him and propped her wrists on his shoulders. His eyes had adjusted to the dimness enough to see that the line of her mouth was twitching, but whether from suppressed emotion or repressed amusement he couldn't tell. She said: "All right, I will."

He started to say, "You will what?" and then realized what he had been snookered into. He thought about that for a long moment, then reached his hands up behind his neck and trapped her hands. He started to lean his body back onto the buffalo robe. She made a couple of futile stabs at jerking her hands free, then laughed as he dragged her down beyond her point of balance. He trusted that his brother-in-law was keeping up his watchdog act in front of the door.

In the evening they sat on the riverbank watching a couple of kingfishers chase each other. They shot back and forth from tree to tree and up and down the bank, settling onto the river for an instant and then charging up into the air again, furiously shaking off the water like wet cats. They looked identical and moved so fast that he couldn't differentiate between the two of them, but he had a sneaking suspicion that the chaser and the chasee alternated from flurry to flurry. He pointed at them and said to Bethsy: "That's us!"

In a tone a touch too cool to be arch, she said: "What is?"

Duncan Cameron came down the bank behind them bringing news. "They sent an envoy over to Fort Gibraltar from Colony House. They claim Miles MacDonell's left Fort Douglas, and they don't know where."

Grant said: "Do you believe them?"

Cameron got an abstract look on his face, as though the concept of believing anyone was open to philosophical debate. Finally he said: "I think so; they're tired of getting shot at for his sake. I wouldn't guess he's run far. Probably gone to ground in one of the farmhouses downriver."

"Should we hunt him out?"

Captain Cameron shook his head. "If we keep making it hot for them, it shouldn't take long before they turn him in themselves—

or make it too hot in turn for whoever's hiding him. I'd say another week, two at most, and we'll be standing on the riverbank waving our handkerchiefs at the lot.''

"Did you hear anything about what happened to the man in Colony House?''

"Which man in Colony House?''

"The one that was screaming.''

"Oh! Yes. John Warren . . . poor fellow. Took it upon himself to give you a dose of the swivel gun, and he put too much powder in it, so when he touched it off the barrel burst and took his hand off. Difficult to tourniquet. I'd guess he'll bleed to death.'' He slapped his hands on his thighs and straightened with a guttural sigh. "Well, I'd best be getting back to Gibraltar. No rest for the witless. I should imagine we'll have a whole raft of them crossing over after today.''

When he had gone, Bethsy said in a passable imitation of Cameron's tone, " 'I'd guess he'll bleed to death.' ''

"It was an accident. And he was pointing his little cannon at us, don't forget.''

"It could just as easily have been my brother. Is that what you'd say then? 'Ho hum, likely he'll bleed to death, tra la la . . .' ''

"Don't be foolish.''

"No? You think John Richards wasn't in there while you were potting away, you and your friends?''

"That isn't the point. Warren did it to himself. John Richards isn't fool enough to go playing with explosives he can't control.''

"No? That makes him rather unique around here, wouldn't you say?''

CHAPTER 45

The week following the attack on Colony House brought more of the same. Anyone who ventured out to work in the fields could expect to be shot at from the bush. The shutters and doors of all occupied homes were pockmarked with bullets. At night, parties of horsemen would gallop past, whooping and singing and firing off their muskets, trampling the sprigs of wheat and barley and potatoes. Adam and Eve, the bull and the cow that had been rafted down from York Factory with the first contingent of colonists, were driven off to make a feast at Frog Plain. Excluding John Warren, though, no one was physically harmed. But every day a few more families or individuals trudged down the path to Fort Gibraltar with their possessions on their backs, to wait for the boats to Upper Canada. No one knew where Governor MacDonell had disappeared to. Duncan Cameron sent word that as soon as the governor surrendered himself into custody, the snipers and night riders would cease.

Sandy was out hoeing his new field early one morning, trying to remember whether his father had ever put in peas this late in the spring in Kildonan. He was leaning on his hoe, striving to fix his recollections, when he noticed something moving on the path along the riverbank. It was a blocky, square-shouldered man walking alone, coming from the direction of the farms at the north end of the colony. The shoulders were so stooped, the walk so aimless and reluctant, that it took him a moment to recognize the governor.

Miles MacDonell stopped where the path touched the corner of the field and looked out over it. Sandy said: "Good morning, sir."

"Hm? Oh, yes. Good morning, Mister . . . Sutherland, isn't it?"

"Yes, sir."

"Um-hm." The governor nodded his head, then clasped his hands behind his back and silently contemplated the hoed clods at his feet. Suddenly he straightened up and forced his lips into a ghastly approximation of a grin. "Making hay while the sun shines, hm?"

"Peas, sir."

"Hm?"

"I'm thinking of putting in peas."

"Ah, peas! Yes. Hm." He pursed his lips and continued nodding. "Have they been giving you much trouble?"

"Not yet, sir, I haven't put them in."

"In? Put what in?"

"The peas, sir. I haven't put them in yet, so they haven't been giving me much trouble."

"Trouble? No—the half-breeds, the North West Company's bully boys, have they been giving you much trouble?"

"Oh. They sneak into the bush and take a few shots at the end of my hoe from time to time. They were roaring about outside the house a few nights ago, so I put a bullet over their heads, just to let them know I have a musket, and they haven't been back. If they had genuinely murderous intentions, they've certainly had enough opportunities, but it is a bit hard on the nerves.''

The governor bobbed his head up and down, looking off into the distance. ''Yes, yes, yes, yes, I suppose it would be. Hm . . .'' He sealed his lips again, then popped them open. ''It was Cameron, you know.''

''Cameron?''

''Duncan Cameron. *Captain* Cameron.''

''What was Captain Cameron, sir?''

''Hm? Oh—that came up with the Pemmican Proclamation, the proclamation that got the half-breeds so upset. That first winter, he used to come down from Bas de la Rivière, drink a cup of wine with me, and give me advice. . . .'' He trailed off and stood nodding his head slowly, gazing at the treetops farther along the point. It didn't appear that he had anything more to say, nor did he seem interested in anything Sandy might have to say. But he made no move to leave.

''Are you going in then, sir?''

''Hm? 'In'?''

''To Fort Gibraltar, sir.''

''Ah! Yes. Hm. Yes, I thought it best.''

''I think it *is* for the best, sir—get it all out in front of the courts and let the magistrates sort it out.'' Sandy was quite aware that ''it all'' was likely to include an indictment of ex-Captain Miles MacDonell's utter failure to grasp the difference between governing and commanding. But if the world was suddenly going to turn itself upside down and make officers pay for their own mistakes, ex-Private Alexander Sutherland was not going to protest.

''Well, hm . . . Carry on.'' The governor squared his shoulders, exhaled, and proceeded at a slow march down the path to Fort Gibraltar.

On the second afternoon following the governor's surrender, Kate was busy pouring musket balls. She'd seen it done once before, and it didn't look all that difficult. The first step was to melt one of the piglets of lead. There was a little, thick-walled iron pot for that purpose, with a spout on one side. When the lead was melted, she poured from the spout into the hole on top of the mold—a cast-iron scissors-handled affair, with a bisectable cube where the scissors blades would be. When she'd set the pot back on the fire and given the lead in the mold a few moments to cool, she held the cube part over a bowl of cold water and pried the handles apart. The cube split open down the middle and out popped an almost perfect little lead sphere.

What with the fire banked up to melt the lead, and the door and shutters latched tight, Kate quickly began to feel the heat. She unfastened the top buttons of her blouse and stripped off her petticoats, but it kept getting hotter.

She refilled the mold and set the pot back on the coals. Then, despite her husband's warning against exposing herself as a target to the outside world, she popped the peg on the shutter and eased it open a crack. She waited a moment, but all was silent. No explosions, no cataclysms. She opened it another inch farther and then swung it wide.

There was a cool breeze off the river, fluttering the tattered remnants of the parchment hide that had been stretched over the window frame. She lifted her hair off the nape of her neck and bent forward.

The face of the shutter was scored with gouges and pockmarks. A couple of musket balls were still embedded. Graced with a sudden inspiration, she tried to pry them loose with her fingernails, but they were in too deep. She popped them out with a knife and took them over to the hearth, bouncing the scrap lead up and down in the palm of her hand.

As she bent forward to splunk them into the rendering pot, there was a distant crackling sound and something flew in through the window, buzzing across her back and past the side of her head. The sensation was much the same as when a hummingbird had once nearly collided with her doing its morning rounds of the wildflowers—the same tiny buffet of the air displaced by a whir-winged body. But this thing flew straight into the wall in front of her face, showering out splinters.

Kate flung herself down on the floor and lay there for a moment, regaining control of her lungs. Then she crabbed her body around to face the open window and crawled toward it. When she reached the wall she stretched her right hand up and flipped the shutter closed, then stood up and refastened the catch.

Someone was approaching the house, shouting on the run. "Kate? Are you in there? Kate . . ." hammering on the door. "Can you hear me? Open the door if you can!"

"Of course I'm in here; where else would I be?" She reached

out to take down the oak bough they used as a bar, but the door was jumping back and forth against it. "I cannot take down the bar with you pounding away on the other side!" The door stopped jumping. She lifted the bough out of its struts, and Sandy burst in, red-faced and breathless, still carrying his hoe.

"I heard the sound of a shot from this direction! Are you hurt?"

"No. I opened the shutter, so they put a shot across my bows—well, across my stern, I suppose, would be more like."

"I told you! So long as this keeps up you must not—"

"I know, I know—but it was so stifling in here, and the heat from the fire and all . . ."

"Better a little discomfort than a musket ball between the eyes."

"You said yourself that if they wanted their bullets to hit us, they would have done so long ago."

He stood his hoe in the corner by the door and slumped down on a stool. "If we give them the impression that we are no longer frightened by musket balls flying past a foot away from us, they are liable to start shaving it finer." He picked up the bullet mold. "What are you doing with this?"

Kate was bending down to take the crucible of lead from the fire. She carried it over to the table and took the bullet mold out of his hand, going on about her business without answering him since it was obvious what she was doing with it. Sandy said: "I have no use for any more musket balls than I already have at present. If you need something to occupy yourself, I could do with some more birdshot for when the ducks come back on their way—"

He was drowned out by a roar of gunfire from outside, accompanied by a wolfish howling. Bullets thudded into the door and the shutter and walloped puffs of dirt down from the roof sods. He leaped up and tore his musket from the pegs set into the chimney-piece. He took a step toward the door and then stopped and lowered his head, letting the musket hang in his hands.

The gunshots and the lunatic chorale carried on unabated for a moment and then trailed off under the approaching onslaught of a burly male voice. "Mister Sutherland? Mrs. Sutherland? Are you safe in there? Hallo the house!" A large hand thudded on the door.

Sandy propped his musket against the lintel post and pulled open the door. Framed by the doorway and backlit by the sun was a heroic figure in red coat, tartan sash, and belted sword. "Mister Sutherland! Mrs. Sutherland! Such a relief to see you have suffered no harm from those villains. They ran off quick enough when they saw me coming." He took off his Admiral Nelson hat to get through the doorway and even then had to stoop. "I trust I have not come upon you at an inopportune time?"

"No, sir, certainly not. Kate, would you boil a pot of tea for Captain Cameron?"

Cameron waved his hand and said: "No, no—I thank you for your hospitable offer, but tea disturbs my bowels. I took the liberty, since I was coming on you uninvited, of providing the refreshments, if you would care to join me. . . ." From the voluminous bosom of his gold-corded tunic, he produced a large, silver-mounted flask.

Kate fetched down two tin cups and set them on the table. "None for yourself, Mrs. Sutherland?"

"No, thank you, Mister Cameron."

"Well, all the more for us, then," pouring a healthy gurgle into both cups. "It is a pity that we cannot drink it as we would back home, with the silver pannikin and the flame, but out here in the wilderness . . . *Shlanje fha*!"

Sandy raised his own cup, said, *"Shlanje mhor,"* and took a small sip, then a larger one. Kate fetched herself a cup of water from the bucket by the door, then sat down at the far end of the table and listened to Cameron going on about the misty hills of home. She tried to quell her distaste for him by dwelling on his obvious pride in his Gaelic heritage, which was no small thing at a time when most of the civilized world regarded a Highlander as something slightly more savage than a Red Indian and a good deal less noble. Unfortunately, that only reminded her of the rumors she'd heard—that Duncan Cameron had never actually set foot in the Highlands.

She might have been able to hold her tongue if her husband hadn't appeared to take him at face value. When it got to the point where she felt she was going to gag if she heard one more 'Och, aye!' or 'Lochaber no more,' she said: "I assume there must be some purpose to your visit, Mister Cameron, since in nearly a year that we have been neighbors this is the first time you have honored us with your presence."

"You are quite right, Mrs. Sutherland, otherwise I would never have presumed to intrude upon you without ever being invited." He refilled his cup and her husband's. "No doubt you are both aware of the *cehlidh* we will be holding at Fort Gibraltar tonight, for those among your friends and neighbors who will be departing for Upper Canada in the morning."

She said: "For the deserters, you mean."

He pursed his lips and shook his head sadly. "Only a woman or a child could use that word so lightly—eh, Private Sutherland? Or was it Corporal?"

"Just Private, sir. They tried promotions on me once or twice, but they did not take."

"That is nothing to be ashamed of—quite the opposite. It is always the private soldier who gets the job done, or that has been my experience. Well, you and I know, Private Sutherland, that 'deserters' is a very hard word to use on poor folk like yourselves that came halfway across the world on false promises—whether false by design or ignorance makes little difference. But despite all they have suffered at the hands of the people who lured them here, I know that somewhere in their hearts there is still a tortured doubt that by going to a safer place they are somehow being derelict to their duty. Well, the sense of duty and loyalty has always been the great strength of our race, but it can sometimes be a curse. So I thought to myself: If only some of those who have chosen to remain could find enough Christian charity in their hearts to come to the *cehlidh* tonight and show that they have no ill will . . ."

Her husband said: "It seems like a small enough thing."

Kate laughed. "Do you not see what he is about? He means to use us to convince the few that might be wavering, or perhaps he even hopes to lure us in at this late date." Cameron was studying the claywork on the chimneypiece. "Do you get a set bounty for every head, Mister Cameron, or is it just pride in your work that makes you want to sweep up every straggler in your net?"

That enameled monument of a head swiveled luxuriously on its pedestal until the dark blue eyes were focused on her. The twinkling charm lights had cooled to a crystalline glitter. "I am afraid I do not take your meaning, Mrs. Sutherland."

"I think you take my meaning well enough. You have already managed to convince two-thirds of the colony to desert, and broke the governor, yet you are still working hard to snatch up the paltry few remaining. Your employers in the North West Fur Trading Company must be very proud of you."

His voice quavering with suppressed indignation, Cameron said: "I do understand that the last few weeks have put a great strain on all of you, but the character your neighbors give you, Mrs. Sutherland, had led me to expect a bit more charity of heart. The stories they tell—of Kate MacPherson nursing the sick on board ship after the doctor died, of Kate MacPherson herding on the stragglers along the long march through the snow from Fort Churchill to York Factory—''

Suddenly he interrupted himself, wrinkling his forehead, and paused in the act of refilling their cups. ''Funny . . . it does seem strange to me, Sandy—I may call you Sandy?—that after a full year of marriage they should still refer to your wife by her maiden name. Perhaps it would have been easier for them to remember if you had changed your name.'' He laughed and winked. ''But it is precisely because of the esteem your neighbors hold you in that I came here today. It would mean so much to them if only Kate and Sandy MacPhers—*Sutherland!* Sutherland''—laughing and rolling his eyes—''were to come by the *cehlidh* tonight for a moment or two, a glass of claret and a cup of tea, a handshake here, a kind word there . . .

''You see, your wife is quite right in her accusations. I do want to see you all away from here, or as many of you as I can spirit away. Her only mistake—quite understandably, I suppose, considering what you have suffered through these last years—is in assuming that my reasons have to do with the North West Company. It has all been for your own sakes, and no true friend of yours would have done less.''

''If you are such a true friend,'' Kate asked him, ''what happened to your promise that the servants of the North West Company would let us alone as soon as Governor MacDonell surrendered?''

''The same thing that happens to all my promises—I kept it.''

''Oh? And what do you call what was going on out there just now when you came to the door? A choir practice?''

Cameron looked at her blandly and said: ''Those men out there were not servants of the North West Company. From the glimpse I caught of them before they ran off, they looked to me to be Indians and half-breeds.''

''They work for the North West Company!''

''I imagine some of them have taken the company's wages for a job of work from time to time, but that does not put them under my command or anybody else's. Oh, I can scare them off when I catch them at some mischief like today's, but the moment my back is turned they will be at it again. And after tomorrow, when I leave with the brigade . . . .''

Alexander said: ''When you leave?''

''Certainly. I promised to escort Miles MacDonell and the others to Upper Canada, or at least as far as Fort William, and the company may well choose to post me elsewhere next year, so I might not return at all. That is the reason I have worked so desperately to get you all away from here. It is difficult enough for me to control the half-breeds, but once I am gone . . ."

He bit his lower lip, paused to assume a graver expression, then leaned forward across the table. "You see, you may think you know the half-breeds, from watching them ride back and forth from Fort Gibraltar and seeing them when they are jovial, but you have never seen them at war. They have spent their lives fighting the Blackfoot and the Sioux and the Assiniboine, and winning—by being more savage than the savages. The half-breeds want you out of here, at any cost. When I am gone, when they see that those of you who remain will not be scared off by threats and harassment . . ." He drew in a long, slow breath and spread his hands across the table-top.

Kate looked across the table at her husband. He was staring at her with a kind of dreamlike horror, as though seeing her in some mutilated memory of El Guerrilla. It took an effort to pull her eyes away and back to Duncan Cameron, who was regarding them both with a credible imitation of tragical commiseration. She said: "It is a remarkable thing, Mister Cameron, that you should feel such compassion and responsibility for people who only shook your hand for the first time ten months ago."

He offered a demurring, self-deprecating shrug and said: "When it comes down to it, have we not known each other all our lives? Are we all not Highlanders together, all banished from the same *shians* and shielings of home? If we do not help each other, who will?"

She said: "I had not known you hailed from Kildonan, Captain."

"Well, Kildonan for you, Lochaber for me, it is still the same fabled Highlands we all long for."

"Really? I would have thought your heart would long for the fabled highlands of Schenectady, New York." That brought his head up. "Do not embarrass yourself further, Mister Cameron, by attempting to deny it. We had it from your own people at Fort Gibraltar."

She had it from nothing of the kind; all she had was a third-hand rumor through Marie Anne Lajimodierre at the Hogmanay *cehlidh* and through Catherine Pritchard since then, but it was worth a shot. Cameron glanced at her husband, who was looking at the tabletop with a relatively impassive expression. Kate knew that he was try-

g to think of a way to tell her to stop embarrassing him that
ouldn't embarrass him further. In the end, he remained silent.

If Cameron had brazened it out an inch further, Sandy would
ve been convinced that his wife was even more of a bitch than
  thought already. Amazingly, what the man did, after turning
rious shades of pink and white, was to recap his flask and tuck it
ack inside his tunic, clap his plumed hat under his armpit, and
ead for the door. He paused there to heft up her husband's musket
d say in English: "I'll just take this with me."

"That you won't!" Alexander bounded up and grabbed hold of

"Perhaps you didn't receive my order for all colonists to surren-
r up their weapons in the King's name?"

"A lot of people have been bandying orders back and forth in
e King's name."

"If you doubt my authority, you can take it up in a court of law."

They jerked the gun back and forth like a couple of dogs on
ther end of a bone. Suddenly it went off with a burst of blue smoke
d sparks, the bullet tearing up through the roof sods. They both
t go of it, and it fell to the floor.

As Sandy stooped to pick it up, Cameron stomped one cavalry
oot down on the midpoint of the barrel and swept his sword out
 the scabbard. It wasn't at all a nickel-plated dress sword but a
ue-black, cutlass-heavy hacking blade with a thin silver line along
e cutting edge. Sandy retreated to the wall and snatched up his
e, cocking it back over his shoulder. They stood brandishing their
eapons, each waiting for the other to move.

Kate ran to the hearth, wrapped her hands in the folds of her
irt, and picked up the little iron pot nestled in the coals. Then
e skirted back around the table, faced Duncan Cameron, and said
  matter-of-factly as she could: "I spent the afternoon pouring
llets for the musket, Mister Cameron. I still have half a pot of
olten lead. This room is too small to dodge us both. Would you
ther be hacked or parboiled? Make up your mind."

Cameron stepped off the musket, letting the sword lower itself
ightly. "Keep it, then, for all the good it will do you." He jerked
e door open. "Only I advise you, for your own sakes—when
uthbert Grant and his friends come calling, you'll be better off
ot shooting back."

He was gone. Sandy waited a moment, then lowered the hoe
d closed the door. Kate scurried back to the hearth and put the
ot down. When she stood up, blowing on her hands, he was still

standing by the door, but his eyes were on her. He said: "Are y(
sure you have no relations to the MacBeths on your mother's side?

In the morning she stood on the riverbank in front of the hou
listening to the pipes come closer, pealing out "The Road to t
Isles" over the Red River and the wild prairie. Sandy had go
down to Fort Gibraltar to say good-bye to his sister. She'd refus(
to go with him to say good-bye to John.

The lead canoe rounded the point with Robert Gunn sitting
the prow, cheeks puffed out like melons and the ribbons flying fro
his bonnet. At the waist of the canoe sat Duncan Cameron, stretc
ing and grinning like an old cat in the sun, with Miles MacDon(
in manacles beside him. Kate stood with her arms crossed watchi
the canoes go by, counting off the people she knew, Jean and Ang
McKay, Joan MacLeod, Catherine Sutherland and John McInty
the Bannermans and the Mathesons and all the others she'd chas(
around the shielings above the Ulidh and bathed the fever sweat (
on the *Prince of Wales*. None of them would look at her.

Toward the stern of the last canoe, John sat stabbing clumsily
the water with a paddle, hopelessly out of time with the voyageu
Her eyes touched on him and recoiled, fixing on to the silver
white column of a birch trunk on the opposite bank. She stared
the tree resolutely, convincing herself that she could make out t
wispy curls of the papery outer skin. The prow of the canoe pok(
in past her field of vision, then the heads of the paddlers and t
passengers. There was an extended instant when she and John a
the birch tree were poised together as three points on a straig
line; then John broke away as the movement of the canoe carri(
him on. Suddenly he turned and bawled, "Katy!" He started
stand, and the steersman pushed him down before he swamped t
canoe. "God keep you, Katy! I will write to you!"

Some manner of thin glass casing burst inside her. She shout(
back: "Stay safe, Johnny! God bless you!" She pressed her han(
to her mouth and tried to hold back the tears, watching the lo
line of canoes glide down the alley of water between the overhan
ing trees until the last one rounded the bend. With them went o
hundred and fifty of Lord Selkirk's colonists; barely sixty remain(
behind.

She turned and headed back toward the house. She was almo
to the door when she saw her husband coming through the scree
of bush that hemmed the base of Point Douglas. He was walkir
very stiffly, as though his neck were shackled to a broomstick. Tw
men on horseback were ambling along behind him, Bostona

gman and another métis, their rifles sloped down lazily across
r horses' necks to point between his shoulder blades.

HAPTER 46

When Chief Peguis stooped in through the tent flap, Bostonais leaned sideways and spat—fortunately missing Ser-
im Lamarr, who was stretched out studying the constellations
he backs of his eyelids. Grant didn't share Bostonais's prejudice
inst the Chief. There was no question that he wasn't pretty—fat
squat and greasy, with only a shapeless flap of skin for a nose.
e nose he'd been born with had been removed many years ago.
re were many theories as to how this might have happened; a
centered around the Indian custom of cutting off the nose of a
use caught in adultery. This was usually visited upon the wife,
there had been exceptions.

ll in all, Chief Peguis's face put Grant in mind of a size fourteen
ccasin that had been boiled in suet and garnished on top with
ned grass stalks. But behind that face was the mind of a cunning
bastard, and Grant was increasingly of the opinion that—friends
enemies—it was much more pleasant to deal with the intelligent
n the alternative.

he Chief settled his bulk onto the buffalo robe across the fire
m Grant. Grant said: "What did they say?"

he Chief reached into the pouch at his belt, took out a folded
ce of paper, and handed it across the fire to Grant. Grant snapped
pen. In four clauses John Pritchard and the others still holed up
Colony House—excluding John Richards McKay, who, accord-
to Bethsy, only wanted to get this foolishness over with and
rn to the Qu'Appelle—laid down their proposals for a truce.
ce the high-sounding phrases had been extracted, the gist of it
s simply "Say, fellas, here's an idea—why don't we pretend
hing unpleasant ever happened and go back to being friends?"
which case, given six months, they would have a new governor
rning out more proclamations.

Grant folded up the paper and dropped it in the fire. He reac
out and dragged his traveling desk across the flattened grass of
tent floor. He unscrewed his ink bottle, loaded a pen, whipped
a clean sheet of paper, and wrote: "1. All settlers to retire fr
Red River immediately, and no appearance of a colony to remai

That was really all there was to say, but he filled out three m
clauses, noting that the Hudson's Bay Company would be allow
to retain a trading house at the Forks, and that all colonists wo
be transported safely out of the territory. He signed his name be
the last clause, then skipped down to the bottom of the page
wrote "the Four Chiefs of the Half-breeds." He handed the pe
William Shaw to sign below his name, then Bonhomme Montc
Rather than wake up Seraphim, he got Bostonais to sign for
fourth.

He pushed the desk aside and wafted the paper back and fo
beside the fire to dry the ink. On the other side of the fire old Cl
Peguis's eyes watched him through the smoke, black within th
oyster folds. Grant said: "Are there enough boats now to take
all?" Peguis nodded, but his eyes didn't move. "Good. Take
back to them"—handing the paper across the fire—"and tell th
they'll be leaving in the morning."

"What if they say—"

"There are no more 'what ifs,' Chief. They've used them
up."

Peguis folded the paper. "I am not your errand boy, Wapp
ton."

"I know that, Chief, and you know that, but you'll take
piece of paper to them nonetheless, won't you?"

"This is a foolish thing you do."

"Is it? Is it? When your grandchildren, and my grandchild
can still ride a horse from the Forks to the lake without being hau
off in chains for trespassing, which of us do you think they'll ca
fool? Now, if you'll excuse me . . . as difficult as it might be
believe, I have a woman waiting for me who's prettier than yo
The Chief laughed.

Outside the tent, the night was alive with singing. The frogs
nightbirds and crickets didn't stand a chance against the wild ch
around the bonfire, ranting along with Falcon and his fiddle. Gr
noted approvingly that the flames were high and bright enough
cast distended shadows of the dancers onto the walls of the te
where the prisoners were being kept. He wanted them to stay scar
In the entire three days since the remaining colonists had be

herded to Frog Plain, they had simply been too scared to do anything foolish. If the prisoners could remain intelligently frightened for just one more night, if Grant could stay alert to every twitch in the wilder of his roaring boys for just a few more hours, it would all be over without anybody dying.

He decided that the bonfire would be the likeliest place to look for Bethsy. He started across the triangle of darkness between the three points of firelight: the prisoners' tents, the cluster of cabins, and the bonfire. Peguis's eyes had made him self-conscious. Grant hadn't been conscious of himself for more than a moment since Duncan Cameron and the brigade had headed downstream. He'd only been aware of the problems that had to be solved, the piecing together of solutions, and the momentum he was riding.

Suddenly he felt something poking into the small of his back. He leaped forward and whirled around. Bethsy was doubled over laughing, jabbing her forefinger into the air. She got enough breath to squeal out: " 'Leap rogue and whore jump . . . and . . .' I can't remember the rest of it.''

"You'd better, it's likely the only ceremony you'll get.''

She clapped her hands on his waist and jerked their torsos together, grinding her shoulders to roll her breasts against his chest. He slapped his right hand on her narrow little bottom, then slid it down over the pneumatic curve, bunching up her skirt and placing his hand between the tops of her thighs. He crooked his arm and picked her up one-handed, propping her against his side. "Come along, I want to check on the guards. . . .'' He set off carrying her by the crotch, delighted by her squeals and by the power in his arms and shoulders. There were limits to his strength, however. After a dozen steps, he had to put her down.

She snatched hold of his hand and tried to drag him off toward the bushes by the river. "Your guards could get along without you for five minutes . . . or a half hour . . . or three or four days.''

"I have to make sure of the rotations. If they stay on too long, they get cranky and might do something stupid.''

"I get cranky, too. You wouldn't want me to do something stupid.''

He yanked her toward him, bent over, then straightened back up with her draped across his shoulder like a sack of flour. As he walked on toward the prisoners' tents, he held her with one hand and with the other started furling up her skirt. "Once they get a look at this, I'll have a hell of a time getting them into the boats in the morning.'' She squealed like an irate piglet and kicked her legs

in the air. It occurred to him that her shrieks might be mistaken by
the prisoners for the voice of one of their own women, so he put
her down again.

Alex Fraser and Joseph Cadotte, an eager young recruit from
along the Pembina, were standing next to the tents with shotguns
cradled in their arms. Grant said: "Hello, Alex, Joseph. How long
have you been standing guard?"

"Not long," replied Alex. "We just sent Deschamps and Machicabou back to the fire."

"Good. Only one more night of this. Well, I suppose I should
get back to—"

"Grant!"

The voice had come out of the darkness, a hoarse, hard rasp.
They all whirled in that direction, the sentries snaking down their
shotguns to firing-from-the-hip positions. A second voice spurted
out in Gaelic: "No, please, Mister Grant, it is only us, we mean
no harm."

Grant pushed down the shotguns. Mrs. Sutherland and her husband came out from the bush cover behind the cluster of tents. Both
were carrying awkward-looking bundles wrapped in HBC blankets. "We did not mean to startle you. We have—my husband has—
something you must see."

"How did you get out there?" Then, before they could reply, he
turned toward the sentries and switched to French. "I thought you
were keeping them within the tents?"

Alex Fraser said: "They must have snuck out while Deschamps
and Machicabou were on."

Joseph Cadotte said: "You'll see, you ask them—I bet they snuck
out there hours ago."

He turned back to the Sutherlands. "What do you have to show
me?"

"You will need enough light to read by."

There was a fire in the open space between the tents, partly to
give the prisoners something to cook on and partly to cast enough
light so the guards would supposedly see anyone trying to slip away.
Grant started toward it. "No! Please—" Mrs. Sutherland headed
him off. "We would rather not . . . not there, where the others
would see . . ."

Her husband said: "It makes no difference to me."

Grant didn't have a great deal of energy or patience left. All he
wanted to do was crawl off under a willow bush with Bethsy and
sleep for two weeks. But there was something horribly wrenching

n the fact that this proud, self-sufficient woman should be pleading
vith him for some insignificant favor. He sighed and turned back
o the council tent. "Come along, then—oh, you might just as well
eave those here," indicating their bundles.

"No! No, they are not heavy."

"Very well, then, suit yourselves. Come along." He waved good
vening to the sentries and started off, trailed by the Sutherlands
nd a surly Bethsy. "This is my wife, or wife-to-be, or . . . damned
:onfusing in a country with no clergy or magistrates. At any rate—
Mrs. Grant, Mister and Mrs. Sutherland."

"How do you do."

"How do you do."

"How do you do."

They walked the rest of the way in silence, except for a clunking
noise from Mrs. Sutherland's bundle—like chunks of wood knock-
ng together. The council tent was empty now, no doubt they had
ll gone out to the bonfire.

The fire had burned down to coals. Grant fed it a few twigs and
ome hunks of spruce. They sat down on the buffalo robes, Grant
nd Bethsy on one side of the fire and the Sutherlands and their
oundles on the other. As the light flared up he could see the end of
a hand-turned spindle sticking out of her bundle and the arc of the
wheel stretching one side of the wool wrapping.

He was thrown for a moment by seeing the Sutherlands in the
ight. Both of them looked scoured to the bone, with haggard lines,
a pink tinge around the roots of their eyelashes, and scared, flitting
:yes. Grant reminded himself that he had been working very hard
o make sure the Sutherlands and their friends were haggard and
:cared, and that it was best in the long run for all of them to remain
naggard and scared.

Alexander Sutherland fished through the neck of his shirt and
oulled out a folded rectangle of moosehide. He handed it across
he fire to Grant. Inside was a folded sheet of expensive vellum
oarchment. Once it had had a wax signet seal on it, two-thirds of
he way down its face, but all that remained now was a pinkish
stain on a portion of the paper. Grant skimmed through the elaborate calligraphy above the traces of the seal, then looked across
he fire at Alexander Sutherland for some explanation.

Sandy said: "Read it!"

"I have."

"Well, then! There you have it."

"There I have what, Mister Sutherland?"

"That is a freehold deed."

"I know. I read it."

"Then there you have it."

Grant handed the paper to Bethsy, wondering what it was Mister Sutherland might be trying to communicate to him. "Uhm . . . forgive me, Mister Sutherland. I am very tired and no doubt I am being excessively obtuse, but . . . there I have what?"

"Well—the rest of them may be tenants of the colony, but *that*"— pointing at the paper Bethsy was studying—"proves that our farm belongs to us outright. You have no right to drive us off."

Grant placed his thumb and forefinger on the bridge of his nose and pinched hard. It didn't help. With a sigh, he took the paper from Bethsy's hands and said: "This appears to have been signed by Thomas Douglas, Earl of Selkirk—"

" 'Appears' nothing," said Sandy, reaching up and taking it from him. "It *is*."

"Very well. And before Thomas Douglas sold said plot of land to you, he got legal title to the land from the Hudson's Bay Company, correct? And the Hudson's Bay Company were granted their property rights by Charles Stuart. Now how did Charles Stuart come by his rights to this country?"

"He was the King!"

"But what made King Charles Stuart's rights take precedence over King Louis Bourbon's or King Frank Hapsburg's or any of the dozen other European Kings who claimed they owned this country? Not to mention the poor red-brown sods who'd been living here since Charles Stuart's ancestors were still painting themselves blue? Quite simply—Charles Stuart's military forces were stronger than everybody else's."

Sandy still didn't appear to get it. Grant crouched down beside him and said: "Do you hear singing?"

"What?" The thin-boned head jerked up, and the hard little blue eyes flicked once at Grant and then darted away.

"Singing—do you hear singing?" He cupped his hand behind his ear and cocked his head.

"Something like singing, I suppose."

"Well, those men singing, and the hundreds of others like them scattered across the *pays d'en haut*, are the strongest military force for thousands of miles. And that makes their rights take precedence over your piece of paper."

Kate Sutherland said: "You cannot fight the whole British army."

"What makes you think we'll have to, or any part of it? Do you

hink the British army is going to ship a regiment into Hudson's
3ay and then row up the Hayes through hundreds of miles of granite
nd muskeg and waterfalls? Or up the Kaministiquia through thou-
ands of miles of the same? Or perhaps you think they will land on
he Pacific Coast and claw across the Rocky Mountains and then
ight their way through the Blackfoot confederacy? It seems like a
ot of trouble for them to go to, considering that not one British
ubject has died at our hands. We intend to allow the fur companies
o continue taking their money out of the *pays d'en haut*, and that
s all the British Empire gives a damn about as far as this country
s concerned."

He was quite sure he hadn't raised his voice, but both the Suth-
rlands had hunched down into their shoulders as though he'd been
creaming abuse at them. Two Dogs Fucking had told him once
hat the only rule worth living by was to try to be as kind to other
eople as possible. He'd always assumed that the "as possible"
eferred to his own limitations of character and patience. He was
eginning to think that it meant "as they will let you." Adopting
what he hoped was a tone of finality, he said: "Tomorrow morning
Chief Peguis's people will get you safely started on your way toward
ack River House on Lake Winnipeg. From there it will be up to
he gentlemen of the Hudson's Bay Company to transport you to
Jpper Canada or back to Scotland."

"Scotland?"

"There is nothing for us there!"

"There is nothing for you here, believe me. The sun going down
omorrow will see not one stick of your colony left standing upon
nother. Your houses will be burned and your crops trampled into
he ground. Within a week the red and green shoots of buffalo grass
nd wolf willow will have painted out the black. By autumn you
vould need a map to find out where your houses stood."

For a moment the only sound was the crackle and hiss of the
uds of flame eating through the twig ends inside the circle of
tones. When Alexander Sutherland spoke, his voice had the same
arched, rustling sound. "Patrick Sellar." He turned and crawled
ut through the tent flap, dragging his bundle of possessions behind
im. His wife followed him.

Grant called after her: "By God, I hope you realize that you
vould have been dead three days ago if it wasn't for me."

"Were you expecting us to thank you?"

He found himself laughing. "Why, yes, when it comes right
own to it, I suppose I was."

In the morning Grant stood on the riverbank and watched the flotilla of York boats and birchbark canoes depart. Chief Peguis posed in the prow of the lead York boat, making a lumpy walnut figurehead. A number of his warriors were salted among the rowing benches, just as flummoxed by the concept of oars as the colonists were by canoe paddles.

Near the stern of the second boat, her unbound hair a blaze of copper in the sun's halo of light, sat Kate Sutherland.

PART THREE

SEVEN OAKS

CHAPTER 47

It looked thin and it smelled thinner, but with a few more hours of boiling down it might pass for barley soup. The barley had been bought from the traders at Jack River House, along with the clan-sized copper kettle, cheerfully totted up at twice retail against the Earl of Selkirk's account with the Company of Adventurers. The mallet to pound the husks off the barley and the hollowed-out log to pound it in had been Kate's husband's contribution. Mrs. Pritchard had built the fire and arranged the quadrangle of stones that supported the kettle. The stripped green bough used to stir the kettle had been Kate's invention. The soup was rendering off bits of bark and filaments of wood in places, but a little essence of poplar wouldn't harm the flavor.

Catherine Pritchard was standing on the other side of the fire, with her son's cradleboard slung from a bough on a spruce tree behind her. She was talking in English—she appeared to have abandoned her half-learned Gaelic as completely as her Indian languages. "In the old ways this would cook with hot stones—make the stones hot in the fire and put them in the water. They name the Stoneys that—the Assiniboines: 'Those People What Cook with Hot Stones'—but it was everybody who did. No other ways to make water cook when all you got to put it in is bark buckets and such. Boy, when those traders first came with the iron pots, you bet there was happy Indian womans. Do your arms tired yet? No? Boy, in the days when I was still a Pied Noir . . ."

Kate didn't mind Mrs. Pritchard's prattle; it blended with the constant whisper of the evergreens and the rattling murmur of Jack River—a fast, clear-water stream more like a Highland river than the muddy Red. She suspected that Mrs. Pritchard's husband didn't encourage her to talk about her Indian past.

". . . and when we couldn't find the buffalo sometimes, when we hunt and hunt and hunt but no luck, and bad hungers, we make

319

a camp and a sun lodge, and the medicine people would dance the Buffalo Dance. And always, then, the buffalo would come to us.''

"Always?"

"Always."

"How long would it take?"

"Oh, a day, a week, a few weeks. They would dance until the buffalo come. It always worked. Do your arms tired yet?''

"Yes." They weren't, but she handed the stick over anyway. She could have kept on stirring until the soup was ready without anyone's help, but that would have been hoarding. A sense of purpose was a precious commodity these days. They had been huddling for weeks under spruce-bough lean-tos or canvas awnings hunched against the palisade of Jack River House. There was nothing they could do but wait, and nothing concrete to wait for except a vague hope that circumstances would move them somewhere else before winter set in.

The fort guns boomed. They did so three or four times a week, whenever a trading party of canoes rounded the bend in the river. It was a courteous ceremonial gesture that also served to point out to the Indians that the fort's artillery was in perfect working order.

This time it wasn't an Indian canoe but a York boat. The crew beached the craft and headed inland, but instead of going through the fort gates they skirted the palisade and came straight toward the ragged camp tacked to the outside wall. At the head of the landing party strode a tall, big-chested man with an upswept wreath of wine-red hair. Catherine Pritchard merely glanced at him and kept on stirring, as though his arrival had been inevitable.

As he had the first time Kate had seen him, Colin Robertson bounded onto an outcropping of rock and struck an oratorical posture. And as before, the scarecrow remnants of Kildonan parish flocked into place in front of him—but this time, instead of thousands, there were only sixty-four.

"Perhaps you remember me from County Sutherland two years ago—for those who don't, my name is Colin Robertson. Lord Selkirk and the Hudson's Bay Company have engaged me to come back to Rupertsland and establish a trading house on the Athabasca—to show those North West Company bastards that we can push just as far northwest as they can. But when I reached the Forks of the Red I realized that there was something far more important to attend to. So I sent the expedition on to the Athabasca and headed here to bring you back."

Someone shouted: "Back where?"

"Back to the colony."

"There is no colony!"

Colin Robertson's eyes and nostrils flared, and he thrust his hands into the pockets of his royal-blue brass-buttoned coat as though to keep them out of mischief. "I can understand your reluctance"— although the impression given was that he didn't understand it at all—"but a great deal has transpired that you do not know of. For one thing, another party of colonists set sail from Stornoway this spring. They will have landed at York Factory by now and should be passing through Jack River in a few weeks. You could wait and come upriver with them, but it seemed to me you'd want to return to the Forks as soon as you can and build yourselves snug new houses before winter sets in."

"So the half-breeds can burn them down again!"

"The half-breeds have cleared off and gone to the buffalo grounds. Now along with the new party of colonists is a gentleman named Mister Robert Semple. He is the new governor of Assiniboia—Lord Selkirk had decided to replace Miles MacDonell even before the unfortunate events of the last few months. Mister Semple is also the new governor-in-chief of the Hudson's Bay Company's operations in Rupertsland. The situation at Red River will be entirely different this year."

"How? It sounds the bloody same to me!"

Colin Robertson picked out the man who had spoken. "For one thing, *I'll* be there with you—and if you do not believe that changes things, little man, come up here and tell me face to face."

It was an unfortunate tack to take for people who regarded a braggart as only marginally higher than a tapeworm, and a bully a few notches lower. John Pritchard bounded up onto the rock beside Colin Robertson and said: "What Mister Robertson means is that he knows the country and the people in it, which Governor MacDonell didn't, which is what led to all the trouble last year. Why do you think the North West Company was so set on keeping me from getting back to join you? Because a little knowledge is a dangerous thing to them. You are afraid this is a doomed enterprise, but I say 'No, we can!' If we just . . ."

Kate scowled and turned her attention back to the soup and the fire that needed feeding. Catherine Pritchard was stirring away with a contented little smile on her face, as though now that her John had taken the floor, it would all turn out right. Mister Pritchard had nominated himself to fill the gap left by Archibald MacDonald. On the day after their arrival in Jack River, Archibald MacDonald had announced that he was heading north to catch the supply ship from York Factory—someone had to tell Lord Selkirk what had happened to his colony. Kate had murmured to her husband: "As the rat said jumping off, 'You folks sit tight, I will just swim over and tell the admiral.' "

The soup was boiling down nicely. The trick was to effect a working compromise between volume and flavor. As far as Kate was concerned, the debate raging on among the spruce trees was just so much gas. They had nowhere else to go. They would freeze or starve to death here; Scotland was out of the question; and it was too late in the year to try for Upper Canada.

Sandy drifted out through the edge of the crowd and came toward her. She was surprised at his appearance. Colin Robertson's speechifying had thrown her back two years. His skin was darker, his hair was lighter, and the devastated landscape behind his eyes was gone—despite the last few months.

He said: "If the soup can take care of itself for a moment, we should see about gathering our things together to go back."

"They are still arguing over it."

"It makes no difference. We have nowhere else to go."

He suddenly looked small and crabbed. There were men in the world who found a way to affect the currents of events rather than allow themselves to be swept along. But the best her husband could come up with was, "We have nowhere else to go."

The chief trader at Jack River House was more than happy to furnish them with a couple of extra York boats to get them out of his jurisdiction. As they were setting off Kate pointed out that they were learning more about inland navigation than farming.

The homogeneous, tangled wilderness she'd traveled through a year ago was beginning to be filled with familiar features. There was the spot a day south of the narrows where the western shore suddenly became prairie while the eastern side stayed woodlands. There was the beach a few days farther on where she'd stood in sheets of rain and told Alexander that she'd marry him. There was Chief Peguis's summer encampment at the mouth of Rivière aux Morts.

August was half-gone by the time the long oars churned them past Frog Plain. Most of the métis cabins were already showing signs of neglect, although a couple still looked occupied. The boats churned on upstream past the places on the west bank where the farms had been. Cuthbert Grant had been right; already there was nothing there but an impregnable tangle of green grown up between

e trees. From somewhere behind Kate a female voice chanted in
almost inaudible monotone: "May your own roof trees be burned
er your heads and your wives and children turned out into the
ow, may you die forgotten in a foreign land and your body flung
to a ditch with no keening or striking of palms or even the howl
a dog to mourn you."

As the boats turned to follow the river along the north shore of
int Douglas, Kate leaned out over the gunwale and peered harder,
it there was nothing to see. She wondered if they were all stone
ad to come back.

Consequently, it was even more startling when the boats rounded
int Douglas and Fort Douglas came into view. Instead of charred
undation logs overgrown with weeds, there was a new pink-log
arracks with a half-finished building standing beside it in the midst
waist-high, nodding fields of wheat and barley, the green already
eeding into gold, and an immense stack of fresh-sawed beams
asoning in the sun. As the boats nosed into shore there was a puff
smoke from a small stone building off to one side, and they
ard the boom of a swivel gun. A bright-hued Union Jack with
BC across its face went skating up the flagpole.

Four young men came marching down the riverbank to meet
em. Kate recognized the big blond-bearded boy in front as John
acLeod, the Hudson's Bay Company apprentice trader who had
en allowed to remain at the Forks to operate the HBC trading
st. His three companions were also part of the HBC contingent
Fort Douglas, but the only one she knew by name was Hugh
nderson.

The awestruck colonists piled out of the boats and congregated
ound John MacLeod and company, who modestly allowed that
e four of them had done all the building and tended the crops and
pt the métis from trampling down Colony Gardens—no more
an any other four young men of singular courage and moral fiber
ould have done in the same circumstances.

John MacLeod pointed out the little fieldstone shed. "When the
lf-breeds set Colony House afire, we retreated to the blacksmith's
ed. We had one brass swivel gun and plenty of powder but no
nnon shot. While Hugh and the other lads were blazing away
ith their muskets to keep the half-breeds back, I rummaged around
e shed and found a barrel of chain. We chopped it into eight-inch
ngths, loaded up the swivel gun, and—what do you think? I looked
or something to shoot at, and there were the two of them, side by
de and not thirty yards in front of me . . ."

John Pritchard said: "Which two of them?"

"Which do you think? Bostonais Pangman and the cheeky one
Grant. I had them cold as mutton—" Suddenly he folded his hand
and cleared his throat. "But enough about us, Mister Pritchard.
How did you fare up at Jack River—"

"No, no, go on. . . ."

"Oh, there's really no more to the story, I've lost the thread.
Did you have fair sailing on Lake Winnipeg?"

"No, go on, what happened? You had the two of them dead
rights and . . ."

"What happened was," Hugh Anderson piped in, grinning, "he
missed them. Hit the ground a good twenty yards in front of them.

"More like ten," John MacLeod corrected frostily.

"Ten, then, if you like, but considering they were only thirt
yards away—"

"Never mind—I put a scare into them!"

"Oh, aye—dirtied their faces with the dust. That showed them.

Colin Robertson caved in the head of a keg of HBC brandy, an
the homecoming got festive. Kate drifted around the edge of th
crowd and found her husband waiting for her on the other side wit
their bundles. She took hers, and they bulled their way down th
weed-choked path. Clouds of midges and mosquitoes rose up ou
of the long grass.

It was the warm, apricot-yellow light of evening, when the su
shone straight on across the face of the prairie. The borders of th
fields were indistinguishable from the bush, although a few whea
and potato plants showed here and there among the weeds. Bu
Grant had been wrong about the house. A sharp-cornered rectangl
of juicy green growth showed clearly where it had stood. The chim
ney hadn't burned entirely, but it had fallen in. Ribs of charre
sticks poked out through the powdered clay.

They stood for a long time looking it over, picking with the toe
of their shoes at the crumbling, ground-level soot of a foundatio
log. Finally Sandy raised his arm and pointed. "We should hav
put the door on the side nearest the river, for the breeze and th
view."

"Then we would have had to run all the way around the hous
to get in and out from the fields, and dig a path around in the winter
If we had set the house closer to the base of the point, we coul
have faced it east and had the angle of the river crossing the fron
door and still have a straight path to the fields."

And our back wall next to all the traffic back and forth along
cart track. Very restful.''

It is not exactly the Edinburgh High Road. If we had built a
ked roof instead of slanted, we would not have had such a piling
f snow and ice.''

You cannot build a peaked roof out of sod.''

We could thatch it, then.''

le turned to face her. "Thatch it with what?''

In case you failed to notice, there are several thousand miles
rairie just over there.''

You cannot live under a thatched roof in a climate such as
''

The Bannermans managed well enough last winter.''

seemed perfectly natural that he should bring his hands up to
them on her shoulders as they bickered, just as it was perfectly
ral for her to put hers on his waist. He said: "Last year we
ted building in June. This is August. If we start putting up a log
se with a thatched roof now, we will still be up there plaiting
ch with the snow drifting in. Besides, a thatched roof in this
ntry would be rife with mice and insects in the summer.''

As if sod is not.''

curious sultriness had come into the air—not an all-consuming
, just a steady, melting warmth. Her knees were stiff from
ding in the same place for so long. As she and her husband
ed down among the sweet clover and twitch grass, she thought
lance over at the base of the field to make sure the trees still hid
t Douglas from the cart track. They did.

CHAPTER 48

Although he'd finished sleeping some time ago, Grant
made no move to get out of bed. He lay still, propped up
ne elbow, watching Bethsy. In the heat of the morning she had
ked her way out from under the covers and was lying on her
k with her jaw hanging slack. Every third breath was a soft

snore, regular as clockwork. Her breasts had definitely grown la
and rounder, ripening. The swelling in her belly was rising nic
The bones of her hips and rib cage were becoming sleeked o
with the subtle building up of fat.

From beyond the blanket partition that divided the cabin,
sephte called: "Cuthbert?" He didn't want to take the chanc
waking Bethsy, so he slipped out from under the sheet and pad
over to the partition. "Cuth—"

"Ssh! I can hear you. What is it?"

"Bostonais's here."

"Tell him I'll come find him later."

From the other side of the curtain came Bostonais's voice: "
there's something I got to—"

"Ssh!" No matter how softly Bostonais tried to speak, the
rumble vibrated through the walls. Bethsy gave out a little sigh
rolled onto her side. Grant whispered at the partition: "All ri,
Get a cup of tea, I'll meet you outside."

He pulled on his trousers, slipped out between the hangings,
a cup of tea from Josephte, and went out into the bright Septem
sunlight. The courtyard of Fort Esperance was bustling v
summer-browned *engagés* and their wives and children, all atte
ing to their various duties in preparing for the coming winter.

Bostonais was squatted on the ground with his back against
front wall of Grant's cabin, blowing into a steaming tin cup. G
sat down beside him. They hadn't seen each other for two mon
since Grant and Bethsy headed northwest from the Pembina,
neither of them said a word, just sat side by side in the soft Septe
ber sun.

At last Bostonais said: "They're back."

"Who's back?"

"Les jardinières."

"Back?"

"Back at the Forks. They're building houses again, planting
dens, cutting down the trees, putting up fences, just like they n
left."

"They can't be."

"They are. I saw them with my own eyes when I went to tr
at Fort Gibraltar."

Grant stood up and walked a few steps out into the yard, t
turned and threw his cup against the wall. "Don't they underst
we could have rubbed them all out in an instant?"

"I don't know—you did all the talking to them. Robertson's with
'em."

"Robertson?"

"Colin Robertson. Maybe you don't know him. He used to be
bourgeois for the North West. Old John MacDonald, Le Bras
Croché, threw him out 'cause he was no good. He's smart, though;
nobody says he ain't smart. Seraphim, Deschamps, some of the
others, Robertson's been sitting down around a keg with them,
talking sweet. He's got some of the Frog Plain boys out hunting
meat for *les jardinières*."

"They wouldn't."

"Why not? A little wage here and there—powder and shot and
satin ribbons don't grow off the trees. The North West Company
don't own us."

Grant headed for the cabin door. "It won't take me a moment
to get my traps together. If your horse is run out, there's a big sorrel
in with my string in the fort herd . . ."

"Hold up. Another day won't change anything. Let me rest my
ass, and we can start off tomorrow." Grant stopped and turned
back. It wasn't at all like Bostonais to want time around human
habitation when he could be pounding a horse across the prairie.
Bostonais looked up from his cup. "And you got things here you
should maybe take care of first." When Grant wrinkled his eyebrows quizzically, Bostonais jerked his head over his shoulder, indicating the interior of the cabin.

Grant had to smile. Bostonais hadn't had much experience with
women and didn't understand that lovers became much more stoical about enforced separations once they were married—even a
marriage *à la façon du pays*.

Bethsy's stoical reply was, "And what am I supposed to amuse
myself with while you're charging off to inspect the troops?"

"I won't be more than a couple of weeks. Josephte's here to keep
you company."

"Josephte? I'd get more company out of a drowned rat!"

"Ssh, she'll hear—"

"I will not 'ssh.' What did you have in mind, Josephte and me
squatting in front of the fire sewing moccasins for you and clucking
away about your sisters' husbands and children while you're galloping your pony up and down the banks of the Red River shooting
at a bunch of poor farmers who don't know one end of a gun from
the other?"

"Nobody's going to shoot at anybody."

"Then why can't I come along?"

"It's a good two hundred miles. In your condition . . ."

"I'm pregnant, not crippled."

"It won't be a Sunday promenade; we want to make Fort Gibraltar in five days." He gave her a pause to back down in, but her expression didn't even flicker. "But if you want to come along, I'd be glad to have you."

"I'll think about it."

They spent the night lying side by side staring at the ceiling and pretending to be asleep. When Bostonais hammered on the door in the morning, Grant sat up and said to her: "Well?"

"Well what? Oh. No, I'll stay." She rolled over and covered her head with the sheet.

On the evening of the fifth day Grant and Bostonais trotted through the gates of Fort Gibraltar. Seraphim Lamarr, who was standing in as bourgeois until Duncan Cameron got back from Upper Canada, was just sitting down to dinner. Grant and Bostonais sluiced the top layer of prairie off their hands and faces and joined him.

Seraphim didn't have to be encouraged to talk about the *jardinières*. "It's all going to be different now with MacDonell gone for good. Mister Robertson told me—"

"*Mister* Robertson?" Grant interjected.

Seraphim shrugged. "Well, a bourgeois is still a bourgeois, don't matter whether he's with the North West Company or the Hudson's Bay or Lord Selkirk's colony. Mister Robertson told me the colony's going to have a whole other governor who should be here any day now with a new shipload of colonists."

"A new *what*?"

"A hundred or so, Mister Robertson says, who set off from Scotland in the spring, so they ought to've landed at York Factory in July. I guess they'll be down here by . . ." At this point, Seraphim's rambling eyes met Grant's, and he trailed off uncertainly. "Yes, well . . . even with that there won't be as many of them as there was last year. . . ." After a slight pause, he cleared his throat and tried again. "Mister Robertson told me that Duncan Cameron told the judges in Upper Canada, when he went to court against Miles MacDonell, that it was us *bois brulé* who did all the shooting and burning, that the North West Company didn't have nothing to do with it."

That threw Grant for an instant, but only for an instant. He said: "Mister Robertson told you that?" Seraphim nodded emphatically.

Grant tried again: "*Mister* Robertson . . . ?" But Seraphim still didn't get it.

A commotion broke out in the yard—shouting and shooting and horses whinnying and rearing. The door flew open, and the troops still resident on Frog Plain boiled in to welcome Wappeston—Bonhomme Montour, Alex Fraser, Joseph Cadotte and the rest. They bellowed jovialities at Grant and Bostonais, but got taciturn nods in return.

Seraphim said: "Well, hum, yes, . . . we should have a regale, eh?" He stuck his head out the door to bellow for an *engagé* to fetch a keg of high wine.

Bonhomme said: "So, what brings you back to the Forks so soon—I thought you'd be digging in to winter on the Qu'Appelle."

"I was, but I heard an ugly rumor that the *jardinières* were back."

Joseph Cadotte said: "Not *back*. It ain't the same as it was. Starch-ass MacDonell never once asked us in to smoke tobacco or to drink a cup of rum. Robertson, now, he's a different man. He knows this colony can't stay here without the say-so of the *bois brulés*."

"I heard an even uglier rumor—that the soldiers of the New Nation who drove the *jardinières* out in June are now hunting food for them."

Alex Fraser slitted his snake eyes and said: "You got no right to say what we should do or we shouldn't."

"Have I said I did? I'm only a *moonias* junior clerk for the North West Company. I don't have all my life invested in the *pays d'en haut*. If you that do are content to trade it away for a few cups of rum and pipefuls of tobacco, that's your choice. I have my own life to attend to."

"You sound angry."

"Angry?" He considered that, then said honestly: "No, I'm not angry." But he was ashamed and disappointed—ashamed of himself for his childish assumption that the wild, free laughter of the *bois brulé* and the brass studs on their gunstocks implied any deeper sense of themselves; disappointed in them that they couldn't live up to his illusions.

Deschamps said: "Tell me, Wappeston—you think there's going to be more of them next summer?"

"I should think so. Why should there not?"

Alex Fraser said: "I'm one reason why not."

Bonhomme Montour shook his head and said: "Sure, now it's

all 'Monsieur Montour, come in to Colony House for a drink,' and 'Monsieur Montour this' and 'Monsieur Montour that,' but what's it going to be when there's another few hundred of them, eh?''

Bostonais growled: " 'Monsieur Montour, get your ass off our property or we'll throw it in jail.' ''

Seraphim said: "Mister Robertson would never—''

"Ha!'' snorted François Deschamps. "I knew Robertson in the old days on Swan River. His first season, the Cree thought he had the heart of Jesus Christ on his watch chain. By the end of the second season, if Le Bras Croché hadn't busted him out, they would have burned the fort and killed everybody in it just to get their hands on Robertson. Funny, too, I remember he used to call métis 'Japans,' I don't know why. . . .''

Grant said: " 'Japan'?''

"Yeah, you know, he'd say, 'Roderick McKenzie has a Japan lady,' when I know for a fact McKenzie's woman is Saulteaux and French.''

Grant said: "I believe it was Mister Robertson's quaint way of saying 'nigger.'''

Alex Fraser said: "Son of a bitch!''

"Well, I suppose it's a name we'd best all get used to. A few years down the road, when the *jardinières* have carved the whole country up into farms with fences around them, there won't be much option for any of us except to work in their fields and chop their firewood.''

Joseph Cadotte climbed up on a chair and said: "I say to hell with the *jardinières* and to hell with Robertson and to hell with the Hudson's Bay Company! I don't care how much they offer to pay me, I'd rather kill meat to rot than sell it to them!''

Grant found himself smiling, upon which the rest of the gathering broke into whoops of laughter. "You go ahead and sell them anything they'll buy, Joseph,'' he said. "You can use the money to buy powder and shot next spring when we come back to level their colony to the ground. And this time they won't be coming back again.''

In the morning Grant and Bostonais rode over to have a look at the new Fort Douglas. There was a full-scale symphony in progress: a percussion section of mallets and axes, the muted string sibilance of scythes and sickles swishing through fields of grain, brass and woodwind input from workers' bellows and grunts and instructions, and a chorale of a Gaelic harvest song that had been old when William of Normandy put up his tents on Hastings Field.

A big-chested man with setter-red hair broke off his conversation with John Pritchard and strode toward them with a welcoming grin. Pritchard just gave them a quick wave and ducked into the larger of the two completed log buildings. In the workmanlike French of Scots traders, the big red-haired gent asked Bostonais how he'd been keeping, what the weather was like out west, and whether he had a mind to do any more hunting for the colony.

Grant didn't have to be told who the red-haired man was, just as he had no doubt that Robertson knew who he was. But he made no attempt to effect an introduction or join in the conversation, and Robertson made no effort to draw him into it. All three of them were perfectly aware that the conversation with Bostonais was merely an opportunity for the other two to size each other up.

Pritchard came back out of the building with the hooks of two tin cups ringed over each forefinger. He gave Grant a big smile in greeting, but Grant only nodded. Robertson handed one of the cups to Bostonais and one to Grant, then took one of them himself and hoisted it in salute. Grant waited while the other three quaffed deep and exhaled heartily, then he turned his cup upside down and poured the rum onto the ground. He said to Robertson: "Next time try blankets and beads."

CHAPTER 49

Kate and her husband were standing behind the back wall of their house, lashing the lower ends of the roof poles to the top log of the wall with lengths of *shagganappi*. For all their talk of high-peaked roofs and riverfront windows, when it came down to it there was only time to throw up a stopgap before winter. It enclosed barely half the ground space of their first house. The walls were unpeeled green poplar logs. The roof would be a low slant of sod.

Mister Pritchard and two of the colony's Orcadian servants were working on the opposite side of the house, lashing the high ends of the roof poles to the top of the front wall. The colony's entire pool of hired labor had shrunk to the few Orcadians who hadn't deserted to Upper Canada. Mister Pritchard had brought these two over to help get the roof on in one day so that Sandy would be free to work on the new Colony House they were trying to finish before the governor arrived.

There were only a few more poles left to fasten before they could start layering the sods on over the framework, which was fortunate for Kate—her arms and shoulders were just about to give way from working constantly at eye level. She gave a last tug to her knot and turned to pick up another length of thong from the pile on the ground.

Sandy had stopped dead in the middle of his knot and turned his head away from her. The work on the front wall had trailed off as well—the two Orcadians and Mister Pritchard had turned in the same direction as her husband. Kate stepped back to peer past him.

On the far side of the fallow meadow that ran up the center of the point, just in beyond the pathway to Fort Douglas, a gray Indian pony stood side on to them. Its saddle pad and headstall were covered with ornate quillwork. Sitting straight-backed and stock still on the saddle was Cuthbert Grant.

There was no one behind him, and he appeared to be unarmed—one surprisingly small hand rested slack and empty on his thigh—but nonetheless Kate felt her heart lurch at the sight of him. There was no discernible expression on his features. He didn't open his mouth to speak. She couldn't think of any words to say to him, and apparently neither could any of the others—despite the fact that John Pritchard was supposed to have been a close friend of his in the North West Company.

They stared at each other across the meadow, which might just as well have been cleft open to the center of the earth. Her vision began to turn in upon itself, as it would when she stared at a single point for too long. The details of his appearance grew sharper. His hair had grown longer since spring. His skin was darker. He had given up his worn riding boots for high-topped moccasins, whose black quillwork was a deep, impenetrable, reflective enamel taken from the fabric of his eyes.

Grant twitched his knee against his horse's side. It turned and walked back into the pathway through the woods and out of sight. One of the Orcadians said: "One of these days somebody is going to put a bullet through that bugger's heart."

Sandy said: "And the next day we will all be turning on spits over slow fires."

Mister Pritchard said in English: "Don't talk nonsense. If we can win the half-breeds over, we can laugh in the face of the North West Company. No, we can! And don't put too much stock in Grant. He has a lot of swagger because of his connections in the Montreal office, but there isn't much substance to him."

In the night, her husband said: "I wish I knew what it is I have brought you back to."

"If I recall, you did not drag me bound and screaming from Jack River."

"I have walked into a number of wars before with my eyes open, and for a good deal less reason than we have here. It is different for you."

She said, "We have nowhere else to go," but once it was said she felt free to quibble. "Do you think there will be a war?"

"I wish I knew. John Pritchard can think what he likes, but he was not in the tent when Grant read us the law. It may be that they went as far as they are willing to go last spring, and now that they see they cannot scare us off, they will leave us alone." There was a long silence. She began to think he'd fallen asleep, but then he said: "You have . . . you have spoke to Grant more than I have. What do you think?"

"He seems to have a kind nature. But then so do you, and you have fought in wars."

"It is one thing to fight in a war and another thing to start one."

"He might well think it is we who have started one, by coming back here. He has a vision of what the people here might live like if left alone."

"God save us from young men with visions."

In the morning he set off to Fort Douglas to work on the new building. He wouldn't be back until evening since a noon meal for the laborers was included as part of the wage agreement. It would save them a little on the debt they were running up with the colony stores for rations.

Kate spent the morning working on the one corner of the roof they hadn't finished sodding the night before. When she finished, he propped the door open—he'd done a better job on the hinges this time—and moved in their possessions from the tarpaulin they'd been sleeping under. Even in this cramped log shanty their worldly possessions made a meager pile—a kettle, a frying pan, a cast-iron pot, an axe, a hoe, a few blankets and bits of clothing, and one unwieldy bundle wrapped in an old shawl. Her three best kitchen knives and her husband's musket—the one they had faced down Duncan Cameron to keep—were now part of some half-breed's armory.

She unraveled the knot in the shawl and let the sides fall. The corners of the old Bible had been blunted, but the binding was still intact. She set it down on the half-packed earth and turned her attention to the spinning wheel.

The dowels fitted into their slots a little loosely; the climate was drying out the wood. But the pieces were all intact, and they did go together. The wheel turned a little crankily, but it did turn. She dragged it along the floor rather than picking it up, since she was sure the legs would drop out if she lifted it, and set it slantwise across the corner farthest from the door. She stepped back a ways and looked at it. Now she was home.

As she was wrapping the Bible back up in the shawl, and wondering where to put it until her husband got around to knocking together a new table, she was taken by a sudden fit of loneliness, just as she had been when it came to finishing their first house on Point Douglas. Even though the population of the colony was a third of what it had been, at this moment in the cluster of buildings that made up Fort Douglas, and on the side-by-side strip farms running north along the river, there would be a constant bustling back and forth from one home to another, neighbors borrowing this or lending a hand with that, while she was cut off and on her own. She reminded herself that her whole life had been a history of wishing for a bit of privacy, from the cottage on Kildonan Burn to the barracks winter on Churchill Creek. She told herself to be thankful that she had a husband who didn't need to bleat with the flock.

She set to work building the first fire in their new hearth. They'd done a more symmetrical job with the framework this time, and she'd learned the knack of molding the clay onto the sticks without a combustible ratio of straw. The surface of the mantel was still soft; a few months of fires would bake it hard. As she cracked away with the steel and flint over the powder of dried leaves, and coaxed the caught sparks into life, she began to hum a Gaelic tune her mother used to sing to the fire: "Sun on the hearthstone, fire in the sky, warm all in this house, ripen the barley, melt away the snow."

Another song broke in from outside, a chorus of lusty male voices. She fed the fire a few bits of spruce branch to keep it happy and went out to have a look. A long line of canoes was winding upriver from the lake. The voyageurs were streaming with ribbons and feathers, roaring their harmonies to the *chanteur*'s call-and-response song, pumping their paddles furiously to reach Fort Gibraltar. Lounged amidships in the lead canoe, his silver-tipped gold mane gleaming against the gold-epauleted shoulders of his scarlet tunic, was Duncan Cameron. He sat up when he saw her, sweeping off his plumed bicorne and clutching it to his breast, and called out to her in Gaelic. His voice carried above the brigade's chorale like the boom of a field gun amid a crackle of musket fire.

"What a delightful surprise to see you here, Mrs. Sutherland. I am so looking forward to another neighborly winter."

CHAPTER 50

The brigade that brought Duncan Cameron back to the forks of the Red also brought Whitehead MacDonell. Whitehead had waited at Fort William while Cameron escorted Miles MacDonell and the bulk of his colonists to Upper Canada. Cameron had been initially delayed by the process of filing charges and countersuits against the ex-governor but had at last been able to arrange matters to his satisfaction—which meant, of course, that Miles MacDonell was relinquished to the jurisdiction of the courts, while he was freed to return to the *pays d'en haut*.

Consequently it was quite late in the season by the time the brigade reached Fort Gibraltar. Whitehead MacDonell was still assigned to the Qu'Appelle district, as were half the *engagés* in the brigade, but by the time they'd wound their way up the Assiniboine the Qu'Appelle would be all but frozen over. So they requisitioned a few dozen horses from the Fort Gibraltar herd and rode west. Along with them rode a gaudy column of horsemen, the métis *jeunes gens* who had spent the summer hunting along the Pembina and would spend the winter in the company's Qu'Appelle posts or dug in with their families in forest cabins. At the head of the column flew the red-and-white flag of the New Nation. Beside the flag bearer rode Cuthbert Grant, Inverness College alumnus, class of 1812.

The two columns made a striking pair of particolored ribbon swatches alongside the curling, black-green satin band of the Qu'Appelle River. When Fort Esperance came in sight, the métis column bounded ahead, leaving the boatmen bouncing up and down in a cumbersome trot. Grant and his *jeunes gens* galloped through the gates of Esperance whooping and firing off their guns. Grant wheeled his horse into a rearing halt in front of his cabin, then stood in the stirrups to watch his wild boys scampering their ponies around the courtyard, leaping off their saddles and back on again at full tilt, hanging precariously by one bent knee to poke their rifles out from under their horses' necks at imaginary enemies.

Josephte was standing in the doorway. He bounced off his horse, gave her a large buss on both cheeks, and then pushed past her into the house. There was no one inside. Josephte said: "She's gone."

His stomach turned over. "Gone?"

"To her brother across the river."

Grant laughed, partly out of exuberance and partly in relief. "Hell of a day she picked to go visiting."

"She's not visiting. She lives there now."

"Talk sense. She lives here."

Josephte shook her head. "Not for two weeks now. She packed up her traps one day and left."

He snatched hold of her arms, jerking her back on her heels. "What had you done? Or said?"

"Me? I know what my position is here—I live on your charity. Do you think I'd do anything to make your wife angry?"

He sprang back out the door and onto his horse. He swung its head around and whipped it out the gates, careening dangerously down the seamed face of the knoll Fort Esperance stood upon. When they hit the flat he galloped straight for the riverbank. They went off the bank at a dead run and splashed hard into the river. The bottom dropped away immediately. The horse tried to swim but floundered helplessly with his weight on its back. He slipped out of the saddle, grabbed the tail as it went by, and let it tow him across.

They came out on the opposite bank downstream, and Grant was back in the saddle before the horse had had a chance to shake itself. He kicked his heels into its ribs and pounded along the valley toward Fort Qu'Appelle.

The gates were standing open, but as he drew closer they began to close. He drove his horse toward the narrowing gap, but the doors swung to just before he got there. He hauled the reins back hard, and his pony's front hooves rammed up against the gates as it reared back squealing. There was a rumble overhead as the three-pounders were run out through the ports, and the creosote smell of the smoldering hanks of rope poised to touch them off.

It all seemed a bit excessive. John Richards McKay popped his head up over the battlements. Grant called: "Good afternoon."

"What do you want?"

"I want my wife."

"Then what do you need the rest of them for?"

Grant's first thought was that he was referring to the two or three charitable young ladies who had consoled the occasional lonely night during his absence from his wife. Then he looked back over his shoulder.

Strung out in a long, straggling line between Fort Qu'Appelle and Fort Esperance was a column of *bois brulé* who had followed Grant from Fort Gibraltar. Some were swimming their horses across the river, holding their rifles and powder horns above the water, some had already crossed and were galloping toward him. The front runners reined their horses in beside him, whooping and waving their weapons, milling around and shouting. As far as they were concerned, their leader had had a sudden inspiration to drive the Hudson's Bay Company out of the valley, and they were just the boys to do it.

Above the palisade, John Richards's face was pale and grim. Grant stood up in his stirrups, clapped his right hand over his heart, and cried out: "O ye topless towers of Ilium, give me back my Helen!"

John Richards blinked, several times. Then his mouth twitched into a smirk, and he said: "You are not exactly my conception of Menelaus."

"Mine neither, believe me."

"Nor Achilles, for that matter."

"Well, when you come right down to it, I don't think your pile of logs is exactly what the blind man saw for many-towered Troy." Bethsy's head popped up beside her brother's. "However, that is the face that launched a thousand ships—or would be if I had a navy."

She called down, not unfondly, "Have you been kicked in the head by a horse lately?"

"I thought I had when I came home and found my wife gone."

"I'm not to be allowed to visit my brother?"

"This seems more like a permanent change of address than a visit."

"How was I to know you'd be coming back?"

"I told you I would."

"You said two weeks. It's been more than a month."

"Things happened."

Her eyes moved away from his to range over the wild troop gathering behind him. "You must have expected me to put up one hell of a fight."

"They followed me home." He settled back in the saddle, but only long enough to disengage his feet from the stirrups. He worked his right knee up underneath him, then brought his left foot up beside it and jacked up slowly until he was standing balanced on the saddle—a delicate operation in wet moccasins. He gave a little jump, caught the rim of the palisade with both hands, and hauled himself up and over.

He put both hands on Bethsy's shoulders, said, "It's good to be home," and kissed her, making a point of pressing her body to his. As the river water in his clothes squeezed through her dress, she squealed and tried to push him away . . . but not too hard.

When he broke the kiss, he picked her up and glanced over the edge of the palisade. Bostonais had stood up on his own saddle and now held his arms out in front of him. Grant swung Bethsy backward to give his arms some momentum and then lofted her over the palisade. This time her shriek of terror was real. Bostonais caught her and dropped down onto the saddle. His horse belched out an astounded grunt, and its hooves skittered and slid, but it managed to stay upright.

No one volunteered to catch Grant. He climbed back over the palisade and slowly lowered himself until he was hanging six feet above the ground. From this rather awkward position, he called up: "Mister McKay, your sister and I would be delighted if you would join us for our homecoming celebration at our establishment across the river . . . later in the day." He let go of the palisade and dropped. On the way down he had just enough time to congratulate himself as a remarkably clever and agile fellow—before his wet moccasins hit the ground and slid out from under him, dumping him soundly on his ass.

He scrambled to his feet and climbed on his horse to much laughter and cheers. Bostonais handed Bethsy over to perch side-saddle behind him, and they headed back to Fort Esperance. This time he crossed the river by the ford.

CHAPTER 51

News that the half-breeds had launched an all-out attack on Fort Qu'Appelle and had only been beaten back after heavy losses soon reached the Forks of the Red, and Colin Robertson retaliated immediately by arresting Duncan Cameron. The logistics of capturing him were simple enough: Cameron went out for a stroll along the riverbank in the cool of the evening, and out of the woods popped six men with muskets. After a few days' incarceration at Fort Douglas, he was set free on his promise that Fort Gibraltar wouldn't be used as a base for attacks against the colony.

It was a hoar-frost day when they let him go. Sandy was at Fort Douglas to fetch some thread for his wife and stumped back home through trees that had lost their leaves but were far from bleak: every twig was enveloped in a starched-white, crystalline feathering of lace.

He jerked the door open and announced: "I heard some news."

"Close the door; we cannot heat the whole country."

She was standing over the table in the firelight, manhandling a knife through a thick sheet of buffalo hide. She was trying to make new shoes for them; the ones they had were falling off their feet. He closed the door and said: "I have some news."

"Do you have some thread?"

"No . . ."

"No?"

"There is no thread to be had."

"No thread? What are we to do when our coats fall apart—run through the snow naked?"

"They sold me this." He pulled the springy article out of his pocket and it uncoiled in his hand. It was two inches wide and a yard long, a white belt with a sickly sheen to it. "It is a buffalo sinew."

"I cannot sew with that, look at the width of it!"

339

"They say it peels off." He pinched his thumbnail in at one edge and pulled. A strand about the thickness of heavy thread separated itself and peeled down the whole length. "They say it is stronger than any thread."

She took it from him and tried it with her hands, then shrugged and went back to carving the hide. Sandy waited for her to ask him about his news. When she didn't, he tried again: "I said I heard some news."

"What is it?"

"Lord Selkirk has come to North America."

The effect was quite satisfactory. Kate reeled back from the table and put her hands to her mouth. The color in her cheeks, the light in her eyes suddenly blossomed. It had the singular effect of separating her from the other constants in the background of his life. She said, "Where is he?" as though she were about to reach for her shawl and start for the door.

He laughed. "I would not be running out to have a word with him just yet. He is in Montreal, or on his way there from New York. He will set out for here in the spring."

She said, "Thank the Lord," then clamped her eyes shut and bowed her head.

He didn't much care for that. It offended him that she and all the others could go on blithely praying and quoting their Bibles after their ministers had sold them out for a few acres of land.

He went back outside and spent some time collecting deadfall in the woods along the point. The ground was orange and crunchy with frosted leaves. The sky and the river were slate blue. Late in the afternoon the snow began to fall. He was standing on the south bank of the point, gazing upriver through the white haze gently wafting down, when two large objects glided into view.

They were canoes, one trailing the other. There were two paddlers in the first one, the bow paddler with a blanket shawled over its head like an Indian woman. There was a clutch of children at the midthwarts. The second canoe had no paddlers, only shadowy low humps like the backs of huddled invalids or corpses. There was a towline running from the stern of the first canoe to the prow of the second.

The paddler in the stern suddenly waved his arm high overhead and called: "Hallo, Sutherland!"

It was Jean Baptiste Lajimodierre. The cowled paddler in the bow was Marie Anne. Last spring, before the trouble started, they had gone south to spend the summer hunting in the Pembina hills.

ey were coming back to winter in their cabin on the Assiniboine
. were stopping at Fort Douglas to see if they could get a better
ce for their pemmican from the colony stores than at Fort Gi-
ltar.

Colin Robertson was decidedly jubilant to see Lajimodierre. He
d been trying to find someone to carry dispatches to the Earl of
kirk in Montreal. Robertson felt it imperative that the Earl retain
oop of soldiers from the garrison there to accompany him when
came west in the spring, both for his own safety and for the
vival of the colony. The circuitous route that had taken John
tchard safely around the north edge of the North West Compa-
s private preserves had also taken him six months. If the dis-
ches were to arrive in time, whoever carried them would have
travel east through the Kaministiquia country in the dead of
iter.

Jean Baptiste Lajimodierre and Colin Robertson closeted them-
ves in a back room of the new Colony House. Eventually they
ck a deal, part of which called for Marie Anne and the children
be housed at Fort Douglas at the colony's expense for the dura-
n.

The Sutherlands were part of the little group assembled to see
i off. It seemed to Sandy that when Lajimodierre kissed his wife
od-bye, Marie Anne turned her mouth aside so that his mustache
y brushed her cheek. Colin Robertson handed over a packet of
ers, which Lajimodierre tucked into the breast of his blanket
t. Then he snatched his rifle and swung up into the saddle of a
ttish-looking spotted pony. He winked and grinned at Sandy.
ou take care for *ma femme*, eh?" But the expression in his eyes
ied his jaunty words. Sandy had seen that look before, right
er an order to fix bayonets.

Lajimodierre clucked his pony into a westward trot. It seemed
ad strange to ride west to go east, but a few miles on was the
ssage of the Assiniboine, where Lajimodierre planned to cross
river and cut southeast to the Pembina, then from there head
aight east along the old Indian route to Rainy River.

As he rounded the corner of Colony House, Lajimodierre swiv-
d in his saddle to wave good-bye. Dutifully, Marie Anne called
er him, "*Adieu, mon amour*," then turned and walked away
hout looking back.

As they returned to their shanty on Point Douglas, Sandy said:
he gives him very little reason to hurry back."

"Only a wife and three children."

"I meant that she said good-bye with a bad grace."

"Why should she not? Her family is in Montreal. She has n
seen them for ten years because her husband says the journey is t
long, and off he goes now on a whim."

"A whim? Did it cross her mind that he might not come back'

"Why should he not? Because she did not hurl herself down a
chew the ground when he said good-bye?"

"Because he might not make it."

Kate came to an abrupt halt in the middle of the path and turn
on him with a suspicious expression. "Mister Lajimodierre knov
how to live off the country, why would he not make it?"

Sandy hadn't thought that part out, all he had to go on was t
expression in Lajimodierre's eyes when he'd waved good-bye. '
seems obvious—the North West Company does not want the colo
here, Lajimodierre is carrying a message to advise Lord Selkirk
bring troops, and his route lies through a thousand miles of w
derness where the only inhabitants are the North West Compan
traders and the wild Indians who do business with them. And the
are so many plausible explanations if he should disappear."

"I do not think it is possible that Marie Anne would have act
so cool toward him if that was the case."

"Perhaps he pretended different because he did not want her
worry."

"Then it seems hard to call her a hard bitch for not worrying

Sandy was certain there was a flaw in her reasoning, but
couldn't find it—which to him was a perfect illustration of her m
annoying habit. Within a few days, however, he felt ashamed
having bickered with his wife over the Lajimodierres' situatic
news began to circulate that the North West Fur Trading Compa
had offered a reward of twenty pounds in gold to anyone w
brought in Jean Baptiste Lajimodierre to a North West Compa
post—or any portion of him large enough to identify. Long af
that, Sandy learned from one of Colin Robertson's clerks that Je
Baptiste had demanded a written guarantee that his wife and ch
dren would be paid a handsome pension for the next ten years if
disappeared en route.

On a snowy afternoon in October, Kate and Sandy stood
either side of Marie Anne on the crest of the riverbank in front
Fort Douglas. Marie Anne held baby Henri—who was almost l
enough to stand on his own—while La Prairie and La Reine sto
on either side of her, each clinging for security to one petticoa

dded leg. Beyond them, the entire populace of the Selkirk colony
s lined up across the front of the fort.

Without a piper, the feeble best they could do when the York
ats rounded the point was to give three cheers in the English
anner. The prows crunched in through the ice lacing the shore,
d the front-bench rowers scrambled out to haul them onto
d. A good two-thirds of the crew and passengers were familiar
es, neighbors and relatives from Kildonan parish who had been
rt of the scarecrow flock on DunUlidh beach but hadn't been
ld enough or desperate enough to ship out two years ago.

One man in particular was easy to identify by the deference the
ers showed him and the way he headed straight up the bank to
lin Robertson without waiting for anyone else to establish prec-
ent. Governor Semple was a tall, prematurely balding man with
ck lips and an air of perfect confidence that was too placid for
rogance. Trailing the new governor were two authoritative gen-
men who paused every few steps to survey the land with a mili-
y eye, nodding thoughtfully to each other.

Once Robert Semple had been identified, all eyes on the bank
turned to the boats, searching for the second man they'd been
iting to see: their minister. The Earl of Selkirk and his agents
d promised from the beginning that a clergyman would be brought
Red River and a kirk built for him to preach in.

He wasn't there. As a stopgap, the presbyters had sent a deacon
the name of James Sutherland, who was empowered to perform
ptisms, weddings, and funerals. Sandy wasn't terribly distraught
their lack of a minister and would have been just as happy without
e deacon. After the Clearances he would have preferred to muddle
ng forever without benefit of clergy. But there was no question
at it was a great disappointment to many of the others, in partic-
ar his wife.

Kate was entangled in a gaggle of grown women who'd reverted
sight to the rag-tag girls who had chased each other up and down
ldonan Burn. He pried her loose and took her aside. "Would it
ease you if I was to ask Deacon Sutherland to perform a marriage
remony for us? We did not have the blessings of the kirk the first
ne."

"I thought you no longer cared for such nonsense as kirks and
essings."

"I asked if it would please you." She looked as though it would.

CHAPTER 52

His wife's screams brought Grant to his feet, but once there, there was nothing he could do but stand flexing his hands and staring at the back of the door. Falcon said: "That's good—the louder they yell, the more it takes their mind off it."

Grant sat back down, a bit embarrassed. Falcon had been through this three times before, and it was only his first. John Richard McKay just sat chewing through the stem of his dead pipe. They were sitting on a buffalo robe on the floor of the trading house with a pitcher of high wine and a carrot of tobacco between them.

Falcon said: "Our mothers, you know, when their time came, they just waddled off into the woods and took a stick between their teeth. This next generation, I don't know where they're going to get their toughness from."

Grant picked up his pipe and reached for the tobacco. "Isn't it going on awfully long?" he asked, trying not to sound as nervous as he felt.

Falcon puffed out his upper lip like a bullfrog and widened his hound-dog eyes, then filled the cups again. Another scream tore through from the cabin next door. Grant wondered that a sound sharp enough to slice through two thicknesses of log walls so easily should grind into him like a rusty saw.

He tried not to picture what was going on next door to wring those screams out of Bethsy. He wanted it to stop more than he wanted a child. He could think of nothing he had ever experienced that would give him an understanding of what Bethsy was going through. He wondered if a fight—the running skirmishes with the Sioux, the contretemps with the colony people—were as much of a mystery to her as this was to him. It didn't seem possible. A fight was open and obvious and active. This was just suffering and hanging on while the life inside you tried to kill you on its way out.

Falcon said: "When are you going to quit?"

Grant said, "Quit?" and then realized the question had been dressed to John Richards.

John Richards said: "Quit?"

"Quit the English company."

It occurred to Grant that the nickname was damned handy when came to marshaling the New Nation. They couldn't very well cus hostility on "the whites" since they were all white to one gree or another. But most of their fathers had been either Canaan French or Highland Scots, and both had imbued their children ith a hearty distrust of the English.

John Richards said: "Oh, in twenty years or so I expect I'll retire a chief factor's pension."

Grant said: "That's assuming there'll still be a Hudson's Bay ompany."

"They've managed to survive a century and a half."

"For a century and a half they weren't throwing themselves in ith colonial schemes."

Falcon said: "Cows."

They turned to Falcon, who was gazing vacantly toward the dark-ed shelves of trade goods. He glanced back and gave them a eamy, wine-soaked smile. "When I was sent away to school in ontreal, I used to watch the cows in the fields there. God didn't ake cows, people did. A buffalo is a beautiful, strong thing; I say prayer every time I take its life. A cow has no life to take, it is ly a machine for making meat and milk. The English company d the *jardinières* want to make the *pays d'en haut* into a pasture r the cows to walk in, swinging their bells around their necks and eir udders between their knees. A buffalo was made for running e."

Grant said to John Richards: "You have to decide what you are."

"I know what I am."

"Which is it—a *bois brulé* or a half-assed white man?"

"I am John Richards McKay, nothing more and nothing less."

"I see. Nothing more or less than a tool of the Company of entures Trading into Hudson's Bay."

"And you aspire to a much higher calling—which is to be a tool the North West Company."

Grant shot forward, his right hand clutching for John Richards's roat. He caught himself halfway and eased back down on the ffalo robe. John Richards had fallen backward jerking out of the ay. Grant was still getting used to the fact that he'd grown into a ysical presence that could scare hell out of people.

John Richards sat back up and brushed his blond mop out of his
eyes. Scared or not, he wasn't one to give in to intimidation. "I
that your new method for coping with anything you find disagree
able—rip its throat out? I wish I'd known that before the crofter
came to ask me in County Sutherland whether they had any hope
of surviving in the *pays d'en haut*. I can't help feeling that some o
their blood will be on my hands."

"Their blood won't be on anyone's hands. There are other ways
to clear them off."

"I thought you'd tried all those last spring—you and your col
league Cameron. How long do you think you can go on shooting
over their heads before the whole thing explodes?"

"There are other ways."

A high-pitched, strangulated wailing cut in strong from some
where in the night. It took Grant a moment to identify it as an
infant crying. The instant he did, he started to scramble to his feet
Falcon reached up, snagged the waistband of his trousers, and
hauled him back down. "Wait. They'll come for you when they're
ready."

The three of them sat waiting. Not even Falcon could think o
anything to say. The crying quieted down, then stopped altogether
Grant fumbled around for his pipe. John Richards picked it up and
lit it for him.

The door opened and Grant's sister Mary came in, a few flakes
of snow drifting over her shoulders. Grant dropped his pipe and
stood. She tried to keep her face solemn, but it broke open in a
grin: "You have a son." Falcon stood up and threw his arms around
the proud father, clapping his forearms against his back. John Rich
ards laughed and shook hands with Grant behind Falcon's back.

Grant followed his sister out into the snow and around to the
cabin next door. He scooped up a handful of white powder and
rubbed it into his face, shaking his head like a wet dog. Mary held
the door open for him. He stepped inside and stood waiting—he
had the feeling that he wasn't supposed to initiate any moves on hi
own. Mary pulled the door closed behind them. Josephte came ou
from behind the blanket partition and held it aside. He crossed the
room and stooped through the opening.

The firelight showed Bethsy lying on the buffalo robes that made
up their bed, her gold hair spread out in flickering rays around he
head. He knelt on the edge of the bed. There were hollows unde
her eyes, and her cheeks were pinched in. Her eyes were red. I
looked as if a layer of skin had been scraped off her face.

They had washed her face and combed out her hair, but the roots were still dank with sweat. He reached a hand out toward her cheek. She stopped it in midair by folding back the corner of the blanket. Nestled on her breast was a tiny red wizened being with its eyes shut and its fists against its nose, looking not unlike a lump of recently melted pink wax. Exposed to the cold air, it began to snuffle and wail.

Bethsy lifted up the baby as though it were a great strain on her arms and handed it to him. It started to scream. He settled it into the crook of his left arm and shielded it from the cold with his right. They had bathed it before he came in, but he could still distinguish the cloying tidepool smell of Bethsy's insides.

He made a few tentative clucking and cooing noises at it, rocked it gently, and, miraculously, it quieted down. As that feeble, warm, living morsel nestled into the crook of his elbow, Grant realized that he'd lied to John Richards. He still planned to do his damnedest to avoid hurting anyone, but when his son grew up he was going to inherit a life more free and wild and joyous and self-determined than that of any Highland Chief in the days before Culloden and the Clearances, and Grant would do whatever he had to do to see that happen. They would call him James. The Grants always called their firstborn sons James.

CHAPTER 53

Kate and Marie Anne Lajimodierre and Catherine Pritchard and the next generation of Lajimodierres and Pritchards were all crammed into the snowed-in shanty on Point Douglas. The children squealed and gurgled and rolled about on the floor under the authoritative shepherding of eight-year-old La Reine. Marie Anne and Catherine Pritchard were scraping the wool off an old raggle-edged buffalo hide. Kate was doing her best to card it with the rickety combs her husband had knocked together for her. They had no more teeth in them than her old granny's jawbone, but nails were terribly expensive.

It had all come about because Marie Anne had broken into a fit of hand clapping and sobbing when she first laid eyes on Kate's spinning wheel. "Oh, *le rouet, le rouet*! I have not see since nine year. *Ma mère*, she have one so tall as me. And in the house of *l'abbé* where I live for so long . . . Look on me, to cry *comme un enfant*—for a few bits of wood. But you live life as the wife of a hunter for nine year . . ." So Kate had asked Catherine Pritchard whether it was possible to spin buffalo wool. Catherine Pritchard had never heard of spinning anything and became quite intrigued when she discovered that it was possible for perfectly mortal women to make wool cloth such as that the traders sold for stacks of furs.

The silver ring on Kate's left hand kept getting in her way, but she refused to take it off. Catherine Pritchard said: "How did he get the silver here?"

"It was a shilling, a silver shilling that was in a pocket of his somewhere. He cut out the middle of it and filed it smooth—while I thought he was out hoeing."

Marie Anne said: "When the part come in the wedding for 'this ring I thee wed'—I don't understand the Gaelic, but all Christian wedding are the same—I see Katy, her head go *secousse* when they don't skip it over, and the next thing Alexandre is put on her the ring. So *romantique*. Jean Baptiste was so much like that the first years. Monsieur l'Abbé don't want me to marry to him, *un homme du nord*—but Jean Baptiste was . . ." She stopped scraping the hide and looked off into the distance with an expression of thoughtful lasciviousness. "So in the spring, when the song from the wild geese come down in the night, and Jean Baptiste say he try all he can but he cannot live in the farms and the towns, that he must go back to the *pays d'en haut*, what else may I do? So here I am."

Kate had come to realize that her initial envy of Marie Anne's ease in the wild country had been entirely displaced. Despite the fact that Marie Anne could make herself understood by any Indian east of the Rocky Mountains and feed herself and her children off the country, despite the fact that she had taken everything the *pays d'en haut* could throw at her, she still saw her life in the wilds as a trial to suffer through until the day her husband took her back to the little towns clustered along the island of Montreal. It did explain why Lajimodierre had been so intent on tying himself in with the colony, and why he'd taken on the dangerous journey for the sake of the colony. If there was a settlement in the *pays d'en haut*, he and his wife might both be able to get what they wanted and still keep each other.

The buffalo hide was still only half-scraped, and only half the scraped-off wool had been carded, but there was enough to make a test. Kate scooped together a double handful of wool and headed for the spinning wheel. Catherine Pritchard and Marie Anne put down their side-handled scraping knives and followed her. Mrs. Pritchard knelt down beside the wheel and gazed at it as though it were some alchemist's device. Kate clumped the raw wool onto the spindle, pulled up a stool, and began to pump the treadle. The wheel turned, the spindle spun. She pinched her thumb and forefinger onto a lock of wool whirling near the top of the spindle and gave it a twist. It rolled together and came out as a nub end of yarn. She kept rolling the pads of her fingers together and spinning the wheel. The yarn grew an inch long, two inches long, six inches . . . Catherine Pritchard's eyes bugged out. Marie Anne squealed and clapped her hands together. Then the door flew open, and the yarn broke.

Sandy slammed the door behind him, but it didn't catch. He picked his way to the table, shedding snow onto the floor and the heads of the children. Kate cried, "Look at what you are doing! And the door!"

"Oh, sorry—but that is one of the advantages of a dirt floor. I will be going straight out again." He sloped the oatmeal sack off his shoulder onto the table. "There was no charge for the oatmeal."

"Why?"

He reached above the mantel and took down his new musket, then headed back to the door. "Mister Robertson asked me to help him intercept the North West Company's express. I will be back soon."

He pulled the door shut behind him before she could ask him for details that he didn't know himself and hurried along the path to Fort Douglas. The snow was growing porous, but he knew it was only an illusion. Winter still had a couple of months left in it. Anyone who fastened on to every momentary thawing as a sign of spring would sink inevitably into brooding and despair. Perhaps that was what was happening to his wife.

The main party had already marched away by the time Sandy reached Fort Douglas, and he had to quick march to catch up. They halted in the last skeletal fringe of cover before the cleared space around Fort Gibraltar, and Colin Robertson held up his hand for silence. He looked elated, quivering like a terrier at a rathole. Sandy wondered if it was just coincidence that Mister Robertson had decided to take such a bold stroke while Governor Semple was away familiarizing himself with the Hudson's Bay Company's outposts.

In a parade ground whisper, Robertson said: "Right, then—we'll march in smartly. No running, just quick and businesslike. Follow my lead." They crunched across the hard-packed snow up to the gates. One gate was propped half-open, wedged in the snow. There was no sentry; the Indians, like their civilized brethren on the European continent, only went raiding in the summer.

The dogs penned in the courtyard set up a commotion, but no one came out of the buildings. Mister Robertson set off at a trot straight for the bourgeois's house. He stopped by the door and waved at Sandy and a few of the others, nodding at them as though they knew what to do. Sandy looked to the others, who didn't appear to have any more of a clue than he had. Robertson flung open the door and was through it in one stride. Sandy and two others leaped in after him and took up flank positions with their muskets at advance. Everyone else in the party thundered in behind them and lined up on the wings.

Captain Cameron, out of uniform, was sitting at a table in front of the fire with three half-breeds and a deck of cards. Two of the half-breeds jumped up as though to reach for a weapon or run, then thought better of it when they got a good look at the odds. Cameron folded his cards against his chest and drawled: "If I'd known you gentlemen were so mad keen on whist, I'd've been more than happy to invite you. We could have had a tournament."

Mister Robertson strode forward to the center of the floor and let go with a baritone that rocked the rafters: "You can save your theatrical gestures for the Japanned rabble that are impressed by them. You're under arrest."

Captain Cameron leaned back in his chair and smiled. "I thought we had already performed that charade once this winter."

"It does not surprise me that you see due process of law as a charade, Cameron. You were released in the autumn on your word that Fort Gibraltar would not be used as a base for intrigue or attacks against the Selkirk colony. You have not kept that promise."

"If a game of whist constitutes a threat to your colony's safety, Robertson, I suggest you—"

"Brazen away, Cameron—it's the only card you've ever had. It'll give us some entertainment while we're waiting for the express to come in."

"Are you expecting some correspondence? I would have been delighted to send one of my *engagés* over with—"

"*You're* expecting some correspondence. We'll see what kind of tune you sing when we have the written evidence."

Cameron threw his cards on the table and shot to his feet. "As a British subject—not to mention an officer of the King—my private correspondence is guaranteed inviolate since the days of Magna Charta!"

"Ha—that stung you, didn't it?"

"The North West Company express is an extension of His Britannic Majesty's Mail Service! If you—"

Colin Robertson cut him off in midroar. "To begin, we'll have a look through the papers you already have on hand," he said, and headed for a doorway in the side of the room.

Cameron looked as if he were about to make a grab for him, then settled for bellowing: "I'll have you up for false arrest, forcible confinement, interfering with the royal mails . . ."

Mister MacBeth, one of the contingent of new colonists in Robertson's party, planted himself in front of Cameron. "What you'll do is sit down and shut your gob like a good little prisoner." MacBeth was a white-haired gnome with a kind of squashed-down look about him. He was also an ex–Regimental Sergeant Major from the 73rd, discharged on a life pension after six months in some Rajah's dungeon. The prisoner sat back down.

A moment later Colin Robertson emerged from the side room with a sheaf of papers in his hand. "This may be a long wait. You—Sutherland, MacBeth, and you three—go on back to the fort, I'll send for you if we need relief."

As they were trudging home, Sandy said to Mister MacBeth: "No more 'Misters' once they have you in the ranks."

Mister MacBeth laughed. "Nothing personal to it—I have a feeling that Robertson would address the Prince Regent as 'Hey you, Hanover.' "

One of the other men tramping along with them piped up: "You'd do well to have more respect for Mister Robertson. With him on our side we're going to teach some respect to those half niggers if they're stupid enough to come back this spring."

Sandy looked at Mister MacBeth. Mister MacBeth looked at him. They kept on walking.

The next morning, as he was having his oatmeal, there was a knock on the door. It was Mister MacBeth. "Mister Robertson sent

a message over that they are still waiting for the express. He wondered would we stand a turn at watch and relieve the lads who have
been there all night.''

Sandy bundled on his outdoor clothes, took down his rifle, and
he and Mister MacBeth high-shouldered their way through the
morning bluster.

The three half-breeds around the card table looked a little the
worse for wear, as did the three colony men who'd been guarding
them all night. Mister Robertson and Captain Cameron both seemed
chipper and saucy. Guard duties weren't onerous, simply sitting
around with muskets telling soldiering stories and occasionally escorting one of the prisoners out to the necessary.

Early in the afternoon they heard the distant descant tinkling of
harness bells, then the sound of the fort dogs erupting as a foreign
team lapped into the yard. Mister Robertson stood up and made a
cautioning gesture at Duncan Cameron. There was the sound of
crunching moccasins on the snow outside, then the door was jarred
open and two frost-rimed *engagés* stomped in. They stopped cold
when they saw the muskets pointing at them.

Mister Robertson spoke to them in French, beckoning with one
hand. One of them came into the room uneasily and sat down
without loosening his coat. The other went back outside. Mister
Robertson held the door open and watched him, standing aside
when he returned carrying two bulging hide bags.

Halfway out of his skin with glee, Mister Robertson slammed
the door and dumped the contents of the bags onto the floor. He
knelt by the pile of envelopes and packages and fished among them
feverishly. He snatched one out with a flourish and read off its face:
" 'Mister Alex Fraser, Fort Gibraltar, The Forks . . .' Is there a
Mister Alex Fraser here? Alex Fraser . . . ?'' All the time leering
directly at one of the half-breed prisoners, a young man with hooded
snake eyes and a slit full of teeth for a smile. "Letter for you, Mister
Fraser—from a Mister Cuthbert Grant on Rivière Qu'Appelle. As
I'm well aware of your people's customary shortcomings in the
literacy field, I'll save you the embarrassment and read it for you.

" 'Thirteenth March, 1816, My dear sir, As the express is due
to start tomorrow morning I shall take the liberty of addressing you
a few lines and at the same time to inform you of our countrymen
at Fort des Prairies. You will be pleased to learn that they are all
loyal and staunch and ready to obey our commands. . . .'

"Now what manner of 'commands' might those be, pray tell?

Mister Fraser? Mister Cameron? Can't help me? Well, perhaps Mister Grant will elucidate.

" 'As for the half-breeds of the Churchill River, Mr. Shaw has gathered the whole of them; as they come by water I do not know which time they will be at the Forks. You must know that Robertson's famous Clarke is gone to pot—' "

The recitation came to an abrupt halt. Sandy was sitting behind Mister Robertson, so he saw the back of his neck flush red and swell up like a sheep's bladder. It took Sandy a moment to place "Clarke" as the subordinate Robertson had sent on with the expedition to the Athabasca. By that time Robertson had risen to his feet and stalked over to Duncan Cameron. He said in a strangulated tone: "What's happened?"

"Happened?"

"Don't come the innocent with me, Cameron, you know exactly what I mean. On the Athabasca. To Clarke."

"Ah. It is a sad tale, Colin. I would have thought you'd had the news already—otherwise I surely would have brought it to you. Your Mister Clarke, it seems, failed to bring enough provisions. Of his hundred men, eighty or so have thrown themselves on the mercy of the North West Company. There was an outpost of eighteen, of whom seventeen starved to death. The last one crawled back to the main camp after gnawing the flesh off his dead friends. I believe your Mister Clarke and a handful of others are still gallantly manning your new post, but that was over a month ago—"

Mister Robertson threw the table aside and started for Cameron, his hands pumping themselves into fists. Cameron stood up and said coolly: "Remember there are witnesses here, in case you've anything in mind except a fair set-to."

Robertson stood in place for a moment, then wheeled back to the pile of letters and started tearing them open and shouting out phrases: "Half-breeds are coming forward to clear their native soil of intruders and assassins . . . God forbid they should butcher anyone . . . Glorious news from Athabasca . . . Never to see any of them again in the colonizing way in Red River . . . collected together at Fort des Prairies—should number more than one hundred . . . To remain at the Forks for fear they should play us the same trick as last summer of coming back, but they shall receive a warm reception . . ." He turned back to Cameron, brandishing two fistfuls of letters. "There's enough in here to hang you if one drop of blood gets spilt this summer!" He jammed the letters into his pockets, then jerked his head toward the door. "Come along."

"If you'll give me a moment to fetch my coat . . ."

"You won't be needing it."

Cameron's head snapped around to Colin Robertson. It was the first time ever that Sandy saw Duncan Cameron look afraid. Robertson produced a pair of manacles from his coat pocket and chained Cameron's wrists, then took up a broom standing by the hearth, broke off its end, and thrust the haft in between his elbows and his back.

The afternoon twilight was setting in. The sky was a low thatch of opalescent gray. The earth was a rippled crust of dusky white with a few tufts of bleached yellow buffalo grass sticking out here and there, stretching west to the horizon. Mister Robertson marched in front. Captain Cameron strode awkwardly along behind him with his teeth clenched and the wind billowing his shirt. Sandy and Mister MacBeth brought up the rear, each with a musket crooked in one arm and a mail sack dragging from the left. They delivered the mail sacks and Captain Cameron to Fort Douglas, then went off to their homes.

A few days later Sandy was out chopping firewood, being careful to follow the grain so as not to shatter his cold-brittled axehead, when a dog *carriole* swung down the frozen river toward Fort Douglas. The passenger bundled inside was Lieutenant Rogers, one of the governor's military advisers. The two men jogging along on snowshoes behind it were John Pritchard and Bostonais Pangman. Bostonais ran with his arms hanging down stiffly, a glint of chain between his wrists.

Sandy stuck his axe into the chopping block and ambled over to Fort Douglas to have a look. He got there just in time to be handed a musket by Lieutenant Rogers and told to guard the prisoner. Mister Pritchard and the lieutenant went into Colony House, leaving Bostonais and Sandy standing by the door.

The lieutenant's exuberance carried his report through the walls. He had been placed in charge of the party of colonists who'd been taken south to winter on the Pembina near the buffalo's wooded winter territory. When Mister Pritchard had arrived to collect a load of meat, and had told him of Mister Robertson's exploit at Fort Gibraltar, they had been inspired to capture the North West Company's Pembina post and the métis hunting lodges along Turtle River.

At that point Colin Robertson exploded. "You did *what*? Half a year I've spent cozying up to the half-breeds to save your hides,

nd with one stroke you bloody-minded idiots have undone it all!
Vhose side are you on?'' Then they all started yelling.

Sandy glanced over at Bostonais to see if he understood what
'as being said. It was impossible to tell. He juggled his musket in
nder the crook of his left arm and dug out his tobacco pouch. He
aid, "Mister Pangman?" and waggled the pouch in the air. The
ny black eyes turned in his direction and settled on the pouch.
he eyebrows shrugged up and down to say he could do with a
moke if it was being offered. Sandy handed him the pouch. Bos-
ɔnais dug one hand in through the flap of his buffalo coat—the
ther hand dragged up by the chain—and fished out a short-stemmed
ipe. As he was packing it from Sandy's pouch, Sandy dug out his
wn pipe.

They stood smoking in the white winter sunshine, Sandy listen-
ıg again to the melee inside Colony House. Mister Bourke, the
uartermaster, had joined in, along with Lieutenant Rogers and
Iister Pritchard. They were all yelling away at Mister Robertson,
nd their gist seemed to be that he would see what was what when
ιe governor got home.

CHAPTER 54

Winter was still set in when tents began to spring up around
Fort Esperance, hemming the skirts of the palisade with a
rinoline of clay-whitened buffalo hide. Some of them were the
nts of old Canadian *engagés* who had signed on for one winter in
ιe *pays d'en haut* thirty years ago and had never seen Lachine
gain. They brought with them to Esperance two, three, or four tall
lack-eyed sons. Some of them were of families who had lived as
lackfoot or Sarcee all their lives, who wore breechclouts and leg-
ings and spoke not one word of English or French or Gaelic but
ad heard there was a New Nation they belonged to. Some of the
∘nts were of clumps of young hunters who had left their mothers'
ɔdges or their fathers' forts as soon as they were old enough to
∘nd for themselves and had lived since then in their own small,

wandering bands, dodging and fighting the Plains tribes and danc
ing in scalp shirts to Breton fiddle tunes.

For all the differences, they were already beginning to resemble
each other. The métis women tended to incorporate embroidered
or beaded black velvet yokes or collars into their men's fringed
buckskin hunting shirts. Many of the men wore beaded rawhide
cinches under their knees and elbows to keep their sleeves and
trouser legs from restricting their movements. Virtually all the
women had given up the Indian dress style, where the yoke and
sleeves were a separate piece from the bodice and skirt, but their
beaded-over blouses were hardly European.

But although there were the beginnings of a certain cohesiveness
in style of dress, it was hardly a uniform. Even at the height of the
métis nation's tribal consciousness, if two hunters met at the spring
rendezvous and the pattern of the embroidery on their new vests
turned out to be the same, one or both would sling it off and fling
it into the fire.

Those who came to Esperance were fed and feted by the North
West Company, and the company provided a blacksmith who set
up shop outside the walls to mend cracked spearheads or bent knife
blades. There was a warm spell, and the courtyard of Fort Esper
ance became a saucer of slush-and-mud stew, a thin layer of thawed
ground skating on the frozen base beneath. It was possible to dance
on it, though—mud-soaked moccasins pounding up and down in
the soup around a tepee-high bonfire. The ring of the stockade was
awash with red light except where the green-tinged shadows danced
across it.

Whitehead MacDonell, dressed in his captain's uniform, grabbed
Grant's arm and bellowed over the cacophony of fiddles and sing
ing: "We'd best get it done while they can still see straight."

Grant followed him over to two immense barrels standing in
front of the trading house. He climbed up on top of one and helped
Whitehead up onto the other. It took Whitehead a few minutes to
get everyone's attention. His brigade voice might have had twenty
years of bourgeoising behind it, but he hadn't been born with the
natural gifts of a Duncan Cameron. The fortful of war-painted mé
tis and *engagés* finally quieted down and milled toward them.

"By the authority vested in me as an officer in His Majesty's
Voyageurs Corps, I do hereby commission Cuthbert Grant Captain
General of the Métis Cavalry." The ovation—in French and Cree
and Bungee and Gaelic and gunpowder—was deafening. When
it toned down, Whitehead MacDonell announced, "In token of

ich . . .'' and held down his arm. His attendant junior clerk held
a bundle of red cloth. Whitehead shook it out and displayed a
form tunic decked with more gold braid and black-backed gilt
gging than Duncan Cameron's.

3rant shrugged off last year's tunic and donned the new one.
e crowd went wild. The fastenings couldn't quite meet, so he
it hanging open. He wasn't sure whether they still hadn't been
e to find a tunic to fit him, or whether it was proof of the literary
ceit that a man's chest could swell with pride.

When the second ovation had settled, Whitehead said: ''We
uld also like to present Captain General Grant with this sword.''
vas a cavalry officer's saber with an ivory grip and gold cord
igling from the pommel. Grant drew it from the scabbard and
irished it. The blade was polished steel, reflecting the firelight
: Death's looking glass. The roar came back at him in waves:
/appeston!''

n the morning he woke up in the fourth circle of hell—or perhaps
fifth, his Dante had grown rusty. He tried to struggle through
hout resorting to Mister MacGillivray's remedy but finally
ickled under and poured himself a tot of brandy. It brought him
k to the gates of purgatory, which strongly suggested that an-
er tot would set him free. But he settled for a cup of tea.

Ie sat down at one side of the table and watched his wife feed
ite luncheon to their son while his sister bustled around at the
rth preparing theirs. Bethsy had unfastened the neck of her
use and pulled it open down to her elbows. James was working
iy at her right breast, the whole of the areola crammed into his
uth, one tiny fist absentmindedly kneading the smooth curve of
iide. Her left breast stood waiting, swollen, rich and heavy, with
ardrop tracery of milk dribbling out of the erect nipple.

3rant's eyes traveled languidly up past the plump breasts to her
cate collarbones and shoulders, across the clean lines of her
iat and button chin and half-parted mouth. When he reached
eyes he found them glaring back at him, with something resem-
ig resentment within the heavy-lidded depths. She said: ''I don't
it when you stare at me when I'm doing this.''

Ie recoiled and looked away, then back. ''It's a prettier picture
 you think.''

he door opened and Falcon came in, closing it quickly behind
 before the cold air could penetrate. He said to Grant: ''John

Richards McKay is outside with some others. They want to talk
you.''

"Well, tell them to come in."

Falcon shook his head. "I didn't mean outside the door—outsi
the gates. They didn't want to come inside the fort."

"What? Why not?"

Falcon shrugged. "Some kind of formal business, I guess. Th
asked for Whitehead first, but he took off for Swan River at fi
light. So then they asked me to fetch you."

It was too confusing for Grant, but then so was everything e
this morning. He shrugged on his wolfskin coat and headed for
door. Bethsy called after him: "I'll come, too, as soon as I've
James settled. Don't let John go before I get there!"

Most of the wreckage from last night had already been clear
away. Falcon headed for the gates, but Grant said, "No," a
headed for the ladder leading up to the sentry's walkway. If Jo
Richards wanted formalities, he'd have them.

They were sitting on their horses looking back toward the riv
Grant leaned over the palisade and called: "Good morning, Mis
McKay. What can I do for you?"

All eyes turned to look up at him. John Richards said: "Go
morning. Had a bit of a kick-up last night?"

"What can I do for you?"

"Governor Semple is at Fort Qu'Appelle."

"So I'd heard. If he'd like me to come to tea, he could ha
delivered the invitation himself."

"No, he . . ." John Richards paused and took off his fur ca
Then he looked back up at Grant and launched into what sound
like a composed speech: "The governor has it on good author
that you have in your possession some of the artillery pieces tl
were stolen from the Selkirk colony last spring. He does not inte
laying charges—he is willing to accept that you were under
impression they came into the North West Company's hands
gally. But he . . . orders you to surrender them up to him. Imm
diately."

"*Orders?* He orders me?"

There was a sound from the ladder behind him. Bethsy climb
up onto the catwalk and waved down over the palisade. "Go
morning, John, what a pleasant surprise."

John Richards waved back and said: "You're looking well, de
How are you feeling?"

"Couldn't be better—James actually allowed me a whole h

ght's sleep last night. Though I suppose it had less to do with his
ood nature than that the noise in the courtyard kept him awake for
e first half. Aren't you coming in?''

"No, not today, I'm afraid, thank you. We have to take a mes-
ge back to the governor.'' He looked at Grant. "Well?''

"Tell him his information is correct. If he wants them, he can
ome and get them. He will receive the reception that such conduct
eserves.''

John Richards hesitated, as though he had something more to
y. "Well . . . good day to you, then. Give James a poke on the
in from his uncle John.'' Then he wheeled his horse around and
aded for the ford.

Bethsy said: "What was that all about?''

Grant said: "Your brother's making a mistake, lining himself up
1 the wrong side.''

"The wrong side of what?''

"Don't be obtuse. There are lines being drawn. I'm not the one
ho's drawing them.''

"Then who is?''

Falcon said: "*Notre pays* herself. She's too damned beautiful for
1yone to share her around.''

Bethsy went back down the ladder. Falcon said: "Do you think
e governor'll take you up on your invitation?''

Grant looked across the stockade at the teepee poles showing
ver the points of the western palisade. Smoke was rising up from
em and from the blacksmith's fire, and all around them reverber-
ed the sounds of singing and laughter and guttural voices in the
alects of the Athabasca and the North Saskatchewan. There were
ready more than fifty warriors in the camp and more drifting in
very day. He said: "I shouldn't expect so. Not even a man that
e Earl of Selkirk would appoint as governor could be that stupid.''

Falcon looked up at the sky. It was a cobalt blue with black,
iling rags of clouds—dark and angry, but a pleasant change from
e pallid skies of winter. A wind was whipping up from the south.
e said: "Well, it would be a good day for it.''

"A good day for what?''

"Anything at all.''

CHAPTER 55

Once Bostonais Pangman was yet again in custody, the most fervent desire of the colonial establishment—at least as temporarily headed by Colin Robertson—was to release him without losing face. Robertson offered to let him go on condition that he surrender up the keys for the North West Company's store at Fort Pembina, which Bostonais obstinately refused to do. Not that he had much of a feel for the legal niceties implied—that if he gave them the keys, they could at least claim they had confiscated the stores without forcing either him or the door—but if they wanted the keys, there must be a good reason not to hand them over. After a few days Robertson gave up and told him he'd let him go on condition that he promise to stop harassing the colony. Bostonais said, "Sure," and walked over to Fort Gibraltar, got a horse, and rode west for the Qu'Appelle.

Marie Anne Lajimodierre was on Point Douglas showing Kate MacPherson—as she was still known in the colony—how the Indians cleaned leather. Inevitably, leather garments had worked their way into the colonists' wardrobes. Bits and pieces of the clothing they'd brought from Scotland eventually succumbed to the rough treatment of the last two years, and the few bolts of cloth in the Hudson's Bay Company's stores were priced as luxury items for the Indian trade. Buffalo hides were plentiful but unpliable, but Peguis's people occasionally brought in deerhides and moosehides to trade—increasingly so when they discovered there was a ready market for them. Deerhide shirts and blouses became surprisingly soft and comfortable after they'd been lived in for a few weeks. Unfortunately, however, leather didn't launder.

So Marie Anne had left her children in the care of Catherine Pritchard for a few hours and come over to Point Douglas to show Kate where there was a vein of white clay in their section of river bank. The cleaning really should have been done outside, but the

round was a sea of black gumbo, so she took a sample of clay up
the house and settled for giving an experimental demonstration
side, just so Kate would know how to go about it when the ground
ried.

Kate dug out her husband's worn-out old boots and watched as
larie Anne worked the wet white clay into a section of the leather,
en scraped away the excess. A fair amount of the accumulation
f grease and sweat and dirt came away with it, soaked out as the
lay soaked in. As it dried, the leather took on the matte white of
idian dresses and tents. Kate took her turn, and was squelching
lay through her fingers like a child playing on a mud bank when
er husband came in.

Sandy didn't seem to notice, just leaned against the door frame
steady himself while he exchanged his mud-caked shoes for in-
oor moccasins. He said in Gaelic: "They are at it hammer and
ngs again."

"Who?"

"Who else? Colin Robertson and the governor, Rogers, and the
st of them. Screaming themselves hoarse over whether they should
t Captain Cameron free or whether they should burn down Fort
ibraltar and God knows what else. At the bottom it is always only
at Robertson doesn't like taking orders from the governor."

"I should think not. Governor Semple hasn't been here long
nough to understand what he's doing."

"He is legally the final authority."

"How many times have you told me that what you hated most
out the army was watching idiots in gold braid giving orders to
en who knew their business? Mister Robertson knows the country
id the people in it."

"Your Mister Robertson may know the country, but he's got a
amned sight left to learn about people. Once he's got the other
an down he can't seem to resist rubbing his nose in it, which is
ot a good idea if the man ever gets up again. That habit of Rob-
rtson's is something we're all going to end up paying for if some-
ne doesn't take him in hand."

"Who do you think should take him in hand? *Lieutenant* Rogers,
erhaps? Or that *ensign* of his?" She emphasized the military titles
remind him of the times he'd groused about the governor's proud-
outhed, drink-sodden excuses for military aides.

Sandy didn't flinch, merely stood there staring at her without a
ord.

It was Marie Anne who broke the silence. In a flustered voice, she said, "Excuse me, I must to . . ." standing up and wrapping her shawl around her. *"Mes enfants . . ."*

Kate hurried after her to see her out and thank her. When they kissed each other's cheeks good-bye, Kate's lips came away with the taste of damp salt. It didn't seem possible that there was anything in her bickering with Sandy that could make Marie Anne suddenly long for the return of her husband. Perhaps it didn't have to do with Jean Baptiste at all, but with the fact that—for all that the bombastic goings-on at Colony House were more fun than a Punch and Judy show—those antics were going to determine the future of the colony or, indeed, whether it had one.

CHAPTER 56

Not long after Bostonais arrived at Fort Esperance, he and Grant rode out to the camp of a Cree Chief named Yellow Shirt, who had been known in his youth as Walks Sideways. They spent the night in his tent, smoking tobacco while Grant tried to persuade Yellow Shirt to join in the coming campaign to rub out the colony for good. He wouldn't be persuaded. One of the few things the Plains tribes all agreed on was that it was a good thing to have two fur companies to bid against each other. No amount of argument could convince Yellow Shirt or any of the other Chiefs that it was possible to root out the colony and still leave the Hudson's Bay Company in operation. Yellow Shirt did give his word, though, as the other Chiefs had, that he would not intervene to help the *jardinières.*

In the morning they rode back through a rolling countryside boiling with spring. The surface melt-off had all been sopped up by the earth. What looked from a distance to be a stubborn patch of snow was actually a swath of ground-hugging, clustered flowers. The grass was sprouting up in a thousand subtle variations of green, each shade as fresh and lush and translucent as a baby's skin.

Most of the morning Grant rode in silence, wrestling with a

problem. Finally he said: "There isn't any way around it, you can't come with us."

"Why not?"

"You gave Robertson your word."

"So? So I gave him my word—what's he going to do, paddle my bottom because I told a lie?"

"That isn't the issue. You can't go around giving your word and then breaking it."

"Robertson does."

"Do you have to do everything Colin Robertson does?"

"They all run around lying through their teeth all the time, promising one thing and doing another. Where does that leave us if we try to keep our word?"

"If a man's word doesn't mean anything to him, what does?"

Bostonais gave a disgusted snort and said: "You talk like an old woman."

"You ride like an old woman."

Bostonais lashed at his horse with the dangling tail of his reins. They both leaped into a gallop. About half a mile ahead of them— bobbing up and down with their progress over the uneven ground— was an oak bluff that made a handy mark. The horses laid their ears back, strained their necks forward, and stretched out, at least as eager to win as their riders. Grant's horse had the advantage of carrying less weight, but Bostonais's had longer legs.

Through the last hundred yards they jostled each other for the advantage of the straight line, flailing away at each other with their reins and laughing. Grant's horse edged into the lead. At the last instant before crashing headlong into the trees, they both sheered off, splitting around the bluff and slowing to a walk. When they met up on the other side, Grant said: "That makes it two hundred pounds you owe me."

"Hundred and ninety—remember last time."

It took a few moments of walking for all four of them to get their wind back. Then Grant said: "What exactly did you promise Robertson?"

"I told you—that I wouldn't cause them no more trouble."

"But what *exactly*? What sort of trouble were you causing them when Pritchard decided to arrest you?"

"We were hunting down along the Turtle River. The *jardinières* were hunting the same country. Like usual, they were on foot and we were riding, so they weren't having much luck. So they hired Desmarais to hunt for them. Desmarais's got the best buffalo runner

I ever seen except Le Père, only not so crazy. So after Desmarais had been hunting for them a few days, I took him aside and told him—like any friend would—that some of us weren't such good shots, and maybe sometime soon we might aim at a buffalo and hit his horse.''

"Ah! So what you gave your word to, then, was that you would no longer harass their hired hunters, correct?'' Bostonais gave out a wary grunt. "Well, then, you won't be breaking your word if you come with us to the Forks—we have no intention of interfering with their hunting parties.'' Bostonais gave another grunt, only this time it was decidedly affirmative.

Grant was quite pleased to have that resolved. He wasn't certain what Bostonais would have said if he'd been ordered to stay behind, but the last thing he wanted was to go toe to toe with Bostonais. Strangely, Bostonais seemed relieved as well. For the first time, it passed through Grant's mind that perhaps the last thing Bostonais wanted was a confrontation with him. He wondered if that balance was an essential ingredient in all lasting male friendships.

On the prairie ahead of them, one of Grant's favorite optical illusions began to unfold. On the undulating carpet of hummocks and new green appeared a zigzag scar of deep emerald. As they rode closer it became a shallow rift, then a gully, then a ravine, the earth spreading itself apart and opening. When finally they halted their horses on its edge, below them was the blue-black satin ribbon of The River That Calls, winding through a broad, rich valley that from a mile away wasn't even a sketch line on the face of the prairie.

They had come at the valley from the north, with the thickly wooded south wall facing toward them. They were high above the Hudson's Bay Company's Fort Qu'Appelle, gazing down into it like a bucket floating in a well. The fort and the open plantation in front of it were erupting with activity. Men with muskets were lining the firing ledge and the catwalk above the gates, huddling over the three pounders in the bastions. Between the front gates and the river milled a horde of tiny figures dressed in the flamboyant colors of the New Nation, galloping their ponies back and forth and brandishing their weapons.

Grant kicked his horse hard and charged down the slope. The horse whinnied and squealed all the way down, its hooves scrabbling and skittering on the sheer grade. They hit level ground upright and galloped for the fort. Just before they rounded the corner of the wall, Grant reined the horse in hard, so that they came into the open at an assured, leisurely trot.

It looked like every man from the camp at Fort Esperance had crossed the river. Some were standing in their stirrups trading insults with the men inside the walls. Some were wheeling the cannons captured last year into position and arguing about their loading. Some, the most dangerous ones, were simply sitting their horses quietly, muskets or feathered lances dangling from their hands.

Grant glanced around the field to see if anyone appeared to be even remotely in charge. Alex Fraser was on foot in front of the cannons, pacing back and forth importantly. Behind him on a horse was Bethsy—shouting and gesticulating and wheeling her horse with the turns in his pacing. At one point he turned on her, shouting back and flapping his hands in her horse's face. It spooked and backed away, but Alex kept coming. Just as the horse seemed about to unseat her, Pierre Falcon rode between them nervously.

By this time Grant's horse had carried him up behind the trio. He reined in and called: "Hello, Alex."

All heads turned, and one pair of snaky eyes clicked up to identify him. There was a pause, then Alex Fraser opened his mouth long enough to say, "Hello, Wappeston," and snapped it shut again.

"What are you doing on this side of the river? Did you bring everyone over for a card party? Or just comparing the length of your cannons?"

Alex flourished his arm in the direction of the Hudson's Bay Company fort. "I told them to clear out. They got no right here. If they don't clear out, we'll blow their fort to pieces around their ears. It's our country, and we don't want the Hudson's Bay here." With that, he crossed his arms over his chest, closed his mouth, and jutted his chin forward.

The shouting and collective pacing had stopped. Grant didn't have to look to know that the entire aggregation was focused now on him. Some of them had been camped outside Fort Esperance for two weeks, just waiting. If they hadn't been tired of waiting, they wouldn't have followed Alex across the river.

An eerie giddiness had come over him with the realization that they were teetering on the lip of a massacre. " 'We'? Who exactly is 'we,' Alex?"

"The New Nation."

"Ah, I see. Did the New Nation all get together while I was gone and decide you'd make a better captain general?"

"So the North West Company gave you a sword and a fancy coat, so what? You don't do nothing but talk and talk. If you can't do what the Chief of the métis should do, then—"

"The New Nation has no quarrel with the Hudson's Bay Company as a trading concern, only with its efforts to colonize—"

"Save that horse piss. Everybody knows the only reason you won't fight Fort Qu'Appelle is you're afraid if we hurt your wife's brother, she won't let you lick her ass no more." It was tossed off reactively, with no more thought behind it than there was behind Grant's response—which was to shoot out his right hand, grab a fistful of Alex's shirtfront just under his throat, and lift him three feet in the air.

With every muscle in his arm, every tendon in his shoulder, screaming at him to let Alex go, Grant held him there and said in as languid a tone as he could manage: "You made a mistake, didn't you, Alex?"

When Alex didn't respond, Grant shook him a little and said louder: "Didn't you?" This time Alex nodded vigorously. With a grim smile, Grant let him go, and Alex dropped to the ground, sprawling sideways.

Grant turned his horse toward Fort Qu'Appelle. The assault force that had followed Alex had stopped their galloping and angry gesticulating, but he knew they wouldn't follow him back across the river unless he could avoid making it look like a humiliating retreat. He rode halfway to the gates of the fort and stopped. He called, "Mister McKay!"

John Richards's blond head raised up over the palisade. "Mister Grant." As soon as he heard John Richards's voice, Grant knew why it was right to have reined in where he had. At that distance, in order to hear each other both voices would have to be raised loud enough to be heard by everyone on either side.

"I must apologize for the intrusion, Mister McKay. Some of my friends were under the misapprehension that the continuing presence of your fort here had something to do with the continuing presence of the colony at the Forks. Fortunately, they see now they were mistaken."

"Fortunately for them."

Stupid bastard, thought Grant. Doesn't he have the brains to leave well enough alone? He called out: "Fortunately for all of us, Mister McKay. It is generally the fools and cowards of this world who spill blood unnecessarily; the brave don't have to slaughter each other to prove their bravery."

He turned his horse toward the ford. Some of his *jeunes gens* were already crossing, others were hitching up the guns. Falcon and Bethsy had already crossed—one or both of them had had the

sense to realize that it wouldn't be politic for her to ride over and
pat her husband's hand just now.

Bostonais walked his horse up beside him and growled: "How's
the arm?"

"What arm?" He grinned and nudged curiously at the wrung-
out slab of dead meat dangling from his right shoulder.

CHAPTER 57

The fields on Point Douglas lay black and open and waiting, hoed into furrows. The seeds—wheat and barley and
oats—waited as well, in three rawhide bags hanging from wooden
pegs just inside the doorway of the low log shanty. All the grain
that had lived to ripen after the tramplings and burnings of the
previous spring had been stored in the loft of Colony House over
the winter, then parceled out to each family on the first of May.
Some had planted theirs already; some preferred to wait a little
longer against the chance of a late frost. It had sunk in to them all
by now that winter wheat wouldn't work in a country where the
ground froze eighteen inches deep.

When Kate was in the house alone she would occasionally stand
beside the bags of seeds, dig her hands into the pellet-hard little
golden eggs, and sieve them through her fingers, thinking of the
coming autumn, when there would be a dozen more for every one
they planted and bread every day through the winter.

At the moment her husband was down on the riverbank showing
Mister MacBeth and several of his sons how to catch catfish—
twenty hooks suspended on hanks of fish line tied to a *shagganappi*
rope strung across the Red River. Kate was on the point above,
working with a sickle in the bright spring sun, clearing the alder
shoots and weed growth from the spot where they'd decided the
new house would go. The cramped shanty they'd spent the winter
in would become a shed for tools and snowshoes and, perhaps, on
some grand day in the future, a cow.

Marie Anne Lajimodierre was working next to her, swinging a

second sickle and chattering brightly. La Reine was pulling up handfuls of grass stalks and stacking them in a pile, with her little brothers puttering in her wake pretending to help.

"In Trois Rivières," Marie Anne reminisced, "I so glad all ways when the autumn come, because it did mean Monsieur l'Abbé would let me to go home to the farm of my father to be of help in the sunshine and the fields. Now, one day it was, *mes sœurs*—sisters—and me were make the sheaves in the cut field, and we see there is a man on *le pont* . . . uh, the bridge." The crescent blades whispered rhythmically through the stalks of grass and clover, underscoring Marie Anne's story. "So—there is a man on the bridge, sitting upon his horse, upon *le pont*, and he is half under the shadow from *les arbres*, and he is chewing on a piece of wheat and watch us. And I say to *mes sœurs*: 'Who is that man who have no work except to sit and watch honest girls with their skirts, you know, *levée* for work?'

"So Helene, she go"—straightening her back and raising up on her toes, shading one hand over her eyes—"and I pull her back down: 'Helene, have you *rien dans la tête*, to stare so at a man?' And she say, 'It don't matter, I seen who it is—Lajimodierre, *l'homme du nord*.'" She sighed and switched her sickle one more time through the weeds, then let her arms go slack and said again: "*L'homme du nord.*" She looked up at the sky and let out a long, chest-heavy moan. Then her head slumped forward, and her legs buckled.

Kate went to Marie Anne. She was hunched over on her knees, rocking back and forth with her forearms pressing against her belly, pushing out a grunted litany in French. There were a few words Kate recognized, *maudit* and *merde*, but the rest were indistinguishable.

She crouched down and tentatively put her arm across Marie Anne's shoulders. Marie Anne stopped rocking and let her body slump sideways against Kate's. "It is idiot . . . stupid," she murmured brokenly. "You clear away the ground for the house you will never build. You plant the wheat you will never see come up. Tomorrow, or the day after, the *bois brulé* come down and kill us all."

"They will not."

"No? You think you . . . you . . . you talk to them nice and they tip their hat and ride away? You think your Monsieur Robertson puff up his shirt and they all run? They already kill my husband!"

"Don't say that! You have no way of knowing what may have—"

" 'Don't say that! Don't say that!' Are you so stupid you think if you dig your garden and say, 'Don't say that,' it isn't going to be?" La Reine and La Prairie had come forward, holding Henri upright between them, and stood stricken with awe at the impossible spectacle of their mother in tears, kneeling on the ground. Marie Anne pushed Kate away and pulled them to her.

Kate stood away from them and said: "Do you think none of the rest of us feel the urge to clap our hands to our ears and run screaming into the river? Short of that, there does not seem to be much we can do but keep on building houses and planting gardens."

Marie Anne looked at her as though she were some alien being. The children were crying, not so much for any specific anguish as because it just seemed like the thing to do. Marie Anne said: "It is the truth about you English—"

"English! Who are you calling English?"

"Whatever you call yourselves, it is the same—you feel nothing!"

"Do not tell me what I feel! I have just as much right to self-pity as you do."

"What do you have? I have three children that are not baptized!"

"You great sniveling brood mare—I have no children!"

Marie Anne's eyes flew open, and her mouth tightened into a hard line. Then her lips began to quiver, and a twinkle flickered in her eyes. She said: "Oh, yes? Well . . . well, I have one foot bigger than the other and it make my shoes to fit bad!"

Kate leaned down and hollered: "Well, I am too tall and everyone makes fun of me!"

"Ha! Me, I can't drink wine, it makes me to burp from behind!"

Kate collapsed onto the pile laughing, the two of them hugging each other and gasping for breath, squashing the children between them. The children giggled and squirmed to break away while the grown-ups sputtered ineffectually.

Sandy's head and torso came into view past Marie Anne's shoulder. He stopped and looked away when he saw the two women hugging each other and laughing. Kate had noticed before that intimacy between women seemed to make him uncomfortable. For that matter, any kind of intimacy made him uncomfortable. She let go of Marie Anne and stood up, wiping her cheeks. Her husband came up the rest of the way over the riverbank and said: "There is something happening at Fort Douglas."

She started toward the bank, but he said: "You cannot see much from there. We are going to the fort to have a look."

They made a slapdash little parade, Kate and her husband in the front, followed by Marie Anne and Mister MacBeth, and the younger generation trailing behind. Kate asked: "What did you see that made you think there was something to go have a look at?"

"They are launching one of the York boats and loading it up with provisions. From the look of things, it is no quick jaunt up to the lake that they are making ready for."

The rumor appeared to have traveled through the colony quickly; the path from the upstream farms was clogged with colonists, and a crowd had formed in front of Colony House, a half circle with its points hinged to the riverbank. Midway between the two points was the moored York boat. A crew of Orcadians wound back and forth from a stack of bundles and trunks and sacks of pemmican heaped on the crest of the bank. Laid out beside that was the boat's mast and rigging. Colin Robertson was crouched by the head of the mast, working away at something. A ways apart from the activity stood Governor Semple, Lieutenant Rogers, Alex McLean, John Pritchard, and all the other important or self-important gentlemen of the colony. John Pritchard held a tally sheet and a pen and ink.

Kate soon heard every rumor running around the colony—Mrs. MacBeth said that Mister Robertson was running out on them, George Sutherland told her that Lieutenant Rogers and his aide were being banished for drunkenness, and James Sutherland said that the boat was being outfitted for an expedition to capture the North West Company's fort on Lake Winnipeg.

Colin Robertson finished his business with the mast, found himself a bit of high ground on the lip of the bank, and turned to address the assemblage. "Well, then—it is good of you all to come and see me off. Myself and Mister Semple"—the word "Governor" had vanished from his vocabulary some months earlier—"have decided that I should return to Britain." He paused long enough to let that sink in. "Someone must present the true state of affairs here to the Crown. And someone must escort Duncan Cameron to a place where his crimes can be laid before an *impartial* court." He stressed the "impartial," as if to differentiate between the British courts and those in Upper Canada.

"Over the course of the winter we have managed to clear out most of the troublemakers. But my last piece of advice is that as long as Fort Gibraltar is still standing—"

"Mister Robertson!" The governor cut him off. "You have of-

ered that piece of advice already, and I have told you that there
·ill be no wanton destruction of private property while—''

'' 'Private property'? Do you still think you are dealing with a
onvention of bank clerks or some such? I should have had the
:nse to leave the colony lying in ruins till you got here so you
·ould have seen what those bastards—''

"The behavior of the lawless is no excuse for duly constituted
uthorities to carry on in the same high-handed manner.''

"When you are among wolves," Mister Robertson retorted,
howl!''

The crowd parted, and two Hudson's Bay men came through
scorting a manacled Duncan Cameron, much grayer and more
ubdued than usual. His escort marched him up to Colin Robertson
nd then stood back.

The crew had climbed aboard the York boat and were stepping
a the mast. There was a fine south wind, just waiting for the sail
o be unfurled, but something was already flapping from the head
f the mast. Colin Robertson caught Cameron's eyes with his own
nd then pointedly looked away, toward the top of the mast. Crack-
ag in the wind was an empty pemmican sack. Colin Robertson
aughed and clapped his hands together at the sight.

Duncan Cameron turned and slowly swept his eyes around the
ircle of watching faces. Then he straightened, lifted his chin, and
aid in a voice that was drier than Kate remembered but just as
trong: "In a very short while every one of you will envy me.''

CHAPTER 58

On a bright May morning, Cuthbert Grant kissed his wife
and child good-bye, climbed onto his horse, and rode out
f Fort Esperance at the head of a column of horsemen as dangerous
s the New World had yet produced. They had been waiting inside
ne gates until the watchtower sentry hollered down that the last of
ne York boats from Fort Qu'Appelle had melted into the distance,

ferrying their season's accumulation of pemmican and furs dow
stream to their governor-in-chief at the Forks of the Red.

Once outside the gates, Grant led his troop behind the fort a
up to the plateau of the prairie, then cut east at a rolling, groun
eating lope, paralleling the valley but far enough inland to be i
visible from the river. It was a grand day. The meadowlarks a
red-winged blackbirds were singing, and the sun poured down o
of a cloudless sky. Bostonais rode on Grant's right and Falcon o
his left. Directly behind them rode Alex Fraser, butting in o
stirrup a long willow pole from which the blue-and-white flag
the New Nation billowed in the breeze. It was the same design
the old, time-tattered red-and-white flag, but in sewing a ne
one, the only piece of sturdy cloth Bethsy had had on hand h
been blue. Grant actually preferred it that way: the red seemed
bit bloodthirsty, and the more vociferously Gallic of his followe
preferred their flags blue rather than Britannic red.

The column stretched out behind the flag in threes or twos
fours, depending on individual inclinations. They started singing
song of Falcon's, a sensitive ditty about the time Bostonais's hor
drank a keg of high wine. Bostonais was inclined to hush them u
for fear of alerting the brigade down in the valley, but Grant l
them go. The scouts he'd sent out would give him plenty of warnir
when they came within earshot of the boats.

Every man in the column had asked him at one time or anoth
what they were going to do when they caught up with the boat
Grant would just shake his head and smile. They didn't have
know until the moment it happened, and he didn't want to spoil t
effect with anticipation—it was going to be far too delicious
watch it unfold in front of them like a watchworks music box.

Toward evening one of the outriders came pounding up to infor
him that they were almost parallel with the brigade. Grant sheare
off to the south to take them farther away from the valley, then har
galloped them east until sunset. The York boats would be makin
good time with the runoff-swollen current, but they had to follo
the loops and switchbacks of the river. By the time he called a ha
for the night, they'd left the boats a good four miles behind. The
made a fireless camp on the open prairie, chewed their pemmica
or jerked venison, and rolled into their blankets for the night.
the morning they rode due east until noon, then angled north to th
valley and cut down to the river.

The Grand Rapids of the Qu'Appelle were an abbreviated ve
sion of the *dalles* of the Winnipeg River. A narrow channel of whi

ter boiled through rock ledges and jutting promontories. Boats
d to shoot through one at a time, and wise guides always waited
good ten minutes before letting the next boat in line follow in
se of disaster.

The lead York boat in the Qu'Appelle spring brigade of 1816
ade it safely through the winding sluiceway and shot out of the
ute into a wide, placid channel shrouded with willows. In the
iddle of the channel stood a hump-backed granite boulder mark-
g the tip of a sandbar. On the boulder, his moccasins and trousers
ipping from the wade out, the braid on his captain general's tunic
eaming in the sun, stood Cuthbert Grant with his arms crossed
d his feet planted wide. He uncrossed his arms and leveled a pair
pistols at the eighteen men in the boat.

John Richards McKay stood up at the midthwarts, a startled
pression on his face. He opened his mouth to laugh, and his
other-in-law shouted: *"Levé!"*

The willows all along both banks suddenly sprouted fifty nasty-
oking customers aiming even nastier-looking buffalo guns. Grant
inked amiably and grinned. He raised one of the pistol barrels
ainst his lips in a shushing gesture and pointed at a low point on
e north bank where Bostonais Pangman and Pierre Falcon were
aving the boat in.

Before the prow had quite touched the shore, there were several
ozen chortling half-breeds wading out to hustle the crew ashore
d yank out the cargo. Within a very few minutes John Richards
d his crew were lined up under guard on a meadow behind the
reen of willows, with their cargo of pemmican sacks piled up on
e side and the York boat on the other; giggling like mischievous
ildren, the intimidation squad hunkered back down in the bush
spring the same joke on the next boat.

All eight York boats were taken without one shot being fired.
uring the entire operation, the greatest danger to the soldiers of
e New Nation was that of collapsing into the river and drowning
efore they could stop laughing. Up until the Great Guffaw on the
rand Rapids of the Qu'Appelle, they had been perfectly happy to
llow Cuthbert Grant, since someone had to coordinate the cam-
ign and no one better had come forward. After this, however,
ey would have stormed the gates of hell for him.

Grant had one of the boats put back in the water and sent it
wnriver with a half load of pemmican. There was every possi-
lity that the colonists at the Forks were destitute after the winter.

He didn't want them to starve to death. John Richards McK
wanted to accompany the boat, but Grant wouldn't hear of it.

That night there was a grand celebration with the boat crew
stock of rum. On the following day Whitehead MacDonell car
down the rapids with the Fort Esperance brigade. There were mo
canoes than usual, and some of them carried no cargo at all. T
York boats' cargo was loaded into them. Several of the HBC boa
men, feeling a distinct change in the wind, signed on with the Nor
West Company. The rest were set free to walk back to Fo
Qu'Appelle, toting a couple of bags of pemmican and a sack
nails rescued from the ashes of their boats.

Grant split his force into two halves, one for each bank of t
river. They rode downstream flanking the North West Compa
brigade along the edge of the plateaus—first of the Qu'Appel
valley, then the broader, deeper Assiniboine. When they came
the last shallow crossing on the Assiniboine before the ford at I
Souris, the platoon on the west bank crossed over to link up wi
the others. By now many of them were riding bare-chested, son
of them in loincloths, their bodies daubed with pigment, feathe
wound into their hair. Even the most resolutely un-Indian had go
in for a streak of paint down the bridge of the nose or across on
cheek. They were having the time of their lives, drawing clos
every day to the riveting conclusion that they didn't need to atta
themselves to their mothers' tribes or their fathers' companies
survive.

As they rode east from the brigade's shore camp, Bostonais a
gued with Grant over what he planned to do at Brandon Hous
"What's the good of bringing all them together"—jerking his thun
over his shoulder at the column following behind—"if they ai
ever going to fight?"

"That is precisely the good of it. If we'd only had a few doze
men at the Grand Rapids, the Hudson's Bay men might have thoug
they had a chance and tried to put up a fight."

"We would've took them anyway."

"No doubt, but some of us would have gone down along wi
them. The point of civilized warfare is to gain an objective th
can't be achieved through negotiation. If we can achieve our obje
tives by showing our enemy that he's defeated before he can beg
to fight . . ."

"Card tricks," Bostonais grumbled unhappily. "If you'd to
me we were going flower picking, I might've stayed at home."

François Deschamps, old Deschamps's second son, gallope

ack from his scout position to inform Grant that he could see the
ookout tower of Brandon House over the next stand of trees. Grant
alled a halt and climbed off his horse. There was a low bluff of
rush and buffalo grass nearby, one side of which had tumbled
nder the process of erosion, showing the naked sand beneath.
Grant walked halfway up the wind-smoothed dune and waited there
vhile the others dismounted and gathered around the base. He
insheathed his captain general's sword and drew in the sand a sketch
nap of the layout of Brandon House, assuming that the fort wouldn't
iave changed much since he was courting its chief trader's sister.

Once he'd explained the scenario, and heard those with specific
esponsibilities repeat them back, he allowed them a moment to
:heck their weapons, then gave the order to mount up. The tree
:over along the riverbank came to an abrupt halt about two hundred
vards shy of the east wall of the palisade. They stopped just within
he last fringe of the woods and stood peering out at the sun-
lrenched meadow that would become a killing ground if anything
vent wrong. All up and down the column, brown fingers were
naking the sign of the cross or fingering amulets. A few wise souls
vere doing both.

Grant's heart was working overtime in his rib cage. A tingling,
:rystalline haze had settled over his field of vision, sharpening the
letails of every petal or palisade point while at the same time bind-
ng them all into a conspiratorial universe. Once again he was on
he brink of proving himself a tactical genius or a fool with a ven-
ilated head.

Bostonais nudged his horse up beside him and caught his eye—
:ver hopeful that even at this late hour Grant might have seen the
ight. Grant shook his head and laughed. At the moment, even
Bostonais's bloody-minded obstinacy was deliriously endearing.
No doubt about it, there was nothing like a whiff of death to remind
you how much you'd been enjoying life, or ought to have been.

Grant held himself coiled on the brink for one more exquisitely
precarious instant, then nudged his horse forward at a slow walk.

Bostonais and a dozen others followed behind him; the rest stayed
nidden in the trees with Falcon. Grant drooped his head forward
and persuaded his shoulders to slump inward. They skirted wide
around Brandon House and ambled toward the river—just a pack
of dehydrated hunters crossing the ford to Fort La Souris and pausing to moisten their parched throats along the way.

They plodded wearily down the low ridge of the bank. Grant slid
off his horse and sloshed water over his face. Bostonais and the

others followed his example. In Grant's mind this was where it had all started two years ago—when he'd come back to broaden his acquaintance with Bethsy McKay and found the ford to Fort La Souris clogged with carts carrying pemmican to Brandon House.

He scooped up a handful of silty water to his mouth and counted off the time in his head. Now the tower lookout would have gone back to scanning the horizon, now the sentry at the gate would have slumped back down into the shade, now the men who'd scrambled up to man the bastion guns at the first sign of approaching horsemen would be stumping down the ladder in disgust . . .

He waited another moment longer, then leaped onto his horse, yanked its head around viciously, and whipped it into a gallop. Crouched low over his horse's neck, with his left hand clutching the reins and his right hand whacking the barrel of his rifle against the horse's rump, he drove straight for the open gates of Brandon House. He could hear the hoofbeats and the snorted breathing of the other horses pressing up behind, but otherwise there was no sound, no war whoops, no shouts of encouragement.

The old gateman heard the drumming and jumped up to close the gates, too late. Grant swung his rifle to brush him back as he swept past. As his horse carried him into the courtyard, Grant whipped his head over his shoulder. The blur of movement that caught his eyes would be Bostonais swinging down off his horse in front of the gateman. Alex Fraser and his men would be swarming up the ladders to the east and west bastions, to lift up the cradles of the guns and wrestle them around to point inward.

Out of the blur of log buildings passing by him, Grant picked out the chief trader's quarters with its roofed verandah. A figure was moving rapidly across the shadowed porch toward the front door. Grant hauled back on the reins and vaulted out of the saddle. He hit the ground running and intercepted the figure on the porch, spinning it back against the wall and jamming the muzzle of his rifle up under its chin.

It was John Richards McKay's replacement as chief trader at Brandon House. Grant had the devil of a time catching his breath against the pounding in his chest, but after a moment he said: "Whatever it was you were thinking of doing, honoured sir—don't."

By that time Falcon and Seraphim and the other eighty riders from the woods were pouring through the gates, whooping and laughing and firing their rifles in the air. There would be no inter-ference from Brandon House when Whitehead MacDonell's bri-

gade passed by, and no reinforcements or provisions for Fort
Douglas.

CHAPTER 59

Both the shanty that Sandy and his wife had wintered in
and the first house they'd built on Point Douglas—the one
the North West Company's métis had burned—had been built with
the standard method of log construction: notches cut in each end
of the log to interlock, the logs overlapping each other at the corners
of the building like fingers interlaced at the top knuckle.

There was another method, one the fur trading companies used
in those of their establishments that were built to last. Squared
beams, grooved lengthwise on two sides, were stood upright in
postholes at the corners and midpoints of the prospective walls.
Then beams that were tongued at each end were stacked laterally
between the posts, the tongues slotting into the grooves. It was
immensely sturdier than the old method, it gave more of a feeling
of permanence, and it required a great deal of hoisting and jock-
eying with massive hunks of wood.

Ex-Private Alexander Sutherland and ex-Sergeant Alexander
MacBeth agreed that they would help each other build post-and-
beam houses, provided enough seasoned logs were available. They
walked down to Fort Douglas one afternoon to take a look at what
the woodcutters had stocked up over the winter and to see what
terms the colonial establishment might set for them.

There was more activity about the place than usual, men bumping against each other in every direction. Sandy and Mister MacBeth
joined a straggling line outside of Colony House waiting to speak
to the governor or Mister Pritchard. A York boat was pulled up on
the shore, with a disconsolate-looking crew unloading a few dozen
bags of pemmican. Mister MacBeth said: "Is that supposed to get
us all through till the harvest?"

"No—pemmican is concentrated, but not that concentrated. The
brigade from the west will bring half a dozen boatloads at the least.

This must just be a temporary shipment from Fort Daer on the Pembina, or from Brandon House, to tide us over till the brigade comes in. You will know when that happens—fifty or sixty oarsmen singing at the top of their lungs and the cannons going off on shore now that we have cannons again. Everyone seems to be quite certain that the guns we confiscated from Fort Gibraltar were the ones they stole from us, but to tell the truth they have gone back and forth so many times now no one knows for sure. Did you manage to get enough land cleared to put down all your seed, then?''

''Aye, six bushels of wheat and three of potatoes. We could have planted more, but that was all they would let us draw.''

''Six?''

''Six, and three of potatoes.''

Sandy had only planted half that, and he'd had almost two full seasons' headstart on Mister MacBeth at turning his parcel of prairie into fields. There seemed only one possible explanation and it wasn't something he liked to think of someone he liked and respected as much as old Alex MacBeth. In the lexicon of uncivilized and destructive behavior there were few crimes more heinous than eating seed—no matter how trying it might be to put wheat and potatoes into the ground when Mister Bourke was playing it so close to the vest with their rations. With as much nonchalance as he could muster, Sandy said: ''How much land did you manage to get broken this spring?''

''I have not so good an eye for the measuring of acreages—I came to it late. But I believe I have seven or eight acres planted.''

''Seven or eight? I barely have four . . .''

Mister MacBeth laughed, ''There, I told you I was not so good at this. Straight distance, now, that I can measure—show me a line of march and I can tell you with one look whether it is four miles or three-and-three-quarters, but acreages. . . . Still, I am certain it must be six acres at the least.''

''In one spring? I have been breaking my back three years running and barely have . . .''

''Yes, well, ahem . . .'' Mister MacBeth cut him off and looked away and grew a touch red in the face. ''There is just you and your wife, you see, while . . .'' He rolled one hand through the air to imply the rest. Sandy saw. Mister MacBeth had four sons over the age of fifteen, and even the younger children were big enough to lend a hand. Whatever theorizing the rest of the community might engage in around their kitchen tables, the fact that he and Kate MacPherson had been married for two years with no sign of pro-

ucing children was not something that anyone of any sensitivity
would care to bring up in public.

Governor Semple ambled out onto the broad front stoop, and the
crowd jostled forward expectantly. The governor looked up and
own the line of petitioners and called out: "Alexander MacBeth
nd Alexander Sutherland?"

Before Sandy could start forward, another voice called, "Here,
ir!" and pushed in front of him. It was young Alex Sutherland,
who had arrived with last fall's party of immigrants.

Sandy grabbed his shoulder and said: "Not you, lad."

Alex Sutherland shook off his hand and kept on going. "He said
lexander Suth—"

Sandy snatched a fistful of his shirt and pulled him back. Alex
utherland rounded on him, batting his arm away. He stood a good
alf head taller than Sandy and twenty pounds heavier, but his face
as still peach-fuzzed. When he saw it was Sandy his belligerence
isappeared; he blushed and stepped back. "Oh, I see. Excuse me,
Mister Sutherland." Someone farther down the line laughed at him.
andy felt as though he'd swallowed a spoonful of salt.

He went forward with Mister MacBeth to the front of the line.
he governor said: "You two were looking to buy lumber for house
uilding, or to have it added to your account?"

"Yes, sir."

"If you give me a few days' free labor, you can have all the
umber you need—not all of it squared, I'm afraid, but all sound
nd well seasoned and plenty to choose from. Well?"

Mister MacBeth said: "What manner of labor, sir?"

"I have decided to demolish Fort Gibraltar."

"I thought you had decided not to, sir," Sandy said. "That is,
hen Mister Robertson left, you said—"

"I have decided to demolish Fort Gibraltar." It was repeated
ith authority and a touch of impatience. Sandy knew better than
 ask again.

The demolishing party turned out to be a lot like a Highland fair,
ith the women cooking up noon meals on the greensward while
e men uprooted the palisade logs; squads of children ran wild,
arning the occasional cuff for nearly getting squashed by falling
gs. Some of the women, Kate in particular, joined in when stub-
orn uprights had to be hauled loose with rope and muscle.

The logs were rolled to the bank and floated downstream to Fort
ouglas. Sandy and the MacBeth faction stacked the lumber marked

for their own use—squared timbers from the bourgeois's and *en gagés'* quarters—off to one side, to raft down to their lots when the demolishing was done. The handful of *engagés* who'd still been living in the fort had been shooed out. They put up tents on the edge of the plantation and stood watching the demolition in silence. On the morning of the third day they were gone.

A canoeful of Indians came down the Red looking to do their summer trading. Where the great citadel of Fort Gibraltar should have been, there was only an empty space with white men swarming over it. Their mouths open, they stopped paddling and drifted. Sandy trotted over to the bank and pointed them downstream, shouting: "Hudson's Bay! Hudson's Bay!" They looked skeptically at each other, then back to him. He snatched up the three-striped Hudson's Bay blanket that his wife was sitting on and waved it at them. They continued looking skeptical but paddled on.

The pieces of Fort Gibraltar's palisades were fished out of the water and resurrected around Fort Douglas, now a fort in more than name. Then Governor Semple ordered a few of his men to transform the colony's schooner *Cuchillon* into a gunboat, raising stout wooden barricades over the foredeck and mounting a pair of brass swivel guns in the bow. Everyone in the colony and the Hudson's Bay store lent a hand with all the work, except for the MacBeths and the Point Douglas Alexander Sutherlands—now so called to distinguish them from the new Alexander Sutherland family—who were too busy preparing their free lumber and laying out the sites of their new homes.

The story of Cuthbert Grant's capture of the pemmican brigade and Brandon House had made its way downriver to the colony at large. But when Sandy looked at the foot-thick interlocked walls of the new house rising on Point Douglas, and at the spiked tips of the Fort Douglas palisade, he felt assured that last spring wouldn't repeat itself. When the North West Company brigade came to the Forks this year, saw the walled fort and the solid front of two hundred dug-in colonists, they would realize they'd have to learn to live with each other.

His wife had just brought him a cup of water. He'd been hacking away with an adze, turning a beam end into a tongue in the hot June sun. The two of them were looking at their stack of lumber and the field of broad-leafed wheat shoots beyond it, when John Pritchard emerged from the path through the bush to Fort Douglas.

Mister Pritchard said: "Good day to you. I only stopped by for a moment, I have a message to carry down to all the other farms

he governor has issued an order that all colonists are to sleep
1 the fort from now on. You are free to work on your farms during
he day, but by sunset you must all be gathered within the stock-
de.''

Kate said: ''Why?''

''In case of a sneak attack.''

''In case of *what*?''

''Really, Mrs. Sutherland, you were here last year, I would think
ou would be the last person that—''

''You are quite right, I was here last year, which is why I am the
ast person to run about like a headless chicken when—''

Sandy jumped in before she could work up a full head of steam.
'How long is that to last, Mister Pritchard, the sleeping in the
ort?''

''For as long as the emergency lasts. That is the order.'' With
iat, he took his leave and went on about his rounds. Sandy looked
o his wife and she to him. He knew that the same thought was
assing through their minds—either the governor was crazy, or they
vere.

CHAPTER 60

East of Brandon House the Assiniboine wound through
miles of shifting sand hills and tangled spruce thickets,
rowding back from the banks and making it difficult for horsemen
o act as an effective escort for canoes. It seemed unlikely to Grant
1at either the colony people or the HBC men would attack the
rigade in such terrain. So he led his troop in a straight course
cross the sand hills, leaving Whitehead and the brigade to nego-
ate the river on their own.

They agreed to rendezvous at Portage la Prairie, halfway be-
ween La Souris and the Forks. There was a rumor that Semple
night be planning to ambush the brigade at the portage, but Grant
ound no one there except a handful of métis hunters and the *en-
agés* from Fort Gibraltar. They passed on news of the destruction

of the fort, of the arming of the schooner, and of Colin Robertson's
departure for Britain. This last was particularly distressing to those
who were journeying to the Forks for the express purpose of cutting
Colin Robertson up into little pieces.

They waited at Portage la Prairie for three days until the brigade
caught up with them. The cargo was offloaded and the canoes
beached for maintenance and repairs. The sacks of pemmican were
stacked up in a breastworks in case the rumored attack material-
ized. If it did, the company's cooks would just have to be careful
next winter to pick the lead out before filling their fry pans.

They held an evening strategy meeting next to a smudge fire on
the riverbank—Grant and Whitehead MacDonell and Seraphim and
Bostonais and Falcon.

The original idea behind the campaign had been to set up a two-
part blockade, at Fort Gibraltar and Frog Plain, effectively sealing
off the colony both upriver and down. Without supplies coming in
from the HBC posts, the colony would be starved out long before
their crops had time to ripen. Whitehead's brigade was to have split
itself in two at the Forks, one-half to remain at Fort Gibraltar and
the other to carry on downstream to Frog Plain. William Shaw was
on his way upriver with the English River boys to rendezvous with
Grant at Frog Plain any day now; they might even be there already.
And a contingent of reinforcements had set out from Fort William
as soon as the ice broke on the Kaministiquia.

There was nothing in the destruction of Fort Gibraltar or the
fortification of Fort Douglas that would prevent any of this. The
problem was that it was now impossible for the North West Company to move its canoes past Fort Douglas without a fight. If there
was no one there to meet William Shaw at Frog Plain, and no sign
of the promised provisions and presents from the company, it
wouldn't take long for the English River boys to start drifting away.
If there was no one at Frog Plain to warn the brigade coming in
from Fort William, they might blunder head on into an armed
schooner. And if the Frog Plain end of the brigade wasn't in place,
it wouldn't matter how effectively they sealed off the Forks, the
Hudson's Bay Company could still send in supplies to the colony
from Jack River House.

Bostonais was for forcing a passage. "We got twenty canoes.
Maybe the gunboat takes out two if they're lucky, then before they
can reload we're on top of them and chop them up good."

Grant said: "They can still fire on us from the fort."

"And we can fire on them when they stick their heads up to aim."

Maybe we lose a couple dozen, and we kill half of them. Just makes for less sweat for the paddlers who got to ferry them out of the country when they do give in."

"Which will take twice as long."

"Huh?"

"The plan is to starve them out—if we kill half of them, it will take twice as long."

"We came here for a fight, didn't we? Didn't we?" But Grant knew Bostonais was only grumping after the fact—the one thing his friend couldn't argue against was logic that was more ruthless than he was.

Seraphim proposed that they drift past Fort Douglas at night. "We get a new moon soon. We hug along the east shore—the current behind us, we make no sound but the steering paddle. Those *jardinières'* ears can't hear nothing quieter than a cow fart."

Whitehead MacDonell shook his head. "One canoe, maybe—two at the most. Not enough to make a difference if the sentries don't hear, or to put up a fight if they do—and then the colony's got two more canoeloads of pemmican."

Everyone looked downcast. Grant said: "Why worry about their gunboat and their fort at all?" They all looked at him like he was crazy. "No, look—there are a couple of carts out behind Montour's cabin. We load them up with pemmican and cut straight across the prairie from here to Frog Plain. We can send them back for another load if we need more. Once we're dug in there you can bring the canoes down to the Forks and put up a camp. The *jardinières* won't come out against you with us at their backs." It was a perfectly obvious solution to all their problems.

Grant set out in the morning with the two loaded carts and sixty men, leaving the rest behind with Bostonais to protect the brigade. The plan was to parallel the Assiniboine until they'd crossed Sturgeon Creek, then angle northeast to Frog Plain, passing well inland of Fort Douglas.

The wheels of the carts made a horrible screeching—wooden hubs grinding dry wooden axles. After an hour Grant couldn't take any more and rode as far ahead as he could get without losing sight of the column. Falcon trailed after him. Grant said: "Why can't they grease the wheels on those damned things?"

"No—no good on the prairie. Too much dust comes up. The dust works into the grease, and after half a day you got a lump like stone."

"It must play hell with the axles, grinding them like that."

"So? An axle wears through, you take an axe out to the nearest oak tree and cut yourself a new one. They are extremely beautiful."

"Oak trees?"

"The carts." Grant laughed, but Falcon was serious. "You look, but you don't see! Think—what makes a woman beautiful? Big breasts for feeding children, big hips for birthing them, long legs for keeping up with the tribe when it's on the move . . ."

"White teeth for fighting the dogs for scraps . . ."

"There, you begin to understand."

"Somehow I doubt your wife would."

"Your sister has no sense of humor about some things. But think—what makes a horse beautiful? The same things that make it a good horse—strong legs to run with, deep chest to breathe . . . Same with a dog. So it is with a cart. Since long before I was born, the *bois brulés* have been working out how to make a cart that will take them anywhere on the prairie without roads. They learned to make big, high wheels so the left can go down into a badger hole while the right goes up over a rock and still stays upright; someone else thought of dishing the spokes in to spread the wheels out wider; another one learned that if you wrap wet *shagganappi* around the rim, it shrinks and dries like iron but more resilient. Your cart comes to a river too deep to ford? You knock the pins out, stack your wheels on top, and float across. Something breaks on it? All you need is a stand of trees and an axe and you can make a new part in a day—or a whole new cart in a week. Sun's too hot to travel? Unhitch your pony, prop the harness poles toward the sun, and sleep in the shade till the cool of the evening." Falcon reined in his horse and said: "Here, stop and wait and look again."

They sat their horses off to the side and waited for the carts to pass by. Amazingly, Grant found his eyes lingering on the details of construction Falcon had described, which had once seemed arbitrary and ungainly. In their own weather-worn, axe-hewn fashion they were, in fact, beautifully constructed pieces of adaptive engineering.

Grant stole a glance at Falcon. He was sitting with his eyes slitted appreciatively, plucking at his lower lip with thumb and forefinger and nodding his head as he watched the carts rumble by. Grant laughed, and Falcon turned to look at him, his eyes wide and ingenuous. Grant laughed harder, then cocked his head in an exaggerated acknowledgment of defeat. Suddenly he wondered if he shouldn't have left Falcon behind with the brigade instead of Bostonais. The thought of Falcon getting shot at didn't appeal to him at all. He shook it off—nobody was going to get shot at.

They crossed the mouth of Sturgeon Creek to where they were planning to angle inland. But the ground was still marshy from the spring runoff, so they kept on heading east along the ridge of high ground paralleling the river, waiting for the marsh on the east side of Sturgeon Creek to dissipate. Instead, it blended with the marsh on the west side of Catfish Creek. They crossed Catfish Creek and went on a little farther, hemmed in between the spring marsh on their left and the river on their right.

The original plan for a line of march—northeast between Sturgeon and Catfish creeks—would have formed the baseline of an equilateral triangle, with the Assiniboine and Red rivers as the somewhat wobbly sides apexing at the Forks. As they continued farther east, however, their triangle distorted, drawing them ever closer to the back wall of Fort Douglas.

Grant decided to try the marsh. He waved his arm out to the left and headed inland. The column followed after him. Within a hundred yards the horses had sunk to their bellies, and the cartwheels were mired to the axles. For a moment it looked as if the carts were going to be sucked under and the horses were going to go mad, but Grant managed to get the carts pulled out and turned around. They retreated in a less than orderly fashion to the riverbank.

As they dismounted to scrape off the muck and catch their breath, Grant said to Falcon: "I thought you said these carts could go anywhere on the prairie?"

Falcon pointed at the ground beneath his feet, then inland at the marsh. "Prairie, swamp. Swamp, prairie." He stomped his sodden moccasins on the solid rim of the swamp bowl.

It looked like Grant had no choice but to keep on paralleling the Assiniboine until they reached the eastern border of the swamp basin. He gave the order to remount and kept on heading east. The riverbank rose and fell in a series of crazy dips and ridges. The trail wound through the shaded fastness of the belt of trees. But when it came time to turn inland, Grant knew, they'd be out in the open. It was another mile before the ground back of the bank grew solid. He took twenty men as an advance guard and trotted north out of the trees, leaving the rest to follow along with Falcon and the carts.

He planned to cut due north until they were past the colony, but it turned out that the marsh spread out wider back of the creek mouth, edging them ever closer toward the colony. Ahead and to his right, he could see the lookout tower of the newly palisaded Fort Douglas.

He felt like a spider crawling across a billiard table. At any moment they might see him—they might have seen him already—but all he could do was keep on going. The marsh had pushed his vanguard so far east that they were riding across tilled fields now. Three stooped figures up ahead suddenly straightened and stared. He told half a dozen riders to gallop ahead and take them prisoner before they could run the alarm to the fort.

Barely a mile ahead, the belt of trees pushed east onto the prairie in a crooked finger of burl oak and wolf willow and poplars—Seven Oaks Creek, the southern boundary of Frog Plain. As soon as the carts were on Frog Plain, the New Nation and their allies would have the colony in a vise. They would only have to tighten the screws, and it would be over—neat, clean, final, and bloodless. A confrontation now would be pointless.

CHAPTER 61

The house on Point Douglas had two and a half sections already standing. Each section consisted of six eight-foot beams layered on top of each other, butting into an upright beam at one end and joined at the other by a corner beam. The half section consisted of beams laid down to continue the line of the east wall, then left to fit in a window frame before adding the top beam.

The MacBeths and the Point Douglas Sutherlands had taken the day off to tend to their fields, but Kate seemed to be the only one tending to theirs. Her husband was busy with a mallet and foot-long beam sections tongued at one end, battering and cursing the pieces into an approximation of a snug-set window frame.

Which left Kate to do the weeding. At this time of year, there were only two aspects of weeding that caused her any difficulty. The first was differentiating the tiny green shoots of potato plants from the tiny green shoots of weeds; she still wasn't all that familiar with the range of Rupertsland's wild vegetation. The second was

he stooping. Her lower back didn't seem to be quite as limber as
t once had been. It couldn't possibly be age, she was barely thirty-
hree. She decided it came from sleeping on a wood floor for the
ast three nights with nothing but a blanket beneath her. At least
he and her husband had had a roof over their heads. The governor's
order to sleep inside the palisades had condemned most of them to
makeshift awnings at best, but Marie Anne Lajimodierre had invited the Point Douglas Sutherlands into the cabin that the colonial
establishment had given over to her until her husband returned.

The powdery gray skin of the earth smelled of sunlight, the dank
black moistness beneath of fertility and decay. Kate pulled out another dewy green slip and nipped it in half with her thumbnail. It
seemed incredible that there might have ever been a time in her life
when she'd looked at a plant as an inanimate object. She half expected the weedlings to writhe when she pried them out of the
ground or wrap their tiny fronds around her fingers to fight back.

The sound of her husband's voice behind her startled her. She
hadn't noticed that the malleting and cursing had stopped. He said:
"We had best be getting over to the fort."

It took an effort to drag herself out of her reverie and respond to
him. "Why?"

"A lot of people are hurrying in from the downriver farms, and
there's a good deal of bustling about on the palisade. Something is
going on."

With a grimace, she straightened up, dusted her hands off on her
skirt, and headed down the path with him. No doubt it would just
prove to be a waste of daylight.

Fort Douglas was like an anthill at war. People were running
about in all directions and flapping their extremities. The sense of
it—or as near to sense as Kate could get out of anybody—was that
the half-breeds had arrived, a troop of them riding north along the
western edge of the colony. "Good, let them ride by, then," she
said perfunctorily, "and good riddance to them." But in the root
of her belly something twisted in on itself.

Governor Semple stepped out onto the verandah of Colony House
and had Lieutenant Rogers call for attention.

When all was quiet, he stepped forward and gazed upon the
crowd with a benevolent, calm assurance. "There is no need for
panic. Some horsemen are passing to the west of us, but who they
are and what their business might be here is only conjecture at
present. I intend to go out and speak with them, and to read to
them a piece of paper"—he patted his breast pocket—"which will

put an end to any mischief they might have in mind before it begins
I would like to have a few volunteers to march out with me as a
escort—''

He was drowned out by men hollering their willingness an
throwing up their arms. It seemed to Kate to be the sort of mas
hysteria they were always accusing women of. Her husband's ar
went up as well. ''Have you lost your mind?''

''The sooner we get the governor out there face to face to tal
with them, the sooner we will be rid of all the rumors and imag
nary—''

''Well, let the governor go, then! Put your arm down!''

''I put it up, I cannot—''

''You cannot wait to play tin soldier again.''

''That is not it at all. Better I should go than some boy wh
might panic and start something.''

By that time Lieutenant Rogers was passing through the crow
selecting from the abundance of volunteers. ''You. You . . . an
you—Black Watch, wasn't it? Good man.''

''That should be enough,'' the governor declared. ''I only war
an escort, not a war party. Those of you whom Lieutenant Roge
has selected, please come forward, you will be issued with muske
and bayonets. As for the rest who volunteered—I am extremel
gratified by your show of loyalty and spirit, I shall remember
fondly all my life.''

Sandy started sidling toward the front of the crowd, sayin
over his shoulder: ''There, you see, Kate, we are only going t
talk. . . .''

''Then why the muskets?''

But he was already heading purposefully toward the quartermas
ter doling out muskets and bayonets. She shrieked after him: ''S
you have finally found an army that will have you!'' She was prac
tically cross-eyed with fury. For three years she had believed th
he'd come out of the military immune to all that murderous idiocy
but at the first beat of a drum he was out the door like any glory
eyed eighteen-year-old.

Sandy checked over the musket, buckled on his cartridge belt
and fell into line. They marched out behind the governor in a doub
file of thirteen. The gates thumped shut behind them.

They walked north along the cart track winding through th
woods and around the indentations of the river. Sandy was at th
back of the line. Now that he had a chance to look around him
he realized that he and three others were the only actual colonist

the entire twenty-six. The rest were either employees of the Hudson's Bay Company or employees of the colonial establishment . . . by and large a collection of the loudest, brashest, and most abrasive men in the settlement.

A number of families from the outlying farms came straggling past them, making for the fort, many of them in a state of hysteria. One who was not hysterical was old Mister MacBeth. He had hidden himself in the bush to watch the half-breeds pass by before herding his family up to the fort. The governor stopped to pump him for information. "How many of them are there?"

"Twenty or so in the party I saw, sir, but there looked to be another bunch following behind them. Give me a musket, sir, and I will come with you."

"No, no, no need of that—I have all the men I need."

"At least let me tell them at the fort to send up a piece of artillery. You have no idea what a pacifying effect the sight of a field gun can . . ."

Governor Semple smiled his kindly, confident, man-in-charge smile and patted the old duffer on the shoulder. "No need for artillery, Mister MacBeth, although I appreciate your concern. I am only going to read them a piece of paper," and he patted his breast pocket reassuringly. It suddenly struck Sandy that the governor was going out to "read a piece of paper" with a sword at his hip, a double-barreled gun slung over his shoulder, and a brace of pistols in his belt.

As the governor began to amble down the path again, Lieutenant Rogers gave the order for the escort to march on. Mister MacBeth stood aside and shouted as they passed: "Keep your backs to the river! Form up with a broad front and, whatever else you do, do not let them outflank you!" As Sandy passed by, Mister MacBeth's eyes widened with recognition—and fear.

As they marched on, John Pritchard loudly reassured everyone that there was nothing to fear, that one white man was worth five half-breeds in a fight, and the half-breeds knew it. Michael Heden, the colony blacksmith, said he hoped the half-breeds would be stupid enough to start something so he could teach them a lesson. The governor announced confidently that the day was yet to dawn when a disciplined body of white men couldn't face down a ragtag batch of savages. Sandy reminded himself that there were always idiots in every body of men, that they were just trying to reassure themselves, and that the governor was only going to read out a piece of paper.

There was a horrendous squeaking of cartwheels off to their lef
on the other side of the bush. Shadows of horsemen flitted throug
the trees. The governor stopped walking, and Lieutenant Roge
gave the order to halt. The governor called up his quartermaste
Mister Bourke, and told him to return to Fort Douglas, load one
the three-pounders onto a cart, and bring it up on the double; th
column would wait for him. The order was delivered with the sam
calm authority with which he had assured Mister MacBeth th
there was no need for artillery.

Mister Bourke jog-trotted down the cart track. Lieutenant Rog
ers gave the order to stand easy, although most of the Orcadia
laborer contingent already had their backs against nearby tree
They waited there for a minute or two, the governor staring reso
lutely up the path. Then he murmured something to Lieutena
Rogers, who turned back and shouted: "Fix bayonets! Should
arms and fall in!"

Sandy fixed his bayonet and showed the two Hudson's Bay Con
pany boatmen next to him how to fix theirs. By the time they we
formed up, the governor already had a good head start on then
walking north as though he had never told Mister Bourke that the
would wait for him to bring up the cannon. They had to jog alon
at a good clip to catch up with him. And just as they did, there wa
a loud crack of a gunshot.

Some of the men dropped to the ground. Sandy stood in h
place, waiting for an order that never came. The man next to hi
swung about in all directions, looking for the sniper and almo
skewering Sandy with his bayonet.

A chorus of laughter rippled through the column. It seemed th
Lieutenant Rogers' musket had gone off accidentally. The Lieute
ant grumbled on about shoddy gunsmithing, but Sandy had a stro
suspicion that it was simply a question of a gin-pickled excuse f
a soldier carrying his musket with the hammer pulled all the wa
back instead of at half cock. They re-formed ranks and took u
following the governor again.

CHAPTER 62

Grant had gotten his vanguard safely onto Frog Plain, and was dismounting to see what repairs would have to be effected on last year's cabins to make them habitable again, when a horseman came pounding up from Falcon's contingent to inform him that a body of men was marching out from Fort Douglas to cut off the carts. He leaped onto his horse and galloped back across Seven Oaks Creek. On the other side of the woods flanking the creek was an open meadow, a two-hundred-yard-wide gap in the riverfront woods where a tongue of prairie thrust in. The carts and forty horsemen guarding them were trotting across the meadow. There was no sign of anyone pursuing them.

Falcon assured him that there was a force coming up from Fort Douglas, "coming through the woods. One of them took a shot at us."

Grant sent Falcon on to get the carts across the creek. As soon as they were safely ensconced at Frog Plain and a guard mounted over them, he was to bring the rest of his troop back to reinforce Grant. Grant's vanguard-turned-rearguard lined their horses up on either side of him with their backs to the oak trees that had given the creek its name. Grant checked his pistols, loosened his sword in its scabbard, and cocked his rifle. Then there was no sound but the occasional stamp or snuffle of a horse, the jingle of harness, and the exploding boom of the pulse in his eardrums and the roar of his own breathing.

Out of the fabric of natural sounds—the rustle of grass, the creak of tree boughs, the chirping of birds, the burble of the river—came the muffled tramp of marching boots. The governor and his escort walked out of the cool, dappled shade of the forest path into the full blaze of the sun and stopped about a hundred yards in front of the métis line. The double file behind him split apart to fan out in a ragged skirmish line.

Sandy ended up anchoring the right flank, standing in a clump

391

of white-and-yellow sweet clover, still blinking against the sudden glare of the sun. The river was about fifty yards to his right. The tree cover along this stretch of the bank had petered out; there was only a low hump of silt buildup covered with willow bushes and then the river.

Sandy could see that they outnumbered the half-breeds, but not by many. He stood at attention with his musket on his shoulder, waiting for the governor to take out his piece of paper and begin to read. He seemed to be taking a devilish long time about it. Finally Sandy stood the gun butt on the ground and propped his hands on the barrel just under the bayonet flange. He stared at the half-breeds, they stared at him.

Grant sat silently working his jaw, waiting for Semple to do something. There was a splashing and bush crackling behind him, and Falcon's men started to emerge from the trees, falling in on both wings and widening the line. He found Falcon with his eyes and inclined his head slightly in the direction of the colony line. Falcon began to edge his horse forward. Grant stayed where he was.

A bumblebee droned by in front of Sandy's nose. Another bumped into the back of his hand and bounced off. It seemed the air all around him was thrumming. The métis line was growing broader, twice the width now that it had been when they first lined up, swollen by horsemen coming out of the woods along Seven Oaks Creek. And now the flanks began to edge forward, bending into a crescent formation. Sandy moved back and to his right, trying to broaden their own line and incidentally get himself out of bumblebee heaven.

Grant sat watching Semple. The thin-haired gentleman bristling with weapons in the center of the colony line didn't appear to be about to do anything except continue standing with his arms crossed, looking authoritative.

Grant glanced at both flanks of his line of horsemen. Falcon on the left and Seraphim on the right had pinched their wings forward into a horn-shaped formation, outreaching the line of infantry by a good twenty yards on either side. Grant nudged his horse with his heels and began to walk forward. The whole crescent moon began to move with him. His image of the scenario was that once they'd gotten close enough, he would stop the advance and ask Semple what he wanted, Semple would look at the odds, realize they were outflanked, and turn his men around and march back to the fort.

But as soon as Grant began to move, a good number of the

olony men threw their muskets up to their shoulders and took aim.
Grant stopped his horse. The line stopped with him. Alex Fraser
began to swing his rifle up. Grant barked: "Don't!"

Alex stopped with his rifle half-up and said: "I'm not going to
sit here like a duck on the water and let them aim at me."

"Don't worry, Alex, they shoot like you. As long as they're
aiming at you, you're safe." That brought a few tight-throated
chuckles from those nearby.

Alex said, "You should talk," but he lowered his rifle.

Sandy felt the same itch as the others when the half-breed line
began to move forward, but he kept his musket grounded. When
the men on either side of him raised their muskets to take aim, he
had to wrestle down an urge to scream and fling himself down on
the ground. Miraculously, the half-breeds didn't start shooting. He
stood with his weapon at rest, the perfect parody of an idiot soldier.
He had learned the hard way that the difference between disaster
and triumph wasn't ferocity or armaments or strategy, but the simple ability to load and fire and stand and fix bayonets by the numbers as though the bullets buzzing all around were so many flies on
a parade square.

Not that there were going to be any bullets flying, as long as
everyone remained calm. At any moment the governor was going
to take out his piece of paper and start to read.

One of the half-breeds, dressed in paint and feathers and a loincloth, slid off his horse and began to slink forward through the
ground cover. Michael Heden pointed his musket and shouted for
him to back off. The half-naked half-breed dropped flat on the
ground, and then the tall grass in that direction began to move
against the wind. Heden said: "If anybody talks one of those bush-
nigger tongues, tell him to back off or I'll blow his greasy head
off!"

Grant dug into the pocket of his buckskin trousers—Bethsy was
probably the only woman in the *pays d'en haut* who went to the
trouble of sewing pockets into her husband's trousers—and tugged
out the last survivor of the two dozen white lawn handkerchiefs he'd
brought from Montreal. He handed it to Firmin Boucher, who had
a reasonably level head and a working command of English. "Go
and ask them what they want. Tell them if they don't ground their
arms, we will fire upon them."

Firmin tied the handkerchief to the muzzle of his rifle and trotted
forward, waving it over his head. Grant shouted after him: "Don't

lose that!'' Firmin looked back over his shoulder and winked and grinned.

As Governor Semple walked forward to meet the envoy, Sandy sidled back toward the center of the line to listen. The governor and the métis herald met about ten paces in front of the colony line. The half-breed said: ''What do you want?''

The governor appeared to consider that for a moment, then crossed his arms and replied: ''What do *you* want?''

The half-breed blinked a few times and then blurted: ''We want our fort.''

''Well . . .'' The governor flourished his arm back in the direction of the Forks. ''Go to your fort.''

''You son of a bitch, you know damn well there ain't no fort there. You tore it down!''

The governor grabbed the bridle of the half-breed's horse with one hand and the flagpole gun barrel with the other. ''Scoundrel! Do you presume to use that tone with me?''

The half-breed slid off the other side of his saddle, 'eaving the governor in possession of his horse and musket. There was the sound of a gunshot.

Firmin's horse shied, clearing Grant's field of fire. He heard a gun go off. His forefinger automatically tightened on the trigger. The rifle bucked against his hand, almost tearing his finger off. Just before the powder smoke plumed high enough to block his vision, he saw the governor go down.

There were a couple of sporadic gun cracks, then a staccato explosion as the métis and the colony line all fired at once. Sandy's training made him hesitate for an instant, waiting for the order to fire. Then his mind took charge again, and he brought his musket up, took aim at Grant, who was already sliding off his horse, and pulled the trigger. A cloud of pungent, sooty smoke enveloped him. Before it had cleared he was already halfway through reloading drill.

A voice off to his left called: ''Do what you can to save yourselves!'' It was Governor Semple, both hands clamped over a wound on his thigh trying to hold in the spurting blood. Another man was stretched out beside him with three holes on his shirtfront and one side of his mouth shot away. The Orcadian HBC servant who'd been next to Sandy in the line was lying on his side with his forearms pressed against his belly and his legs pedaling wildly. There was a sudden outburst of cheering. The men who were still standing took off their hats and waved them in the air, pointing toward the métis line. Michael Heden and three others who had started running for the river stopped in front of Sandy to look back. Craning his neck to peer between them, Sandy saw what the cheering was about. Every saddle in the métis line had been cleared of its rider. The exultation only lasted for an instant, however, before it registered in his mind that one ragged volley from twenty-five muskets would not take out fifty men.

Grant was flat on his back in the tall grass, ramming home the load in his rifle, when he heard the cheering. He restrained himself from looking, snicked the ramrod out, and stood up behind the shelter of his horse. They were waving their hats in the air and cheering, but he couldn't understand why. He took aim across his horse's backside, blessing the trainer who had taught it to stand still despite the sound of gunfire. There were fewer targets than there had been. As he pulled the trigger there was a crashing volley from either side of him, as the whole troop leaped back to their feet from reloading.

The three men with Michael Heden who had stopped running for the river right in front of Sandy saved his life. Two of them went down, one screaming and holding the remnants of his shattered knee, the other thrown clear off his feet by the force of half a dozen bullets hitting him at the same time. Heden and the other man—George Sutherland, it was—started running again. Sandy threw his musket up to his shoulder and looked for a target. There was nothing visible except the line of horses and a hat or a leg behind them. Lieutenant Rogers was running toward them, waving his hat wildly over his head and shouting what he thought was the right French word: *"Merci! Merci!"* An arrow tore into his throat at the same time a thrown hand axe took him in the chest. Sandy sighted at the middle of the horse directly across from Rogers's body and pulled the trigger. He had the pleasure of seeing it jerk and fall, he hoped on the man behind it, then he threw his musket down and started running for the river.

His leg seized up on him immediately. He dragged it along, swinging it forward with twists of his body and springing hard with his good leg to keep the momentum going. Sucking in great gulps of air, he asked God why the bobbing surface of the water wasn't getting any closer. By this time Michael Heden and George Sutherland had reached the river and were scrambling into an old canoe that was drawn up in the bushes. He screamed at them to wait, but they pushed off, paddling frantically toward the far shore.

Grant threw down his rifle. The men on both sides of him did the same, tugging out sheath knives or hatchets and ducking under their horses' bellies to charge forward at the remnants. Grant got up on his horse and drew his sword. Most of the colony men were down. The handful that were still on their feet were running, some for the river and some for the trees. Old François Deschamps trained his rifle on one who was running slower than the others, then swept the barrel ahead to lead him and pulled the trigger. The bullet took him perfectly between the shoulder blades and lifted him off his feet. The momentum of his running and the impact of the bullet carried him farther, arms arching back and chest leading in a perfect dive into the earth.

Grant kicked his horse and galloped straight across the meadow for the runners trying to make the trees. Between him and the backs of the escaping men was the gentleman colonist, Mister Alex Mac-Lean, shot up but still on his feet, hunched around the butt of his musket, waving the bayonet point in circles in front of him. He lunged at Grant's horse. Grant twitched the reins to his left, swept the bayonet aside with an upward cut of his sword, and sliced the blade down with a backhand as he went past. It hit something and stuck. For an instant it felt as though either the sword would be pulled out of his hand or he would be pulled out of the saddle, but then the point jerked loose.

He was almost up on one of the running men, just about to cut him down before he plunged into the woods, when he saw something moving on the cart track, indistinct in the leaf-filtered green light and the dappling shadows from the arch of trees. There was a booming crack from that direction and a flash of sparks, then he felt the bullet whacking into his horse's chest.

His horse screamed and fell sideways. He got his feet out of the stirrups and flung his sword away as he hit the ground. The pistols in his sash scraped against his belly, bruising his ribs. One of them worked its way loose just as he stopped rolling. He grabbed it and cocked it with the heel of his left hand. Still not quite sure which end was up, he sighted it down the path, saw a movement, and pulled the trigger.

It was a horse and cart, with three men carrying muskets leading the horse. One of them went down with Grant's pistol ball in his leg. One of the others picked him up to throw him onto the cart bed. The other began desperately to get the horse and cart turned around in the narrow pathway.

A dozen horsemen pounded up behind Grant. One of them leaped down to see if he was hurt—Alex Fraser. Grant said: ''I'm fine

Alex. Get them.'' But by that time the cart had been turned around, showing the muzzle of a cannon poking over the tailgate. The man Grant had wounded was propped against it, sparking a pistol over the touchhole.

Alex and the others scattered to either side of the path, but the explosion never came. The cart rattled away down the track.

Grant recovered his saber, looked to see that his horse was dead, then walked back through the dead and the dying. There were low moans from the wounded colonists that hadn't been discovered yet, screams of terror and pain from those who had been, and the thudding of hatchets. A very young man with soft-looking cornsilk hair was lying in a twisted posture in Grant's path. The jagged tip of a rib showed slick white through the red hole in his shirt, but he didn't seem to mind. Grant stepped over him.

''Mister Grant!'' The voice was husky but strong, coming from somewhere off to Grant's left. He turned toward it. It was Semple, propped up on one elbow with his other hand clutching the top of his thigh. His hands and sleeves, one leg of his trousers, and the flattened stems of grass around him were all black with blood. His face was pallid and glossy.

As Grant walked over to him, he spoke again. The voice was much breathier now, as though it had used up all its strength calling his name. ''You are Mister Grant?'' Grant nodded. ''I believe . . .'' A grimaced intake of breath cut him off, but he started again. ''I believe that I might live . . . if you could take me to the fort.''

It was a startling thought, that some of them might live. He would have to stop the butchering and get Falcon to empty one of the pemmican carts to transport them. ''I will see to that,'' he told Semple.

Falcon was sitting on his horse surveying the carnage. Grant waved him forward and started to walk toward him. He hadn't taken two steps when a voice close behind him growled hoarsely in broken French, ''It's you that caused all this,'' and a gunshot exploded by his ear.

CHAPTER 63

The crackle of gunfire and wind-shredded screams carried upriver to Fort Douglas. Kate set little Henri onto the patch of grass in front of Marie Anne's cabin and stood up. Marie Anne came out of the doorway. Most of the men who had remained in the fort, and some of the women and children, ran to the north wall of the stockade, crowding up onto the firing ledge to see through the trees. Kate and Marie Anne stayed where they were. The sentry in the lookout tower shouted down that he could see a haze of smoke rising over the treetops toward Seven Oaks Creek but nothing more. The rest of them stayed silent, shushing anyone who started to speak, straining to listen.

The gunfire died out, and the fort erupted with voices, shrieking questions and bawling back guesses, all to no purpose except to keep from thinking. Kate stood next to Marie Anne, waiting.

Suddenly the man in the sentry tower shouted down: "The gates! Open the gates! It is Mister Bourke, open the gates!"

The cart rattled through, its horse lathered with foam and hock battered by the prow board. The people on the walls poured down and swarmed around the cart. The men who had opened the gate swung them shut again and hurled the bar back into place, rushing to join the crowd.

Kate crossed the courtyard slowly and stood on the fringes. The swirling hubbub of voices shouting questions at Mister Bourke seemed very far away. Finally a few stronger voices bellowed the rest into silence so Mister Bourke could be heard. He was leaned back against the barrel of the cannon on the cart bed, evidently in some pain. A bloody rag was wrapped around his left leg. He said, "If there had been one of them left to save, I would have stayed and fought to the last. The governor, all the gallant men that marched out with him, they are all dead."

It was as though a strong man had swung a long oak cudgel into her stomach. The breath went out of her, and she sank to her knees.

She rocked forward and put her hands to the ground to hold her up. There were tears in her eyes, but no more than the tears of getting the wind knocked out of her. When she tried to call up images of her husband's features, they were invariably glimpsed over his shoulder in the act of turning away, or of being turned away.

The sounds around her began to penetrate through the seashell roaring in her ears. Some men were crying. Some were blustering hysterically about what they were going to do to the half-breeds in retribution. Over it all wailed the keening of the widows.

Catherine Pritchard was on her knees a few yards away from Kate, chanting an Indian song and scooping up dirt, holding her hands out palm-up in front of her and sifting the dust through her fingers. Michael Heden's wife, Elisabeth, came over to her and pushed her over into a sprawl, shrieking at her in Gaelic: "Stop that heathen caterwauling. Do you think it fools any of us? It is your people that did this."

Kate stood up and pushed Mrs. Heden back. "We *are* her people."

Elisabeth Heden floundered three steps backward before recovering her balance. She threw Kate a look of loathing, then glanced back down to Mrs. Pritchard. Her eyes widened, and she backed away. Kate looked down.

Mrs. Pritchard had a knife in her hand. She took up her kneeling and chanting once again, but instead of filtering dust through her hands she began to score the backs of her forearms with the knife, the red blood oozing out against the brown skin. Kate took the knife away from her, then wondered whether she was doing her a kindness or not. It might be easier after all to feel an exterior pain. If only she could find one strong enough to penetrate.

Mister MacBeth stepped in front of her. "Mrs. Sutherland, I know there is nothing anyone can . . . well, I would just like to say that I have been privileged to know a number of good men in my time, and your husband was among the best of them. But I suppose you do not need me to tell you that. I am sorry for your loss."

She nodded politely and moved to step around him. Then she was shrieking and howling and flailing her arms. Mister MacBeth took hold of her and pinned her arms to her sides. The wails settled down to low grunts passing out with each exhaled breath. She stood slack but upright, her chin resting on the top of his squat little gnome's head. Though her eyes still streamed they were wide open, staring straight into the distance.

For all Mister MacBeth's soothing noises and his round paws patting her back, she knew that he misunderstood. She wasn't crying for her husband's death, but for what she had made of his life.

CHAPTER 64

As the gunshot exploded behind him, Grant either threw himself forward onto the ground or was thrown forward by the bullet striking, he wasn't sure. He lay there for a moment taking inventory of his body parts. Incredibly, they all seemed to be whole. From the volume of the report, it had gone off no more than three feet behind him. Nobody could miss at that range.

He turned his head around. There was another head at ground level not six inches from his own, the eyes staring wide and unblinking through a sparse hedge of grass stalks. A gout of thick, fresh blood dangled from one corner of the mouth.

Grant sat up. It was Robert Semple, with a hole torn in his chest that hadn't been there before. Machicabou, one of the Fort des Prairies faction, was walking away blowing spent powder grains from the priming pan of his trade gun.

A horseman stopped beside Grant. The beadwork on the moccasin was Mary's crocus pattern; that made it Falcon. Grant took hold of the stirrup leather and hauled himself to his feet. All around him came the sound of laughter and joyous shouts, punctuated by the moist hacking of hatchets and knives. There was no one left to kill: the soldiers of the New Nation were cutting up the dead. One was making a collection of trigger fingers; another was waving a heart on a bayonet over his head; a third had popped out a corpse's eyes and was replacing them with another dead man's balls.

Impossibly, there was something familiar about the scene, something that resonated of comfort and domesticity. It was the prairie after a buffalo run, with the women and children butchering the carcasses where they lay.

He looked up at Falcon. Falcon's eyes were swollen and black, his lips drawn back from the tips of his teeth. It was impossible to tell whether the riveted expression on his face came from elation or revulsion. His lips were moving ritualistically, chanting something inaudible.

Grant looked out at the carving ground. In a way he could understand it. From the crack of the first gunshot they had hurled all their ferocity and endurance into what they thought would be the battle of their lives, and it had all been over in a moment. He let his body drop sideways, still holding on to Falcon's stirrup strap with one hand, and scooped up his saber. He swung himself back upright, opened his mouth, and let out a great bull-roaring bellow that surprised him with its power: *"Stop!"* They stopped long enough to turn and look at him, glazed eyes over bloody hands. "Even the Sioux leave it to their old women to chop up the dead. Seraphim, you and Deschamps find some shovels and some more hands and bury these men."

Old Deschamps started to say, "I don't dig holes for . . ." Grant turned toward him. Deschamps ducked his head down and raised his hands in the air. They cleaned their knives on the grass and drifted back to their horses. Grant didn't know what he would have done if they hadn't stopped. He did know that he had been dragged by a wild horse through a swamp of blood, and there were still warm bits of tendons writhing between his teeth.

He let the saber hang slack in his hand and leaned against the warm barrel of Falcon's horse. One of his soldiers was coming his way, herding a spare, light-haired white man with his rifle. The white man was shouting in English: "Cuthbert! Mister Grant! You know me! Tell him you know me!" There wasn't a mark on him. The only possible explanation was that he had thrown himself onto the ground and pretended to be dead. "I always did my best to treat you fairly, Mister Grant, you and all your people. Tell him that. Please. You don't want to kill me."

The words didn't really register except as a meaningless babble of fear. It was John Pritchard. Grant said: "Take him to Frog Plain and hold him prisoner." Pritchard started to blubber his thanks. Grant turned away quickly. If Pritchard had thrown himself at his feet, the sword would have pinned him like a frog on a spike.

Falcon still had that curious trancelike look. His lips were moving with no sound coming out, his eyes were still abstracted, but now his head was bobbing up and down rhythmically. It suddenly struck Grant that Falcon was making up a song.

Alex Fraser came across the meadow leading an unfamiliar bay pony with Grant's saddle and harness on it. He said: "Jumps High went down in the shooting. You need a horse, so you might as well take his.''

''Who else went down?''

''No one, except for a couple of other horses that got hit.''

Grant sheathed his sword and climbed onto the saddle, then kicked his horse toward the line of trees marking Seven Oaks Creek. The creek was still near its spring height, the water lapping up to the horse's belly and tickling the soles of his feet through his moccasins. He stopped the horse in midstream and slid off. The water was cold and clean. It swept him off his feet. He grabbed the horse's tail and hung suspended in the current. He breathed in a gulp of water, retched, then heaved his guts out.

He ducked his head under the surface and held it there. He came up gasping, grabbed a handful of mane, and pulled himself back onto the saddle. Jumps High had had a good horse. It stood anchored in the stream until Grant clucked it into motion again.

The sun hadn't touched the horizon yet, but its rays were too weak to burn the water off him. By the time he reached the cluster of cabins on Frog Plain, he was shivering. Someone had thought to build a fire, and he squatted down beside it. Joseph Cadotte came by and draped a blanket over his shoulders.

The soldiers of the New Nation drifted across the creek in twos and threes with their souvenirs, bayonets or bloody shirts or other things Grant didn't want to know about. The fire grew larger. The clumps of men around it kept shifting, as one group would tell each other of their individual exploits in the victory, then split off to find other groups they hadn't traded stories with.

For all their experience in tribal wars, and all their tough talk on the ride from the Qu'Appelle, most of them had been apprehensive at the thought of fighting Europeans. The only white men they had known in their lives—excluding the voyageurs, who were a strange hybrid race of their own—had been their fathers and officers of the fur companies. They couldn't quite believe that it had been so easy.

The only words Grant spoke from the time he sat down by the fire until long after dark were to tell Seraphim to break out the rum. The three kegs packed in among the pemmican were to have been parceled out slowly during the coming blockade, but Grant told Seraphim to break them all open now. Someone brought him a brimming tin cup. He sat sipping it, watching dead men writhe in the flames.

Firmin Boucher crouched down beside him. ''Here, I told you I wouldn't lose it.'' He held out a dark-colored rag—Grant's handkerchief, now less white than green and red-black with grass stains and blood. Grant took it and thanked him. Firmin beamed and bobbed his head and moved away. As soon as he was out of sight Grant threw it into the flames.

It caught on a twig end and hung out of reach of the flames, the hem scorching and curling slowly. Grant wondered if the blood was Semple's. Finally the scrap of linen flared up, flaking away in fragile black wisps. It was Semple who'd come looking for a fight— or if not, it was hard to imagine what he'd thought he was up to. Either way, there was nothing Grant could have done to stop it. Brooding wasn't going to help anyone. He couldn't change it, but there might be a way to use it.

He stood up and threw the blanket off his shoulders. "Where's Pritchard?" he asked Seraphim.

"With the other prisoners."

"What others?"

"The three *jardinières* we saw in the field when we were riding from Catfish Creek."

He'd forgotten about them. He said, "Fetch Pritchard," then called Alex Fraser over to stand beside him.

The hours that had passed since the shooting stopped certainly hadn't done anything to calm Pritchard's fear. Even in the firelight his face was still chalky white. Good, thought Grant. That would make things easier. The noise around the fire quieted a little as a few of the celebrants stopped to eavesdrop.

"Good evening, Mister Pritchard. I am going to send you and the other prisoners back to the fort."

"Thank you, thank you. I won't forget this."

"Don't thank me yet. It is going to be up to you to see whether what happened this afternoon is the end of the bloodshed or only the beginning. If the fort is surrendered up to me by noon tomorrow, I will see to it that everyone in it is transported safely out of the country. If we have to take the place by storm, we will butcher every man, woman, and child."

"You wouldn't—"

"You saw how much mercy we showed this afternoon."

Alex Fraser gave Pritchard his best snaky smile and said: "Robertson said our skins are black. We can show you our hearts are even blacker."

It was a bit self-conscious for Grant's tastes, but Pritchard appeared to be affected. Grant actually had no intention of storming the fort. If they didn't surrender, he would wait for Whitehead to establish the upstream end of the blockade and carry on with the plan of starving them out. But if he took advantage of the terror Semple had provided him with, it just might be possible to put a quick end to the whole business.

When Pritchard and the other prisoners were gone, Grant returned his attention to the celebration. The stories had petered out; by now they all knew each other's anecdotes by heart. They started singing old voyageur songs. After the third or fourth, someone called for a song from Falcon. He stood up by the fire with a shy, sly smile and began a melody they'd never heard before.

It was in the style of a canoe song, with a call-and-response couplet in double waltz time to start the verse. They fell into that quickly enough, bellowing out the repeat line without thinking about what they were singing. Then, when they began to catch on, there were howls of delight and applause and shouts of encouragement.

All the relevant details of the day were there in eleven verses: the New Nation's attempts to avoid bloodshed, the governor's Napoleonic delusions, the first volley from the invading *jardinières* that almost killed the métis envoy. When the whoops and applause at the end had died down, they made him sing "La Grenouillière," as he called it—French for Frog Plain—again and then again, until they all knew it as well as he did.

The moon rose and set, the kegs were emptied and the effects of the rum wore off, but they still stayed gloriously drunk. There were only a couple of hours of darkness left when, one by one, the victors of La Grenouillière crawled away from the fire, rolled themselves in their blankets, and fell asleep.

Grant looked across the dying embers at Falcon. Falcon raised his empty cup in salute and said: "The names of La Grenouillière and Cuthbert Grant are twined together forever."

It was impossible to tell whether it was a toast or a curse.

CHAPTER 65

It was late at night, but the children still hadn't been undressed and put to bed. Little Henri was asleep at the foot of Marie Anne's bed. La Reine and La Prairie were bustling around helping their mother pack clothing and household things into bundles.

Kate was sitting on a pile of blankets in a corner, with her forearms on her knees and a cup of tea that had gone cold in her hand. It had been more than two years since she had last lain down to sleep without Alexander Sutherland beside her. She shifted her attention from the empty bedding to Marie Anne. "What are you doing? Can I help?"

Marie Anne dropped the pot she had just taken down from its hook above the hearth. It clanged hollowly and bounced on the floor. She turned around quickly and fluttered her hands. "Me? I am only . . . I thought to, if we need to go from here, to be ready—if we need to. Sit you. No need to help." She seemed strangely evasive. Her eyes refused to focus on Kate directly. But then no one's eyes had focused on her directly since midafternoon, except those of the other widows.

The door jarred open and Catherine Pritchard thrust her head in. "Mrs. Sutherland! You come quick. Your man—they shout at the doors of the fort—prisoners from the *bois brulés*. My John and your man, too." She gestured frantically at Kate to follow and then was gone, leaving the door open.

Kate's body wanted to get up and run after her, but she made it stay where it was, afraid that she had misinterpreted Catherine Pritchard's words to mean what she wanted them to mean. She looked to Marie Anne for a clue, but Marie Anne was still standing with her hands twined together, chewing on her lower lip.

She ran back over what Mrs. Pritchard had said. There was no other way to interpret it. Suddenly she jerked her body forward and stood up, forgetting about the tea cup. It fell out of her hand, spilled

406 Alfred Silver

down across her skirt, and clattered onto the floor. As she stood looking down at the mess, Marie Anne waved her toward the door. "Go! Go you—I will do it." Kate started running.

On the far side of the dark courtyard was a small fire for the gateman to warm himself by—as sultry as June days might be, the nights were still cold. There were others besides Kate running toward it. On the far side of the fire the Pritchards stood wrapped together, shadowing two men behind them who were having their hands pumped and shoulders slapped by the sentries.

As soon as Kate had gone through the doorway, Marie Anne snatched up a blanket-wrapped bundle in one arm and the sleeping Henri in the other. She hissed at La Reine and La Prairie to take the other bundle between them and follow her without making a sound. She slipped out the door and around to the side of the cabin.

A Saulteaux from Chief Peguis's band had come to her in the afternoon while the fort was still in the throes of panic from the news of the massacre. Peguis had learned that the métis were soon going to descend on the fort, set it on fire, and kill everyone who wasn't burned alive. The Chief didn't have enough warriors to stop them, or preferred not to try, but he could save the family of his old friend Lajimodierre. If they could get down to the riverbank that night, there would be a canoe and paddlers waiting for them.

In the north wall of the palisade behind the governor's big house, there was a postern gate no larger than a shed door. There was no need to mount a sentry over it since it was securely barred from the inside. Marie Anne put down her bundle and reached for the bar. Henri started to cry, only soft gurgles and whines to start with, but she could feel him working up to an outraged wail. Cooing and rocking had no effect. She ripped open the fastenings of her blouse and crammed a nipple in his mouth. He had been fed barely an hour ago, but he settled down to suckling in his sleep.

She tried to raise the bar one-handed, but it was too heavy or too tightly lodged in the brackets. She whispered at La Reine and La Prairie to put down their bundle and help her. With the three of them straining against it, it popped out, one end clunking against the fort wall as it fell and the other thumping down on La Prairie's toe. He yelped and accused La Reine of doing it deliberately, and she launched into counteraccusations. Marie Anne shushed them both and then stood breathing shallowly, straining her ears to listen for any sign of an alarm.

She asked herself what she was afraid of. Most of the people in

Fort Douglas were friends of hers, or at least friendly acquain-ances, and Jean Baptiste's suicidal venture had planted them all squarely on the same side. But they might be less friendly if they found her sneaking away and leaving them to their fate. She shooed away the onrush of guilt by telling herself that there was nothing that she could do to save anyone else and that her first duty was to save her children.

She led them through the gate. Outside, there was nothing but shadows, except off to her right where the moon glimmered on the surface of the river. She hurried off in that direction, leaving the eastern gate hanging open.

The night was full of sounds, crickets and nightbirds and, carried by the wind, a distant ghost of the hellish choir celebrating its victory downriver. Her breath panted in and out in time with the beating of her heart. A deep, guttural voice suddenly growled out of the shadows. She froze. It came again. *"Kiche Omachew Kisk-wao!"*—"Great Hunter's Woman."

A sloping mountain of shadow detached itself from the general gloom. The moonlight showed her the beautiful, mutilated slab of Chief Peguis's features. Two of his men scooped up La Prairie and La Reine and the bundle they carried between them. Peguis wrapped his hand around her arm and battered his way through the thicket of willows clothing the riverbank along the shoulder of Point Doug-las. There were two other Saulteaux waiting there, steadying a ca-noe in the water.

La Reine and La Prairie were loaded in. Peguis splashed Marie Anne into the water, wading toward the prow. She couldn't seem to get any air into her lungs, no matter how hard she sucked. The black shadows patching the slick surface of the river began to blur. Her head lolled, and she crumpled sideways into the muddy wa-ter. Even as the river closed over her, two big arms were under her, lifting her up into the canoe.

Chief Peguis climbed in after her, and they shot off for the east bank. There was a large, dark object moving across the surface of the river—a canoe crossing over from the opposite shore. The shapes of the three men paddling it suddenly disappeared as they ducked below the gunwales, letting the momentum carry them past the Saulteaux canoe. Marie Anne wondered if they might be métis taking up their positions for the assault on the fort. She crossed herself and said a prayer that it might not be so.

* * *

Kate was almost to the gatekeeper's fire when another woman came running from the opposite side of the courtyard and cut in front of her, shouting: "Sandy! Sandy!" It was Mary Sutherland, wife of the other Alexander. One of the two men shadowed by the Pritchards broke away and ran to meet her. They collided and flung their arms around each other.

By now Kate could see that the other man behind the Pritchards was Robert Bannerman, standing with his wife. She stopped running and stood in the shadows, watching.

Catherine Pritchard left her husband's side and came over to her. "I am so awful sorry, Mrs. Sutherland. I heard his name called from the gate, and I oughta have thought . . ."

Kate nodded and turned to go back to Marie Anne's cabin. The sentry over the gates suddenly shouted to open them again, that there was another group of survivors outside.

She moved forward as the great beam was lifted down again. The left gate was pushed open and Michael Heden came through, followed by George Sutherland and John Matheson. Then the gate was swung shut and the bar lifted back into place.

She listened to see if they had anything to say about her husband. It seemed that Heden and George Sutherland had got away from the battlefield in an old canoe that had been left on the bank, paddling across to the opposite shore. John Matheson had swum across. They'd stayed hidden in the bush until dark, then carried the canoe south until they could cross over to the fort.

John Matheson squinted across the firelight into the gloom. "Katy? Katy MacPherson?" She started to turn away. He came around the fire and caught her arm. "Did Sandy make it back?"

She shook her head, not trusting herself to speak, and tried to pull away. He held on and said: "He made it into the river with me, but he could not swim strong enough to get across. Because of his leg, I suppose—I believe he was not wounded at all. The current carried him downstream. He might still be alive, washed ashore farther down."

She didn't know what she was supposed to do with that, whether it was information that she should be grateful for. She'd been hurled back and forth too many times in the past few hours, her responses were all worn out. She murmured something polite and walked back quickly to the safety of Marie Anne's cabin.

There was no one there. She wondered whether Marie Anne might have moved into one of the rooms in the laborers' barracks to leave her to herself but didn't trouble much with worrying over

an explanation. Things simply happened. She sat down in her corner with her knees up and the heels of her hands pressed to her
temples.

When the dawn light started poking through the seams in the
shutters, she struggled to her feet, working the circulation back into
her legs. Whether she had slept at all she couldn't say, nor whether
she was awake now. There were no edges to anything.

She went out into the dewy morning. It looked as though no one
had done much sleeping. A group of people were arguing in English near the front gates—John Pritchard and Michael Heden and
a few others. As she passed by them, she heard Mister Heden say:
"We have enough food for two weeks. They'll never stick it out
that long. They don't have any backbone. If they hadn't jumped on
us without warning yesterday, we would have . . ."

By that time she was at the gates, focusing her attention on the
bar and the big iron brackets that cradled it in place. It was a rough-
adzed oak beam eight inches square and twelve feet long. She didn't
have a prayer of lifting it out by herself.

Mister Pritchard excused himself from the arguing committee
and came over to her. "Is there something I might help you with,
Mrs. Sutherland?"

"Yes, thank you, Mister Pritchard. If you would be so good as
to take hold of that end of the beam and I will take this one . . ."

"What for?"

"What for? So I can open the gate and get out."

"You can't go out there."

"I have to look for my husband. I have been waiting all night
for the sun to come up so I could—"

"Oh, Mrs. Sutherland, Mrs. Sutherland . . ." He shook his
head and took his lower lip between his teeth as though to keep
from weeping. "You don't understand, you mustn't go out there."

"You don't understand. My husband is—"

He took hold of her elbow with one hand and started walking her
way from the gates. "Now, now, Mrs. Sutherland, you come along
with me. Mrs. Pritchard will have a pot of tea on the hearth . . ."

She looked over her shoulder at the receding gates. Suddenly it
occurred to her that they were hinged to swing outward. She jerked
out of Mister Pritchard's grasp and ran back. He followed her at a
steady, methodical walk, calling after her in a soothing tone, "Come
along now, Mrs. Sutherland . . ."

She squatted on her heels and got the palms of her hands under
the left end of the beam. Then she straightened her legs, holding

her back stiff. The bar edged upward. Mister Pritchard started running toward her, finally realizing what she had realized—that since the gates swung outward she didn't have to lift the bar all the way out of both brackets. By that time she had raised it far enough to clear the top of the left bracket. She bumped the gate with her shoulder, and it swung ajar. She let the beam drop, skipped over it, and slipped through the opening. Once out in the open, she hiked up her skirt in both hands and ran for the woods on Point Douglas.

One thing about the stilt legs God had cursed her with, she had always been able to outrun all the girls she'd grown up with, and half the boys. With the wind whistling past her ears and the green grass flying by, she felt fourteen again. For a moment there was no yesterday and no death, only Katy MacPherson's long legs carrying her through the blur of the world. She could hear the struggle in Mister Pritchard's voice between his fear and his sense of responsibility: "Mrs. Sutherland! Please, you mustn't! Mrs. Sutherland!" Then she was into the trees. She ran a few steps farther, dodging around poplar trunks and hazel wands, then slowed to a halt and sank to her knees. Her legs might still be fourteen, but her lungs had put on a couple of decades while they weren't looking.

CHAPTER 66

The smell of hot tea and the feel of the sun warming his eyelids coaxed Grant into wakefulness. Whoever had draped the blanket over him while he slept hadn't done him any favors; it had wrapped itself twice around his leg and once around his throat, and he came close to strangling himself before he got it untangled.

Someone had had the presence of mind to build a fire on last night's embers. A bowed green sapling hung over it, bent double by the weight of a bubbling pot suspended from the end. The other sleeping bodies that had ringed the fire had disappeared, except for a cross-legged Indian with a face like a slab of meat left in the sun too long and two holes where his nose should be. Chief Peguis did

ot look particularly amused at waiting for some young pup to
inish his beauty sleep.

Grant sat up slowly. He hadn't had more than one cupful of rum
he night before, but it felt as though every cell in his body had
een peeled off and squeezed dry, then glued back together. Ele-
ating his head expanded his range of vision. Slightly behind Peguis
nd off to one side sat Louis Nolin, one of the free hunters from
cross the river. A few other Saulteaux stood farther back, confer-
ing in low voices with Firmin Boucher and Alex Fraser. The rest
f his troop were putting up tents and refurbishing the roofs of last
ear's cabins.

The tin cup he'd been drinking from last night was lying beside
im. He shook the dew out of it and dipped it in the pot, then
ooked around to see if there was one to offer the Chief. The Chief
hook his head and waved his pipestem bearer forward. Grant fum-
led in his pockets for his tobacco pouch and handed it across the
ire. The pipestem bearer went through the entire formal ceremony,
y which time Grant had taken in enough tea to come awake.

Once the pipe had been around once, Chief Peguis spread his
ands out oratorically and said: "The outcome of the battle you
ought yesterday, Wappeston, may make your footsteps light and
he morning air taste sweet to you, but you must not forget that
here are many others who this day sits heavy on because of that
ame battle."

"I believe that's the usual way of things with battles." Rude or
ot, he wanted the Chief to come to the point. What with just
vaking from a long sleep and the sudden ingestion of warm liquid,
here was a very unpleasant pressure building on the left side of his
bdomen.

"The widows and brothers of the dead whites are afraid that you
vill kill them, too, if they venture out of their fort. Yet it weighs
eavy on their hearts to think of their dead warriors lying naked to
he sun and the ravens."

"They aren't. I had them buried yesterday."

"It wasn't done well. The wolves or the dogs dug them up again
n the night."

"I see. Uhm—if you would be good enough to excuse me for a
noment, Chief, I'm afraid there is a bit of urgent business I must
ttend to. Only a moment"—he rose gingerly to his feet—"and
hen we can continue this conversation at our leisure."

"The bladders of young men are not what they were in my day."

"What is, Chief, what is?"

He headed into the woods along the riverbank, waving Firmin
Boucher to follow him. As he watered down the lee side of a cot-
tonwood, he asked Boucher if there had been any word from Pritchard in the fort. There hadn't been. The sun still had a long way
to climb before the ultimatum he'd given Pritchard last night expired, but he had thought Pritchard was too scared to wait it out
that long.

He stuck his head in the river, shook off the excess, and went
back to Peguis and Louis Nolin. He said: "I will send a cart with
you over to where their dead are lying, and a few men to help you.
Load as many of the bodies onto the cart as you wish, and take
them back to their friends and families for a proper burial."

"It is good to see that Wappeston is as generous as he is strong.
That is a rare thing in the young."

Grant inspected the Chief's features for any trace of irony; there
was none. As far as he was concerned, he wasn't being generous
at all. If Pritchard and the others in the fort were having trouble
making up their minds about whether to leave or to try and hold
out, the sight of a few hacked and mutilated corpses might help
them come to a decision.

The delicious smell of roasting prairie chicken wafted on the
breeze. Grant sent Boucher off with the Chief and Nolin, then followed his nose around to the other side of the cabins, where Falcon
and Deschamps were supervising a cooking fire and a network of
improvised spits.

They had only done a cursory job of the plucking, and he burned
his fingers on the crackling skin, but it was a delightful change from
the pemmican they'd been living on since leaving Esperance. He
stood by the fire cutting off pieces with his knife and juggling them
from hand to hand until they cooled enough to pop into his mouth.
His hands and lips were soon slippery with grease. As he chewed
he gazed off to the west, across the silvery green undulations of
grass rolling on to the foundation of the sky. It was said that the
buffalo herds had grazed here in the days before the whites started
burning off the grass and building farms. They would come again.

Just below the soft bellies of the clouds, a hawk skimmed languidly through its hunting circles. He thought how pleasant it would
be to sit with James on his knee and point out the hawk, tell him
what kind it was and whether it would dive to kill like a falcon or
swoop along the surface of the ground cover like an owl. He would
have to start learning before James got old enough to ask the questions. Soon the Hudson's Bay Company would be cured of its de-

usion that it could have the *pays d'en haut* all to itself, and everyone could go back to living their lives.

The men squatted around the cooking fire began to stand up and turn toward the river. Grant came out of his reverie and turned around to see what they were looking at. Joseph Cadotte was herding a white woman up from the riverbank. She was tall and angular, with red-gold hair disheveling out of its plaits. There was something unnatural about the listless, careless way she placed her steps, like a sleepwalker or someone plodding on miles after the body's resources have been exhausted.

The requisite remarks and commentary began to well up from the men around the fire. Grant was going to shush them, then let it go. Even if she'd managed to pick up a few bits of French and Bungee, it wasn't likely to be those bits. He planted himself in front of her and said in Gaelic: "Mrs. Sutherland." She didn't reply. "Is there some way I might be of assistance to you?"

"You could tell your followers to let me alone. I have to go along the riverbank to look for my husband."

"Your husband? Did he get trapped outside the fort yesterday?"

"He marched out of the fort yesterday."

Grant brought his right hand up to shield his eyes and closed them, grinding his eyelashes into the sockets with his thumb and forefinger. He reminded himself that he was not responsible for the Highland Clearances or the Earl of Selkirk's schemes, or for the fact that the Sutherlands hadn't taken the opportunity to leave last year, then opened his eyes again. "I am truly sorry, Mrs. Sutherland. Some of the bodies are being disinterred at this very moment, but believe me, it would be best to leave him where he lies."

"He was not killed in the fighting, I know it."

He tried to adopt a soothing tone. "Mrs. Sutherland . . ."

"I am not some hope-silly woman! One of the men who was here said he saw my husband get safely into the river, but the current swept him downstream."

"I see. The river could have carried him for many miles, though, before he fetched up on shore. He might well have drowned."

"Do you think I have not thought of that? I did not come here to ask for your sympathy or your advice—were it my choice, I would not have come here at all. I merely want to go along the riverbank to see whether my husband is dead or washed up on the bank somewhere hurt and helpless and alone."

"I will send a squad of men with you to help you look."

"No—if you were my husband huddled away in the bush some-

where and you heard a squad of horsemen hunting for you, would
you call out to help them find you?''

"Point taken. Well, I will at least send one man along to escort
you." She opened her mouth to object, but he threw up his hand
and cut her off: "Mrs. Sutherland, several dozen of the men who
rode here with me yesterday are rambling about fishing or hunting
or looking for something else to amuse themselves with. Do you
wish to be dragged back here again by every one of them you
stumble across?'' He didn't think it necessary to spell out the other
obvious possibilities.

He called Falcon away from the cooking fire and explained the
situation to him in French, switching back to Gaelic to say to Kate:
"This is my brother-in-law, Mister Falcon. He will see that you are
left alone. I would go with you myself, of course, except that there
are so many other calls upon my time just at present. I pray that
you find Mister Sutherland alive and unharmed.''

Her eyes snatched hold of his like grappling claws; they held fast
but couldn't seem to penetrate. In a subdued, confused voice, she
said: "How can you be so cruel one day and so kind the next?''

"Perhaps it is not me that changes, Mrs. Sutherland, but the
days.''

Late in the morning Grant was down on the riverbank by the
mouth of Seven Oaks Creek with Seraphim and Alex Fraser, scouting out positions for mounting a blockade in case Fort Douglas
didn't surrender. Seraphim said: "But you said if they didn't surrender we'd storm the fort.''

"So I did. Do you know what grapeshot is?''

"No . . . something for a cannon?''

"Did you ever hear of an occasion when the Blackfoot stormed
a trading fort in their country?''

"I don't think so . . . sometimes they pick off a trading party
but I never heard of them storming a fort.''

"They know what grapeshot is.''

Boucher called from the other side of the trees on top of the
bank: "Monsieur Grant?''

"Down here!''

"It's Pritchard, he just walked over from the fort.''

Mister Pritchard was standing by the cooking fire with his arms
crossed. Grant came up behind him and said: "Well?''

Pritchard appeared to have been expecting more of a preamble.
When it became obvious that Grant wasn't going to give him one

he made a stab at providing his own: "The people in the fort wish to avoid further bloodshed . . ."

"That is very wise of them."

"But . . . they're afraid of what might happen to them once they're in your hands."

"They are in my hands now."

"Yes, of course, but . . . you understand what I mean, Cuth— Mister Grant. They're afraid of what might happen once we've given up all our defenses."

"I told you what will happen. You will all be allowed to leave peaceably. If there aren't enough boats at your fort to accommodate you all, I'm certain that Peguis will be more than happy to sell you a few canoes. I would say that your most logical destination would be Jack River House—the gentlemen of the Hudson's Bay Company should feel at least a minimal responsibility. From there I don't care where any of you go—so long as you don't make the mistake of coming back here. If you do, you will find a very different reception than you did last year."

"What about our property?"

"Property?"

"Our personal possessions."

"Ah. You will all be free to take whatever's yours, of course. But any articles that are the property of the Governor and Company of Adventurers Trading into Hudson's Bay, or of the Selkirk colony, will be held here pending certain damage suits that are still before the courts." Pritchard tried to interject. "*That* is the way things are. Any personal possessions that can't be fitted into the boats will be inventoried and accounted for at a later date."

Pritchard scuffed at the ground with the toe of his boot and said: "And what of . . ." His voice dropped down to a mumble.

"What of the what?"

"The women."

"Which women?"

"In the fort, the . . . wives and daughters of the colonists and so on. Once they have no protection, you understand . . ."

Grant didn't at all, until it suddenly hit him that what Pritchard meant was "the white women." He started to laugh, out of disbelief if nothing else. He said: "What is it that puts the idea into white men's heads that white women have something so unique between their legs that the men of every other race can't stop slavering after it?"

Seraphim said: "Don't worry, we won't rape your women."

Alex Fraser said: "Except Heden's wife." Seraphim laughed which didn't help matters.

Grant said: "You have my word that if you surrender up the fort no harm will come to any of you."

"But how can we be sure?"

"I said you have my word!" Pritchard actually cringed and backed away. "If it will make you and your women feel safer, I will sleep in front of the fort gates and be your watchdog. I don't believe that there are any further details to negotiate. I will write up the articles of surrender and deliver them to the fort for you to sign."

Pritchard groped momentarily for something to say, then turned and walked toward Seven Oaks Creek and the path back to the fort, his head down and his shoulders hunched. There was no rum left in the camp, but by midafternoon most of the contents of the governor's cellar had managed to find its way to Frog Plain. The celebration would have been tumultuous regardless. The entire summer's campaign had been accomplished in twenty-four hours without Whitehead MacDonell's brigade, without the English River contingent, without the North West Company's reinforcements from Fort William—by the boys of the west alone, and the miraculous Mister Grant.

CHAPTER 67

Kate tripped on a protruding tree root and fell, skinning her hand on a rock, then discovered that she couldn't get up again. Her arms and legs had no strength in them. While she'd been scrambling over deadfalls and shore rocks, wading through shallows in places where the thickets pushed out into the water, the shadows of the trees had revolved to the north and were now lengthening eastward onto the river. She hadn't put anything into her stomach but a few scooped-up palmfuls of river in more than twenty-four hours.

She decided to rest where she was for a moment before going

n. She was lying in a low basin on the bank, thick with the smells
f sun-warmed silt and dank crawfish pools. There was a crackling
n the bush behind her. Mister Fall-Coe, the gentleman Mister Grant
ad sent to accompany her, broke through the tangle of willow
ushes and thistle. He had kept up with her all along, walking the
orses on the inland side of the riverbank jungle, paralleling her
rogress along the bank, or helping her onto the saddle of the pony
e'd borrowed for her and leading it over the rare stretches where
he bank was clear.

He crouched down a few feet away from her, looked at her and
hen out across the river, puffing up his upper lip contemplatively.
Ie let the air out with a soft pop and said in English: "If the current
ad wash him up any farther north from here"—he shook his head—
'he would have be in the water many hours."

"The other bank! We can cross over and go back along the other
ank."

"You said yourself he couldn't get across. Even if he did, he
vould have hear you calling."

She worked her way up onto her knees and paused there before
ackling the next stage in the ascent. "But if he was too weak to
hout across to me . . ."

The hound-dog eyes settled on her sadly. "What good do it do
or him if you kill yourself, too?" He offered her his hands and
elped her to her feet. He put his arm around her waist and sup-
orted her up the steep slope of the bank to the horses waiting in
he trees. She managed to raise her foot into the stirrup, but the
nud-slick sole slipped out again. She had some difficulty bending
er leg up that high a second time. Mister Fall-Coe bent down and
ifted her foot into the stirrup, then put his hands on her hips and
oosted her onto the saddle. He climbed onto his horse, took hold
f her horse's reins, and started back.

She sat slumped forward with her hands propped on the horse's
houlders, the gentle side-to-side rocking of its walking motion
ulling her to unconsciousness. All the hours of wrestling her way
long the riverbank had settled nothing. She still had no idea
vhether he was alive or dead. In her weariness, she accused herself
f wishing she'd found his corpse, just to bring an end to the agony.

Even when they came out of the soft green light of the woods
nto the full hammer of the sun on Frog Plain, it barely registered
n her. The bustle and shouting as they rode past the métis en-
ampment were buffered, unreal. When the horses dipped down
he bank of Seven Oaks Creek, she came back to herself enough to

tell Mister Fall-Coe that he could leave her now, she could wal[k]
from here. He said: "No, I take you to the edge of the plantatio[n]
of your fort. To ride back won't take me long."

The meadow on the other side of the creek still bore traces o[f]
the day before. Patches of grass and clover lay flat, the stalks ben[t]
or broken. Clusters of flies buzzed over rich black deposits of drie[d]
blood. A long mound of freshly turned earth bisected a stand o[f]
wild roses. Mister Fall-Coe urged the horses into a trot until the[y]
were back in the cool air of the woods on the other side of th[e]
meadow. They had gone about halfway along the cart track to For[t]
Douglas when he suddenly vanished off his horse.

Kate blinked at the empty saddle a couple of times, then looke[d]
down at the ground. A muddy scarecrow of a man was sitting o[n]
Mister Fall-Coe's chest, holding a fist-sized rock in one grimy claw[.]
He was struggling to jerk his wrist out of Mister Fall-Coe's grip s[o]
he could get a clear swing at his head and at the same time wa[s]
gasping words at her over his shoulder: "Run! Get away! I wil[l]
follow after!"

She slid awkwardly off the horse and grabbed hold of the han[d]
holding the rock, pulling backward as Mister Fall-Coe pushed[.]
"No! Leave him be. He was helping me. We were looking fo[r]
you."

He fell over onto his back, his chest heaving. He was shivering[.]
His eyes were red and sunken, shifting blankly back and fort[h]
between her and Mister Fall-Coe. His voice came out a croak[:]
"Looking for me?"

"John Matheson said you had been carried down the river. [I]
went to look for you. Mister Grant sent Mister Fall-Coe to help.['']

"Grant?"

She raised up his shoulders and propped them against her lap[.]
He had no more strength to him than a bundle of sticks and string[.]
His clothing was damp and clammy; the cold seeped in throug[h]
her skirt. She kissed the top of his head and pressed the palms o[f]
her hands against his cheeks and swore to herself that she woul[d]
never speak a cross word to him again.

She held him for a long time, crooning bits of Gaelic lullabies[.]
His breathing began to slow. His shivering abated somewhat. Mis[-]
ter Fall-Coe and the horses had slipped away. Alexander said: "Yo[u]
are safe, then? Did they not attack the fort?"

"No, they did not. How did you come to be here? If the rive[r]
carried you downstream from where the fight was . . ."

" 'Fight'? It was no more a fight than . . ." He couldn't seem[

to find a fit comparison. "But the river did carry me downstream from there. By the time I could thrash my way back to the shore, I was north of their camp. I waited for them to finish their celebrations and go to sleep, then I waded along the shore. I lay down under a thicket, and I suppose I slept. I heard horses and looked out onto the path here, and there you were with that . . ." He let his breath out in a long hiss and slumped against her.

After a moment he rolled his shoulders around so he could look up at her. He took hold of her hand and put it inside his shirt over his chest. He said: "Can you feel that?"

"Feel what?"

He gave her a quirky sprout of a smile. "That curious thumping."

"Of course I can, it is—"

He put his hand to her mouth to silence her, then reverently traced one fingertip along the border of her upper lip. "I have my heart back again."

CHAPTER 68

For all of one day and half the next, Grant sat at a table set up beside the gates of Fort Douglas and made a list of every item in the colony that the deportees wouldn't be able to carry with them, from cannonballs to teacups. Next to each entry was listed the name of the individual owner or "Property of the Honourable HBC." The lists were written out on the backs of printed sheets of Bible school lessons that John Pritchard had brought with him from Montreal, for the edification of future generations of colonists that would never be. Pritchard sat at the table beside him, copying out a duplicate for Lord Selkirk and the Hudson's Bay Company. As each sheet was completed, Grant inscribed across the bottom in his discreetly businesslike hand, "Received by Cuthbert Grant, Esquire, Clerk, The North West Fur Trading Company."

The number of articles inventoried was edging up toward seven thousand when Bostonais rode in, crusted with dust from the ride from Portage la Prairie. He walked his horse over to the table and sat there looking down at the piles of papers. Grant set his pen aside and leaned back in his chair. Bostonais said: "Is that how you killed two dozen of them, then—you added them to death?"

"Didn't you know the pen is mightier than the sword?"

"Wouldn't surprise me. Swords ain't much good for close in."

"And besides, it was only twenty-two."

Pritchard said: "Twenty-three." Grant shrugged. Given the state of confusion in the colony, probably no one would ever know for certain.

An aggrieved note crept into Bostonais's voice. "I thought you weren't going to fight them?"

"I didn't plan to. Would I have left you behind if I thought there was going to be a fight? Where else would I find such a tempting target to draw the enemies' fire and at that same time such a reliable obstruction for me to hide behind?"

Bostonais let out a slightly mollified grunt, then said: "Can't you offer a man a drink?"

"I can't, actually. We polished off the governor's stock last night. I'd've thought Whitehead would have had the decency to send over a couple of barrels when he got news of what we've accomplished here."

"Couldn't fit them on my horse. The brigade set out this morning. Should be here late tomorrow. Dry night tonight, I guess."

"Not at all. The tail ends of a season's worth of trading liquor are sitting in the Hudson's Bay store. Once I get the inventorying done, we can roll them over to Frog Plain and bash their heads in."

Pritchard said: "That liquor is the property of the Hudson's Bay Company!"

"I am well aware of that, Mister Pritchard. If you'll but look on the appropriate sheet, you'll see that it says 'Two kegs High Wine and One of Brandy, Property of the Honourable HBC'—and there at the bottom, you see, 'Cuth-Bert-Grant-Es-Quire'? That is my signature. You really must pay more attention, Mister Pritchard."

"That does not give you the right to—"

"Your employers, or landlords, or whatever you choose to call them, can take it up with my employers."

Bostonais's eyes had shifted over to Pritchard, two small black gleams deep within the shadow of his hat brim. Nervously Mister Pritchard went back to shuffling papers, and after a moment Bostonais returned his attention to Grant and said: "Whitehead said to keep them all in the fort till he gets here."

Pritchard jumped in frantically: "You said we could leave as soon as this is done. You gave your word. We're set to leave tomorrow morning."

Grant said: "Whitehead will be here tomorrow evening. One day more or less . . ."

"If Whitehead MacDonell gets here first, not one of us will leave this place alive."

"Really, Mister Pritchard, I realize you've had good reason to grow a trifle overwrought over the last few days, but—"

"Maybe the plan at the beginning was only to chase us out, but after Seven Oaks—Whitehead can finish off the colony and say it was the Indians, or it was you, and the North West Company didn't have anything to do with it. Do you think William MacGillivray wouldn't give him his partnership after that?" Grant sighed and turned away. It was ridiculous to argue with someone in a state of mind like that. Pritchard grabbed his shoulder. "What means more to you—your word or your orders from the North West Company?"

Grant looked down at the hand on his shoulder. It fell away. Pritchard switched to a calmer tone, pasting a confidential smile across his face. "Don't you see what Whitehead's planning to do, Mister Grant? If we're still here when he arrives, he can represent it as though we surrendered to him and not to you. He means to take all the glory from what you've done over the last few days for himself."

Whether that insulting attempt at manipulation was more indicative of Pritchard's low opinion of Grant or his high opinion of himself, it was still difficult not to pick him up by the throat and shake him like a terrier shakes a rat. Nevertheless, there was no denying that his fear of Whitehead was real—whether he was afraid for the population of the entire colony or only for himself.

Grant looked down at the inventory sheets stacked in front of him. It had all turned into an inextricable tangle of images and voices tearing him in different directions. In his mind, he shrieked at all of them: "I'm twenty-two years old, what do you want from me?" That felt better.

He said to John Pritchard: "I said you can leave in the morning; you can leave in the morning."

"Thank you." But instead of going back to the inventory sheets, Pritchard sat there twisting his pen between his fingers, looking down at the tabletop.

Grant said: "What else?"

"When I . . . retired from the company, to turn my hand to farming, they made me sign a bond for a thousand pounds that I wouldn't engage myself in the fur trade any longer, or interfere with the company in any way. You know that there are a number of men in the company who'll look for any excuse to get back at me for deserting to the other side, as they see it, even though I've never—"

"What do you want?"

"You see, if I only had some sort of . . . statement from you, some sort of testimonial—you know I always treated you fairly . . ."

Grant snatched up a scrap of paper, stabbed his pen into the inkwell, and scribbled: "John Pritchard has behaved honourably toward the North West Company. Cuthbert Grant." He flapped it in the wind to dry it, then held it out by one corner so he wouldn't have to touch Pritchard's hand when he took it.

He didn't dislike Pritchard, which only made his sniveling and hand licking all the more sickening. He realized that it was very easy to pass judgment—after all, *he* wasn't at the mercy of a pack of painted warriors who had just butchered twenty-some of his friends. But he liked to think that even if that were the case, he would manage to comport himself with dignity. Pritchard made him question that. Perhaps that was what had made it so difficult to keep from lopping off Pritchard's head when he had been dragged whining and scratchless from beneath the mounds of dead at Frog Plain.

Pritchard folded up the piece of paper and tucked it into his shirt. Grant said: "Go tell Bourke and Heden that if they don't have the rest of their goods out in five minutes, I'll seal these up as totaled."

Bostonais watched the one-time bourgeois trot off, then leaned out from his saddle and spat. "We won't have any peace as long as one of those dogs is left alive."

CHAPTER 69

At first no one in Fort Douglas seemed to notice that Marie Anne Lajimodierre and her children had disappeared; and by the time they did, there were enough other crises to cope with without worrying about a woman who'd had eight years in Rupertsland to learn how to look after herself and her children. Kate had to see that her husband got enough rest and food to recover his strength before they started north. She also had to bundle together their possessions yet again to load into the boats for Jack River.

By the morning of departure, her husband was enough himself again to take an oar in one of the York boats. Kate sat beside him on the rowing bench, clutching her blanket-wrapped bundle of spinning wheel parts and Bible and spare clothing. The Selkirk colony was once again a ragged flotilla of patched York boats and old canoes.

As soon as they'd rounded Point Douglas, Kate began to regret that they hadn't gone in one of the canoes. The passengers and paddlers in the canoes faced forward, so they didn't have to watch the plumes of smoke grow up out of their homes behind them. She could have turned herself around on the rowing bench, but the rowers didn't have any choice, so she stayed where she was.

In the places where the woods on the west bank grew sparse enough to see the open prairie beyond, she glimpsed a lone rider trotting along parallel to the boats. On the eastern shore were two riders—Bostonais Pangman and the Mister Fall-Coe who had helped her find Sandy. The lone rider was Cuthbert Grant. He had promised them a safe departure, and he was going to make sure they got one.

A few miles north of Seven Oaks Creek they passed a meadow on the west bank called Image Plain. There was a low knoll there that jutted out slightly into the river. Grant rode up onto the knoll and stopped his horse. He stayed there, silhouetted against the distant trees of smoke spreading their crowns into the sky, until the boats rounded a farther bend and the wooded banks closed behind them.

On the third day of their progress north, as they were passing into the delta at the foot of Lake Winnipeg, they ran head on into the North West Company brigade from Fort William. Another day and they would have been safely out onto the lake. The brigade forced them in to shore. Even if they'd had any spirit left, there was no sense in putting up a fight against a hundred armed *hommes du nord*. The brigade men had already heard the story of what the half-breeds had done at Seven Oaks—news traveled with remarkable speed through the scattered family bands of Indian hunters—and they were eager to prove that they would have performed just as valiantly if they'd been there.

The bourgeois of the brigade was a man named Archibald Norman MacLeod, who was coming west to fill Duncan Cameron's place at the Forks. It was he, in fact, as a major in His Majesty's Corps of Voyageurs, who had cosigned Captain Cameron's commission. He said now that he'd been appointed justice of the peace for the Indian territories by the courts in Lower Canada, so that it was his duty to take depositions about the recent events at Red River.

He held them there for three days, interrogating most of the colony men and bullying any whose statements incriminated the North West Company in any way. When he finally let them go, he held on to John Bourke, Michael Heden, and John Pritchard, saying that they would be transported east to face charges of assault and false arrest. The embarkation was accompanied by the screams of Elisabeth Heden, shrieking for her husband from the lead York boat, and John Bourke, who had been dumped unceremoniously onto the bales of cargo in one of the North West Company canoes with his festering leg bent under him. Catherine Pritchard sat on the rowing bench in front of Kate, with one child in her arms and another in her belly, gazing silently at her husband on the shore.

As the refugee flotilla was sailing north down Lake Winnipeg, a wandering band of Saulteaux found three naked white men on a spit of land in Rainy River, three-quarters starved and swollen over with insect bites. Several of the Saulteaux were acquainted with Kiche Omachew—the Great Hunter—but they didn't recognize him until he got enough of his voice back to identify himself, and even then there was some debate over whether this croaking, sprung-ribbed old wreck was truly Jean Baptiste Lajimodierre or just a

razy man who thought he was. Lajimodierre explained to them
ow he'd carried dispatches to the Earl of Selkirk in Montreal, the
stounded Earl asking if he'd walked all that way—"No, most of
1e way I ran." On the way back, Lajimodierre had hooked up with
 couple of old friends heading back to the *pays d'en haut*. They
ot ambushed one night and dragged to Fort William where the
North West Company men had kept him until he told them what he
new of the Earl of Selkirk's plans; then he and his companions
ad been stripped naked and driven out into the bush. The Saul-
eaux explained to him in turn what had happened at the Forks of
1e Red, as they'd had it from a family of Cree who'd heard it from
1e of Peguis's band—that the half-breeds under Wappeston had
escended on the colony, burned it to the ground, and rubbed out
ll the whites down to the last squalling infant.

When he was well enough to be moved, Lajimodierre convinced
1em to take him downstream to the Hudson's Bay Company post
n Lake of the Woods. The master of the post there was quite happy
 outfit him on credit, after which Lajimodierre left his friends
nd the Saulteaux who had saved them and drifted west from Lake
f the Woods alone. The wooded rocklands around the lakes had
ever been the true *pays d'en haut* to him, only a transitional ter-
tory between the Canadas and the horse country of the open prai-
e. But now he found something soothing in the spruce-scented
alf-light, in the padding of moss under his moccasins, in the clear,
lack trickling streams and cowled pools. He knew he would have
 go out into the harsher light eventually, but for now he preferred
1e comfort of the shadows. He grew accustomed to the taste of
1oosemeat rather than buffalo, and to the songs of loons at night
istead of wolves.

He entertained fantasies of revenge for the first few weeks, but
hom was he supposed to kill? Every agent of the North West
`ompany? Every half-breed within a hundred miles of the Forks
f the Red? Or himself for taking Marie Anne away from the house
f Monsieur l'Abbé in Trois Rivières?

It was autumn by the time he'd reached the joining of the Pem-
ina River and the Red. He persuaded a Cree Chief there to part
"ith a good horse in return for the traps he had never used; the only
illing he'd done all summer had been to feed himself.

He headed north along the Red. He didn't want to go back to the
orks, yet he knew he'd have to face his memories eventually, and
e owed money and needed to outfit himself for winter. The night
efore he'd left last autumn to carry the dispatches to Lord Selkirk,

he'd buried a pouch of gold coins near the east bank of the Red
out behind a tumbledown old hunter's cabin that he and Marie Anne
had lived in for a season before he'd built the cabin on the Assini
boine. The arrangement he'd made with Lord Selkirk in the spring
meant that the land the cabin was on now belonged to him, but tha
was meaningless now.

The sinking sun and the trees around the cabin were the same
burnt orange. There was smoke coming from the chimney hole
and someone had propped up the caved-in sections of the roof and
patched in new sod. He had an impulse to sheer his horse off into
the riverside bush and wait until nightfall. In the dark he could ge
his gold and be gone without the horror of contact with another
human being.

He took hold of himself and walked his horse in closer. A child
came around the corner of the cabin and stopped. Lajimodiern
jerked hard on the halter, and his horse stopped. He knew it wasn't
reasonable to be angry at the child for bearing a resemblance to hi
lost La Reine, but it seemed like a particularly cruel trick. The
child's eyes grew wider. She put her hand to her mouth and
screamed. The cabin door flew open and a woman came out. It was
Marie Anne.

In the valley of The River That Calls, Bethsy McKay had jus
taken her squalling son out of her sister-in-law's arms when the
boom of the fort's cannon rocked the cabin walls. She thrust Jame
back at Josephte and rushed for the water basin, tearing off he
blouse. With her face and hands and neck dripping wet, she trie
to brush her hair, towel off her torso, unfasten her skirt, and get th
fresh dress down from the wall peg all at the same time. She'd bee
through the same performance three times in the last week. Ever
salute to an incoming party might mean that her husband was home

She took James from Josephte and ran out the door. Smoke wa
still rising over the gun bastions flanking the gates. The *engagé*
were swarming up onto the catwalk, waving their hats in the air an
shooting their muskets at the clouds. There were answering gun
shots, whoops, and the pounding of hoofbeats coming from th
flats to the west of the knoll Fort Esperance sat on. The drill Beths
had developed for a party of horsemen was to stand in front of th
cabin and wait for their leader to come through the gates. If it ha
been an incoming canoe brigade, she would have gone out throug
the gates and waited within view of the riverbank.

He was just as likely to be traveling by canoe as on horseback

From the stories and rumors that had made their way back over the summer, he had been ranging from the Forks of the Red to Lake of the Woods, sometimes leading a troop of horsemen and sometimes accompanying the North West Company's canoe brigades. Many of the men who'd ridden east with him in the spring had already drifted back through the Qu'Appelle, telling stories of what had happened at the Forks. But there were many other, more shadowy stories of the months after La Grenouillière, of kidnappings and murders and assaults. It was impossible to tell how many of them were true and exactly how her husband fitted in with them.

A spotted horse galloped through the gates, clods of earth kicking up from its hooves. Its rider's face was lit up like a beacon, laughing with joy. In the best gallant *jeunes gens* style, he brought the horse to a rearing halt in front of her, stepping down off his stirrup while his hands were still hauling back on the reins.

He bent forward, wrapped his arms around her thighs just under the swell of her hips, and lifted her off her feet. She squawked: "Careful of James, you'll crush him!" But it was only for form; the strength in his shoulders and arms and upper back was terrifyingly assured and controlled.

He was still laughing, kissing her mouth and her cheeks and her neck and their son and then back to her mouth. He leaned his head back to get a good look at her. She searched the big-boned, browned face for any evidence of whether the worst of the stories she'd heard had any truth in them—a hardening around the mouth, a killer's coldness in the eyes—any sign that would identify a lover who had gone away for seven months and come back changed. She found she couldn't see a change from the man who'd left her in the spring, because the man who was holding her in his arms was someone she had never met before.

PART FOUR

SACRIFICIAL LION

The snow was waltzing down on Rainy River. John Tanner—or Shaw Shaw Neba-se, as he'd been called for the greater part of his life—came paddling through the wafting flakes, freighting his harvest of wild rice and Indian corn to Mister Tace's trading post on Rainy Lake. Behind him followed a second canoe with Red Star of the Morning and their two infant daughters and Netnokwa, the Ojibway medicine woman who had adopted him many years ago. When he was eight years old the Shawnee had snatched him from outside his father's cabin on the Ohio—not much against his will since his father had had a liberal hand with a cane—and he'd been traded north from tribe to tribe as a slave and a curiosity. Netnokwa had taken a sudden fancy to the idea of having a white son, and what Netnokwa took a fancy to she usually got.

The haze of snowflakes began to thin. The squared-off blot of Mister Tace's stockade grew out of the ragged spruce trees on the shoreline. There were snowdrifts piled up against the base of the palisade, which seemed strange since on the rest of the countryside the snow was melting as it touched the ground, leaving only a slick, gleaming residue.

Tanner had spent too much of his life as a nomad hunter to argue with his senses. Whether there should be snowdrifts there or not, his eyes told him there were. If he'd grown up in the environment he'd been born into, he might have stopped his canoe and tried to puzzle out an explanation. As it was, he kept on paddling. An explanation might or might not choose to present itself to him in the course of time. Either way he would still have to carry his harvest through the hip-high snowdrifts to do his trading with Mister Tace.

As his canoe came into shore, he saw that they weren't snowdrifts at all, but a collection of the low, peaked canvas tents the traders used. Tanner had never seen so many in one place. Men were moving among them, some in white shirts and white trousers,

431

others in red coats. None of them showed any inclination to hel
beach the canoes.

By the time Tanner, Red Star of the Morning, and Netnokw
had gotten the harvest and the children and the gear unloaded an
the canoes drawn up on shore, a delegation had emerged from th
fort gates to greet them. Among others there was a red-coate
soldier and a blocky, square-cut man in a black coat. The block
man raised his hand in sign-language greeting and said: "H
Friend!" Then he thumped the palm of his hand against his chest-
"We friends!"—and extended it in a grand, sweeping flourish-
"Friend!"

Tanner said: "Where is Mister Tace?"

The soldier began to laugh, although he tried hard not to. Th
blocky man turned red and replied stiffly: "Mister Tace has bee
transported to Fort William to wait for the spring when he an
William MacGillivray and the rest of the North West Compan
brigands will be taken east to stand trial. I am Governor MacDone
of the Selkirk colony."

The soldier said: "We into the fort should go, to talk with a roc
above our heads." There was something more than a little eccentri
about the way he pronounced the words.

Tanner said: "My corn'll get wet. I brought it in to trade, alon
with them baskets of rice."

The soldier said, "We will help you them move," and shoute
over his shoulder in a harsh, spit-consonanted language that Tanne
had never heard. A squad of soldiers trotted down from the ten
and snatched up everything in sight that looked remotely portable
One of them even made a lunge for the babies in their cradleboard
until Netnokwa and Red Star of the Morning scared him off.

Tanner and his family followed the line of soldiers bearing the
belongings into the fort. The blocky man, whose name Tanner ha
heard as M'Dolland, pointed to a cabin in the northeast corner c
the stockade. "Your women and children may house themselve
there. Come into the trading office, where we can talk."

Tanner repeated the gist of that to Netnokwa and Red Star of th
Morning in Ojibway. Neither of them changed their expression
but Tanner could tell that they didn't like it any better than he did
By all established patterns of trading etiquette, natives should hous
themselves outside the palisade in their own tents. After his trans
lation Tanner added: "If you take off your wet moccasins, put dr
ones on, and don't take the babies off their cradleboards."

He went into the bourgeois's cabin behind the man who calle

himself the governor. Like everyone else in the *pays d'en haut*,
Tanner knew that Wappeston and the half-breeds had rubbed out
the colony at the beginning of the summer. It seemed a bit suspect
for an obviously unmurdered white man to suddenly appear on
Rainy Lake claiming to be the governor of Selkirk colony.

They offered him a cup of white wine and a twist of tobacco for
his pipe. He took them both and sat down on the floor. The soldier
and the "governor" looked at each other, then lowered themselves
awkwardly to sit cross-legged in front of him. He puffed on his pipe
and sipped from his cup and thought for a moment, translating the
thoughts in his mind from Ojibway to English, then said: "If Mister
Tace ain't here, who's gonna buy my corn and rice?"

The soldier said: "We! We have need of provisions."

The blocky-faced man said: "Captain D'Orsennens is with the
Des Meurons Regiment of Foot, late of His Britannic Majesty's
forces in the Canadas, now serving under Lord Selkirk. We mean
to march overland to Fort Douglas and take it back from the North
West Company to hold until Lord Selkirk comes from Fort William
in the spring. We need—"

"You ain't English," Tanner pointed out to the captain.

"No, we are Swiss the most, and some Germans."

It sounded extremely suspicious to Tanner. Why hadn't the captain and his soldiers gone home to Swissland now that the war with
the Americans was over? And why would a bunch of Swiss and
Germans have come across the ocean to fight for the English King?
His English vocabulary, more or less frozen at the age of nine,
didn't include the word "mercenaries," and none of the Indian
dialects he knew had an equivalent. He kept his reservations to
himself, though, considering it impolitic to point out the holes in a
man's story while a bunch of his friends were standing around
behind him holding muskets.

The blocky man who'd called himself the governor said: "We
have to get to the Forks of the Red River without losing the element
of surprise. We hear there is an overland route that the Indians use,
that doesn't go past the North West Company posts on the Winnipeg River and the lake." Tanner nodded. "Could you guide us
here?"

"I could make you a road straight from here to Harshfield's front
door."

That seemed to puzzle them. They exchanged a number of confused comments and queries before they finally ciphered out that
Tanner's "Harshfield" was Archibald Norman MacLeod, the new

bourgeois at the Forks of the Red. Tanner had a great deal of difficulty with European names. The closest he ever came to Captain D'Orsennens was "Tussenon," and he always heard Miles MacDonell's name as "M'Dolland."

Once they'd sorted out what Tanner had said, the captain and the governor clapped their hands on his shoulders and called one of the soldiers over to refill his cup and his pipe. The captain said: "And so when shall we leave?"

"Soon if I was you. Winter's gonna clamp down hard any day now. But I'd like for you to trade me powder and shot and goods for my rice and corn before you go."

They both looked puzzled. The governor said: "Before 'you' go?"

Tanner ran the phrase over in his mind to see if he'd missed something. He said again: "Before *you* go."

The captain said: "But you said you can make for us a road straight in to the commandant's bedroom door."

"Yup. Oh!" Tanner began to laugh, and they glanced sideways at each other and then back at him. He said: "You asked me could I and I said I could and you thought I meant I was gonna." They still couldn't seem to see the humor. He calmed himself lest they grow offended.

The governor said: "Why wouldn't you?"

"Why would I?"

That seemed to stump them for a moment. Then the governor said: "The great white Chief Selkirk, who is my Chief, was given his authority by the great King across the water. The North West Company have broken the great King's law—many of his laws. By helping us you would be helping the great King, and his laws."

"So?"

They offered to pay him ten pounds in gold, then upped it to twenty, then added in a barrel of rum, and then upped it to anything he wanted out of the stores at Fort Douglas. He didn't want any part of it. Once he'd traded in his rice and his corn he'd already have everything he needed. He didn't fancy spending the winter trudging over open prairie leading a gang of foreign soldiers who, as far as he knew, had never seen a snowshoe before. He fancied even less the idea of turning the entire North West Company against him. The governor and the captain began to grow exasperated, so Tanner said he would think about it and excused himself to see to his family.

He explained the situation to Netnokwa and Red Star of the

Morning and solicited opinions as to how they might be able to sneak out of the fort without leaving their harvest behind. Netnokwa said: "We won't have to sneak away at all if you guide them where they want to go."

"You always said we shouldn't get on one side or the other in the fur companies' wars."

"Things change. My medicine tells me you should do what they ask."

Tanner had never quite worked out whether he had any faith in Netnokwa's medicine. Much of her reputation as a medicine woman came from her visions of hibernating bears. She would announce to whatever band they were traveling with that she had had a dream of a snow-covered cutbank or mounded deadfall in a specific direction from the camp. They would find it looking exactly as she'd described it, and underneath it there would always be a hibernating bear waiting to be turned into a feast and bear's grease and a warm robe and decorative claws. One night when the rest of the band had been asleep, Tanner had heard Netnokwa slipping out of the lodge. He had sneaked out behind her and trailed her for miles across the countryside, watching from the shadows as she poked sticks into snowbanks and sniffed at fallen trees. The next morning she said that she'd had another vision.

The captain and the governor were very happy when Tanner announced that he'd decided to guide them. The only decision he'd actually made was that doing what Netnokwa wanted him to do was better than getting a sore head from arguing with her.

There were enough horses in Mister Tace's corral to accommodate half the soldiers plus Tanner and his family. The plan was to ride west to Rush Lake, then bring the horses back for the other half of the troop. As they were saddling up to start out, Captain D'Orsennens said to Tanner: "Should you not leave your women here in the fort to join with them after all is over? If from this Rush Lake we have to walk, they may have trouble keeping pace with my men."

"Maybe at first, but they'll get used to slowing down for you."

There was a Saulteaux camp at Rush Lake. They stayed there four days while the horses were relayed and the Saulteaux women whipped up forty pairs of snowshoes. Then they set off due west across a few hundred miles of new snow toward the joining of the Pembina River and the Red. The men of the Des Meurons Regiment weren't accustomed to short rations and sleeping in the snow—enlisted soldiers could be forced to march on weevily hardtack, but

wise generals kept their mercenary regiments cozy and well fed,
Captain D'Orsennens had to run through every gambit from flattery
to fistfights to keep them from mutinying.

Forty days after leaving Rainy Lake, they reached the juncture
of the Pembina and the Red and took the North West Company fort
there. "Taking" it consisted of marching in through the open gate
and informing the handful of old hunters in residence that their fort
was now the property of the Governor and Company of Adventurers
Trading into Hudson's Bay.

They left a few of the soldiers there, along with Netnokwa, Red
Star of the Morning, and Tanner's baby daughters, and headed north
along the Red. A day south of the Forks they cut northwest and met
up with Peguis and twelve of his warriors and the young Saulteaux
from Rush Lake whom Tanner had sent on ahead to arrange the
rendezvous.

The Chief was camped in the shelter of the high north bank at
the passage of the Assiniboine, the first shallows upstream from the
Forks. With the river frozen over, any crossing place was as good
as another, but the passage was an easily identifiable place to meet
within striking distance of Fort Douglas or Fort Gibraltar or whatever it was the North West Company had decided to rename it.

The governor and the captain and Tanner hunkered down beside
Chief Peguis to debate strategy in comfort, with a spruce-bough
lean-to at their backs and a snug fire in front of them. No one
seemed to have thought beyond the moment when they were all
assembled and ready to launch their attack. They all kept proposing
half-baked inspirations to each other, then talking themselves out
of them and lapsing into silence. Whenever Tanner tried to interject
his own ideas, they would turn to him with the glazed expression
of adults humoring someone else's idiot child, then go back to their
own conversation as soon as he finished.

Tanner was particularly disappointed in Peguis's dismissal of
him. He'd known the chief since the days when Peguis had a nose.
It was Tanner's adoptive brother, Netnokwa's son, who'd bitten it
off. Peguis had tried to intervene in a free-for-all fight in which
someone had bitten off Tanner's brother's nose. At the bottom of
the pile of flailing bodies, Tanner's brother had mistaken Peguis for
the man who'd bitten his nose off, and bit his nose off. He'd apol-
ogized, and Peguis had said: "I am an old man; it is only a short
time they will laugh at me for having no nose."

The strategy meeting finally broke off with a brilliantly innova-
tive plan. Tomorrow morning they would all march over to the fort

line up in front of it, and tell the men inside to surrender. Tanner
rolled into his buffalo-robe cocoon and elbowed his snow mattress
furiously, expressing his opinion to Louis Nolin, Peguis's Canadian
friend: "I told them I could make them a road right to Harshfield's
bedroom door, but will they let me? No. They want to line up in
front of the fort in broad daylight and see if Harshfield's got any
cannons. We could sneak over there tonight and be over the walls
before they got out of their beds. You and me could do it alone. A
gang of old women could do it. But will they listen to me? Oh, no,
they—"

"Why don't we, then?"

"Huh? Why don't we what?"

Nolin took his pipe out of his mouth and spat in the snow. "Do
it alone. You and me. Now."

"Oh, I don't know about that, there's—"

"They won't even have sentries out. It's gonna be so damned
cold tonight the wolverines are staying home. You said you and me
could do it—or were you just farting out your mouth?"

Tanner threw off his buffalo robe, stood up, and said: "Let's go,
then." Much to his surprise and consternation, Nolin got out of
bed and started strapping on his snowshoes.

They had gone a few hundred yards out of camp when they
realized they were being followed. Tanner turned around, hoping
to find the governor or the captain come to order them back. Instead
he found a dozen of the soldiers. The lead one said in thickly ac-
cented English: "We hear when you talked. Good. We come, too.
Bugger D'Orsennens. We finish it now."

They trekked east along the frozen Assiniboine. The cold was
the brutal January kind that worked its way into the bones, but at
least the riverbanks sheltered them from the wind, and it was the
wind that would turn exposed skin black and shear away the flesh.
But the soldiers didn't grumble, and there were no signs of weariness, despite the fact that they'd marched all day and hadn't slept.

They were nearly at the Forks when Tanner spotted a spruce tree
about three times his height among the naked oaks and willows
along the crest of the bank. He pointed it out to Nolin, and the two
of them climbed up the slope and went to work felling it with their
hand axes. The lead soldier left the huddle at the foot of the bank
and followed them up. He said: "I think Christmas has long gone
past already."

Tanner grunted, "Huh?" and carried on with his chopping.

"The *tannenbaum*—why do you do with the tree? I thought we go to take the fort."

Nolin grunted, "Stand away," and gave the trunk a push. Once it was down Tanner lopped off the crown where the stem narrowed thinner than the span of his thumb and forefinger. Nolin was already at work amputating branches, some snug to the trunk and some leaving a stump a handsbreadth long.

The soldier suddenly said: "So! Maybe you not are so"—revolving one mittened hand around his ear—"after it all, yes?" He helped them tote their new-made ladder to the bottom of the bank. The soldiers carried it in relays until they reached the Forks, then Tanner waved them all up to the top of the bank. They crossed the stretch of wind-hardened snow that once had been Fort Gibraltar and slipped into the skeletal shadows of the trees on the other side. The path that had run north from Fort Gibraltar to the colony was still a clear line through the bush but drifted over with snow.

Tanner waved them to a halt just before the sparse cover of the woods came to an abrupt end. Around the black mass of the fort was a white swath spidered over with a network of blue-shadowed paths. A few wisps of smoke curled out of the chimneys beyond the walls.

Tanner shook off his moosehide mittens and thawed the knot on his snowshoe bindings with his hands. Nolin pointed to the southwest corner of the palisade and whispered, "Blacksmith's shed," jumping one hand over the wall of the other. Tanner nodded, slipped his rifle out of its covering, and checked the load. The soldiers were peeling the coverings off their muskets. They had started the trek from Rush Lake with their naked muskets on their shoulders, but even the dimmest of them had only needed one try at clapping unmittened hands onto gun metal that had been exposed to a few hours of winter winds to set them scrounging up a piece of blanket cloth or an old pelt to fashion into a rifle scabbard.

Once they'd taken off their snowshoes and unlimbered their guns, Nolin and three of the soldiers picked up the ladder and Tanner led the rush across the clearing. They loped toward the corner that Nolin had pointed out, moccasins and boots thudding softly into the snow, fourteen pairs of lungs panting the cold wind in and out. There wasn't a sound or a sign of life from the fort walls.

Tanner went up the ladder first, the soles of his moccasins gripping the scaly stumps. The roof of the blacksmith shed was below him, flush to the stockade wall. He dropped onto it and then to the

ground, rolling and coming up with his rifle in his hands. No one
had sounded an alarm.

Nolin and the soldiers came down one at a time behind him—a
muffled thump and a grunt, then the dry rustle and crunch of footsteps in the snow. Once they were all down there was a long moment of hesitation, then they started forward in a kind of huddled
hedgehog formation, bristling with musket barrels that swung to
aim at every imagined sound.

They came out from between two rows of sheds into a wide
central square. Tanner went from building to building, guessing
which were occupied, looking for traces of smoke from the chimneys and listening for log-wall-filtered snoring. He set a couple of
soldiers outside each door he thought might have life behind it.
Once they were all in position he held up his hand, the lead soldier
barked a command in German, and they all burst through their
separate doors at once.

One factor Tanner hadn't considered was that the interiors would
all be lightless voids. A few shins got bruised on bedsteads, a few
chairs got overturned, but after some scuffles in the dark the North
West Company men were all herded out into the moonlight half-
dressed and still half-asleep. All except for Harshfield. Tanner told
the soldiers to put their prisoners into one cabin and guard them,
then he went looking for Harshfield.

He finally found him in a corner room of what had been Colony
House, just as the sky was beginning to lighten. He was bunkered
in behind his bed with a pair of pistols poking over the coverlet.
Tanner managed to convince him that there were twelve Swiss mercenaries in the courtyard who would be more than happy to use his
belly for bayonet practice if he pulled the triggers.

Chief Peguis and the captain and the governor showed up at the
front gates with the rest of the war party shortly after sunrise and
took charge. The captain and the governor didn't quite shower Tanner with the gratitude and congratulations that he thought he'd had
a right to expect. If anything, they seemed a trifle brusque, almost
miffed. At least Chief Peguis, when he wasn't keeping up his stoic
red Chief front for the benefit of the governor and the captain,
extended Tanner a good deal of winking and grinning, as though
something more than a little amusing had just taken place.

Harshfield fought and threatened and howled that he was a duly
constituted justice of the peace representing the Governor in Chief
of the Canadas. Finally, to get a little peace, the captain had him
bound hand and foot and thrown out into the snow. After a period

of time Tanner pointed out to the captain that Harshfield would probably freeze to death if they left him out much longer, so the captain sent a couple of soldiers to carry him back in. He did seem a good deal cooler, except that he growled at Tanner once he'd started to thaw: "If you were an honest man, you would have told me when I saw you in the fall that you'd joined sides with my enemies."

Tanner said: "When you came to my lodge in the fall and I was kind to you, I couldn't see the ashes of your brothers' houses on your hands."

CHAPTER 71

Bostonais was lying on his back in front of the hearth with James crawling all over him like a kitten on a Newfoundland dog. Falcon was propped up on one elbow on a buffalo robe on the floor, his eyes glazed and his breathing shallow, stuffed practically comatose with venison and wild rice and snowshoe hare stew. Grant was leaned back against the warm clay mantel, sucking in through his nostrils a savory dessert course of sage- and venison-flavored air.

Bethsy and Josephte and Josephte's son, John, were clearing the debris off the table. Falcon's first two children were rolling about underneath it gurgling threats at each other. The third was sitting on Mary's knee getting his feeding. Little Jean Baptiste was six months older than James, but James had already been weaned. The custom of the Plains tribes, and consequently of many métis women, was to breast-feed their children a good deal longer than Europeans generally did, sometimes up to two or three years old. This was partly due to the belief that as long as they were suckling a child they couldn't get pregnant again and partly due to the fact that a nomad society living on wild game didn't have the time or materials to fuss with a separate menu for infants. Grant wasn't sure whether Bethsy's break with custom meant that she was eager to have more children, that she didn't want her breasts to lose their shape, or whether it meant nothing at all.

Grant was on again about what had become his favorite topic since the colony was removed—the buffalo hunt. The established practice of scavenging around the edges of the Plains tribes' hunting grounds didn't fit with his vision of the métis nation's destiny, and consequently his own. Not that he'd given up his plans for a rising career in the North West Fur Trading Company. He saw himself as a kind of feral Medici, alternating between the boardrooms of the east and the wild splendor of the *pays d'en haut*. He said: "Using carts instead of packhorses, we could bring back ten times the volume of meat."

Falcon took the floor with a growling belch. "We do that all the time, to move meat from fort to fort."

"No, what I mean is to take the carts out onto the prairie where the herds are."

"In case you forgot, a cart ain't the best way to travel if you don't want to attract attention."

"But if forty or fifty carts traveled all together . . ."

Bostonais extricated James's fingers from his mustache and said: "How do you figure forty or fifty axles squealing together ain't as likely to be heard as one or two?"

"If you're traveling in that large a group, who cares if some wandering war party hears you? They won't want to take you on."

Bostonais rolled his eyes skeptically, but he didn't reply. Bethsy came over from the table and sat down in front of the fire, curling her legs beneath her and leaning her head on Grant's knee. Bostonais suddenly raised a forefinger and opened his mouth as though to speak. But before he'd said a word, the door flew open and Joseph Cadotte burst in, slamming it quickly against the blowing snow. He said: "They took the fort."

Grant said: "Who? What fort?"

Falcon said: "And where did they take it?"

"The fort at the Forks. Miles MacDonell and Selkirk's—"

There was a curious roaring sensation and a blackness. Grant realized that he was on his feet and that he'd been shouting, although what the words were he couldn't say. Bethsy was slowly righting herself from the sprawl that his leaping up had dumped her into. Everybody in the room seemed to be studiously avoiding him. He said to Bostonais: "You were right—we won't get any peace as long as one of them is left alive."

Bostonais grunted noncommittally. Grant turned to Cadotte "Did they sneak back down from Jack River?"

"No. It wasn't the *jardinières*. It was soldiers—I guess some of the soldiers that Selkirk brought to Fort William." Like everyone else in the *pays d'en haut*, Grant knew that Selkirk had brought a troop of soldiers from the Canadas and captured Fort William. But he'd expected them to stay there until the ice thawed on the Kaministiquia, by which time William MacGillivray's connections in the colonial government would have descended on the Earl of Selkirk with a frigateful of writs. "I got a letter for you, too—from Mile MacDonell. That's why he let me go, so I could bring it to you."

"Good Lord, of course—you've just come all that way. You must be half-frozen. How thoughtless of me. Come sit by the fire. Jo sephte—do pour out a cup of brandy for Joseph. How long have you been traveling?"

"Six, seven days, they ran together. I lost a dog by Montagne à la Bosse, so that slowed me down."

Once Cadotte had been made comfortable, Grant opened up MacDonell's letter. It was respectful, it was conciliatory, it suggested that Seven Oaks had been more the fault of the North West Company than the métis, and it assured Grant that if he came to Red River to discuss a resolution to their differences, he would not be detained or harmed.

Grant refolded the paper and batted it against the back of his hand. The year that MacDonell had spent shunting through the courts in the Canadas appeared to have taught him something about diplomacy. Grant didn't believe the closing assurance for a moment. He said to Cadotte: "How many soldiers are there?"

"Twenty."

He turned to Falcon: "How many *jeunes gens* do you think we could get together overnight?"

"Thirty, maybe forty."

"Good. We'll start for Red River in the morning."

"There aren't enough *carrioles* at Esperance."

"There's enough horses."

"Horses? Ride to Red River in January?"

"MacDonell and his soldiers must have walked at least that far from the east. Are you telling me they can get around better in our own country than we can? If we stick to the ridges where the snow thin, the horses won't founder."

Bethsy said: "Let me go with you."

He laughed and tweaked her ears. "How would you keep the air out of your face with your ears frozen off?"

She pulled her head away and said quietly: "I can't keep on knowing you by hearsay." She said the words as though he were supposed to attach some significance to them, but at the moment he had a good many more immediate concerns to attend to.

In the morning he kissed her and James good-bye and rode off at the head of his hastily assembled troop. A bitter two weeks later they trotted into Fort La Souris, forty shaggy-coated men on shaggy ponies, looking like the frost giant's bastard children by a Shetland centaur. There was another packet waiting for him there from Miles MacDonell, a ribboned proclamation and a letter. The letter was worded in the same conciliatory tone as the last one, respect edging over into flattery. It repeated all the assurances of the last letter and introduced a proclamation that had been issued by the governor in chief of the Canadas last year, ordering all loyal subjects in the Indian territories to cease and desist any acts of violence and to surrender up those who had been guilty of them in the past.

Grant turned his attention to the proclamation. He was leaning against the fieldstone mantelpiece of the bourgeois's house in Fort La Souris, reading by the light of a cheery blaze. When he'd read to the end, he announced to Falcon and the others in the room, *'Voilà encore une des proclamations Sacrés,''* and tossed it into the fire. The governor's letter followed hard on its heels.

He let his forty intrepids thaw their bones in front of the hearths of Fort La Souris for a few days, then saddled up again. A half day's ride east of the Forks they came to a sprawling, snow-cloaked cabin on the north bank of the Assiniboine. Grant stopped his troop thirty yards from the front of the house and called out: "Lajimodierre!" There was no reply.

The house was definitely occupied; smoke was pouring out of the chimney. Cadotte had told him that the Lajimodierres had moved back into the place after Jean Baptiste's return in the fall. Grant called again: "Lajimodierre!"

A shutter opened a little ways, not far enough to let them see the person behind it. Lajimodierre's voice called: "What do you want?"

"I want to talk to you. Come out for a moment."

There was a pause, then Lajimodierre called back: "I can talk to you just fine from here."

"If we wanted to harm you, a few log walls wouldn't stop us. Come on out where you can talk to me like one man to another

instead of like a gopher to a fox. I don't have any grudge agains
you.''

''Your friends in the North West Company seem to think the
do.''

Grant laughed. ''I suppose they do, but from what I hear they'v
already taken it out on you. You can probably consider yourse
fortunate that that was before anyone quite knew just how muc
damage your splendid job of postal delivery was going to cause
But it's a little late to nail you to the barn door after the horse
bolted. Come out and talk.''

The shutter closed. A moment passed, then the door opened an
Lajimodierre came out, shrugging into his coat. Grant dismounted
handed the reins to Bostonais, and crunched forward across th
snow to meet Lajimodierre halfway. He tugged off his mitten, shoo
Lajimodierre's hand, and said: ''You're not hunting on the Pembin
this winter?''

Lajimodierre shook his head. ''I thought I'd stick close to hom
I got a trap line out. Good cold winter.''

''I would've thought MacDonell would have hired you to hun
provisions for his soldiers.''

Lajimodierre blinked, but his expression didn't change. ''No
they got more provisions stored in the fort than they can eat ove
the winter. Once in a while I bring in a few rabbits I snared, 'caus
MacDonell's got a taste for them, but they don't need me to fee
them.''

''Ah. Well, I suppose the fort was stocked with rations for a
entire complement of *engagés*, and now only has to be shared o
among a few mouths. . . .''

Lajimodierre shrugged. ''Not that few. Must be a hundred
so.''

Joseph Cadotte had said twenty. If Lajimodierre was lying, h
was doing it artfully; there had been no pause taken to formulate
lie, nor had he jumped in too quickly, as so often happened with
lie prepared ahead of time.

Lajimodierre looked up at the sky, scratched his beard, and saic
''Looks like snow.''

''Yes, perhaps. Well, I suppose we'd best be pushing along. I'
glad to see you bear no lasting ill effects from your ordeal. My be
regards to your lovely wife.''

''And to yours.''

Grant headed back toward his winter warriors. Bostonais leane
down to hand him the reins of his pony, but Grant walked on pa

him to Joseph Cadotte's horse. "Joseph, how many soldiers did you count when they took the fort?"

"Forty, maybe fifty."

With great difficulty, Grant resisted the impulse to drag him off his pony and shake him till his teeth rattled. "Back at Esperance you said twenty."

"Twenty, forty, sixty"—Cadotte shrugged—"what's the difference? We can take them."

"The *difference* is . . ." Grant caught hold of himself and walked back to his horse. The difference was that this wasn't a question of taking anyone in an open fight. Even if Lajimodierre had been doubling the truth, there was no way fifty Swiss mercenaries were going to be intimidated into surrendering their cozy fort to forty frost-bitten métis. And any attempt at drawn-out siege warfare in January could only end one way: with the New Nation slinking home with the stump of its froze-off tail between its legs.

He swung up onto his horse, stood in the stirrups, and announced: "We're riding back to La Souris." Over a week of feasting and drinking at Fort La Souris, he could gradually disseminate the impression that he'd intended from the first for this to be no more than a reconnaissance mission. After a few fatted calves and hogsheads, they'd find the ride back to the Qu'Appelle a little easier to bear. The company could foot the bill. Joseph Cadotte could tote it up and present it to Whitehead MacDonell.

In March, when the cold began to ease off, Grant started east from the Qu'Appelle again, this time with sixty men behind him. They picked up another twelve from the isolated cabins of free hunters passed along the way. Some were barely older than boys, still living under the roofs of their ex-voyageur fathers and Indian or métis mothers. In some cases, the parents tried to hold them back. The recruiting process now involved more threatening and cajoling than it had the year before.

They set up camp in the hollow where Catfish Creek joined the Assiniboine, and Grant sent Cadotte over with a letter for Miles MacDonell, demanding that he surrender the North West Company traders he was still holding prisoner. The reply that came back was from the old Miles MacDonell of the pemmican proclamations, bristling with references to "the heinous murders and depredations of the summer past" and "the aforementioned General Order of the Governor in Chief of British North America," and threatened that if Grant did not surrender himself up to Lord Selkirk's duly

appointed governor of Assiniboia, "you shall find to your regre
that I have the force to take you into custody, willingly or no—d
not imagine that I will hesitate."

Grant hummed to himself happily as he thawed some snow in
tin cup next to the fire and stirred in some powder of ink. Th
suspension wasn't entirely successful, a bit clotty, but serviceabl
enough to write:

> Sir, your threats you make use of we laughed at them and yo
> may come with your forces anytime you please. We shall b
> always ready to meet you with a good heart, you shall see m
> to-morrow morning under arms. I dare you to come out wit
> your forces. Since you will not come to any reasonable term
> you may do your worst and you may perhaps have reason t
> repent your expressions and folly. As for your General Order,
> shall believe it when I see the original. I am, Sir, your humbl
> servant
>
> Cuthbert Gran
>
> P.S. Please excuse this ink and scrawl.

He wanted to add a P.P.S.—"Now art thou MacDonell, now ar
thou what thou art by nature as well as by art!"—but restraine
himself. He gave it to Falcon to deliver over to the fort, then spe
the afternoon sitting in an oak tree with Bostonais, the two me
pointing out to each other the natural features of the countrysid
along the likeliest marching route from Fort Douglas—willo
copses, snowed-over deadfalls, and hidden ravines.

But the soldiers didn't come the next day or the day after tha
and finally Grant was forced to admit that the governor wasn
coming out to play. Perhaps the parallel to the last governor wh
had marched out to teach the métis a lesson was so obvious tha
even MacDonell couldn't miss it. Or maybe the captain of the me
cenaries had pointed out to him the idiocy of abandoning thei
warm safe fort for a fight in the snow. Or perhaps Grant's "I dar
you" had been too transparent.

For two days a blizzard raved across the plain above their littl
hollow. When it had blown itself out they dug out of their tents an
found that they'd lost five horses. They'd had to dig to the botton
of their pemmican stores, and game was scarce. The boisterous
wild-blooded war party that had ridden east from the Qu'Appell
was eroding rapidly into a ragged batch of grumblers huddling o
their days around the campfires. Too late, Grant realized that the

night be more than coincidence to the fact that all their past exploits had happened in the spring and early summer, when the energy that had been buried alive for six months burst out and all things seemed possible.

He had done the one thing he was most afraid of doing—led his *jeunes gens* into a confrontation they couldn't win. There would be no disguising this foray as a reconnaissance mission. He hesitated a few days longer on the chance that something might break, but he knew that if he waited too long to lead them back to the Qu'Appelle, they would start to drift away despite him.

As they were packing the tents and saddling up for the long ride back, Alex Fraser came bounding over to him, bright-eyed with inspiration. "They only got a few soldiers holding Fort Pembina. We can ride down there and kill the soldiers and take the fort back."

Grant tried to grasp what possible advantage there would be in that, but he couldn't figure it out. If they took Fort Douglas, the little fort on the Pembina would inevitably surrender, but Mac-Donell and his soldiers would stay battened in on the Forks even if the earth opened up and swallowed Fort Pembina whole. Finally he gave up trying to puzzle it through and asked: "Why?"

"Better'n coming all this way for nothing."

"What?"

"Better'n coming all this—"

"I heard you. We are not barbarians."

CHAPTER 72

At Jack River House on the northern end of Lake Winnipeg, Lord Selkirk's Red River colonists eked through the winter in the same kind of makeshift huts they'd thrown up on the edge of Hudson's Bay three years before. News reached them of Lord Selkirk's capture of Fort William and Miles MacDonell's recapturing of Fort Douglas, but what bearing either event would actually have upon their future no one could say.

Some of the men, including Sandy Sutherland, found work on

the construction of the majestic wooden sprawl that the Hudson'
Bay Company was building to replace Jack River House. Although
it hadn't been officially christened yet, the new fort was already
known as Norway House, after the Norwegian carpenters the com
pany had brought across the ocean to construct it—big, rawboned
fair-haired men whose first response to the obviously Norse "Sud
erland" had been an enthusiastic outpouring of Norwegian.

Although they were hundreds of miles north of the Forks of the
Red, the winter was actually less cruel because the dense-packe
forest of scrub spruce gave some shelter from the wind. The soun
of the needled boughs soughing against each other joined with th
raucous croaking of the immense ragged-feathered ravens flapping
back and forth from the rubbish heap behind the fort.

Spring came later in the year than at Point Douglas, and less
explosively. Although the transition was just as immediate, the pre
dominance of evergreens meant that the landscape's change in colo
from winter to summer wasn't as drastic.

A few weeks after the ice on the river had broken, Kate went ou
into the bush with Catherine Pritchard to gather fiddleheads an
then wandered away from her with John Bheag—not so *bheag* any
more—strapped over her shoulder in a willow-frameworked hide
pouch. Catherine's back was already occupied with baby Janet.

Behind a stand of ground-hugging kinnikinnick was a fern sprig
that looked to be the right variety, and Kate crouched down t
inspect it. It was a succulent yellow green, without the red that ha
tinged the last wrong one she'd picked. The shape was right, too—
a tight-curled spiral, like a pressed ram's horn, but then so were al
new fernlets. She reached down and parted the moss with her thumb
and forefinger to get at the base of the stem, releasing a sweet, dar
smell of earth and decay—dank and yet fresh. John Bheag squirme
and complained under her arm. She clucked what she thought migh
be soothing sounds at him, nipped through the fern stem with he
thumbnail, and went to find his mother.

Catherine Pritchard wasn't hard to locate, even in a hummock
spruce forest with spring growth crowding against the trees. Sh
kept up a running stream of chatter, in Blackfoot and Bungee an
English and French and even the occasional mangled scrap o
Gaelic, to herself and Janet and the red squirrels and whoever els
might be in earshot. That was the major reason Kate had decide
to wander off alone. It seemed a bit silly once she'd finally gotte
a few hours away from Jack River House, which had been the ful

scope of the world for so many months, not to be able to hear the birds for the incessant chatter of another human voice.

Catherine Pritchard was bent double over the trunk of a fallen fir tree, harvesting the fern shoots on the other side. She straightened when she saw Kate and sat down on the log. Kate came forward and held out her green prize in the palm of her hand. Mrs. Pritchard took it, looked at it, then wrinkled her forehead sadly and shook her head. "No—this one would taste . . ." She screwed up her nostrils and stuck out her tongue, then giggled at herself and blushed, covering her little white teeth with her hand.

Kate found it a source of constant wonder that such a child should have two children of her own. What was even more wondrous was that she managed to maintain such dewy ingenuousness despite the fact that she hadn't seen or heard from the father of her children for almost a year, ever since the North West Company brigade carried him away.

Mrs. Pritchard reached into a bulging rawhide bag and pulled out a picked fern sprout. "See? See the different?" Kate nodded, although for the life of her she couldn't see it. "You take, to look and see."

Kate took the model fiddlehead and went back to combing the undergrowth, although this time she stayed within Catherine Pritchard's general vicinity and tried to hold up her end of the chatter. But she really wasn't all that good at it. For three decades she'd worked to suppress the inclination to blather without purpose or intent. And now, of course, she simply couldn't—except when she was angry. Eventually she gave up trying and drifted farther afield again. Mrs. Pritchard's merry gabble sank into the background with the burble of the river, and the bird song and bough creakings rose to the fore.

Suddenly Catherine Pritchard let out a shriek. Kate bolted for the nearest climbable tree without pausing to look behind her, as she'd been instructed. After several tries she managed to get herself and young John Pritchard up onto the lowest limb. There were still no bear noises from behind her, so she stopped to look back before trying to climb any higher.

The limb she was on was high enough to see over the tops of the bushes between her and Mrs. Pritchard. Mrs. Pritchard had been caught and held, but not by a bear. She was entangled with a fair-haired man—and when they disentangled themselves long enough to look at each other before falling to again, Kate was pleased and astonished to see that the man was Mister Pritchard.

Her first instinct was to sneak back to Jack River House and leave them to each other. She could get details later. But she still had their son strapped to her back, and at the moment he was voicing his dissatisfaction at the jostling and twig battering he'd just been subjected to.

Kate climbed down, slung him around to her front and quieted him, then tracked forward through the bush as surreptitiously as she could. John's parents were still twined together. Mrs. Pritchard was crooning in one of her Indian tongues, and her husband was saying: "Now, now . . . in English—English, now . . ." He looked up and caught Kate coming through the junipers.

She took off the baby bundle and handed John Bheag forward. "Here is your son."

"Look at the size of him!" Mister Pritchard took him out of her hands, enthralled with ogling and goo-gooing. It seemed an appropriate opportunity to leave quietly, but before Kate had quite gotten away Mister Pritchard swung his head around and announced: "I've come to bring you back, Mrs. Sutherland."

"Back?"

"Back to your homes on Red River, all of you."

Although it was what she'd been praying to hear for eleven months, once it was said she felt a terrible dismay. Some part of it must have shown on her face, for he immediately cried: "No, we can! Lord Selkirk is at Red River by now with a full regiment of soldiers. I came with them from Fort William as far as Bas de la Rivière, then they swung south up the Red, and I came here to bring you back. By the time we make our way to the Forks, Lord Selkirk will have the situation well in hand. There is nothing to be afraid of."

In the evening she sat with her husband by the canvas door flap of their spruce log shelter, feeding clumps of grass and green leaves into the smudge fire to keep the bugs away. After a long silence, Sandy said: "I had meant to wait to talk of this until the end of the summer. You see, by then the building will be done here, and the Norwegians will be going north to York Factory to take the company ship out from York Factory to Stromness. Out of the money I have laid away from my winter's wages, we could buy passages for ourselves."

"Why would we want to go to Stromness?"

"From there we could take a passage on the first ship bound for Upper Canada. It seems a long way round, crossing back and forth over the ocean, but neither one of us knows enough about the wilderness to do it overland. Even with all that passage money paid out, we should still have enough left over to give us some kind of a start in Upper Canada, take a leasehold on a piece of land . . ."

"We already *own* a piece of land, on Point Douglas."

"It will make us a fine cemetery. Can you not see that each year the half-breeds and the North West Company have gone further? The first year they merely burnt us out and sent us away. But we came back, so the next year they killed twenty-two men before driving us off. What would it be this year? If you were them, do you not think you would be growing awfully weary of having us at their mercy and sending us away and then watching us come back again?"

"But Lord Selkirk is there now."

"Do you think they will be any more frightened of his coronet than they were of Robert Semple's piece of paper?"

"He has soldiers with him."

"How many? A hundred? Two hundred? How long do you think they would last? A soldier of the line is considered a dead shot if he can hit a man-sized target fifty yards away one time out of three. I saw what happened at Seven Oaks. They would . . . marching out with fixed bayonets in their red coats . . ." There seemed to be too many thoughts trying to push themselves out of his mouth at once. Sandy grew flustered and frustrated, and finally resolved it by yelling: "Would you seek to read *me* lessons about soldiering from all your long campaigns?"

Her temperature shot up, but she forced herself to keep quiet and just sat gazing across the clear rill of the river. The sun had dipped low enough to seep the first tinge of blood into the blue. At last her husband sighed and said much less belligerently, "That seems to be always the way with me. I get the impulses of human speech so jumbled together that all I can do is make animal noises. If you would like, I could try to list all the reasons why pretty European soldiers would be next to useless fighting the half-breeds, but you could just take my word for it. I might be willing to go back and fight if there was something to be gained by it. But they do say that suicide is a sin."

A bird started singing in the distance, a complex, trilling melody with grace notes so tightly packed together that they tumbled over one another and harmonized. Some meadowlark had overshot the prairies and nested in a clearing among the spruce thickets. There was nothing mournful in the song that might account for the hollow ache inside her. It was homesickness. But there had never been a meadowlark along Kildonan Burn. It was a sound she knew only from summer evenings on Point Douglas. She said: "After all you learned over the winter about building with wood, we could make a fine house this time."

"They have trees in Upper Canada. If anything, too many of them, from what I hear. We can make just as fine a house there."

"You were always so dead set against Upper Canada, right from the time Robert Gunn and my brother started parroting Duncan Cameron. What have you learned new that changed your mind about the place?"

"Nothing. All I know for certain about Upper Canada is what I knew then—that it is civilized enough to have magistrates and landed gentry. That is why I had no wish to go there—not after the Clearances. Not after I came all the way across the ocean to live free. But I am not strong enough. It is true that in Rupertsland there is no rooted-in system of magistrates and bailiffs and landowners to abuse us, neither is there one to protect us." He paused for a moment, then sighed wearily. "Perhaps I would still chance it if it was only me. I would have nothing to lose. One thing to be said for frontline soldiers, if there is a final disaster, they rarely have to live with the consequences. But you would."

"It is not up to you to decide what chances I want to take. I can decide that for myself."

"We neither of us can decide for ourselves anymore. We are no longer two people."

"You might try listening to yourself on that one."

He said indignantly: "I have been thinking of you all along."

"You have not. You have been thinking for me." She let that sit with him for a moment. She could see that if they argued much further, they would no longer be arguing over which was the best decision, they would only be arguing to win. She said: "It does seem to me that there is no need to pay out all that money on ship passages back and forth across the ocean. If we went back to Red River with Mister Pritchard, we could buy passages on one of the North West Company canoe brigades going to the Canadas. I am certain they would be more than happy to transport us out of Rupertsland. At the very worst, it could not cost us more than half of what all that ocean voyaging would."

He rubbed his chin and said: "That does make good sense. Very well, we will consider it settled, then."

She nodded, although in her mind the only thing that was settled was that they would get back home to Point Douglas. Then they would see.

CHAPTER 73

The third time in the year 1817 that Cuthbert Grant rode out from Fort Esperance to the Forks of the Red River, he rode in front of a hundred horsemen, all rambunctious with the joy of their sudden release from winter's imprisonment, running horse races up and down the sides of the column. Bethsy rode beside him, James bouncing on the pommel of his father's saddle or snoozing in a pannier behind his mother's. They established camp at the passage of the Assiniboine under a high bank that would protect them from artillery.

Twenty-five of the Des Meurons mercenaries marched over from Fort Douglas under a white flag. The inhabitants of the camp assembled in a kind of slouching crescent formation with the soldiers lined between the tips of the horns and Grant, Bethsy, Bostonais, and Falcon at the boss.

Captain D'Orsennens took three folded sheets of paper from his dispatch pouch. He started with the most beribboned and seal-adorned, unfolding it and reading in his parade-ground voice and eccentric pronunciation. Not surprisingly, it was another proclamation, but a very different one from all that had come before. This one hadn't been issued under the dubious authority of the governor of the Selkirk colony, or even the governor in chief of Upper and Lower Canada, but by the imperial Parliament of the Prince Regent in London. It ordered all British subjects in Rupertsland to cease and desist all acts of aggression involved in the mercantile war *now*. A royal commission was on its way to investigate the crimes that had already taken place.

Captain D'Orsennens refolded the proclamation carefully and replaced it in his dispatch pouch, then unfolded and read out his other two pieces of paper. These, which were much shorter and less elaborate, were warrants for the arrest of Joseph Cadotte and

Cuthbert Grant. Once they'd been read out, D'Orsennens put them back with the proclamation and marched across the narrow patch of prairie between the mercenaries' line and the apex of the métis crescent. Grant stood with his arms crossed, watching the lines around the captain's eyes growing steadily sharper, waiting for the sudden gleam of returning sanity. It didn't come. D'Orsennens marched right up to him, took hold of Grant's left arm above the elbow, and tugged it forward as though to lead him away.

Grant swung his arm out, sweeping the hand off. The captain stumbled backward, his arms pinwheeling to maintain his balance. Grant drew one of the pistols from his sash and pulled back the hammer. The air was filled with a loud rustling and staccato clicking as the men around him cocked their own guns. The mercenaries leveled their muskets, a straight line of round black dots above the gleam of bayonet points. Everyone was moving very slowly and deliberately, like toy figures in jelly. If they started shooting, both sides would be firing into a densely packed mass ten paces in front of them, and Bethsy and James were in the middle of it.

Captain D'Orsennens recovered his balance and stood trapped between the two lines, flicking his eyes between his soldiers and Grant. At last there was a gleam of recognition that he was not confronting some unruly batch of rioters with an uncivilized bully for a ringleader. It was a little late.

In as calm a voice as he could muster, Grant said, "If you will withdraw your soldiers from the camp now, and return to your fort, Mister Cadotte and I will surrender ourselves into your custody in two days' time, to answer all accusations against us."

Captain D'Orsennens took about three seconds, to give the impression he was thinking it over, then marched his men away. Not even Bostonais complained that Grant had sidestepped that fight.

Bethsy was especially tender to him that night. When they were lying side by side looking at the stars through the smokehole at the apex of the tent, she said: "Do you think they'll hold you in custody for long?"

"In custody?"

"At the fort, after you and Joseph give yourselves up."

"Oh. No, not long at all, since I'm not going in."

"You told the captain . . ."

"If I hadn't told him that, my dear, you and I would not be lying here—we would be lying outside shot to *rubaboo* with the wolves and the ravens fighting over the pieces. I doubt there would have been enough of our men left alive to give us a decent burial. Certainly there wouldn't be any of theirs left.''

"You gave him your word.''

"MacDonell gave me his word in three separate written dispatches that he had no intention of laying charges against me. D'Orsennens marched in here under a flag of truce—to my knowledge a truce doesn't include leveling muskets at someone and placing him under arrest. I'm quite certain that D'Orsennens knew I was lying, but it gave him an excuse to get the hell away before we all got butchered.''

She didn't say anything, but it was obvious from her posture that he hadn't exactly put her at ease. He said: "If I were to surrender, the instant I got across the threshold MacDonell would clap me in irons, throw together some kind of trumped-up tribunal, and hang me from the gates. Only a fool attempts to act honorably with dishonorable men.''

"You didn't use to talk like that.''

"I didn't use to know that self-appointed Moses figures like MacDonell believe they have a divine dispensation to employ any perfidy they choose against the Canaanites. If I'd truly wanted to respond in kind, I would have waited until they'd turned to march away and blown the lot of them to hell with one volley.'' That didn't appear to satisfy her, either. He could spend all night trying to explain what she would never understand if she wasn't going to take him on faith to begin with. He rolled over and closed his eyes, but neither one of them slept.

In the morning he got an explanation for MacDonell's abrupt reversion to high-handed policy: the Earl of Selkirk had started south from Bas de la Rivière with another fifty of the Des Meurons mercenaries and seven British regulars. Those seven soldiers of the line had been the only troops the Earl had managed to pry out of the governor in chief of His Britannic Majesty's North American colonies, thanks to concerted pressure from William MacGillivray and assorted friends of the North West Company. And those seven soldiers had been assigned to him for one reason only—because no reasonably ambitious member of the foreign service wanted a dead peer on his hands without having provided at least some token protection. Selkirk, with just that token bodyguard, could have been neutralized if there hadn't been a leftover regiment of out-of-work Swiss mercenaries pawning their buckles in the taverns of Montreal. As soon as MacGillivray had got word of that, the North West Company had descended to outbid him. They'd managed to hire away a portion of the regiment, but Selkirk had hung on to the rest.

From his base camp on the Assiniboine, Grant had no trouble at all keeping track of events inside Fort Douglas. The soldiers weren't much for taking care of themselves, so MacDonell had had to hire métis hunters and cooks and laundresses. Grant knew almost before MacDonell did that Chief Peguis was bringing in his warriors to formally ally themselves with the colony. Grant saw that the word got around to the other tribes. A Cree chief named Sonnant drifted into the camp at the Assiniboine with a war party of his own. Up until now the Plains tribes had avoided choosing sides in the companies' war, but now that the Saulteaux had made a move, all bets were off. Grant made a number of grand speeches to Sonnant and presented him with his sword. He could always get another.

The Earl of Selkirk arrived at Fort Douglas, and his private army dug itself in. The North West Company was again faced with the problem of getting its harvest of furs and provisions out past Point Douglas. There was no moored gunboat like last year, but MacDonell kept bonfires burning on both sides of the river all night long and lined the banks with mercenaries. Finally, the North West Company—in the person of Angus Shaw, a partner whose son William had been one of the original half-breed lieutenants—struck a deal. The Earl was perfectly willing to let the North West Company brigades go by and pass out of the country so long as no one who had taken a hand in the depredations of last year—and in particular a certain Cuthbert Grant—went with them. The brigade set off, with all the North West Company officers in the vicinity piled on board, leaving the armies of the New Nation and the Selkirk colony staring at each other across a swatch of open prairie.

The evening after the brigades embarked, Grant was sitting on the bank of the Assiniboine with Bethsy, watching James paddle in the mud. He hadn't had much time for either of them over the past few days, but he had made a point of telling Bethsy to expect that when she'd said she wouldn't stay at Esperance this time.

He pulled a stick of driftwood out from between two rocks and whacked the mud with it. He said: "It doesn't make sense. For four years the company has been telling me—telling us—that if we don't stand together and drag this colony out by the roots, the country will be stolen away from us. But here we have Selkirk and his soldiers firmly ensconced in their fort, and the whole pack that we banished last year merrily rowing back from Jack River—and sud-

denly the company seems perfectly content to let them stay in possession of the Forks so long as they don't interfere with the orderly
pursuit of business.''

"That surprises you?''

"You can't deny that there's a certain graphic inconsistency in—
Of course! In strategic terms the first necessity is to see to it that
the provisions get to the outposts, and once that's been accomplished we can turn our attention to rooting out the colony. I don't
see why Mister Shaw couldn't simply have explained that to me to
begin—''

Bethsy scooped up James and carried him wailing up the bank.
Grant asked where she was going. She said: "Don't forget he's
only a child. If left to himself, he'll flounder in out of his depth.''

Word came out that the Earl of Selkirk was negotiating a treaty
with Chief Peguis, the first Indian land treaty west of the Great
Lakes. Selkirk wanted to secure every possible facet of legitimacy
for his colony. There was a certain controversy, though, that Selkirk
didn't know about—namely, that the Sioux and Cree and Assiniboine who had been spearing each other back and forth across the
Forks of the Red for generations didn't quite know how a Saulteaux
Chief like Peguis got the right to sign the land away.

Bostonais Pangman saddled up his horse one morning to ride
over to Peguis's camp and have a conversation with him. Grant
asked him if he wanted any company. "Naw. We'll just have a little
talk, old Peguis and me.''

Bostonais walked his horse into the circle of wigwams on the
meadow behind Fort Douglas and called one of the women to bring
him a burning twig from her cooking fire to light his pipe. He sat
on his horse blowing smoke rings. The Chief's pipestem bearer
came out of the council lodge and said that the Chief would be glad
to welcome him inside. "Nope. I'll wait.''

The Chief let him wait for as long as it took the sun to move half
its width across the sky, and then he came out. "Ho, Bostonais,
my cousin!''

"Chief.''

"Why do you not come in and smoke tobacco? The sun is hot.''

"Naw. Too much talk for not much to say.''

"What does my cousin Bostonais wish to say to me?''

"Heard about your treaty. Sonnant, Kayajieskabin, some other
Chiefs, they heard, too. Makes them sore here—'' He whomped
one boulder paw against the left slab of his chest.

"It makes my heart sore, cousin, to hear their hearts are sore.

Why does it make them sad that I make peace with the Silver Chief
Selkirk?''

Bostonais leaned down to knock his pipe out against the side of
his stirrup and murmured: ''If you keep squirting shit out your top
hole, I'm going to guess you're standing on your head and turn you
over. You know why they're sore.''

Peguis rubbed his upper lip under where his nose used to be and
said: ''The earth is wide, cousin. Who can say from one day to the
next where the land of one Chief ends and another begins? The
Miskouseipi has many Chiefs who claim to own it.''

Bostonais scratched the mouthpiece of his pipe against his chin
and said: ''Seems to me we got a problem. Also seems to me if
there wasn't any Saulteaux, there wouldn't be a problem.'' He put
his pipe back in his pouch, turned his horse around, and walked it
out of the camp.

In his next parley with Lord Selkirk, Chief Peguis announced
that there were other local Chiefs who should be consulted on the
treaty. In the end, five Chiefs drew their pictographs at the bottom
of a piece of paper that guaranteed them an annual payment of two
hundred pounds of tobacco, in exchange for which they ceded to
Lord Selkirk the land on both banks of the Red River and the
Assiniboine as far inland as could be seen from under the belly of
a horse on a clear day.

On the afternoon of the fifth of July, the Earl of Selkirk marched
his soldiers out of Fort Douglas and lined them up in parade order
along the green crest of the riverbank. Half a dozen *canots du nord*
rounded the tip of Point Douglas. A shirt-sized Union Jack flapped
at the prow of the lead canoe. A handful of red-coated soldiers
were dotted in among the gaudy voyageurs.

Captain D'Orsennens snapped his soldiers to attention. The Earl
and Governor MacDonell strode down to the landing stage to welcome the royal commission.

The canoes didn't swerve toward the landing stage. The paddlers
didn't alter their stroke. The passengers didn't turn their heads to
the bank. The canoes skimmed straight on by. They landed a couple
of miles upstream at the Forks and established a camp on the open
ground where Fort Gibraltar had stood. In the evening an envoy
arrived at Fort Douglas to inform the Earl that the commission had
set up shop at the Forks and would begin taking depositions in the
morning. Another envoy bore the same message to the métis camp
on the Assiniboine.

Grant didn't like it. It was patently absurd that a handful of men should roll in from two thousand miles away, sporting fancy titles bestowed by some gilded authority another three thousand miles away, and presume that the wild nomads of the plains would lay down their guns and come twisting their hats for approval. The disturbing part was that a great many of his *jeunes gens* seemed eager to do just that.

For two days he listened to the stories of those returning from giving their depositions. Each one was progressively more impressed with this manifestation of interest from the outside world, progressively more eager to be judged. On the evening of the second day he started packing up his traveling gear and instructed Bethsy to do the same. "I've given the order to break up camp and head back to the Qu'Appelle. There's nothing more we can do here at present."

"What about the commissioner?"

"What about him? He has no power over our comings and goings. The sooner everybody realizes that, the better."

"But you haven't given your deposition yet."

"I have no intention of giving a deposition. Do you think if I don't, the commissioner will snap his fingers and a British army will materialize out of the ground and come chasing after us?"

She hesitated for a moment, then said cautiously: "If you have done nothing wrong, you have nothing to fear."

He threw the pannier he was packing onto the floor and said: "I have done nothing wrong. And if I had, it would not be up to some stranger to pass judgment on it, dropping in out of the clouds onto a country he's never seen before. The royal commission is a royal irrelevancy."

"Doesn't it seem that by running away you make yourself appear guilty?"

"To whom? To you? Do you want to get in on the judging? Do you imagine that the month you've spent lolling about in this camp and the rumors you heard back on the Qu'Appelle give you a perfect knowledge of what happened here last year?"

"Am I an irrelevancy as well?"

"Of course not. You're the mother of my son." He realized after the fact that that didn't exactly convey the impression he'd intended. He put his hands on her shoulders. "By which I mean that you are the great love of my life, otherwise you wouldn't be the mother of my son." That didn't seem to do it, either. But there were a lot of things outside their tent that had to be attended to if he hoped to get the column on the move by morning. He kissed her on the forehead and went off to attend to them.

By the time the sun had worked its way up half its ascending arc, they were halfway to Portage la Prairie. Grant rode in front as always, with Bethsy to his left holding James, and Falcon and Bostonais on either side of them. Behind them, the blue-and-white standard snapped overhead on the pole Alex Fraser carried. Behind that rode the cavalry of the New Nation.

In front of Grant the prairie rolled away in its early summer green, not yet cooked brittle by the sun. It seemed as though his body and his mind had grown encrusted with cobwebs during the long weeks crouched on the bank of the Assiniboine. The clean wind and the jouncing thrust of his horse were finally sweeping them away. If he wished to, he could let his horse's hooves keep chewing up the miles, past the headwaters of the Qu'Appelle and up to the High Plains, picking up the brothers and cousins and uncles of the hundred dark-eyed, laughing boys behind him. He was certain there wasn't a force between Red River and the Shining Mountains that could stand against them. He was quite sure there wasn't one man in all the wide world, up to the fat Prince Regent himself, who wouldn't be getting the better of the bargain by changing places with him.

Firmin Boucher galloped up from the rear of the column. "There's someone behind us, riding hard, trying to catch up."

"Go back and see who it is. Don't get yourself shot."

Near noon Boucher came galloping up again. "It's Mister Coltman, the commissioner."

"Alone?" Grant eased his horse to a walk. The thudding of hooves behind him slowed and softened. "What does he want?"

"He asks could we go back to the Forks—at least them that haven't yet told him their stories about what happened last year. He says he knows we have to go and hunt to feed ourselves, but he's got to start back east soon or the freeze-up's going to catch him on the Ottawa. He says if we go back, he'll make Selkirk give us supplies out of the fort for the time we stay."

"He says a great deal for a man who isn't here."

"Well, his horse was tired, so I told him to walk it slow and breathe it out and I'd get you to stop and wait."

By now Grant had halted, and the riders behind had clustered forward to surround him and Boucher. Grant said: "Unfortunately you'll have to inform him that he's winded his horse for nothing. I have nothing to say to his royal commission."

François Deschamps said: "I haven't told him what I know yet."

Falcon said: "It does seem a shame if he's willing to go to all the trouble to ride that hard to catch us and make Selkirk feed us, that we can't give him a few days."

"Suit yourselves. I feel no obligation to explain myself to strangers."

He flicked his horse lightly with his reins. The horsemen in front of him jostled aside to let him pass, and Bethsy followed along behind. Bostonais and Falcon fell in, along with Alex Fraser and a handful of others, but even some of them kept glancing back over their shoulders. There was a sudden drumming of hoofbeats that receded as three-quarters of the column galloped toward the royal commissioner. Grant narrowed his eyes to keep the wetness from overtopping the brims of his lower lids.

CHAPTER 74

Kate was working the companion oar to her husband's on the half-waterlogged relic of a York boat that had been salvaged from Jack River to round out the complement of boats needed to ferry them back. The long stretch and pull through her arms and back gave a pleasant feeling of aliveness, but she couldn't keep at it for longer than an hour at a time. Oversized or not, there still wasn't man's bulk to her bones, so her muscles had to work harder and tired more quickly. They had only a few miles left to Fort Douglas, though, and she'd decided she could keep it up until then.

Suddenly Sandy stopped rowing. She followed his lead, levering her oar out of the water and resting it on the oarlock. Sandy had craned his head over his shoulder to look at the shore. The other men were still rowing. The steersman hollered at the Point Douglas Sutherlands in his Orkney Gaelic: "What are you doing?"

"What are *you* doing?" Sandy shouted back. "We still have several miles to go yet."

The steersman, leaning hard against his sweep to angle them in toward the shore, said: "I am only following Mister Pritchard." The lead boat, with John Pritchard in the prow, had already beached its nose and was being drawn up onto the sandy bank of Frog Plain, just south of Seven Oaks Creek.

The rest of the rowers shipped their oars now as the momentum of their last stroke carried them in to shore. The men on the bow benches leaped out and hauled the prow up onto the bank. Sandy turned around to look inland but stayed poised in a crouch with one knee on his bench and one hand clutching the gunwale, staring fixedly at the grassy meadow and the woods flanking the creek as though he expected something to leap out of them. Kate put her hand on his arm. It felt as though the muscle were about to jump off the bone.

He twitched his arm out of her grip and vaulted over the gunwale, landing only a few steps from where he'd leaped into the river with bullets whizzing past his head. John Pritchard was standing at the crest of the bank, staring at the long, low mound of stones in the middle of the meadow. Sandy grabbed his shoulder and spun him around, shouting in English: "Pritchard! What the hell do you think you are about landing us here?"

Mister Pritchard looked to be a bit taken aback by his own reaction to the place. He murmured a bit dazedly: "You're right, of course, I never should've . . . it was . . . it was not my idea. There were arrangements made. And the fact is there are only one or two of us here who were there—that is, here then, that is . . . Come along, there's someone coming to meet us." He turned and called down at those who were still lingering by the boats: "No, no—leave your baggage in the boats. They'll be towed to the fort later."

Kate took her blanket-wrapped bundle nonetheless, and her husband's bundle of clothing and hand tools and rag-wrapped fiddle. She carried them up the bank and handed his over to him. He seemed a touch ashamed now of the reaction he'd had and was trying to put a stoic face on it. It had caught him by surprise. His reaction to the place had caught her by surprise. She would've thought that all his years of soldiering would have steeled him to such memories—except in fever dreams. She liked him a little better for proving them mistaken.

The flotsam of the boat train trailed behind Mister Pritchard in a ragtag, drawn-out procession, across the meadow and into the woods, past the weeded-over patches between the trees where stumps of charred clay chimneys showed through willow wands and stands of fireweed. The first field their path intersected was ex-Sergeant Alex MacBeth's. They all stopped there. Instead of the riot of wild growth they had expected, there was a half acre of green-white barley nodding knee high in the sunlight.

From the far side of the field a lone man came wading through the rippling green toward them. He was tall and thin, with silver hair and a trace of a stoop. He was wearing a travel-abused blue broadcloth cutaway coat with a white frilled neckcloth spilling over his waistcoat. Kate dug her fingers into her husband's arm.

No one said a word, and for a moment no one moved except the man walking toward them. Then one man put his hand up to his head and tugged his bonnet off, then another and another. The women drew their shawls up to cover their heads. Some of it might have been the bred-in crofters' knee jerk to a laird, but the fact was that this was the one man in the world who had held his hand out to them when they had been driven off their crofts and left to starve. Most of them wouldn't have been much more awed if Jesus Christ had come walking across the Red River to greet them.

He shook hands with Mister Pritchard and then moved forward to the nearest of his colonists, who happened to be Sandy Sutherland. The Earl extended his hand shyly and said in Gaelic: "Thomas Douglas, of Selkirk."

Sandy shook the hand gingerly, as though afraid it might break, and fumbled out: "Alexander, Sutherland, sir . . . of Point Douglas."

"Welcome home, Mister Sutherland." The Earl turned to Kate. "And you would be . . . ?"

"Catherine Ma—*Sutherland*, sir." She gave him a clumsy curtsy when he took her hand. She let go of his hand quickly—it felt as soft as a swan's wing and made her ashamed of her callused-padded paw. It didn't occur to her that the feel of her hard-worn hand might make the Earl ashamed of his life of privilege.

The crowd pressed forward and surrounded him, jamming tightly against each other but leaving an open circle an arm's length wide around him. They reached out their hands across it: "Alexander MacBeth, sir, regimental sergeant major, Seventy-third, retired." "Eppy Bannerman, milord." "John Matheson, Your Lordship."

He no longer shook their hands, merely allowed his to be pressed, giving out quick, curt nods and inarticulate syllables from behind tightly closed lips. Anyone with any delicacy now avoided letting the Earl's eyes catch theirs, glancing away when his gaze drifted in their direction and only moving back to him when his had traveled

on to someone else. That way they could look their fill at him and
he at them without either of them having to acknowledge the tear
streaming down his face.

They were all given temporary billets at Fort Douglas until they
had settled themselves onto their home farms—excepting, of course,
the Point Douglas Sutherlands, who would be lodging at Fort
Douglas but had only come back to find passage to Upper Canada.

Kate was crossing the parade square when she saw Marie Anne
coming out of one of the barracks buildings, carrying a sheaf of
loose papers in one hand and a pen and ink bottle in the other. She
called to her, but Marie Anne kept on walking. She hurried after
her and called again. Marie Anne stopped and squared her shoulders, then turned around to face her. Kate reached out her hands
to grab Marie Anne's, but since they were filled she took hold of
her forearms instead. The elbows jerked back as though to pull
themselves free. Kate said: "You are safe!"

"*Oui*—yes." There was something artificial in the sound of her
voice. "So are you, too—safe."

"And Jean Baptiste?"

"Oh, yes. He, too, is safe. He did . . . *rètourne*, at the autumn."
Her head kept bobbing sideways, looking over her shoulder, although Kate couldn't see anything particularly interesting to look
at beyond the polyglot bustle of soldiers and newly returned colonists. Suddenly Marie Anne seemed to come to some decision and
focused her eyes squarely on Kate for the first time. She blurted:
"There was no thing else I could do. What would you do? There
was my children. Peguis, he telled me *les bois brulés* were kill
everything here. What else would I to do?"

"Else? When? Do what?"

"When I snucked away. After La Grenouillière. I would not be
able to save you, but my children, yes. What would you do?"

Kate began to understand. She said: "Of course. What else could
you do?" But it came out stiffly. She let go of Marie Anne's elbows
and looked down at the sheaf of papers. "What are the papers?"

"I am make a *pétition*, to your Lord de Selkirk, to give to us a
church and priests. Les Des Meurons, the soldiers, many of them
are Christians—Catholics—so I go to them to put their names on,
too. They are to stay here now, les Des Meurons, because your
Lord de Selkirk give them lands to farm here, so from now we do
be safe all way."

They stood there awkwardly, looking past each other, trying to think of something else to say. Marie Anne said: "So now what do you do? Do you mean to stay here on yourself . . . alone?"

"Alone?"

"What I mean to say"—Marie Anne looked down—"do you mean to make your farm alone . . . a widow?"

"A widow?" Kate didn't mean to sound as though she were mocking her, parroting everything she said, but she couldn't understand what Marie Anne was trying to say. Suddenly it came to her. "Alexander! No, he came back safe. I found him, the day after you—"

"He was not kill?"

"No."

Marie Anne flung her arms around her neck, papers and all, spouting a cascade of French that was much too fast for Kate to follow, except for *le bon Dieu* and *ma chère Katerine*.

At last Marie Anne let go of her and stepped back, smoothing out her papers. "Well, I must go on now—more name. I am politics now, yes?"

Kate nodded and said: *"Tu es politique."*

Marie Anne blushed and bobbed her head. They went their separate ways.

Kate carried on to the sway-backed old troop tent that she and her husband had been appointed to share with the MacBeth tribe. There was no one there. The MacBeths would probably be upriver looking over their property and assessing the damage. Sandy might have gone to Colony House or any of a dozen other places, but there was one place she hoped he had gone.

She went out through the fort gates and turned north along the cart track through the woods. The little path that used to wind off it onto Point Douglas had vanished under spear grass and thistles. But someone had turned off in that direction recently. Two parallel lines showed clearly through the thigh-high growth, grass stalks bent outward where the legs had brushed them aside and broken where the feet had come down. She followed the trail onto the tongue of land that had so imperceptibly wormed its way into her heart.

Just in past the first stand of trees, the trail suddenly veered off to the left. It led into a circle about eight feet in diameter. The grass was thoroughly beaten down, as though the circuit had been walked several times. She couldn't make sense of it until she realized that this would be approximately the spot where they had made love on coming home from Jack River last summer.

She followed the trail where it wound away from the circle, feeling a bit of a blush warming her cheeks. He had continued on up the point, to the low log shed they had lived in for one winter. The half-breeds hadn't bothered to burn it, merely left it to collapse under the workings of the seasons. With no one living in it to perform the day-to-day repairs and maintenance, the door had fallen off its hinges and the roof sods had sprouted into a weed bed slanting in crazily at the middle.

Behind the shanty was the stack of squared beams meant for the new house. The outer ones were bleached and cracking from a year of lying unattended. The corner of the house that they had managed to get up last spring had been pulled down, likely by horsemen looping ropes up over the tops of the post beams. Grasses and sweet clover and hazel wands stood tall between the tumbled beams. The tangle of growth was reft with a complex system of bent and broken stalks; he had walked back and forth a good deal between the house site and the stacks of lumber. He had turned over one of the fallen beams, showing a damp, matted, brown and gray and slick white bed where a few crawling things were still wriggling to escape from the light.

She followed his track on toward the river. When she reached the crest of the bank she saw him, crouched on a flat rock among the cobbled mud of the shoreline, peering intently into the reeds. Most of their property's riverfront made up the lee shore of the current's bend around the point, leaving a broad fringe of water reeds and bullrushes with a bed of lily pads floating beyond.

As she picked her way down the bank, he turned his head and held up his hand in a shushing gesture. She took off her shoes and came closer cautiously, wet clay oozing up between her toes. He motioned her to bend down beside him and pointed into the shallows.

Barely six feet in front of them, under a canopy of arcing cattails, was a bird with a black-and-white barred back, riding very low in the water. It had red eyes, a satiny green-black head, and a black saber beak. The green of its cowl wound down around its speckled throat like a band of ribbon on a jeweled choker. It was peering intently into the muddy water, but a pair of fuzzy chicks kept paddling in under its chin and distracting it.

The mother bird arched her neck and cracked open her beak, showing a flicking, pointed tongue, and flung out a wild, warbling woodwind laugh that echoed back maniacally. Kate had heard loons sing before, she had even heard them harmonizing with the wolves and each other on the lakes around Jack River, but never from six feet away in broad daylight. It startled her so completely that she lost her balance and fell backward, letting out a stupid little whoop. When her eyes opened again from the impact blink of smacking down on wet clay, the loon had swung her tail toward them, and the chicks were clambering up onto their mother's back. It shot off into the reeds and disappeared.

Sandy stood up laughing, despite the fact that he had to brace his right knee with both hands to get back on his feet. Once he was up he offered her his hand, and they went up the bank. He sat down on the stack of beams, plucked a stalk of grass, and rolled it back and forth along the tips of his teeth. She sat beside him. He said, "You know that . . ." and then trailed off, although his eyes stayed focused into the distance and his fingers kept rolling the grass stalk.

After a minute or two had passed in silence, she said: "I know that what?"

He shifted the grass stalk into the corner of his mouth and said, with some effort: "You know that I do not much like going back on my stated word, no more than you do . . . and I am afraid that this is going to seem to you like I am bobbing back and forth like a cork in a bucket . . . but since we are here now . . . and since the half-breeds and the North West Company seem to have decided now to leave us to ourselves . . . and since Lord Selkirk seems to have put the colony on a firmer footing than ever it was before . . . and since the crops that were left in the fields last year appear to have reseeded themselves . . . well, I have been thinking that perhaps we might just as well stay on here, for at least one more year, and see if we can make a home here."

He moved the grass stalk back to the middle of his mouth and rolled the end of it back and forth across his tongue. She thought of saying, "Oh, have you now?" and making him talk her into it. She thought of saying, "Whatever you think is best, dear,"—she could always laugh about it with the other women when they traded stories of married life. What she did say was: "Why do you think I persuaded you to come this way to get to Upper Canada instead of taking the ship from Hudson's Bay?"

He stopped rolling the grass stalk between his fingers, then took it out of his mouth and tied it into a bow. He said: "I do hope that in years to come you will grow to appreciate the wisdom of the decisions I have made for us."

CHAPTER 75

Commissioner William B. Coltman heaved his not inconsiderable bulk onto his stumpy little legs and commenced to stump around on them. The latest colonist to walk over from the fort to give a deposition droned on in his Gaelic-lilted English, the pen nib of the clerk on duty scratched across the foolscap, the flies buzzed, and the river rippled along maddeningly—maddeningly because it would not do at all for a royal commissioner to rip off his pantaloons and boots and waistcoat and hurl his barrel-bellied body buck naked off the bank, no matter how hot the sun or how dusty dry the air. The clerks had followed his instructions and set up their traveling desk in the shade of the only tree in the vicinity large and leafy enough to be worthy of the name. But over the course of the morning the shadow had shortened and swung away from them.

It was supposed to have been a two-man commission, but Lieutenant Colonel Fletcher had dropped off at Sault Ste. Marie, along with the bulk of the military escort. Coltman didn't mourn the loss. Whether Lieutenant Colonel Fletcher had been driven to drink by insanity or driven insane by drink, the result was still a revolting human being—although it did leave him to do the job of two men on his own.

For four weeks now he'd been taking depositions concerning shootings, kidnappings, river piracy, fistfights, forcible confinements, wholesale arson, and a list of grandiose proclamations issued in the name of every trumped-up assumption of legal authority the human mind could fabricate. They had been having themselves a high old time out here in the fur country, no question about it. The clerks had recorded verbatim the statements of bald-faced liars, befuddled paragons of honesty, and not a few individuals who would have found a way to convince themselves that they were the injured parties if they'd sold their children to a whoremaster for beer money. When the day's depositions were done he would spend the evening compiling them all into a massive report that would eventually be submitted to Sir John Sherbrooke in the Colonial Office in London, adding a terse marginal note here and there such as: "Michael Heden's memory does not appear to be entirely trustworthy."

The pattern that had emerged so far was labyrinthine, a tangle of clearly drawn paths leading to a large void at the center. The void went under the name of Cuthbert Grant. Grant was at Fort La Souris. Coltman had sent him numerous invitations to come and testify, but there had been no response. Coltman had considered riding to La Souris, but there was every possibility that Grant would be gone by the time he got there, or would refuse to see him, or would put a bullet through his head, which would be perfectly in character according to some of the depositions.

With or without a deposition from Cuthbert Grant, Coltman knew he'd already done a thorough enough job to secure himself a judgeship when he got back to the Canadas. That was the only logical reason for a man of his mature years to have dragged his impressive belly across two thousand miles of the nastiest traveling this side of the Limpopo. The purpose of the royal commission was to amass information, and he'd certainly done that. But Billy Coltman was something more than a mere amasser of paper—he was a disentangler and a puzzle solver who delighted in examining the quirkier facets of human interaction.

In the distance he could see two horsemen riding in from the west, the heat waves alternately elongating them or squashing them flat. It was a damned deceptive country. At first glance it seemed that any large object moving across the prairie was as inescapably nailed to the eye as a cue ball on a billiard green. Then suddenly the object would vanish, dipping down into an unseen gully as though the earth had taken a notion to unbutton itself for an instant and then just as quickly fastened itself closed again.

Coltman had a sudden curious sensation about those two riders. And he didn't trust curious sensations—they usually proved to owe more to digestion than premonition. He stumped back to his camp stool and dragged it over to the tree trunk so he could sit in the shade and have something solid to lean against.

By the time the last colonist had finished his halting recollection of the second arrest of Duncan Cameron, the commissioner had become insensible to anything except the smell of roast duck wafting over from the cooking fire. He thanked the good man on behalf of the Crown and bustled over to the muslin-sided tent where he took his meals.

He was in the act of kissing adieu to the last of the good Bordeaux when he saw his corporal of the guard come marching across the meadow escorting a dusky young man in a resplendently quill-worked fringed jacket. The young man was marched up to the front flap of the awning, and then the corporal said, "Wait here," and stooped to get his bearskin busby through the awning.

The young man said: "No."

The corporal of the guard stopped cold in midstoop. He disentangled his busby from the awning and turned back to the young man, who said in a perfectly level, calm voice: "I am willing to abide by formalities, but don't give me orders."

The thrill that went up Coltman's spine was exactly the same as when a brook trout leaped at his hook after a day of fruitless casting. He bolted out of his chair and scooted his little legs over to the entrance flap. "That will be all, Corporal. Thank you."

"Sir, this gentleman was—"

"Thank you, Corporal."

The corporal of the guard saluted smartly and marched back to his post. The commissioner turned his gaze upon the young man. The young man looked back at him. Coltman knew that the muslin scrim between them, combined with the fact that the young man was standing in the sun while he was shadowed by the tent roof, would make him by far the hazier figure. Which meant that he had a few seconds to give him a good going over without being offensive.

The young man was somewhat above average height, a good half a head taller than Coltman even in moccasins. There was a deceptive breadth and depth to his upper body that made him appear shorter from a distance and a springiness in the way he held himself that contradicted the weight. The head was quite large, the features regular and smooth but heavy-boned. The eyes were quite black and opaque, with an almost ingenuous directness to them that might easily be read as insolence—especially by someone who expected deference from those of tenderer years or darker complexions. All in all, the initial impression was contradictory, to say the least.

Coltman pushed the entrance flap aside with his left hand and stepped outside with his right hand extended, saying: "You would be Mister Grant."

Grant shook his hand. Surprisingly, Coltman found Grant's hand not much larger than his own. "You would be Mister Coltman."

"It's an honor and a pleasure to meet you at last." A flicker crossed Grant's face. Coltman footnoted: 'Suspicious of flattery;

hought they said he was twenty-three?', but carried on: ''I thought
here were two of you.''

''Two of me?''

''I saw two riders coming in from the west. Wasn't that you?''

Grant grinned, the naked flash of a naïf's good humor. ''You
lon't miss a great deal, do you?''

''Far too much, invariably.'' Coltman was pleased nonetheless,
hen wondered who was flattering whom.

''The other rider was my associate, Mister Pangman.''

''Peter Pangman—that they call Bostonais?''

''Just so. He's waiting for me elsewhere.''

''He would be perfectly welcome to wait here in the camp. My
·rderly would be delighted to furnish him with such poor comforts
.s we have at our disposal. For that matter, I am almost as eager
o interview Mister Pangman as you.''

''Perhaps at a later date—Mister Pangman had other affairs to
ttend to today.''

''Ah. Are you pressed for time, then?''

''Not immediately. Mister Pangman won't be expecting me to
ejoin him before dusk. I don't imagine he'll become impatient
efore nightfall.''

''You don't trust me, Mister Grant.''

''I don't know you, Mister Coltman.''

''Well, do come in out of the sun. I'm afraid I was just saying
he obsequies over the last ounce of Bordeaux. We'll have to make
o with vin ordinaire.''

Twilight was setting in by the time Grant got up to leave. There
vas more than one dry-bottomed wine bottle lolling on the table.
Coltman was a bit leery of what he might find in the last few pages
·f the deposition—during the last hour Grant had insisted on pour-
ıg wine out for the recording clerk as well. But he could face that
ı the morning.

The commissioner walked out under the stars—bright against a
obalt glaze in the eastern cosmos—to clear his head before turning
ı. There was no question that he'd been charmed and delighted by
is afternoon with Mister Grant, and disarmed by his complete lack
·f evasiveness. There was no question that Grant was an extremely
:eductive young man. The question was whether he was a seducer.

If Grant was, in fact, as forthright and generous-hearted as he
ppeared to be, then he was as much a victim of circumstances and
1anipulation as the men he'd killed at Seven Oaks. Some of the
·ther crimes he was accused of, such as the cold-blooded murder

of a Selkirk colonist named Owen Keveney, just didn't fit into tha
scenario, but it was within the realm of possibility. If, however
Grant's performance over the course of the afternoon had been a
lie fabricated to disarm and charm the royal commission, the
Cuthbert Grant was the most diabolically accomplished Machia
vellian cutthroat that this royal commissioner had ever seen—and
he'd met a few in his time.

For his own purposes, Coltman would have been more than con
tent to spend a long period of observation unraveling the knot. A
his time of life it was quite a pleasant surprise to stumble across
such a baffling and intriguing specimen. Unfortunately, Sir John
Sherbrooke and the Colonial Office needed a concrete recommen
dation immediately. If they meant to have any hope at all of ending
these embarrassing disruptions in a territory that was supposedl
under their jurisdiction, they would have to come up with a policy
for Cuthbert Grant. The influence he had over the half-breeds and
Indians was remarkable; although he himself had pointed out to
Coltman that there was a vast difference between influence and
control. So far as Coltman was concerned, given a self-willed, self
sufficient population roaming free and armed across a stretch of
open country roughly the size of the European continent, "influ
ence" was about as much as anyone was going to get.

At this point, though, all that the royal commission could hon
estly report was that Cuthbert Grant was either a very frank and
ingenuous young man or a very nasty bit of goods indeed, although
either way he was undoubtedly a very dangerous individual. Colt
man suddenly stopped his riverbank pacing, cocked his head to one
side, and played that thought back again. When it came right down
to it, he didn't have to solve the puzzle of young Mister Grant in
order to make his recommendation to Sherbrooke, because either
way the recommendation would be the same. In the current situa
tion in the *pays d'en haut*, Grant was the ace of trumps, and the
Colonial Office couldn't afford to leave him shuffled loose among
the pack. If he couldn't be co-opted into their own hand, he would
have to be eliminated.

Grant and Bostonais made a leisurely jaunt of the trip back to
La Souris, camping early in the evening and rolling out of their
blankets long after the sun was up. On the afternoon of the third
day they were riding through the sand hills, pretty and treacherou
country of scrub oaks and grassy sage clinging to shifting dunes
What had been a solid trail last year might now be drifted over with

ine sand that a horse's hooves sunk into and slid through. A few
wrong turns and a traveler could find himself in the middle of a
desert where the sand had won out completely.

There was a flock of sandhill cranes along a marshy stream,
striding tall and dignified and stabbing at the ground for frogs. They
stopped their horses and sat watching the big birds. Bostonais said:
"So, what do you think?"

It took Grant a moment to figure out that Bostonais wasn't asking
about the cranes. Over the past couple of summers, Grant had lost
touch with Bostonais's habit of letting a conversation trail off and
then picking it up again ten miles farther on. They had been talking
over Mister Coltman's proposition. The commissioner wanted Grant
and Bostonais to accompany the witnesses, plaintiffs, and defen-
dants he was taking back to Montreal for a series of hearings sched-
uled over the winter. Grant shrugged and said: "He promises the
trials will be fair and impartial."

"Do you trust him?"

"It's difficult to judge on such short acquaintance. But he is a
skeptic, so . . ."

"A what?"

"A skeptic. Someone who would introduce his father as 'This
is the man who my mother tells me is . . .' "

Bostonais grunted somberly, then said: "I never been to Mon-
real."

"It's something to see."

"But not worth getting hung for."

"That doesn't seem likely. Mister MacGillivray will be more or
less a codefendant."

"You could get your money, too."

"My money?"

"Your father's money, that MacGillivray has."

Even after four years of close acquaintance Grant was still occasionally caught off guard by the amount of information stored
away in the elliptical mind of his taciturn friend. It had been two
years since Grant had reached his majority and mentioned to Bostonais in passing that he would eventually have to get around to
taking charge of his inheritance. Anyone in the civilized world
would have laughed in Grant's face if he'd tried to tell them that an
inheritance of approximately ten thousand pounds had temporarily
slipped his mind. But the fact was that the money wouldn't have
made much difference to his life out here; he could hardly spend
his clerk's salary from one year to the next. And there had been a

few more immediate concerns to occupy him. But now that Bos
tonais had brought it up, a journey to Montreal at this point woul‚
be a perfect opportunity to get the matter resolved.

Some miles farther on, when the sand hills had given way to th‚
Assiniboine River valley, Bostonais said: "So we'll go, then, wha
the hell."

"I don't know."

"Why not? A free trip out east, with the government and th‚
company to look after us. And all those poor, pale Canadian wome‚
who all their lives have thought a wild *homme du nord* is one o
those packhorse canoe paddlers—until we get there."

"You're forgetting that I have a wife and child to think of."

Bostonais lapsed into a silence and then said as they rode dow‚
toward La Souris, "No, I don't forget that."

Late the following night, when Grant peeled his skin away fron
Bethsy's and rolled back gasping—seven nights apart can do won
ders for a marriage—she said: "Why don't you go?"

"Are you that eager to get rid of me?"

"Don't be an idiot. It will be a terribly difficult winter for me
But it will be worth it to have this settled."

"To have what settled?"

"The question of whether you've done anything wrong."

"The courts in Canada can't tell me that. There's no questio‚
that I've made mistakes from time to time, but I know—when a‚
the circumstances are taken into account—that there's nothing
need to be ashamed of."

"But in terms of the law . . ."

"The law can't touch me here. And I have to think of you an
James."

"Well, think of us, then! Think of James. Don't you think it wi‚
have some kind of effect on him, growing up with the unresolve‚
question of what kind of a man his father is?"

"I should think he'll be able to work that out for himself withou‚
the help of some magistrate two thousand miles away. Can you?'

"Of course I can." She was crying. "Why are you so afraid ‚
going there?"

"I'm not." He pulled her close and snuggled the side of her fac‚
against his chest. The warm tears pattered down onto the hollo‚
above his collarbone. He kissed the silky baby hair at her templ‚
and said: "I'm only afraid of leaving you alone."

"We'll be all right. Pierriche will be nearby, and Mary, and Josephte, and John Richards will be just across the river. We'll be here safe when you come home."

The projected expenditures of the royal commission had to be expanded by the cost of four *canots du nord* and paddlers to transport the witnesses and prisoners to the east. As the flotilla roistered downstream past Fort Douglas, the Earl of Selkirk and Miles MacDonell stood on the bank glaring at the scandal in the lead canoe. Lounging beside the commissioner, with no sign of restraints or remorse, was the "prisoner" Cuthbert Grant. The pair of them were chatting amiably. Cuthbert Grant was quite the most entertaining accused mass murderer with whom Billy B. Coltman had ever gone a-boating.

CHAPTER 76

Kate managed to separate herself from her husband discreetly, slipping away while he was engrossed with old Mister MacBeth, debating the finer points of roof thatching from their amassed expertise of blind guesswork and implication. As soon as she was safely away she charged straight for the gates of Fort Douglas.

The trip took her some time and required a certain instinct for navigation. The entire expanded community of colonists, mercenaries, free hunters, and Saulteaux were in the process of gathering on the green bank in front of Fort Douglas to bid farewell to the Earl of Selkirk. And as she got closer to the gates the press of eager bodies grew thicker, slowing her progress to a series of short advances. If she couldn't get in through the gates before Lord Selkirk came out of them, it would be too late.

A gap suddenly opened in front of her, showing a clear lane through to the open gates. Kate rushed through it. Just before she broke out of the crowd, a woman in the group on her left stepped backward, and Kate rammed into her.

The woman yelped and stumbled, scrambling to keep from dropping the baby in her arms. Kate grabbed her shoulders to steady her, then kept on going, throwing out a quick apology. The look the woman tossed over her shoulder was more amused than affronted.

They were all still elated by the two announcements the Earl had made the day before. The first was that he was changing the name of the Selkirk colony to Kildonan, since he felt that the credit for the colony's survival lay more with the Kildonan refugees than with himself. The second was that he had struck out all the colonists' leasehold contracts and granted them their farms outright. It was that which had brought Kate Sutherland née MacPherson bulling through the crowd and into Fort Douglas instead of keeping to her place beside her husband.

Fort Douglas was largely deserted, most of its inhabitants having left for the riverbank. A group of a dozen men was just starting across from Colony House toward the gates—the Earl and Miles MacDonell, Captain D'Orsennens and Mister Pritchard, and other functionaries. Kate intercepted them and said: "Pardon me, Lord Selkirk, if I could ask you for only a moment of your time . . ."

Governor MacDonell said, "As much as the Earl would like to, he doesn't have time to say good-bye to each of you individually," and moved to step around her.

Lord Selkirk said, "I doubt that a moment one way or the other will make much difference by the time we get to Montreal," and turned to Kate. "Forgive me, madam, I should know you all by name, but with such a short time here among you . . ."

"Kate Sutherland, sir."

John Pritchard said to the Earl: "Her maiden name was Mac-Pherson."

The Earl's milky-blue eyes lit up. "Katy MacPherson! How fortunate to have come upon you at the eleventh hour. Lady Selkirk would have been quite displeased with me if she'd learned I'd spent six entire weeks here without conveying her best regards to you."

"To me?"

"She is a great admirer of yours. Archie told us a number of stories about how you helped him with the typhoid patients on the ship after poor Dr. La Serre passed on, and with the march from Churchill to York Factory."

It took her a moment to figure out that "Archie" was Archibald MacDonald. She was a little miffed at the notion of her having "helped" him, but then again, considering the manner she'd habitually used toward him, it was a bit surprising that he'd begrudged her any credit at all.

Governor MacDonell snapped open the casing on his pocket watch. "We had best be getting started, sir, if we hope to reach—"

"Now, Miles, this good woman asked me for a moment of my time, and all that I have done so far is to take up a moment of hers. Now, Miss MacPherson—that is, Mrs. . . . ."

"Sutherland, sir."

"Sutherland, of course. What is it you wished to speak to me about, Mrs. Sutherland?"

"Well, sir—yesterday, when you granted clear title to all those who had been leaseholders, sir . . . ?"

"Yes?"

"It was a grand thing to do, sir, and generous, but . . ." There was suddenly a piece of dry straw caught halfway down her throat. She moistened her mouth and tried to swallow it away.

The Earl said gently: "But . . . ?"

"But, you see, sir, my husband already owned his piece of land—*our* piece of land. He bought it outright before we left DunUlidh, for ten pounds cash money. Not that I begrudge the price, sir, and not that I begrudge the people you granted theirs to yesterday, but it does not seem quite . . . it does not seem quite . . ."

"Fair? You are quite right, Mrs. Sutherland. It does puzzle me, though, that Mister Sutherland hasn't come forward with this."

"My husband . . . is a very proud man, sir."

"Ah." The Earl turned his attention to Governor MacDonell. "I had thought that all the arrangements were for leaseholders?"

"Colin Robertson decided to make an exception in this case."

Mister Pritchard said: "Mister Sutherland had spent ten years with the Black Watch. He was invalided out after Corruna."

"Ah. Then he has good reason to be proud. Well, Mrs. Sutherland, I believe you have a valid point concerning the inequity of the situation. The question is how to correct it?"

She waited a moment for one of the others to offer a suggestion, then said: "Actually, sir, I had thought of something . . ."

"I had the curious premonition, Mrs. Sutherland, that you might have."

"You see, sir, over the last few years my husband and I—the same as everybody else here—have worked up a debt to the colony accounts, for provisions and such. My husband made some wages over the winter working on Norway House, but after outfitting ourselves to start again here and paying off as much of the debt as we

478

could, there is still six pounds or so we owe. Now if we could take the ten pounds my husband paid for the land and put it against our account, so that instead of six pounds or so in debt we had four pounds or thereabouts in credit . . . And it would not be as much of an expense to you as though you paid out ten pounds in currency for recompense, and . . .''

The Earl held up his hand. "I believe you have hit upon the perfect solution. Mister Bourke, you'll see that this is—"

The quartermaster said: "Yes, Your Lordship."

"Good. And now, Mrs. Sutherland, I'm afraid you must excuse us if we hope to get a start while the day is still ahead of us."

"Yes, sir. Thank you, sir." She stood aside.

As soon as they had gone past her she became appalled that she could have been so graceless as to have had five minutes face to face with the man who had done so much for her and all she could do was berate him about ten pounds owing to her husband. But there was nothing she could do about it now.

She hurried out of the gates and around the edge of the crowd to where her husband was standing. He said: "Where did you sneak away to?"

"I had to use the necessary in the fort."

"You were gone long enough to build one."

"Would you rather I just squatted down behind a thistle?"

The crowd fell silent as the Earl and his entourage made their way down to the waiting York boat. The boat was only to ferry the Earl, Governor MacDonell, Captain D'Orsennens, and an escort of soldiers to the opposite shore, where Jean Baptiste Lajimodierre was waiting with a string of horses. They would take the southern route through American territory rather than following the North West Company's canoe route.

Lord Selkirk stepped one foot up onto the prow, then stopped and turned back. He seemed to be as much at a loss as to what to say as his transplanted crofters. All words seemed inadequate. Finally he called out in a reedy voice: "Good-bye. God bless you."

Kate murmured, "God bless you," in response as everyone else did, a soft flutter like the beating of a flock of small wings.

As the Earl climbed into the boat and the rowers pushed it out into the stream, a high, clear tenor voice near Kate began to sing:

Speed bonny boat like a bird on the wing,
Onward the sailors cry.

She looked around for the singer. It was Sandy, flushed so red that the skin on the bridge of his nose glowed like parchment stretched in a windowframe. But he kept on singing, and soon others joined in. By the time he hit the next refrain, there were a hundred voices singing with him.

Carry the lad born to be King
Over the sea to Skye.

When the boat reached the opposite shore the Earl clambered out and turned back to wave. Miles MacDonell stood beside him grimly looking at his watch. They had never sung for him.

After the Earl had disappeared into the woods there was a moment of shuffling silence, and then the crowd began to break up and drift back to their homes. Old Mister MacBeth passed by the Point Douglas Sutherlands, trailing his broad-shouldered brood. As he passed he winked and said: "Aye, Sandy's the lad."

Kate cooked their evening meal of whitefish, new potatoes, and wild onions on their own hearth in their new house. The front and back walls were twenty feet wide and six high. The side walls were sixteen feet wide up to a height of six feet and then gradually tapered narrower to the roof tree eight feet higher. The walls were built of foot-square beams tongued and pegged into upright posts at the corners and midpoints. The floor was packed earth. There was no furniture to speak of, but that would have to wait until the roof was done. At present it consisted of a sketchy latticework of lashed-together green poles.

When Kate had done cleaning up the dishes, she went out to help her husband with the thatch. Over the last few days they'd been sickling down stacks of tall grass, combing out the leaves and detritus, soaking the stalks and flailing them flat, then tying them into bundles with hanks of *shagganappi*. Sandy was up on the roof now, lashing the bundles of thatch onto the poles. He had worked his way across the lowest pole on the south wall, which had been set to project the hem of the thatch beyond the rim of the wall. In County Sutherland the custom had been to end the eaves flush with the top of the wall, which made for seepages of rainwater and melting snow.

Kate handed him up a few armfuls of bundled straw and then clambered up the ladder of poplar branches lashed between two barbered saplings. She took a few bundles and a length of thong to the opposite end of the pole he was working on and tried to arrange

herself into a secure position. As she worked she looked down
between the roof poles at the cozy home beneath her, thinking of
various locations for the bed and the table and wondering whether
she'd chosen the best corner for her spinning wheel.

She tied off the bundle of thatch, making sure it had a good
overlap on the finished layer, and took out her stubby knife to cut
the end off the knot. Her husband called: "Snub it off as tight as
you can. Once we run out of *shagganappi* we will have to tie the
rest with plaited straw."

"Would it not be easier to buy another green hide from the
storehouse and cut more thong?"

"Certainly, but we are deep enough in debt as it is. We might
have the money to spare when the harvest is in, but by that time we
had best have this long done or we will have soggy sleeping through
the autumn."

It seemed like the perfect opportunity to tell him, but she hesitated. She told herself that she had only done the sensible thing,
and that she'd have to tell him eventually. She said: "We are not in
any debt."

"Six pounds, three shillings, and four pence may not seem like
any debt to you, and I will grant you that it is nothing compared to
what some of the others owe. But I did not come all the way across
the ocean to indenture myself to an endless round of debts and
interest payments."

"We have no debts to pay. If you go over to the fort and look in
Mister Bourke's account book, what you will find next to your name
is almost four pounds in credit."

"Have you had another one of your dreams, then? I do not remember you doing much thrashing about last night—no more than
usual. . . ."

She told him what she'd done. Quite early on in the story he
stopped working on the thatch and just listened. When she came to
the end he said nothing, merely sat there in silence. She thought
perhaps she hadn't made herself clear and started to tell it again.
But at the first syllable he jerked up into a crouch and climbed
stiffly down.

She thought he might be going to Fort Douglas to look in the
ledger for himself. Instead he headed in the other direction, toward
the stand of wild woods covering the tip of the point. She called
"Where are you—"

He whirled back, his right hand making a chopping motion
through the air. The violence of the movement stopped the words

n her throat. He said: "You have shamed me." Then he turned
nd walked away.

CHAPTER 77

As the first cold white splotches mottling the roofs and
gardens of Montreal broadened and thickened into a knee-
deep quilt, the residents of the streets next to a certain dignified
stone building gradually became resigned, if not inured, to sleeping
with their pillows over their heads three nights a week. But even a
six-inch thickness of goosedown couldn't shut out all the drunken
caterwauling and lascivious invitations ejaculated at any female
between the ages of twelve and sixty who passed by. The general
opinion concerning the four comparatively peaceful nights of the
week was that three were leapfrogged for recuperation and the fourth
was respectfully given over to mandatory chapel services.
   The grand old stone building was the courthouse with its floors
of holding cells. The reveling crew was made up of the prisoners
from the *pays d'en haut* currently undergoing hearings regarding
charges brought against them by the Earl of Selkirk. The lascivious
invitations that so offended female passersby—they didn't need to
speak Cree to get the gist—had at first been extended only to particularly pneumatic-looking specimens over fifteen and under thirty;
but as the winter wore on, the boundaries wore down—more as a
result of ennui than any libidinous pressures. Every month or so
the weekly consignment of rum was accompanied by a dozen
women from the waterfront taverns and a piper or a couple of fiddlers to warm up cramped muscles. All amenities flowed from the
beneficent hand of the Honorable William MacGillivray, who was
facing the same charges but had been released on his bond.
   In response to complaints concerning the encrimsoning of the
fairer ears of this fair city, the spokesman of the prisoners—a certain Cuthbert Grant—insisted that the blame lay entirely with the
governor of the jail. The prisoners had repeatedly petitioned for a
billiard table, and no billiard table had as yet been forthcoming;

there was simply nothing else to do but drink and play cards and lean out the windows hollering lewd suggestions at anything in a skirt, including a few irate officers of the Royal Highland Regiment.

At the moment, Grant was leaning against the bars with Bostonais. There was nothing to be seen outside the window but the snow wafting down and the blurred forms of the buildings on the far side of the square. One more tot of rum and the inside of the cell would start to blur again as well. There was a card game going on between two banks of bunks. Even Bostonais's passion for cards had cooled.

Someone called out, "Wappeston, read us something out of the bible," prompting a general clamor. Grant waited until it had built to a gratifying pitch before weaving over to his footlocker and extracting a thick morocco-leather portfolio.

The "bible" was Grant's collection of the printed works that had come out of the propaganda war that Lord Selkirk and the North West Company had been waging against each other through intermediaries. There were reams of pamphlets and sheafs of letters to the *Montreal Gazette* and two entire hardbound full-length books. Both books represented themselves as factual accounts by disinterested writers seeking only to inform the public, but one had been authored by a sodden hack and the other by a cousin of Lady Selkirk's. Grant had had to ferret that information out for himself; neither of the books sported author's biographies.

Grant sat on his bunk and flipped open the portfolio. The print kept sneaking in and out of focus, and individual words kept bisecting themselves like amoebae, but he knew the more amusing sections by heart. He began with a selection from the Selkirk faction's book, the chapter headed "The Deposition of Michael Heden." It was peppered with rousing gems such as "half Indian bastard children of North West Company traders," and its description of the "dastardly sneak attack at Seven Oaks" could always be counted on to rouse a few howls of outraged laughter.

When the last sleepy, bearded head had settled down upon its pillow and the last candle had been blown out, Grant lay down, but he didn't sleep. While it didn't seem to bother any of the others, the fact remained that the North West Company's publications were just as full of distortions and half-truths as those of the other side. It was as though once the battle had been joined in print and in the courts, both sides dropped any interest in the truth and became interested only in hiring better liars than the other side.

He told himself that he was being childish and that it was an inevitable offshoot of the adversary system of law. And he had seen for himself how slippery an article the truth could be. John Pritchard and others had testified that at Seven Oaks Semple's men had waved their hats in the air as a token of surrender and then had been shot down. Grant had known that the hat waving had been elation at the illusion that the métis had all been killed. But after enough conflicting testimony, after the advocates had argued it back and forth, after running back over his own memory until it was worn smooth, he was only prepared to swear that they had waved their hats in the air—perhaps in triumph, perhaps in surrender, perhaps to fan away the mosquitoes.

From the bunk beside his, Bostonais rumbled over the surrounding snores: "Some of them are almost going to miss this place after tomorrow."

Grant said: "I won't." Tomorrow was the last day of preliminary hearings, when the magistrates would decide whether any of the charges warranted a true bill of indictment and a trial.

"Whatever we ain't drank we leave for the guards, hm? They been good fellows."

"No wonder. They've probably made more off Mister MacGillivray's bribes than their wages."

"Figure we'll have to pay anything in fines?"

"Perhaps. If so, I'm sure the company will contribute."

Bostonais grunted and rolled over. Grant rolled over as well but still couldn't sleep. Whenever he brought out the bible these days, it brought him back to the same inexplicable item. In both books and several of the pamphlets, there were references to a letter that William MacGillivray had written to one of the other partners upon hearing the news of the massacre at Seven Oaks. It was a private letter sent by the North West Company's express, but it had inevitably been intercepted—during those months, mail packets, private papers, and dispatches were being intercepted in all directions.

In the letter, Mister MacGillivray expressed his great regret and sorrow that "the Indians" had butchered Governor Semple and his brave men, lamented the fact that the colonists hadn't heeded his advice to be less high-handed with the natives, and concluded with a weary assumption that the North West Fur Trading Company would undoubtedly be blamed for it somehow, "despite the fact that there were none of us within two hundred miles of the place." The letter was quoted extensively in the print salvos fired from both sides during the last few months, to illustrate either the North West

Company's innocence or perfidiousness, depending on which livery the writer wore.

As on so many nights before, now that that letter had been brought back to mind, Grant ran over and over the same path of reasoning, trying to sort out some rational explanation for how Mister MacGillivray could have come to write it. Invariably, the chain would lead Grant to the same not-quite-seen, leering sphinx that made him suddenly sheer off. He would find himself back where he'd started, with the links he'd so carefully assembled scattered all around him. Once again he began to piece them patiently together.

The smell of brewing tea and the slap of oatmeal into bowls informed Grant he'd been sleeping. The faces hovering over the table in the dawn light looked severely chastened from the night before. The *pays d'en haut*'s version of epicureanism—''Drink as much as you can whenever you can''—served them well enough back home, where the pattern of life provided its own restraints. But if some of them didn't get out of jail soon, they were going to be permanently crippled.

Once they'd taken a bit of semisolid food and trooped out to and back from the snow-capped bank of privies in the exercise yard, Grant led the shambling, gray-faced parade along the corridor to the courtroom. They would return to life quickly enough if the verdicts came out as expected. The foundations of the Montreal taverns had better be anchored firmly in the rock.

An even larger crowd than usual was crammed into the courtroom. Montreal hadn't witnessed such a prolonged winter's entertainment in years. The Earl of Selkirk and his lady were in their usual pew, looking even more pinch-faced and purse-mouthed than usual. The last few months had been a strain on them. The Earl was mired in legal problems of his own, facing a raft of charges from his capture of Fort William. On top of that, the current proceedings had been undertaken entirely at his own expense. As was usual in such cases, the plaintiff had to pay all court costs up until such time as the Crown returned a true bill of indictment and proceeded to trial.

The Selkirk faction had entered these hearings fully prepared to face a certain amount of corruption, a certain inevitable bias on the part of courts housed in the home base of the North West Fur Trading Company. But they'd had no conception of the power wielded in Montreal from the homes and offices of the Mac-

Gillivrays, McGills, et al.—and the education they were receiving was beginning to put a strain on their egalitarian principles. Even Lady Selkirk, by nature a gracious and sweet-tempered woman, had grown so exasperated as to recently remark, "Who would have thought the scum of Scotland would aspire so high?"

A robed official emerged from the wings and commanded all to rise. The tribunal of senior magistrates sailed in in their wigs and robes and ribbons and took their places on the bench. The congregation, like obedient toddlers waiting patiently for a pushy dowager's posterior to connect with the sofa, gratefully squeezed themselves back onto their seats. The clerk announced that the court was in session.

The lead tenor of the bewigged trio began to read out their findings. "In the matter of the charges against the Honourable William MacGillivray, the court finds insufficient grounds to proceed."

Grant shifted his gaze from the Earl of Selkirk—white knuckles on the head of his walking stick—to the princely profile of the aforesaid "Honourable" beneath its Byronic crown of red-gold curls. The flicker of a nod in response to the verdict didn't even shake one curl. He had probably known what the court's findings would be before the court did.

"In the matter of the charges against Peter Pangman, known as Bostonais, resident of the Indian territories, employed by the North West Fur Trading Company as an interpreter, the court finds insufficient grounds to proceed to an indictment. In the matter of the charges against Joseph Cadotte . . ."

The litany went on and on, without a variation in the formula. Grant had to shush the rest of the boys in the dock to keep them from laughing out loud. As it was, there were a number of stifled sputters and grins, and Boucher was chanting "insufficient grounds" under his breath after every name.

Grant glanced over at the Selkirks. The Earl was practically translucent with rage. The attorneys banked in front of him were chalky and still. Suddenly Grant was afraid that Mister MacGillivray had gone too far. The North West Company might own the city of Montreal and most of the magistrates in the Canadas, but if the Earl of Selkirk were to stand up in the House of Lords armed with a blatant case of perversion of justice . . .

"Cuthbert Grant"—the magistrate's voice brought him back to the immediate—"late of the cities of Inverness and Montreal and currently residing in the Indian territories, employed as a clerk by the North West Fur Trading Company. In the charge against you for the murder of Robert Semple, Governor of Lord Selkirk's colony of Assiniboia, this tribunal returns a true bill of indictment and orders you to be bound over to the courts for trial. In the charge against you for the murder of Owen Keveney of the aforesaid colony, this tribunal finds a true bill . . .''

There were four other charges, assault and arson and so on, but Grant barely heard them. His eardrums and the walls of the court were pumping in and out like the inside of a heart. He looked across the room at the Earl of Selkirk. The Earl looked mollified, if not exactly pleased. He wrenched his eyes away and looked for the Honourable William MacGillivray. Mister MacGillivray had taken his leave.

CHAPTER 78

"In the matter of the murder of Owen Keveney . . .''

Near the end of the summer of the fight at Seven Oaks, Owen Keveney was sitting in his canvas tent pitched near the birch-bark and reed mat wigwams of an Ojibway camp on a bend of the Winnipeg River. He was propped on his camp cot with his chin in his hands and his stomach in an uproar, glaring at his brass-bound portmanteau and traveling desk stacked at the foot of the cot. There ought to have been a rifle and an axe and a pistol case leaned up against them, but the nasty bastard voyageurs who'd been escorting him to Fort William had confiscated those when they'd abandoned him. Someday they would pay for that—with interest. At the same time they'd confiscated Keveney's weapons, they had also disarmed the Indian guide, Joseph, who'd kept pointing his musket at him and saying, "Boom!" and laughing; but Owen Keveney wasn't the kind of man to let a little thing like evenhandedness stand in the way of a good grudge.

They were all going to pay, along with their North West Company masters, as soon as Keveney'd got the papers in his portmanteau and traveling desk to Fort William. The Earl of Selkirk was in control at Fort William now—which was the main reason that the

Canadians had dumped him by this backwater and scuttled back for Bas de la Rivière—and the Earl was going to be extremely interested in the North West Company mail packet that had come into Keveney's possession. Although the letters had been written and dispatched long before the half-breeds rode to Seven Oaks, they contained indisputable evidence that the partners of the North West Company knew what was coming and, in fact, were engineering it, just as they had engineered the disaster on the Athabasca. The letters also contained inquiries, from one bourgeois to another, about the feasibility of murdering Lord Selkirk in the wilderness and making it appear to have been an Indian ambush.

There was a scratching on the tent flap. Or at least Keveney thought he heard a scratching at the tent flap; it was difficult to say for sure, what with the white water roar from the river. The sun had shifted around to the back of the tent, so there were no shadows on the front wall. The scratching sound came again, and the flap fluttered slightly. Keveney said: "Who's there?"

The flap was pushed aside and an Indian girl stooped in, holding a small birchbark bucket. She said something in Ojibway, or at least he assumed that's what it was. In four years in the Indian territories he hadn't learned one word of their jabber. He had damned well earned English, so could they. He said: "What do you want?"

"Food."

"I got no food."

She tentatively thrust the container toward him. It was filled with a murky white liquid that gave off a strong odor of fish. So she wasn't asking for food, she was offering it. He gagged as the fish taste worked its way to the back of his throat. He hadn't been able to hold anything down for three days—some kind of bloody flux or digestive fever, which was the other reason the Canadian boatmen had dumped him here.

The odor coming off the Indian girl didn't help. She had smeared her body with rancid animal grease, which most of them seemed to do. Apparently they thought it would keep them warm and keep the bugs from biting. If an insect's sense of smell was anything like his, Keveney felt sure it did the job admirably.

He would have to down something sooner or later. He reached out and took the container from her, swirling its contents suspiciously. It had the appearance of heavily watered, curdled milk, with a few flecks of something solid floating in it. The girl ducked her head and lifted off one of the many strings of beads and thongs hanging around her neck. It turned out to have a spoon of hollowed-

out horn hanging from the end of it. She wiped it on the skirt o
her deerskin dress and offered it to him. He shook his head and
dug through his gear for his own spoon.

The fish broth didn't taste that bad—hardly tasted at all, in fact
despite its vicious odor. He slurped it in through his teeth and too
another look at the girl. She couldn't have been more than twelve
or thirteen. She looked to have loaded herself down with every bi
of finery she owned, over her powwow dress and moccasins. Sh
pointed at him and said: "Hussen Bay man?"

He shook his head. "I am an officer of Lord Selkirk's colony o
Assiniboia."

She wrinkled her forehead and shook her head. "No Assini
boine. Ojibway."

"No. Me Selkirk's man. Sell-kirk. Red River." He pointed hi
spoon in what he figured was a westerly direction.

She shook her head again and said: "All dead. *Bois brulés*
T-boom." She made the motion of firing a gun.

"Not me. Starch-ass Semple sent me up to Fort Albany in th
spring to fetch down some calves. Like some damned herd boy
Damned lucky for me, though." He spat out a fishbone and too
another spoonful.

"You . . . kill man?"

"No! I told you, I wasn't there!"

"Mans say . . . Ojibway mans say . . . you . . . " She made a
hitting motion with both fists. "Kill mans. English River."

"That's a damned lie. That trumped-up Justice of the goddam
Peace McLellan made it up for an excuse to arrest me and ship m
to Fort William. It's true I did give a few of those goddamned boa
rowers a good knocking on the head, but who wouldn't? Staving i
a boat on a rock any damn fool could've seen from half a mile off
losing calves in the bush and then pretending they don't understan
the King's English . . . If any of their skulls got broke, it was jus
where they were cracked to start with."

A sudden fishy belch shot up his throat and exploded behind hi
nose. He thought for an instant he was going to spew, but it settle
down. He handed the birchbark bowl back to her, wiped the spoo
off on the corner of his blanket, and put it away. He looked back a
the girl. Given a good scrubbing she wouldn't look half-bad. Young
but they started them young in this country; old enough to bleed
old enough to butcher. He put on his best smile and said: "What'
your name?"

There was a burst of gunshots and yelling from outside. The

girl's head whipped around toward the tent flap. He crab-walked to the entranceway and peered out.

A batch of Ojibway had run down to the bank, firing their tin-plated trade guns in the air and whooping. There was a long *canot du nord* approaching from downriver, the paddlers driving their blades furiously against the churning current. Hunched forward in the prow like a vulturous figurehead was the Indian, Joseph, with a musket cradled in his arms and a tartan plaid draped over his shoulders like a shawl. The canoe passed by Keveney and veered in to the landing place. Besides Joseph there were three others who weren't helping the crew with the paddling: Archibald McLellan, an ex-sergeant of the Des Meurons named de Reinhardt, and the half-breed Grant.

The sight of Joseph unsettled Keveney's stomach again. He lurched over to an amber mossbank and sat down. The Indian girl followed him out of the tent. She said: "You go . . . other mans?"

His stomach was churning and cramping. Sweat oozed from his forehead. He found it difficult to breathe. Suddenly he lunged at her. "What did you put in the soup? Are you trying to poison me?" She backed away quickly. He dove forward off the mossbank and caught her by the ankle. She fell, squealing when her elbow hit a rock. "Did they pay you to poison me? Is that what—"

She kicked out with her free foot and caught him on the base of the neck. His grip loosened, and she jerked her ankle free, leaving him holding an empty moccasin. She scrambled up to her feet and scuttled off toward the camp. He sat up and looked at the moccasin. It melted over his hand like warm butter, bleached deerskin worked so soft that it held no shape except where the beaded flower on the toe gave it some stiffening. He tossed it in the river, and the current swept it out of sight.

The canoe had landed. A few of its occupants were picking their way across the rocks toward him. He thought of getting up and running, but he'd never survive in the bush without a gun, and he doubted he could even stand upright with his innards tying figure eights. Besides, if the North West Company insisted on shipping him off to the Canadas on some trumped-up charge, they would only be providing him with a perfect opportunity to stand up in front of a judge and start reading the papers in his portmanteau.

The leader of the landing party was big Grant, dressed more Indian than white, still sporting the habitual cocky half smile that Keveney looked forward to wiping off with the papers in his trunk. Behind him came de Reinhardt, rigged out in full sergeant's fig,

parade sword and all. Whenever his hirers wanted to make them
selves appear official, they'd tell de Reinhardt to haul out the bi
jous.

Grant said something in French to the voyageurs trailing behind
and they went to Keveney's tent and started pulling out the stakes
Keveney said: "Here then—that's private property!"

"I'm perfectly aware of that, Mister Keveney, so I assumed yo
wouldn't want to leave it behind when we take you away."

It seemed to Keveney that there was a certain harassed ton
beneath Grant's accustomed arrogance. Apparently the news of th
capture of Fort William had put a boot into the hive. "What if
don't want to go anywhere?"

"You don't appear to be in much condition to resist."

"Where are you taking me?"

"You'll have to take that up with Mister McLellan. All I'm con
cerned with is getting up to Rainy Lake, where we can discover i
there's any truth behind some of the more extravagant rumors tha
have been circulating lately."

Keveney laughed. "Oh, they're true all right, boy. You Nort
West bastards have been having your way pretty free, haven't you
Well, now you've got the Earl of Selkirk to contend with." H
turned to de Reinhardt. "Looks like you picked the wrong side.'

De Reinhardt just gazed stolidly over his head. But there was
side to the Earl of Selkirk's coup that Keveney hadn't considered
The capture of Fort William had effectively lopped off the Nort
West Company's head, leaving the reactive nerve bundles—such a
Archibald McLellan—to thrash about on their own.

The voyageurs encountered some difficulty in folding up the cam
cot until Grant showed them how the hinge catches worked. The
they shouldered up his gear and headed down to the landing place
Keveney walked with a bend in his middle to keep his belly fror
exploding. De Reinhardt offered him the crook of his arm, an
Keveney took hold of it, hobbling along like somebody's grand
mother.

McLellan was poking at the hull of an Indian canoe drawn u
beside the *canot du nord*, dickering with a couple of Ojibway.
bargain was struck. McLellan said: "Joseph, de Reinhardt, Mainvill
take him"—pointing to Keveney—"in this"—pointing at the smalle
canoe—"and follow along." The half-breed Mainville flipped th
Indian canoe upright and walked it out into the water. The voyageu
started loading Keveney's gear into the *canot du nord*.

"Here then—those are my things!"

McLellan turned on him, the red splotches on his cheeks burning redder. "I know that, you shit-faced mick! I have to distribute the load."

Keveney shouted back at him: "I've locked those cases shut, I'll know if you've tampered with them!" Instead of escalating the shouting match, McLellan merely turned away. Suddenly Keveney felt cold.

The *canot du nord* made better headway against the current and gradually left the smaller boat behind. Mainville and Joseph and de Reinhardt seemed unconcerned. The distant roar of the *dalles* grew steadily louder as they approached, the river foaming through narrow rock channels. They would have to portage there. Keveney was looking forward to the opportunity to hunker down in the bushes. The fish soup had primed a pump deep in his bowels, and it was taking all the concentration he could muster to keep it from gushing out. They were still a ways downstream of the portage when he realized he wasn't going to make it. He called to de Reinhardt to put him ashore. Joseph said, "No, no," pointing ahead. "Not far now."

Mainville, paddling from the stern, suddenly bellowed out a string of French imprecations and steered them in toward land. Joseph was laughing and holding his nose. Keveney stepped over the gunwale before the prow touched the shoreline, splashed out through the thigh-high water, and ran into the bush, unbuttoning his trousers while casting about frantically for a convenient deadfall.

When he returned to the canoe they were all out on the shore. Mainville was sitting on a rock looking at the water. De Reinhardt was waiting nearby with his arms crossed. Joseph was standing a little apart, with his arms straight out in front of him, one hand wrapped around the muzzle of his musket and the other on the pommel of his paddle. Keveney said, "I hope you all had yourselves a good laugh," and walked to the waiting canoe.

Something struck him at the base of his neck where the Indian girl had kicked him, something infinitely stronger. He was thrown forward across the canoe. A bomb had gone off inside his ear. There were sparks in his right eye, and the smell of burning hair. He wanted to cough, but nothing would come out. He tried to breathe, but nothing came in. He could hear a choking sound coming from under his chin. Something hot and sticky rolled down his chest.

His head lolled to one side. Over his shoulder he saw a red-clad arm with something extending from it, something that flickered in the sunlight. The sword went into his back under the shoulder blade, scraped against a rib, and came out in front. De Reinhardt jerked it out again. Keveney flopped on the canoe like a frog with a pin through it. He felt the point of the sword piercing the muscle on his back again, then something burst.

They stripped the body and threw it into the bush. The bears and crows would do the rest. They caught up with the second canoe where they'd camped for the night on the other side of the portage. McLellan went through the pockets of the dead man's clothes and came up with the key to the portmanteau, but not the one to the traveling desk. Grant pried it open with his knife. The two of them sat up late into the night reading through the packets of papers and feeding them to the fire.

They didn't get through them all. In the morning, McLellan filled the pockets of his coat with stones before climbing into the canoe. He read through the rest of the papers en route, wrapping them around stones one by one and dropping them over the side.

When they came to Tace's post on Rainy Lake, they got firsthand accounts that verified the rumored disaster at Fort William. It was apparent that Selkirk had too many soldiers with him for their handful of men to accomplish anything. They headed for Bas de la Rivière, leaving de Reinhardt behind at Tace's post. There was the odd chance that he might be able to get a shot at Selkirk when he came down Rainy River. He was also becoming decidedly odd.

De Reinhardt grew odder as summer moved into fall, living off by himself in the bush, wandering into Tace's store from time to time for supplies. When D'Orsennens and Miles MacDonell arrived with their expeditionary force, he surrendered himself to his old captain with a palpable feeling of relief. He wanted to confess.

CHAPTER 79

"Last will and testament of Mister Cuthbert Grant. Seventeenth March, Eighteen hundred and eighteen. Before the undersigned Public Notaries duly Commissioned and . . ."

The voice accompanying the scratching of the pen was a pleasant baritone, with a bit of a rasp from a first-thaw cold and a slight Welsh lilt. Grant was sitting on the broad window ledge of the jailer's office, with his back against one wall of the frame and his knees propped against the other. His right temple and cheekbone were pressed against the pleasingly cold, thick, wavy glass through which he looked out at the eroding snowdrifts in the exercise yard while Mister Owen Griffin's raspy Welsh baritone warmed the room. The jailer was Welsh as well—Gwyn Owen. Seemed to be a lot of Welsh going around these days.

". . . being in perfect sound health memory and understanding as appears to us the said Notaries by his words and actions but considering the Certainty of death and the Uncertainty of the time thereof . . ."

What was certain was that de Reinhardt had been sentenced to hang for the murder of Owen Keveney. It wasn't likely that the courts were going to stop at de Reinhardt. The curious thing was that, try as he might, Grant simply couldn't remember whether he'd known what was going to happen to Keveney before de Reinhardt came down the portage path carrying a blood-soaked wad of clothes.

"First . . ." The syllable resonated from Mister Griffin's chest, like the first word of a speech, but then he trailed off into silence. He gave a distinctly artificial cough and repeated: "First . . ."

Grant said: "First?"

"Yes, sir—the first clause? If the preamble is to your satisfaction, we can go on to . . ."

"Ah. Yes, of course."

Another moment passed in silence. Then Mister Griffin said: "Well, it is customary to—"

"I suppose," Grant interrupted, trying to be helpful, "that we had best start with any liens there might be against the estate, funeral expenses, outstanding debts, and so on. . . ."

"Just so." The pen went back to scratching in time with Mister Griffin's self-dictation. " 'First, the said testator doth Will and require that all his just and lawful . . .' "

Grant had no idea how much might have been drawn out of the estate over the years to pay for his education and so on. It had been one of the things he'd been planning to discuss with Mister MacGillivray during his stay in Montreal, but Mister MacGillivray hadn't made himself available for discussion.

"Second?"

"My son, James."

"Natural son?"

"Not unnatural."

Mister Barron, Mister Griffin's partner, began to laugh politely
at this bit of wit on the part of their client. Something in Grant's
face choked it off. Grant dictated: "To my son, James Grant, the
sum of three thousand pounds. To his mother, Elisabeth McKay,
five hundred pounds for her own use and benefit and at her own
disposal."

It was so clear to him now that what he would miss most about
his life was Bethsy and James. So much of the time they might have
had together he had chosen to squander, charging around trying to
build himself a place in the outside world. He wondered if there
had ever been such a fool in the history of humanity. He supposed
there might have been a few, but none of them were present to
dispute the title.

"Any further bequests?"

"The remainder of the estate to be divided between my nephews,
John Wills, Junior and François Morin, Junior." He had other
nephews, Pierre Falcon's sons, but the problem there was that Mary
and Falcon bred like rabbits—if he added in shares for them, the
pieces were going to end up too small to be of any use. And Falcon
could provide for his own children. Josephte's husband was dead,
and Marguerite's François had a reputation, even among the métis,
for being no good with money.

"And now, Mister Grant, if you have no more clauses to insert
. . . the question of executors?"

"John Stuart, of New Caledonia in the Indian territories"—it
was with the Stuarts in Grantown-on-Spey that Grant had spent his
summers between terms at Inverness—"and William MacGillivray,
of Montreal."

"*The* Mister MacGillivray—MacTavish, MacGillivray and
Company?"

"The same." There was a certain neatness to it—as the executor
of the estate of Cuthbert Grant, Junior, Mister MacGillivray would
be legally bound to pry the original bequest loose from the executor
of the estate of Cuthbert Grant, Senior.

When he looked back on the long chain of betrayals, Grant didn't
blame MacGillivray so much as himself. He had been so eager to
please. The North West Company had bred him and raised him as

a tame wolf cub, then set him loose in hopes that he would lead the pack for his masters' purposes. It had worked a treat. And now the final brilliant stroke was to throw up their hands in horror and throw him to the hounds.

" '. . . and signed by the said testator in the presence of us the said Notaries who have hereunto also subscribed our Names in his presence and in the presence of each other these presents being twice read to him according to the law.' "

Mister Barron leaned forward to take the pen from Mister Griffin and witness the document. Mister Griffin jerked the pen away from him, whispering: "We can't witness that he's signed it until he's signed it." Mister Barron grunted and leaned back in his chair. "Mister Grant . . ."

Grant climbed down from his window seat and read the document. The neat, professional march of words across the page looked misty and indistinct no matter how much he blinked his eyes. So this is where it ends, he told himself—no barbaric splendor of a kingdom in the west, no revered throne in the boardrooms of the east, no dynasty of grandchildren playing about the feet of the great man. It did have its amusing side if one's tastes leaned toward irony.

For once, however, he failed to see the humor of it. Mostly he just felt sick inside—sick of himself. He was leaning over the table with his hands resting on the rim when suddenly he wrenched his back straight and flung the table. It went up in the air, executed a neat flip, and came down flat on its head with a report that shook the room, papers and pens and ink bottles scattering.

Grant said: "Give me a pen and some paper." Both Mister Griffin and Mister Barron had scuttled off to the far wall. Neither of them replied. He took hold of the table to lift it back onto its feet. "Did you hear me? A pen and paper—or do you think because speak Cree I won't know what to do with them?"

The door opened and Mister Gwyn Owen, the jailer, stuck his head in to investigate the crash. "My apologies, Mister Owen—a little accident with the furniture. No harm done, no need for alarm." Mister Owen closed the door again. Grant snapped his fingers impatiently, waving the notaries forward.

Mister Griffin began to edge in off the wall, saying: "If there is some dissatisfaction with the document, we will be glad to—"

"No, no, not at all—splendid piece of work. Pen and paper, please. I want you to deliver a note for me. Add the time and trouble to my account."

Mister Barron retrieved the ink bottle from a corner, leaving half its contents on Mister Owen's floor. Mister Griffin took a fresh sheet of paper from his portfolio and drew a clean pen from his case. Any firm expecting to do business in the town of Montreal soon learned that although the manners of *les hommes du nord* might not pass in the more exclusive circles, their money certainly did.

Midpoint across the sheet of vellum, Grant wrote, "The Honourable William MacGillivray—Urgent, Personal, and Confidential," then flapped it in the air to dry the ink, flipped it over, and started on the other side:

> *My dear sir,*
> *So often in the past when I have found myself out of my depth*
> *you have proved the source of sound and patient and, might I*
> *say, fatherly advice. I have drawn on the account of your kind-*
> *ness and your greater wealth of experience so many times that I*
> *have hesitated to do so again. But soon I shall be called upon to*
> *account to a court of law for my part in the unfortunate acts of*
> *violence that have so marred these last few years—and not merely*
> *a court of law, for are there not eyes as far away as the Colonial*
> *Office in London turned on our humble doings?*
> *The dilemma that I find myself in is that, while on the one*
> *hand there are so many hitherto hidden circumstances that would*
> *cast my past actions in a different light, on the other hand I*
> *hesitate to entangle other parties who might have inadvertently*
> *influenced those actions.*
> *I should consider it a great mark of favour on your part if you*
> *could see your way to come to me here this afternoon, as I cannot*
> *come to you. I realise, though, that you have many calls upon*
> *your time. If you cannot disentangle yourself from other affairs,*
> *I shall have to blunder through as best I can. I can only beg t*
> *be remembered, as in all matters, as your humble servant,*
>
>   *Cuthbert Grant*

He folded the sheet of paper over twice, leaving an open seal on the obverse side of the address, and asked Mister Griffin if he had such a thing as a seal and sealing wax about him. Mister Griffin sounded a bit miffed as he replied: "I should hardly think that would be necessary; as a duly sworn notary public, it is assumed can be trusted in confidential matters."

"In your vast and varied experience, Mister Griffin, you mus

ve discovered that there are, regrettably, some people on this
rth whose trust and confidence can prove distinctly detrimental
one's health.''

Mister Barron produced a stick of sealing wax from his waistcoat
cket.

It was just after two when the great slab of a door at the end of
e corridor of cells crashed open. Grant knew because he checked
s pocket watch. Two pairs of boot heels echoed along the corridor
d stopped at his cell door. There was a jangle of keys, the door
vung open, and there entered the heroically proportioned form of
'illiam MacGillivray in fawn-colored trousers and a beaver coat.
ne stride carried him halfway across the cell, a broad smile on
s face and his right hand extended. "Well, Cuthbert!"

"Well, William." The smile flickered out. If he'd been expect-
g "Mister MacGillivray," Grant thought grimly, he should have
arted with "Mister Grant."

The jailer cleared his throat discreetly, said, "I'll be just outside,
r," and started to pull the door closed behind him.

MacGillivray stopped it with his hand. "No need to wait—I may
e a while. Go on back to the guardroom. I'll call you when I'm
ne.''

The jailer didn't quite tug on his forelock, but the effect was the
me. Once his footsteps had faded down the corridor, Mister
[acGillivray turned to Grant. "Well now . . ." It looked as though
e were about to say "Cuthbert" again, but he didn't. "So many
eeks have passed since last I saw you.''

"It's very good of you to have responded so quickly to my note."

"How could I do otherwise? You know I've always had the great-
t concern for your welfare. I deeply regret that business and fam-
y matters have so occupied my mind of late that I've been
eglecting to call." He slipped off his massive coat, the silk lining
iding smoothly over the broadcloth beneath. He slung it up over
e rail on the upper bunk and sat down on the lower beside Grant.
Now, how might I best advise you?"

"Let's start by my advising you that if my case goes to trial, I'll
ill my guts.''

Mister MacGillivray flew to his feet, his boardroom bellow
uncing off the walls: "Don't take that tone with me, sir!"

Grant didn't so much as blink an eyelash, despite the fact that
e old boy could still put on a pretty good show. "With all due
spect, Mister MacGillivray, sir—you would be well advised to
sten to me regardless of what tone I care to use." He wasn't nearly

as confident as he sounded, but Mister MacGillivray closed hi
mouth, crossed his arms, and waited. "Once broken down to it
essential elements, the situation is quite simple. I don't want t
serve a prison sentence, and I certainly don't want to hang. Yo
don't want it to come out that those nasty half-breeds in the north
west have only been doing what 'the Honourable William Mac
Gillivray' encouraged them to do.

"My case is due to go to trial in a few days. They're bound t
convict me on one charge or another. When I am called upon t
testify, I intend to do so with my whole heart in the grand old kir
manner, and I shall not stop testifying until I have unburdened m
soul of every trace of sin I've committed or seen or heard of sinc
the day I stepped off the ship from Inverness. So it would seer
quite obviously a matter of no debate whatever that neither you nc
I want me to stand trial."

Mister MacGillivray stroked his side-whiskers and said: "At th
particular juncture, however, that does seem difficult to avoid."

"I think not. Get me bailed. Two or three hundred pound:
whatever it takes—perhaps as much as half a year's interest on m
father's estate. I'll slip out of the city and forfeit the bond. If an
officers of the law care to pursue me into the *pays d'en haut*, it
be their own lookout."

"Jumping bail would look like an admission of guilt."

" 'Guilt' has become a rather nebulous concept of late, wouldn
you say?"

"They refused to grant you bail at the preliminary hearing."

"I don't recall that the company's lawyers put up much of a figl
about it. But then, of course, at that time you were assuming I'd g
to the gallows quietly, like a gentleman."

"Can you truly believe I would sell you that way?" Evidentl
Grant's expression made the question rhetorical. Mister Mac
Gillivray's eyes actually misted over. He blinked and looked away
up to the high, barred bit of window that gave the cell a glimpse c
sky. He said with an anguished sigh: "All the time you've been i
here we have been fighting feverishly to keep them from movin
your trial to Quebec or Kingston—Selkirk thinks he'd have more c
a chance of a conviction outside of Montreal. We've been movin
heaven and earth to find a way to save you."

"I've found a way."

"But to bolt like that . . . wouldn't it be best for you to have i
settled once and for all, to clear your name? Isn't that why yo
came here in the first place? If we could arrange to have it tried i

front of an amenable magistrate, if we could guarantee a verdict of innocent, couldn't you see your way clear to stand trial without bringing anyone else's name into it?''

"And what if the judge didn't live up to your guarantee? I wouldn't be in much of a bargaining position after the fact.''

"Do you distrust me that much?'' The tone was genuinely injured. Grant was flooded for a moment with memories. After all, it was Mister MacGillivray who had taken him under his wing when his parents were dead, who had chosen to send him to Inverness when a few cursory years in parochial school were good enough for any other half-breed, who had given him a better leg up in the company than his own father could have.

He looked straight at the great man's wounded blue eyes and said: "You misunderstand me. I trust you implicitly to look out for my own welfare as though it were your own—so long as I remind you that it is.''

"You've grown into a hard man, Cuthbert.''

"I've had hard teachers, Mister MacGillivray.''

"Selkirk would scream bloody murder if he got a whiff of a bail application. He'll be out of the city for a few days near the end of the week—traveling to Quebec for an interview with the governor in chief. . . .'' He reached for his coat. Grant took it and helped him on with it. "I'll see that you're provided with a draft to draw on against the money from your father's estate. I'd hoped to get the entire estate signed over to you while you were here, but of course that's out of the question now.''

"Of course.'' The words grated across the roof of his mouth like ground glass.

Mister MacGillivray flung open the cell door and bellowed: "Jailer!'' He turned back to Grant. "Well, Cuthbert, I'd hate to think we parted on ill terms.''

"So would I, sir.''

"You realize that the step you've decided to take may exile you from civilization forever?''

"It beats the hell out of being exiled from life.''

"Well, you're your father's son right enough—once he'd got his mind set in a certain direction, there was no turning him. He'd have been proud to see the man you've grown into, by and large. Well . . .'' He stuck out his hand. "Good luck to you.''

Grant took it. "And to you, sir.'' MacGillivray's hand enveloped Grant's completely, casting him back to the days when the great man used to tousle his hair and ask him what he'd learned in school.

Now, though, Grant was quite sure that if he exerted all his strength, he could crush MacGillivray's meaty hand into bone chips in aspic.

The jailer came down the corridor and escorted Mister MacGillivray back out to the open air. Grant flung himself down on his bed and blew the stale air out of his lungs. He felt as if he'd just gone three falls with a team of Bostonais Pangmans.

Two days later, at the morning sitting of a certain magistrate whose home was mortgaged to Todd & McGill, bail was granted to Mister Cuthbert Grant for a surety of two hundred pounds. Grant went straight from the courthouse to the nearest ostler's and hired a horse for the day. He trotted languidly through the melt-slick streets of Montreal, then kicked the horse into a canter when he got out into the farm country. He rode the length of the Island of Montreal to the little chapel of Ste. Anne de Bellevue, where the outward-bound canoe brigades stopped to pray for a safe return.

The next day the horse was returned to the ostler by an itinerant farmhand who'd once been employed by the North West Company as a voyageur. He told the ostler he'd found the horse wandering in a field and had taken a guess as to its owner. He wouldn't even accept the shilling the ostler offered him as a reward—merely doing his Christian duty as any honest man would . . . well, perhaps a tot of rum, then, if monsieur insisted. . . .

CHAPTER 80

Although the harvest from the fields that had seeded themselves hadn't been monumental, there was actually a certain amount of grain left over after all the fields on Point Douglas had been sown. The Point Douglas Sutherlands waited for the new crops to come up, waited until the green stalks grew tall and heavy headed and the blue began to burn out from the mated colors of sun and sky, and then decided it was safe to eat the surplus seed.

Behind a shed in a corner of Fort Douglas was a quern, a form of grinding mill older than the Old Testament: two roughly circular stones set on top of each other, one dished inward and the other outward. A hole was bored through the middle of the upper stone, which was revolved back and forth by means of two wooden handles set opposite each other, rather like a two-handled saw.

Kate and Marie Anne were kneeling on opposite sides of the quern, alternately pushing and pulling on the handles. Catherine Pritchard knelt to one side, funneling handfuls of wheat into the feeder hole. Kate had tried to teach them a quern song but hadn't had much success. Marie Anne got them singing a weaving song from Trois Rivières. The rhythm wasn't quite right, but the other two had a better ear for French than Marie Anne had for Gaelic. When they'd sung that one out it was Mrs. Pritchard's turn. It took some coaxing; with each passing year she became noticeably more reluctant to refer to her Indian childhood. Finally she came out with a song in Blackfoot. They learned it phonetically, sang it through with her a few times, then asked her what it meant.

"When you take away where the same word goes over and over and all such, it means: 'There was a woman who married a buffalo dropping, but he had a medicine pipe between his knees.' "

Kate and Marie Anne laughed so hard they had to stop turning the quern. Mrs. Pritchard blushed furiously, and Kate and Marie Anne had to do a lot of coaxing to reassure her that she hadn't committed some horrible faux pas. Even then she didn't seem entirely convinced.

Without the rumble and rasp of the quern, they began to hear a strange, distant whirring sound somewhere to the west. A number of men hurried over from Colony House and climbed up onto the firing ledge on the west wall of the stockade, pointing over the palisade and shouting questions at each other.

The three women stood up and headed for the ladder in the near corner of the palisade, Marie Anne and Mrs. Pritchard pausing to take up their newest crop of infants.

The line of men had become so dense that they had to squeeze their way onto the catwalk. Beyond the few scattered trees behind the fort stretched a perfectly typical summer day. On the prairie the soft mauves and yellows shifted among the greens, dancing with the breezes. Overhead a few owl-white clouds butted across the bolt of blue. But there was another cloud—a long, dark, snake-like shape writhing its way out of the west. From its color and from the drizzle lines hazing down from it, Kate assumed it must be a rain cloud, but she had never seen a cloud that shape, nor one that low.

Catherine Pritchard said an Indian word, apparently groping fo.
a European equivalent. Marie Anne said, *"Sauterelle?"* and made
a kind of gnashing motion with her front teeth and fingertips. Mrs.
Pritchard nodded enthusiastically and made a stab at repeating
"sauterelle."

Kate said: "What does it mean?"

"Les sauterelles—they are . . . mmm—the locusts."

The only impression that called up was of the Reverend James
Ross thundering from the pulpit of Gaillable Kirk about "a plague
of locusts." Kate had imagined they were some sort of biting insec
in the Bible lands, not in the wilds of North America.

Catherine Pritchard said: "They are nuisance, messy, but of no
real hurt. Birds like it when they come, big feast. But sometime
they make the buffalo go away, for they eat of the grass."

"The birds?"

"No, the . . . *sauterelles*?"

Marie Anne nodded. "Just so—*les* locusts."

"They eat the grass?"

"Yes. The seeds, the leaves, the . . . everything."

The same thought hit all three of them at the same time. They
piled down the ladder and herded together the scattered member-
of the Lajimodierre and Pritchard broods. Then they ran out of the
fort gates together and split off in three different directions—Mrs.
Pritchard running north along the cart track with her arms full o
children, Marie Anne bustling La Reine and La Prairie and the
others down the riverbank to their canoe, and Kate flying along the
woods path to Point Douglas and the fields of wheat and barley
fattening in the sun.

She was almost through the bush when the sky went black. Sud
denly she was in the midst of a whirring, humming fog so thick i
blotted out the sun. The particles that composed it whirled and flew
in all directions, batting into each other and into her, caroming of
and crunching underfoot. They settled onto her shoulders and
hopped off or settled into her hair and stayed, dropping down the
neck of her blouse. Some of them were as long and thick as he
little finger. She yanked her shawl up to cover her head and kep
on running, holding one arm up to shield her eyes.

Something flew into her mouth, legs scrabbling on her tongue
and wings rattling against her palate. She spat it out and clampe
her jaws shut. Her right foot came down on a writhing carpet an
slipped in the crushed-out juice. She fell hard on her back. The ha
of bodies from the sky began to settle on her. When she put the

palm of her hand on the ground to lever herself upright, it came down on a seething mass of carapaces and wings and antennae. She jerked her hand away and set it down on another place—but that place was covered, too. She pressed down hard and pushed herself to her feet, wiping her hand on her skirt.

The cloud seemed to be thinning. She began to see bits of sky and trees again through the whirling haze. At first she thought she had come to the edge of the swarm, or that it was moving on. Then she realized that it was settling.

The sun came out again. She discovered that she was standing on the edge of their barley field. Her husband was flailing away at the plants with an old blanket. There were green-black tumors sprouting out of the barley heads and the stalks and the ground around them, heaving and crackling, feeding. The individual components of the growths looked exactly like the harmless grasshoppers she might see bouncing across her yard on any given summer day. Some were long and rangy, some were short and chunky. Their sleek, jointed armor ranged from yellow to green to black, with gleaming, luminous, symmetrically forked designs ornamented in contrasting colors.

Sandy paused just long enough to turn his ravaged, red-eyed face to her and roar: "Help me!"

She stripped off her shawl and waded in among the barley, flailing away at the locusts. But it was no use. They could flail at them, they could strip them off the plants with their fingers, they could crush them in their hands by the cupful; the creatures still kept eating, crawling over the bodies of their dead to get their mandibles around the next seed. The robins and blackbirds were stuffing their craws fiendishly, but it made no difference to the swarm.

Sandy said: "There is no hope. We must try to save what we can for seed."

"I will fetch sacks."

They were in the house as well—pattering down the chimney and hopping off the hearth. She threw a few sticks of kindling onto the coals, hoping the smoke might keep them out, and yanked a handful of empty bags off a peg in the wall.

Outside, she handed half the bags to Sandy. They worked from one end of the field to the other—breaking off half-ripened barley heads, scraping off the locusts, whipping their laden hands in and out through the drawstring openings so the insects couldn't get in. In the end, they only half filled two small sacks. They went over to start on the wheatfield.

By the time they'd gathered all the seed they could save, the sun
was bleeding out into the brief summer night. They sealed themselves into the house. Kate built up the fire to cook supper, although
the thought of swallowing anything made her want to retch. Suddenly she remembered the bag of flour she'd left sitting by the
quern.

Sandy had lit the wick of their foul-smelling tallow lamp and
was prowling about the floor killing locusts. She went to the door
and said: "I have to go to the fort to fetch something. The grain
was grinding . . ."

"You left it there?"

"I only thought of saving what we had here."

"I suppose I would have done the same. Go! God knows we will
need every speck we can scrape together now."

The locusts were spread thinner now, and most of them were off
the path among the wild grass. When she reached the fort the shadows had lengthened and were beginning to meld together. The bag
of flour was still sitting by the quern, but she saw that she'd left the
mouth open. Inside was a mass of gorging bodies. She went to the
quern; perhaps there would be a few handfuls of half-crushed grain
between the stones.

Over the feeder hole of the quern there was a squirming lump of
carapaces, shouldering each other out of the way to crawl down the
tunnel to the treasures inside. She wrapped both fists around the
nearer handle and put her shoulders into it.

CHAPTER 81

On the lee side of a bend in the Qu'Appelle River three
miles below Fort Esperance, the Terror of the Plains sat
naked on a slime-skinned underwater rock with only his dripping
head and his hands above the surface. He was attempting to shave
his face in a palm-sized metal traveling mirror. The razor scraped
and snagged continuously, and the cup of lather kept falling off the
rock it was balanced on—forcing him to scramble after his badg

rtail brush—his hobbled horse had chosen to empty its bowels on
he edge of the bank upwind, but the only thing that stood a chance
of scratching the shiny surface of his joy was the question of whether
ae could sing through the three final verses of "Jock Hock's Adventures in Glasgow" without losing the rhythm between razor
strokes or severing his windpipe.

After a last once-over in the mirror, he shook his head underwater, then stood down off the rock and walked in deeper, letting
the current scour the last traces of dust from his body. He climbed
out onto shore warily, watching the rocks for crawfish.

There were clumps of bright yellow flowers growing among the
shore reeds, too broad and heavy for their drooping stems. He
wondered what they were called and how long they bloomed.
He was planning to learn those things now. It was time he started
devoting more attention to his mother's legacy—this country and
the people who belonged in it.

He let the sun and the breeze dry him while he turned his attention to the gear piled beside his saddle. He picked up his stiffjointed traveling clothes, whose smell had seemed so innocuous
until he'd bathed himself, and tossed them in the river. From one
saddlebag he took out a blanket-wrapped bundle and unrolled it.
Inside were the presents he'd bought at Fort William for his family—a tiny pair of Ojibway beadwork moccasins, a silk shawl, and
a leather-bound copy of Lord Byron's "Childe Harold's Pilgrimage." This last-named item was more than a bit dog-eared. He'd
had to pry it out of the private library of one of the clerks at a price
that would have brought British booksellers storming Lake Superior
by the shipload.

Tamped down in the bottom of the saddlebag were a few other
bundles of cloth. He shook them out: a swan-white linen shirt and
lace neckcloth and a pair of doeskin trousers. They were irreparably
rumpled, but the general effect would hold. Unfortunately he had
no replacement for the battered riding boots he'd worn since Montreal. Over the shirt he drew on the fringed and quillworked jacket
Bethsy had made for him. He went to the river to have a look at his
reflection. No doubt about it, he was a damned good-looking fellow.

There were a lot of fire-red lilies in the meadow bordering the
bank. Once he'd saddled his horse, he took his knife and cut an
extravagant number of them, along with a smattering of yellow
flowers for contrast. He tucked the presents into his shirt, settled

the flowers into the crook of his left arm along with his rifle, an swung up into the saddle.

It was a difficult decision whether to gallop full bore into For Esperance or saunter in casually. He settled on the languid ap proach. They would have had no word that he was coming; he' ridden straight across country from Lake Winnipeg, leaving th incoming brigade weeks behind him. The last news Bethsy woul have had of him was when Eostonais and the others came home i the spring, leaving him locked in the Montreal jail with two murde charges hanging over him.

Despite his best intentions for a dignified entrance, once th palisades of Esperance crept into view, his horse caught his moo and speeded up. He careened through the open gates barely keep ing his seat—six months lounging in a jail had softened him some what. He heard the shout of recognition from the sentry over th gate, but he didn't look back or slow his horse, merely gallope straight for the shake-roofed cabin in the southeast corner of th stockade. He reined the horse in hard just before they were due t crash into the front door.

The door was closed, and no one was out front. On a day lik this, he thought, James should be playing outside. Perhaps he' missed them; they might have gone out on the prairie with Falco or John Richards. He hopped out of the saddle, bounced to th door, and threw it open.

A man he'd never seen before was sitting at the table, which wa closer to the door than it was supposed to be. The curtain that ha separated his and Bethsy's sleeping area from Josephte's was gone along with all the things that had hung on the walls. Four beds wer ranged along the wall opposite the hearth, like a barracks for e gagés. Grant brought his eyes back to the man sitting at the tabl and said: "Who the hell are you?"

"Who the hell are *you*?"

"Cuthbert Grant."

"Jesus . . ."

"Close enough." Leaving his left arm to hold the flowers, h brought his rifle up and cocked it one-handed. With the full exten sion of his right arm behind it, the muzzle almost touched the ti of the *engagé*'s nose. "Where is my wife? And my son? And m sister and her son?" The *engagé* sat stiff and speechless with h mouth half-open, staring cross-eyed into the mouth of the rifl "Where?"

"I . . . I don't know."

"He doesn't know."

The voice came from behind Grant, in the doorway. He turned his head slightly, just far enough to be able to see over his shoulder and keep an eye on the *engagé* at the same time.

Pierre Falcon was standing in the doorway. He didn't greet Grant or extend his hand, just said: "It's a bad omen for the day to kill a stranger before noon."

"I hadn't heard that."

Falcon shrugged. "May be just an old wives' tale, but that's what they say."

Grant raised the rifle over the *engagé's* head, then brought his left hand up to ease the hammer down. He turned back to Falcon and said: "Where are they? What's happened?"

"Josephte and John are with me—or with Mary, up where I'm camped on Rivière Tremblante—I just came in today for powder. Bethsy and James . . . no one knows where they are."

"What? I don't understand."

"I don't understand it either, but that's what's happened. They're gone. Since late spring. She went out riding one day, with James perched in front of her. They never came back."

"What? Didn't anyone look for them? Couldn't you—"

"Of course we looked for them." Falcon kept his voice deliberate and calm. "Every man from both forts was fanned out across the country for two days. We thought maybe her horse had gone down, or maybe the Sioux or Assiniboines . . . But then Josephte started to notice there were little things gone from the house, things someone would take if they weren't planning to come back."

"What the hell is that supposed to mean?"

"I don't know. It means whatever it means. I can only tell you what I know. And that's all I know. Nobody knows anything more."

"We'll see." He stepped to the doorway. Falcon put his arm across it, gripping the doorpost with his hand. The furrows around his eyes grew deeper. He had the look of a man with a knife stuck in him.

"Wappeston, you won't find out more by pushing guns in people's faces. Nobody knows."

Grant moved Falcon's arm aside and went out into the sunlight. He snatched up his horse's reins, threw the flowers aside, and put his boot into the stirrup. Then the man he was going to see came trotting through the front gate—John Richards McKay, his horse's hocks still dripping from the ford. He rode over to Grant and dismounted. He looked down at the scattered flowers, then back up

to Grant and said: "I told our sentries to keep an eye out for you,
just in case."

"Where is she?"

"I don't know. If it were anyone except my sister, I wouldn't
think it possible; you know how you can't break wind around here
without everyone in both forts inquiring after the state of your digestion. But no one knew she had any intention of leaving until she
was gone. And all that we know now is that she is gone."

"Two days of looking and then you just throw your hands up?
Your own sister!"

"There wasn't a trace. Wherever she went, she hid her trail
well."

"That's ludicrous. Why would she do that?"

"If you were running out on Cuthbert Grant, would you want
him to be able to find you?"

Grant reached out and took hold of John Richards's throat with
his right hand. The flesh underneath the jaw was soft against the
webbing between his thumb and forefinger. The pulse in the jugular
veins thumped rhythmically against the pads of his fingers. If he
squeezed hard enough, maybe everything would go away.

John Richards didn't try to fight back, merely held his hands up
slackly in front of him. Falcon didn't try to pull Grant off, merely
placed one hand lightly on his shoulder. Grant let go. John Richards
leaned against his horse and got his breath back, then croaked
"*Quid est demonstratum,*" and reached into one of his saddlebags
for a square-shouldered quart bottle. He drew the cork out with his
teeth and handed it to Grant.

It was the genuine article, shipped at God knew what expense
from some spring-fed glen on the far side of the world. After a
couple of deep pulls, Grant passed it on to Falcon, who took a
tentative swig and handed it back to John Richards. John Richards
looked around the courtyard and said: "I could think of more amenable places to drink." Grant realized that every man, woman, and
child attached to Fort Esperance had come up with some innocuous
task to perform within eye- and earshot of what had been the cabin
of the Grants.

The three of them rode to a camping spot upriver where the
willows shaded the bank. When the bottle got low John Richards
fished about in his saddlebag and produced another. Grant suggested they should root out Bostonais to help them drink it, but it
turned out no one knew where he was. He'd come back with the
brigade in the spring but then had disappeared. It was nothing of

of the ordinary for Bostonais to take off on his own for weeks at a time, although this time it was starting to add up to months.

Partway into the second bottle, the gears that had been grinding up Grant's insides moved apart and lost their teeth. They would grow back.

CHAPTER 82

The Kildonan colony spent the winter at the Hudson's Bay Company's Fort Daer on the Pembina River. If they could make it through until summer living on what they hunted, the seeds they'd managed to save from the locusts could save them. Over the course of the winter they learned that if one grew hungry enough, buffalo guts could be edible, that a buffalo head could be boiled for soup, that buffalo hooves could be rendered down into a paste with some nutritional value.

When spring came, they learned why the Sioux called the Pembina country the Hair Hills. Every thorn bush and rough-barked tree, every object that bore even the slightest resemblance to a scratching post, became covered over in clumps and wisps of winter-weight buffalo wool. In the interim before the day of departure down the Red to the Forks, Kate managed to stuff half a dozen empty pemmican sacks to take home to her spinning wheel.

Despite the fact that the house on Point Douglas had only been secured with a stick shoved through the latchstring to keep the door from blowing open, there had been no intrusions over the course of the winter, save for a few mouse nests in the thatch and a bit of fraying on a corner beam where a porcupine had tried a taste.

They started seeding as soon as the fields were dry enough to walk on, risking the chance of a late frost in their desperation for an early harvest. The plants survived and came up fast and healthy. By mid-June they were tall and green and succulent. That was when the other seeds began to hatch.

Every female locust in last year's swarm had dug a shaft into the ground and emptied her hundreds of eggs into it before she'd died or flown on. The eggs had lain dormant through the winter and the spring, but the summer sun warmed the earth enough to hatch them. They crawled blindly upward toward the warmth, pushing through the pellets of earth until they broke out into the light. First there were only a few scattered green-black freshets bubbling up here and there between the furrows. But soon the entire surface of the fields was boiling with them.

They ate the seeds, they ate the leaves, they ate the stalks, they ate the bark off the trees. When there was nothing left to eat, they died. Their bodies lay ankle deep over the ground, blanketing the river, clogging the streams and fouling the water, putrefying in the sun. The Point Douglas Sutherlands spent three days shoveling dead locusts into the sacks that they had planned to fill with grain and dumping them into the river. Even when the river finally ran clear again, the shore rocks were still littered with insect bodies all the way down to the lake. There was no seed saved this time.

Fortunately the half-breeds and the Indians started trailing into Fort Douglas with the proceeds from the spring buffalo hunt, and the fishing on the lake was good. But when the snow came again the Kildonan people had no choice but to trek back to Fort Daer. On a brisk day in November, Sandy and Jean Baptiste Lajimodierre were trailing a wind-blurred hoof track through the snow. Excluding the sighing of the wind and the occasional crack of a cold-split branch, the only sounds in the entire pallid, sparkling universe were the muted crunch of their snowshoes and the hissing of the empty toboggans following on their leashes.

Sandy strained his ears against the sibilant whistle of the wind and his eyes against the churned-up track ahead, trying to hear what Lajimodierre was hearing and to see what he was seeing. According to Lajimodierre, they were following two buffalo, a bull and a cow, but Sandy couldn't tell how he knew that. He told himself not to feel too inadequate—Lajimodierre had been born with a vocation, had found it young, and had been practicing it for a quarter of a century.

They came to the base of a wooded rise. Lajimodierre took off his snowshoes, uncovered his rifle, and moved forward in a crouch, leaving his toboggan behind. Sandy followed suit. As they approached the crest of the ridge, they both plunked down on their elbows, shrugged off their fur hats, and poked their eyes up over the lip of snow. Two big hump-shouldered creatures grazed on the slope below, pushing at the snow with their noses to get at the buried grass, a bull and a cow. Lajimodierre winked at Sandy, a much as to say: "Call me lucky," although luck didn't appear to have much to do with it, then looked to the priming of his rifle.

They waited for the bull to move out of the line of fire and for the cow to turn her shoulder toward them. Then they both rose and fired at the same time. When the smoke cleared the cow was sliding down the slope on her side, her legs kicking spasmodically. By the time they'd reloaded, the snow ploughed up by her slide had banked high enough to stop her.

The bull hadn't run off. He was nudging at her body with his nose, trying to work his head under her as though to lift her onto her hooves. Lajimodierre stood and waved his cap in the air and shouted to scare him off. Instead the buffalo charged at them, pounding up the ridge in that peculiar sideways-sighted gallop. He came about half the distance, then stopped and shook his horns at them. Then he turned, trotted down to the cow with his tufted tail high in the air and went back to nuzzling at her.

Lajimodierre gave a disgusted grunt, raised his rifle, and put a bullet behind the bull's left shoulder. The bull shuddered and turned to face them, standing over the cow with his head slung low. They each put two more bullets into him—or at least Sandy was relatively sure he'd hit him both times. The bull just stood there. Finally Lajimodierre said, "He's finish, just too dumb to fall down," and started down the hill, mumbling, "Damn waste, too heavy to haul back, too tough to eat if you ain't starving, waste of powder, waste of bullet, waste of him, waste of time . . ."

Sandy said: "Have you ever seen that happen before?"

"Hm?"

"A bull like that with a cow—trying to help her up rather than running away?"

"Oh. Sometime they will, in the rutting season."

"I thought the rutting season was the summer?"

"Mostly. There are more buffalo in the *pays d'en haut* than there are people in all the continent. When you get into that many numbers, only a fool or a schoolteacher will tell you that every one of them is going to act the exact same."

They both had to put their shoulders into the bull before he finally crashed over on his side, throwing up a cloud of snow. Sandy went back to fetch the toboggans and their snowshoes while Lajimodierre started the butchering. While they were carving up the cow, Lajimodierre said: "The colony people want me to guide some men down to Prairie du Chien, on the Mississippi, to buy grain for seed and bring it back for the spring. It will need a dozen men or so. Why don't you be one of them?''

"How far is it?''

"Don't know, I never go that way before. I think maybe two, three month walking down. Coming back we take boats.''

"Would you not be better off taking younger men? My knee . . .''

"Most of them will be young men, but they ain't no good without a few with fiber in their bones to show them how. When all them young men will get tired and want to quit, you will still be humping along on that bad knee, shame them into going on.''

It was obvious that Lajimodierre wasn't paying a compliment, merely making a statement of fact, which made it all the more complimentary. Sandy said: "I would have to speak to my wife about it.''

She said: "Could they not find a younger man to—''

"I am barely thirty-four years old, hardly doddering into my grave!''

She shushed him. They were bundled in their makeshift bed in their corner of the cabin they shared with a dozen other winter refugees from the colony. The corners were the least snug sleeping places, especially the two flanking the door, but at least they gave the illusion of privacy. He continued in a calmer tone: "Jean Baptiste seems to think I would be of some help to him.''

"Must you go?''

"Somebody must. We need the seed the same as everyone else.'' He didn't mention that it was also an opportunity for him to feel that he was capable of doing something that actively affected events, instead of standing by and letting them wash over him.

She said matter-of-factly: "I suppose you must, then.''

They lay side by side gazing at the fire shadows flickering on the rafter poles. She reached out and moved her hand across his belly. It seemed perfunctory and awkward, a case of what they were supposed to do on the eve of a long separation. They went through the motions.

On the morning that their little troop lined up to leave, she stood in front of him with her hands on his shoulders, her cheeks red with the pinch of the wind, a few wayward strands of hair floating like copper ribbons against the glinting white field behind her. She tugged at the buffalo-wool muffler she'd knitted for him, tucking it in snugly, and said: "Come back.''

It took them most of the winter to reach the American settlemen of Prairie du Chien, four hundred miles to the southeast. They froze, they starved, they lost their way in blizzards, they all lost their tempers more than once, but they didn't lose one man. They had to wait a month in Prairie du Chien for the river to clear before starting back. They used the time wisely, filling in the hollows between their ribs and dickering out the maximum tonnage of wheat, barley, oats, and rye they could get in exchange for the thousand pounds they were authorized to spend. When spring came they loaded their sacks of seed onto flatboats and headed up the Mississippi.

It was June by the time they made their last shore camp before the Forks of the Red River. They were traveling in canoes now; they had left the flatboats behind when it came time to portage from the Mississippi River system to the Red. Their complement had been filled out by a half dozen young Ojibway aglint with avarice for all the riches Lajimodierre had promised in the name of the colony and the Hudson's Bay Company. They spent the last hour of twilight scrubbing out shirts and draping them over bushes to dry overnight, trimming each other's beards by firelight, and scrubbing themselves in the muddy river.

With Point Douglas only one day upstream, Sandy noticed the return of a curiously flayed feeling that had died down to a subconscious murmur over the months away. It felt as if there were indelible patches on him where he had no skin, in the places where he and Kate MacPherson had grown together.

Lajimodierre plunked himself down on the other side of the smudge fire and lit his pipe. Sandy said: "Looks like we made it."

Lajimodierre grinned and said: "Surprised the hell from me." He took the pipe out of his mouth, winked, and said: "I think you been a lot of different thing in your life, and now you are another one—*un homme du nord*."

As they passed by the Forks and came within sight of Point Douglas, Sandy strained his eyes trying to pierce the rippling green curtain masking the south shore of Point Douglas. Through a gap in the foliage he glimpsed a patch of black that suggested Kate had already weeded and furrowed the fields in preparation for the seed. When it came down to it, he supposed that the only real cause he had for concern about leaving her alone was that she might have discovered she could do a better job of things without him.

The fort guns banged out a salute. The long slope of the bank in front of Fort Douglas was covered with people. As the canoes hove into shore they burst into cheers and applause. Sandy scanned the

514 Alfred Silver

crowd, expecting that she would have planted herself in the fron
rank to welcome him. He couldn't find her. He picked out Mari
Anne Lajimodierre, standing beside a tall woman with the swolle
silhouette and swaybacked posture of advanced pregnancy, but Kate
was nowhere in sight.

Mister MacBeth and his oldest boys formed part of the crew tha
waded out into the shallows to steady the canoes and help with the
unloading. Mister MacBeth took hold of Sandy's forearm to give
him a hand out of the boat, clapping him on the back with his othe
arm.

As Sandy stepped over the gunwale he nodded at Mister MacBeth
abstractly, his eyes still on the crowd. They returned to Marie Anne
Lajimodierre, since that was most likely where he would find hi
wife. They passed over the pregnant woman standing beside he
and then suddenly jolted back.

His left foot was still in the canoe, leaving him tottering precar
iously on one leg. He lost his balance and pushed his left foot dow
hard to recover. It tore straight down through the bark and into th
water. Mister MacBeth caught hold of him and steadied him. Sand
pulled his foot back out through the hole, and the river came gush
ing in behind it.

There was an instant of panicked scrambling by all hands, bu
since the sacks of grain had already been safely unloaded, it a
became a grand joke. Sandy walked away from it, past boisterou
volunteers shouldering the cargo out of the other boats, past colon
officials gravely shaking hands with Lajimodierre as though the
had somehow been responsible for the success of the expedition
As he came to the top of the bank, she moved toward him, wit
the one-leg-at-a-time pregnant walk that seemed so alien on her
He put his hands on her shoulders but couldn't think of anything t
say. He edged forward, gingerly settling his forearms around he
back, and rested his cheek against hers. She said, "I won't break,"
and clasped him to her almost hard enough to pop his ribs.

When he could breathe again he took a half step back to look a
her. The planes under her cheekbones had filled out. Her eyes ha
a placid assurance. He said: "When will . . . ?"

"Mrs. MacBeth figures mid-August."

There was no trace in her of the shyness that had taken hold o
him. He well knew that the self-assurance she generally showe
the world was more a facade than anything else. But the self
possession she had now was different. Whatever uncertainties sh
might still be harboring in her mind and her heart, her body knew

that the world was revolving around it. He said: "If I had known in November, I never would have left."

"If I had known in November, I never would have let you."

He took her arm and walked her home, her waddle matching his limp. His mind kept edging off toward a simple computation, but he managed to hold it off until they were almost to the house. Then he gave in, feeling like the lowest scoundrel that had ever graced a trash heap but unable to stop himself. Without moving his fingers to give it away he counted back nine months from August.

CHAPTER 83

The trees were sparsely boughed and set closely together, black colonnades against the cool moonlit white of snow. The irregular avenues of white clicked shut and reopened like magic lantern slides as the progress of Grant's horse along the path altered his vantage point. Grant could see his breath in the air, but he didn't feel the cold.

The squared-off black cabin was suddenly in front of him, a blue trace of smoke fingering out the chimney. He slid down off his horse silently and walked forward, angling his moccasin toes first into the snow to knife the crust instead of crunching it.

He stopped in front of the door and unbuttoned his coat. There was a muffled sound from the other side of the door—a woman's laugh, low and languid. He tore open the door and drew the pistols out of his sash at the same time, surprising himself with his own dexterity.

The hearth fire cast more light than he would have expected. He could see them clearly, lying on a bed of buffalo robes and striped white blankets. Bostonais had his back to the door and was propped up on one arm, twisting his head over his shoulder to look back. Between Bostonais's naked, slab-muscled torso and his arm, her face peered out. The blankets were wreathed in disarray. One pretty, slender calf was draped across the small of Bostonais's back.

As she opened her mouth to scream, Grant put a bullet in it. An instant later he twitched the forefinger on his left hand, firing through her ankle into Bostonais's spine. As Bostonais bowed back from the impact, Grant's right forefinger twitched again. Impossibly, the pistol fired without reloading. He didn't question it but just kept pulling the triggers. The pistols kept firing, pounding two-ounce lumps of lead into rib cages, bellies, backs, elbows, eyes . . .

Grant wrenched himself bodily out of the dream. His head hit the ground. It was a warm, moonless summer night. He was camped in a stand of poplars by a lake, with his coat rolled up for a pillow. He wasn't camped alone; there were a good many other sleepers dotted around him. One of them—Cadotte, it was—had raised his head and was peering at him groggily—he must have made some sort of sound when he'd jerked himself out of the dream. He made a dismissive gesture with his hand, and Cadotte laid his head back down.

Grant dug his flask out of his gear and shook it hopefully against his ear. He was rewarded with a happy little splashing. He crawled away from his bed and hunkered down beside the embers of the fire. After a long slug of rum the world began to steady itself. He was ashamed that he could imagine such a thing of Bostonais, even in a dream. The only link that existed between Bethsy and Bostonais was their mutual disappearance; there had been no concrete word from either of them in the two years since he'd returned from Montreal. In that time there had been rumors of Bostonais: someone had seen him stretched out with a hole in his back, someone else had seen him very much alive in the foothills of the Rockies, someone else had heard that he was guiding for the British along the Columbia River. There had been no word at all about a fair-haired métis woman with a black-haired child.

Grant's head gave a sudden sideways jerk like a terrier flinging a rat over his shoulder. He had buried Bethsy long ago, in Madelaine Desmairais of the soft, taut thighs, and buoyant Janet MacDougal, and Buffalo Wallow Woman, and several others besides. He had spent that first summer searching as far west as Fort des Prairies before he'd asked himself whether he wanted to spend the rest of his life looking for a woman who didn't want him to find her.

It was a bit of a strain on coincidence that Bostonais should choose to disappear at exactly the same time, but that was hardly enough to justify the kind of nightmare Grant's subconscious had just produced. In a country as big as the *pays d'en haut*, it was perfectly possible for a loner like Bostonais to disappear for years without choosing to. And there were lots of reasons why he might have chosen to that didn't have anything to do with James and Bethsy. After Frog Plain and the hearings and all, it was understandable that a man might want to remove himself from the companies' spheres of influence. Grant occasionally planned to do that himself, on those days when he tricked himself into thinking he had something else to go to.

When he thought back he couldn't come up with even a hint of any special tenderness between Bethsy and Bostonais. They had always been polite but distant; two sides of Grant's life that didn't mesh. But then again, perhaps that distance had been something they'd imposed on each other for his benefit. . . .

The morning birds began to sing, the morning breeze off the lake began to rustle the leaves, the camp began to stagger to its feet. There was a single, surreptitious splash from the bank that no one but Grant seemed to hear. Some poor muskrat had woken up several mornings ago to find fifty fur trade men camped on the roof of its den. Grant had a pretty good idea of its underwater entrance, but he preferred to see the muskrat beat the odds.

It was all Colin Robertson's fault that they were there. He had returned last summer from escorting Duncan Cameron to the British courts. Cameron had stayed in Britain, not because he was constrained by the courts—his charges had been dismissed—but because he had stumbled across a gold mine. He was suing the Earl of Selkirk for false arrest.

The last couple of seasons had been a trade-off of both companies plagiarizing Grant's invention of nabbing the opposition's brigade when the boats were spat out helpless at the foot of white water. For three days now, Robertson and the HBC's Athabasca brigade had been perched at the upstream end of the grand rapids of the Saskatchewan River while Grant and Whitehead MacDonell and fifty métis waited at the place where the Saskatchewan flowed into Lake Winnipeg. Robertson knew they were there; they knew he was there. He was too low on provisions to turn back. And they weren't about to throw in their hand and go home just because some wandering Bungee bigmouth had spoiled the surprise.

The whole business put Grant in mind of a schoolyard fight in which neither of the combatants was particularly interested—a played-out grudge kept alive for the benefit of the spectators. They would slug it out as a matter of form.

The camp got up and prepared breakfast, although Grant preferred to drink his. Halfway through the morning the word came down that Robertson had finally given in to the inevitable and started downriver. The York boats emerged from the rapids one at a time, the métis on the banks pointed their rifles at them, the oarsmen raised their hands in the air, the boats were reefed ashore and the cargoes unloaded, Colin Robertson delivered his standard tirade about North West Company pirates, Whitehead MacDonell produced a crumpled warrant that one of the company's justices of the peace had scrawled on the back of an inventory form—all in all they walked through their parts in a workmanlike manner.

There was the obligatory issue of rum to the victors. Grant passed up the celebration—though not the rum—and spent the afternoon taking inventory of the confiscated cargoes of furs. There was a certain appreciable irony in the legal question of who had just stolen what from whom. Since the fall of Quebec, the Hudson's Bay Company had been squawking that their charter gave them monopoly rights to all the fur country draining into Hudson's Bay. These furs came from the Athabasca, which—as Sir Alexander Mackenzie had proven thirty years ago in one of the mad voyages he was knighted for—drained north to the Frozen Ocean through Mackenzie's River of Disappointment, a thousand miles west of the bay. Not that either company could pretend to give a cup of whore's piss about legalities anymore, except to appreciate the ironies.

In the evening Grant sat upwind of the smudge fire jawing with Whitehead and Robertson. Robertson wasn't a bad fellow to pass the time with, so long as one kept reminding him that one wasn't about to be intimidated by the size of his voice. At the moment, said voice was holding forth on the current stage of the trade war. "The imperial government's had a bellyful. So've the shareholders. Four percent dividends last year. Four percent! Can't marry off your sunk-chested daughter to a Duke at four percent. All those poor decaying bloodlines going begging. What was your profit last year?"

Whitehead MacDonell said: "Six percent."

"Balls. I know for a fact it was three and a half."

"Then why'd you bloody ask?"

"To see how much you'd bloody lie. The talk in London now is of a merger."

Grant said: "A what?"

"Mirr-jirr! It means 'to join together.' I thought you'd learned English in that starch-assed college."

"I thought you'd learned self-preservation in the *pays d'en haut*."

"At any rate—the shareholders and the Colonial Office can squawk for a merger all they want, Selkirk'd never stand for it."

Whitehead said: "Mackenzie'd never stand for it either. He hates Selkirk's lily-white guts."

Robertson wrinkled his forehead. "Roderick McK . . ."

"Roderick? Roderick's a puppy—I mean Old Sir Blood-and-Whiskey Two-Oceans Himself. First white man across to the Pacific fifteen years ahead of Lewis and what's-it. I mean Alex-the-Great. Mackenzie. He still thinks Selkirk robbed him of thirty thousand pounds."

"So what? Mackenzie hasn't been a majority shareholder since back in the days when—"

"Back in the days when La Bras Croché threw you out of the company."

Robertson flushed red and looked as if he were going to take a swipe at Whitehead. Instead he just said: "Best stroke of luck that ever happened to me."

Grant unscrewed the cap of his flask and passed it around. Whitehead took a healthy swig, wiped his mouth with the back of his hand, and said: "Maybe Mackenzie don't own a majority, but he owns enough. And you know as well as I do he'd swim across the Atlantic and rip out MacGillivray's liver with his teeth if the Montreal partners pushed through a merger."

Robertson shrugged and said: "So I suppose then we'll just keep on squeezing each other's throats until your North West Company goes under."

Whitehead said: "Until your Hudson's Bay Company does."

Grant laughed. "Until you both do."

They both spun their heads around to face him with galvanized expressions. He couldn't stop laughing.

CHAPTER 84

 On a warm spring day in the village of Pau in the south of France, the Earl of Selkirk—his health and his fortune broken by his enemies—coughed out his life in the arms of his wife. Three weeks later, in the Pass of Killiecrankie, Sir Alexander Mackenzie's coachman hauled the horses to a halt at the sound of his master's frantic rapping on the carriage roof with his goldheaded cane. The carriage door flew open and the titanic knight lurched out, his face mottled, gasping for breath. His foot slipped on the step and he died in midair.

In the shade of an awning made from two poles and an old tarpaulin, Grant sat dandling his daughter on his knee. Maria by Wappeston out of Madelaine Desmairais. Madelaine Desmairais had been out of both their lives since early in the spring, breaking métis tradition by weaning Maria at six months.

Maria cooed and giggled and wrapped her pudgy fingers around her father's thumb. "Lucky for you," he told her, "that your father has a widowed sister. Left to his own devices, he would have kept you in a cage and fed you table scraps till you were big enough to get out and hunt for yourself." She rolled her eyes at him and dribbled her tongue out of the corner of her mouth, then let go with a belch that would have done credit to a bull moose at a sulphur springs. "Ever the coquette, hm?"

Josephte and Maria's cousin John were out picking saskatoons. The lord of the manor should have been inking in the account book or stacking away the bags of pemmican that had been brought in yesterday, but it was far more calming to sit on a keg in the shade and breathe in the sweet scent of the sage. That was why he'd decided to take this isolated little post on the prairie instead of moving up to chief clerk at La Souris or Bas de la Rivière. There it would have been impossible to escape the ongoing plots and counterplots between the companies, the incessant bustle of humanity drowning out the world around them. But the life he'd chosen had been too isolated for Madelaine. Perhaps she would have stuck it out if he had ever managed to convince her that she meant more to him than a consolation prize. But she never did believe him . . . which was hardly surprising considering it wasn't true.

The isolation and solitude that had driven Madelaine away had brought Grant back to himself. And after several years of relatively sober reflection, he had reached a point where just the sound of words like "tribe," "nation," "race," "company"—or any of the other contrivances that divided people up into teams and determined right and wrong by the colors the players wore—made his throat heave.

Not that he didn't intend to keep working for the company—after all, a man had to do something. He intended to give the company a day's work for a day's wage, and to one day retrieve his inheritance from MacGillivray, but his only ambition now was to live in the *pays d'en haut* while it still lasted.

A rider was approaching slowly, the only moving figure on the entire sand-griddle face of the earth. In point of fact, the horse was probably moving at a brisk trot, but he had a lot of distance to cover.

The rider stopped; there was a sudden starburst of light, winking on and off, and then the horse came on again at a brisker pace. Grant realized it was John Richards McKay, using his brass pocket telescope to scan the horizon.

Along with the recognition came a sickly wrench and an immediate surge of adrenaline. It annoyed him; he'd thought he'd resolved all that years ago. Yet all it took was the sight of Bethsy's brother riding toward him, and he was thrown back. He tried to dismiss his fancies, telling himself John Richards was undoubtedly just dropping by for a jaw and a jar. His fancies responded that Fort Qu'Appelle was a hundred miles away, and John Richards hadn't jaunted over once in all the time he'd been here. Grant then decided it was probably business; John Richards was bringing news of the forthcoming merger between the North West and Hudson's Bay companies. His romantic fancies countered by asking why an employee of the Hudson's Bay Company would be sent to bring news to Cuthbert Grant?

There was a wind coming up, one of those dry prairie winds that scales the skin off your lips. Grant stepped out from under the awning as John Richards kicked his horse into a canter for the last few hundred yards. "Good day, Mister McKay."

"Good day, Mister Grant," as though he hadn't just ridden a hundred miles to see him.

"Bit of frost?" He fingered his chin—his erstwhile brother-in-law had let his beard grow in, and there was a dappling of white hairs in the goatee area.

"Not a bit—just a summer's worth of sun bleaching out the blond."

"Ah." He held out the little bundle he'd been concealing in the protection of his arms. "If I recall, you haven't met . . . ?"

"No, I don't believe I've had the pleasure."

"Mister McKay—Miss Grant, Miss Maria Grant."

"A pleasure, Miss Grant," bowing from the saddle.

Miss Maria Grant crossed her eyes and sputtered, then arched her back to show off her private parts. "I told her you were an old friend of the family, so she decided not to dress."

"Charmed, I'm sure."

"Dry ride?"

"Dreadful. Yesterday I had to resort to water."

Grant shuddered and said: "I think I might have something to wash the taste out of your mouth." John Richards got off his horse and followed him inside.

Grant filled two tin cups with high wine from the bunged keg under the counter. He pushed one across to John Richards, then led the way through the stock shelves to the living quarters behind. He set his cup down on the table and started to bundle Maria back into her moss bag, then realized the moss hadn't been changed. "Damn. Sit down, sit down—this won't take me a moment."

He shook out the old moss into the hearth and relined the beaded velvet baby bag with clean moss from a rawhide sack, crushing in a few leaves of wild mint. "So what brings you out so far from the oases of human habitation? Excluding, of course, the mercurial delight and elevating wisdom of my conversation. . . ."

"You mean of *my* conversation, and the obligation I feel to spread its benefits around."

" 'Spread it around' seems the appropriate terminology."

"They've finalized the merger."

"Thank Christ. I was beginning to think the companies were going to end up like a couple of bull elk with their antlers locked together in a death grip. Just let me get Her Highness safely tucked away"—keeping her arms inside the mouth of the bag with one hand while the other laced her in—"and we'll drink to it. What are they going to call the new company?"

"They'll keep the Hudson's Bay name to avoid having to renegotiate the charter."

"Are they keeping the system of wintering partners and profit sharing?"

"Yes . . . to a certain extent. . . ." He trailed off. For a man who'd come to impart good news, he seemed strangely reluctant to part with it.

Grant picked up his daughter, bundled her over to the little squared-off hammock hanging at Josephte's eye level, and trussed her into the pocket. Then he went back to the table and picked up his cup. "And now that I've fulfilled my maternal obligations . . .

To the Governor and Company of Adventurers Trading into Hud

son's Bay. . . . Well, I wasn't struck by lightning, so I suppose we can drink.''

John Richards had to be cajoled into clinking cups and only took a perfunctory sip. Grant downed a healthy draft and stood for a moment, feeling the first drink of the day warm the walls of his stomach. Then he sat down across the table from John Richards. "So who is the governor going to be—or are they sticking with a board of directors? How are they organizing the districts? I want to know it all.''

"I'll tell you all that, if you wish"—John Richards appeared to be dragging the words out of himself—"but you might find it all somewhat . . . abstract.''

"Abstract?" Grant laughed. "I realize that the majority of my activities in the *pays d'en haut* don't fit into what might normally be termed commerce, but that doesn't mean I've completely lost touch with—''

"No, that isn't what I meant by 'abstract.' ''

Grant was eager to hear what he did mean, but once John Richards had taken the floor he seemed unsure what to do with it. Grant waited, and finally John Richards went on, his eyes focused on the tabletop. "You see, when I said that the majority of the officers and employees of both companies would be absorbed into the new one . . .'' He raised his eyes to a point between Grant's eyebrows. "I didn't mean that you would be one of them.''

It was a textbook sucker punch. If it didn't actually rock Grant back in his chair, it left him every bit as numb. The old void, the one he'd thought he'd sealed off successfully—the childhood terror that, in the end, all his elders' praise and high expectations would prove to be mistaken—suddenly opened wide and sucked him down. He got his breath back, tossed down another cup of wine, and said in a gravelly, brittle voice: "How many others?''

"Others?''

"Yes, how many others were let go? Simply as a matter of reference, you understand—so I will know whether I finished in the bottom third of the class or half or ten percent . . .''

"Well, a great many of the voyageurs won't be engaged again next season, since the supply route through Hudson's Bay is—''

"Don't play silly-ass games with me. You know that isn't what I meant. I mean company men.''

"Sam Black. And you.''

"That's all?''

John Richards looked into his empty cup and nodded stiffly.

Sam Black was a vicious lunatic who had murdered a number o
Indians and had only been saved from precipitating a score of ma:
sacres by last-minute interventions and miraculous good luck. Th
North West Company had been trying to rid itself of him for year:
As Grant let the significance of it sink in, John Richards said: ''C
course, there were also a number of Hudson's Bay Company facto:
who were already on the brink of retirement, and a few of the Nor
West Company's wintering partners who preferred to be bought o
rather than—''

''It didn't have anything to do with abilities, did it?''

''What?''

''The decision to exclude me; it didn't have anything to do wi
whether I was competent to do the job or not?''

''Of course it didn't. You were a . . . a gesture of goodwill o
the part of the North West Company's negotiators.''

Grant felt a momentary wave of relief and warmth, but then th
rest of it broadsided him. A guttural roar burst from his ches
''What?'' He was almost out of his chair and across the table; th
only thing that held him back was that his target was John Richard.
''What am I supposed to do? I can't go back east—I have a coup
of murder warrants hanging over my head. I have a daughter and
widowed sister and a nephew to look after—how am I supposed t
support them? How am I supposed to live? Am I supposed to p
on a breechclout and paint my face and spend the rest of my li
chasing buffalo with bows and arrows? What the hell am I suppose
to do?''

John Richards didn't appear to have an answer; he was hunche
forward staring into the tabletop again. Grant kicked his chair acro
the room and then crossed his arms to trap his hands under h
armpits. Without turning to look at John Richards—he didn't tru
himself—he said: ''That's why they sent you, isn't it?''

''Pardon?''

''That's why they sent you, instead of one of the others.''

''Well''—John Richards cleared his throat—''you do have th
reputation . . .''

Grant paced around the room and found himself beside Maria
hammock. She was still sound asleep, snoring away like an o
duty cherub. Grant ghosted one fingertip down her tiny bud of
nose. ''Wake up and tell your papa what he's going to do.''

He moved away from her, back to the table, and filled his c
from the pitcher again. This time he took the whole cup down
once, inhaling and exhaling briskly to cool his throat. He turne

around, caught John Richards's eyes, and smiled at him—not a
created or planned smile, merely the natural emanation of the heat
rising inside him. He said: "Excluding, of course, the logical option of butchering the lot."

John Richards didn't smile back.

CHAPTER 85

With the harvest and the threshing done, Sandy and Mister
MacBeth and his sons took a couple of carts down to the
lake to cut timber and build cribs to burn limestone. The Hudson's
Bay Company was buying lime for mortar in the immense new Fort
Garry they were building on the site of Fort Gibraltar. What wasn't
sold to the company could be used for whitewashing houses and
taking the hair off hides.

After a week alone in the house with baby John, Kate still wasn't
used to it. It seemed remarkable, considering that she and her husband could go days without exchanging more than a few pragmatic
monosyllables. She kept feeling that she was off balance somehow
or planting her foot wrong—as though she'd run a long three-legged
race and was taking her first steps after the finish.

Not that John wasn't plenty to occupy her. He had recently ascended to the toddling stage and was galvanized by the miracle of
self-propulsion. There were times she could barely keep up with
him.

The cheese form was spewing off more whey than usual, already
overflowing the pan beneath it. As she ran back and forth to the
clump of rocks stacked beside the front door, for weighting the
follower to tamp the form down, John kept planting himself in front
of her. She was developing a fairly reliable alarm keyed to her lower
peripheral vision—any dark blot around knee height meant she was
about to trample her son. His barley-beard-blond baby hair had
quickly molted to a vivid black like her father's; strange how it had
skipped a generation.

Over and above her own clattering and bustling, and John's occasional outburst, rang an incessant, plaintive wail of longing and pain from Bessie's house next door. She had tried to explain to Bessie, when she and John had gone to visit in the morning, that relief was on the way if she'd just be patient, but it hadn't helped. Bessie's home was a hundred yards farther up the point, in the refurbished old shanty in which Kate and Sandy had passed the winter between the first destruction of the colony and the summer of Seven Oaks. They had spent an entire week this past spring primping it up in preparation for the day Bessie came to live with them. It was Kate who had decided to call her Bessie, although she'd pretended to her husband that it was just a whim. Only Catherine Pritchard and Marie Anne Lajimodierre knew the secret of the name. She had christened her after Elisabeth Heden in hopes that Bessie would live up to the name, since Mrs. Heden was a great cow.

Kate pushed open the door and reached for the last rock in the pile. The bustling back and forth would have been easier if she'd left the door open, but she was afraid John might try to help while her back was turned and get his little hand crunched between two rocks. Bessie's bawling grew louder. Robert MacBeth, the ex-sergeant's third son, had promised to bring his bull around that evening, but it was a difficult concept to communicate to Bessie.

The world outside the door was as piebald as their cow—slick blots of white where last night's light snowfall hadn't melted off, dappling fawn-colored whorls of frost-dead matted leaves, and veins of stark black naked earth. Through the denuded trees, Kate saw a family of Indians traveling north along the cart track in a little caravan of three furry ponies. The second and third ponies had travois dragging from their withers, which toted their possessions just the way Kate's father used to transport baskets of potatoes down to market at DunUlidh. In front of the crossed poles of the travois frames slumped a woman with a baby on her back and a boy about twelve years old. In front of them rode the buckskinned paterfamilias, leaning far back on his saddle pad to tilt a leather bottle into his mouth. The new Hudson's Bay Company had said it was going to eliminate alcohol from its list of trade goods, but the policy had yet to be initiated.

She closed the door, carried her rock back to the table, and clunked it on top of the others filling the cheese bucket. She sat down to catch her breath, and John planted himself in front of her. "Want Da."

"Your father will be home in a few days, dear."

"Want Da!"

"Now, Johnny . . ."

"Want *Da!*"

"Johnny, please, I cannot bring your father home any sooner than—"

"No. Da. Want *Da.*"

Suddenly she wondered whether his "Da" might not be referring to his father at all. Over the summer, Sandy had gotten into the habit of spending the quarter hour or half hour before his lunch or supper of sawing out tunes on his fiddle. Since John had gotten into the habit of standing upright, however precariously, he'd stood beside his father's chair swaying from side to side or bouncing from foot to foot waving his arms in the air in approximate time to the music. "Da" could just as easily mean "dance."

She took a stab at singing, clapping her hands in time, a song in Gaelic:

> *I pluck the smooth yarrow that my body shall have more elegance,*
> *That my lips shall have more heat in them,*
> *That my voice shall be like a sunbeam,*
> *That my lips may be like the juice of strawberries . . .*

John began to giggle and shuffle from one foot to the other like a bear cub, flapping his paws in the air.

> *That I may be an island in the sea, a star when the moon wanes,*
> *a staff to the weak walker;*
> *So shall I wound every man, but no man will wound me . . .*

Bessie's bawling suddenly doubled in volume, with a shrill shift in pitch. Another voice broke in at the same time, vibrating the house logs, lower than Bessie's in pitch but much louder in volume—a chesty, bellowing roar. If Robert MacBeth had brought his father's bull around, he would have knocked at the door. The only explanation was a bear.

Sandy had taken his new fowling piece with him, but his old musket still rested on its pegs above the mantelpiece. He kept it loaded but not primed. Kate sprang up and snatched the musket and its powder flask, then sprinkled a pinch across the priming pan, spilling as much as she got in. As she headed for the door, John clutched at her skirt. She twitched it aside. "You stay inside, John."

"Bup Maa . . ."

"You stay inside!"

She flung the door shut behind her and ran around the hous
her homemade shoes skating and skittering on the frost-sli
ground. As she ran, she wrenched the hammer back through bo
clicks, holding the musket out in front of her. She had a vague id
that the barrel might explode if she'd put too much powder in t
pan, then told herself that her hands were shaking so much it wou
be blind luck if there were two grains left in it by the time she
crossed the yard.

The bawling of the animals grew suddenly louder—the horri
discordant clamor of the hunter and the helpless. But if Bessie
voice was still that strong, the bear wasn't ripping at her vitals y
As Kate rounded the corner of the shed, her foot came down on
patch of wet snow and slid away from her. She tried to stea
herself but ended up skidding to the ground. The gun butt hit t
earth at the same time she did, and the charge went off with a cra
and a flurry of soot, kicking her arm down and skinning the bac
of her fingers.

Both animals at the shed wall jumped at the explosion, but ne
ther of them ran. Bessie couldn't; she was haltered to a po
Clamped to her back was a vast, black, shag-furred beast, its fro
paws raking at her ribs—claws gleaming in the sun—and its beard
jaws closed on her spine. . . . It had horns, though. Bears did
have horns. And what Kate had seen as blue-black claws in the fi
jolting, smoke-blurred glimpse were slick black hooves gleami
in the sun. What she had taken to be the broad, blunt ends of
front paws were the curly black pantaloons of wool above its fo
hooves. Its coat—no, definitely "his" coat—was dripping w
droplets of ice gleaming like crystal pendants on the tips of
curls. Both Bessie and the buffalo had their necks arched and th
eyes rolled back. His tight-furred, gold-tinged haunches were qu
ering and gyrating back and forth like a snapped whipsaw.

Kate got to her feet and tried to shoo him away while still keepi
her distance. He paid no mind. She picked up the rifle and extend
it at arm's length, prodding at the buffalo's flank with the muzz
He shifted his back hooves slightly but kept on plugging away
time to surprisingly human-sounding grunts that weren't only co
ing from him—Bessie seemed shockingly disinclined to be rescue

There was a sudden peal of laughter from behind her. Kate turn
around. Two of the junior clerks from Fort Garry had ridden in
the yard with hunting rifles propped across their saddle bows. O

f them raised his gun to his shoulder. She shouted, "No!" and hrew her arms up, placing herself between them and the animals.

The other clerk took hold of the rifle barrel and pushed it down. "Don't be a fool, James—you'll hit the cow."

"Oh, of course. Sorry, madam."

"Wait till he finishes and climbs down," the second clerk continued, "then we'll have a clean shot."

"Of course." James nodded. "Let him go out with a smile on is face."

His partner winked at him. "Isn't that how you'd like it?" Then e turned back to Kate. "We saw him swimming the river, madam. Never heard of one so close in."

James murmured thoughtfully: "Must be some cow. . . ."

Kate held her position in front of the lovers with her arms splayed ut to make a wider screen. She wasn't quite sure whether she was rotecting them from bullets or from prying eyes. She glanced back ver her shoulder periodically to make sure the bull was still busy. His horns could rip her open with one shrug of his head.

More people started trickling into the yard, mostly men who'd een working in the fields of Colony Gardens. There was a smattering of women and children, who turned their heads aside to vatch out of the corners of their eyes. There were a good many tifled snickers and a lot of solemnly choking faces reddened to ursting. Kate blushed for Bessie.

There was a loud, deep thump behind her, and she turned to ook. The buffalo had all four hooves back on the ground. He was uzzling at a patch of snow to get at the grass. Bessie was calmly rinding her cud as though nothing had happened—but her contemplative lowing had lost its plaintive note.

A murmuring bustle rose out of the crowd as the two junior lerks and every other man who'd brought a rifle looked to their weapons. Kate edged closer to the bull and shouted: "Leave him e! This is our property!" It didn't appear to have any effect.

"The first man of you that cocks his piece shall never cock a iece again."

The voice carried over the crowd like a baritone trumpet. It was e big Indian Kate had seen idling northward with a bottle in his outh. He had a brassbound horse pistol in each hand. She could e now that he wasn't beardless like most Indians, but rather rudely shaven—uneven shadings of blue black here and there. It as Cuthbert Grant.

She turned around to face the bull and moved forward tenta-

tively, waggling her hands in front of her. "Shoo, get away fro
here. Run along while they're busy arguing over you." He turne
up one dark, glinting eye but kept on cropping the frozen gras
She swallowed a couple of times and took another half step fo
ward, clapping her hands together. "Shoo, boss, go along wi
you, back where you came from."

He jerked his head up sideways to his humped shoulder, lettin
out a bass snort that sent her springing backward. But the sno
turned out to be a signal of retreat rather than attack. She followe
after him, yelling nonsense syllables and fluttering her skirt wi
both hands. He trotted toward the river, showing the white rims
his eyes when he glanced back at her, lowing like the king of a
steam trains with a chest cold, tassel-ended tail sprung high. Sh
chased him down the bank and into the river. He swam with on
his shoulder boss and knobbly black plank of a face showing abo
the water. The opposite shore was the Lajimodierre's property. Je
Baptiste Lajimodierre wouldn't feel the need to shoot inedible o
bulls outside his front door to prove his prowess as a hunter. Ju
why she should be so concerned over the fate of a randy buffa
was a bit beyond her. She supposed that he had, in a way, just ma
himself part of the family.

When she came back up the bank the crowd was still there. Th
junior clerks were sitting on their horses with their lower jaws b
tween their knees at the realization that the man with the pisto
was Cuthbert Grant. Michael Heden was raging and waving h
hoe over his head in Grant's direction. Another man was shoutin
something about "murdering bastard!" Grant himself had lowere
his pistols and was sitting in his saddle with his eyelids droopin
lazily, as though he didn't give a damn whether they attacked an
tore him to pieces or not.

Kate called: "Mister Grant!" He raised his eyes. "It has bee
so long. Would you be so kind as to come in and have a cup of t
with me?"

The corners of Grant's mouth curved up. He nodded a bow
acquiescence and jogged his pony with his knees. The horse pranc
around in a circle to turn its head toward the house. There was
small figure beneath its hooves.

"Maa!"

"Johnny!"

Grant appeared to fall sideways out of his saddle, but an insta
later he had swung back upright. Both pistols were clutched in h
left hand now, his fingers just barely encompassing both barrel

Tucked into the crook of his right arm was a tiny black-haired boy, his terrors vanishing at the wonder of his new vantage point. Kate didn't doubt that John would feel safe nestled in that arm; it had once supported his mother's weight without a sign of strain.

She headed for the door of the house on Point Douglas. Grant walked his horse behind her, talking earnestly with John in Gaelic: "I believe we have not met before. My name is Grant. And you? John Sutherland, is it? A pleasure to meet you, Mister Sutherland."

When they came to the door, Grant handed John down to her. "Did I or did I not tell you to stay inside?" she said. He began to wriggle in her arms and snuffle. "Now there is no use in crying over it, but were it not for Mister Grant, you might have been trod into the ground. You frightened me half to death. Next time I tell you to stay inside the house and out of mischief, you *will*, will you not?"

"Mm-hm," nodding his head tearfully.

"There, no need to say another word about it." By that time, Grant had dismounted and followed them into the house, pulling the door shut behind him. "Do sit down, Mister Grant." He threw himself carelessly onto one of the split-bough chairs that Sandy had built last winter. It did not quite smash to flinders, but it definitely shuddered.

With John under her arm, she went to the hearth and stirred up the fire beneath the kettle. "I will just put John down for his nap while the water is boiling."

"Where is Mister Sutherland—Mister Sutherland, Senior, that is. . . ."

"He has gone down to the lake to burn limestone."

"Ah."

John squirmed and fussed, but she tucked him into his cradle securely. Sandy hadn't had a clear concept of how fast children grew; either he would have to build a bigger cradle soon, or John was going to go through life with his chin melded to his knees. When she stood up from kissing John's eyes shut and turned back to the table, Grant was staring at her. The big black-silvered mirrors of his eyes, always metallically opaque, had suddenly misted sheer. He said hoarsely: "How could I have been such a fool? . . ."

The fire had grown uncomfortably warm. She stirred the burning sticks apart, took the kettle off, and poured boiling water over the cobbled tea leaves in the pot. She said: "I am sure we all have been from time to time."

He stood up, shaking his head slowly, his eyes wide and luminescent. "All the years I spent galloping after idiot girls . . . and all my self-congratulations that I could feel such generous-hearted sympathy for my vanquished enemies . . . all the time it was *you*, it was always you. . . ." He reached for her. She started to back away but stopped when his fingers touched her shoulder blade. He cupped his other hand to her waist, the warmth emanating through the fabric of her blouse.

There were deep-carved lines around his eyes that hadn't been there when she'd first seen him on the riverbank in front of Colony Gardens. His body had grown thicker and heavier. He was no longer the overgrown pretty boy; he was a time-battered man of no more beauty than it took to suck the air out of her lungs. He eased his arms around her and said in a broken whisper: "Kate Ruadh . . ."

In her entire adult life no man had ever had to bend his head down to kiss her mouth. He smelled of woodsmoke and leather and sweat and rum and tobacco and clean linen. He was Grant of the hundred horsemen, elegant and feral, the courtly leader of the wild hunt, and she was his Kate Ruadh—Red Kate MacPherson—the true wife of his heart, who would reign as *Ban mhorhair* of whatever principality he chose to carve out for her.

She heaved herself fiercely out of his arms, found her breath and her bearings, and said with a vehemence that surprised her: "And what of your wife, then?"

"My wife?"

"Or do you not dignify her with that name? I mean the mother of your children, who I saw following behind you along the river-bank—reeling back out of your saddle sucking the dregs from a bottle."

He blinked at her. "That was my widowed sister, Mrs. Wills."

"Then what of my husband?"

"After all the suffering I have already caused him, I would not for the world . . . But love does not choose where . . ."

"*Love?* Do you think *love* is something of first glimpses across a dancing floor, or a flirting trick of the moonlight? I lived for two years day and night with my husband and cooked his meals and washed his dirty linen before I learned that I felt something more for him than duty—and then it was only because I thought you and your bloody-handed friends had chopped him into bits. He and I have worked eight years to build something in our hearts as solid to the touch as this house. Oh, it may not be grand to look at, Mister Grant, but it is fit for us, and the winds do not shake it."

John was crying. She bustled over to him. By the time she'd lulled him, Grant was at the door. "Mister Grant! Please . . ."

He turned back momentarily with his hands in front of him and his eyes on the floor. She hadn't seen before how shabby he'd become. "Excuse me, Mrs. Sutherland, I have made a fool of myself. I should be getting back to the rock I crawled out from under. . . ."

"No, please . . . you have not drunk your tea."

He laughed.

"Do stay a moment." She pulled out a chair for him. He came back reluctantly and sat. She bustled with pouring the tea and sat across from him. "Mister Grant . . ."

"*Must* you call me that?" A pained grin furrowed his face. "The foot-pounds of energy I have expended in my life to get people to call me that . . ."

"You are a grand man—no, please, listen to me. . . . When I am withered and ancient and dried up—next year or the year after—and the young people pity me, I will get an unseemly glint in my watery eye from time to time—'Whatever can Granny be thinking of?'—I will be thinking back to this day and the glorious fact that—shriveled granny or not—there was a time once, for a moment, when Cuthbert Grant thought he loved me."

A voice called from outside the house: "Hello home! Jean Baptiste, when your wife finds out you were . . ." Sandy opened the door and stopped abruptly.

She stood up quickly. "I thought you would not be back until Thursday."

"So did I. We had good luck with the wind."

"Oh. Did Mister Lajimodierre meet up with you?"

"No—I saw the horse outside and thought . . ." He didn't move from the doorway, standing with his bag of tools over one arm and his axe and sleeping roll and fowling piece slung under the other.

Kate took them from him, set them down, and shut the door. "Mister Grant had just—"

"Da!" John was standing in his cradle flapping his arms and bouncing his bare belly.

Sandy stooped beside him and ruffled his hair. "How is my John? Been a good boy?"

"Heega donner!"

"Pardon me? Now, now—talk slow, John . . ."

"Hee! Gawdawn! Err!"

"He got on her?"

John chortled and bobbed his head and clapped his hands together: "Bumpata-bump!" Then he covered his mouth with one hand and flicked his eyes from corner to corner, whispering: "Won sposa see!"

Kate said: "Bessie went into heat and a buffalo bull got to her before Robbie could bring Goliath around."

"Ah. Well, you finish your nap, John. I will be here when you wake."

"A pair of junior clerks from Fort Garry," Kate went on, "and Michael Heden and other mighty hunters would have shot the buffalo in the midst of it, despite my trying to stop them, if Mister Grant had not happened by."

Grant said: "He was too old and tough to eat, and his hide too thick to work. Besides—we creatures of the wild must stick together. Well, my sister will be waiting for me. Thank you for the cup of tea, Mrs. Sutherland. Good day, Mister Sutherland." He bowed and took his leave.

Kate turned to her husband. "Well, I suppose you have not eaten since breakfast?" He grunted. "We may as well have an early supper." She went to the vegetable bin, loaded three fat turnips into the hammock of her apron, scooped up her paring knife, and came back to the table. "Did it go well? No one got their skins lime-burned?" He didn't even grunt this time. She went to work with the paring knife—which was itself pared down to a sliver by incessant grinding. They would soon have to buy another.

Sandy hadn't sat down. In a barely audible, rigidly contained voice, he said: "When was he here last, then?"

She looked across the table at him. His eyes were trained on the rafters. She set down two of the turnips and started peeling the other, the mauve-white skin winding off in an orange-backed ribbon. "Who?"

His pale eyes lowered themselves to impale her like a specimen under glass. "Your Mister Grant, of course. Who else?"

"What? Never. I would have said if—"

"Why? Why would you need to? You know you can take me in easy enough. You led me by the nose right from the first with your 'Oh, Mister Sutherland, I am with child, I fear I must do away with myself if no man will marry me.' "

"What? I never said that!"

"No, no—you were much too clever to say it outright. But you knew I was too soft-hearted—soft-headed—to leave you to your fate."

"If you think, after all this time, you can get me to believe that

the only reason you asked me to marry you was because I was
pregnant . . .''

"You never *were*. Until John."

"I thought I was."

"Oh, aye—Katy MacPherson with all her reading and writing
and English never learned to tell if she was pregnant."

"Everyone thought I was."

"*I* thought you were. That was all that counted to you."

"Do you think so much of yourself to believe that I would—"

"Not *me*. You never wanted *me*," thumping the flat of his hand
against his chest. "It was this place. You knew I was the only man
who owned his land outright. You saw the deed."

"What?"

"On the ship. When I was delirious with the fever. You so much
as admitted it."

"What? Have you thought . . . all this time . . .?"

"Do you think I had no idea why you had to gouge the money
out of Lord Selkirk when he made all the farms freeholds? It was
so you would not feel that all your machinations had got you no
more than anyone else in the end. You think you are so much
cleverer—that no one is capable of wiping their own ass unless you
push their hand for them."

"Not *no* one—just you!" she said. "You can pretend that it is
beneath you to look out for yourself because I do it *for* you. You
made me feel like some penny-grubbing bitch for saying a word
about it to the Earl, and you so pious—but you spent the money
well enough once I had got it for you."

"Piousness has never been my strong suit. I leave that to the
Bible readers and psalm chanters and all the rest of the canting
hypocrites who feel free to lie and scheme and cheat six days of
the week because their souls get saved each Sunday."

"I know that without you telling me. If it was up to you, your
son would get raised half heathen."

"Half?" He moved closer, a sly smile on his face. "I would not
say *half*. I would say by the dark look of him that John was born a
quarter heathen, if I have the bloodlines of your Mister Grant
right."

Kate swept her right hand up and across at him, and the paring
knife slashed his arm. She felt it cut and let go of the handle. The
knife flew across the room and clattered in the distance. He looked
down at his slit sleeve—a black line as straight and pristine as a

razor cut, but with a red ooze weeping down from it that spoile
the symmetry.

John was bawling from his cradle. She hesitated, then starte
around the table toward Sandy. He hissed at her through his teeth
"Stay the hell away from me!" and went out the door.

She took John up in her arms, jogged him up and down and fe
him some kind of nonsense to quiet him, then boiled and mashe
half a turnip and fed it to him with some smoked fish mixed i
She sat by the fire with her hand in front of her face—the pal
cupped over her nose and the four fingers pressing their tips int
the corners of her eyes.

She remembered Bessie—even with the one need satisfied th
afternoon, she would still need her evening's milking. She told Joh
to stay inside and went out without her shawl. The sun was dyeir
the sky red and purple. She unknotted Bessie's halter and led h
into the byre. The air inside the cowshed was thick and warm wi
the smells of straw and manure and milk. From the hayloft tw
yellow eyes flared down at her—MacCrimmon II. With the succe
of last year's harvest a plague of field mice had descended, so th
freight in the spring's York boat brigade had included a few litte
of kittens. No one else had wanted the coal-black one.

Something stirred and sat up behind MacCrimmon. It was Sand
straw matted in his hair. He came down the ladder awkwardly, h
lame knee stiff and his cut arm limp. He had ripped the sleeve o
his shirt to wrap around it. The rag bandage was black with bloo
but it was clotted. A quarter inch to one side or the other and sh
might have sliced an artery. She reached her hand out tentative
and said: "I might have killed you."

"Were I you, I would have."

CHAPTER 86

 George Simpson was extremely displeased. The blizza
had turned the world into a white, biting haze. He w

cold and hungry and stiff from riding, but he disdained to allow discomfort to disturb his inner equilibrium.

His displeasure stemmed from his impression that the guides—so-called—had lost their way. When they broke camp in the Swan River valley to cut across country, they had assured him they'd reach Fort Hibernia on the Upper Assiniboine by nightfall. The sky was growing gray, and they had yet to stumble over an escarpment bearing any resemblance to the Assiniboine valley. The possibility of freezing to death was what he found most displeasing.

At the age of thirty-three George Simpson had already ascended to governor of the northern department of the newly amalgamated Hudson's Bay Company, and he had every intention of becoming governor of the entire trading territory in British North America in the not-too-distant future, provided he had one. When the merger took place, Simpson had been the right man at the right time—extremely able, but without a history that would make him distasteful to the officers of either of the old companies. Not many illegitimate sons of Scots governesses found themselves riding such currents. It seemed damned idiotic to waste such an opportunity by freezing to death on his first tour of inspection.

The wind had shifted to hurl snow crystals directly into his face, or—more likely—the guide was wandering in circles and had turned them into the wind. He wasn't by rights a guide at all, only the most senior of the porters. The original guide, a half-Indian Canadian, had indulged in sarcasm one too many times, and Simpson had told him that he wasn't going to take any more of his damned cheek.

"Cheeks?" the man had replied. "You want cheeks? You can kiss mine," and he'd climbed up on his horse and headed down the Swan River valley. How was anyone supposed to enforce discipline with a work force that would just as soon live off the land as draw wages?

The gray blot of the porter/guide ahead of him grew darker and larger and more distinct. He had stopped his horse and was standing in the stirrups with his eyes closed, which was probably just as effective a method for him to find the way as any, given the efficaciousness of his performance so far. Simpson stopped his horse beside him. "What are you doing?"

"Woodsmoke."

They followed the "guide's" nose to a horseshoe copse of pine trees. Snuggled in against its lee shoulder was a teepee with half a dozen hobbled ponies browsing in the snow. The tent turned out to be occupied by three rustic gentlemen named Deschamps, Cadotte, and Fraser.

There was plenty of room in the tent, and the occupants made the governor's party welcome, even more so when the governor instructed his cook to serve out a regale from the packhorse keg and to add what he deemed appropriate from the private stores into the stewpot bubbling over the fire. The inside of the tent was surprisingly toasty, if smoky, and Simpson soon found himself willing to believe that there might be some ordering principle overseeing the cosmos after all.

It turned out that they had found their way into the Assiniboine valley after all, but some ways south of Fort Hibernia. Deschamps, Cadotte, and Fraser had just left there yesterday, on the return leg of a journey from Fort Pembina.

Simpson's ears pricked up at the mention of Pembina. A recent piece of secret information had made Pembina a particular problem. The forty-ninth parallel of latitude had been settled on as the international boundary between British North America and the American Republic. Not long ago, an American army survey team had come west to sight out the border. The mouth of the Pembina River, with its two forts and surrounding cluster of métis habitation, was on the American side. After a hundred and fifty years of trade wars, the company was at last about to settle into placid enjoyment of its monopoly charter, only to discover that there was a rival trade base perched just beyond British jurisdiction. The survey team's findings weren't public knowledge yet, and the London committee of the company would be very appreciative toward any enterprising employee who came up with a way to neutralize Pembina before the secret got out.

The conversation between Simpson's porters and their hosts went on in the old fur-trade polyglot of Indian dialects, Canadian French, English, and Gaelic. ''Pembina'' was repeated several times, along with another word that sounded something like ''Watson.''

The sky had cleared again by morning. Simpson's party set off north along the frozen river. Simpson said to his interpreter: ''Our kind hosts of last night must have had some very particular business in Fort Hibernia, to bring them all the way north from the Pembina and back in the depths of winter.''

The interpreter shrugged as though to suggest that there was no accounting for his people's wandering whims. He added: ''They went to visit a friend.''

''Ah. The Mister Watson they spoke of?''

The interpreter shot him a sidelong glance, then looked away and nodded. Simpson was quite pleased with himself. In future the interpreter would always be uncertain how much of a native conversation his employer understood. It was best to keep these people on their toes.

By midafternoon they could see the good old Union Jack flapping on the flagpole of Fort Hibernia. There were a good many Indian tents pitched on the snow-covered plantation, upward of a dozen. The posts that Simpson had visited already rarely saw more than two or three small family bands at a time come trading in winter.

The chief trader was gratifyingly taken aback by the arrival of the governor of the northern department. No one had expected to see him until spring—which was, of course, why he was making his inaugural inspection tour now. Simpson got himself washed and brushed, changed into a clean suit of clothes, and then settled in with the books.

They were confusing. Not that they didn't balance, as well as might be expected between inventory takings. But the volume of furs and provisions incoming and trade goods outgoing was triple that of any comparably sized post. He had his dinner brought to him in the counting room and continued going over the ledgers.

He still hadn't found a mistake of sufficient magnitude to explain t when the music started up in the servants' mess next door. The chief trader was laying on the obligatory kick-up in his honor, and Simpson would have to put in an appearance. He decided it was ust as well—better to get a clear-eyed look at them in the morning—and left the books open as they lay. No one would have the emerity to touch them.

The jovialities had been arranged along customary lines. A clutch of fiddlers stood sawing away in one corner, with an old man banging on an Indian drum. A barrel of high wine and a keg of rum stood in the opposite corner by a stack of tin cups. A riot of moccasined, beribboned half-breeds and Home Guard Indians jigged and jostled, with a few booted Orcadians salted here and there. Some of the younger squaws were quite fetching in a north woods, feline sort of way. Simpson considered picking one of them out but decided against it.

After the obligatory introductions and a few moments of desultory conversation with the chief trader's immediate subordinates, the governor of the northern department considered his convivial duties satisfactorily performed. The chief trader delegated a clerk

to show the governor to his quarters and the first warm bed he
seen in a week.

But before they'd quite gotten through the door, another fixe
item of fur trade festivities broke out in front of them. There was
sudden outburst of shouting and a flurry of movement, and tw
large, dark men in buckskin trousers and wool shirts had their hane
on each other's throats and were flailing away with their free limb
There wasn't room to skirt around them. At any instant one of the
might get his hand on a weapon, or it might escalate into a full
scale free-for-all. Either way, it would be some time before orde
was restored. It was deplorable, but there was simply no point i
trying to reason with these people when their blood was up.

Simpson had resigned himself to going back for another cup
punch and waiting it out when another half-breed stepped up to tl
two grapplers, thrust his arms between them, and flung them apar
They began to spring up off the floor to go at him, then both stoppe
as though they'd run into a wall. He was a large man—although n
insurmountably larger than either of them—tall and thick-cheste
He looked from one to the other and spoke to them in an India
dialect, in a tone that wasn't so much angry as disappointed. The
murmured back at him in the same tongue. One of them—a nast
looking specimen with a mass of scar tissue sunken in over his rig
eye socket—actually scuffed the toe of his moccasin on the floo
Simpson was quite sure he heard the name "Watson" among the
murmurings.

A moment later the two were apologizing to each other as we
as to "Watson," and the three of them were heading over to tl
barrel corner with their arms around each other's shoulders, laug
ing. As the clerk ushered him across the courtyard, Simpson co
sidered asking him who Mister Watson was, then decided again
it.

After a good night's sleep he was at the books again. The r
markable totals still held up in the cold light of day. After supp
in the officers' dining hall, after the pipes and port had come o
and the cooks had cleared the dishes, after the junior clerks a
interpreters had discreetly made their exits, Simpson leaned ba
and said to the chief trader: "I don't mind telling you, sir, that yo
returns this season are remarkable—astronomically higher than a
other district. How have you managed it?"

The chief trader shrugged happily, as though to imply that he
only applied himself to the best of his abilities, as he assumed tl

chief traders of other districts had applied themselves to the best of theirs.

"Not that," Simpson continued, "I mean to suggest that the other districts' returns have been less than adequate. Quite the opposite. In fact, gentlemen"—surveying the senior clerks and traders gathered around the table—"I would venture to predict—although I don't like to count my chickens—but I think I can safely predict that once the returns for this year have been laid before the London committee, all doubts about the wisdom of the merger will be laid to rest."

"I wouldn't count my chickens."

The voice had come from somewhere behind the governor's chair. Simpson looked over his shoulder. A man was standing by the hearth, his upper body in shadow and his quillworked moccasins and fringed trousers flickering red from the firebox. The clipped pronunciation of his English was quite unusual, given the nature of his costume and complexion. "Do you doubt my computations, sir?" asked Simpson.

"Not at all. I believe the returns for this year will be enormous. But things have been known to change quickly in the *pays d'en haut*."

"I don't like riddles, sir, any more than I like talking to shadows."

The man moved forward into the light. It was the big half-breed from the night before, the mysterious Mister Watson. There was something in his manner that Simpson found annoying—not precisely insolence, more a lack of deference, which amounted to the same thing as far as the governor of the northern department was concerned. Simpson said: "I don't believe we've had the pleasure of an introduction. . . ."

The chief trader said reluctantly: "Mister Simpson, Wappeston."

Simpson heard the extra syllable this time and was relieved he hadn't embarrassed himself by saying: "Watson, isn't it?" There was something decidedly downcast about the chief trader's manner, not unlike a man at a dinner party who has discovered that his hostess sat his wife and mistress side by side and finally, just as dessert is being cleared away, has heard the fatal "I don't believe we've met. . . ."

Simpson extended his hand. "How do you do, Mister Wapa . . . Wapum . . ."

"No need to torture yourself with Cree pronunciation, Mister

Simpson. The name I inherited from my father—just as you have inherited the Swan River trade that he inaugurated—is Grant.''

It all fell into place in an instant. Simpson never even considered the possibility that it was any other Grant. "I thought you were no longer on the lists, Mister Grant.''

"I'm not. I've been kindly allowed to winter here.''

"You see,'' the chief trader said in some evident pain, "when Mister Garry came through last season, to sort out the merging, he allowed as Mister Grant could be quartered here. And in fact, the returns we've had, as you were just commending us on, have a lot to do with Mister Grant. He has so many friends that prefer to come here rather than—''

"Ah.'' Simpson smiled at the chief trader, quite aware that one of the few advantages he'd inherited was a pair of eyes so glacially blue they made a husky dog's look cordial. "In fact, then, your returns are so high because the natives of neighboring districts come here. Now, Mister Grant, you were about to set your riddling into plain speech. . . .''

"Not immediately—or I presume that you would prefer I should not.''

"You *do* presume, sir.''

"I presume that the American army's astrolabes function accurately.''

Simpson shifted his eyes from Grant to the chief trader. The chief trader stood up, yawned, and said: "Well, we all have an early morning. . . .''

When they were alone, Simpson said to Grant: "Now perhaps you'll be so good as to tell me exactly what you're alluding to, if anything.''

"Pembina.''

"Pardon me?''

"Mister Simpson, I do appreciate your reluctance to trade trumps for hints, but I think we can save a good deal of dancing around— as amusing as that might be—if I simply point out that the American surveyors had to hire guides and cooks and teamsters and interpreters, and—perhaps even more to the point—even commissioned officers get cold and lonely at night camping out under the stars.'' He poured himself a cup of claret and sat down. "Some friend from Pembina came up to see me. . . .''

"Cadotte and Fraser and Deschamps.''

Grant threw back his head and laughed. It cut against Simpson' grain, but he found himself grinning. There was something impos sibly disarming about a man who exploded with delight when you stole a trick from him. Grant saluted him with his cup, quaffed it down, and went on: "Just so. The gentlemen you seem to know—I won't ask how—brought me a proposition. Like many others in the *pays d'en haut*, they are extremely anxious about the fact that they and the country are now the exclusive property of one company. Doesn't leave much room to negotiate. They think it would be possible to start up a rival enterprise, operating out of Pembina."

"That would take a good deal of capital."

"Not at all. They have already discussed it with a number of American traders operating down the Mississippi who said they'd be delighted to buy any amount of furs that could be rafted down to them."

"How did your friends propose to accumulate furs in the first place? It seems unlikely that the American traders would be willing to advance a season's worth of trade goods on credit. So, as I said, it would take a lot of capital. . . ."

"As I said, not at all. There are enough trade goods stored in the Hudson's Bay Company's depots at Pembina and the Forks to outfit the most ambitious enterprise for at least two seasons."

It was Simpson's turn to laugh. "No doubt—but how do your friends propose to get their hands on them?"

Grant leaned forward and refilled both their cups, then set down the pitcher and raised his eyes to look directly at Simpson. The governor of the northern department stopped laughing. Grant went on: "The gentlemen from Pembina seemed to think that I was just the man to head that sort of enterprise."

"What did you tell them?"

"It seems to me that the gentlemen from Pembina, like so many others here, have failed to see—in their not ungroundless fears—that there are other implications in the merger. It seems to me, Mister Simpson, that it is no more in the company's interest than it is in the interests of the Cree or the *bois brulés* to encourage further immigration. One can't harvest furs out of wheatfields."

"How did you respond to their proposition?"

"I believe that what we both want—the company and the native populace—is for the *pays d'en haut*—pardon me, Rupertsland—to remain in its pristine state for as long as possible. Were that in fact to be the case, it would be better for the gentlemen from Pembina to remove themselves from American territory and settle under the company's wing. The most that anyone can ask is to cope with the

circumstances existing in one's own lifetime. But then''—Grant
looked at the governor of the northern department with a smoldering sad smile—"I have been wrong before.''

"It does seem to me, Mister Grant, to be a great waste to leave
someone of your obvious abilities outside of the company's operations. I think it would be in everyone's best interests if I were to
suggest to the London committee that you are a resource that should
not be left to languish. Although, I hope you understand that—
given the past—the odds are rather stacked against you.''

"When you come down to it, Mister Simpson, the odds are
rather stacked against us all.''

EPILOGUE

 "Ssh—Gran's sleeping.''
          "No, she's not.''
"She is too.''
"Is not.''
"Is too.''
"Is not—she ain't snoring, is she?''

Kate's eyes snapped open at that. Margeret and little Katy were
squatting on the rag-twist rug beside her downstairs bed, playing
with the dolls their grandfather had whittled and painted for them.
Christy and Morisson were helping their mother set the table for
supper. Hugh and Donald and their father and grandfather were at
the washstand by the door, scrubbing off the portion of the west
field they'd worn home, arguing over whether to take the hay up
tomorrow or hope for another day of sun.

Kate was finding it an increasingly long and convoluted path
back to the waking world, whether from her afternoon lie-down, a
moment sitting in the sun, or a night's sleep. Coming back to the
family also meant coming back to the pain—not only in her never-
mended hip, but also in her fingers and knees and elbows. All her
joints had become lined with sand. It was only when her eyes were
closed that she could leave the pain behind, hiking over Ben Grian

with her long legs swinging free and her unbound hair waving copper wings in the wind.

Sandy and her favorite grandson, Hugh, came over to help her into her chair. Hugh did most of the lifting. Although Sandy tried to be attentive, he no longer had the strength in his back. His hands were still clever enough to whittle and tinker, though: the wheeled chair had been his own invention. When she'd come to the end of the two-month sentence in bed to which the doctor had condemned her after she'd slipped on the kirk steps, John and Janet and the children had made a ceremony out of Sandy wheeling in the old armchair he'd converted.

At the supper table, John said the grace in Gaelic out of consideration for his parents, as he did many things, including leaving the head and foot of the table for them to preside over. Looking down the long colonnade of children filling their plates with beef and turnips and potatoes and fresh garden greens, Kate decided that the pain was worth it.

After supper Hugh wheeled her chair outside and eased it along the path to the necessary. The chair rattled and squeaked, but not alarmingly—the ruts were worn in well by now. Sometimes Hugh had to wheel her back and forth three or four times over the course of an evening. She liked to pretend that it was only because she was forced to be so sedentary, but she knew that she was wearing down. Things were bound to after eighty-seven years' hard wear.

It was unfortunate that Hugh had got saddled with this chore. Young people were so squeamish about bodily functions. But he never complained. When he'd helped her to stand and handed her her stick, she stood blinking at him for a moment, trying to reconcile her Christmas-born boy with this sun-browned young man who smoked tobacco and shot buffalo and rode like a wild Indian.

When she hobbled back to her chair Hugh was nowhere in sight, so she settled down to wait for him. Saber-winged nighthawks skimmed the treetops, calling to each other. MacCrimmon the Eighth padded across the yard and into the bush, pausing to stretch himself awake for his night's adventures. On the other side of the Red, windows were winking alight. She could just make out the outline of the lone, dark toolshed on Point Douglas.

The Point Douglas Sutherlands had moved their home to the east side of the river after the flood of 1852. Or, rather, it had moved itself. When they'd made their way back from the high ground, Point Douglas had been swept clean. But they'd found their house standing four square and strong on the other side of the river, in a

stand of elms next to the Lajimodierres. It had been easier to row
back and forth to work the fields on Point Douglas than to build a
new house.

As Hugh was wheeling her back to the house, he said: "You
knew old Grant, didn't you, Gran?"

"Old Grant? Which Grant?" There was old Ben Grant who'd
worked at MacDermott's store and Hamish Grant who'd had the
place next to the MacBeths . . .

"Mister Grant."

"Ah." In Red River lexicon there was only one "Mister Grant,"
although how the "old" had got in there was another question.
"We were acquainted with him, your grandfather and me."

"Henry Pritchard told me he had two wives. Is that true?"

"More than two, from what I understand."

"At the same time, I mean. They had two bedrooms, and when
Grant came home at night he'd hang his hat on the door of the one
that . . . uh, whose turn it was."

"That does not seem very likely." Not that she would've put it
past him, but the Catholic church stood directly beside the big white
house in Grantown on Phantom White Horse Plains, and during
the early years the priest had lived in Grant's home. It didn't seem
likely that even Cuthbert Grant could have got away with . . . Then
again . . .

"What's funny, Gran?"

"Funny?"

"You were laughing."

"Was I, dear? Oh, old people will do that sometimes as their
minds unravel."

Hugh swung the chair around to bump her up the steps backward
and pull her through the doorway. As he wheeled her around to
face into the room, she knew immediately that something wasn't
right. In the half-circle panorama before her were all the elements
of a normal domestic evening—Margeret and Katy were helping
their mother with the dishes, Donald was carrying James and Roderick up to bed, Christy was rocking Mary Ann Bella's cradle.
Except that all of them had managed to place themselves around
the edges of the room, as though flung out to the walls and corners
by some centrifugal force. Sandy and John were sitting on either
side of the dinner table at the center with the teapot between them,
staring fixedly at the walls.

She said: "I believe I will take my tea now, dear." Hugh wheeled
her to the table, then padded back to the door and went outside.

She sat waiting for her husband or her son to pour her a cup of tea. Neither of them even looked at her. John said, crisply and politely: "You're not giving this any serious thought at all, Father."

"*I* am not? What do you propose to feed the children on?"

"We would still have the garden plot and the barn stock."

"Do you think you can support a wife and ten children on that?"

"Might I have a cup of tea, please?" Sandy threw her a look of irritation, then dropped his eyes and poured a cup.

As she was ladling in maple sugar from the bowl, he said: "Your son wants to sell Point Douglas."

John looked to the ceiling for patience. "Must you always explode things out of all proportion? In the first place, we don't own Point Douglas, only half of it. Secondly, I'm not proposing to sell it off all at once, but to parcel it up into building lots and sell the lots off one at a time."

She said: "Why would anyone wish to buy a little plot of land when there are thousands of miles of empty prairie?"

"It isn't going to stay empty for long. The frontier of civilization is catching up with us, and the company can't hold it back."

"Civilization?" Sandy hooted. "Is that what you call that Canadian gang of saloon keepers and thieves—civilization?"

"Good Lord, Father, they aren't thieves, just businessmen."

"Businessmen? Is that what they call them these days? We used to have other names for them. I have seen them in their thousands, and they never change. They make nothing, except money. They love nothing, except the portraits of themselves they plan to pay someone to paint for them. They know nothing, except . . . well, there is no 'except' to that one, is there?" Suddenly he dropped the note of anger. "Oh, Johnny, perhaps you cannot stop them, but you must not become one of them."

She was surprised by the vehemence, the note of pain, in his voice. John appeared to be as well. "Da, I'm not going to change, but the country is changing. There's going to be an influx of population here, and of business, there are going to be opportunities, and someone is going to take advantage of them."

"They are only opportunities to cheat yourself."

"Cheat myself? I've gone over and over the figures a hundred times. Do you want me to show you—"

"It has naught to do with *figures*," slapping his hand on the table. "What you have here is worth more than any profit you can make by selling it away. If you were to have gone back and told my father, or your mother's father, that you and your children had grown

up in a place that had more people in it than Golspie and Brora and
DunUlidh put together, but you had never seen a padlock or a
politician or a landlord or a press gang, and that the people in this
place, who kept watch on each other's herds and rescued each other
from blizzards and danced at each other's weddings, were Catholics
and Free Kirkers and High Anglicans and English and Highlanders
and French and half Indians and Swiss—any old man of the old
country would have thought you'd fallen into a *shian* and come back
enchanted or mad. Would you sell that?''

John said gently: ''It only seems to you that what's coming is
worse than what was because you were young then.''

''No. I was young when I was a soldier, but I do not miss those
days. I was young in the Highlands, but I would never have gone
back. I will give you the benefit of one doubt, though. Perhaps the
Red River settlement is just a place like any other. But the golden
light I've seen it in these fifty years was not because they were my
younger days. I spent those fifty years in the company of Kate
MacPherson.''

Little Katy was up first the next morning and brought her grand
mother her tea, perching on the end of the bed. ''Granny, did you
know Mama's afraid of you?''

''She is not.''

''She said she was.''

''*Was*, dear. Way back when she was no older than Hugh is
now—well, not much older—and was only your father's intended.
You see, your grandfather and I were good friends with your moth
er's grandfather, old ex-Sergeant MacBeth, and he was known to
. . . exaggerate a mite in his stories of the bad days when we first
came here. So your poor mother thought your grandfather and I
were a good deal more daunting than we really are, and here she
was coming to live with us! So on the last night of the wedding
week, I took her aside and told her the story of the day Duncan
Cameron came to threaten us in our first house on Point Doug
las . . .'' She went through the story of Cameron drawing his sword
and Sandy raising his hoe, and of snatching up the pot of molten
lead. ''And when the door closed behind 'Captain' Cameron, your
grandfather turned to me and said: 'Are you sure you have no
relation to the MacBeths on your mother's side?' 'And now, see,'
I said to your mother, 'I have, on my daughter's side.' ''

''But why did Grandda—''

"Janet!" John called from the top of the stairs. "Would you come up here, please?"

Kate looked toward the stairwell and then back to her grand-daughter. Something was wrong: when the children were around, John always called Janet "Mother."

Janet called Margeret over to take charge of stirring the oatmeal, then hurried across the room and up the stairs. Kate handed her teacup back to Katy and said softly: "Would you just reach me down my shawl, dear . . . thank you."

John came down the stairs slowly, hesitated at the foot, and then crossed toward her bed. He stopped beside it, looking down but not quite at her. He opened his mouth and then closed it again, as though he had no idea what was required of him, which was unusual for John. She said: "I will not be able to climb the stairs."

He knelt down, put one arm under her knees and the other under her back, and lifted her with no apparent effort—nothing left of her but hollow bones and parchment. The stairwell was narrow and boxed in, with a turn near the top. She tucked in her head and her legs as well as she could and swayed upward step by step with her arms around her son's neck.

The rest of the children were clustered in the doorways of their rooms. Since the last time she'd been upstairs, someone had nailed up an *Illustrated Magazine* reproduction of "The 42nd Highlanders Charging into the French Redoubt at Corunna" on one wall of the hallway. The children were growing too big to be all crammed into three bedrooms, she thought. Now they would have four.

John had to do some maneuvering and sideways shuffling to fit through the doorway at the end of the hall. It hadn't occurred to her how much the room would have changed once all her things had been moved downstairs. There was an old tin trunk pulled over next to the bed now, with an oil lamp on top of it and a spread-eagled book and his pipe. It was a wonder he hadn't burned the house down around their ears.

When her eyes got to the edge of the bed, they skipped over it to Janet standing on the other side. They caught a residual image of a small man lying on his back with the bedclothes pulled up to his chin. Janet said: "That's how John found him. His eyes were closed already."

Kate nodded at her and said to John: "Sit me down on the bed."

He did. She turned to each of them and nodded to tell them they could go away. They did, closing the door behind them.

Now she turned her head to gaze at him. He looked so frail. But then he always had—as frail as one of those tiny dun-brown birds that sit fluffing their feathers in a blizzard while the grizzly bears hide in their dens. Was it death that made his skin so gray, or had it already gone that way with age and she hadn't noticed? She would have to shave him and comb his hair.

The sob burst out of her breast without warning, doubling her over and spewing spray out of her eyes and nose and mouth. She clutched the rim of the bed to steady herself. The howl echoed back from the walls. Another tore itself out of her, and then another. She forced her jaws shut and held her breath for a moment, quieting herself so as not to frighten the children.

She pivoted on her good hip and lay down on her side next to him. With her head on the pillow beside his, the arches of her feet still cupped up against his soles—he had shrunk as much as she had. She looked down at the side of his neck, gristled and bristly with gray wire-end whiskers. She snuggled her head down in the hollow of his shoulder. It was cold, with no throbbing of a pulse inside it, no rising and falling of breath, just the pasty hardness of dead skin on cold bones.

It wasn't possible there could be such a change just from the stopping of the mechanical processes of heart and lungs. It had to be that Sandy Sutherland had been taken away somewhere to wait for her, leaving this empty husk behind. But if that was all that had happened, why did she feel so desolate?

She whispered into his ear: "I will not pray for you. If you were right about the church, there is no one to pray to. If you were wrong, I never knew a human soul that needed prayers less."

In front of Kildonan Church, which stands within a short wall north of the mouth of Seven Oaks Creek on the west bank of the Red River, there are several ranks of tombstones aligned at a different angle from all the others that came after. The newer graves were laid out in relation to the squared boundaries of the church yard, but when the first stones were put in, the only baseline that existed was the face of the church. In among them is a white stone with straight-chiseled lettering that snow and wind and moss have eaten almost smooth. But it is still possible to pick out the inscription:

In memory of Alexander Sutherland
who departed this life
July 13th 1867
aged 83 years
Also
of his beloved wife
Catherine MacPherson
who died December 7th 1867
aged 86 Years

AUTHOR'S NOTE

This section is likely only of interest to insomniacs and history fanatics and the compulsively curious and those who might find some amusement in a living writer embarrassing himself by confessing the stunning depths of his naiveté . . . or perhaps I'm splitting hairs. The preceding story and the people in it have been a particular fascination of mine for over a quarter of a century, ever since the little hairs on the nape of my neck started doing the goosebump two-step at the first skeletal description in Canadian history class of the incident in which twenty-two men died on and around the swatch of ground that became the backyard of the house I lived in when I was six years old. Consequently, when the opportunity came up to write this book, I saw no need to "dramatize" the historical facts—although I knew that there were plenty of gaps that would have to be filled in and fleshed out since the *pays d'en haut* in the first decades of the 1800s was hardly awash with journalists recording every minute happenstance for posterity.

My intention from the first was to write what Josephine Tey referred to, in her most excellent *The Daughter of Time*, as "the almost respectable form of historical fiction, which is merely history-with-conversation, so to speak . . . an imaginative biography rather than an imagined story." One of the few principles I have left after several decades of making a living by entertaining is that if you're going to ride on the backs of dead people, the least you can do is not tell outright lies about them. And if there is an afterlife, the last thing I want to do is find myself facing an outraged Cuthbert Grant . . . or perhaps the second last, now that I consider the possibility of an irate Kate MacPherson. . . .

A number of scholarly historical books had already been written on the Selkirk colony and Seven Oaks. I imagined I could nail down the details of events by culling my way through them (some of you with prior experience in these matters are already snickering behind your hands). The more historians I waded through, the more dismayed I grew. Three times out of five they contradicted each other, not only as to who had done what to whom and why, but where, when, and how. It might not have been quite so disorienting if it wasn't that they were all set down in tones that suggested Moses had lugged the rough drafts down off Sinai. So I figured what I would do is skim through a selection of original source material to determine which of the historians was correct and carry on from there. (Those prior-experienced types I mentioned earlier have now broken into bellows of guffawing, and some are falling off their chairs.)

Where was I? Oh, yes, original sources. There are several dozen firsthand, eyewitness, swear-on-the-Bible accounts of the harassment campaign in the spring of 1815, leading up to the first destruction of the colony. Some of them are depositions taken down by the justices of the peace employed by the North West Company. Some of them are depositions taken by the justices of the peace employed by the Hudson's Bay Company. Some of them are journals scribbled by candlelight in Colony House after a year of dodging bullets. Some of them are journals revised twenty years after the fact by retiring HBC officers looking to show the company why they were owed a better pension. Some of them were recorded slightly after the fact, just long enough for the witness to have mulled over the events and determine which slant of memory would cast him or her in the best light. Some of them are letters from Miles MacDonell and his staff to Lord Selkirk, explaining how the whole sordid mess had been caused by everybody else screwing up. And all of that applies to the year *before* Seven Oaks, which is when things really begin to get convoluted.

Faced with the above, I would like to be able to say that I experienced nothing akin to unseemly panic. I had promised to myself and others—some of those others with check-signing authority—that I was going to write a story out of the past that did not play shell games with history, and here was history itself thimblerigging away like a cigar-smoking octopus known as Doc. I must confess to a momentary, shifty-eyed impulse to simply slide back into the grand old tradition of slapping a few historical names onto a page and spinning them into whatever fiction took my fancy—who would know the difference?

But then I let the gift horse's lips smack back together and took a step back. Serious jigsaw puzzlers will tell you—they've told me—that only a *moonias* tries to fit the pieces together by guessing how their colors fit into the overall picture; a genuine player pay far more attention to the patterns of their edges, the tongues and grooves and contradictory outcroppings and orifices. Here I was fuming away because I couldn't find a clear-visioned account—whether original source or scholarly revisionist—when I should have been delighting in the fact that the prejudices on all sides were relatively easy to define. If you have one picture of a scene taken through a green lens and another through a red lens, overlaying the' two of them should give a relatively clear spectrum. None of which is science, of course, but what came out in the end felt much more three-dimensional to me than any single snapshot through an objective observer.

I suppose that the above-selected implement from Mister Occam's razor case, and the strop that follows, have specifically to do with a certain Colonel Billy B. Coltman, he of the eponymous royal commission. Call me zany, but I found a certain reassurance in coming across someone who'd been hired as an impartial observer and who ended up being equally vilified by partisans of both sides. It was to Coltman's commission papers and one other source that I finally traced down the origins of a certain known historical fact that almost crippled this book before it was begun.

I wanted to set up the structure of the book as it starts now—with Grant leaving Montreal at the same time Kate MacPherson and Sandy Sutherland were being driven out of the Highlands. Unfortunately, the Kildonan Clearances took place in 1813, and every history book that mentions Grant says that he came west in 1812. The books written in the 1960s took as their authority the books written in the 1950s, which took as their authority . . . etc., etc. Finally I traced it back to two original sources, one of them being a reference to the deposition Grant gave to the royal commission, in a letter from Coltman to Sir John Sherbrooke. The reference is to Grant mentioning that he was first put in charge of a NWC outpost "at the tender age of nineteen." Since Grant was born in 1793—month and day uncertain—simple arithmetic adds nineteen to 1793 and determines that he came back to the *pays d'en haut* in 1812. Simple arithmetic doesn't take into account that if Grant's birthdate was in October, November, or December, he could've been nineteen and in charge of a trading post after coming west with the brigade of 1813. While no one of any credibility ever called Grant a liar—and no one of any description ever did so to his face, at least not twice—everything that's known about him suggests that he was perfectly capable of weighing the relative dramatic merits of "when I was a few weeks shy of my twentieth birthday" and "when I was nineteen."

Before I go on to the second proof of every historian's dating, a small footnote to the detail-conscious retentive . . . It may seem strange to you—it did to me—that Coltman's reference to Grant's deposition wasn't checked against the deposition itself. The index of the papers of "The Royal Commission Appointed to Look into the Recent Depredations in the Indian Territories" lists the deposition of Cuthbert Grant—the central document in the report, as Grant was the central figure in the events—as "disappeared."

The second piece of evidence used to prove that Grant went west in 1812—excluding the fact that other historians said so—is a note in the North West Company ledgers at the end of that year, transferring his account and wages to the northern department. It might well mean that he had already gone, or it might mean that he was about to go—a bookkeeping practice in preparation for a transfer in the coming fiscal year. I believe accountants still maintain something resembling the same procedure in modern times.

I hope that the specific examples above give some idea of the process that was used throughout the entire book. Listing all the details and decisions involved in the layering on of flesh over the scraps of old bones would fill another couple of books. In the places where there were no traces left at all, I simply made it up, although I'm pleasantly surprised on looking back that a high percentage of the personal histories are based on verifiable evidence. It's amazing what you can find out about people from parish records and third parties' diaries.

After all my grumbling about misinformation in supposedly factual history books, it would be remiss of me not to point out that there was also a good deal of very solid and painstaking work done before I came along, without which it would not have been possible for me to even consider writing a book such as this. I have my own prejudices and preferences, but for what it's worth, I thank them all.

I can't claim that I've read every book or parish record or crumbling-paged journal or scrutinized every microfiche and every gravesite. The higher the bonfire is fed, the wider the dome of darkness grows, and the sparks still shoot off into it and disappear. There comes a time to stop scrabbling through the cold for deadfall and hunker down.

As for the traces that remain outside of libraries and archives . . . Current Scottish Tourist Board brochures describe the Sutherland

Highlands as a delightfully unspoiled wilderness where a hiker can roam all day without seeing a human habitation. Near Golspie is a cairn to Canada's first prime minister, dedicated by Canada's thirteenth prime minister, both of them descended from crofters who were driven off by the countess of Sutherland. The city of Winnipeg and the surrounding countryside for hundreds of miles are dotted with streets and roads and lakes and towns and edifices named after the people in this story (Falcon Lake, etc.). I'm told that Sandy Sutherland's fiddle is somewhere in the attic of a distant descendant's house, just off Grant Avenue. When asked about Kate Sutherland, members of the Selkirk Association will grow a little vague, and then their eyes will gleam: "Oh! You mean Kate MacPherson!" My favorite monument of all stands next to Seven Oaks Creek. It is a plinth supporting a bronze bust of Chief Peguis. The bust is of a lean but robust, high-boned, venerably noble savage, with intense, far-seeing eyes planted squarely on either side of a long, straight, commanding, aristocratic nose.

Grant and the Sutherlands remain somewhat shadowy figures in both academic and popular history. Histories tend to be written from a "point of view"—official or revisionist, racial or political. Although in the years following this story the Point Douglas Sutherlands and Cuthbert Grant were continually thrust into the forefront of events, they became increasingly more difficult to slot into any point of view or thesis because—Ah, but that's, as Mister Kipling used to say . . .

ABOUT THE AUTHOR

Before embarking on his present career as author of historical novels about the Canadian frontier, ALFRED SILVER was a playwright, actor and songwriter. In 1983 and 1984, he was Playwright in Residence at the Manitoba Theatre Center. Although his novels are based on the lives of real people and meticulously researched, Silver's primary goal is to tell a good story.

Silver grew up in various locations across the Canadian prairies including Winnipeg, and claims as one of his boyhood backyards the site of the Seven Oaks Massacre. He is recently married and now lives in Toronto.